Richard Matheson on Screen

Richard Matheson on Screen

A History of the Filmed Works

Matthew R. Bradley

Foreword by Richard Matheson

McFarland & Company, Inc., Publishers
Jefferson, North Carolina, and London

LIBRARY OF CONGRESS CATALOGUING-IN-PUBLICATION DATA

Bradley, Matthew R., 1963–
Richard Matheson on screen : a history of the filmed works /
Matthew R. Bradley ; foreword by Richard Matheson.
p.   cm.
Includes bibliographical references and index.

ISBN 978-0-7864-4216-4
softcover : 50# alkaline paper ∞

1. Matheson, Richard, 1926–   2. Novelists, American — 20th century —
Biography.   3. Screenwriters — United States — Biography.   I. Title.
PS3563.A8355Z57   2010   813'.54 — dc22   2010029770

British Library cataloguing data are available

On the cover: Poster art of Vincent Price in *The Last
Man on Earth, 1964* (AIP/Photofest), Charlton Heston in
The Omega Man, 1971, and Will Smith in the 2007
I Am Legend (both Warner Bros./Photofest)

Manufactured in the United States of America

*McFarland & Company, Inc., Publishers
Box 611, Jefferson, North Carolina 28640
www.mcfarlandpub.com*

To Gilbert,
who always believed,
and to Tom,
the Host with the Most.

Acknowledgments

As a labor of love, this book represents the contributions of many more people than the one whose name appears on the cover. I would therefore like to thank the following, in no particular order (and, I hope, without excluding anybody).

For permission to reprint portions of previously published work, either mine or their own: Jo Addie, Tony Albarella, Robert Arnett, John Baxter, Steve Biodrowski, Jeff Bond, Richard Chizmar, Mark Dawidziak, David Del Valle, Stephen Farber, *Firsts The Book Collector's Magazine*, Graeme Flanagan, Martin Grams, Jr., Barry Hoffman (Gauntlet Press), Alan Jones, Dick Klemensen, Christopher Landry, Ted Newsom, William F. Nolan, Lee Pfeiffer (www.cinemaretro.com), Mark Phillips, Jim Pierson, Paul M. Sammon, Scarecrow Press, Peter Sobczynski, Michael Stein (*Filmfax*), Kate Stine (*Mystery Scene*), and Tor/Forge Books.

For sharing their reminiscences: William Peter Blatty, Ray Bradbury, Keith Dinielli, Keir Dullea, Anne Francis, George Clayton Johnson, Hank Jones, Ali Matheson, Richard Christian Matheson, Kevin McCarthy, Michael McGruther, William F. Nolan, Chris Ryall, and the late George Baxt, Bob Clark, Jerry Sohl, and Dennis Weaver.

For providing material and/or information without which this book would be significantly less complete: Jo Addie, Don Cannon, Greg Cox, Tom Flynn, Martin Grams, Jr., Barry Hoffman, Hank Jones, Brian Kirby, Marion Korsmeier, Doug Menville, William F. Nolan, Lee Pfeiffer, Paul M. Sammon, Dan Scapperotti, Paul Stuve, Joe Tura, and my special heroes, Gilbert Colon and the late Brian G. Ehlert.

For putting up with me and my obsession during the whole process: my mother Jean, my wife Loreen, and my daughter Alexandra. I love you all. Too bad Dad didn't live to see this get finished...

For graciously critiquing portions of the manuscript and/or providing invaluable other guidance: Jo Addie, Brian Boucher, Gilbert Colon, Greg Cox, Mark Dawidziak, and Tom Lisanti.

For being my partners in Matheson scholarship as this and other books evolved simultaneously: Paul Stuve (who has earned not only extra-special thanks but also combat pay as my valiant photo editor) and Stanley Wiater.

For moral support and other kindnesses too numerous to mention: R.C. and Ruth Matheson.

For fellowship and encouragement: Chris Blake and Fred Pennington.

And, for everything, Richard Matheson.

Table of Contents

Acknowledgments   vii

Foreword by Richard Matheson   1

Introduction   3

THE FILMS

The Incredible Shrinking Man (1957)	9	*Scream of the Wolf* (1974)	192
The Beat Generation (1959)	17	*The Morning After* (1974)	194
The Twilight Zone (1959–1964)	21	*Icy Breasts* (1974)	197
Other Episodic Television	49	*The Stranger Within* (1974)	199
House of Usher (1960)	78	*Trilogy of Terror* (1975)	201
Master of the World (1961)	85	*The Strange Possession of Mrs. Oliver*	
Pit and the Pendulum (1961)	89	(1977)	207
Night of the Eagle (1962)	94	*Dead of Night* (1977)	209
Tales of Terror (1962)	101	*The Martian Chronicles* (1980)	212
The Raven (1963)	107	*Somewhere in Time* (1980)	219
The Comedy of Terrors (1963)	112	*The Incredible Shrinking Woman*	
The Last Man on Earth (1964)	117	(1981)	228
Fanatic (1965)	123	*Twilight Zone—The Movie* (1983)	231
The Young Warriors (1968)	127	*Jaws 3-D* (1983)	239
The Devil Rides Out (1968)	130	*Loose Cannons* (1990)	242
"It's Alive!" (1969)	137	*The Dreamer of Oz* (1990)	245
De Sade (1969)	141	*Twilight Zone: Rod Serling's Lost*	
Cold Sweat (1970)	146	*Classics* (1994)	248
The Omega Man (1971)	149	*Trilogy of Terror II* (1996)	249
Duel (1971)	155	*What Dreams May Come* (1998)	252
The Night Stalker (1972)	162	*Stir of Echoes* (1999)	257
The Night Strangler (1973)	169	*Blood Son* (2006)	262
The Legend of Hell House (1973)	177	*My Ambition* (2006)	262
Dying Room Only (1973)	185	*I Am Legend* (2007)	265
Dracula (1974)	186	Other Unproduced Projects	269

Bibliography   273

Index   281

Foreword by
Richard Matheson

My friend Matthew has been working on this book for more than a decade. I am not only grateful for his labors but stand in awe of his creative patience and determination. During that decade plus — 11 years to be exact — he also did yeoman artistic work on my book *Duel & The Distributor* and on *The Twilight and Other Zones*, both edited by guess who? Hint: He also did the majority of editorial work on *The Richard Matheson Companion*. If he wasn't already my friend, he would certainly be my loyal ally.

I have only to add that this book, *Richard Matheson on Screen*, is a meticulously thought-out history of my script work for the past (good lord, *that long?*) 50+ years. All done with care and good taste, presented with carefully constructed chronology and commentary.

Matthew, in the course of the book, also interviews and quotes various friends and fellow screenwriters whose career paths crossed mine (Ray Bradbury, William F. Nolan, George Clayton Johnson, Jerry Sohl) and a host of actors, directors *et al.* Again, all of it presented with care and honesty.

In brief, well done, my friend! I doubt if there will be any Richard Matheson on screen during the next 50+ years. However, if there is, I will certainly look to Matthew Bradley to prepare another remarkable tome on the subject.

Introduction

Many books have been written about the lives and works of various authors, poets, and playwrights, and as many if not more about an equally wide variety of movie and television stars, directors, and producers. But it is rare for entire books to be devoted to screenwriters, which is symptomatic of the short shrift they often receive in all but the most erudite discussions of filmmaking. While Richard Matheson has enjoyed a formidable and richly deserved reputation in the literary world since his first professionally published short story, "Born of Man and Woman," appeared in the summer 1950 issue of *The Magazine of Fantasy and Science Fiction,* he has also occupied a unique, and arguably as important, place in the cinema and television of the fantastic for more than fifty years. Beginning with *The Incredible Shrinking Man* in 1957, Matheson's cinematic *oeuvre* epitomized and in many ways propelled an overall renaissance in horror, science fiction, and fantasy films, a genre that had been in a significant decline since the Golden Age horror films of the 1930s and '40s were supplanted by the mostly mediocre science fiction films of the '50s.

Matheson was prominent among a group of authors who brought to the screen a renewed emphasis on literary adaptations and such neglected elements as plotting, dialogue, characterization and atmosphere. One of them, William F. Nolan, has written extensively of their personal and professional relationship. He noted in "The Matheson Years," a "profile in friendship" in *The Richard Matheson Companion* (2008), that they were introduced in February of 1954 by Charles Beaumont, "also a young struggling author soon to become a leading member of what *L.A. Times* critic Robert Kirsch would call 'the Southern California School of Writers.' Eventually, we would all be named as active members in this regional 'school': Matheson, Beaumont, Ray Bradbury, Robert Bloch, and William F. Nolan. There were others, down the years, but we five were the 'creative center' of the group." Also known as the Matheson Mafia (as Bloch called it in his autobiography), the Green Hand, the California Sorcerers, or simply "the Group," it had no formal members; the circle also included Harlan Ellison, George Clayton Johnson, Ray Russell, Jerry Sohl, and Theodore Sturgeon, all of them screenwriters as well as authors.

With few precedents (e.g., H.G. Wells scripting *Things to Come* and *The Man Who Could Work Miracles* in 1936), the involvement of established literary figures affected the genre's development as much as the syndicated *Shock Theater* package of classic Universal horror films, and the color remakes begun by England's Hammer Films with *The Curse of Frankenstein,* in that *annus mirabilis* of 1957. Their literary credentials notwithstanding, no other member of the Matheson Mafia (who often collaborated and/or adapted one another's work on the large and small screen) equaled his success at screenwriting, with more than thirty feature-length screenplays and teleplays, plus forty-odd episodes of some twenty television series, produced over the ensuing decades, garnering a number of awards. Matheson's scripts have been directed by such seminal genre filmmakers as Jack Arnold, Roger Corman, Jacques Tourneur, Terence Fisher, Steven Spielberg, and Joe Dante, while his work on Rod Serling's classic series *The Twilight Zone*— which included many of the show's most memorable episodes — and with Dan Curtis helped set the standard for televised horror, science fiction, and fantasy.

"I always wanted to write for the movies," Matheson told Robert Arnett in a lengthy and insightful 1998 interview that was published in *Creative Screenwriting*, along with a biographical essay by Christian K. Berger. "They were so attractive to me because of their immediacy. I mean there's nothing like reading a good book, but a film hits you right in the face.... I remember the first time I really saw a scary movie, I talked my mother into taking me to see *WereWolf of London* [1935], with Henry Hull, and when he turned into a werewolf I literally flopped down into the aisle and crawled out and stood up. My mother came out and said, 'I told you [you] shouldn't see a picture like this.' [Laughs] I mean, she didn't want me to listen to *Let's Pretend* on the radio.... I remember, when I first started to work in Hollywood, sitting at the writers' table and thinking, 'Oh boy, this is going to be so inspiring, they're all going to talk structure and writing character.' And all they talked about was their investments. Or going to the horse track. Or what girl they had the night before.... You write for your own pleasure. You don't write for an audience out there who will give your [*sic*] money."

Born to Norwegian immigrants in Allendale, New Jersey, on February 20, 1926, and raised in Brooklyn, Richard Burton Matheson has lived in California since the 1950s. He has received the World Fantasy ("Howard") Award for his novel *Bid Time Return* (1975) and his *Collected Stories* (1989); the Howard and Bram Stoker Awards for lifetime achievement; the Hugo, Edgar, Christopher, and Golden Spur Awards; and two Writers Guild of America Awards. Bradbury has called him "one of those who have moved imaginative fiction

Richard Matheson in 1951.

from the sidelines into the literary mainstream," and Matheson notes that among his biggest fans is Stephen King. "Stephen has always claimed that my writing was a great inspiration to him. It's nice to have been able to influence someone like that. Stephen has brought up my name in a very nice way on many occasions, so he certainly doesn't keep the fact that I've influenced him a secret. I think that Stephen's success is great," he told James H. Burns in an interview (part of which appeared in *Rod Serling's The Twilight Zone Magazine*) quoted in *Richard Matheson: He Is Legend*, a 1984 "illustrated bio-bibliography" compiled by Mark Rathbun and Graeme Flanagan.

In 1998, King told *The New Yorker*'s Mark Singer, "The people who taught me the most about being a novelist were Max Brand and John [D.] MacDonald and Richard Matheson and James M. Cain. Their work was always about story and at the same time there's a poetry to their books." His other tributes to Matheson have been many and varied, including the dedication to his novel *Cell* (2006), shared with filmmaker George Romero. According to Stephen J. Spignesi's *The Lost Work of Stephen King*, he praised Matheson's novel *The Shrinking Man* (1956) as a "tour-de-force" and his Poe adaptation *Pit and the Pendulum* as "one of the most frightening (and artful) movies ever made" in "King's Garbage Truck," a 1969–70 column for the University of Maine student newspaper, *The Maine Campus*. Spignesi also notes that King chose the first half of his Richard Bachman pseudonym, which he created in 1977, in Matheson's honor, and named *I Am Legend* (1954) and "Prey," respectively, among his ten favorite fantasy-horror novels (with *The Shrinking Man* as a runner-up) and short stories or novellas in J.N. Williamson's *How to Write Tales of Horror, Fantasy and Science Fiction* in 1987.

Three of Matheson's four children are also writers. "I don't know whether I inspired them," he said modestly in an interview with me for the Gauntlet limited edition of *What Dreams May Come*, "but they were exposed to it. When they grew up, they saw me at it all the time. They saw that you could make a living at it, which is something that most families don't. If someone wanted to be a writer, the practicality of it would seem so remote. My younger son had a girlfriend for many years, ten years I think, and when she first came into our family, she had a talent. I remember reading a little term paper she wrote. But I encouraged her very much, and she'd seen that it was feasible to make a living at writing. Today she is a very successful writer. I had a much harder time than my children, though, because I was not exposed to this. If I was exposed to anything it was, 'Gee, do you really want to do that? Do you really think that's practical?' Or, as the Irish mother of one of my friends was wont to say, 'When you gonna go to woik?' Others would say, 'How long are you going to give it?' That's a phrase I think that many young creative people hear, and they should logically just shut their ears to it."

An acclaimed author in his own right, Richard Christian ("R.C.") Matheson collaborated with his father on several unproduced scripts and what became *Loose Cannons*, and with Tom Szollosi on *Three O'Clock High* (1987), *It Takes Two* (1988), and episodes of various television series, before adapting Dean Koontz's bestseller *Sole Survivor* into a four-hour 2000 miniseries for the Fox network. Christian ("Chris") Matheson scripted *Bill & Ted's Excellent Adventure* (1989), *Bill & Ted's Bogus Journey* (1991), and *Mom and Dad Save the World* (1992) with Ed Solomon (who scored a hit in 1997 with *Men in Black*), then proceeded to cowrite *A Goofy Movie* (1995) and *Mr. Wrong* (1996). On his own, he adapted Francess Lantz's novel *Stepsister from Planet Weird* (2000) for the Disney Channel. A veteran of the top shows *Moonlighting* and *Growing Pains*, Ali Marie Matheson has written for the series *So Weird*, on which she her husband, Jon Cooksey, were both executive producers. They also collaborated on the Disney Channel movies *Halloweentown* (1998) and *Halloweentown II: Kalabar's Revenge* (2001), and have contributed to various incarnations of the *Rugrats* franchise for Nickelodeon.

Of his own upbringing, Matheson told *Fangoria*'s Paul M. Sammon, "[T]here really was nothing in my family background to account for my subsequent interest in fantasy and science fiction ... [but] I happen to believe that your interests are not all the influence of environment. I believe that you're born with a certain predilection towards the things you have an interest in. For example, when I joined the library at the age of seven, the first book I borrowed was something called *Pinocchio in Africa*. From there I just automatically gravitated towards the huge volumes of fairy tales they had then. And [in 1935] I started writing little poems and stories for a local newspaper, *The Brooklyn Eagle*. They would give little gold stars as payment, which could later be cashed in for a toy or something. So I guess you could say I began my writing career under a golden star." After graduating from Brooklyn Technical High School in 1943, with an eye toward an engineering career, Matheson enlisted in the Army. But following his military service in World War II and a June 1945 medical discharge (due to trench foot), he earned a Bachelor of Journalism degree from the University of Missouri in 1949.

Having made an immediate impact with "Born of Man and Woman" (also the title of his first collection, published in 1954), Matheson moved to the Los Angeles area and began selling stories in a variety of genres, recalling in Nolan's *Firsts* magazine article "Collecting Richard Matheson" that "I was trying everything, just selling where I could with no thought of building a reputation in any one field." In 1952, he met and married Ruth Ann Woodson, a divorcée with a young daughter. The next year saw the appearance of both his first son, Richard, and his first two novels, the crime thrillers *Someone Is Bleeding* and *Fury on Sunday*. But even with the income from cutting out airplane parts at Douglas Aircraft and critical praise for his third novel, *I Am Legend*, he had trouble staying afloat. Writes Nolan, "Beset by financial problems and not at all sure of his future as a writer, Matheson returned to New York with his family and rented a small house on Long Island. He had just enough cash to carry him through the two and a half months it would take him to write one more novel. If the novel didn't sell, he would give up the idea of a fiction career and go to work for his brother [Robert]."

Fortunately, that novel was *The Shrinking Man*, whose sale to Universal-International not only launched Matheson's screenwriting career but also enabled him to permanently return to Los Angeles — and full-time employment as a writer. Affectionately nicknamed "Mr. Paranoia" by his children, he candidly discussed the origins, and the very real effects on his life and art, of that potentially crippling (although fortunately not debilitating, in his case) psychological condition in the introduction to his *Collected Stories*, wherein he also described the leitmotif of all his work as "the individual isolated in a threatening world, attempting to survive." In many of his classic novels and stories, he begins by introducing an element of the *outré* into a rigorously realistic situation, then examines its logical ramifications in lean and evocative prose, ensuring verisimilitude through the accretion of specific and believable details. Explaining George Clayton Johnson's characterization of his work as "coffee and cakes" horror, Matheson said to Douglas E. Winter in *Faces of Fear*, "You know, where people are sitting around the kitchen table having coffee and cakes, and the werewolf is battering at the window."

It may seem odd that Matheson, who had established himself in the SF community by selling his first story at the age of twenty-three in 1949, would graduate to writing novels outside it, but as he noted in an interview with me, "When I came to California in 1951, I stayed with William Campbell Gault, who wrote detective novels, and I became a member of the Fictioneers. They were primarily Western and mystery writers, so I thought, 'Hell, I'll try one, too. I could use the

Richard Matheson in 1986.

money.' That's why I wrote those two books, then I just went back to what I was always interested in." As Gault himself recalled in an essay published in *He Is Legend*, "I had enjoyed his short stories, and when he came out to California, I met him at the bus station in Santa Monica. I forget how long he lived with us, not long. I got him a job at the Pacific Palisades Post Office where I had worked, but he soon tired of that and got a much better paying job at Douglas Aircraft in Santa Monica. He tried at that time to get some studio acceptance as a writer without luck. So he moved back to New York. Naturally, as soon as he was three thousand miles away, the studios wanted him."

One early supporter became a close colleague and friend, as Matheson related in *Robert Bloch: Appreciations of the Master* (1995):

> Kindness. It is the word which comes to mind most readily in seeking to recapture the essence of Robert Bloch. And, with it, inevitably, *thoughtfulness*. I was witness to a prime example of these two qualities before I even met him. I had read his stories, of course, and aspired to achieve some small measure of his skill and imagination. Which made what he did for me such a source of total wonderment. Having read a limited number of my stories — there *were* only a limited number because I was just starting out as a writer — he wrote a long, carefully delineated, astonishingly generous article about my work, titling it (this really flabbergasted me) "The Art of Richard Matheson." To a novice writer, it was an injection of gratification and excitement I had never anticipated and which I will never forget.

Bloch later expanded the very same article into his introduction for *Born of Man and Woman*.

The versatile Matheson's output on page and screen far exceeds the realms of the fantastic. His two dozen novels include other works of crime fiction (*Ride the Nightmare* [1959], *Passion Play* [2000], *Camp Pleasant* [2001]), Westerns (*Journal of the Gun Years* [1991], *The Gun Fight* [1993], *Shadow on the Sun* [1994], *The Memoirs of Wild Bill Hickok* [1996]), thrillers (*7 Steps to Midnight* [1993], *Now You See It...* [1995], *Hunted Past Reason* [2002]), and mainstream fiction drawing on his World War II experiences (*The Beardless Warriors* [1960], *Hunger and Thirst* [written in 1950, but not published until 2000]). Screenwriting credits likewise range from *The Young Warriors* (based on *The Beardless Warriors*) and the highly regarded telefilm *The Morning After*, with Dick Van Dyke as an alcoholic, to biopics of the Marquis de Sade and Oz creator L. Frank Baum, plus episodes of *Wanted: Dead or Alive*, *Philip Marlowe*, *Combat!*, and *The Alfred Hitchcock Hour*. And his long-standing interest in metaphysics, psychic phenomena, and the "supernormal" has resulted in the nonfiction books *The Path: Metaphysics for the '90s* (1993), *Mediums Rare* (2000), and *A Primer of Reality* (2002).

But Matheson is inevitably best known for his work in the genre of horror (although he prefers the term "terror"), science fiction, and fantasy, which thus forms the primary focus of this book. Wherever possible, I have included his own comments on these films and programs, drawing heavily on my extensive interviews and correspondence — from which all quotations are taken, unless otherwise attributed — with Matheson, his friends and fellow writers. Portions of this book have previously appeared in other forms in *Fangoria*, *Filmfax*, *Outré*, *Mystery Scene*, and *The New York Review of Science Fiction*; in limited editions of Matheson's *I Am Legend*, *Hell House*, *What Dreams May Come*, and *Noir: Three Novels of Suspense*; in *Duel & The Distributor* and *The Richard Matheson Companion* (revised and updated as *The Twilight and Other Zones: The Dark Worlds of Richard Matheson*), both of which I edited or co-edited; and on the now-defunct Scifipedia website.

One of the most prolific screenwriters to come from a literary background, Matheson has been able to bring his own work to the screen with an unusual frequency; I have also discussed those instances in which it was adapted by others, devoting a separate section to every English-language feature film, TV-movie, or miniseries written by Matheson or based on his work. These entries are arranged in chronological order according to original release or airdates, while for simplicity's sake I have grouped episodic television into two additional sections (also chronological), one devoted solely to the original *Twilight Zone*, and inserted them at the most logical point, although they naturally parallel his feature-film career. The credits, broadcast dates, and synopses for specific television episodes can be extremely difficult to obtain, but exhaustive efforts have been made to document them as thoroughly as possible.

THE FILMS

The Incredible Shrinking Man

(Universal-International, released February 22, 1957 [New York City], April 1957 [general]) DIRECTOR: Jack Arnold; PRODUCER: Albert Zugsmith; SCREENPLAY: Matheson, Richard Alan Simmons [uncredited], based on Matheson's *The Shrinking Man*; MUSIC [uncredited]: Irving Gertz, Henry Mancini, Hans J. Salter, Herman Stein; MUSIC SUPERVISION: Joseph Gershenson; TRUMPET SOLOIST: Ray Anthony; MAKEUP: Bud Westmore; SPECIAL PHOTOGRAPHY: Clifford Stine; OPTICAL EFFECTS: Roswell A. Hoffman, Everett H. Broussard. Black and white, 81 minutes. CAST — Robert Scott Carey: Grant Williams. Louise Carey: Randy Stuart. Clarice Bruce: April Kent. Charlie Carey: Paul Langton. Dr. Thomas Silver: Raymond Bailey. Dr. Arthur Bramson: William Schallert. Carnival Barker: Frank J. Scannell. Nurses: Helene Marshall, Diana Darrin. Midget: Billy Curtis. KIRL-TV Commentator: John Hiestand. Giant: Lock Martin [scenes deleted]. Joe the Milkman: Joe La Barba. Midget: Luce Potter.

Widely regarded as one of the finest SF films ever, *The Incredible Shrinking Man* won the Hugo Award — given annually by the World Science Fiction Society (WSFS) and named in honor of Hugo Gernsback, "The Father of Magazine Science Fiction" — for Best Dramatic Presentation in 1958. That same year, Matheson was the guest of honor at the WSFS's World Science Fiction Convention (aka Worldcon). As he told *Fangoria*'s Paul M. Sammon, "*The Incredible Shrinking Man* was the start of my screenwriting career. And it also proved something that I'd always felt about screenwriters 'breaking in' in Hollywood. You see, before *The Shrinking Man* was published, I had lived out here in Los Angeles, and I'd been trying to sell some scripts for television, for shows like *Dick Powell's Zane Grey Theater*. But nothing was happening. It was just a nightmare; constant excitements and disappointments. But when I had [the novel] published and Hollywood wanted to buy the rights to it, I stipulated that I would have to do the screenplay before any kind of deal was closed. And that was that. I still feel this is the easiest way for a writer to break in."

He added in a *Filmfax* interview with me, "I think that was the only way you *could* do it unless you got hired, through some means that I was never privy to, as a contract writer. I had a friend named William R. Cox, who was a Western writer, and when I joined ... the Fictioneers in 1951, he was working at Universal. He was making like $375 a week, you know, doing any kind of assignment — we just thought he was like a god, with the kind of position he had." Cox's credits include *The Golden Blade, The Veils of Bagdad* (both 1953), and *Tanganyika* (1954) for Universal, as well as such series as *Broken Arrow* and *Bonanza* in later years. "He was always rambling about doing 'tits and sand' movies, which were Yvonne De Carlo desert pictures and everything. It was just an assignment thing, anything that came along. I always had the feeling that I had to have a book to sell that they wanted to do that I could use for leverage." Said leverage came in the form of *The Shrinking Man*, a brilliant paranoid fantasy that—like its oft-filmed predecessor, *I Am Legend*—was issued as a paperback original by Gold Medal and inspired by a movie that Matheson had seen some years earlier.

As Matheson told James H. Burns in *He Is Legend*, "I got the idea for *I Am Legend* when I was 17 years old in Brooklyn and saw [a revival screening of] *Dracula* [1931].... Then I went to a movie when we were in California that had Ray Milland, Aldo Ray and Jane Wyman in it [*Let's Do It Again* (1953), a musical remake of Leo McCarey's Oscar-winning screwball comedy *The Awful Truth* (1937)]. There was a scene where Ray Milland was leaving Jane Wyman's house in a huff and he accidentally put on [Tom Helmore's] hat which went way down over his ears. It just suddenly occurred to me, 'What would happen if a man put on his own hat and that happened and he realized that he was shrinking?'" His finances at an all-time low (a sobering situation his daughter Bettina recalled in a tribute for *The Richard Matheson Companion*), he returned to New York in 1954 and wrote *The Shrinking Man* in the cellar of a house he had rented in Sound Beach on Long Island. He also used the house as his story's setting, so that he did not have to keep notes on his protagonist's surroundings.

Universal-International quickly acquired the rights for its house science fiction expert, director Jack Arnold. During his days as a U-I contract director, Arnold proved himself equally adept at juvenile delinquent films (*Girls in the Night* [1953]), crime dramas (*The Glass Web* [1953], *Outside the Law* [1956]), and Westerns (*The Man from Bitter Ridge* [1955]), but it is for his science fiction films that he is best known, as one of the genre's only true stylists of the period. In his pioneering overview *Science Fiction in the Cinema: 1895–1970*, John Baxter singled him out as "the great genius of American fantasy film," noting that "from 1953 to 1958, reaching across the boom years, Arnold directed for Universal a series of films which, for sheer virtuosity of style and clarity of vision, have few equals in the cinema." *It Came from Outer Space* (1953), *Creature from the Black Lagoon* (1954), *Revenge of the Creature* and *Tarantula* (both 1955) were all produced by William Alland, who left U-I late in 1957, later returning there on a picture-by-picture basis to work with Arnold once again on a pair of romantic comedies, *The Lady Takes a Flyer* (1958) and *The Lively Set* (1964).

While the SF films he made with Alland in many ways epitomized the monster movies then saturating the genre, Arnold transcended most of his contemporaries through the almost Hitchcockian use of atmospheric natural settings, which gave his films a genuine sense of menace. Several were shot in 3-D, with *It Came from Outer Space*—which was based on an original treatment by Bradbury—and *Revenge of the Creature* respectively marking the short-lived format's first and last use by U-I in the 1950s. *The Incredible Shrinking Man* was Arnold's second collaboration with another of the studio's staff producers, Albert Zugsmith, who had supplanted Howard Pine, the producer of *The Man from Bitter Ridge*, on Arnold's second Western saga, *Red Sundown* (1956).

"Few established science fiction writers have written for SF film," Baxter states, "and those that have, such as David Duncan and Jerome Bixby, seldom had distinguished writing careers. An exception is Richard Matheson who, after producing a number of successful novels and short stories, turned to the film field with the same skill and imagination he had shown in the magazines. It is from his novel *The Shrinking Man* that Matheson adapted the script for Jack Arnold's next film, *The Incredible Shrinking Man*, a fantasy that for intel-

Grant Williams and director Jack Arnold on the set of *The Incredible Shrinking Man* (Universal-International, 1957).

ligence and sophistication has few equals. Written with Matheson's usual insight and directed with persuasive power, this film is the finest Arnold made and arguably the peak of SF film in its long history.... More formally planned than his other films, containing many images of great visual power and beauty, *The Incredible Shrinking Man* is Jack Arnold's masterpiece, interpreting Matheson's script with ferocious precision." Arnold directed three more films for Zugsmith, but while *The Incredible Shrinking Man* may be his greatest achievement, it was their only foray into SF, and the collaboration never matched the alchemy he achieved with Alland.

Interestingly, Matheson was already back in California and working on the script several months before the book's 1956 publication. In a September 30, 1955, letter that was excerpted by Paul Stuve in *The Richard Matheson Companion* (and written on U-I letterhead), he told his advanced writing professor from the University of Missouri, William H. Peden, of his "big news for the year—that the above studio has bought my book *Shrinking Man* and I am at the moment in the act of preparing a screenplay for it. Sounds so simple when you write it down. Words fail sometime. They do in this case. They fail to indicate what a tremendous thrill it was to get such news." As ever, though, he was averse to repeating himself: "Oddly enough, I now temper this delightful news with the report that I feel bored. Going back to an already finished work seems dull. I wish I were doing something new. Even with all this money coming in I feel tempted to go home and write stories again.... I want to do more movies but only once in a while. Most of the time I want for my books and stories.... I am going to try to do a good job on the picture so I'll have a chance to pick and choose in the future."

The film opens with the vacationing Robert Scott Carey (Grant Williams, who had appeared in both *Red Sundown* and *Outside the Law*) sunbathing on a boat owned by his brother and boss, Charlie (Paul Langton), and playfully persuading his wife, Louise (Randy Stuart), to go below and bring him a beer. When the boat passes through a strange, glowing mist minutes later, Scott is alone on deck. He thinks nothing of the episode at the time, but six months later Scott finds himself losing weight and height, attributed by Dr. Arthur Bramson (William Schallert, later seen as a priest in Matheson's *The Beat Generation*) to overwork and errors in previous physical examinations, respectively, until X-rays spaced several days apart confirm the grim truth: In an unprecedented case, he is shrinking day by day. Bramson sends Scott to the California Medical Research Institute, where weeks of testing by Dr. Thomas Silver (Raymond Bailey) indicate a gradual loss of nitrogen, calcium, and phosphorus due to a rearrangement of the molecular structure of his cells, caused in turn by the effects of radioactivity (which is deduced to have been in the mist) on an insecticide to which Scott was subsequently exposed.

In a longer version of Sammon's interview, published in *Midnight Graffiti*, Matheson said, "Isaac Asimov once even wrote a whole article explaining how Scott Carey wouldn't uniformly shrink at a seventh of an inch a day. Hell, what did I know?... I spoke to [Dr. Sylvia Traube] who worked at the Columbia Presbyterian Medical Center, and asked her what could possibly affect the growth system. The insecticide is what she came up with. I just came up with the radioactivity..." George Lucas, Steven Spielberg, and James Cameron all attested to the influence this premise had on their generation in Richard Schickel's TCM documentary *Watch the Skies! Science Fiction, the 1950s and Us* (2005). Lucas observed, "To get even smaller—I mean, you already feel small as it is, so for any young person who's trying to grow up, to say, 'What's going to happen [is], we're going to sprinkle you with magic atomic dust and you're going to get smaller and even less powerful, and as a matter of fact, there's nothing we can do to stop this.' So it's like stripping away all sense of power. You're completely helpless. That was an extremely frightening idea for a young person."

When Charlie's ad agency loses a major account, Scott can no longer be kept on salary and, with his debts steadily mounting while the doctors attempt to develop an antitoxin, is forced to accept Charlie's suggestion that he sell his story to the media, which dub him "The Incredible Shrinking Man." At a carnival—where scenes of a giant played by Lock Martin, best known as Gort in *The Day the Earth Stood Still* (1951), were reportedly deleted—he meets a midget, Clarice Bruce (full-sized actress April Kent), with whom he enjoys a brief period of happiness as the antitoxin temporarily halts his diminution, but after it resumes he must move into a dollhouse. In Matheson's favorite sequence, Scott is menaced by the family cat, Butch, which knocks him into the cellar. The horrified Louise believes him to have been devoured whole.

Although he never became a major star, Williams quite ably portrays the perplexity, bitterness, fear, frustration, and desperation of this slowly dwindling Everyman. Adds Baxter, "The gradual disintegration of Scott Carey's life and hopes is beautifully conveyed, perhaps most significantly when, after visiting baffled doctors for the last time, Scott's wedding ring slides from his diminished finger. Soon after, his marriage collapses, and only his cat provides any comfort. Yet it is the cat that finally precipitates his plight by driving him into the cellar. Inexorably the process continues, and, as Scott changes, the familiar world assumes new significance, an effect which Arnold and Matheson, by careful 'planting,' make appear even more convincing. The changing role of the cat, from prop to companion to menace, is especially well managed." Williams went on to make more genre films such as *The Monolith Monsters* (1957), which was cowritten by Arnold and directed by his former assistant, John Sherwood (who had also completed the Gill Man trilogy with *The Creature Walks Among Us* the previous year), *The Leech Woman* (1961) and Robert Bloch's psychological thriller *The Couch* (1962).

The optical effects by Roswell A. Hoffman and Everett H. Broussard are variable, with shaky matte lines in certain shots and Louise convincingly confronting her waist-high husband in others. The special photography with which Clifford Stine enlarged the tarantula that Scott confronts in the cellar involved techniques that he and Arnold had used in *Tarantula*, and remains impressive. Living in a matchbox and subsisting on mousetrap cheese, stale cake and droplets from a leaky water heater (actually water-filled condoms), Scott vows to dominate his domain despite nearly drowning when the water heater floods the cellar, and at last dispatches his fearsome arachnid adversary by impaling it with a pin in a tense and utterly unforgettable climactic confrontation. Ultimately, in a metaphysical and surprisingly non-commercial ending, Scott has shrunk sufficiently to enable him to walk out of the cellar through the wire mesh of a window screen and onto the lawn outside, where

Scott Carey (Grant Williams) faces his arachnid adversary in this promotional shot for *The Incredible Shrinking Man* (Universal-International, 1957).

he continues to dwindle, presumably to microscopic and then sub-atomic size, while contemplating the eternal mysteries of nature's creation and the brave new world that now awaits him.

As Baxter concludes, "Intriguing though one finds the philosophy of *The Incredible Shrinking Man*, there is more interest in the remarkable control with which Arnold shows Scott Carey's physical and emotional metamorphosis. [Alexander Golitzen and] Robert Clatworthy's art direction provides believable out-of-proportion sets [with set decorations by Russell A. Gausman and Ruby R. Levitt], but Arnold places Williams in them with complete skill. Scott sprawled on a grating after the cellar has been flooded, just part of the debris left behind; the towering edifice of the steps up which he must struggle, the enormous flaming creature that the boiler becomes, the dusty chunk of cake and the careless pile of sewing things in which he finds weapons and tools; impeccably engineered, these settings became completely convincing. The battle with the spider and with the cat are also remarkable, his final dispatch of the former counting among the great moments of film, but in the end it is with Scott, the tortured yet triumphant victim, that we are most in sympathy." Seldom has an SF film so effectively combined ideas and images, both of which are presented therein with a consummate artistry.

Despite the studio-imposed title (and, in the narration, an equally inexplicable expansion of the protagonist's name, given simply as Scott Carey in both novel and credits), Matheson's script hews fairly closely to its source, although omitting the Careys' young daughter, Beth, and downplaying Scott's unfulfilled sexual longings, which result in a morbid obsession with Beth's teenaged babysitter. The most significant change was one of form rather than content, with the novel's unusual structure — which prefigured the elegantly intertwined narratives of such subsequent films as Francis Ford Coppola's *The Godfather Part II* (1974) and Sergio Leone's masterpiece *Once Upon a Time in America* (1984) — dropped in favor of a more straightforward, conventionally chronological approach. After a one-page prologue in which Carey passes through the mist, *The Shrinking Man* begins *in medias res* with him already trapped in the cellar, and alternates between recounting the circumstances that brought him there, with flashbacks demarcated by his progressively shorter measurements, and chronicling what he believes will be his last week of life before he eventually dwindles to nothingness.

In *Directed by Jack Arnold*, Dana M. Reemes provides a useful chapter on the making of *The Incredible Shrinking Man*, including extensive remarks by Arnold himself, in which he reveals many of the methods used to integrate rear-projection footage, matte work, and the oversized sets and props (the latter created by Floyd Farrington, Ed Keyes, Whitey McMahon, and Roy Neel). There are also behind-the-scenes production photos and several storyboard sketches, of which Arnold told Reemes,

> For a story like [this], where the effects were such an important aspect of the story, my storyboard was invaluable to those very talented people in the special effects department. Every department head would know exactly what I wanted and there would be no misunderstanding or lack of knowledge about what I [was] going to do. When I got to a scene they were prepared for me, they knew what I wanted and the effect I wanted to achieve. It was precise and economical. That was the only way I could make it for under a million dollars, I knew exactly what I wanted. This is where my background and training stood me in good stead.... [W]e had to use our imagination because we didn't have money.

Reemes reveals that for the spider sequence, tarantulas of nearly six inches across were flown in from Panama, their movements photographed on a normal-sized basement ledge set and carefully timed. Then, Williams was photographed on huge sets of the wall, the web, and the ledge — which made him appear only one inch tall — from 250 feet away to match the perspective of the spider footage, with his own movements synchronized to the tarantula's by the beats of a metronome. The two images were later wedded by Clifford Stine and his team. But the book borders on hagiography when Reemes writes, "One can hardly speak of Jack Arnold's *contribution* to *The Incredible Shrinking Man*; to the extent that such a thing is possible in an intrinsically collaborative medium like film, it is *his* movie. Arnold was regarded with some deference as U-I's science-fiction expert, and received little interference from producer Albert Zugsmith, who had little idea what the project was all about. The only problem was with regard to the film's ending. To anyone casually familiar with the works of Lao-Tzu or Plotinus the ending is logical and edifying, but this was not the case with the studio executives." As Arnold (who died on March 17, 1992) told Reemes,

> The studio wanted a happy ending [in which] the doctors find a serum to reverse the shrinking process, Carey is reunited with his wife, and they live happily ever after. I had quite a to-do with them, as such an ending is not at all right for this film.... I wanted a kind of metaphysical ending; it was based on my own personal religious feelings, my ideas about God and the universe. I may be a minority of one, but I think what we did with this scene — and the way Grant Williams played it — was highly effective. In my opinion it is visual and cinematic. Anyway, Universal trusted me and said, "Let's test your ending." The first preview went so well they decided to release the film with my ending, and it was very successful. Some people were shocked by the ending, however, and there are still some who don't like it. They felt that the ending came somewhere out of left field, but many liked its poetry. For better or worse, I take the credit — or discredit. The ending was entirely my idea.

Reemes adds, "And so it is. Mr. Matheson's novel (and screenplay) has no such ending." Yet such assertions are at best misguided, and at worst disingenuous.

Aside from equating God with nature — hardly a herculean intellectual leap — Arnold's ending mirrors Matheson's quite closely, as a direct comparison reveals. Carey's closing narration (which, amusingly, is misquoted by Reemes) ends, "I had thought in terms of man's own limited dimension. I had presumed upon nature. That existence begins and ends is man's conception, not nature's. And I felt my body dwindling, melting, becoming nothing. My fears melted away, and in their place came acceptance. All this vast majesty of creation, it had to mean something, and then I meant something, too. Yes, smaller than the smallest, I meant something, too. To God, there is no zero. I still exist." In fact, this echoes almost verbatim the pertinent passage in the novel, which reads, "He'd always thought in terms of man's own world and man's own limited dimensions. He had presumed upon nature. For the inch was man's concept, not nature's. To a man, zero inches meant nothing. Zero meant nothing. But to nature there was no zero. Existence went on in endless cycles." In short, story *and* ending are Matheson's alone, although admittedly they have been brilliantly realized on the screen by Jack Arnold.

Agreed Matheson, "It is the ending of the book. There is too much voice-over narration in it, a lot of which I didn't write. It was a bit overdone.... Well, a lot of that was Henry Mancini. You know, at Universal, they wrote scores on the production line. One man would be in charge of it, and then three or four composers would be writing the music, and one of them would ultimately have their names on it. Mancini was one of them, Herman Stein was another. So, I don't know whose surge of orchestral grandeur that was.... [*The Incredible Shrinking Man*] was their top earner along with their two big war pictures, *Away All Boats* [1956] and *To Hell and Back* [1955]. It also got nice reviews.... Obviously, when he got small, that was fascinating to watch. And I guess you had to use the tarantula [instead of the black widow spider that figured in the novel], that was the only essentially showbiz spider you could use then [*laughs*]. But my favorite sequence was ... when he was being routed out of the dollhouse by the cat.... That was about 35 cats all together. One cat would do one thing, another could do something else, and so on," as he recounted in his *Midnight Graffiti* interview with Sammon.

John Pym's *Time Out Film Guide* calls this "one of the finest films ever made in that genre. It's a simple enough story.... But it is what Richard Matheson's script ... does with this basic material that makes the film so gripping and intelligent.... A pulp masterpiece." Matheson told me, "Richard Alan Simmons did a revision on it, and then I, I thought at the time brilliantly, prepared my argument against him having any kind of credit at all. Years later, getting to know him a little better, I think he just was nice to me and backed off, and said, 'Yeah, let him have his own credit.' Because he did a number of major scenes in it, like the paint can scene and everything, that was all his. I mean, it was still pretty much the same story, it was just altering one scene, one setup for another." Prolific writer-producer Simmons later worked extensively in television, garnering Emmy Award nominations for *Columbo* and an episode of *The Dick Powell Theatre*.

Matheson elaborated on the challenges — and restrictions — of his first screenwriting assignment in William Johnson's *Focus on the Science Fiction Film*: "The only limitation I had was that it was my first screenplay and I was working in a new form. I picked it up rapidly, however, and it turned out quite well. Unfortunately, the producer I was working for had a very commercial mind and weakened the script considerably, notably in the area of character. I am not sure that the film would not have been better if it had followed the form of the novel, which was to tell the front story in the form of flashbacks. But this kind of thinking was totally alien to Universal Pictures in those days and there was no way to do it other than in a straight narrative — which had the weakness of telling which caused me to scrap that form of telling when I wrote the novel. The story is quite weak in the beginning and I was not able to go into the character story in any depth because I had to 'get to the good stuff' as soon as possible — whereas, if I had *started* with the 'good stuff,' the audience would have accepted more character depth study than they got."

He added to Robert Arnett in *Creative Screenwriting*, "I didn't really think much of it for a long time, until I finally thought, it's very unusual for its time, very interesting visually, and certainly has an ending that's totally atypical of what they were doing then. Jack Arnold did a very nice job of directing that. I wrote a sequel to it, but they never filmed it. They had all these wonderful huge pencils and chairs and everything. It made an awful lot of money for its time. It cost about $800,000 and it made millions. But they didn't make the sequel. It was called *The Fantastic Little Girl*. The adjectives were always added by the producer, Al Zugsmith.... [Years later] I thought they were going to remake *The Shrinking Man*, and I said, well, good, I'll do the script, only I'd like to use the time sequence that I have in the book.... It turns out they were going to do *The Incredible Shrinking Woman* and that they were going to turn it into a comedy with Lily Tomlin. And even that I wouldn't mind, as I have said, if they had turned it into a *really* funny comedy. But they turned it into a lousy comedy." As of this writing, a second comedic remake, possibly to star Eddie Murphy, has long been in the planning stages.

Genre favorite Mara Corday, a Universal contract player who had appeared in Arnold's *Tarantula* and *The Man from Bitter Ridge*, passed up the chance to appear in Matheson's screenwriting debut, as she told Tom Weaver in *It Came from Weaver Five*: "They wanted me to play the wife, and by that point I was fed up to my eyeballs with screaming and Indians. I thought, 'When is my break going to happen? When am I going to be offered something with more substance?' The title was *The Incredible Shrinking Man* and it was all Grant Williams, all the way through it. The role of the wife was a thankless role. I told my agent, 'There is no way I am going to do this. I don't care if they suspend me or *what* the hell happens.' So [producer] Al Zugsmith approached me — he took it *very* personally. He said, 'One day you are going to get down on your knees and wish to *God* that you had done this film. This is going to be an enormous breakthrough.' I said, 'Sure, sure.' Well, maybe he was right [*laughs*] — it would have been nice to have been associated with it, because it *was* another classic.... [But] it did nothing for Randy, nothing at all." In point of fact, Randy Stuart's sole remaining film role was in *Man from God's Country* (1958).

Hailed by *Entertainment Weekly* as one of the fifty greatest SF works, this was Arnold's last major contribution to the SF cinema, followed only by *The Space Children* (1958), a preachy anti-war parable that reunited him with Alland at Paramount, and the dismal *Monster on the Campus* (1958), which like *The Leech Woman* was produced by Joseph Gershenson, Universal's musical supervisor. Arnold then worked exclusively in other genres, including the unusual Western *No Name on the Bullet* (1959), with Audie Murphy; the delightful comedy *The Mouse That Roared* (1959), featuring Peter Sellers in three roles; the Bob Hope vehicles *Bachelor in Paradise* (1961) and *A Global Affair* (1964); and a pair of blaxploitation films starring Fred Williamson, *Black Eye* (1974) and *Boss Nigger* (1975). He also directed several TV-movies and many episodes of a wide variety of series, including the Sherwood Schwartz sitcoms *Gilligan's Island* and *The Brady Bunch*, as well as producing both the short-lived show *Mr. Terrific* and *The Sid Caesar, Imogene Coca, Carl Reiner, Howard Morris Special* for CBS. The latter received the Emmy Award as Outstanding Variety Special for the 1966–67 season.

Ironically, as Matheson observed to William P. Simmons in *Cemetery Dance*, "The phrase *Incredible Shrinking* has become part of the American language," seen in everything from innumerable news headlines to Lisa Passen's children's book *The Incredible Shrinking Teacher*, whose protagonist is reduced in stature by a combination of prune pudding, kidney bean cookies, and Brussels sprout juice. A somewhat more mature homage appears in *Hable con Ella* (Talk to Her, 2002), Pedro Almodóvar's film — an Oscar winner for his original screenplay — about the one-sided conversations carried on by two men, Benigno Martín (Javier Cámara) and Marco Zuluaga (Darío Grandinetti), with a pair of women lying comatose in hospital beds, Alicia (Leonor Watling) and Lydia González (Rosario Flores). In a sequence that *Leonard Maltin's Movie Guide* calls "outrageous and unforgettable," Benigno recounts seeing a silent film, *Amante Menguante* (Shrinking Lover), whose overweight hero, Alfredo (Fele Martínez), runs afoul of "an experimental diet formula" created by his scientist girlfriend, Amparo (Paz Vega). When she is unable to find an antidote, he consigns himself to her vagina while she sleeps.

The Beat Generation

(aka *This Rebel Age*; MGM, released July 3, 1959) DIRECTOR: Charles Haas; PRODUCER: Albert Zugsmith; SCREENPLAY: Matheson, Lewis Meltzer; MUSIC: Albert Glasser; MAKEUP: William Tuttle. Black and white, 95 minutes. CAST— Sgt. Dave Culloran: Steve Cochran. Georgia Altera: Mamie Van Doren. Stan Belmont (aka Hess): Ray Danton. Francee Culloran: Fay Spain. Louis Armstrong and His All-Stars: Themselves. Joyce Greenfield: Maggie Hayes. Jake Baron: Jackie Coogan. Art Jester (aka Arthur Garrett): Jim Mitchum. The Singer: Cathy Crosby. Harry Altera: Ray Anthony. The Singing Beatnik: Dick Contino. Marie Baron: Irish McCalla. The Poetess: Vampira [Maila Nurmi]. Dr. Elcott: Billy Daniels. The Wrestling Beatnik: Maxie Rosenbloom. Lover Boy: Charles Chaplin, Jr. The Beat Beatnik: [Norman "Woo Woo"] Grabowski. Father Dinelli: William Schallert. Dancer: Regina Carrol [aka Gelfan].

The success of 1957's *The Incredible Shrinking Man* enabled Jack Arnold and Albert Zugsmith to work with higher budgets and one of U-I's biggest stars, Jeff Chandler, on their next two films the same year: *The Tattered Dress*, a courtroom drama, and *Man in the Shadow*, a contemporary Western costarring Orson Welles (whose superb *Touch of Evil* [1958] Zugsmith also produced). Moving to MGM, they enjoyed another hit with the "troubled youth" classic *High School Confidential!* (1958), a seemingly bizarre project for the prestigious studio. It starred Russ Tamblyn, Jerry Lee Lewis, and such soon-to-be Zugsmith regulars as blonde bombshell Mamie Van Doren, the "Platinum Powerhouse"; her then-husband, bandleader Ray Anthony; and Jackie Coogan. Although it proved to be his last film with Arnold, this charted the course of Zugsmith's subsequent career as an exploitation filmmaker, which in 1959 alone encompassed four films for MGM: *The Beat Generation* (later reissued as *This Rebel Age*), *Girls Town* (aka *The Innocent and the Damned*), *Night of the Quarter Moon* (aka *Flesh and Flame*), and *The Big Operator* (aka *Anatomy of the Syndicate*).

Directed by Charles Haas — as were *Girls Town, The Big Operator,* and the producer's earlier *Star in the Dust* (1956), all starring Van Doren — *The Beat Generation* featured Zugsmith's trademark eclectic cast, including not only *High School Confidential!* alumni Van Doren, Anthony, and Coogan but also Fay Spain, Vampira (aka Maila Nurmi), "Slapsie" Maxie Rosenbloom, Charles Chaplin, Jr., Jim Mitchum (son of Robert), and Louis Armstrong. Irish McCalla, who after a stint at Matheson's own onetime employer, Douglas Aircraft, had achieved international stardom as comic-book heroine Sheena, Queen of the Jungle, in an eponymous 1955 syndicated series, played Coogan's wife, Marie Baron.

McCalla told Herb Fagen in a *Filmfax* interview that she "was offered the lead, but I turned it down because it had a rape scene.... I told Mr. Zugsmith that I couldn't take the part because my blouse would be ripped off in the scene. I felt there was the Sheena image to preserve, and there was another matter as well. I had two young boys and I didn't want them to be ashamed of their mother. He said, 'Irish, this rape scene will be done in good taste!'... I said, 'Mr. Zugsmith, how can you rape somebody in good taste?'" Her other films range from *Hands of a Stranger* (1962), an uncredited adaptation of Maurice Renard's oft-filmed novel *The Hands of Orlac*, and Richard E. Cunha's cult classic *She Demons* (1958) to *Five Gates to Hell* (1959), written, produced, and directed by James Clavell, later the best-selling author of *Shogun*.

Also novelized by Zugsmith, *The Beat Generation* opens with Louis Armstrong and His All-Stars performing the title song in the Golden Scallion, the Beat coffeehouse where Stan Belmont (Ray Danton, soon to guest-star in Matheson's award-winning *Lawman* episode "Yawkey") quotes Schopenhauer and tells his female companion Meg that she must "play it like cool.... You've gotta live for kicks, right here and now. That's all there is." Calling himself "Arthur Garrett," he insinuates his way into the home of bored housewife Joyce Greenfield (Maggie Hayes) by pretending to be a friend of her traveling salesman husband Charley,

Opposite: **Poster art for *The Beat Generation* (MGM, 1959).**

and then brutally assaults her, adopting the *modus operandi* of another local rapist known only as The Aspirin Kid and planting evidence to suggest that she was actually acquainted with her alleged attacker. While walking away from the scene of the crime he encounters Sgt. Dave Culloran (Steve Cochran) and blithely accepts the LAPD detective's unwitting offer of a lift. After spotting an ad for Hess Foods on the seat of the car, Stan introduces himself as Stan Hess, whereupon he proceeds to elicit such personal information as Dave's address and marital status, which he writes down in a small notebook.

Betrayed by his unfaithful first wife, Dave periodically interrogates his devoted second wife, Francee (Fay Spain), about her whereabouts while he is working. He is deeply suspicious about the credibility of the rape victims whose cases he investigates, which leads his veteran vice squad partner, Jake Baron (Coogan, also the film's dialogue coach), to deduce that Dave has a hatred of women. Based on a composite sketch of the rapist, Stan's friend Art Jester (Mitchum) is picked up as a possible suspect and released. Stan calls Dave as "Garrett," offering to give himself up, but while the two vice cops wait in vain for Stan to meet them at the Golden Scallion, he effects an entrance into the Culloran house and rapes Francee, once again making it appear that she willingly allowed him to enter. This seems to confirm all of the tormented detective's worst fears about women, and to sow further confusion, Stan blackmails Art into using the Garrett name and M.O. in an attempt to rape recent divorcée Georgia Altera (Van Doren). Her ex-husband Harry (aptly played by Anthony, whose soulful trumpet solo was heard over the opening credits of *The Incredible Shrinking Man*) arrives before Stan can attack her.

Georgia is exactly the kind of woman Dave suspects the other victims of being: She begins a relationship with Art, whom she still knows only as "Garrett." The Cullorans, though they have long wanted children, become further estranged when Francee clashes with Dave over her intention to obtain an illegal abortion, after learning that she is carrying what might be the rapist's baby. Hounded relentlessly by Dave, as are the other rape victims, Georgia at last agrees to identify Garrett and brings Dave to the Malibu "beach pad" presided over by Stan, who knocks him unconscious and takes them both prisoner, intending to kill the detective under cover of the beatniks' "regular Sunday night hootenanny." Georgia persuades Art that Stan is dangerously crazy, and so he releases them. Dave must extricate himself from the over-eager beatniks (including former world light heavyweight champion boxer Maxie Rosenbloom) before the aquatic final showdown, during which he suppresses his desire to kill the speargun-wielding Stan. All ends well when the latter is apprehended, proclaiming that "women are filth," while Dave is reconciled with Francee and their newborn daughter.

Rarely seen today — perhaps mercifully so — *The Beat Generation* is dismissed in *Halliwell's Film and Video Guide* as a "bankrupt exploitation melodrama, not easy to sit through." Matheson concurs, noting in a 1992 letter to me, "It was on TV a few weeks back and I thought I'd record it just to have a copy of it. I couldn't even sit through the whole thing, it was so horrible. I used the tape for something else, anything would have done, a rerun of *Hee Haw* or something. I still remember Al Zugsmith going through my script and, every place where the word 'police' or 'policeman' was located, he penciled it out and wrote in 'fuzz.' A man of great talent. One would never know it but when I first began to work on it, it was based on a *Cosmopolitan* article by some judge about a true-crime case in which a man hitchhiked, found out, in conversation, about the man's wife, address, etc. Showed up there, was admitted because he clearly 'knew' the husband, then robbed, raped and usually murdered the woman. It was Zugsmith's inspiration to add the Beat Generation to it. Unqualifiedly stupid." It appears that the film still has never been released on home video in any format.

Reunited with Haas on *Platinum High School* (1960), Zugsmith then directed Van Doren in several films, including *The Private Lives of Adam and Eve* (1961), which began as a Matheson screenplay, *Adam and Eve*. "Wasn't a bad script," he added in his letter. "After Zugsmith finished with it and made [co-director] Mickey Rooney the Devil, it wasn't so good. I also wrote a sequel to *The Shrinking Man* called (by Zugsmith) *The Fantastic Little Girl*. They thought of cashing in on the big receipts of *The Shrinking Man* and still had all the big sets and props. Never came to fruition. Probably better that it didn't. I also wrote a script [*Voyage to Lilliput*] based on [Jonathan Swift's] *Gulliver's Travels* in which a boy was Gulliver. Then, after *Around the World in 80 Days* [1956] was such a hit, I did—at Zugsmith's request—a long outline in which Gulliver was David Niven and a Lilliputian soldier was the guy who played Passepartout [Cantinflas]." *Call for Small*, also written for Zugsmith, was a television series idea about a tiny adventurer, based on *The Shrinking Man*.

Matheson reportedly fought to retain his credit on the film after a substantial rewrite by Hollywood veteran Lewis Meltzer, who contributed to *High School Confidential!* as well as Otto Preminger's *The Man with the Golden Arm* (1955); he apparently took no such action on *The Private Lives of Adam and Eve* (credited to writer Robert Hill). Discussing the latter with *Femme Fatales'* Dan Scapperotti, Van Doren noted that Zugsmith "was famous for getting all the beautiful women in Hollywood in his movies. He was always a step ahead of everyone and he was always having problems getting the seal of approval [from] the Catholic Church and the Legion of Decency.... You have no idea what women went through. It just wasn't fair. Every time I did a scene that had an evening gown or something a little bit revealing, I had somebody from the Hays Office standing there looking [on] to see if everything was all right. It was ludicrous." In a separate *Femme Fatales* interview, Van Doren told Marc Shapiro that, having recently been separated from Anthony, she immediately hit it off with Steve Cochran. "The first time I met Steve was in the very first scene I had with him. It was a scene where I opened the door and he was standing there with this gun in his hand and I was like 'Oh my God!' He was so mean-looking and so sexy. He just bowled me over. We didn't have to do or say a thing. We just looked at each other and that was it. We started dating immediately. In fact, we were all over each other on the set."

Ten years after making her film debut here, Regina Carrol (*née* Gelfan) appeared in *Satan's Sadists* (aka *Nightmare Bloodbath*, 1969), which began a long collaboration with another notorious exploitation filmmaker, Al Adamson, encompassing a dozen films and a twenty-year marriage ended by her death of cancer in 1992. In David Konow's *Schlock-O-Rama: The Films of Al Adamson*, Regina said of her unbilled role in *The Beat Generation* as a dancer with several lines, "We wore a lot of black clothes and looked and acted real tough.... The movie set is like a temple for me and the director is God. I wait for direction, to reach inside the depths of myself. I truly enjoy acting, the feelings that you touch upon. Trying to bring out all the truth and beauty and to share that with an audience." Carrol presumably had to dig deeply to find the "truth and beauty" in the likes of Adamson's *Dracula vs. Frankenstein* (1971), *Brain of Blood*, *Blood of Ghastly Horror* (both 1972), *Black Heat*, and *Blazing Stewardesses* (both 1975).

The Twilight Zone (1959-1964)

"Early in 1959," Matheson wrote in his introduction to the anthology *The Twilight Zone: The Original Stories*, "Charles (Chuck) Beaumont and I were invited to see the pilot film ['Where Is Everybody?'] for a new CBS series to be entitled *The Twilight Zone*. Chuck and I were, naturally, aware of Rod Serling and his outstanding writing accomplishments in television ('Patterns,' 'Requiem for a Heavyweight,' etc.). What we didn't know was how very nice a man he was and how pleasant it was going to be to work with him and his producers for the next five years, first Buck Houghton, then Herb Hirschman, then Bert Granet. And what we could not possibly have foreseen was how successful the show was going to be, what a cult phenomenon it was destined to become." Conspicuously absent from Matheson's list of pleasant producers is William Froug, who succeeded Granet during the show's fifth and final season and was, to say the least, not simpatico with Matheson, Beaumont *et al.*, canceling a number of teleplays — already approved by Granet — that they had completed or were in the process of developing.

Among these was Matheson's "The Doll." "I think I wrote it for Bert Granet," he recalled in an interview with me for *Filmfax*, "and then Bill Froug, the producer who took over, didn't like my writing. As a matter of fact, when I was collaborating with Chuck Beaumont, I made the mistake of saying, because I didn't like to go out, 'I'll do the first drafts, and you go out and do the office meetings.' So because of that, everybody got the impression that I was like the retarded country cousin he was supporting out in the sticks. And Froug, the producer who we did *Philip Marlowe* for, was totally convinced of that. Anyway, he didn't like my *Twilight Zone* script at all." Another Group member and frequent *Twilight Zone* contributor, George Clayton Johnson, also ran afoul of the new regime when at Froug's behest his teleplay "Tick of Time," which he had adapted from his story "The Grandfather Clock" (later published in Johnson's collection of *Twilight Zone Scripts and Stories*), was drastically rewritten by Richard DeRoy as "Ninety Years Without Slumbering" (12/20/63). "The Doll" was finally produced, twenty years later, as an Emmy-winning episode of *Amazing Stories*.

Froug's dubious legacy notwithstanding, Matheson's work as one of the principal *Twilight Zone* writers ranks collectively among his finest. When Serling won a then-unprecedented fifth Emmy Award for Outstanding Writing Achievement in Drama on May 16, 1961, he expressed his thanks to "three writing gremlins who did the bulk of the work: Charles Beaumont, Richard Matheson, and George Clayton Johnson." That was Serling's second Emmy for the series in as many seasons; his widow, Carol, recalled in her preface to *The Original Stories* that upon receiving the first he had told Matheson and Beaumont, "Come on over, fellas, we'll carve it up like a turkey." Yet while Beaumont is cited as second only to Serling in the number of scripts he wrote for the series, many of the twenty-two episodes credited to him were the result of an unusual arrangement that postdated his early collaborations with Matheson. Teleplays for various shows (e.g., *Naked City*, *Route 66*) were ghostwritten, co-written and/or based on unpublished original material by such friends and fellow fantasy writers as Johnson, Jerry Sohl, and John Tomerlin.

As Johnson told me in an interview for *Filmfax*, "Beaumont had a very strange group of friends, and each one of his friends had his own kind of power, but a number of them, like OCee Ritch or Bill Idelson [who had a small role in Matheson's episode 'A World of Difference'], contributed material to *The Twilight Zone* pseudonymously. At the same time, Beaumont was submitting a script to *Wanted: Dead or Alive*, the Steve McQueen series, 'Angels of Vengeance' [4/18/59], which they bought and made. It has an original script by me, which Beaumont rewrites based upon a discussion between the two of us, with Beaumont taking the credit and collecting the money and giving me, I think at the time, $600, which was an enormous sum to me, for being the first-draft guy on that and not taking the credit.

Anything to try to get some writing done, to get some experience, to get things sold, not to fight for these credits, to understand the business, to be willing to make a deal and stick with the deal.... As I watched Beaumont, I could understand how an office sort of worked if you were a writer." Johnson later made the same arrangement on the *Twilight Zone* episode "The Prime Mover" (3/24/61).

Sohl (who died at the age of eighty-eight on November 4, 2002) was one of the Group members to pay Beaumont tribute in the latter's *Selected Stories*, edited by Roger Anker and later reissued as *The Howling Man*: "Chuck was the kind of person who could go in [to see a producer] and absolutely flabbergast you. He'd do what you'd call 'Blue Sky'—he'd pitch this story and no one would say that's no good, because they'd be so fascinated with Chuck. He had this ability to absolutely overpower you with what it was that he was doing. The trouble with most writers is that they may be good writers, but they can't sell themselves in television. Chuck Beaumont was able to do both; plus he could deliver the goods when the chips were down." But, as Bradbury added, "He overloaded himself; then had to farm the extra work out to his friends. I think there's a similarity here to Rod Serling—Rod could never resist temptation. In other words, you've been neglected a good part of your life and no one is paying attention to you, and all of a sudden, people *are* paying attention: They're offering you jobs here and there. And the temptation is: Jeez! I never had anything. I better take that because it may not last!"

Matheson told Marc Scott Zicree in *The Twilight Zone Companion* that Beaumont "was my best friend for many years. We wrote together for a period of time when we first went into television (until we decided that we would do better each going solo) and acted as 'spurs' to each other creatively. I had sold my first collection of short stories [*Born of Man and Woman*] before Chuck, which spurred him on to get his first collection [*The Hunger and Other Stories*]. We both wrote 'mainstream' novels about the same time [*The Beardless Warriors* and *The Intruder*, respectively]. We both went into TV at the same time. We both wrote films in the same period of time. There was competition but only of the friendliest sort." He added in an interview with me for *Filmfax* that they "had a similar take on fantasy, I think. It's been mentioned before, but I never made any social commentary in my *Twilight Zones*. They were all just stories and character studies, whereas very often [Serling's] had a social commentary, and I don't think Chuck Beaumont did that, either. I think his were just plain stories, too, because when we were in print, with the stories we wrote for magazines, that's what they were.

"[Beaumont and I] were both already well established in the magazine field, we knew how to write that kind of story, and we were very adaptable. We could fit the *Twilight Zone* pattern almost instantly, which as I've said many times was a very specific pattern. The pattern is: a teaser that gets your interest, and then Rod making a comment, and then your first act with a cliffhanger, and then to your ending, which hopefully has a surprise.... Once, [writer-producer-director] Dan Curtis [a longtime television collaborator of Matheson's] and I were going to do an anthology series, and I got boxes—I think I still have them somewhere—of *The Magazine of Fantasy and Science Fiction* and found, I would say, zilch stories that fit that pattern. Most of them don't. Most of them just sort of start out gradually. You know, very often it's like, 'I met this man on a train, and he told me a story about how his Uncle Dudley had something horrible happen to him,' and the last line is, 'And there was Uncle Dudley with a moth's face,' or something. But they didn't do that approach, where you just [start off with a] bang, and I didn't do it either. You have a little more time when you're writing a short story."

In an interview with me for *Outré*, Ray Bradbury noted, "I knew Rod Serling for many years before he started his series. He came over to the house back in the late '50s, and he told me he was going to have his own TV series. I said, 'Well, if you're going to have a TV series, you'd better bone up on all the best fantasy writers.' So I gave him copies of books by Roald Dahl and John Collier, Richard Matheson, Charles Beaumont, and some of my own books, of course. I said, 'Read these and you'll know what the field of fantasy and science fiction is like, hunh?' So he read all these books, and he hired some of the writers, or if he didn't hire them he bought the story rights to some of the short stories, and started his series." Bradbury was hired to adapt his story "I Sing the Body Electric!" during the program's third season, but after inviting his closest friends over to his home to watch the broadcast, he was shocked to find a crucial scene missing. To make matters worse, a second teleplay he had written for Serling, based on his story "Here There Be Tygers" (which he later adapted as a 1990 episode of his own anthology series, *The Ray Bradbury Theater*), was ultimately unproduced.

As Carol Serling recalled in *The Original Stories*, "Rod Serling freely admitted that he was unabashedly a great devotee of tales of horror, fantasy, and the supernatural. He grew up reading Poe and Lovecraft, so that when CBS gave him the green light to the new series— *The Twilight Zone*— he sought out the master fantasy storytellers of his day.... It was only natural that Rod would turn to Beaumont, who, as someone once said, actually lived in the Twilight Zone. Chuck, in his enthusiasm at the time, said that if the series was successful, 'the dream of every green-blooded fan would come true and for the first time we'll have decent science fiction and fantasy available on a regular basis.' And natural, too, that Rod would call upon Matheson, a writer of great variety and strong plots whose excursions in the genre were well known. [Richard] remembers his years of working on the series as some of the most enjoyable writing assignments of his career. Each man's work was different, but the chemistry was right and from this alliance came one of the most successful and creative series ever to hit television." The show's enduring reputation after many decades certainly bears out this assessment.

"What keeps *The Twilight Zone* so popular, of course, are the stories," Matheson added. "The concepts, which intrigue and excite and amuse and terrify and half a dozen other wonderful emotions. The story was all in *The Twilight Zone*." Of the fourteen teleplays collected in *Richard Matheson's* The Twilight Zone *Scripts* (1998), edited by Stanley Wiater, six were based on his published short stories, as were two additional early episodes adapted by Serling from his work: "And When the Sky Was Opened" (based on Matheson's story "Disappearing Act") and "Third from the Sun." "How did I, personally, feel about the transition of my stories from prose to film?" he continued in *The Original Stories*. "My favorites, in general order of preference, are 'Steel,' 'Death Ship,' 'Nightmare at 20,000 Feet,' 'Night Call,' 'Little Girl Lost,' 'Mute,' then the two Rod adapted. Pure ego at work on these last two, although I certainly appreciate the problem Rod faced in expanding what is essentially a short-short story ('Third from the Sun') into a full half-hour program; and, as a matter of fact, 'Disappearing Act' was not really adapted at all, only the smallest aspect of its premise being used [for the teleplay]."

"[Serling] may have bought the stories before I even saw the pilot," Matheson told Wiater.

But I think that if I had known I was going to be working on the show, I would have tried to do the scripts myself. At the time he was starting out, I knew he was reading through a massive amount of material. He must have picked out those two stories. I'm just guessing, but maybe that was why Chuck Beaumont and I were called in to look at the pilot. To see if we could do original scripts as well.... I believe Rod had in mind — as I believe Gene Roddenberry had in mind later with *Star Trek* [to which Matheson and many of his friends also contributed scripts] — to use all the top writers in the fantasy and science fiction field to write for the show. And in both cases, as I understand it, they didn't have much success in that area. There were only a few people who ever worked out.... Beaumont and I were very visual writers [and] wrote stories that tried to grab the reader immediately. Which fit into the *Twilight Zone* pattern of having that little teaser at the beginning. Our stories usually had a surprise ending. If not, they had an ironic ending that was still completely appropriate for *The Twilight Zone*.

Asked (in Sammon's *Midnight Graffiti* interview) about assertions that Serling was a plagiarist, he said, "When I started writing ... all these science fiction magazines were around, and I started reading them and every anthology I could get a hold of. Naturally, when I later started to write some stories, I would start repeating some of the things that I had just trash-loaded my mind with. And Serling was not familiar, that I know of, with fantasy and science fiction at all when he started the series. So he had to read all of this stuff to get himself familiarized with the whole area. And I think, because of that, you just unconsciously start repeating themes and ideas. And the demand on him for scripts! I mean, Chuck Beaumont and I wrote quite a few, but out of hundreds of *Twilight Zone*s Rod Serling wrote most of them.... I don't think he ever took anything that wasn't his, deliberately. I can say that because he once did a script, and I called to their attention that it was an idea I had submitted to them. And he felt terrible about it, and they paid me some money. To my knowledge, I was the only one they ever paid like that. Because he didn't want me to feel that he had taken my idea."

Matheson closed his introduction to *The Original Stories* by recalling "Rod Serling and my good friend Charles Beaumont. Rod, as noted, could not have been a nicer man. To me, he was always kind and thoughtful, supportive, helpful, and a joy to know and work with — not to mention his awesome talent. And Chuck Beaumont was a scintillating light in my existence during his all-too-brief a span. Funny, charming, a challenging delight to be with — and also an awesome talent. I miss him. I miss his lovely, wonderfully good-natured wife, Helen. I admire, to this moment, the talent and resourceful courage of their four children — Chris, Cathy, Elizabeth, and Greg [who died in 2002] — who were left, far too early, with the need to grow into maturity without their parents." Beaumont died on February 21, 1967, chronologically thirty-eight but aged prematurely by a degenerative condition (probably Alzheimer's or Pick's Disease); the frenzied juggling of projects that required so many ghostwriters was, in part, an effort to defray his enormous medical bills. Yet even in so brief a lifespan, Beaumont left a rich legacy on page and screen that has made him a true immortal in the fantasy genre.

In his foreword to *The Twilight Zone Scripts of Charles Beaumont, Volume One*, edited by Roger Anker, Matheson wrote that the ages of their respective children were "almost synchronous: Chris Beaumont with our Tina, Cathy Beaumont with our Richard, Elizabeth Beaumont with our Ali and Greg Beaumont with our Christian." Helen Beaumont suffered from cancer and outlived her husband by barely four years, leaving their youngest child an orphan at only seven. Added Matheson, "We were their foster parents for a while. Actually, we were talking about the possibility of the four of them coming to live with us. We had four children already and it seemed like a tremendous undertaking, because suddenly we were going to have to rush and build extra rooms and everything. Later, they chose to stay in their house in North Hollywood, with us overseeing it. Through all of this, Chris was a total wonder. At his age — in his late teens — he was unbelievable; the guy has lived three lifetimes of responsibility." The story of Chris's struggle to obtain guardianship of his siblings was fictionalized in Randal Kleiser's telefilm *All Together Now* (1975), to the script of which Matheson made uncredited revisions.

A veteran of the series *Buck Rogers in the 25th Century* and *Wonder Woman*, Alan Brennert served as the executive story consultant and was a frequent contributor to the mid–1980s *Twilight Zone* revival; he noted in his introduction to *New Stories from the Twilight Zone*, edited by Martin H. Greenberg, "What Serling was — in addition to being one of the greatest television writers of all time — was a canny producer who brought individuals with their own talents and visions into his playroom, and let them run loose. Over time the series seems to be a homogenous whole, but look closely and you'll see that there were at least three very distinct subgenres of *Twilight Zone* stories — humanistic parables like 'Eye of the Beholder' and 'Changing of the Guard,' most of them written by Serling; darker, moodier pieces like 'The Jungle' and 'Shadowplay [*sic*],' hallmarks of Beaumont's writing; and inventive, plot-driven stories which, as Marc Scott Zicree has put it, are so involving that you have to keep watching to find out *what happens next*, and those were and are the domain of Richard Matheson." The episodes are listed in order of production (according to Zicree).

"The Last Flight"

(February 5, 1960) DIRECTOR: William Claxton; PRODUCER: Buck Houghton; TELEPLAY: Matheson; MUSIC: stock [all cues composed by Bernard Herrmann]. CAST— Flight Lt. William Terrance Decker: Kenneth Haigh. Maj. Gen. George Harper: Alexander Scourby. Maj. Arthur Wilson: Simon Scott. Air Vice Marshal Alexander Mackaye: Robert Warwick. Corporal: Harry Raybould. Guard: Jerry Catron. Jeep Driver: Paul Baxley. Truck Driver: Jack Perkins. Stunt Pilot: Frank Gifford Tallman.

Directed by William Claxton, who made several low-budget Westerns and the genre film *Night of the Lepus* (1972), Matheson's first *Twilight Zone* teleplay — which was also one of his first solo script credits for any show — concerns Flight Lt. William Terrance Decker (Kenneth Haigh), Royal Flying Corps, who becomes lost while returning from a patrol over France in 1917. When Decker at last touches down after flying through a strange white cloud, he is still in France but inexplicably finds himself at an American air base in 1959. Placed in custody, he learns that Mackaye, a comrade whom he believed was killed in action because of his (Decker's) cowardice, survived to become an air vice marshal and is due at the same air base for an inspection that very day. Realizing that Mackaye must have survived through his own intervention, and that his strange odyssey through time has given him a second chance to prove his courage, Decker breaks free and takes off again in an effort to save Mackaye, a task which the Americans learn he completed at the cost of his life when the marshal (Robert Warwick) arrives and recalls the noble sacrifice of his downed colleague.

The first non–Serling script produced, "The Last Flight" was pitched to Serling and Houghton in a single sentence. Its multi-leveled initial title was "Flight"; similarly, as Martin Grams, Jr., notes in *The Twilight Zone: Unlocking the Door to a Television Classic*, Matheson's teleplays "Young Man's Fancy" and "Spur of the Moment" were previously called "The House" and "Pale Rider," respectively. "Night Call" was originally entitled "Long Distance Call," as was the short story from which Matheson adapted it (which, in turn, was originally published without his preferred title as "Sorry, Right Number" in the November 1953 issue of *Beyond Fantasy Fiction*), but that obviously had to be changed because of the second-season episode "Long Distance Call" (3/31/61), written by Beaumont and William Idelson.

Matheson's "In the Nick of Time" was later shortened to "Nick of Time," while in perhaps the most complex of these titular round-robins, Serling's script "And When the Sky Was Opened" began life as "The Aftermath" before reverting to Matheson's original title, "Disappearing Act," during production, and then was copyrighted as "When the Sky Was Opened" (minus the "And") the day before it debuted.

The plagiarism issue dogged *The Twilight Zone*, leading to a series of letters (excerpted by Grams) in which Serling cited two of Matheson's works as examples of innocently repeated themes. "Disappearing Act," he said, was strikingly similar to Philip MacDonald's story "Private — Keep Out!" (which Serling misidentified as "No Trespassing"), a debt that Matheson readily acknowledges, while "Flight," according to Serling, was "down-the-line almost a twin" to "One for the Book," written and directed by *Lights Out* creator Wyllis Cooper in 1948 for his radio series *Quiet, Please!* Serling also alluded to lawsuits directed at Beaumont, Matheson, and Johnson based on material they had written for the show. On a related note, radio legend Arch Oboler threatened legal action over alleged similarities between Matheson's 1971 TV-movie *Duel* and his 1942 *Lights Out* script "What the Devil?" (which Oboler adapted into an unproduced *Twilight Zone* teleplay in 1963). "He claimed that when I was a child, I had heard [his] radio program ... in which the guy is chased by a car, which the Devil is driving. His contention was that it lingered in my memory all those years," Matheson told me in 2008.

"And When the Sky Was Opened"

(December 11, 1959) DIRECTOR: Douglas Heyes; PRODUCER: Buck Houghton; TELEPLAY: Rod Serling, based on Matheson's "Disappearing Act"; MUSIC: Leonard Rosenman. CAST — Lt. Col. Clegg Forbes: Rod Taylor. Maj. William Gart: Jim Hutton. Col. Ed Harrington: Charles Aidman. Amy Riker: Maxine Cooper. Bartender: Paul Bryar. Nurse: Sue Randall. Medical Officer: Joe Bassett. Girl in Bar: Gloria Pall. Investigator: Logan Field. Officer: Oliver McGowan. Mr. Harrington: S. John Launer. Nurse Two: Elizabeth Fielding.

As Matheson stated, little remained in this teleplay beyond the basic premise of "Disappearing Act," his tale of an aspiring novelist whose acquaintances and very identity begin to vanish piece by piece (presented as entries from a school notebook found next to a half-finished cup of coffee in a Brooklyn candy store). In the three-volume Edge Books edition of his *Collected Stories,* Matheson provided editor Stanley Wiater with a brief commentary for each, noting that this one was inspired by "Private — Keep Out!" (published in the first issue of *The Magazine of Fantasy*, then minus the "and Science Fiction," and in Fletcher Pratt's 1951 anthology *World of Wonder*). MacDonald's story "was about a guy in a restaurant, and some stranger comes up to him and tells him his identity has been lost, and all he has now is a few scraps of papers and photographs to prove that he really had an existence. And I think it ends when the guy goes to the restroom, he comes back and the man has disappeared. So my story was without a doubt a similar idea. And I love that last sentence [his ends, "I'm having a cup of cof"] — it came to me as I wrote it. And I burst out laughing, because I thought it was so perfect."

He added in an interview with me for *Filmfax*, "Actually, ["Disappearing Act" and "Third from the Sun"] are the only two stories I sold them for many years, because I wanted to just do original [teleplays] and hold onto my stories, and then later on I sold some of the stories, because all my early [scripts], if you notice, are originals.... [Serling's "Third from the Sun"] was okay. That was closer to my story. I mean, it was a very short short story. They had to expand it.... [It was first published] in *Galaxy Science Fiction*. I got all of fifty dollars for it. I was thrilled. I remember walking on Third Avenue with a friend of mine, and he just couldn't believe it. 'Fifty dollars for a short story! Whoa!'" One of several stories in which Matheson's protagonist is a desperately struggling writer, "Disappearing Act" may have seemed quite close to home when it debuted in *Fantasy and Science Fiction* in March of 1953, the same year its fledgling author's own first novel and first son would appear. "I think if it was filmed as written, it would be great ... [but] there was no point [in trying to adapt it personally], because I didn't own it. I sold the story to *The Twilight Zone*. I would have liked to [write the script myself]."

Serling's script concerns the crew of the experimental interceptor X-20, which disappears from the screen for twenty-four hours during a space flight. While Lt. Col. Clegg Forbes (Rod Taylor) and Maj. William Gart (Jim Hutton) survive a crash-landing in the Mojave Desert, Forbes insists that the two were accompanied by his best friend, Col. Ed Harrington, of whom Gart denies any knowledge. Forbes relates that after calling his parents and having them deny his very existence, like some ill-fated George Bailey in an SF version of *It's a Wonderful Life* (1946), Harrington (Charles Aidman) vanished from the bar where they were sharing a beer, and now Forbes can find no evidence that he ever lived, or anyone who remembers him, including Forbes's puzzled girlfriend Amy Riker (Maxine Cooper). Australian-born Taylor, who later appeared in the thriller *36 Hours* (1964) and such genre films as George Pal's *The Time Machine* (1960) and Alfred Hitchcock's *The Birds* (1963), is suitably intense as Harrington's theory—that they were not meant to return from the flight—is borne out with grim inevitability, their front-page newspaper photograph altering as each astronaut fades away, one by one.

First-time *Twilight Zone* director Douglas Heyes, whose subsequent episodes include Matheson's "The Invaders," later wrote and directed films ranging from the notorious *Kitten with a Whip* (1964) to the critically panned 1966 version of *Beau Geste*, and created the short-lived William Shatner series *Barbary Coast*, which ran on ABC during the 1975–76 season. Serling and Houghton "both were extremely encouraging as to finding unusual and new ways to do things," Heyes told Zicree. "They didn't say, 'Stick to the script,' to me or to any director. They'd say, 'Think of something to make it *Twilight Zone*, to make it unusual.' ... Originally, [Taylor's] disappearance or the feeling that he was going was written as a very painful experience, but I decided to make it a very *euphoric* experience. Instead of playing it for terror or agony—everything had been fear up till then, fear of disappearance, fear of the unknown, and so forth—I said to Rod Taylor, 'Let's play this as if this is the most marvelous thing that ever happened.' We took an angle on him and we lowered the camera as he was talking, so the effect was that he seemed to be rising while he was talking [with Maj. Gart]."

Much has been made of the extraordinary roster of actors and directors whose work brought the *Twilight Zone* scripts to life, but another key contribution came from the show's crisp, atmospheric photography, which when seen in all its glory in the uncut clarity of DVD is impressive indeed. George T. Clemens, who photographed this episode and all but one of Matheson's own teleplays for the first three seasons (the exception was "A World of Difference," shot by Harkness Smith), won an Emmy Award for Outstanding Achievement in Cinematography for Television for his work on the series in 1961; he also received nominations in 1962 and 1963, sharing the latter with Robert W. Pittack. Both had been working in Hollywood since the early 1930s, and Pittack—previously nominated in 1956 for the Ann Sothern series *Private Secretary*, and again in 1957 for "The Glorious Gift of Molly

Malloy" (9/23/56), an episode of *General Electric Theater*— photographed all of Matheson's scripts for the fourth and fifth seasons of *The Twilight Zone*, except for "Steel," which was also shot by Clemens.

In *As Timeless as Infinity: The Complete Twilight Zone Scripts of Rod Serling, Volume One*, the show's associate producer, Del Reisman, related to editor Tony Albarella, "George was just marvelous. He had a sense of an 'other world' kind of situation, particularly in lighting. You always felt you were in another part of the forest. You were somewhere else. He was brilliant. He was very tough on the set, by the way. He was a real, wonderful veteran cameraman — as they were called in those days, a cameraman — and he knew what could be done. He knew the time that it would take to set up and light. He knew what his schedule was and Buck was very strong on scheduling. Clemens was really a great strength on the set. He had a wonderful combination of old moviemaking savvy and art." Before turning to television, Clemens began his 20-year career in feature films as an uncredited camera operator on *Dr. Jekyll and Mr. Hyde* (1931) and, according to Albarella, he came out of retirement to photograph the lion's share of *The Twilight Zone*'s 156 episodes. After working on one more series, *Twelve O'Clock High*, he retired for good, and died at the age of ninety in 1992.

Gauntlet publisher Barry Hoffman wrote a variation on "Disappearing Act" entitled "An Island Unto Himself" for *He Is Legend: An Anthology Celebrating Richard Matheson* (2009), a collection of prequels, sequels and other tales inspired by Matheson's work that was edited by Christoper Conlon. The original story was also used, uncredited, as the basis for "*O Acidente*," an episode of the Brazilian anthology film *O Impossível Acontece* (aka *Believe It or Not*, 1969) that was written, produced, and directed by Rio-born C. Adolpho Chadler (aka Cícero Adolpho Vitório da Costa Chadler), who also starred. The remaining two segments of this Portuguese-language film were produced by Daniel Filho, who also directed one of them, "*Eu, Ela e o Outro*" (which he wrote with Gilvan Pereira), while the third, "*O Reimplante*," was written and directed by Anselmo Duarte. "I'd never heard of that," a surprised Matheson responded when he was told about Chadler's unauthorized version, which appears to be unavailable in English. "I'll have to tell my agent — they probably cheated me out of some money. Hell, all I could get out of that would be a cup of coffee, probably," he joked in *Filmfax*.

"Third from the Sun"

(January 8, 1960) DIRECTOR: Richard L. Bare; PRODUCER: Buck Houghton; TELEPLAY: Rod Serling, based on Matheson's story; MUSIC: stock. Cast — William Sturka: Fritz Weaver. Carling: Edward Andrews. Jerry Riden: Joe Maross. Jody Sturka: Denise Alexander. Eve Sturka: Lori March. Ann Riden: Jeanne Evans. Guard: Will J. White. Loudspeaker Voice: S. John Launer.

Clocking in at fewer than ten pages, and reflecting Cold War anxieties, Matheson's second published story, "Third from the Sun," appeared in the October 1950 issue of *Galaxy*. It is rigorously nonspecific in its details as it depicts a pair of families fleeing their world in an unauthorized space flight, hoping to preserve "the future of life itself" by avoiding a global war that they think is inevitable. Its twist ending, subsequently done to death in SF films such as *Voyage to the End of the Universe* (the English-language version of Czechoslovakian writer-director Jindrich Polák's *Ikarie XB 1*, 1963) and Mario Bava's *Terrore nello Spazio* (Terror in Space, aka *Planet of the Vampires*, 1965), reveals their destination to be a small planet near a moon, "third from the sun" (i.e., Earth), in another solar system. Serling's teleplay admirably expands the story, both backtracking from Matheson's minimalist original, by showing more of the preparations prior to the spacecraft's departure, and increasing the tension, by pushing up the time frame from an apocalyptic conflict that is envisioned within a few years to one that is expected in a mere forty-eight hours, on what Serling's opening narration calls "the eve of the end."

Shot by Oscar-nominated veteran Harry Wild with off-kilter camera angles, the episode follows scientist William Sturka (Fritz Weaver) as he plots the eleven-million-mile flight — whose destination Serling spells out more overtly than Matheson — with his friend, pilot Jerry Riden (Joe Maross), and reveals the plan to his wife and daughter (soap stars Lori March and Denise Alexander, respectively). Serling adds an extra element of suspense in the form of Carling (well played by ubiquitous character actor Edward Andrews), an oily government stooge who gets wind of the plan and begins a sadistic game of cat-and-mouse with the nervous conspirators, intercepting them at gunpoint as they are about to board the spacecraft. They subdue him to prevent him from turning them over to the authorities. Unlike many neophyte *Twilight Zone* directors, Richard L. Bare (who cast his wife, Jeanne Evans, as Riden's wife, Ann) had already established himself with such feature films as the crime dramas *Smart Girls Don't Talk* and *Flaxy Martin* (both 1948) and the Western *Return of the Frontiersman* (1950) before segueing into television. Bare went on to direct Matheson's "Nick of Time" in the second season.

Matheson modestly recalled the creation of "Third from the Sun" in his *Collected Stories* commentary for Stanley Wiater: "I had just gotten out of college, and I was living at home with my mother. I used to go to the YMCA in downtown Brooklyn to swim. And I would sit in their library to write. On this particular day I had one big piece of yellow paper. I wrote real small. I did the entire story on both sides of this one sheet of paper. I thought it was such a clever idea — little did I know because I had never written 'science fiction' and knew nothing about it. Of course it wasn't clever at all." In the story, both couples conveniently have one child of each gender, but by establishing that their destination is already inhabited, Serling sidesteps the issue of the need to propagate the species once they have arrived, and makes the Ridens childless. Story and script both include the nice human detail of having characters comment on the absurdity of cleaning up dishes and locking doors in houses to which they know full well they will never return. Although the car in which they ostensibly travel to the ship is obviously sitting inside a soundstage, the episode is otherwise visually impressive.

In *As Timeless as Infinity*, Bare recalled, "[T]he objective in the scenes that led up to the climax was to avoid betraying Serling's secret that we were actually watching members of another planet preparing to come to ours. It was decided to use conventional-looking, -acting and -sounding players, living in conventional Earth-like surroundings; but they would be treated differently with the camera. I ordered the widest-angle lens that Metro-Goldwyn-Mayer Studios had, a 17.5mm 'bug eye.' I told [Wild] that I wanted this lens used exclusively, even on the close-ups. I explained I wanted the distortion that this lens gave everything and suggested that [he] work out unorthodox sources for the lighting, sources that would bring an unusual aura to the film. In addition to this, every camera setup was cocked to one side or the other, which further served to take away the feeling of normalcy. What I was striving to do was protect Serling's surprise ending and yet give the feeling of oddness so that when the picture was over, the audience would understand why the 'kooky' camera treatment was used." In one scene, a card game is shot first in a 360-degree pan atop a glass table, and then upward through it.

Fritz Weaver told Albarella that this "was my first film ever, of any kind. I didn't know a thing about it. I had some small success on the stage that year and I guess the casting people paid attention, dumb luck for me. In my naiveté, I thought all filming was going to be like that: wild, improvisational, with imaginative texts that took you out of the ordinary. Alas, it did not turn out that way." Added co-star Alexander, "Doing the show as an actor was great fun. The cast was all so caring about the project. We took great pleasure in the twist at the end of the tale, and felt we were making something truly unique that would engage the audience.... I loved watching *The Twilight Zone* as a kid but I had no idea how big the audience was, how well-regarded the show was in our profession and the extent to which it was lauded. 'Third from the Sun' was such a terrific show and everyone I knew loved it, so to be a part of it was a thrill. As I matured, I became more and more proud to have been in that episode." In *Danse Macabre*, Stephen King calls this "the episode which marks the point at which many occasional tuners-in became addicts. Here, for once, was something Completely New and Different."

"A World of Difference"

(March 11, 1960) DIRECTOR: Ted Post; PRODUCER: Buck Houghton; TELEPLAY: Matheson; MUSIC: [Nathan] Van Cleave. CAST—Arthur Curtis, Gerald Raigan: Howard Duff. Brinkley: David White. Marty Fisher: Frank Maxwell. Nora Raigan: Eileen Ryan. Sally Phillips: Gail Kobe. Sam Endicott: Peter Walker. Marian: Susan Dorn. Kelly: William Idelson. Film Technician: Joe Norden. Silent Bit Parts: Chester Brandenburg, Beryl McCutcheon, Jerry Schumacher.

Matheson's next *Twilight Zone* effort was directed by Ted Post, who went on to work with his former *Rawhide* colleague, Clint Eastwood, on the big screen in *Hang 'Em High* (1968) and *Magnum Force* (1973), and whose genre credits also include *Beneath the Planet of the Apes* and the TV-movie *Night Slaves* (both 1970), the latter based upon the novel by Matheson's friend, Jerry Sohl. Like many of the best *Twilight Zone* episodes, and indeed much of Matheson's best work, its premise is deceptively simple: When businessman Arthur Curtis (Howard Duff) is inexplicably unable to make a telephone call from his office, he suddenly hears a voice behind him call out, "Cut!," and turns around to find himself on a movie set, being addressed by director Marty Fisher (Frank Maxwell) as "Gerry." Matheson keeps the viewer off-balance: Has a flesh-and-blood Arthur Curtis been wrenched into a new reality, or has an actor named Gerald Raigan fled from an unhappy marriage by slipping completely into his role as Curtis? Duff escapes back to *The Private World of Arthur Curtis* just as its set is being struck, while in another reality, the perennially beleaguered Gerry Raigan has vanished forever.

Matheson's introduction to his *Collected Stories* offers a parallel: "I found personal escape in writing. Instead of imbibing drink [as his father, Bertolf, had], I imbibed stories: became addicted to fiction. Instead of turning to religion [as his mother, Fanny, had] I turned to fantasy. In the Freudian sense, the manifestation of my escape was fantasy itself; a re-structuring of the world into more acceptable form. The creating of a new world of imagination in which I could work out any and all troubles. A therapeutic battlefield on which I could confront my enemies (my anxieties) and — in relative safety — deal with them in socially acceptable ways. In this manner, was I able to prevent this paranoia from damaging my personal life by releasing it, in safe bursts, through my stories. Writing into existence a many-layered realm of fantasies — most of them fear-oriented — then sealing it off from my private world. To use a simile: the vessel contained excess steam — I discovered an outlet by which to release that steam — the vessel did not rupture but prevailed." So what Gerry literally did, creating a world of his own to escape a threatening life, Matheson metaphorically did, to ease the pressures of his.

Beaumont's third-season teleplay "Person or Persons Unknown" (3/23/62), in which a man awakens to find that no one close to him knows him and all evidence of his existence has vanished, is a variation on the same concept. According to Martin Grams, Jr., Matheson's episode was spoofed on episodes of such shows as *Saturday Night Live*, *Mad About You*, and *Eerie, Indiana*. The creative use of a "wild" wall that could be removed while off-camera enabled Post to create an establishing shot that shows all four walls of Curtis's office, then pans over to the movie crew that is photographing Raigan. As the screenwriter told Stanley Wiater in *Richard Matheson's* The Twilight Zone *Scripts*, "I remember how the director had told me he arranged that special shot so that he could do it all in one camera movement. He had them move the wall away quietly so he could move the camera around and reveal all these people on the soundstage standing behind Howard Duff's character. I love ideas like that. It was a perfect *Twilight Zone* opening."

"A World of His Own"

(July 1, 1960) DIRECTOR: Ralph Nelson; PRODUCER: Buck Houghton; TELEPLAY: Matheson, based on his "And Now I'm Waiting" [uncredited]; MUSIC: stock. CAST— Gregory West: Keenan Wynn. Victoria West: Phyllis Kirk. Mary: Mary La Roche.

Matheson introduced an element of self-conscious whimsy with the last episode of the show's first season, in which "one of America's most noted playwrights," Gregory West (Keenan Wynn), discovers that he can bring characters to life by dictating descriptions of them into his tape recorder, and then banish them with equal ease by cutting off and throwing that section of tape into the fireplace. Interestingly, Matheson's consecutive and similarly titled *Twilight Zone* teleplays "A World of Difference" and "A World of His Own" both feature protagonists who create their own reality in order to escape from shrewish wives, but with diametrically opposite tones; in West's case, he finds solace by conjuring up the character of Mary (Mary La Roche), the warm and affectionate woman of his dreams. Director Ralph Nelson had won an Emmy Award for the *Playhouse 90* production of Serling's "Requiem for a Heavyweight" in 1956 and, after making his theatrical debut with the 1962 film version, went on to guide Sidney Poitier and Cliff Robertson through their Oscar-winning performances in *Lilies of the Field* (1963) — for which Nelson also received a nomination — and *Charly* (1968), respectively.

The waspish Mrs. Victoria West (Phyllis Kirk, who as Matheson told Wiater "fumbled around with" his dialogue, which was a rarity for the show) spies Mary through the window of her husband's office, but by the time she enters in a jealous rage her rival has vanished, and Victoria not surprisingly refuses to accept West's explanation of how his characters have gradually taken on a life of their own. She threatens to have him committed; when West produces an envelope containing the snippet of audiotape on which *she* appears, Victoria arrogantly tosses it into the fire and vanishes. Serling, in the first of his trademark on-camera appearances after having narrated all of the season's previous episodes, dismisses the story as "ridiculous nonsense," and West then banishes him as well! The father of screenwriter Tracy Keenan Wynn and the son of actor Ed Wynn — with whom he had worked in the small-screen "Requiem"— Wynn made a career out of such memorable character roles as a Shakespeare-promoting gangster in George Sidney's *Kiss Me Kate* (1953) and Colonel "Bat"

Guano in Stanley Kubrick's *Dr. Strangelove* (1964), and here plays the quiet, henpecked husband to perfection.

Matheson's original outline for this episode (based on his unpublished story "And Now I'm Waiting," which finally made its debut in the April 1983 issue of *Rod Serling's The Twilight Zone Magazine*, and concerned a writer who brings his characters to life with tragic results) was considered too dark, so he redid the script in a lighter vein. He himself wrote an as-yet-unproduced mystery-suspense play, *Magician's Choice*, in the 1970s and later revised it into his novel *Now You See It....* "We were on the very verge of [a Broadway] production," he told Mark Rathbun. "We had as director Robert Altman, we had a cast of Jack Palance and Susannah York and Paul Dooley — and then Altman had a play on Broadway, *Come Back to the Five and Dime, Jimmy Dean, Jimmy Dean*, and it got such horrendous reviews that we all panicked..."

Almost twenty years after its first appearance, "And Now I'm Waiting" finally saw publication in book form in Matheson's *Off Beat: Uncollected Stories* (2000), edited with an introduction and invaluable checklist by William F. Nolan. As with Rod Serling's loose adaptation of "Disappearing Act," little beyond the basic concept of conjuring characters into existence made the transition from page to screen. The narrator, David, arrives in response to an urgent summons from his sister, Mary, at the home she shares with her husband, an arrogant writer whom Matheson mischievously names "Richard," and who explains to David that the woman with whom Mary alleges he has been unfaithful is Alice, a character from his last novel come to life, although in this case, no Dictaphone is required to give her existence. Richard demonstrates his power to David by summoning Alice, sends her out of the room, and then conjures up a ten-foot cobra to dispose of Mary. Alice inadvertently becomes its victim instead. After David orders Mary to drive to safety, the remorseful Richard causes the house to burst into flame, forcing David — who realizes that he too is one of Richard's characters — to await a fiery fate with him.

"Nick of Time"

(November 18, 1960) DIRECTOR: Richard L. Bare; PRODUCER: Buck Houghton; TELEPLAY: Matheson; MUSIC: stock. CAST— Don S. Carter: William Shatner. Pat Carter: Patricia Breslin. Counter Man: Guy Wilkerson. Mechanic: Stafford Repp. Desperate Man: Walter Reed. Desperate Woman: Dee Carroll. Customer: Bob McCord.

A pre-*Star Trek* William Shatner plays Don S. Carter, a superstitious honeymooner stranded by car trouble in the little town of Ridgeview, Ohio, with his new bride Pat (Patricia Breslin). As they wait out the repairs in the Busy Bee Café, Don begins feeding pennies into the Mystic Seer, a fortune-telling machine sitting atop a napkin holder. After a phone call confirms its apparent prediction that he has secured a promotion, he becomes obsessed with the machine and convinced of its infallibility, unable to tear himself away until Pat at last convinces him that he controls his own fate. Matheson's simple yet thought-provoking script — considered one of his best in any medium — cleverly demonstrates how coincidence can make the vague prognostications of a cheap novelty seem unerringly accurate. It ends with a characteristic twist as another couple, "permanently enslaved by the tyranny of fear and superstition," takes their place, frantically asking the machine if they can leave Ridgeview.

Matheson, who has frequently praised the performances and chemistry of the two leads, recalled the episode's real-life origins in an interview with me for *Filmfax*. "My wife and I were in a coffee shop in the San Fernando Valley, and there was this little answer machine that answered yes or no.... And so I just thought, 'Oh, that's an interesting idea.'" Because the episode was conspicuously free of overt "action" or special effects, the acting and the direction by Richard L. Bare, previously of "Third from the Sun," were forced to fill the void and did so admirably, most notably with the repeated and effective close-ups of the bobbing, grinning devil's head atop the machine and with the trademark intensity of Shatner's performance. As he compulsively pumps penny after penny into the Mystic Seer, producing card after card with their cryptic yet (to him) crystal-clear messages, Don truly appears to be a man obsessed with his fate, while Pat's fears for his future and his sanity seem both amply justified and believably embodied by Breslin.

Matheson added to Wiater, "I also liked the way it didn't follow the basic premise of a typical *Twilight Zone* in terms of a teaser, and Rod saying, 'Something strange is going to happen...' It came on so gradually — Shatner's involvement with this fortune telling machine. It was so logical at first. Pat Breslin, the actress who played his wife, reacted just perfectly throughout. And it had a great little moral — and a real nice zapper at the end.... It had a happy ending only in the sense that the main protagonists have gotten away. Then you have this second couple ["desperate man and woman" Walter Reed and Dee Carroll] — you don't really know them — but they're a reminder that what has happened to them *could* have happened to our protagonists. If I have a choice, I'd prefer an ironic ending to an unhappy ending, but most of the time you end up with both. I think that's very common in fantasy, horror, and science fiction. You don't really give them a 'happy' ending. Nine out of ten of these kind of stories are going to have a dark or downbeat ending." Grams notes that this episode was alluded to in Shatner's guest appearance on *The Fresh Prince of Bel-Air*, "Eye, Tooth" (5/13/96).

"The Invaders"

(January 27, 1961) DIRECTOR: Douglas Heyes; PRODUCER: Buck Houghton; TELEPLAY: Matheson; MUSIC: Jerry Goldsmith. CAST — Woman: Agnes Moorehead. Voice of Astronaut: Douglas Heyes.

"The Invaders" was a *tour de force* for actress Agnes Moorehead, whom Orson Welles had successively recruited for his Mercury Theatre troupe; directed in *Citizen Kane* (1941) and *The Magnificent Ambersons* (1942), with Moorehead receiving the first of four Academy Award nominations for the latter film; and co-starred with in *Journey into Fear* (1942) and *Jane Eyre* (1944). Matheson's teleplay provided her with a non-speaking role at which very few actresses would probably have leaped: a poor, drab, and hungry old woman whose farmhouse is suddenly, and literally, shaken by the arrival of a diminutive flying saucer — actually one of the models from the oft-cannibalized classic *Forbidden Planet* (1956) — that crashes onto her roof, complete with its crew of tiny astronauts. Virtually the entire episode consists of her mute battle with these Lilliputian spacemen; one can see the seeds of Matheson's later short story "Prey" (memorably filmed in *Trilogy of Terror*) and its short-statured but relentlessly lethal Zuni doll, before the ending reveals the ship to be from Earth and the astronauts as normal-sized human beings facing a titanic, and ultimately triumphant, adversary.

Moorehead displays an impressive range of emotions as she matches wits with these tiny "invaders" — aptly compared to Michelin Tire Men in a conceptual drawing by director Douglas Heyes, reproduced in *As Timeless as Infinity* — from perplexity at the impact of the ship's arrival, to disbelief at finding it on the roof, to terror as its occupants shoot her with undersized, but clearly painful, ray guns. While obviously no mental giant despite her great size relative to the astronauts, even drooling open-mouthed at one point, she shows resourcefulness and tenacity as she topples, barricades, bludgeons, and burns her tormentors, eventually laying waste to their ship (which we then see is marked "U.S. Air Force Space Probe No. 1") with a kind of primitive hatchet and reducing it to smoldering wreckage. Ultimately, even though we have now learned that *she* is in fact the "monster," the episode leaves us in sympathy with this nameless woman, aided by the effective direction of Heyes and the anxiety-inducing strings of Jerry Goldsmith's taut score, and thus we share in her sense of triumph and relief when she realizes she has at last bested her alien foes, "the tiny beings from the tiny place called Earth."

While this is among his best-known *Twilight Zone* episodes, Matheson told me in an interview for *Filmfax*, "I would have liked it if ["The Invaders"] had gone faster. In that and the Buster Keaton thing ["Once Upon a Time"], I had a lot more material—more going on between her and these little critters because the opening I find, to this day, unbearably leisurely.... It takes forever before she hears the noise on the roof, and then it takes forever for her to get up there. I think [the opening] probably could have been cut in half, or by a third.... And I didn't like the little [spacemen], those little roly-poly things [manipulated and voiced by Heyes himself].... I had them appearing so—just flying past your eye or your attention. They had little space things that made them fly, and you would just see them and then they'd be gone. They weren't just wobbling around." With its twist ending similar to that in "Third from the Sun," it was important that the final revelation of the story's alien setting not be telegraphed, necessitating that the interiors of the cabin be as primitive and generic as possible.

"I remember Doug ... telling me that Agnes Moorehead wondered where her part was, because there was no dialogue," the screenwriter added in *Richard Matheson's* The Twilight Zone *Scripts*. "The reason the script contained no dialogue was because then you'd know she wasn't from Earth. But the original concept was to do a script without any dialogue. It's interesting to have a concept like that, and then to follow it to its conclusion. One of my first *Lawman* scripts was called 'Thirty Minutes.' And the entire story took place in thirty minutes." Matheson's *Collected Stories* commentary for "Prey" reveals that the episode's similarity to that story and its subsequent screen incarnation was not coincidental. "I had originally submitted the story—or at least a similar premise [then entitled "Devil Doll," according to Grams]—to *The Twilight Zone*. And they rejected it because they thought it was too grim. So I turned it around into a science fiction story—and it became 'The Invaders' ... because it's the same damn story—except here there's only one doll. Later on I wrote the premise as the short story called 'Prey' and *Playboy* bought it," he stated to Wiater.

"Young Man's Fancy"

(May 11, 1962) DIRECTOR: John Brahm; PRODUCER: Buck Houghton; TELEPLAY: Matheson; MUSIC: Nathan Scott. CAST—Virginia Laine Walker: Phyllis Thaxter. Alex Walker: Alex Nicol. Jim Wilkinson: Wallace Rooney. Henrietta Walker: Helen Brown. Alex (age 10): Rickey [*sic*] Kelman.

The first of Matheson's three third-season episodes to be produced, "Young Man's Fancy" opens as thirty-four-year-old Alex Walker (fortysomething Alex Nicol) and his bride of twenty minutes, the former Virginia Laine (Phyllis Thaxter), arrive at his late mother Henrietta's house to arrange for its sale before departing on their honeymoon. But after the realtor, Jim Wilkinson (Wallace Rooney), arrives, Alex announces that he wants to reconsider selling the house, which has remained unchanged for twenty-five years and is full of Henrietta's presence, including her ubiquitous photos, a broken radio playing her favorite song, "The Lady in Red," and appliances and furnishings that revert mysteriously to their antiquated counterparts. When the ghostly Henrietta (Helen Brown) finally appears and is confronted on the stairs by Virginia, who has been trying to wrest Alex from her grasp for twelve years, she sadly reveals that this return to the past is not her doing but that of her son. Alex reverts to his boyhood self (Rickey Kelman) while his defeated wife makes, as Serling's closing narration says, "a retreat back to reality."

German-born director John Brahm, whose English-language credits include the genre films *The Undying Monster* (1942) and *The Mad Magician* (1954), was reportedly hired by Houghton on the basis of two psychological thrillers starring Laird Cregar, *The Lodger* (1944) and *Hangover Square* (1945), and oversaw an even dozen *Twilight Zone* episodes, more than any other director. Despite Brahm's contribution, Matheson told me in an interview for *Filmfax*, "I liked all of that [one] until the last few minutes.... Alex Nicol could have been a little better, but Phyllis Thaxter was a wonderful actress.... Actually, you know, they should have upped [the character's] age [to match Nicol's]. It would have been a better point, that he had waited so long to marry. I never thought of that; it just struck me.... [The mother] looked more like Stella Dallas. She should have been scary-looking. You know, she's a ghost. It should have been like *The Uninvited* [1944]. I still get chills when I watch that."

In the prologue to *Richard Matheson's* The Twilight Zone *Scripts*, the screenwriter told Stanley Wiater of a long-standing dilemma:

> [W]hen I write a script, I see it *precisely* in my head. Then, when it appears on television or on the screen it couldn't possibly — or almost never — be exactly what I've seen in my brain. Once in a blue moon that happens, and then it's astonishing. But most of the time the results vary. As it would have to be — because other people are doing their work; interpreting your script in their own way. So very often I've had a sense of disappointment in what I saw. But then, after a while, I lose that feeling of "Well, it should reflect my script *exactly*." I begin to look at the collaborative effort for what it is, and then I begin to appreciate it more. Of course, the closer the finished episode came to what I originally visualized in mind, the more I liked it. But after that need to see my brainstorm directly reflected faded, then I could look at each episode on its own terms, and appreciate it for the values given to it by the other people involved.
>
> I have no distinct recollection of this story being inspired by something from my past.... [It] was just an interesting idea; sort of a dark version of trying to regain the child within you. This character literally regained the child within himself. This was what he wanted all along. In reality, you try to find a youthful aspect of yourself that can help you with your current life. But my character didn't want any of that; his current life was irrelevant and detestable to him, he just wanted to go back and be a kid all over again. Literally. And this kid was so selfish he brought back his own mother to be in on the process. No happy ending there.... When you get the premise of a story — if you tell it honestly — you know from the outset whether it's going to have a happy ending or not because you have to be true to it. Too often, characters go through horrendous situations in a given story, and suddenly at the very end they tack on a happy ending — and it's totally false. I don't write unhappy endings just for the sake of writing unhappy endings, but it's just they often go with the story; they stay true to the premise.

The dramatic limitations he cites admittedly place "Young Man's Fancy" among his lesser episodes.

"Once Upon a Time"

(December 15, 1961) DIRECTOR: Norman Z. McLeod, Les Goodwins [uncredited]; PRO-
DUCER: Buck Houghton; TELEPLAY: Matheson; MUSIC: William Lava. CAST—Woodrow
Mulligan: Buster Keaton. Prof. Rollo: Stanley Adams. Jack—Repair Man: Jesse White.
Prof. Gilbert: Milton Parsons. Clothing Store Manager: Warren Parker. Policeman in
1890: Gil Lamb. Policeman in 1962: James Flavin. Second Policeman in 1962: Harry
Fleer. Fenwick: George E. Stone. Men in Cars: Beau Anderson, Dave Armstrong, Jack
Clinton, Hank Faver, Jim Turley. Boy on Skates: Jim Crevoy. Utility Man in Car: Bob
McCord.

Having met legendary comedian Buster Keaton through his friend William R. Cox,
Matheson was inspired to try to get him into a *Twilight Zone* episode, a wish that was
fulfilled when Keaton made his only appearance on the show as "Woodrow Mulligan, a disgruntled citizen of Harmony, New York, 1890," employed as a janitor by Professor Gilbert
(Milton Parsons). Outraged by the noise, the high cost of living, and the bicycles racing
through the streets, Mulligan borrows Gilbert's newly invented time helmet, hoping to find
some peace and quiet, and travels to 1962 (at which point the footage shifts from silent to
sound). But the trends that horrified him have only intensified, and as his thirty-minute
window of opportunity to return dwindles, the helmet is damaged. He meets Rollo (Stanley
Adams), an electronics scientist and history buff who takes him to Jack's Fix-It Shop, but
once the proprietor (Jesse White) has repaired the helmet, they struggle for its possession
and are drawn back in time together. Woodrow is delighted to discover that Rollo is just
as disappointed with "barbaric" 1890 as he had been with 1962, and sends him safely back
into the future.

Matheson told Wiater, "I probably first mentioned the idea to the producers, and they
said, 'If you can get Keaton, sure.' I don't think I would have tried to get Keaton's interest
until I was sure that [they were] willing to do it. It had to have been that way, because the
script was designed for him." Certainly the presence of Keaton, reduced to the likes of
Pajama Party (1964), *Beach Blanket Bingo* and *How to Stuff a Wild Bikini* (both 1965) in
his last years, augured well for Matheson's second comic episode, as did that of Norman Z.
McLeod, whom Houghton recruited from semi-retirement. But while McLeod had directed
the Marx Brothers in *Monkey Business* (1931) and *Horse Feathers* (1932) and W.C. Fields in
It's a Gift (1934), Matheson was again disappointed when it came to seeing his work realized
on the screen. "I had so much *more* going on in the script. Though in this case I suspect the
budget would not allow all the situations to be filmed. I had an extended scene in a supermarket; I had him riding a bicycle through a car wash. All sorts of things. So they redid it."

"I don't know who wrote the scene in the repair shop [directed more than a month
later by an uncredited Les Goodwins], but it was just interminable, I thought." Noted
Grams, "In the initial draft, Rollo and Mulligan spend most of the 1962 scenes running
about in a food market, with Rollo making the adjustments and corrections during the
comedic scenes.... Rollo needed to purchase a replacement for a television tube, which was
installed on the helmet. The police officer who was spending time looking for Mulligan,
catches up to the time traveler in the store, and when Mulligan explains to Rollo that he
brought a chicken with him, just by holding it, Rollo disbelieves him and runs out of the
food market." After principal photography, the decision was made to print only two out of
every three frames in the 1890 sequences, thus giving them a jerky feel that evokes early
cinema, as does William Lava's piano score. The screenwriter added in *Richard Matheson's
The Twilight Zone Scripts*, "To go forward [in time] is pure science fiction, and it's just a

lot of technology. So it's interesting only in that light. Whereas, going *back* in time — immediately there are intense emotions involved with it."

"Little Girl Lost"

(March 16, 1962) DIRECTOR: Paul Stewart; PRODUCER: Buck Houghton; TELEPLAY: Matheson, based on his story; MUSIC: Bernard Herrmann. CAST— Ruth Miller: Sarah Marshall. Chris Miller: Robert Sampson. Bill: Charles Aidman. Tina Miller: Tracy Stratford. Tina's Voice: Rhoda Williams.

Six-year-old Tina Miller (Tracy Stratford) awakens her father Chris (Robert Sampson) with her crying. Her frightened voice (that of adult actress Rhoda Williams) is clearly audible from beneath her bed but she is nowhere to be seen. After Chris has summoned his physicist friend, Bill (Charles Aidman), to try to help them, the family dog, Mack, races under the bed and vanishes as well. Theorizing that Tina has slipped into the fourth dimension, and that Mack went after her in an attempt to rescue her, Bill outlines the invisible opening in her bedroom wall, has her parents urge Tina to let Mack lead her back home with his sharper canine senses, and anchors Chris by holding his legs while he enters the fourth dimension to pull them both to safety in the nick of time, just before the gap closes. Directed by actor Paul Stewart, a fixture for forty years in films ranging from *Citizen Kane* to *S.O.B.* (1981), this was Matheson's only *Twilight Zone* episode to be scored by Alfred Hitchcock's frequent collaborator, Bernard Herrmann (who, like Stewart, made his film debut with *Kane*), and the first that was personally adapted from his own published stories, as were all but one of his subsequent teleplays.

"I preferred writing originals," he recalled in *Richard Matheson's* The Twilight Zone *Scripts.* "Maybe it was because Ray Bradbury didn't like to sell his short stories to television at that time [possibly because of his unhappy experience in adapting 'I Sing the Body Electric!' for Serling], and I preferred not to myself. But in many ways, writing an original is easier because it's conceived directly for the show, and therefore you don't have to make any corrections or alterations to take a short story and make it into a *Twilight Zone* episode. I had submitted at the time the stories of mine that I thought would be appropriate, and those I didn't have to 'pitch' because the material was already there. I would only pitch the originals. Also, it was easier to get the producers interested in an original idea than it was in a short story, because the structure of the short story might need too much alteration, whereas an original script could be tailor-made for the show.... By [the show's fourth season] I was accustomed to throwing my stories [some of which had been written and published since he began working on the show] in 'the hopper' — which of course they paid for — but in the beginning I preferred to do originals."

Although ultimately pleased with Stewart's efforts, Matheson was distressed at the direction of his previous episodes, as he revealed in a letter to Houghton on January 6, 1962 (quoted in *The Twilight Zone: Unlocking the Door to a Television Classic*): "I feel that I must, at this point, raise a brief, polite ruckus as to the treatment my stories have gotten in the past year or so. What brings this on is my admiration for [Lamont Johnson's work on] 'Nothing in the Dark'; which we all saw last night. I feel that I have gotten considerably less on my last three scripts. I thought that Douglas Heyes did a bad job on the Agnes Moorehead story, setting a draggy pace and allowing her to gorge herself on the scenery. I am not too pleased either with 'Young Man's Fancy,' as I feel that Brahm missed a lot of values, that Alex Nicol was badly miscast and that [Richard L.] Bare spoiled the ending.

[According to Grams, Bare shot some revisions to the closing scenes that were not used.] Finally, I feel that the Buster Keaton show descended into absolute monotony in the second act and was, generally, badly directed. For these reasons I would like to — urgently — request that Lamont Johnson direct 'Little Girl Lost.'"

Of the inspiration for his story, first published in the October-November 1953 issue of *Amazing Stories*, he recalled in an interview with me for *Filmfax* that "our older girl, Tina [Matheson used the first names of his wife and her child by a previous marriage, whom he adopted, in both story and script] ... was crying, and I went into the room. Actually, the apartment [in Venice, California] was so small, it was just a wooden army cot that she slept on at that time. I felt around the bed and she wasn't on the bed, and I thought, 'Oh, my Lord, the poor kid fell on the floor,' then I felt on the floor, she wasn't there. When I felt under the bed I couldn't find her. Finally I found her — she had gone under the bed and rolled all the way to the wall, and that's where I found her, and then of course the diabolical writer's mind, you know, after the kid stops crying you think of a story." In *The Twilight Zone Companion*, he praised the performance of Aidman (who had played Harrington in "And When the Sky Was Opened," and would later replace Serling as the narrator of CBS's ill-fated *Twilight Zone* revival during the mid–1980s) but noted, "The fourth dimension could have been a little stranger."

Creating that fourth dimension presented a special challenge in which the crew was aided by Herrmann's effective score, which appropriately echoed his work on an earlier "otherworldly" adventure, the 1959 adaptation of Jules Verne's *Journey to the Center of the Earth*. Mark Phillips and Frank Garcia related in *Science Fiction Television Series* that an art director walked in with the script and showed Houghton a page where it said, "INTERIOR: LIMBO." [As Houghton recalled to Phillips and Garcia,] "He asked, 'What's that supposed to be, Buck?' I said, 'It's up to you.'" The art director went off and created a fourth dimension for the episode. "He broke his neck to make a limbo set. That's challenge and response. That's what the scripts were full of." Many later remarked upon the similarity between this tale and *Poltergeist* (1982), co-written and co-produced by Steven Spielberg, in which five-year-old Carol Anne Freeling (Heather O'Rourke) is pulled by restless spirits into another dimension, although her disembodied voice can still be heard, and must be guided back to this one and retrieved by her parents.

In a letter to me, Matheson wrote, "The wife [Sarah Marshall] was a little over the top but okay. She was Herbert Marshall's daughter. I'd forgotten that Bernard Herrmann did the score. He was so great. I was just admiring his *Psycho* [1960] score the other night on AMC. All with strings too.... [Stewart] became a proficient TV director in his later years. As did Ray Danton [who] starred in the *Lawman* script I wrote ['Yawkey']. He was excellent. On the *Poltergeist* resemblance, it's there. Steven Spielberg asked me to send him a cassette of 'Little Girl Lost.' Later he sent it back. I was never told by him of the resemblance ... between the two. When the film came out, people all kept telling me they'd made my story into a movie. Others urged me to sue. I'm just not the type. Especially against a multi-million dollar outfit [such as Metro-Goldwyn-Mayer, in the case of *Poltergeist*].... Anyway, later I was given [the job of co-writing] the script for *Twilight Zone — The Movie*, then hired as the creative consultant on *Amazing Stories*. I think Steven was paying me back for *Poltergeist*. I guess. Too bad I didn't get a piece of *Poltergeist*. It made a nifty sum. Ah, well."

A more amusing homage appeared in "Homer[3]," a segment of *The Simpsons*' Halloween episode "Treehouse of Horror VI" (10/30/95). Hiding from his dreaded sisters-in-law behind a bookcase, Homer sees his hand pass through a seemingly solid wall. "That's weird," he

The family dog, Mack, leads Tina Miller (Tracy Stratford) through the fourth dimension in "Little Girl Lost" on *The Twilight Zone* (CBS-TV, 1962).

says. "It's like something out of that *Twilight*-y show about that zone." Then, fearing discovery, he decides, "I'll take my chances in the mystery wall," whereupon he enters the third dimension. As his disembodied voice calls for help, the nerdy Professor John Frink traces the outline of the portal *à la* Bill in the original, and various other Springfield residents invoke *Poltergeist* and *Tron* (1982). Bart ties a rope around himself and plunges through in a rescue attempt, but Homer is sucked into a black hole and emerges in the live-action "real world," where he is last seen going into an erotic bakery.

"Mute"

(January 31, 1963) DIRECTOR: Stuart Rosenberg; PRODUCER: Herbert Hirschman; TELE-PLAY: Matheson, based on his story; MUSIC: Fred Steiner. CAST— Cora Wheeler: Barbara Baxley. Sheriff Harry Wheeler: Frank Overton. Edna Frank: Irene Dailey. Ilse Nielsen: Ann Jillian [misspelled "Jilliann" in closing credits]. Maria Werner: Eva Soreny. Prof. Holger Nielsen: Robert Boon. Frau Fanny Nielsen: Claudia Bryar. Tom Poulter: Percy Helton. Prof. Karl Werner: Oscar Beregi. Man at Bus Stop: William Challee.

"Mute" was one of two hour-long *Twilight Zone* scripts written by Matheson during the fourth season. "In the story [originally published in the 1962 anthology *The Fiend in You*, edited by Charles Beaumont], the young telepath is a boy," Matheson pointed out in *The Original Stories*; "in the script, she became a girl, I don't recall why. And that little girl has become, in real life, the most-exotic Ann Jillian, who has lately played a ghost and Mae West on television. A far cry." Jillian received three Emmy Award nominations during the 1980s, while Stuart Rosenberg, like many of the younger *Twilight Zone* directors, went on to enjoy at least intermittent success on the big screen. His feature credits include the Paul Newman vehicles *Cool Hand Luke* (1967) and *The Drowning Pool* (1976), the commercially successful but critically pan-ned genre entry *The Amityville Horror* (1979), and the fact-based prison drama *Brubaker* (1980).

In a prologue, the teleplay establishes at the outset what is only gradually revealed in the story: Four married couples in Germany, having accepted the proposition that humankind possesses a latent telepathic ability that can be rekindled, reside in separate, secluded locations and apply the same principle in raising their own children entirely without speech. Orphaned when the house where she was raised outside the town of German Corners, Pennsylvania, is destroyed by fire a decade later, twelve-year-old Ilse Nielsen (Jillian)— whose surname appears in many of Matheson's scripts and stories — is taken in by kindly Sheriff Harry Wheeler (Frank Overton) and his wife Cora (Barbara Baxley), who mourns their drowned daughter, Sally, and comes to love Ilse. Unaware that crude verbal input is acutely painful to Ilse and also threatens her telepathic abilities, the well-meaning Wheelers put her in school, where a harsh teacher, Edna Frank (Irene Dailey), forces her to speak. By the time Karl and Maria Werner (Oscar Beregi and Eva Soreny) arrive from Germany, Ilse has lost her gift, and yet found the love her coldly clinical parents denied her.

"I never thought of it having an unhappy ending," Matheson told Stanley Wiater. "It's true her parents were kind to her, but she was more or less like a test case to them.* Whereas with the people she was going to live with now — although she may have lost her telepathic ability — she was going to be in a loving home. Marc Zicree didn't think that was a happy ending either. But I think it is. Better to grow up in a loving home than to have a sixth sense. There have been too many miserable people who have been psychic.... I wrote [the original short story] 'Mute' in a deliberately professional way. Most stories I get an inspiration, and sort of dash it off before I redo it in another draft. This one I did very methodically."

---

*Indeed, he raises this very concern in the opening sequence of the teleplay, which is set in Dusseldorf in 1953, as Frau Werner asks Ilse's father, Prof. Holger Nielsen (Robert Boon), "Do we have the right to impose this — study on our children? Even those unborn?... We offer them no choice in the matter. Is that *just*?"

"Death Ship"

(February 7, 1963) DIRECTOR: Don Medford; PRODUCER: Herbert Hirschman; TELEPLAY: Matheson, based on his story; MUSIC: stock. CAST—Capt. Paul Ross: Jack Klugman. Lt. Ted Mason: Ross Martin. Lt. Mike Carter: Frederick Beir. Ruth Mason: Mary Webster. Jeannie Mason: Tammy Marihugh. Kramer: Ross Elliott. Mrs. Nolan: Sara Taft.

Seeking inhabitable worlds for an overpopulated Earth to colonize in the year 1997, the three-man spaceship E-89 (in reality another leftover from *Forbidden Planet*), commanded by Capt. Paul Ross (Jack Klugman), is cruising above the thirteenth planet of star system 51, planning to take specimens, when Lt. Ted Mason (Ross Martin) spots something glittering down on the surface. Thinking they may have discovered evidence of an alien race, Ross, Mason, and Lt. Mike Carter (Frederick Beir) land and are shocked to find a wrecked duplicate of their own ship with the bodies of three identical crewmen inside. Mason and Carter conclude that they themselves are dead, while Ross stubbornly insists that they are in fact alive, so there must be a logical explanation. Theorizing that they have passed through a time warp, and that the wreck represents only one possible future for the crew, Ross argues that if they do not take off again, they cannot crash. Mason and Carter, unlike the captain, have people waiting for them back on Earth; they point out that the ship's supplies of food and energy will not last long on the cold surface of this harsh alien planet.

While staying true to his original story, first published in *Fantastic Story Magazine* in March 1953, and retaining much of its dialogue almost verbatim, Matheson also augmented it significantly for the new hour-long format by adding a twist reminiscent of Ray Bradbury's "Mars Is Heaven," which Matheson later dramatized in his teleplay for the NBC miniseries version of *The Martian Chronicles*. When Carter and Mason experience visions of meeting deceased friends and relations back home on Earth, Ross decides that both those and the wrecked ship are telepathic illusions created by the planet's indigenous beings to discourage colonization. But after taking off safely to test this theory, he insists they return, only to find the same wreck and realize that their ship is "a latter-day *Flying Dutchman*." Matheson noted in *The Original Stories*, "I liked this one very much, thought the direction by Don Medford fine, the three lead performances by Jack Klugman, Ross Martin and Frederick Beir excellent, emotionally moving." A feature film version, *Countdown*, has been announced.

"Death Ship" achieves a high level of intensity with a trio of strong performances by the leads, particularly that of Martin (best known as James West's sidekick, Artemus Gordon, on *The Wild Wild West*); the actor drew upon his feelings toward his own daughter, from whom he was then separated, in the emotional scene where he is reunited with his deceased child. Herbert Hirschman, who succeeded Houghton at the start of the season (and was in turn succeeded by Bert Granet after leaving in mid-season), had the MGM special effects department create expensive shots of the ship landing and taking off. Simple but convincing split-screen shots, betrayed only by differences in lighting, depicted Mason and Carter gazing down in astonishment at their own corpses inside the wreck.

Although admired by Matheson and many others, "Death Ship" was not held in high esteem by Klugman, who told *Filmfax*'s Tony Albarella, "I hated it from the beginning. It was too technical with all that jargon, and there was the [split-screen] trick photography so you had to stand still. I never liked that program, but a lot of people still talk about it. I had two guys who were crying all the time.... There was more filmed; you don't know how much they cried. I said to Ross [Martin], 'Jesus Christ, it's like acting with Joan Crawford!' I mean, he never stopped crying!" Klugman's distaste may stem partly from an incident with director Don Medford on the earlier *Twilight Zone* episode "A Passage for Trumpet" (5/20/60), in which they disagreed over the way Klugman played a scene and Medford, a good friend at the time, was overruled by Serling. "Because of that, Don and I [were never close again]," Klugman told Albarella. "I lost jobs, but it was the best money I ever lost. I was a coward in every other area, but not with my acting. I will not compromise my acting. It became my best friend.... Don Medford was a wonderful director. He had won all kinds of awards; he was good with cameras. Wasn't good with actors, but he was good with cameras."

Matheson told Stanley Wiater in *Richard Matheson's* The Twilight Zone *Scripts*, "I don't know whose idea it was to go an hour, whether it was CBS or Rod's. I was not unhappy with my two one-hour episodes. But it wasn't *The Twilight Zone* structure any more. I think the producers felt that it was the lesser of all the seasons simply because it did not follow the typical *Twilight Zone* pattern." He added in an interview with me for *Filmfax* that the hour-long format "was really a terrible idea for a *Twilight Zone* season, because that just was not the flavor of *The Twilight Zone*, and we were all glad it went back to a half-hour for the last season.... I did some of my best work in the last season. I kind of like ["Death Ship"], actually, because it had such a good cast, and it had a lot of honest emotion in it, so it wasn't bad at all. The other [hour-long] one ['Mute'] wasn't too bad, but that one ... was a long story," and thus required no new material to expand it to the longer format.

"Spur of the Moment"

(February 21, 1964) DIRECTOR: Elliot Silverstein; PRODUCER: Bert Granet; TELEPLAY: Matheson; MUSIC: Rene Garriguenc. CAST—Anne Marie Henderson: Diana Hyland. Mrs. Henderson: Marsha Hunt. John Henderson: Philip Ober. David Mitchell: Roger Davis. Robert Blake: Robert Hogan. Reynolds: Jack Raine.

Matheson's final four *Twilight Zone* episodes were produced back-to-back by Bert Granet, who, as Matheson told Wiater, "was very, very good to work with; I liked working with him a lot after Buck Houghton [and Herbert Hirschman] left the series. I liked both of them, but anyone would be a little uneasy after four seasons about getting a new producer. It worked out extremely well, though. He was a very nice man, very knowledgeable. It was very rewarding working with him. But I never worked with William Froug, who later replaced him. As soon as he came on — I was out.... When he got control of *The Twilight Zone* in its last year, I believe he was the one who canceled one of my previously accepted scripts ['The Doll']. Which in hindsight I'm glad he did, because years later it was done for *Amazing Stories*, and there it really turned out beautifully.... I don't know why he felt that way about my work, but that's how it was. If Bert Granet had stayed as producer, I probably would have written a couple of others. I mean, Granet was the one who chose 'The Doll.' But as I've said, I'm just as glad Froug dumped it..." Granet had been a writer and producer in Hollywood since the early 1930s.

The last teleplay written by Matheson for the classic *Twilight Zone*, "Spur of the Moment" was his only original script in the fifth season, which contained more of his favorite episodes than any other. It opens in 1939 as eighteen-year-old Anne Marie Henderson (played by Diana Hyland, some ten years her senior) is pursued on horseback by "a strange, nightmarish figure of a woman in black." Anne, who was forced by her parents (Philip Ober and Marsha Hunt) to break her engagement to the penniless but romantic David Mitchell (Roger Davis) in favor of a stodgy investment broker, Robert Blake (Robert Hogan), is terrified of the figure, soon revealed as an embittered, impoverished, and alcoholic Anne herself, returning from a quarter century hence in a vain effort to change her own past. As the present-day Anne tells her widowed mother, "I was warning myself not to marry the wrong man," but in an inversion of the standard romantic cliché, we learn that she did indeed marry her "true love," David, who has proceeded to run their estate into ruin. Matheson opined to Wiater.

> Probably more people than not go by the heart rather than the head. Which is perfectly understandable at that age. And they often make *terrible* mistakes. But who could expect a young person to calculatedly figure out which of two suitors was the best one?... I love that title! She married on the "spur of the moment," really. She married from emotion. And there was also the spurs of the person riding the horse.... Titles are very important, and it's really nice if you can get a good one. As a writer, I prefer to have the title occur to me instantly — even sometimes before I do the story. It colors how I approach the story, and I feel much more comfortable.... I realize, in re-reading this script, that it must have been too short. I don't know who added the extra material seen in the finished film — the scene with her mother and the aged, dissolute David — also the flashback to the engagement party. Maybe *I* did although I don't have those extra pages. A fitting conclusion to my days on the show — scenes added from, I choose to presume, *The Twilight Zone*.

Unfortunately, as with "Young Man's Fancy," what finally reached the screen fell far short of the scriptwriter's vision. Matheson was disappointed with the treatment his script received from the director, in this case Elliot Silverstein, a veteran of live theater whose other credits include three previous *Twilight Zone* episodes, and occasional feature films such as the Westerns *Cat Ballou* (1965) and *A Man Called Horse* (1970). "I like that kind of story [about the unexpected effects of traveling through time], and the only thing I didn't like was that I thought in the beginning they gave it away," Matheson told me in an interview for *Filmfax*. "You know, you should not have seen her face when she was chasing the young girl [who turns out to be her younger self]. It should have just been a scary figure in black in the background."

"Steel"

> (October 4, 1963) DIRECTOR: Don Weis; PRODUCER: Bert Granet; TELEPLAY: Matheson, based on his story; MUSIC: [Nathan] Van Cleave; MAKEUP: William Tuttle. CAST — Steel Kelly: Lee Marvin. Pole: Joe Mantell. Maynard Flash: Chuck Hicks. Battling Maxo: Tipp McClure. Nolan: Merritt Bohn. Maxwell: Frank London. Voices in Crowd: Larry Barton, Bob Peterson, Edwin Rochelle. Announcer: Jimmy Ames. Men in Crowd: Slim Bergman, Lou Cavalier. Maynard Flash's Handler: Bob McCord.

Matheson's avowed favorite among all of his *Twilight Zone* episodes, "Steel" was faithfully adapted from a story that was originally published in the May 1956 issue of his most common outlet, *The Magazine of Fantasy and Science Fiction*. It is set, perhaps a trifle unrealistically, in 1974, six years after the legal abolition of prizefighting, when only robot fighters are permitted into the ring. Battling Maxo (Tipp McClure), a decrepit and obsolete B2 model, arrives in Maynard, Kansas, with his manager, ex-heavyweight fighter Steel Kelly (Lee Marvin), and handler, Pole (Joe Mantell), for a six-round semi-final against the local favorite, a B7 unit known as Maynard Flash (Chuck Hicks). The desperate Steel is relying on this lopsided contest for sufficient funds to give Maxo a proper overhaul. Trouble begins when the trigger spring in Maxo's arm breaks, leaving him out of commission. Steel's contract is good only if he delivers a fight, so he impersonates Maxo in the ring. He is predictably and brutally beaten in the first round, yet puts up enough of a fight to receive half of the promised $500.

Already a *Twilight Zone* veteran from the third season's "The Grave" (10/27/61), Lee

Marvin later won an Oscar for his dual role in *Cat Ballou* after playing numerous heavies—most notably in Fritz Lang's *The Big Heat* (1953)—and went on to become one of the screen's legendary tough-guy heroes. His best-known films include such macho classics as Richard Brooks's *The Professionals* (1966); Robert Aldrich's *Attack* (1956), *The Dirty Dozen* (1967) and *Emperor of the North* (1973); and John Boorman's *Point Blank* (1967) and *Hell in the Pacific* (1968). An interesting counterpoint to Serling's own "Requiem for a Heavyweight," with Marvin perfectly cast and Van Cleave's jazzy score eminently appropriate to its boxing milieu, "Steel" was the only *Twilight Zone* episode directed by Don Weis, who would begin alternating with William Asher on the rapidly declining *Beach Party* films the next year. And as Matheson told me in an interview for *Filmfax*, the title once again had a double meaning: "'Steel' refers to the strength of his personality plus the fact that these [robot prizefighters] are made out of steel."

He added in his *Collected Stories* commentary, "I had a lot of trouble with [the story]—the beginning of it reads like a pastiche of Hemingway—but finally I caught on and got my own style back. It's the story of a man who is just so determined that things work out that he will put his own life on the line.... [I]f I had written it when I was much younger I would have had him knock the robot out—which of course would have been insane. But it made a wonderful *Twilight Zone* ... Lee Marvin was really fantastic." His face perpetually sheened with sweat, Marvin embodies Steel's nervous energy with constant motion as he talks to the corpulent fight promoter (Merritt Bohn), to whom Matheson mischievously gives the name of Nolan. As Serling says in his closing narration, "No matter what the future brings, man's capacity to rise to the occasion will remain unaltered. His potential for tenacity and optimism continues as always to out-fight, out-point and out-live any and all changes made by his society, for which three cheers, and a unanimous decision, rendered from ... the Twilight Zone." A feature film version, entitled *Real Steel*, is now in production.

"Night Call"

(February 7, 1964) DIRECTOR: Jacques Tourneur; PRODUCER: Bert Granet; TELEPLAY: Matheson, based on his "Long Distance Call" (aka "Sorry, Right Number"); MUSIC: stock. CAST—Elva Keene: Gladys Cooper. Nurse Margaret Phillips: Nora Marlowe. Miss Finch: Martine Bartlett. Voice of Brian Douglas: Ken Drake.

According to Martin Grams, Jr., "Night Call" was originally set to premiere on the evening of November 22, 1963, but—like the regularly scheduled programs on all networks—was canceled due to coverage of John F. Kennedy's assassination, and was postponed until the following February. It was, as Matheson observed in *The Original Stories*, "the only *Twilight Zone* helmed by that master director of the genre, Jacques Tourneur; my doing, I am happy to say. At least, I forcefully suggested the idea to Bert Granet and he hired Tourneur. A wondrous talent, Jacques Tourneur. He should have been hired to do far more than he was able to do in his lifetime." Tourneur had directed *Berlin Express* (1948), which Granet produced, and eight weeks after "Night Call" wrapped, he began shooting Matheson's *The Comedy of Terrors*. His impressive résumé included such classics of the genre as producer Val Lewton's *Cat People* (1942), *I Walked with a Zombie* (1943), and *The Leopard Man* (1943), as well as the decidedly Lewtonian *Night of the Demon* (aka *Curse of the Demon*, 1958). "Also," said Matheson of this episode's legendary leading lady, "who could ask for a better performer than Gladys Cooper?"

Cooper—who soon earned her third Oscar nomination as Best Supporting Actress for *My Fair Lady* (1964), and had previously appeared on *The Twilight Zone* in Johnson's "Nothing in the Dark" (1/5/62) and Beaumont's "Passage on the *Lady Anne*" (5/9/63)—stars as Miss Elva Keene, a crippled maiden lady living "alone on the outskirts of London Flats, a tiny rural community in Maine." Tourneur's atmospheric direction and Robert W. Pittack's moody photography are essential to the episode's effectiveness for, as in the Lewton films, suggestion is all when Miss Keene begins receiving mysterious phone calls in which she hears at first nothing, and then a faint male voice that is eventually traced by the phone company to a fallen wire that landed in Valley View Cemetery on the edge of town. Matheson's original story "Long Distance Call" ends as Elva waits in terror after the voice says, "I'll be right over," while in "Night Call," she visits the cemetery and finds the wire lying on the grave of her fiancé, Brian Douglas, who died in the 1932 crash that crippled her—after she insisted on driving. But now, to Elva's great regret, he says that he will obey her earlier, unwitting admonition to "leave me alone."

In *Richard Matheson's* The Twilight Zone *Scripts*, he noted, "To give the woman some sort of characterization, some sort of 'arc' as they say (I hate that word!), I created this new ending to make the surprise be that *she* was the one who was responsible for all this. Her own selfishness. I liked the new ending a lot better, actually. It was simple human nature which did this to her. I always prefer that kind of approach to fantasy or terror or whatever. She had done this to him while he was still alive [he was thrown through the windshield when Elva hit a tree], and, even dead, he still had the habit of doing exactly what she told him.... Jacques was a wonderful director. The producers were uneasy about hiring him. The feeling was Jacques was a motion picture director, and he would not be able to successfully accomplish ... the short shooting schedule of a television show. Especially just a half-hour show. As I've mentioned a number of times, he was *so* organized. Looking at his scriptbook where all his notes were so meticulous—he knew ahead every single thing he was going to do. It's my understanding he shot the shortest shooting schedule of any *Twilight Zone* episode, which was 28 hours."

Not surprisingly, Matheson had been an admirer of the Lewton films since the 1940s, as he told Robert Arnett in *Creative Screenwriting*:

I liked Val Lewton a lot, because of the subtlety of his pictures. The first one I ever saw was *Cat People*. They were frightening and yet they were very subtle. I even wrote a letter to Val Lewton, at the time I think I was seventeen years old, saying I think I figured out some of your tricks, how you scare people. One of them being that you lead the eye all the way to say the right hand side of the screen and then suddenly have something jump out from the left hand side of the screen. Another one was to have a very long period of silence suddenly broken by a loud noise, whatever, the nickering of a horse, or in *Cat People*, the hiss of a bus stopping by a curb, it makes people jump out of their skins.... I don't know whether I learned the elements of how to frighten people in films from these, but they certainly helped. They're so simple that I'm always incredulous that more people don't know about it.

For instance, I did a *Twilight Zone* with Bill Shatner where he's on an airplane ["Nightmare at 20,000 Feet," which Matheson had hoped to have Jacques Tourneur direct as well]. The camera moves slowly to the window and he rips open the curtain and you see this horrible face. It couldn't be more obvious and yet everybody remembers that. And, of course, I always read fantasy, but I came from a mundane type of environment and my taste for fantasy or terror was informed by that mundane environment. I never thought of exotic cities or creatures or anything like that. Just what could happen under the most mundane of circumstances and be frightening.... These Val Lewton pictures, they're still with me, the wonderful moods he evoked, the way they frightened you and the tasteful way in which he presented these things. Oh, I forgot to tell you, when I wrote him he answered me. He said, "My editors, Robert Wise and Mark Robson, were delighted that you liked our pictures and that you figured out our little tricks."

Like Robson, Wise worked with Welles and became a director under Lewton's aegis with such classic genre films as *The Curse of the Cat People* (1944) and *The Body Snatcher* (1945).

"Nightmare at 20,000 Feet"

(October 11, 1963) DIRECTOR: Richard Donner; PRODUCER: Bert Granet; TELEPLAY: Matheson, based on his story; MUSIC: stock; MAKEUP: William Tuttle. CAST— Bob Wilson: William Shatner. Julia Wilson: Christine White. Gremlin: Nick Cravat. Flight Engineer: Edward Kemmer. Stewardess: Asa Maynor. Police Officer: Dave Armstrong. Passengers: Slim Bergman, Estelle Etterre, Madeline Finochio, Ed Haskett, Hath Howard, Bob McCord, Beryl McCutcheon, Jean Olson.

Easily Matheson's best-known episode of *The Twilight Zone*, and his last to be produced, "Nightmare at 20,000 Feet" benefits from a strong star turn by William Shatner as Bob Wilson, a salesman who is flying home with his wife after being discharged from the sanitarium where he was recovering from a nervous breakdown, the onset of which took place on a similar flight.* Despite being frequently lambasted for chewing the scenery as Captain James Tiberius Kirk in *Star Trek* (ironically, a prime example might be his dual role in Matheson's sole episode "The Enemy Within") and its follow-up films, Shatner here delivers a superbly nuanced and calibrated performance, every bit the equal of his effective one from "Nick of Time," his only other *Twilight Zone* appearance.

As they fly through a storm, Wilson repeatedly spots a grotesque humanoid figure on the wing, but each time he tries to point it out to his wife Julia (identified as Ruth in the script and other sources, and played by Christine White) or a crew member, it vanishes and later reappears, revealed in one shocking moment with its face at the window when he suddenly slides open the curtain. Seeing the figure — which, due to the budgetary limitations on William Tuttle's makeup, a bemused Matheson later compared to a panda bear — tampering with the cowling on one of the engines, Wilson equates it with the mythical gremlins that supposedly plagued Allied pilots during the war. Convinced the plane will crash if it is not stopped, he takes a gun from the holster of a sleeping policeman. Wilson straps himself into his seat, opens the emergency exit, and is nearly sucked out by the decompression as he blasts away at the gremlin. When the plane safely reaches the ground he is forcibly restrained and considered a madman with a unique method of attempted suicide until, as the closing narration tells us, the tangible evidence of the damaged wing is found, vindicating him at last.

In an interview with me for *Filmfax*, Matheson discussed the differences between story and script: "I must have cut about 5,000 words out of it [before it was published]. The story [originally] starts a lot before that moment — he's in his office, he's in the cab, it goes on just establishing the mental state he's in.... [Shatner's character] had *had* a nervous breakdown; in the story, he was in the *midst* of a nervous breakdown, but that's why he himself, I think, doubted, wondered whether he was going crazy, seeing this thing out there, and then he realized that it wasn't so, that it was really out there." Matheson has also praised Shatner's performance, particularly the moment when he realizes that the reassuring flight engineer (Edward Kemmer, previously the star of TV's *Space Patrol*) is only humoring him. Up-and-coming young director Richard Donner, who according to Zicree confronted enormous

---

*In the original story, Wilson is traveling alone, and the only evidence of instability is his impulse to kill himself with the pistol he carries aboard the plane in his overnight bag — an idea that was less farfetched when "Nightmare" was published in the 1961 anthology *Alone by Night* (edited by Michael and Don Congdon, the latter Matheson's literary agent) than it would be in a post–9/11 climate.

logistical difficulties in filming the episode, went on to spectacular commercial success as the director of *The Omen* (1976), *Superman* (1978), and four *Lethal Weapon* films to date, and as the executive producer of such disparate hits as *The Lost Boys* (1987) and *Free Willy* (1993).

Matheson has often expressed disappointment at the appearance of the gremlin, and had hoped that "Nightmare at 20,000 Feet" could also be directed by Tourneur with the same actor, Nick Cravat (who, according to Matheson, bore a marked resemblance to the gremlin as described in his story), in a dark suit and minimal makeup. Cravat and his childhood friend, Burt Lancaster, had formed an acrobatic act that made many vaudeville, nightclub, and circus appearances; when Lancaster broke into the movies, he brought Cravat with him to costar in Tourneur's *The Flame and the Arrow* (1950) and many others, including Cravat's last film, *The Island of Dr. Moreau* (1977). In a lecture at Sherwood Oaks College (excerpted on the DVD of *The Twilight Zone: The Definitive Edition, Season 5*), Serling said he took great pains to have a blowup of the gremlin placed outside the window when making a flight with Matheson some weeks after the episode aired, only to have it blown away by the prop wash before Matheson opened the curtain. (Matheson calls the account apocryphal.)

Perhaps more than any other individual episode of this beloved anthology series, "Nightmare at 20,000 Feet" has succeeded in penetrating the national consciousness during the past few decades, with Matheson's gremlin recently rendered as a 12" *Twilight Zone* figure by Sideshow Collectibles (as was the spaceman from "The Invaders"), and has become the subject of a wide variety of homages. Shatner also appeared in the genre telefilm *The Horror at 37,000 Feet* (1973), directed by *Twilight Zone* veteran David Lowell Rich, and on *Cosby* in "Pilot, Not the Pilot" (11/10/97) as a maniacal airline passenger. The November 15, 1997, issue of *TV Guide* featured a survey of "doomed-airliner drama" TV-movies, including *The Crash of Flight 401* (1978): "Shatner plays a National Transportation Board inspector who determines that a blown lightbulb was partly to blame (not a gremlin on the wing)."

In 1999, Shatner earned an Emmy nomination as Outstanding Guest Actor in a Comedy Series for his work on NBC's *3rd Rock from the Sun* (coincidentally echoing the title of the Matheson-based "Third from the Sun"), opposite two-time Oscar nominee John Lithgow, who had played the leading role when "Nightmare at 20,000 Feet" was remade as part of *Twilight Zone — The Movie*. *3rd Rock* starred Lithgow as Dick Solomon, who poses as a human college professor but is really the commander of a group of aliens sent to study Earth people and their customs. Shatner's first appearance in the recurring role of the often invoked, but hitherto unseen, "Big Giant Head" inspired an ingenious in-joke during the third season's final episode, "Dick's Big Giant Headache" (5/25/99). Unaccustomed to human form, the "supreme leader of the galaxy" (aka Stone Phillips) arrives drunk and disheveled at the airport after traveling to East Rutherford, New Jersey, by mistake. When asked how his trip was he answers, "Horrifying, at first. I looked out the window, and I saw something on the wing of the plane." The astonished Dick responds, "The same thing happened to me!" (More recently, Jude Law lampooned "Nightmare" in a 2010 *Saturday Night Live* sketch.

Like "Little Girl Lost," this episode was spoofed on *The Simpsons*, hilariously rendered as "Terror at 5½ Feet" in the Halloween special "Treehouse of Horror IV" (10/28/93). Bart introduces each of the segments (the others were "The Devil and Homer Simpson" and "Bart Simpson's Dracula") with a painting, in a parody of Serling's subsequent *Night Gallery* hosting chores. En route to Springfield Elementary School, a panic-stricken Bart tells the bus driver, "Otto, you've got to do something — there's a gremlin on the side of the bus," whereupon Otto knocks the AMC Gremlin that is driving in the next lane off the road. As the fearsome apparition begins removing one of the wheels, none of the other passengers aboard the school bus sees it or is willing to believe Bart's story. He at last opens the emergency exit and uses a flare to dislodge the gremlin, which is picked up off the road by the Simpsons' well-meaning but overly pious neighbor, Ned Flanders. As Bart is being sent to the New Bedlam Mental Hospital despite the demonstrable damage to the bus, he sees the gremlin taunting him, mischievously dangling Ned's still-speaking head outside the window of the ambulance.

"Nightmare at 20,000 Feet" was one of several episodes briefly alluded to on *Futurama*, the second animated series from *Simpsons* creator Matt Groening, when *The Twilight Zone* was spoofed as *The Scary Door* in "I Dated a Robot" (5/13/01). Another variation appeared on yet another Fox comedy, *The Bernie Mac Show*, in the special Thanksgiving episode "Tryptophan-tasy" (11/27/02). Playing a thinly fictionalized version of himself, the eponymous stand-up comedian has taken custody of his sister's children Jordan (Jeremy Suarez), Bryana (Dee Dee Davis), and Vanessa (Camille Winbush). The episode shows Bernie experiencing nightmares while suffering from indigestion after overindulging in undercooked turkey. Following the first dream, in which he and Jordan appear as clay animation characters in "Cartoon Land," Bernie refuses to give Nessa money to go to the mall, and then slips into a reverie in which he and his wife Wanda (Kellita Smith) are en route to a kid-free vacation, only to reenact Matheson's scenario with a vengeful Nessa as the gremlin, disposed of when she flies off after the cash proffered by Bernie.

In *A Critical History of Television's* The Twilight Zone, *1959–1964*, Don Presnell and Marty McGee note that the episode "was even parodied in ... *The Looney Zone* [*Looney Tunes* #30, July 1997]. Sylvester the Cat is the troubled passenger who looks out at the wing and sees Tweety Bird instead of a gremlin. Tweety tries to sabotage the wing with a hammer, acetylene torch, and a jackhammer. Sylvester tries to stop Tweety, but is sucked out the window and found clinging to the rudder when the plane makes an emergency landing. And, like the previous incarnations of the troubled acrophobe, he is taken away in a straitjacket. The title of the segment: 'Nightmare of 20,000 Tweets.'"

Zone's status as a multimedia phenomenon is demonstrated not only by such omnipresent homages, but also by its many manifestations over the years, including a radio series for which Dennis Etchison adapted many of the original scripts. Matheson was involved in three additional incarnations: the 1983 feature-film version; the mid–1980s CBS revival; and a 1994 TV-movie, for which he scripted a rediscovered treatment written by Serling for one of his own abortive attempts to mount a *Twilight Zone* feature film.

Other Episodic Television

Like many Group members, Matheson plunged enthusiastically into the burgeoning medium of television after the success of *The Incredible Shrinking Man*, and co-wrote many of his early efforts with Charles Beaumont. "We were very close friends," he said in an interview with me for *Filmfax*. "When we joined this agency [Adams, Ray, and Rosenberg] together, it was such a strange new world out there that we decided to work together. We collaborated on a lot of different shows. We did a couple of Paladins, *Have Gun—Will Travel*, *Philip Marlowe*, the Steve McQueen thing about the bounty hunter [*Wanted: Dead or Alive*], we did a lot of them. We knew each other, our families knew each other, our kids knew each other." They decided from the outset, however, not to collaborate on *The Twilight*

Zone. "There was no need to, because that was our field," he told Stanley Wiater in *Richard Matheson's* The Twilight Zone *Scripts.* "The other fields — Westerns, detective — we were really not that familiar with, although I did six *Lawman* scripts on my own.... But this was the area of expertise that we both had, so it would have been crazy for us to collaborate on *The Twilight Zone.*"

Matheson and Beaumont did co-write one feature film within the genre, *Night of the Eagle* (aka *Burn, Witch, Burn*), and although no longer writing teleplays together, they joined forces for one of two Group efforts to create a new series in the *Twilight Zone* mold. In his commentaries for the teleplays in *The Twilight Zone Scripts of Charles Beaumont, Volume One,* editor Roger Anker incorporates and expands upon much of the biographical material from his introduction to the *Selected Stories,* and quotes a letter written by Beaumont: "I have a show of my own called *Out There* which I'm trying to launch, but it keeps blowing up on the pad," he wrote around the spring of 1960. "I don't know why, but I'm not surprised, for that is the Hollywood way, ten and a half times out of ten. Ray Bradbury, Bob Bloch, Dick Matheson, Jerry Sohl, Ray Russell and others pitched in and supplied twenty scripts, all of them first-rate and ready to shoot. We all thought that this would goose a network into an immediate okay for production; but no. For two and a half months vast enthusiasm, plenty of talk and no action. Still, *Twilight Zone did* make it, and imitation is a way of life here, so perhaps somebody will wise up."

Matheson also attempted to create a television counterpart to *Galaxy,* wherein editor Horace Gold had published five of his stories, including "Third from the Sun," "Lover When You're Near Me" (May 1952), "Shipshape Home" (July 1952), and "One for the Books" (September 1955). As he told Paul Sammon in *Midnight Graffiti,* "I wrote a pilot with [James Bond screenwriter] Richard Maibaum for a science fiction series, *Galaxy,* that David Gerber, who does *Police Story,* was the executive producer for. We were going to use nothing but the best, the most classic science fiction stories, which we did in the pilot. And Horace Gold was involved in that too [as the story editor].... There was to be a [story by Arthur C.] Clarke, and an [Isaac] Asimov — I had others, too, but they just weren't interested." According to Rathbun and Flanagan, he adapted "Lover When You're Near Me" and "The Holiday Man" (*Fantasy and Science Fiction,* July 1957), but as he added to J.N. Williamson in the anthology *Masques,* "In reading through [the stories], we discovered that the science fiction short story world is a rather bleak one. The power of most of the stories comes from the power of hopelessness."

In his afterword to Jerry Sohl's *Twilight Zone* scripts, Johnson tells of another ill-fated venture: "I vividly remember walking along the curved corridors of the starship *Enterprise* with Jerry Sohl, Theodore Sturgeon and Richard Matheson, talking about the future. We'd each been hired by Gene Roddenberry to write episodes for his new series *Star Trek,* and been given the run of the premises. We were taking advantage of his generosity to familiarize ourselves with the workings of the ship — a grand tour of the starship's standing sets. Jerry was writing 'The Corbomite Maneuver' [11/10/66], Sturgeon, 'Amok Time' [9/15/67], Matheson, 'The Enemy Within,' and I was working on 'The Mantrap' [*sic*; 9/8/66]. However, as we walked along, instead of being caught up in the fantasy of being aboard the spaceship, we were still lamenting the death of Rod Serling's *Twilight Zone....* As we looked into the forced perspective of the engineering section ... Jerry brought up an idea we had discussed earlier — why not team up to get a series of our own, some kind of half-hour fantasy series like *The Twilight Zone*?" Sohl also suggested using the title of Sturgeon's 1958 collection *A Touch of Strange* for the new series.

The four friends formed a corporation called The Green Hand, with Johnson as its president, intending to create entire new series for various networks. Matheson picked up the story in a separate *Filmfax* interview:

> We got together, we incorporated, we had this big, beautiful suite of offices in Beverly Hills, we had an office at Metro-Goldwyn-Mayer, we were meeting with the top bigwigs in all these studios, we had some wonderful ideas. Unfortunately, Jerry Sohl and I were the only ones who did much writing. The other two — you know, Ted Sturgeon [was] one of the really great writers in the field, science fiction *and* fantasy, but he didn't really do that much for The Green Hand, and so we never got anything down on paper that went anywhere, and finally I just backed out of the whole thing. We had a manager for the thing, and we were paying him $250 a week at that time, which was quite a salary, and then later, after I had backed out, they found themselves in trouble with the IRS and found out that this guy had been continuing to pay himself, even though the whole thing was kaput.
>
> You know, it was fun; we used to meet at each other's houses, and they would smoke pot. I didn't, but I probably got high just on the fumes. We had some wonderful ideas. I remember one day walking from Metro to a coffee shop and back with George, and before we had gotten back to the studio he and I had plotted out an entire movie, which would have been very fascinating, but we never wrote it.

According to Johnson, Michael Eisner turned down their proposal for *A Touch of Strange* when he was a vice-president in charge of development at ABC. Sohl, who wrote for many of the same series as Matheson, told the author in *Filmfax*, "We went in to see [the network executives], and they didn't seem to understand us at all. We seemed to be oddballs to them. Whenever they visited with anyone it was usually singly, and when they saw us four ... come in and invade their office, they seemed to be overpowered and stunned and open-mouthed, and they would never buy anything that we were selling. We'd go to the coffee house afterwards and talk about the meeting that we'd just had and say, 'They just don't seem to understand television [or] what people want.'

"They particularly did not seem to understand the project, or what we were driving at. If you have something that you're presenting on television, you can't do it exactly the way life is, you have to do it in some other way, and your writing has to be implicit rather than explicit.... The things that we offered to them were very well thought-out. We were not newcomers to the medium. We were established writers who'd written books and short stories and were prize-winners and all that sort of thing, but it didn't seem to make any difference to them. It just really surprised us all, so we finally gave up, collapsed The Green Hand, and went our separate ways." Sohl told *Starlog*'s Edward Gross that their other abortive projects included *Hunter, E.T.* (no connection with Steven Spielberg's film), *Gestalt Team*, and a series about an android.

Notwithstanding the failure of The Green Hand, Matheson has created a diverse body of work on the small screen outside of *The Twilight Zone*. Although information on some of his earliest credits in episodic television remains elusive, every effort has been made to cover these other contributions to the medium as thoroughly as possible.

Studio 57 (DuMont, 1954–55; syndicated, 1955–58): "Young Couples Only" (9/3/55) was an episode of this anthology series sponsored by Heinz 57 Varieties, which aired for one season on the dying DuMont network and then was syndicated. Almost certainly the very first Matheson adaptation of any kind, it is based on "Shipshape Home," which concerns a writer named Rick, who initially dismisses his wife Ruth's tales of massive engines below the basement of their suspiciously affordable apartment building and of a third eye on their sinister janitor (compared to Peter Lorre), saying, "You read too many fantasy pulps!" But the entire block is actually a disguised craft that soon whisks the residents off into space. In his *Collected Stories* commentary, Matheson related, "I lived in an apartment with my mother at the time. Originally I think the title I had on it was 'The Janitor Had Three Eyes.' It may be that ... Horace Gold put the title 'Shipshape Home' on it. That's possible. We lived on East 7th Street in Brooklyn, and the apartment house was across the way. That was when we had these apartment buildings which were like seven, eight, nine stories high."

In a note to me, he made an interesting addendum regarding one of his many unfilmed scripts: "After I wrote *The Incredible Shrinking Man*, I was hired to expand ... 'Shipshape Home' into a feature film. It didn't work out [but earlier] they made it into a half-hour show which I also think I saw one summer; not so good." Despite his dismissive reaction, veteran screenwriter Lawrence Kimble's adaptation is quite faithful, with offscreen spouses Barbara Hale (*Perry Mason*'s Della Street) and Bill Williams as Ruth and Rick, the latter now a cartoonist instead of an author. In a delightful casting coup, Lorre himself—later to appear in three Matheson movies—plays the alien janitor collecting his "perfect physical specimens." Directed by Richard Irving, a future Emmy nominee for the series *The Name of the Game* and *Quincy M.E.*, "Young Couples Only" featured the young Robert Quarry, best known for playing the title role in *Count Yorga, Vampire* (1970), and Dani (aka Danny Sue) Nolan as the Thompsons' equally ill-fated friends and neighbors, Phil and Marge. Ubiquitous character actor Paul Bryar rounded out the cast as Johnson, the friendly local cop who turns out to be an alien as well.

Richard Diamond, Private Detective (CBS, 1957–59; NBC, 1959–60): Matheson wrote one or more teleplays, for which I have no details, of this half-hour series starring David Janssen. It was produced by Dick Powell (who had played the character on radio from 1949 to 1952) for his Four Star Productions. Mary Tyler Moore originated the role of Diamond's contact "Sam," shown only from the waist down.

Now Is Tomorrow (c. 1958): Because it never aired, it is difficult to date Matheson's "Thy Will Be Done," the half-hour pilot for an abortive anthology series hosted by Charles Bickford and created by associate producers Burton Rosen and Harvey Bennett, the latter a mainstay of the *Star Trek* films. Made by Roncom Telefilms, it was released on video in the "TV's Magic Memories" series by Moviecraft, which identifies it as a 1958 production (there is no onscreen copyright). Rathbun and Flanagan list it as 1960. The unusual assemblage of talent includes director Irvin Kershner, best known for *The Empire Strikes Back* (1980); Ernest Laszlo, the Oscar-winning cinematographer of *Ship of Fools* (1965); Robert Culp, then starring in the CBS series *Trackdown*; and actor Sydney Pollack, later an Oscar-winning producer and director. As host Bickford tells us, it concerns "the most difficult assignment in the history of mankind.... A hundred thousand other men were tested for it and rejected.... The careful choice was necessary. The year of preparation was necessary, even though the assignment is only for six months, because the man you are looking at will be given the authority to destroy the world."

Capt. David Blair (Culp) reports to his new commander, Col. Hilyard (Simon Scott, seen in several Matheson teleplays), who plays a Presidential message underscoring his "grave responsibility." Blair next meets his fellow captains, including Stein (Pollack), Ward (Warren Vanders), O'Neal (David Garcia) and the slyly named Russell (Jack Hogan), Beaumont, Johnson and Nolan (John Lassell). On a daily two-hour watch, each sits alone at a console with a world map and a key that can be turned from "peace" to "war" to launch missiles against the enemy (unnamed, but presumably Soviet) in the event of a major incident. "If the moment should come when action is required," he is told, "there'll be no time for argument or discussion. The decision will have to be made by one man, instantaneously." One by one, Captains Ward, Russell, Johnson, and Beaumont all drop out due to the unbearable strain, which begins to tell on Blair until, after he hysterically responds to an alert by turning the key to "war," it is revealed that the men are actually in space, unknowingly undergoing another test. Hilyard recites the Lord's Prayer as he sits at the genuine key and wonders, "Who will watch over me?"

This rarity understandably rates no mention in most sources, yet ironically it conformed more closely to Matheson's vision than usual. "I never went into direction, I never wanted to," he told Arnett. "I always said either I would be a total wimpy washout that everybody would walk over or I would turn into a Nazi; I would become so unpleasant, because when I write a thing I know exactly what I want. The reason I get disappointed when I see a film, even if they're good, is it's not what I visualized.... I did a pilot once that Irvin Kershner directed, [a] long, long time ago, and it was amazing to me because it was as if he had looked into my head. He did the script *exactly* as I had visualized it. That's very rare, though. Usually you have to think, 'That's not the way I saw it' and then, over a period of time, it's another way of looking at it." Provided with a videotape of "Thy Will Be Done," Matheson expressed some reservations after seeing the pilot again for the first time in forty years, but added, "I don't blame [Kershner], he did a good job. I think the script just wasn't as good as I remembered it. He did a fine job, and the acting was fine.... I think they just did the one pilot [episode]."

The D.A.'s Man (NBC, 1959): Matheson and Beaumont wrote "Iron Mike Benedict" (2/14/59) for this short-lived half-hour crime drama produced by *Dragnet*'s Jack Webb. John Compton plays former private eye Shannon, who infiltrates mob operations as an undercover investigator in New York City, and reports to assistant D.A. Al Bonacorsi (Ralph Manza). According to the synopsis on tv.com's episode guide, "Shannon is on the streets of Manhattan, this time pretending to be a Bowery bum, to investigate the deaths of two drifters, whom a bar owner just happened to have insurance policies on." Perhaps the ultimate archivist of Matheson's work, William F. Nolan reports that he and Beaumont wrote a second script for this series, but I do not know the title or whether it was filmed.

Buckskin (NBC, 1958–59): For this half-hour Western about Annie O'Connell (Sallie Brophy) and her young son Jody (Tommy Nolan)—who interact with guests and locals at their Buckskin, Montana, boarding house — Matheson and Beaumont wrote "Act of Faith" (3/23/59), in which, per the Classic TV Archive website, an "aloof, mysterious, Bible-quoting stranger" stirs up the town.

Markham (CBS, 1959–60): Matheson shared the story credit with Beaumont for "The Marble Face" (5/23/59), an episode of this half-hour series that starred Ray Milland as wealthy lawyer-turned-private-eye Roy Markham. It was directed by Bretaigne Windust (a veteran of *Alfred Hitchcock Presents* who died shortly afterward) and scripted by John Kneubuhl. Apparently originated by Beaumont and Matheson under the title "Spirit Unwilling," the episode guest-starred character actor John Hoyt as Thornton Delaney, a crooked attorney who conspires with a phony medium to murder his wealthy client, Agnes Morton, and replace her with an actress (Katherine Squire), concealing the fact that Delaney has been embezzling from the Morton estate. Before her death, however, Agnes invited Helen (Betty Lynn), a niece who had not seen her since childhood, to come and live with her. When Helen appears, the panic-stricken conspirators decide to eliminate the impostor, but the latter is saved by the intervention of Markham and his assistant, John Riggs (Simon Scott, who soon left the show, later appearing in Matheson's "The Last Flight").

Wanted: Dead or Alive (CBS, 1958–61): Steve McQueen took an important step on the road to fame as Josh Randall in this half-hour Four Star Television series and consolidated his stardom with another Western, John Sturges's *The Magnificent Seven* (1960), during the show's run. Directed by series regular Donald McDougall, later a desultory contributor to such genre shows as *Star Trek* and *The Night Stalker*, "The Healing Woman" (9/12/59) was scripted by Beaumont, who shared the onscreen credit for the story of this second-season episode with Matheson. Tom Summers (Mort Mills, memorable as the cop in *Psycho*), who has hated doctors since his father died in surgery, is furious when Josh finds his son, Carey (John Collier), stricken with acute appendicitis and seeks medical help. Josh must convince Tom's wife Amanda (Virginia Gregg) to let Dr. Langland (James Westerfield) treat Carey, instead of medicine woman Mag Blake (Helen Kleeb).

Philip Marlowe (ABC, 1959–60): Matheson and Beaumont contributed scripts (for which I could find no details) to this half-hour series produced by William Froug, later of *The Twilight Zone*, with Philip Carey as the famed private eye. "Towards the end of 1958," notes Al Clark in *Raymond Chandler in Hollywood*, Chandler "was approached by two NBC producers, Mark Goodson and Bill Todman, requesting permission to use his character Philip Marlowe in a TV series of that name, and to adapt and paraphrase Chandler material to the requirements of the individual programs. Uncharacteristically, he agreed. Chandler's regard for television was about equal to his fondness for Hollywood: He detested it with the kind of automatic-pilot relish W.C. Fields had once reserved for children and water....

Marlowe kept up his quirk-count by having an apartment overlooking the harbor at Newport Beach and a cabin cruiser to assist in the occasional maritime investigation. 26 episodes were filmed—employing directors like Irvin Kershner, Arthur Hill [*sic*] and, on a more regular basis, Gene Wang—then sold by NBC to ABC..." The program debuted just months after Chandler's death on March 26, 1959.

Have Gun—Will Travel (CBS, 1957–63): For this half-hour series starring Richard Boone as hired gun Paladin, Beaumont and Matheson wrote Ida Lupino's third-season episode "The Lady on the Wall" (2/20/60) and, according to Rathbun and Flanagan, the apparently unfilmed teleplay "The Joust." Hanging over a bar in the ghost town of Bonanza, the painting of a beautiful woman is all that reminds old-timers Elmer Jansen (Ralph Moody), Rafe Adams (Hank Patterson), Ezekiel Becket (James Stone), and Double G. Phillips (Perry Ivins) of happier days, and when it disappears, they suspect

Steve McQueen as Josh Randall in a promotional shot for *Wanted: Dead or Alive* (CBS-TV, 1958–61).

Ida Lupino directs Richard Boone as Paladin in an episode of *Have Gun—Will Travel* (CBS-TV, 1957–63).

Paladin. Learning that saloon owner Jack Foster (Howard Petrie) had sold the canvas to Armand Boucher (Ralph Clanton), Paladin identifies the culprit as Foster's elderly employee, Miss Felton (Lillian Bronson), who reveals that she was the model and original owner, and after she refuses the dealer's offer of $50,000, it is restored to its rightful place.

Bourbon Street Beat (ABC, 1959–60): Matheson co-wrote "Target of Hate" (3/7/60) for this hour-long Warner Bros. series inspired by the success of the same studio's *77 Sunset Strip*. Matheson wrote the story and shared script credit with William L. Stuart on the episode, directed by the prolific Leslie H. Martinson, in which Rex Randolph (Richard Long) is lured to a spurious meeting while his offices are taken over by assassins, each played by an up-and-coming Hollywood actor: Dale Wellington (Richard Chamberlain), Buzz Griffin (James Coburn), and Artie (John Marley). Wellington believes his father was framed and driven to suicide by a crusading journalist now hosting a political rally across the street. As they hold Rex, his partner Cal Calhoun (Andrew Duggan), Rex's his friend Gloria (Saundra Edwards), and their assistant Kenny Madison (Van Williams) prisoner, Wellington learns that his father was not only guilty, but also silenced by employees Buzz and Artie, thus enabling Rex *et alia* to divide and conquer.

Cheyenne (ABC, 1955–63): For this long-running one-hour Warner Bros. Western series, which had a notoriously tumultuous production history, Matheson provided the teleplay for "Home Is the Brave" (3/14/60) from a story by George Waggner (quirkily credited as "george waGGner"), the cinematic jack-of-all-trades who had produced and directed *The Wolf Man* (1941). Directed by Emory Horger, previously the dialogue director on Waggner's production of *Gypsy Wildcat* (1944), this fifth-season episode finds the peripatetic Cheyenne Bodie (Clint Walker) arriving in White River with orders from the Army to bury Private Cole Prescott, only to be told by Sheriff Dan Blaisdell (Brad Johnson) that the town council has voted against allowing the decorated war hero's interment. Council chairman John Thompson (John Howard) sends the hulking Pete Windsor (Mickey Simpson) to warn off Cheyenne, who learns from Cole's widow Maria (Donna Martell) that Cole was a half-breed driven by bigotry into enlisting. Despite a legal loophole that might enable Cheyenne to circumvent the council, violence holds sway until the cavalry arrives to escort Cole's remains to Arlington Cemetery.

"They always had trouble — they had to find six-foot-nine villains, because [Walker] was like six-foot-five," Matheson told me in 2008. He also recalled working on "The Last Hour of John Butler Hickok," which was reportedly an abortive 1962 *Cheyenne* episode that never reached the script stage. "I was doing that for a show that the guy who produced *Lawman* [Jules Schermer] was doing. I remember talking to him and saying, 'You know, I'd like George C. Scott to play this part,' and he said something like, 'George C. Scott could play a midget if he wanted to.' I don't recall Jules Schermer becoming a producer on *Cheyenne*, but after they cancelled *Lawman* [see below], maybe he did." (That same year, Schermer did in fact produce "A Man Called Ragan" [4/23/62], an episode of *Cheyenne* in which Walker's character did not appear, and which was eventually spun off into the show's short-lived replacement, *The Dakotas*, with Larry Ward starring as Marshal Frank Ragan.) Asked if the similarity between the names "John Butler Hickok" and Wild Bill Hickok — about whom Matheson has written several times — was more than a coincidence, he answered, "Yeah, of course. It *was* Wild Bill Hickok."

Lawman (ABC, 1958–62): Surprisingly, Matheson wrote more teleplays (six) for this half-hour Western series — starring taciturn John Russell as Marshal Dan Troop of Laramie, Wyoming, and Peter Brown as his young deputy, Johnny McKay — than for any other program except *The Twilight Zone*. "One of the first things I ever did for television, even before *The Twilight Zone*, was for the Western series *Lawman*," he recalled in an interview with me for *Noir* of his first script for the Warner Bros. show, then in its second season. "It was called 'Thirty Minutes' [3/20/60] and it took place in a half-hour. I like to do that [writing in a limited time frame], and I thought, 'The shorter the period of time I can make it, the better.'" A longtime Western enthusiast, Matheson had published such oaters as "The Conqueror" (*Bluebook*, May 1954) and "Too Proud to Lose" (*Fifteen Western Tales*, February 1955), and later used a pair of hitherto unsold stories (eventually published in his 1993 collection *By the Gun*) as the uncredited basis for *Lawman* episodes, including "Thirty Minutes," which he adapted from "Of Death and Thirty Minutes."

The short story concerns a high-strung outlaw named Jake Warner, who kills the proprietor of a barroom and his older son (the latter recognized him from a wanted poster), then holds all the remaining occupants hostage while demanding that the sheriff clear the street outside for his getaway in thirty minutes. Jake shoots several more before being gunned down by a saloon singer, Jeanie Foster. Directed by Robert T. Sparr, a sometime television editor and writer as well, this episode featured frequent heavy Jack Elam as Jake (his last name understandably altered to Wilson), and transposed the action to the show's frequent setting of the Birdcage Restaurant & Saloon. When cowboy Len Eaton (John Clarke) recognizes Jake, McKay is in the Birdcage and tries to intervene, exchanging fire with Wilson; both men are wounded. After killing Len, the outlaw forces Troop to clear the street and disarm. Luckily, the unconscious McKay revives as Jake is about to kill his boss, and distracts him with a shot from inside the saloon. Troop recovers his gun and finishes the job.

Matheson received the Writers Guild Award for the first of his four third-season episodes, "Yawkey" (10/23/60), directed by old Hollywood hand Stuart Heisler. Arriving in Laramie, Yawkey (Ray Danton) states his intention to meet Troop in the street and kill him, refusing to say why. At the appointed hour, the legendarily fast gun says, "It's a nice day to die, marshal," and is shot down while pulling the trigger on an empty gun. He reveals as his life ebbs away that he'd grown weary of being challenged and chose Troop, whom he knew by reputation, to help him commit suicide.

Heisler also directed Matheson's "Samson the Great" (11/20/60), which concerns a pugnacious prizefighter (Mickey Simpson, previously seen in "Home Is the Brave"), and an offer of fifty dollars to anyone who can stay in the ring with him for two minutes, thus forcing Troop to curtail his antisocial behavior with fists rather than firepower.

Deputy McKay takes center stage in "Cornered" (12/11/60) when he is forced into a fatal confrontation with the feared Jed Barker (Frank DeKova, later Chief Wild Eagle on *F Troop*). Next McKay must endure public pressure from the people of Laramie to face up to Jed's presumably vengeful son Jim (Tom Troupe), only to learn that Jim hated his father and desires a showdown no more than McKay. Matheson's short story "Little Jack Cornered" ends on a more somber note, with protagonist Jack Haskell also killing Jed Baladine's younger brother Kirk, who he later realizes was terrified of him, and then waiting apprehensively for the inevitable challengers to his now-legendary prowess with a gun; this recalls Gregory Peck's titular Jimmy Ringo in *The Gunfighter* (1950). Sharing the real-time structure of "Thirty Minutes," director Robert B. Sinclair's "Homecoming" (2/5/61) evokes the classic *High Noon* (1952) as Troop awaits the arrival of an escaped convict, Frank Walker (Marc Lawrence, also the director of "Cornered"), who vowed vengeance on the lawman when he was imprisoned. Walker reveals that he is now terminally ill and wants nothing more than to die with his family.

In his first of three Matheson teleplays, horror icon and Shakespearean John Carradine was well cast as the impoverished, alcoholic Geoffrey Hendon in season four's "The Actor" (5/27/62), staggering into the Birdcage with a gunshot wound and accepting the aid of proprietor Lily Merrill (Peggie Castle) in this episode, directed by future filmmaker Richard C. Sarafian. Little more than a supporting player here, Troop tries to save Hendon when Martha Carson (Mary Anderson) willfully misconstrues his intentions toward her as inappropriate,

Marshal Dan Troop (John Russell), Lily Merrill (Peggie Castle), and Johnny McKay (Peter Brown) on *Lawman* (ABC-TV, 1958–62).

and urges her husband Bill (Warren Kemmerling) to gun him down. Troop shoots the pistol out of Bill's hand, but Hendon is mortally wounded by Martha herself. After urging Troop to "let her freedom, if freedom it is, be in some small measure my tribute to the many, many women I have truly wronged," he delivers his own epitaph, courtesy of the Bard, dying with a beatific smile as the patrons applaud his final performance. "With great imagination, [director Richard C.] Sarafian ended the story with a closing curtain, in recognition of Hendon's theatrical life. I don't think I'd ever seen that before, certainly not in a Western," an admiring Matheson says.

"When I was in the hospital in England during the war," he told *Midnight Graffiti*'s Paul Sammon, "I used to read two Westerns a day.... I was very happy with [*Lawman*]. Almost more happy than any other show I had worked on in the early days of television, because of the producer, Jules Schermer. He had very strong control over the show. He liked my writing, he used good directors, he never changed anything. So I ultimately had about six episodes on that show, and they all turned out extremely well." Group member John Tomerlin was even more heavily involved with the series, and told Christopher Conlon in a *Filmfax* interview that Matheson "recommended me to the producer. I ended up doing a dozen originals and a couple of rewrites. Westerns were fun because you could write about virtually any subject — capital punishment, racial prejudice, political corruption — and people wouldn't object because they didn't recognize what you were doing. All they saw were white hats and black hats. You had to be careful about some content, though; this was just after the McCarthy affair, and story editors were still asking, 'Are you now or have you ever been...?'"

Thriller (NBC, 1960–62): For the second season of this hour-long anthology series hosted by Boris Karloff, Matheson adapted "The Return of Andrew Bentley" (12/11/61) from a story by August Derleth and Mark Schorer. John Newland starred as Ellis Corbett and, as he did while hosting ABC's allegedly fact-based supernatural series *One Step Beyond*, doubled as the director. Ellis and his wife Sheila (Antoinette Bower) visit his aged uncle Amos Wilder (Terence de Marney), who tells the couple he is about to die, and that as his only living relative, Ellis will inherit his house, on the condition that he remain there at all times and make frequent checks of the burial vault where Amos is sealed after his death, which is ruled as a suicide by Dr. Weatherbee (Philip Bourneuf). Terrified by the ghost of Andrew Bentley (played by Reggie Nalder, the *Nosferatu*-like vampire in 1979's *Salem's Lot*), a sorcerer killed by Amos, the Corbetts, Weatherbee and the Rev-

A portrait of Reggie Nalder as the sorcerer from "The Return of Andrew Bentley" on *Thriller* (NBC-TV, 1961). Photograph courtesy of the Paul M. Sammon Collection.

erend Burkhardt (Oscar Beregi, later seen in Matheson's "Mute") must find and destroy Bentley's body in order to stop his familiar (Tom Hennesy), a low-budget Lovecraftian demon, from inhabiting Amos's remains.

Beaumont and Sohl adapted the work of H.P. Lovecraft, who profoundly influenced Bloch and Derleth, in *The Haunted Palace* (1963) and *Monster of Terror* (aka *Die, Monster, Die*, 1965), respectively, but Matheson never did. "He wasn't my kind of writer — too heavy," he said in an interview with me for *Filmfax*. "Heavy stuff. You know, he'd spend fifty pages talking about some Eldritch horror that is so horrible to describe that he can't possibly do it, and then in the last ten pages he describes it. I mean obviously, the man was brilliant, I just don't care for that kind of writing.... I spoke to [Newland] a lot of times about some scripts for *One Step Beyond*, which I would have enjoyed doing. He was a very good actor....[but] I didn't like what was done to the *Thriller* script. They redid it. There was a lot more humor in my script. The attitudes [of Ellis and Sheila Corbett] were sort of like those of Bill Shatner and his wife in 'Nick of Time,' and then little by little they became frightened, because something really frightening was going on. But the show *Thriller*, the whole thing had a Lovecraft atmosphere to it."

The short story appears in *Colonel Markesan and Less Pleasant People*; in their introduction, Derleth and Schorer wrote, "The stories in this collection grew out of a felicitous collaborative effort in the summer of 1931 [during which] the method of work was this — the basic outline for each story was set down by Derleth, the entire first draft then written by Schorer, [and] a final revision made by Derleth [who then] prepared the story for submission — usually to *Weird Tales* [wherein 'The Return of Andrew Bentley' was originally published in September of 1932] or *Strange Tales*." Writing in 1966, the authors added with refreshing modesty, "One of these stories — 'The Return of Andrew Bentley' — it might be pointed out, achieved a sort of modest fame by its inclusion in Bennett Cerf's Modern Library anthology [from 1944], *Famous Ghost Stories*, and more recently entertained an even wider audience on television — but the remainder saw the light of day only briefly and then sank back into oblivion."

Associate producer Doug Benton told Alan Warren, the author of *This Is a* Thriller*: An Episode Guide, History and Analysis of the Classic 1960s Television Series*, "When [producer] Bill Frye was put on the show after the original producer [Fletcher Markle] had made a mess of it, I came over to work for him as I had on *General Electric Theater*. The first thing I did was call Richard Matheson, and he said the man who knew this particular genre was Charles Beaumont; they were both satellites of Ray Bradbury's. As it turned out, it wasn't the right sort of thing for Matheson. And Chuck Beaumont said he didn't want to do television [although both did contribute to the series]; he said, 'Look, I just got a feature picture [to write].' He said, 'Call Forry Ackerman, and get his complete file of *Weird Tales*. He just bought it from me.'... We had a whole legal staff tracking the authors down, and we paid them two or three times as much as they were paid for the stories in the first place." Added Matheson in *Midnight Graffiti*, "I didn't pick [the story]. It was assigned to me.... The music in that episode ... was great. [Morton Stevens] did a fine job on that."

Matheson's desire to achieve a dynamic similar to that in "Nick of Time" led him to create the character of Sheila Corbett, who has no literary equivalent. Otherwise his adaptation (one of eighteen *Thriller* episodes based on short stories from *Weird Tales*), or at least the version that was ultimately broadcast, is relatively faithful to the Derleth-Schorer original, with a few interesting exceptions. The episode, for example, raises the dramatic stakes in several ways, with Amos insisting that Ellis spend "twenty-four hours of every day" at the house, rather than "most of your time"; Bentley's third manifestation makes the elderly caretaker, Jacob (Ken Renard), literally drop dead of fright in the television version, whereas earlier the knowledge of his return merely made Jacob head for the hills. When Ellis first surprises Bentley outside the vault in the story, he springs forward and seizes Bentley's hand before being knocked unconscious, only to find "the unmistakable first two joints of the little finger" clutched in his own hand when he awakens. When Bentley's body is burned, the familiar does not vanish until Ellis has retrieved the fragment of Bentley's finger and thrown it into the flames.

Benton recalled in *This Is a* Thriller, "John Newland was an absolute genius at staging things. He'd come on the set and say, 'You stand there and you do this and you do the other thing,' and all of a sudden it would be four o'clock and you'd be going home. Actors liked working for him, because they thought they were doing what they liked, when they were actually doing exactly what *he* liked. And then, at other times, John would get bored. He was like the little girl in that rhyme: 'When he was good he was wonderful, and when he was bad he was horrid.'" Newland, who appeared opposite Tom Conway's Bulldog Drummond in two 1948 films, was then a prolific television director, whose genre credits include the TV-movie *Don't Be Afraid of the Dark* (1973) and episodes of *Star Trek, Night Gallery,* and *The Sixth Sense*. Considered *Thriller*'s high point, his "Pigeons from Hell" (6/6/61) also featured Renard, and was based on a story by Conan creator Robert E. Howard; Stephen King notes in *Danse Macabre* that "some say it was the single most frightening story ever done on TV," although he nominates Newland's "I Kiss Your Shadow" (3/25/62), an episode of *Bus Stop* based on a Robert Bloch tale.

Combat! (ABC, 1962–67): Matheson utilized his pseudonym Logan Swanson for the premiere episode of this wartime drama, "Forgotten Front" (10/2/62). It was based on a story by Jerome Coopersmith and directed by Robert Altman, a series regular and World War II veteran who was later slated to direct Matheson's oft-postponed stage play *Magician's Choice*. Matheson told Mark Rathbun in *He Is Legend* that the pen name Logan Swanson "comes from my wife's mother's maiden name, Logan, and my mother's maiden name which is actually Svenningsen, but in this country it was changed to Swanson. He came into being when they had the first script for *Combat!* [rewritten]. They sent me a copy of my script, and I called them up and said, 'You sent me the wrong script.' And they said, 'No, no, that's it.' And it was so grotesquely altered that I didn't want anything to do with it. I called the Writers Guild and said, 'Look, I don't want my name on this.' And they said, 'Listen — if you don't have some credit on it, you lose residuals and everything.' And I was supporting four children, so discretion took the better part of valor there, and I invented Logan Swanson."

In point of fact, the pseudonym dates back at least as far as the March 1957 issue of *Alfred Hitchcock's Mystery Magazine*, which contained two of Matheson's stories, "The Children of Noah" and "I'll Make It Look Good" (later retitled "A Visit to Santa Claus"); he could only use his real byline on one of them, so the latter wound up as Swanson's first known credit. "Good old Logan Swanson," he laughed in *Richard Matheson's The Twilight Zone Scripts*. "I always wanted to write a short story about a writer sitting in a fancy restaurant, and this seedy guy in rags comes in and sits at his table. And his eyes are all red, and he hasn't slept for days, and it turns out to be the writer's pen name — who is miserable because he got stuck with all the stuff the successful author didn't like." Stephen King wrought a variation on this same idea with *The Dark Half*, filmed by George A. Romero in 1991, in which an unsuccessful author tries to "kill off" his literary alter ego, a writer of violent bestsellers who then manifests himself as a flesh-and-blood killer. "He's written so much crap, Logan Swanson," Matheson told Sammon in *Midnight Graffiti*. "That man's career has been abysmal."

As filmed, the episode begins with a four-man team being wiped out by a booby trap in an abandoned French die works, where they have been sent to guide artillery fire toward a German cannon, and replaced by King Company mainstays Sgt. Chip Saunders (Vic Morrow), Pvt. William G. "Wild Man" Kirby (Jack Hogan), Doc Walton (Steven Rogers), and Pfc Paul "Caje" Lemay (Pierre Jalbert). Found taking refuge in the same building is English-speaking Corp. Carl Dorffman (Albert Paulsen), a reluctant German soldier and former carnival magician who quickly develops an unlikely rapport with Doc, to the extent that when the medic stumbles and drops his carbine while guarding him, Dorffman casually picks up the fallen weapon and hands it back to Doc with the barrel pointing toward himself. Aided by Altman's taut direction and the crisp cinematography of rookie Robert B. Hauser (who would shoot Matheson's *The Night Strangler* a decade later), the episode depicts the crisis of conscience Caje undergoes when an approaching German tank forces them to withdraw across the Vire River, and he must weigh the possibility that Dorffman might reveal the plans for their advance on the following day.

Matheson added an ironic postscript in an interview with me for *Filmfax*. "The funny thing is that Robert Blees, the producer, was so full of praise when I went in to be introduced to people, and I guess he must have done [the rewrite], since he was a writer. [Robert J. Shaw is also credited in some sources, but not onscreen.] It was just changed so much, I really thought it was somebody else's script, and that's why I [used the pseudonym].... But then I met Blees at a party many, many years later, and for the first time said, 'Why did you do that to my script? Why did you change it so much?' And he said, 'We didn't change it.' It was like George Orwell at work." Blees had been a screenwriter since the 1940s, with credits including Jack Arnold's *The Glass Web* and *High School Confidential!*, and as a producer was already a veteran of such shows as *Bonanza* and *Bus Stop*. Among his mostly undistinguished genre efforts are the features *The Black Scorpion* (1957), *Screaming Mimi*, *From the Earth to the Moon* (both 1958), *Whoever Slew Auntie Roo?* (1971), *Dr. Phibes Rises Again*, and *Frogs* (both 1972), as well as the Dan Curtis telefilm *Curse of the Black Widow* (1977).

The Alfred Hitchcock Hour (CBS, 1962–64): Based on Matheson's 1959 novel, "Ride the Nightmare" (11/29/62) was the first of his two teleplays for Hitchcock's long-running anthology show, which shuttled back and forth between CBS and NBC in thirty- and sixty-minute incarnations. In an interview with me for *Noir*, he said, "It was only an hour long, which means with twelve minutes off [for commercials] it was only forty-eight minutes, which was a little short for a novel. It had Hugh O'Brian and [John] Cassavetes's wife, Gena Rowlands.... Norman Lloyd [a sometime actor who played the title role in Hitchcock's *Saboteur* (1942)] produced it." After seeing it for the first time since 1962, he added in a letter, "Very nicely done and it's nice to know that, once in the long ago, Gena Rowlands was in something I wrote." It was directed by Bernard Girard, who began his Hollywood career as a screenwriter.

Christopher Martin (O'Brian) receives a threatening phone call from Fred (Jay Lanin), who soon breaks into Chris's Los Angeles home and is killed with his own gun in a struggle, but not before revealing that he had identified the former Chris Phillips from a magazine photo and that his old friend is a fugitive from justice. This comes as quite a shock to Chris's wife Helen (Rowlands). When she learns from a newspaper that Fred was one of three recently escaped convicts sentenced to life imprisonment for a 1948 murder, Chris explains that he had acted as the lookout while Fred, Adam (John Anderson), and Steve (Richard Shannon) were robbing a jewelry store, and then lost his nerve and fled when he heard a police car coming, not knowing at the time that they had killed the jeweler. After burying Fred in the hills, Chris is accosted by Adam and Steve, who demand that he deliver $4,000 in "traveling money" to them in Latigo Canyon. When he returns home he discovers that they have kidnapped Helen as insurance. In an appropriately Hitchcockian touch, he is buttonholed by talkative neighbor Mrs. Anthony (Philippa Bevans) while on line at the bank to make a withdrawal.

"There's a scene [in the novel] which sort of has a British quality to it," Matheson said in the *Noir* interview, "where he is in agony in the bank waiting to take some money out, and this woman comes up who he's been working with on a musical charity, and wants him to talk all about it, and he's dying inside. That's the sort of the thing the British do, and that's nice suspense." Adam tries to take the money without freeing Helen, so Chris grabs his gun and forces Adam to lead him to the shack where Steve is holding her. After effecting her release and dropping Steve in a shootout, Chris runs out of ammo and must flee with Helen. Chris starts a brushfire that kills Adam and, with Helen, climbs the canyon wall to safety just before the police arrive. Matheson's otherwise extremely faithful teleplay eliminates the character of their daughter Connie, who in the novel is taken hostage instead of Helen.

It also simplifies a more elaborate climax (later dramatized in the feature version, *Cold Sweat*), in which a badly wounded Steve forces Chris to return to town for a doctor, and tells Helen to keep him awake while Adam, who wants to flee into Mexico, waits for Steve to pass out.

Swedish stage and screen actor Alf Kjellin, who also appeared in such American films as *Ice Station Zebra* (1968), directed "The Thirty-First of February" (1/4/63), which Matheson adapted from the 1950 novel by Julian Symons. As he noted in the *Noir* interview, however, he later substituted his Swanson pseudonym "because they changed it so much. I didn't like what they did to the script. I've seen it — I may even have a copy of it — and it just doesn't add up the way I think my script did. It's an interesting novel." Certainly, Matheson must have seemed an appropriate choice to adapt a psychological suspense tale in which a man who has lost his wife under somewhat suspicious circumstances is driven into a paranoid frenzy by the Kafkaesque machinations of an anonymous tormentor. Offsetting this grim storyline is a very pointed satire of the advertising industry, in which Symons himself had been a copywriter like his protagonist, Andy Anderson (transformed into an industrial designer in the script). The novel, already brief at barely 200 pages, also includes several digressions regarding his childhood and the baroquely colorful characters in his low-rent neighborhood.

The finished episode hews fairly closely to the main plotline as Andy (David Wayne) explains at an inquest that on the evening of February 4 he heard a thud and found his wife, Valerie (Kathleen O'Malley), dead at the bottom of the cellar stairs, where the light bulb had burned out. Although the D.A. (Stacy Harris) asks why a book of matches was found nearby, her death is ruled an accident. When Andy returns to work on the 25th, a series of strange occurrences begins: His desk calendar is periodically changed back to the 4th, to the perplexity of his secretary, Maggie Wright (Bernadette Hale); Sgt. Kress (William Conrad) produces an unsigned letter suggesting he murdered Valerie; and Andy finds a letter apparently written by her to an unknown lover, evidently one of his own colleagues. Confiding in an attractive co-worker, Molly O'Rourke (Elizabeth Allen), Andy theorizes that the lover is trying to force him into a confession, assuming he had heard about the affair and killed Valerie in a jealous rage, and that the newly hired young Peter Granville (William Sargent) has been brought in to spy on him. Andy also reveals that he suffered an emotional breakdown from battle fatigue during the war.

Bringing Molly back to his house, where his romantic overtures are not entirely unwelcome, a drunken Andy bitterly describes Valerie as "a dull, drab, cold woman [with] no taste, no refinement," but insists that he did not kill her. Yet while Molly is helping Andy to bed, he sees Valerie's face superimposed on hers and tries to strangle the terrified young woman before coming back to his senses. Scored by Robert Drasnin, the show reaches its climax as the increasingly unstable Andy, whose calendar now bears the nonexistent February 31 date, has a falling-out with his boss, Mr. Vincent (Staats Cotsworth), and returns home to find the night of the 4th recreated with a dummy in Valerie's place, prompting the crazed Andy to attack the accusatory Kress. Assisted by Granville, an undercover colleague, Kress had persecuted Andy, believing as his literary counterpart, Inspector Cresse, states that, "A policeman is like God. He wants to know the truth. And he's bound to believe that any means are justifiable — any means, do you understand me? — if he can find the truth through them." Tragically, his "unorthodox methods" have driven an innocent man insane.

In *Midnight Graffiti*, Matheson recalled an encounter with Hitchcock around that time: "Once, it looked like I had the screenplay assignment on *The Birds*, and I met with him," he told Paul Sammon. "He is, I guess, a very shy, kind of withdrawn person. See, there was supposed to be my agent and his agent there as a kind of buffer, but there wasn't. There was nobody, just he and I. And I screwed myself out of the job in the first ten seconds by saying, 'I don't think you should show too many birds, Mr. Hitchcock.' [*Laughs*] I was looking at ... Daphne Du Maurier's story, which is a fantastic thing. I wish they had followed it.... I told Hitchcock, 'You know, I think the more birds you show, the less frightening it will be.' Again, it's my idea that terror is what you don't see, it's what you imagine.... I think that the only really scary scene in *The Birds* ... was when they were alone in the house, and Hitchcock had the birds outside all around them. Pecking at the door, rattling at the windows — you just hear those strange electronic sounds at the same time. Wow! But the rest of them are just sort of spectacle scenes [and] it just takes too long to get to the birds." Evan Hunter got the writing job.

Bob Hope Presents the Chrysler Theatre (NBC, 1963–67): For the fourth season of this anthology series, Matheson wrote "Time of Flight" (9/21/66), which according to Rathbun and Flanagan concerns "a private detective hired to protect an informer from vengeance [who] seems certain to fail in his task — until he is aided by a group of emissaries from the future." The pilot for the proposed series *Race Against Time*, it was directed by television mainstay Joseph Sargent, a multiple Emmy winner whose few features include *Colossus: The Forbin Project* (1970) and *The Taking of Pelham One Two Three* (1974). "They did a nice job on that," Matheson recalled in an interview with me for *Filmfax*. "[Jack] Klugman played the guy from the future [Markos], but then the lead [Al Packer] was Jack Kelly.... I liked him, and I liked Juliet Mills, and they kept the humor in it. I thought Sargent did a nice job. I don't know whether they kept [the episodes of the program] on tape, or burned them afterwards. They destroyed so many wonderful television shows."

Star Trek (NBC, 1966–69): Matheson's sole contribution to this seminal SF series was "The Enemy Within" (10/6/66), in which a transporter malfunction splits Kirk into his good and evil selves. It was directed by Leo Penn, a blacklisted sometime stage actor and the father of Sean and Christopher Penn. As veteran actor Don Eitner recalled in Mark Phillips and Frank Garcia's *Science Fiction Television Series*, "I played the good/evil camera double for Bill Shatner. I'm kind of the King of B Movies. I fought the *Queen of Blood* [1966] with Dennis Hopper, and I was a soldier eaten by a giant grasshopper in *Beginning of the End* [1957]. But I never worked harder than I did on *Star Trek*. It was a very exacting schedule. I had to rehearse both 'characters.' Bill was very pleased with the results. The cast was very dedicated. Bill even challenged some of the logic of the scenes.... Things were worked out and it turned out to be a terrific show." The fifth episode in order of both broadcast and production, this also introduced the famous "Vulcan nerve pinch," added by actor Leonard Nimoy as a suitably sophisticated method for his character to render the evil Kirk unconscious.

A contamination of magnetic ore causes the *Enterprise's* transporter to malfunction during a specimen-gathering mission on the planet Alpha 177, whose temperature reaches 120° below zero. After engineer Montgomery Scott (James Doohan) beams Kirk back aboard the ship and escorts the shaky-looking captain from the transporter room, a strange alter ego materializes. The double demands brandy from Dr. Leonard "Bones" McCoy (DeForest Kelley) and almost rapes Yeoman Janice Rand (Grace Lee Whitney). Scotty shows Kirk and Spock (Nimoy) a "savage, ferocious opposite" that appeared a few seconds after a docile animal indigenous to Alpha 177 — in reality, a small dog with a horn and antennae appended — was beamed aboard the *Enterprise*, and explains that because of the risk of a similar duplication, he dares not beam up the landing party led by Sulu (George Takei).

The double's existence and the suddenly indecisive captain's concomitant innocence are acknowledged at last, and Kirk orders his doppelganger taken alive, sensing that the latter's death could cause his own. But the wily double, who is identifiable by the scratches Yeoman Rand left on his cheek, covers them with makeup before Spock subdues him with a Vulcan nerve pinch. Kirk's power of command continues to wane while Scotty races to repair the transporter and rescue the landing party, which faces a frozen death below as night falls and the temperature on the surface of the planet plummets. Although Scott succeeds in reversing the process to reintegrate the divided alien dog, Bones grimly intones, in another famous first for the newborn *Star Trek* series, "He's dead, Jim." Planning to go through the transporter together despite the risk, Kirk frees the double, who knocks him out, scratches his face, switches clothes with him and assumes his identity, ordering the ship to leave the planet's orbit. The real Kirk recovers, faces down his hysterical alter ego on the bridge, and persuades him that they will both survive when the transporter is repaired and reunites them, as they do.

Later converted into short-story form in James Blish's *Star Trek 8*, this episode was singled out as a favorite by both creator-producer Gene Roddenberry (in a 1991 *TV Guide* cover story on the show's twenty-fifth anniversary) and Shatner. Matheson told Sammon, "I didn't do more because I wasn't too happy with the way it had turned out. There was a case where a script was altered without my consent or knowledge.... [Years later] I was called in, as was every other writer in town, on [the first *Star Trek* feature film]. And my one suggestion was that they turn [Arthur C. Clarke's] *Rendezvous with Rama* ... into a *Star Trek*. I think that's a marvelous novel. Clarke is, to me, the best science fiction writer in the world." He added in his *Collected Stories*, "I had submitted other ideas to Gene ... and he never chose any other beside the one that was done."

Cinefantastique's Sue Uram discussed "The Enemy Within," and addressed the psychological underpinnings of Matheson's script, in her episode guide to the "classic" series: "Matheson superbly points out that all human beings have various character and personality traits which allow them to function. Removal of all evil from a personality may cause the formation of an incomplete person. Matheson looks at the Id and the Ego leaving the viewer to act in the capacity of the Superego. The splitting of Kirk into two separate, psychologically incomplete individuals in the transporter incident results in a temporary impairment of his decision-making ability. Happily, his full capacities are restored upon the reuniting of his two selves." Matheson's script was published in *Matheson Uncollected: Volume One* in 2008.

In *Star Trek Memories*, Shatner noted, "The writer's ten-to-twelve page story would arrive, and Gene [and associate producers] John D.F. Black and Bob Justman would all comment upon the feasibility and potential of the project. A round-robin of memos on the subject began.... Once the basic story had been approved, the writer would go off and spend the next several weeks hammering out the first draft of his full-blown script. When that was complete, it would be handed in, run through the mimeo machines, read by [the trio], then ultimately discussed in a whole new round of interoffice memos." He quotes one from Black to Justman regarding Matheson's script: "I would like to state that I feel there are too many speaking parts and extras in this story. If there were a great need for many speaking parts, I would understand it, but this is not the case. Also, how about letting some of our regulars have some of the speaking parts that are necessary to the story? Such as SULU and SCOTT. On the first page of the teaser, do we need to establish 16 crew members down on the surface of the planet? Five lives are important too. Sixteen lives are more than I feel we can afford for this segment."

Talking to Robert Arnett in *Creative Screenwriting*, Matheson elaborated on his dissatisfaction with the episode's uncredited rewrite: "If you have twenty, thirty characters and you can just keep jumping from one to the other, the difficulty is trying to bring it all together and tie up the strings at the end, [but] my script ... just completely investigated the aspect of [Kirk] having a negative and a positive character. Roddenberry added the element of some of the crew stuck down on the planet and they couldn't get up because the transporter wasn't working. It was all right, but it took away, for me, from the interesting thing, which was: Here's the captain with his negative and positive in the ship at the same time and all the different things you could get into. The old A story and B story — I'm not a B story person. I hate B stories.... If I'm in an interesting situation, I don't want to go away from it, I don't want something else to happen, I want to stay with it. But, it can be done. We were watching *The Bridge on the River Kwai* [1957] the other night and they succeeded, they had different things going on at the same time and it was fascinating. You have to be really adept at that, and want to tell the story that way."

The Girl from U.N.C.L.E. (NBC, 1966–67): This single-season spy spoof spin-off from *The Man from U.N.C.L.E.* starred Stefanie Powers as the eponymous April Dancer, Noel Harrison as her partner Mark Slate, and venerable character actor Leo G. Carroll, repeating his role as the head of the United Network Command for Law and Enforcement

April Dancer (Stefanie Powers) and Vic Ryan (Denny Miller) at the mercy of sword-wielding eccentric Honore Le Gallows (Claude Woolman) in "The Atlantis Affair" on *The Girl from U.N.C.L.E.* (NBC-TV, 1966).

(U.N.C.L.E.), Alexander Waverly. Best known today as Roman Castevet in Roman Polanski's *Rosemary's Baby* (1968), Sidney Blackmer played Teddy Roosevelt more than a dozen times in his fifty-odd years on stage and screen, and guest-starred in Matheson's teleplay "The Atlantis Affair" (11/15/66), which, as Matheson told me in an interview for *Filmfax*, "was much more ambitious [than what was shot]. It had to do with Atlantis and everything, you know, [that] obviously they could not afford to do, and [producer] Doug Benton [who had been the associate producer of *Thriller*] had to sort of prune it down to size to fit them, so I don't even remember it." Formerly the first assistant director or production manager on several of Matheson's *Twilight Zone* episodes, E. Darrell Hallenbeck helmed this and many other entries from both of the *U.N.C.L.E.* series.

A cryptogram leads Prof. Henry Antrum (Blackmer) to the entrance to a portion of Atlantis that survived the continent's destruction, and to quartz crystals that can combine the rays of the sun into a beam 1,000 times more powerful than a laser. Both are on the Caribbean estate of Honore Le Gallows (Claude Woolman), an eccentric who abhors progress and resides in a seventeenth-century *milieu*. U.N.C.L.E.'s opposition, Thrush, has taken an interest due to the crystals' potential use as weapons, so Antrum is repeatedly captured by Thrush — which has compelled the cooperation of Le Gallows by threatening his livelihood — and rescued by April and Mark with the help of Vic Ryan (ex–Tarzan Denny Miller), an apolitical local entrepreneur whose rented truck becomes a casualty of the conflict. Khigh Dhiegh, memorable as the brainwashing scientist in John Frankenheimer's *The Manchurian Candidate* (1962) and later as Jack Lord's archenemy Wo Fat on TV's *Hawaii Five-O*, plays Thrush agent Col. Frank Faber, who destroys the tunnel and flees with the crystals, only to be blown to smithereens when the crystals are exposed to, and activated by, the sun.

Late Night Horror (BBC, 1968): In *The BFI Companion to Horror*, Tony Mechele calls this "a six-part taped color BBC series, mixing fine performances with classic stories" (which included Robert Aickman's "The Bells of Hell," Roald Dahl's "William and Mary," and Arthur Conan Doyle's "The Kiss of Blood"). "No Such Thing as a Vampire" (4/19/68) was based on Matheson's tale, published in *Playboy* in October of 1959, about a man who uses the fear of the undead to trick a superstitious servant into disposing of the rival for his wife's affections with a wooden stake. Andrew Keir, who starred as the fiendishly clever cuckold, Dr. Gheria, was a strong presence in Hammer genre films like *Dracula — Prince of Darkness* (1966), *Quatermass and the Pit* (aka *Five Million Years to Earth*, 1967), and *Blood from the Mummy's Tomb* (1971). Directed by *Doctor Who* veteran Paddy Russell, the episode costarred Meg Wynn Owen as Alexis Gheria, Peter Blythe as Dr. Michael Vares, and Thomas Gallagher as Gheria's unwitting puppet Karel. It was written by Hugh Leonard and not, as some sources allege, by Matheson, who later adapted the story in the TV-movie *Dead of Night*.

According to Colin Cutler's comprehensive online *Illustrated Gazette* article devoted to this episode, which was the BBC's first production in color, "No material is known to exist at either the BBC Archive or in private hands." Director Russell had previously worked with writer Leonard and producer Harry Moore on the BBC's *Thirty-Minute Theatre*, and as she told Cutler, "I vividly recall the corrections needed to color balance the new studio cameras. My comment to the technical operations manager that faces in Transylvania did go green occasionally was not appreciated! Having come from live television, I always recorded in sequence, with as few breaks as possible. Not only did this keep the expensive editing down, but I also felt it gave an 'edge' to the performances."

Journey to the Unknown (ABC, 1968–69): Many of Hammer's early hits were theatrical adaptations of radio and television series and serials, but as Tom Johnson and Deborah Del

Vecchio note in their invaluable *Hammer Films: An Exhaustive Checklist*, "Because of Hammer's success at the box office, there was really no need until the late sixties for the company to become seriously involved in television. However, Hammer's success in the theaters began to wane a bit, and the company's association with 20th Century–Fox led to the production of a television series, *Journey to the Unknown....* [T]he series went into production at Elstree Studios and lasted through most of 1968. In all, 17 stories were filmed by producer Joan Harrison, who had made her mark on *Alfred Hitchcock Presents* a decade earlier. The episodes featured performers who were recognizable to American audiences and premiered on the ABC network on September 26, 1968. The series ran until January 30, 1969, but made little impact in America." The episodes "Miss Belle" (10/24/68) and "The New People" (11/14/68) were based on short stories by Beaumont.

As Robert Bloch wrote in his delightful "unauthorized autobiography" *Once Around the Bloch*, "In a moment of folly and madness [Harrison] asked me to join the team in London.... The first script I turned out was an adaptation of my own story, 'The Indian Spirit Guide' [10/10/68]. It met with favor and they asked for another story of mine, subject to approval by 20th Century–Fox's resident geniuses back home on Pico Boulevard. Word was not forthcoming; apparently some of the geniuses were doing a long lunch. Since I was on salary, it was suggested I adapt [Matheson's] 'Girl of My Dreams' [12/5/68] ... which they already owned." Although Matheson had previously written several scripts for Hammer, his story — published in *The Magazine of Fantasy and Science Fiction* in October of 1963 — was adapted by Bloch and Michael J. Bird; it was directed by Peter Sasdy (as were the Beaumont episodes).

American actor Michael Callan, whose credits include the genre film *Mysterious Island* (1961), stars as unscrupulous London-based photographer Greg Richards, a kind of reverse blackmailer who extorts money in exchange for specific information that allows people to prevent various catastrophes, seen in precognitive dreams by his reluctant and emotionally dependent wife, Carrie (Zena Walker). When she dreams that the son of wealthy Mrs. Wheeler (Jan Holden) will be run down by a van, Greg thinks he is onto the big score at last and plans to flee the country. After the guilt-ridden Carrie gives Mrs. Wheeler the information for free, Greg fatally injures her during a violent altercation, only to learn from her dying breath of his own impending murder, the time and location of which are now unknown. Matheson related to Stanley Wiater in his *Collected Stories* commentary, "Well, I believe I wrote that story very carefully, too. I seem to have written quite a few stories very carefully. I liked the idea that for once the really rotten guy gets his comeuppance. And the girl isn't doing it out of viciousness; she just can't help it. And why they didn't later ask me to adapt it myself for television I don't know."

Night Gallery (NBC, 1970–73): Directed by Jeannot Szwarc, "Big Surprise" (11/10/71) was one of two teleplays Matheson adapted from his stories for the second season of Rod Serling's less successful anthology series, which initially consisted of hour-long episodes with several segments of varying lengths. A sinister-looking old man, Mr. Hawkins (John Carradine), tells teenager Chris (Vincent Van Patten) that if he and his two companions dig a hole in a certain spot in Miller's Field, "there you'll find a great big surprise." Eventually abandoned by his impatient young friends Jason (Marc Vahanian) and Dan (Eric Chase), Chris perseveres in the hope of finding gold, only to uncover a coffin-shaped box from which a winking Hawkins emerges and says, "Surprise!" In our *What Dreams May Come* interview, Matheson said, "The story that they made 'Big Surprise' from was published in *Ellery Queen's Mystery Magazine* [in April 1959]. They didn't put the last sentence in, and that was the question at the end. They retitled the story, 'What Was in the Box?,' and they had people write in to guess what the kid found."

When seen in reruns, the segment ends with an effect that recalls Ambrose Bierce's "An Occurrence at Owl Creek Bridge," cutting back to Chris meeting Hawkins once again and then running away, presumably to avoid the terrifying fate that he has foreseen. "That may have been [producer] Jack Laird's idea," Matheson told me in *Filmfax*. "I don't remember doing that.... [The story] just seemed like an interesting idea. I guess if you had to explain it, you'd say it was the guy's ghost.... The other one ['The Funeral,' from a humorous story in *The Magazine of Fantasy and Science Fiction*'s April 1955 issue] they sort of did the way I wrote it. I think I did several other [teleplays], but they didn't get made. They were adaptations of other writers' stories. They did that — all of their stuff was adaptations, except for the little five-minute things, which I guess were like little jokey things, but I had nothing to do with those. There were certain producers who just really didn't like what I did. I don't think Jack Laird cared for what I did, just [like William Froug], who took over as the producer [of *The Twilight Zone*]..."

Gerald Sanford, a longtime television writer and producer who served as the show's story editor for the first two seasons, recalled in Phillips and Garcia's *Science Fiction Television Series*, "Jack Laird was the strangest human being who ever lived. I was told, 'No one can work for Jack. He's impossible.' He would get into these violent, dark moods and scream and throw things. He never hurt anybody, but he was a total loner. He didn't relate to the people at Universal, but he loved working on *Night Gallery*. He did everything — wrote, directed, acted and picked costumes — but he rarely left his office. He even slept overnight there. In the morning I'd find him asleep on the couch.... Laird was a talented writer. It wasn't his show, but he had total control. NBC was in awe of Rod, but Jack simply tolerated him. He often used Rod as a cover to get things done. The executives at Universal considered Jack a genius, and they left him alone." Alvin Sapinsley, who wrote six scripts for the series, told Phillips and Garcia, "The guiding hand of *Night Gallery* was not Rod's but that of Jack Laird. Rod was the creator and host, and he read all of the scripts, but he had very little control or influence."

In "The Funeral" (1/5/72), directed by John Meredyth Lucas, Morton Silkline (Joe Flynn), the proprietor of Silkline's Cut Rate Catafalque, is delighted at the arrival of Ludwig Asper (Werner Klemperer), a well-heeled customer to whom "the cost is of no importance," until he learns that Asper himself is the intended object of the exequies. "I never had a proper going off," Asper smoothly explains. "It was catch-as-catch-can, you might say; all improvised. Nothing — how shall I say? — *tasty*." After assuring Silkline that he is completely in earnest, and that a friend of his will speak at the service, the fang-baring Asper menacingly commands the proprietor to remove all mirrors from his funerary establishment, flying off in the form of a bat. Silkline is relieved at the eventual departure of Asper's boisterous guests — including the count (Charles Macaulay), who delivers the address; Ygor, a hunchback (played by the scenery-chewing Laird himself); Jenny (Laara Lacey), a crone; and Bruce (Jerry Summers), a werewolf. But then an alien arrives and says, "A friend recommended you to me."

On the package in which Asper provides payment, Silkline's first name is shown onscreen as "Morton," as it is in the short story and teleplay, yet in a slip, he clearly introduces himself to Asper as "Milton" in the dialogue. The only significant difference between the story and teleplay (later published as a Gauntlet chapbook) is the content of the oft-interrupted count's flowery funeral oration. In the story, it reads, "Good friends, we have gathered ourselves within these bud-wreathed walls to pay homage to our comrade, Ludwig Asper, whom the pious and unyielding fates have chosen to pluck from our existence and place within that bleak sarcophagus of all eternity. And thus, we collect our bitter selves about this, our comrade's bier; about this litter of sorrow, this cairn, this cromlech, this unhappy tumulus, this mastaba, this sorrowing tope, this ghat, this dread dokhma ... *Requiescas in pace*, dear brother. The memory of you shall not perish with your untimely sepulture." Amusingly, Matheson had already recycled this same speech almost verbatim, to be delivered by the addle-brained undertaker played by Boris Karloff in *The Comedy of Terrors*, and rewrote it for the television episode.

According to Scott Skelton and Jim Benson, the authors of *Rod Serling's* Night Gallery: *An After-Hours Tour*, the circular ending eventually imposed on "Big Surprise" was one manifestation of the indignities to which *Night Gallery* was subjected when it was mutated into a more desirable thirty-minute series for syndication. Many segments were severely cut or padded with miscellaneous footage, some of it shot expressly for that purpose; and in addition to repeating the opening scene at the end, the syndicated version of "Big Surprise" also reveals such Procrustean tampering with a plethora of stock shots from *The Birds*. "Well, that's Universal," Matheson told me in his interview for *What Dreams May Come*. "The [executive] producer of *The Incredible Hulk* one time cut in about, oh, half to two-thirds of *Duel*.... [Steven] Spielberg was not too happy about it." Footage from Universal's 1974 disaster films *Airport 1975* and *Earthquake* was also used in the first-season *Hulk* episodes "747" (4/7/78) and "Earthquakes Happen" (5/19/78), respectively. (The latter was coincidentally scripted by Richard Christian Matheson and his writing partner at that time, Thomas Szollosi.)

"Once a series has been cancelled, it's like carrion," director Szwarc told Phillips and Garcia. "The vultures do what they want. I never saw the episodes in syndication, but I'm sure the overall result was awful." To add insult to injury, episodes of another series, *The Sixth Sense*, were shoehorned into the syndication package.

But *Night Gallery's* woes had begun even earlier, with Serling (who outlived it by only two years) trying to have his name removed, even though his episode "They're Tearing Down Tim Riley's Bar" (1/20/71) was nominated for an Emmy as Outstanding Single Program. To its credit, the series boasted the involvement of such future filmmakers as Spielberg (who directed one segment of the 1969 pilot film and the first-season episode "Make Me Laugh" [1/6/71]), Szwarc, John Badham, and *Star Trek's* Leonard Nimoy (who made his directorial debut with "Death on a Barge" [3/4/73]), as well as *Twilight Zone* veterans Douglas Heyes and Ralph Senensky. It also featured adaptations of works by genre authors Lovecraft, Derleth, Algernon Blackwood, R. Chetwynd-Hayes, C.M. Kornbluth, Fritz Leiber, Clark Ashton Smith, A.E. van Vogt, and Manley Wade Wellman.

"The ratings were not great but generally good for its [Wednesday] time slot," recalled Szwarc in *Science Fiction Television Series*. "The demographics were excellent, and the audience it attracted was very loyal." But their loyalty was put to the test when the show was moved to an unpopular Sunday night slot and cut from 60 to 30 minutes in its third season, during which it was abruptly cancelled. Added Szwarc, "Some of *Night Gallery's* previous material had come from some of the best authors of the genre. The shortening of the format hurt, and there were no more interesting mixtures [the majority of the third season consisting of single-story episodes]. The whole thing became monochromatic.... Perhaps its weakness was that it tried to embrace too wide a range. It never found its specific *Zone* like *Twilight* did.... It was too different and too original. Neither the network nor the studio ever understood it. Although the people who worked on it were passionate about the show, its very sophistication and literary quality turned the people in power off. The series never had any champions among the network or studio executives." It does, however, have a devoted fan following.

The show is also fondly remembered by many of its participants, like Vincent Van Patten, who recalled his experience working with John Carradine. "I had a lot of respect for him," he told Jim Benson. "Before shooting 'Big Surprise,' my father [actor Dick Van Patten] told me, 'You're going to be working with John Carradine. He was in *The Grapes of Wrath* [1940] and he's one of the greatest actors of all time. Just listen to his *voice*.' My father had built him up as a wonderful actor, which he was, but I didn't feel intimidated by him. I had been under contract at Universal as a child actor since the age of nine, and when you're a kid actor, I don't think *anybody* intimidates you." Szwarc — the show's most prolific director, with 22 segments — told Scott Skelton, "John was marvelous. That one was supposed to be set in the country. I found this place on the back lot and I used negative space [composing the frame so that something in the foreground blocks the view of an unwanted element, such as a telephone pole, in the background]. We ended up with a piece that looked like it was shot in the Midwest."

Ghost Story (NBC, 1972–73): Matheson's pilot episode, "The New House" (3/17/72), earned him a "Developed for Television by" credit on all episodes of this hour-long anthology series, but he wrote no additional scripts. "I don't even know whether I was asked," he told

Winston Essex (Sebastian Cabot) outside Mansfield House on *Ghost Story* (NBC-TV, 1972).

me, discussing the series in two separate interviews for *Filmfax*. "I think I first met [executive producer William Castle] because I was up for writing *Rosemary's Baby*, and then he hired Polanski to direct it, and of course Polanski, being a consummate writer, insisted on writing it.... So then we talked about this script and the series, and like an idiot I said, 'You know, you could shoot it down at the Coronado Hotel [outside San Diego].'... And at the time I was just starting to work on my novel *Bid Time Return*, which became *Somewhere in Time*, and setting it there, and he just picked up on it immediately, and shot his openings to the series down at the Coronado, and I thought, 'Oh, God, I've screwed myself!'"

Adapted from the short story by Elizabeth Walter, which appeared in her 1965 collection *Snowfall and Other Chilling Events*, Matheson's script was directed by John Llewellyn Moxey and featured Barbara Parkins, David Birney, Jeanette Nolan, and Sam Jaffe. Parkins had just worked with Moxey and Hammer screenwriter Jimmy Sangster — soon to become a story editor for the series — on the TV-movie *A Taste of Evil* (1971); her other genre credits include *The Mephisto Waltz* (1971) and *Asylum* (1972). Matheson told *Midnight Graffiti's* Paul Sammon that Castle "was a very nice man. I had no problems with him at all. They liked the script I did for them, they did the script as I wrote it.... It wasn't that bad. But *Ghost Story* was a doomed idea. I mean, how many ghost stories can you tell? Later in the season they changed the title and concept to *Circle of Fear*," including tales of suspense as well as the supernatural.

After greeting Castle — who makes a Hitchcockian cameo — the series' host Winston Essex (Sebastian Cabot) introduces viewers to Eileen Travis (Parkins), who is expecting her first child, and begins to hear ghostly manifestations as soon as she and her husband John (Birney) move into their newly constructed home on Pleasant Hill, including laughter that seems to emanate from the statue of a young woman bought at an antique shop in town. After being told by her housekeeper, Mrs. Ramsey (Nolan), that the house may have been built atop a cemetery, she learns from DeWitt (Jaffe), an expert in local history, that the hill was the site of a gallows torn down in 1779 due to the uproar over the execution of Thomasina Barrows, a nineteen-year-old orphan and Revolutionary War widow who lost a baby at birth and was condemned for stealing a loaf of bread. During a violent storm that delays John from returning home, Thomasina tricks Mrs. Ramsey into leaving by posing as Eileen, then appears in an attempt to claim the newborn Caroline. Soon afterward the baby's sinister laughter suggests that Thomasina — who before her execution had laughed insanely and vowed to find "a home from which no one could ever evict her again" — has done just that.

Racconti di Fantascienza (Tales of Fantasy, 1979): Evidently based on Matheson's story of the same name, first published in *The Magazine of Fantasy and Science Fiction* in November of 1954, "*L'Esame*" (The Test, 1/31/79) was a segment of this genre anthology series from the celebrated Italian filmmaker Alessandro Blasetti; it also featured stories by Beaumont, Bradbury, Murray Leinster, Robert Sheckley, and others. As Matheson told Wiater in his *Collected Stories* commentary, "I just thought, 'What if, in the future, old people had to pass a mental test in order to be allowed to live?' (I presume because the population was overcrowded.) Editor Tony Boucher was very impressed with that story; he thought I was awfully young to have such an insight into parents-and-children relationships. In the end, I had some very poetic last couple of lines. I think it was adapted into a multi-story Italian film by producer Carlo Ponti. I never saw it, so I never saw how it turned out or maybe they never even made it. But that's what I was told." Although the series appears to be unavailable in English, a clip from it has been posted on YouTube, and this is presumably the adaptation to which Matheson referred.

The Twilight Zone (CBS, 1985–87; syndicated, 1988): Matheson returned to episodic television after a 14-year hiatus by adapting "Button, Button" (3/7/86) from his story for the first season of this ill-fated *Twilight Zone* revival, from which his colleague Harlan Ellison resigned as creative consultant due to network interference. Published in the June 1970 issue of *Playboy* (which was second only to *The Magazine of Fantasy and Science Fiction* as an outlet for Matheson's short fiction), the story concerns Norma and Arthur Lewis, who are sent a mysterious push-button unit and told by Mr. Steward, a representative of an unnamed organization, "If you push the button, somewhere in the world, someone you don't know will die. In return for which you will receive a payment of $50,000." While Arthur refuses even to discuss the possibility, Norma becomes so obsessed with pushing the button that she eventually gives in to temptation. After she learns that Arthur has died in a subway accident, leaving her $50,000 due to a double indemnity clause in his life insurance policy, Steward telephones her and says, "My dear lady, do you really think you knew your husband?"

The television version featured one-time Brat Pack member Mare Winningham, later an Academy Award nominee for *Georgia* (1994), as Norma and Brad Davis, the star of Alan Parker's Oscar-winning *Midnight Express* (1978), as Arthur. Basil Hoffman played Steward, whose offer had been suitably sweetened to $200,000, presumably due to the effects of inflation. But despite the casting and the involvement of Hungarian director Peter Medak, best known for the British black comedies *A Day in the Death of Joe Egg* and *The Ruling Class* (both 1972), Matheson found the episode — in which the couple is of a much lower socio-economic standing than in the story — sufficiently disastrous that his pseudonym Logan Swanson got the screenwriting credit. "The first *Twilight Zone* series was by far the best one," he said in *Richard Matheson's* The Twilight Zone *Scripts*. "The revived series was a little *too* ambitious, and I think by trying to do something new and bigger they lost the flavor. Some of them were well done, some of them weren't. When they did my story 'Button, Button' though, I thought they did an abominable job.... They loused it up," he lamented to Stanley Wiater.

Here, Arthur is a stuttering, henpecked husband and Norma a slovenly, shrewish wife already fixated on their financial straits, while the middle-class literary Norma desires a trip to Europe and a cottage on the Island. "It was crappy, it was a piece of junk," Matheson added in an interview with me for *Filmfax*. "It was just miserable. I wish I had been able to get that one away from them, like Spielberg was able to get 'The Doll' away from them. I could have done a much better job on the script, and I'm sure they would have done a lot better job on the production. They revised [my] script, and then did a bad job on it." In the new ending, Steward returns to reclaim the unit and pay Norma after she has pressed the button, assuring the couple that a person did die and the unit will be reprogrammed and offered to someone else "whom you don't know," as the camera zooms in on a tight close-up of Norma's eye, implying that she will be the next victim. Gary A. Braunbeck contributed a sequel called "Everything of Beauty Taken from You in This Life Remains Forever" to *He Is Legend*; writer-director Richard Kelly's film adaptation of the original, *The Box*, was released in November 2009.

Kelly told *SCI FI Wire*'s Patrick Lee, "I spent several years trying to figure out how to adapt this into ... a feature where there's a way to present the setup from the short story. It felt like it could be the first act of an entire film, and it felt like something that was sort of asking to be resolved, in my mind. But resolved in a way that hopefully was still very faithful to the spirit of what I believe.... Matheson [meant] that the pushing of the button ... it's the key to the downfall of man." He added on Ain't It Cool News that "in the episode ... Norma was a shrew and he was a weasel; they were kind of annoying and selfish. I didn't want that to be the case at all with the film; I wanted them to be extremely likable and extremely intelligent people, characters you really care about. But even those characters can be tempted by this dilemma. That's part of ... Steward's agenda, which is revealed at the end of the film. If this is ultimately some sort of test that's being conducted on humanity, they would seek out the best and brightest examples of humanity. They would choose and try to snare people who would be least likely to commit an act of violence."

Amazing Stories (NBC, 1985–87): More than two decades after it was written for the original *Twilight Zone*, "The Doll" (5/4/86) became the first of two consecutive Matheson episodes during the debut season of executive producer Steven Spielberg's attempt to revive the half-hour anthology format, which ran concurrently with the new *Zone* but was cancelled two months earlier. Boasting an impressive array of talent, ranging from filmmakers Martin Scorsese and Clint Eastwood to newcomers Phil Joanou and Mick Garris, the show was also a virtual family affair for Matheson, with both his daughter Ali Marie (who wrote the second season's "Lane Change" [1/12/87], on which, he notes, "I helped her a little with the surprise ending, but it was her story") and his son Richard contributing scripts. Sensing his niece's disappointment with the gift he buys from Mr. Liebemacher (Albert Hague), lonely bachelor John Walters (John Lithgow) brings the doll home, then learns that its model, spinster schoolteacher Mary Dickinson (Annie Helm), not only matches the persona he created for it, but also had herself bought a doll in *his* image from Liebemacher (German for "maker of love").

When invited to contribute, "I told the producers about the old script," Matheson told Wiater, "and they read it and loved it. I think they approached the owners of *The Twilight Zone* and asked if I could have the rights back to the script [published in *Rod Serling's The Twilight Zone Magazine* in June 1982]. So they gave it to us and it was done for *Amazing Stories*. It turned out great!... This all goes back to my 'non-relationship' with producer William Froug, who never cared for my writing. The 'Doll' situation is ample evidence of that. They had an entire script, but Froug just didn't like it. Fortunately, *Amazing Stories* was later able to get the rights to it. I made a few improvements to the script—I hope—but it was pretty much the same script, because there was no short story to adapt.... Fortunately, Spielberg and his creative people were as inclined to sentiment as they were the scary stuff." Directed by Phil Joanou (as was R.C. Matheson's *Three O'Clock High*), the episode won Lithgow—for whose role Matheson and Granet had envisioned Martin Balsam—an Emmy as Outstanding Guest Performer in a Drama Series, and was part of the ersatz telefilm *Amazing Stories: The Movie II* (1987).

Adapted by Matheson from his short story (which, according to Martin Grams, Jr., had been considered and rejected, along with "The Test," for the original *Twilight Zone*), "One for the Books" (5/11/86) was directed by Lesli Linka Glatter. After idly scanning the blackboard in a French classroom at Pierpont University, janitor Fred Elderman (Leo Penn, who had directed Matheson's *Star Trek* script "The Enemy Within") awakens the next morning inexplicably fluent in French, to the confusion of his wife Eva (Joyce Van Patten), and soon absorbs the knowledge of every department he visits on his nightly rounds. He later collapses in pain after entering the library. While Dr. Arthur Fetlock (Nicholas Pryor) theorizes that some form of telepathy is enabling him to utilize his full learning potential, Fred offers his own explanation: "My brain is like a sponge." Ultimately a UFO summons him to the stadium and drains the knowledge with a light-beam. In his *Collected Stories* commentary, Matheson said, "I've never seen the episode, so I don't know if they used my last line ['I been squeezed'], which I liked a lot. I found the entire concept very humorous." (The line was used.)

"I have no idea [how Penn's casting came about]," Matheson related in an interview with me for *Filmfax*. "I just met him on the set, and talked to him briefly. A very nice man. He lived next door to my son Richard [for] three, four years, and Richard got to know him quite well. A very sweet man.... You know, Sean Penn's mother, Eileen Ryan, was in my Howard Duff *Twilight Zone* ['A World of Difference']." In the second and final season of *Amazing Stories* (during which Matheson *père* served as a formal creative consultant), Richard Christian wrote "Magic Saturday" (10/6/86) as an original solo effort and then adapted the show's last episode, "Miss Stardust" (4/10/87), from his father's work with Thomas Szollosi. Based on a humorous story from the Spring 1955 issue of *Startling Stories*, in which Matheson paid affectionate tribute to his friend William Campbell Gault, "Miss Stardust" was directed by Tobe Hooper, who enjoyed early hits with *The Texas Chain Saw Massacre* (1974), Stephen King's *Salem's Lot* and *Poltergeist*, but whose career has since slid into episodic television, plus the likes of a much lower-rent King adaptation, *The Mangler* (1995).

A decided change of pace for some of those involved, the episode concerns down-at-the-heels p.r. man Joe Willoughby (Dick Shawn), whose work on the Miss Stardust beauty pageant is disrupted by the Cabbage Man (song parodist "Weird Al" Yankovic), a vegetative alien who cites a prior contest of the same name to demand either a change in the title or "representation." When the latter takes the form of contestants from Mars, Venus, and Jupiter, judges and audience alike are bemused by the extraterrestrial entries. The Cabbage Man threatens interplanetary vengeance if each of them is not awarded first prize, so it is up to Joe and his trusty secretary Miss Schroedinger (Laraine Newman) to save the Earth by providing an unexpected solution. "Well, it was kind of bizarre, with these bizarre creatures and everything, and I guess that's why [Hooper was hired]," Matheson told me. "You know, it's like people associate me with scary stuff. They don't realize I've written a lot of comedies, a lot of funny stuff, so obviously the man has tastes to do more than one type of thing, and that just gave him an opportunity.... I got a kick out of what Richard and Tom did with [my story]."

Speaking of his efforts as a creative consultant for *Amazing Stories*, Matheson continued in an interview with me for *Filmfax*, "I enjoyed it very much. My agent called it 'The Gig of the Year.' What [led to the formal position] was, I would read a bunch of their scripts and ideas and make notes on them, and then we would go to a big general meeting in this big boardroom at Amblin [Entertainment, Spielberg's production company], and Spielberg would be there, and the two guys [Joshua Brand and John Falsey] who created that funny series about Alaska, *Northern Exposure*. They were the story editors [and supervising producers] when I went to these meetings. And [production executive] Kathleen Kennedy would be there, and we would just talk. There was a whole pile of stuff up on the bar, bagels and cream cheese and all that delicious stuff, and then we would just work for two, three hours discussing these things, and then we'd go out on the deck and they'd have a big catered meal, so it was great. And I guess they liked what I contributed to these meetings, so they hired me to come and do it on a weekly basis [during the show's second season]."

In a 1996 letter to me, Matheson discussed another kind of consulting in which he was then involved: "I have been doing some work at Disney Imagineering as consultant on a ride they are planning (if they can get the approval and the money) for Epcot in 1998. Called *Space*. It has been a lot of pleasure for me although I know as much about space as my cat. But I gave them some ideas they kind of liked. So we'll see." He also revealed, in his *Collected Stories* commentary for "The Wedding" (originally published in the July 1953 issue of *Beyond Fantasy Fiction*), that at least one of his scripts for Spielberg's series was never filmed. "It occurred to me that it would be funny to write a story about someone who was hopelessly superstitious through the entire courtship. While their fiancée was totally baffled and dubious about their actions. In the end of course the whole situation flips over, and the one who wasn't superstitious succumbs to superstition immediately. I later adapted it for the television series *Amazing Stories*, as a matter of fact. As I recall I don't think they cared for the ending. I tried to do another ending, but ultimately it just didn't work."

Mick Garris, who also served as story editor for *Amazing Stories* and later became one of the foremost interpreters of Stephen King's work on the screen, recalled in Phillips and Garcia's *Science Fiction Television Series*, "In the second season, we did a weekly round table where people would talk about the scripts and critique the ideas. Bob Zemeckis, Bob Gale, Steven [Spielberg], myself, Michael McGill, Richard Matheson, a whole bunch of people, and it was really exciting! Really intimidating at first to a newcomer like myself.... I think the main reason *Amazing Stories* didn't work for the audience was they never knew what to expect each week. One week would be an animated show, another week would be [a] kid-oriented fantasy show, another week a dark thriller. It really was scattered in its approach, and there was no Alfred Hitchcock or Rod Serling, or any identifiable core to the series other than a trip into the fantastic.... You had reliable filmmakers who, most of them, haven't really worked in television, even to this day, taking feature-quality production values and making television.... There was some really good talent discovered on the show. Steven used it as an opportunity to try people out..."

Discussing the short-lived show's conspicuous failure in his *Creative Screenwriting* interview with Robert Arnett, Matheson added, "They were given too much leeway. A million dollars, I think, for a script for ... a half-hour show. Jesus. One of the nicest things I ever had done was the one called 'The Doll' with John Lithgow. It was a lovely piece of work, just lovely, so simple. But a lot of them I just didn't care for, especially in the first season. They seemed very slipshod. I think they only lasted two seasons. If they hadn't had a commitment for two seasons, I don't think it would have made even that. Hopefully, with my consulting, it got a little better in the second year.... [Spielberg] had a number of ideas that I red-penciled. I said I didn't like them, which I don't think pleased him. He did that one, that was an hour, about the people on a bomber ['The Mission' (11/3/85), scripted from Spielberg's story by Menno Meyjes]. And the kicker to the whole thing was that the guy draws tires on the damn airplane. That's not the way to resolve something like that, it's very unsatisfactory."

The Outer Limits (Showtime, 1995–2000; SFC, 2000–02): Matheson never contributed to ABC's beloved 1963–65 SF anthology series *The Outer Limits*, but came close, according to second-season story editor Seeleg Lester. "I would've loved to have had Richard Matheson," Lester recalled in David J. Schow's book *The Outer Limits Companion*. "In fact, he called one day on behalf of Charles Beaumont, and said, 'Can you get Beaumont an assignment? *I'll* write it if I have to.' But Beaumont was a horror writer, and what he submitted to us was just not usable." Donald S. Sanford did, however, revise Beaumont's unfilmed script into "The Guests" (3/23/64), an episode of the original series, which also featured teleplays by Sohl and, most notably, Harlan Ellison. During the second season of Showtime's cable revival, "First Anniversary" (2/16/96), amusingly credited to "Richard Matheson, Sr.," was adapted by Ali Marie Matheson with her spouse and writing partner, Jon Cooksey.

Directed by Brad Turner, a veteran of the new *Twilight Zone*, the hour-long episode expands the eight-page story, published in *Playboy* in July 1960. Financial consultant Norman

Glass (*Max Headroom*'s Matt Frewer) enjoys an idyllic year married to Ady Sutton, a sexy widow (Michelle Johnson, the voluptuous vixen of *Blame It on Rio* [1984]). Just after their anniversary she becomes first inexplicably repugnant, and then completely intangible, to his senses of taste, smell, and touch in succession, and ultimately the horrified Norman discovers that he and his friend Dennis (Clint Howard) have married hideous alien shape-shifters, whose ability to cloud men's minds breaks down after a year. Richard Lewis, one of the executive producers of the *Outer Limits* revival, told *Cinefantastique*'s Frank Garcia, "That was 'It's too good to be true!' Clint Howard and Matt Frewer are two regular Joes ... and they have two stunningly beautiful women, and you wonder, 'What's wrong with this picture?' And that's what's wrong with the picture. The women weren't real. They weren't human. Why would these two attractive, seemingly intelligent women fall for them?"

In an interview with me for *Filmfax*, Matheson related, "I had been approached by Mel Tormé's son [Tracy] to work on *Sliders*, and I've been in to talk to Chris Carter of *The X-Files* because he has said that he was inspired by the two Kolchak movies [*The Night Stalker* and *The Night Strangler*]. He sent me a bunch of scripts to read, but whether he really wanted me to work on them, I don't know. Of course, he certainly didn't need me. And *Outer Limits*, too. I went in to talk to them, and I just didn't want to do it, so that's why — I was supposedly collaborating with Ali and her husband on that show, but I did nothing. I just let them do it completely. They didn't need me at all.... It just baffled me how they could do it so well ... I mean, I wouldn't even have submitted [the story], because it was so short..." He added to Arnett,

> Working on series television is just something I haven't done in such a long time. As a matter of fact, I don't think I ever worked on series television. It was always anthology shows. *Twilight Zone* was an anthology show. *Lawman* had running characters, but [no continuing plots, so] it was really an anthology, with a different story every week....
>
> The hour form to me is really very difficult. It's almost like a bastardized form, because in a half-hour you can [present] a beginning, middle, and end, [the] one-act idea, very easily. In two hours you can tell a full story. In an hour, you can neither tell the one-act story or the full story.... What I would be best at, as I was when I was a consultant on *Amazing Stories*, is to read ideas coming in and be able to ferret out the good ones from the bad ones and give ideas to the ones that are halfway there to make them better. I could read scripts and make comments. David Vogel, who was the producer on the last season of *Amazing Stories*, asked me if I wanted to be a consultant for him at Disney. I met with [George A.] Romero last year and ... gave him an idea for a script, which was something I was going to make a novel out of [*Something Outside*], but I figured I'd never do it, and it's a very good idea, so I let him have it. He'll write it, or somebody will write it. I'm not going to write it. I will talk to them about it, make suggestions, and read the script when they're done. [This proposed project remains unfilmed.] Making comments, that's really what I'm best at.

Masters of Horror (Showtime, 2005–07): Eighteen years after "Miss Stardust," R.C. Matheson was reunited with Tobe Hooper on another adaptation of his father's work, "Dance of the Dead" (11/11/05), for the first season of this anthology series that paired up major genre authors and filmmakers.* First published in *Star Science Fiction Stories No. 3* in 1954, "Dance of the Dead" depicts a post-apocalyptic 1997 as 18-year-old Peggy — against her mother's advice — accompanies a trio of twentysomethings to a sleazy St. Louis nightclub. There, the horrified girl witnesses "the loopy's dance," in which a corpse writhes up on the

---

*R.C. also scripted "Mad House" (*Fantastic*, January-February 1953) for a third season that unfortunately never materialized.

stage after being injected with the distillation of a germ gas found during World War III to cause spastic gyrations of the dead, referred to as a Lifeless Undead Phenomenon (LUP). "I never submitted it to *The Twilight Zone* because it was too ghastly. But I really worked hard on that story to get the language right and make full use of my descriptive powers," Matheson told Wiater in his *Collected Stories* commentary.

Expanding the story to fit the show's hour-long format also increased its ghastliness for the new century, with LUP necrophilia, topless moving corpses tossed into Dumpsters to be immolated, and gruesome special effects makeup by Greg Nicotero and Howard Berger, plus Robert Englund of *A Nightmare on Elm Street* (1984) fame well cast and suitably slimy as the emcee of the Doom Room. Because "fresh plasma engenders and reinvigorates the drama of the performance," he buys blood stolen from elderly pedestrians by Jak (Jonathan Tucker, the second lead in the 2003 remake of Hooper's *Texas Chain Saw Massacre*) and Boxx (Ryan McDonald), who bring their equally depraved friend Celia (Lucie Guest) and a reluctant 16-year-old Peggy (Jessica Lowndes) to the nightclub. In both versions, Peggy surrenders to this macabre milieu, but in the show she recognizes one of the "dancers" as her older sister Anna (Melena Ronnis), and then learns that their mother, Kate (Marilyn Norry), a war widow, supported them both by selling Anna, who was dying of an overdose. R.C. also added a vicious coda in which, after burying Anna, Peggy provides Kate as her replacement loopy.

Matheson visited the disturbing Doom Room set in Vancouver, and was duly appalled; all agreed that the emcee was a post-apocalyptic Joel Grey from *Cabaret* (1972), and Hooper also wanted to evoke *A Clockwork Orange* (1971), to which he pays a brief visual homage. R.C. added in his DVD audio commentary, "I thought of the world in which the story takes place ... and I thought that by exploring it a bit, it would further paint the backdrop that the characters are plunged into. I began with the kind of ghastly successor to napalm, which is a weapon that I call 'blizz.'... [I]t's some kind of a fast-acting, almost instantaneous flesh-eating composition..." Flashbacks foreshadow Kate's ruthless idea of family values as she locks the guests out of the house when a blizz attack devastates Peggy's birthday party.

House of Usher

(aka *The Fall of the House of Usher*; AIP, released June 22, 1960) DIRECTOR-PRODUCER: Roger Corman; SCREENPLAY: Matheson, based on Edgar Allan Poe's "The Fall of the House of Usher"; MUSIC: Les Baxter; MAKEUP: Fred Phillips; SPECIAL EFFECTS: Pat Dinga, Ray Mercer. Color, 79 minutes. CAST—Roderick Usher: Vincent Price. Philip Winthrop: Mark Damon. Madeline Usher: Myrna Fahey. Bristol: Harry Ellerbe. Ghosts: Bill Borzage, Mike Jordan, Nadajan, Ruth Oklander, George Paul, David Andar, Eleanor Le Faber, Geraldine Paulette, Phil Sylvestre, John Zimeas.

House of Usher began a long and fruitful association between Matheson and American International Pictures, founded by James H. Nicholson in 1954 as the American Releasing Corporation. By all accounts, Nicholson's vice-president Samuel Z. Arkoff, an attorney by training, was the "bad cop" who negotiated the deals, while Nicholson was the "good cop" whose specialty was creating AIP's outlandish titles and ad campaigns, and with whom Matheson struck up a particularly cordial relationship. It eventually extended beyond the producer's departure from AIP to his first — and last — independent production. As Matheson told me in an interview for the Gauntlet limited edition of *Hell House*, Nicholson "was a very nice man. He was sort of my friend in court ... [and] I dealt mostly with him.... He always liked what I did, and we got along very well."

In its use of color, Gothic horror, classic literary sources, and relatively low budgets, AIP's highly successful series of Edgar Allan Poe adaptations served as an American answer to the Hammer horror revival that was then underway. Roger Corman directed the first eight, half of which were written by Matheson and one, *The Tomb of Ligeia* (1964), by Robert Towne, then still in his twenties. Charles Beaumont worked on the other three: *Premature Burial* (1962), written with the late Ray Russell; *The Haunted Palace*, which took its title from the poem by Poe, but was primarily based on H.P. Lovecraft's novel *The Case of Charles Dexter Ward*; and *The Masque of the Red Death* (1964), which was rewritten by R. Wright Campbell and incorporated Poe's story "Hop-Frog" as well. Corman's team also included Vincent Price, who starred in all but *Premature Burial*; art director and production designer Daniel Haller, who later directed AIP's more overt Lovecraft adaptations *Monster of Terror* (adapted by Sohl from "The Colour Out of Space") and *The Dunwich Horror* (1970); and cinematographer Floyd Crosby, who won an Oscar for the semi-documentary *Tabu* (1931).

A living legend in the film industry, Corman has directed more than fifty low-budget independent motion pictures, thirty-three of them for AIP; produced and/or distributed hundreds more for his own companies, New World Pictures and Concorde-New Horizons; given a generation of major filmmakers their first big break, on one or both sides of the camera; and even acted in occasional films. Long before there was a Sundance Institute for independent filmmakers, there was an unofficial "Corman School" whose many prestigious alumni include Peter Bogdanovich, James Cameron, Francis Ford Coppola, Joe Dante, Jonathan Demme, Dennis Hopper, Ron Howard, Gale Anne Hurd, Jonathan Kaplan, Jack Nicholson, John Sayles, Martin Scorsese, Towne, and countless others. Associated with AIP since its inception, Corman became disillusioned with the company over changes made by Jim Nicholson to four consecutive films without his knowledge or approval, and after making *Von Richthofen and Brown* (aka *The Red Baron*, 1971) for United Artists he took a hiatus from directing to get married, start a family, and found New World, which he then sold in 1982.

Born on April 5, 1926 — 44 days after Matheson — Corman recalled in his autobiography *How I Made a Hundred Movies in Hollywood and Never Lost a Dime* (written with Jim Jerome) that he was assigned to read Poe's "The Fall of the House of Usher" at Beverly Hills High, and then asked his parents to buy him Poe's complete works. Decades later, his octet of adaptations would incorporate an even dozen of Poe's poems and stories.

House of Usher marked quite a new direction for a company then better known for the likes of *I Was a Teenage Werewolf* (1957). At the time *House of Usher* seemed decidedly risky indeed, with its period setting and thematic elements (e.g., overtones of incest) perhaps poorly suited for AIP's largely teenaged audience. Shot in Eastmancolor and CinemaScope, *House of Usher* was a deliberate attempt to upgrade AIP's product, with a larger budget and longer shooting schedule than their previous monochrome co-features, and was based on a literary classic no doubt familiar to said audience from endless English classes, one which not coincidentally happened to be in the public domain. Price — who eventually starred in seven films scripted by Matheson — had gained critical acclaim for *Laura* (1944) and stardom in such genre films as *House of Wax* (1953), *House on Haunted Hill* (1958), and *The Tingler* (1959), while Matheson was already a respected science fiction and fantasy author with seven novels, several short story collections, and two screenplays to his credit. These included the indirect inspiration for one of AIP's biggest successes, *The Amazing Colossal Man* (1957), since

Arkoff noted in his autobiography *Flying Through Hollywood By the Seat of My Pants* (written with Richard Trubo) that the film was a deliberate inversion of *The Incredible Shrinking Man*.

Until Matheson's advent, AIP had relied on a trio of screenwriters that included Arkoff's brother-in-law Lou Rusoff, whose prodigious output included eight films — *Day the World Ended, The Phantom from 10,000 Leagues, The Oklahoma Woman, It Conquered the World, The She-Creature, Runaway Daughters, Girls in Prison* and *Shake, Rattle and Rock* — released by AIP in 1956 alone. Adding to the familial atmosphere (Corman's younger brother, Gene, was also a producer, and Nicholson later married AIP star Susan Hart) was the aforementioned R. Wright Campbell, who wrote Corman's directorial debut, *Five Guns West* (1955), and whose brother William acted in several AIP films, including Coppola's early effort *Dementia 13* and Corman's *The Young Racers* (both 1963).

The third leg of AIP's pre–Matheson screenwriting tripod was Charles B. Griffith, who is best known for Corman's black comedies *A Bucket of Blood* (1959) and *The Little Shop of Horrors* (1960). His range also extended to Westerns (*Gunslinger* and *Flesh and the Spur* [both 1956]), rock 'n' roll (*Rock All Night* [1957]) and bikers (*The Wild Angels* [1966], *Devil's Angels* [1967]). In *Faster and Furiouser: The Revised and Fattened Fable of American International Pictures*, Griffith told Mark Thomas McGee of his ire when he learned of Matheson's

Roderick Usher (Vincent Price) shows Philip Winthrop (Mark Damon) portraits of his depraved ancestors in *House of Usher* (American International, 1960). Photograph courtesy of the Paul M. Sammon Collection.

hiring: "I was working on something, possibly *Little Shop of Horrors*, in the other office and I could hear [Roger] making a deal on the phone for Richard Matheson. And I said, 'Why'd you go outside for a writer?' He said that Matheson had a reputation. They were going to go with color and CinemaScope. It was irritating because I saw that he was making a value judgment based on how much people were making and *he* was the one making policy. He said that no screenwriter who gets less than fifty thousand [per] script is any good."

There may be some poetic justice here, for according to McGee, it was Griffith who was initially hired to write the Matheson-inspired *The Amazing Colossal Man*, although he soon left because of artistic differences with producer-director-special effects technician Bert I. Gordon. (According to Griffith, "He wanted to dictate. Demanding bad dialogue. Horrible clichés.") However, as McGee adds, "Matheson was not paid fifty either. He got five, plus five percent of the net profits. Every time he got a statement from AIP the price of the picture went up. Years later, after having scripted half a dozen pictures for the company, he got tired of the company's creative bookkeeping.... He called Arkoff 'a shark.'" As Matheson explained to me in an interview for *Filmfax*, "I had a percentage of the net on all the pictures, and I was getting nothing, and I knew I would never get anything. And so they finally talked me into selling all my percentages to them for $10,000. Which at the time was $10,000 more than I'd have made anyway. But then when all this residual stuff started, if I had held on to them, I would have done much better."

In the first part of an AIP overview by Randy Palmer, David Del Valle, and Steve Biodrowski in *Cinefantastique*,* Corman recalled, "[Matheson] was originally signed by Jim [Nicholson]. Jim had read several of his works. I had seen pictures he had written and several works as a short-story writer and novelist. I would meet with [Matheson] before doing the script and discuss it, but then when he did the script I would leave him alone. I would get a first draft and discuss it, then a second draft, and so forth.... It was truly a wonderful moment. It was exciting. It was one of those rare films where we had both the critical acclaim and the box office success, so we could sit back and see it coming from all directions." Despite the warm welcome from both audiences and critics, however, he added that, at the time *House of Usher* was made, there was no thought of filming more Poe: "It was never decided to do a series. Each time we said, 'All right, we'll do one more,' until it became unwittingly a series."

Certainly none of the previous films appearing on Corman's admittedly diverse résumé (e.g., *Apache Woman* [1955], *Sorority Girl* [1957], *Teenage Cave Man* [1958], *The Wasp Woman* [1959]) prepared anyone involved for the enthusiastic critical and commercial reception afforded to *House of Usher*. "They were totally floored by the success of it, they didn't expect it at all," Matheson told me. "It ran all summer, it was running on a double-bill with *Psycho*, it made all kinds of money, and they were just going to do it as a one-shot, and then they started doing the whole cycle of pictures because of that. Then after that, except for [*Tales of Terror*], it got further and further away from Poe. I mean, we did *The Raven*, which is a poem, which I turned into a comedy. But they always say 'Edgar Allan Poe's *The Raven*,' you know.... Then they would do a book adaptation of the screenplay, so it would be '*The Raven*, by Edgar Allan Poe,' and it would be a story that had nothing to do with [the poem]. And nobody ever knew it; unless they were familiar with literature, they wouldn't even know it was based on a poem."

---

*According to this article, Poe's title was shortened to *House of Usher* so that it would fit on theater marquees. Some television and home video prints do show *The Fall of the House of Usher* onscreen.

In his introduction to *Visions of Death: Richard Matheson's Edgar Allan Poe Scripts, Volume One* (2007), Corman wrote, "I had been directing low-budget movies for about five years when I decided I was ready to move on to better scripts and bigger budgets. To that end I had convinced [Nicholson and Arkoff] to back me in a picture I wanted to make from Edgar Allan Poe's 'The Fall of the House of Usher.' It was a classic story I had first read in high school and had always loved, except it would be a real gamble for AIP to make, because at the time they were a very small company. They had never spent anything near what the picture eventually cost, which was almost $300,000."

Corman shot in CinemaScope, at AIP's insistence, although he acknowledged in his DVD audio commentary that the widescreen format might not have been well-suited to a film set largely within the confines of a house: "I used ... a wide-angle lens, in order to give a feeling of greater depth and greater size to what was essentially not really that big a set." He added in *Visions of Death,* "When we went to the prop houses to rent the set decorations, we tried to get objects that made the sets look as accurate as possible—within the confines of our limited budget. I was very much a believer in what we called 'articulation of the surface'—which was to fill the surface of the set with as many objects as we could get, such as antique furniture with ornate carvings, paintings, statues, candelabra and so forth."

As the film opens, Philip Winthrop (Mark Damon, now a prolific producer himself) travels through an unnaturally desolate New England landscape—filmed at the site of a

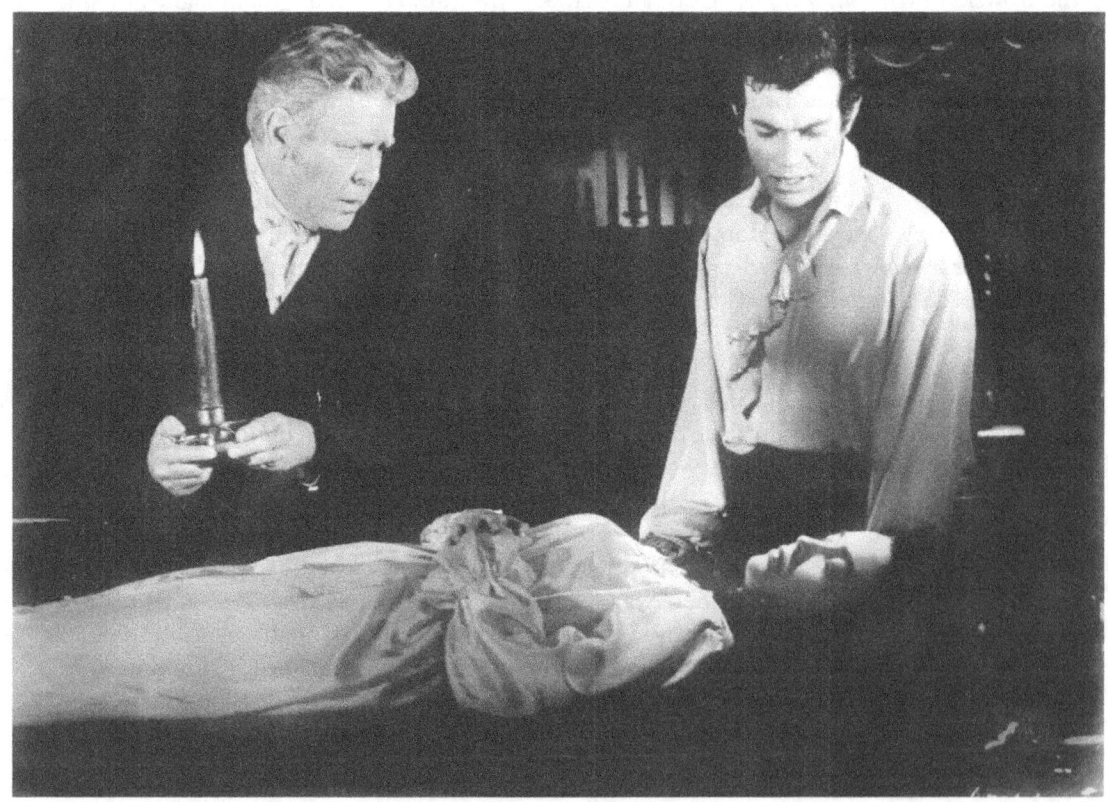

Philip mourns Madeline Usher (Myrna Fahey) as faithful family retainer Bristol (Harry Ellerbe) looks on in *House of Usher* (American International, 1960).

forest fire in the Hollywood Hills the day before. His destination: the remote, crumbling home of the prematurely white-haired Roderick Usher (Price) and his sister Madeline (Myrna Fahey), both of whom "suffer from a morbid acuteness of the senses." Philip has come from Boston, where he had met and courted Madeline, but Roderick tries to send him away, forbidding the lovers to marry because he believes "the Usher line is tainted." When the sickly Madeline apparently dies, Roderick conceals from Philip the fact that she was subject to cataleptic trances. Roderick entombs her in an attempt to ensure the end of that line, but Madeline awakens, claws her way out of the coffin, and maniacally throttles Roderick. Unlike the story, the film ends with an accidental blaze that literally brings the house down on the Ushers and their faithful family retainer, Bristol (Harry Ellerbe), as Philip escapes.

Regarding the fiery climactic footage, Corman wrote in his autobiography, "Just by chance, we located an old barn out in Orange County that was going to be demolished by developers. We asked the owner: 'Instead of demolishing it, how would you like to burn it down? But burn it down at night and I'll be out there with fifty dollars and two cameras rolling.' He agreed. That's how we got the incredible long shots of the Usher house burning.... I covered this with two cameras, which seemed like a major production back then. Today, you cover something like that with five. We got some really strong stuff— the burning rafters coming down, the flames shooting higher and higher. That sequence would stand up to almost anything done today." Never dreaming that people would one day be able to watch the Poe films back to back and notice its recurrence, the ever-economical Corman used the same footage in three subsequent entries in the series.

Excepting the climactic fire, Matheson's primary alteration from the original story was to change the dynamics among the three main characters. The story's nameless narrator — who becomes Philip in the film — is a boyhood friend of Roderick's who has not seen him for many years, and hopes to alleviate the "acute bodily illness [and] mental disorder which oppressed him." The reader is left with the impression that the narrator not only has never met Madeline, but also was unaware of her existence until he arrived at the House of Usher in answer to Roderick's urgent summons, although it is later established that Madeline and Roderick are twins. Citing the film as one of his more challenging adaptations, Matheson told the author in *Filmfax*, "Poe was difficult ... 'cause his stories were not exactly page-rippers. ['The Fall of the House of Usher'] is very brooding and ruminating, and not too much plot, not too much movement or dialogue.... I put in a romance with the guy who comes to the house, whereas I don't think that was the case at all in the story.... The first one I got really into. I wrote an extremely complex outline for it, I analyzed Poe and everything, and it turned out very well."

As Corman added in his introduction to *Visions of Death*, "Dick was paid $5,000 and a share of the profits, and he did a very good job, turning in a literate screenplay that I was very pleased with. It was clear we had found the ideal writer to adapt Poe to the screen. I soon discovered that one of the great beauties of working with Dick was that his first draft would always be very close to the final draft. I have spent so much time working with other writers who will go through a first draft, a second draft, then on to a third draft, only to realize that you're still not there yet. With Dick, we would usually have one discussion outlining what the film was going to be about, do a treatment, and then he would go off by himself and come up with a first draft that was almost ready to shoot. Usually, the most we'd ever need to do would be a dialogue polish. With the possible exception of John Sayles, I don't think I've seen that in another screenwriter.... [Y]ou may notice that we did trim some brief dialogue sequences from the final scripts. As with most writers who have a background in short stories and novels, Dick had a tendency to overwrite slightly in the dialogue, but it was always a matter of very minor editing."

Staff composer Les Baxter recalled in *It Came from Weaver Five,* "I felt very privileged ... to do the Poe films, because they were not 'C'-horror movies, they were classic pieces of literature.... I'm very pleased to have those among my credits. I did so many of these films for James Nicholson.... It's too bad he had an early demise, because he would have been doing ... *Star Wars* [1977] and *Raiders of the Lost Ark* [1981] and so forth.... He chose me to write the music and gave me *absolute* carte blanche.... [I had] an old castle, and Vincent Price with a strange disease where he hears things from the dungeon and is sensitive beyond belief to touch and sound. Which was an actual illness, I understand.... [W]hat more could I ask for? It was a composer's dream.... [*Usher*] was very sensitive for a horror film. In this particular one, horror had a great deal to do with senses — Vincent Price's sensitive skin, his relationship with his sister who was buried alive and scratching on her coffin. The music was very much on the sensual side — in *some* scenes, almost to the point of passionate, the string writing. Unfortunately, it's under dialogue and sound effects, but it still can be heard."

House of Usher reflects Corman's interest in psychoanalysis (which he was then undergoing), the inner workings of the psyche, and dream interpretations. As he told Lawrence French, the editor of *Visions of Death,* "I think Poe was among the first writers to work with the concept of the unconscious mind. The work Freud was to do a little later was part of what was happening at the time — in the late nineteenth, and early twentieth century — but as an artist Poe was simply a little bit in advance of Freud. Most artists work partially from their conscious, and partly from their unconscious. But with Poe, it was almost as if he had an open door into his unconscious. And since there are no eyes into the unconscious, I felt its workings would best be expressed through non-reality. On that basis, I decided to build all the sets and shoot everything interior, on studio soundstages, since I wanted to show the interior world of the mind. Previously, most of my films had used actual locations, but for the Poe films I went in the other direction and tried to make the sets very stylized." The Ushers (Price and several uncredited extras) also taunt Philip in a color-drenched dream sequence. Scenes like this soon became a beloved series staple in Corman's Poe films.

Among the house's more memorable furnishings are portraits of the Usher ancestors, whose depraved history Roderick recounts to Philip. Previously the art director on AIP's *The Brain Eaters* (1958), Burt Schoenberg (aka Shonberg) provided the paintings (and furnished others for *Premature Burial*). Schoenberg was, according to Corman's audio commentary, "a very strange young painter, who was having something of a vogue in ... post-beatnik, pre-hippie coffeehouses and art galleries in Hollywood. I commissioned all of these paintings, and everybody at the end took one as a memento.... I took the portrait of Vincent Price for myself.... I think [Schoenberg] conveyed very well the spirit of the [film], in which we are showing recognized people, but we're showing them through a distorted vision, possibly the distorted vision of the artist, who is picking up the distortion within the minds of the people."

In *Visions of Death,* Matheson added, "I commissioned [Schoenberg] to do a painting of Atlantis as it would look today. He did a beautiful painting for me that I gave to my son. He also did some nice paintings for Chuck Beaumont. The problem with the paintings he did for the movie was that they didn't look like they were from that time period. I don't think anyone would have painted them in that style in the nineteenth century. I wonder what happened to those portraits?... I did get to keep one. I got the matte painting they used for the house itself. But now I don't know where it is." The publication of Matheson's first two Poe scripts confirms his frequent observation that they were shot almost verbatim, except for some trimming of the dialogue. "I would generally act the part out myself while I was writing it, to see if the lines played right.... I carefully sculpted every word, to make it sound just right. It would play better for the actors that way. Then, when the actors went to read my dialogue a lot of them may not have read it well, but at least they read my dialogue," he told Lawrence French.

The subsequent efforts of Corman, Matheson *et alia* notwithstanding, Poe has, by a popular critical consensus, probably never been treated better on the screen than he was in *House of Usher*. Phil Hardy's *Overlook Film Encyclopedia: Horror* called the film "a minor masterpiece, surprisingly faithful to Poe.... A magnificently *coherent* film that is often dismissed as pure decoration, it shows a remarkable care for detail." The *Time Out Film Guide* enthused, "Price is his usual impressive self ... but it is Corman's overall direction that lends the film its intelligence and power.... Matheson's script is also exemplary: lucid, imaginatively detailed and subtle." *Leonard Maltin's Movie Guide* noted that Poe's story has been "filmed several times before and since, but never this effectively; a great tour-de-force for Price," while *Halliwell's Film and Video Guide* praised the picture's "tense and spectacular finale."

Master of the World

(AIP, released May 31, 1961) DIRECTOR: William Witney; PRODUCER: James H. Nicholson; SCREENPLAY: Matheson, based on Jules Verne's *Robur le Conquérant* (Robur, the Conqueror, aka *The Clipper of the Clouds*) and *Maître du Mond* (Master of the World); MUSIC: Les Baxter; TITLE SONG LYRICS: Lenny Addelson; SUNG BY Darryl Stevens; MAKEUP: Fred B. Phillips; SPECIAL EFFECTS: Tim Baar, Wah Chang, Gene Warren; PHOTOGRAPHIC EFFECTS: Butler-Glouner, Inc., Ray Mercer; SPECIAL PROPS AND EFFECTS: Pat Dinga. Color, 104 minutes. CAST—Robur: Vincent Price. John Strock: Charles Bronson. Prudent: Henry Hull. Dorothy Prudent: Mary Webster. Phillip Evans: David Frankham. Alistair: Richard Harrison. Topage: Vito Scotti. First Mate Turner: Wally Campo. Crewman Weaver: Steve Masino. Crewman Shanks: Ken Terrell. Crewman Wilson: Peter Besbas. Talkative Townsman: Gordon Jones.

In writing *Master of the World*, Matheson was faced with the task of combining Jules Verne's novel *Maître du Mond* with his earlier *Robur le Conquérant* (Robur, the Conqueror), in which Verne created an airborne variation on his own Captain Nemo. Like Nemo, the charismatic character introduced with his submarine, the *Nautilus*, in Verne's *20,000 Leagues Under the Sea*, the film's Robur uses his revolutionary airship, the *Albatross*, to make war on war itself. According to Phil Hardy's *Overlook Film Encyclopedia: Science Fiction*, "Script and direction are both surprisingly lightweight, perhaps because the problem of unifying the mood of the two novels was so great. The first (published in 1886) sees Robur as a visionary and idealist, the second (published in 1904) marks Verne's growing disenchantment and conceives of its hero as a clumsy, power-hungry megalomaniac. These tensions are repressed in the film in favor of an atmosphere in which adventure dominates." AIP clearly aspired to the success of Disney's *20000 Leagues Under the Sea* (1954) on a much smaller budget (albeit large by AIP standards).

"That was a *biggie* for American International, all of half a million dollars!" Matheson told me in a letter. "[Charles] Bronson was completely out of place. Strange man. The only person I ever knew who was immune to Vincent Price's charm; Price was undoubtedly the

Robur (Vincent Price) regards — from front to back — his soon-to-be adversaries Dorothy Prudent (Mary Webster), Phillip Evans (David Frankham), Prudent (Henry Hull), and John Strock (Charles Bronson) amid the wreck of their balloon in *Master of the World* (American International, 1961).

nicest man I ever met in the business. Actor anyway. Totally charming. Bronson? The first morning I went in to watch shooting, I walked up to him and introduced myself as the writer of the film. 'Oh, don't talk to me,' he said and walked away. I really seethed. I guess he must have thought it over because, later, he came over to me and said, 'I hear you're quite a good writer.' 'I am,' I said coldly and walked away from him. Then later, I had second thoughts and, after lunch (during which Price told me that he had given up trying to get along with Bronson) I approached Bronson and said, 'Why don't we try again?' We got into a brief conversation at the end of which he said, 'I hope you don't mind if I play [Strock] like a Polish coal miner.' I laughed and thought we had broken the ice. The next morning, I said good morning to him and he walked past me without a word. I gave up at that point."

He added in *Midnight Graffiti*, "I have a very quick temper.... If someone rubs me the wrong way, and I can tell it immediately, because I have an antenna, I will respond immediately. I remember [William Witney] ... who was going to direct *Master of the World*. Obviously, he didn't understand the script, had no feeling for it, and was making these comments. And immediately I was bristling and speaking to him in a very cold, cutting tone of voice.

And Jim Nicholson knew it and tried to calm me down.... Anyway, most of the people I have worked with may have their faults, but I haven't had any trouble with them to a large degree.... I'm sure that it is an extrasensory thing. I mean, some of it is obvious, of course. You can hear the tone of someone's voice, you can hear the words they speak, but you can also pick up antipathy in other ways.... The only thing that happens is, after you leave, the committee system shows up ... and they just do a lousy job. The actual creation of a script, the actual revision of a script, that's usually pleasant. The unpleasant part comes when you go to see the screening, and you say, 'Oh, Jesus. What have they done?' That's what happens most often."

Certainly the film would have benefited from a surer directorial touch than that of Witney, who was a veteran of Republic Westerns — including no fewer than 27 with Roy Rogers — and serials (many of them co-directed with John English); he displayed no particular affinity for this genre. Equally damaging is the obvious use of anachronistic stock footage from Zoltan Korda's *Four Feathers* (1939) and Laurence Olivier's *Henry V* (1944), including a shot of London from the latter with the Globe Theatre clearly in view. Second-billed Bronson, who had his first starring role in Corman's *Machine-Gun Kelly* (1958), appears acutely uncomfortable as Robur's taciturn antagonist, John Strock. But AIP mainstay Vincent Price cuts a suitably commanding figure as Robur, and the special effects by Tim Baar, Wah Chang, and Gene Warren of Project Unlimited are generally passable, with the *Albatross* model an admittedly impressive miniature.

In *Robur le Conquérant,* Verne's imaginary "aeronef" is constructed of treated and compressed paper around a hundred-foot-long ship's deck, suspended and propelled by horizontal and vertical screws, respectively. ("The *Albatross* might be called a clipper with thirty-seven masts," he notes, hence the first novel's alternate title of *The Clipper of the Clouds.*) Able to attain altitudes up to 8,700 feet, with a top speed of 120 miles per hour, the *Albatross* "could make the tour of the globe in two hundred hours" — and indeed much of the novel, written in Verne's characteristically discursive style, is little more than a glorified travelogue interrupted by occasional snatches of dialogue. (This is demonstrated by such chapter titles as "Across the Prairie," "Through the Himalayas," "Over the Atlantic," and so on.) By the time of *Maître du Mond* — in which Verne switches to the first person, with the new character of Strock as narrator — Robur has created a new machine, the *Terror,* a kind of combination *Albatross* and *Nautilus* with which he tries to dominate the world by land, sea, and air. It is finally destroyed when struck by lightning.

The movie is set in 1868. Strock is sent by the Department of the Interior to Morgantown, Pennsylvania, to investigate apparent volcanic activity inside the Great Eyrie. He flies over its unscalable crater in a balloon with a munitions manufacturer, Prudent (Henry Hull), Prudent's daughter Dorothy (Mary Webster), and her fiancé, Phillip Evans (David Frankham). After the balloon is shot down by Robur, they awaken as his prisoners aboard the *Albatross.* Once Robur raids London, the horrified captives vow to destroy the airship, even at the cost of their own lives. When Robur drops anchor to repair damages he has incurred while trying to stop an African war, Strock plants a bomb in the armory. Jealous of Dorothy's growing affection for Strock, Phillip knocks him out and flees down the anchor rope with the Prudents. Strock recovers in time to climb down and cut the rope with the repentant Phillip's help, while Robur and his loyal crew go down with the stricken ship, as did the crew of *Nautilus.*

According to Mark Thomas McGee's *Faster and Furiouser,* Project Unlimited — which later provided the memorable (if economical) special effects for *The Outer Limits* — sent a letter to the Academy of Motion Picture Arts and Sciences to ask that their *Master of the*

Strock, Prudent, Phillip, Dorothy, and Robur aboard the *Albatross* in *Master of the World* (American International, 1961).

World work be given Oscar consideration: "*Miniatures*: The *Albatross*, Jules Verne's airship, as the star of the film had to be shown in its entirety and functioning in all aspects. To have built a radical life-size model 200 feet long would have been a physical as well as a financial impossibility. A scale model was constructed which was complete in all respects, 39 practical [rotating] propellers, mechanized trap doors, rocket devices, controls, etc. The only life-size portion built was the rear deck. In the miniature, puppet figures duplicated the live figures on deck for long shots. The balloon was handled the same way as the *Albatross* and for the same reasons. *Optical Effects*: Intriguing color effects of oil and fog — and revising quality of period black and white shots. Made several colorful inserts for special effect."

Les Baxter scored more than forty AIP pictures, including *The Comedy of Terrors* and all of Matheson's Poe films. "Baxter claimed that the secret to writing music for horror movies was to put notes where they didn't belong," wrote Mark Thomas McGee. "Unfortunately, he seemed to use this same approach for his non-horror scores." "One of my favorite scores that I did was *Master of the World*," he told Tom Weaver. "I think [it] has some good melodies and some lovely orchestration in it. Again, I had carte blanche — here I had Jules Verne and Vincent Price and airships going around the world, so we managed a lot of interesting orchestration. Pre-John Williams work. I have been said to have influenced all of these guys in their work. Unfortunately, 'influenced' is a *kind* word. There's an awful lot of copying that goes on that makes me a little bit unhappy. I hate to hear my stuff quoted directly on the screen."

Halliwell's Film and Video Guide correctly labeled *Master of the World* an "aerial version of *20000 Leagues Under the Sea*, with cheap sets and much use of stock footage.... [S]ome scenes however have a certain vigor," while *Leonard Maltin's Movie Guide* said simply, "very well done." A more mixed message came from the *Time Out Film Guide*, which called it "a pleasantly ludicrous children's fantasy movie, with a talented production team making the most of a low budget.... [T]he film's imaginative use of stock shots and its garish line in nineteenth century hardware are admirable." The screenplay superbly shows off its author's adap-tive abilities as it skillfully synthesizes Verne's two novels, the second of which is espe-cial-ly lacking in narrative thrust. Matheson cleverly conflates, transposes, and recombines elements from both books and expands an extremely minor character into the obligatory love interest.

This was actually Matheson's second attempt at adapting Verne after interpolating Nemo into *The Deadly Powder of Thomas Roch*, a teleplay written for Albert Zugsmith in the 1950s, based on Verne's *Facing the Flag*; it is not known whether this is related to *The Kingdom of Nemo*, an unproduced pilot that Matheson wrote with Beaumont. And, according to Robert Skotak, writing in *Filmfax*, a follow-up to *Master of the World* featuring Nemo was planned: "The 1970 MGM film *Captain Nemo and the Underwater City* actually owed its existence to a ... project entitled *Captain Nemo and the Floating City* [that] Corman had developed in 1963 with the screenwriters R. Wright Campbell and Harold Yablonsky. Art director Daniel Haller [*Master of the World*'s production designer and associate producer] provided preliminary designs, including a flying ship and a multi-tiered city. Plans were made to shoot underwater sequences at Marineland in Southern California." Unfortunately, MGM's final product, on which Campbell shared screenwriting credit with Pip and Jane Baker, suffered from uninspired direction by James Hill and the miscasting of the otherwise estimable Robert Ryan as Nemo.

Pit and the Pendulum

(AIP, released August 12, 1961) DIRECTOR-PRODUCER: Roger Corman; SCREENPLAY: Matheson, based on Edgar Allan Poe's "The Pit and the Pendulum"; MUSIC: Les Baxter; MAKEUP: Ted Coodley; SPECIAL EFFECTS: Butler-Glouner, Inc., Ray Mercer, Pat Dinga. Color, 81 minutes. CAST— Don Nicholas Medina, Sebastian Medina: Vincent Price. Francis Barnard: John Kerr. Elizabeth Barnard Medina: Barbara Steele. Catherine Med-ina: Luana Anders. Dr. Charles Leon: Antony Carbone. Maximillian: Patrick Westwood. Maria: Lynne Bernay. Nicholas as a Child: Larry Turner. Isabella Medina: Mary Menzies. Bartolome Medina: Charles Victor.

Although AIP and Corman had not set out to start a Poe series, the stunning success of *House of Usher* made it inevitable that they would adapt another story, for which they once again recruited Price, Matheson, Baxter, Crosby, and Haller. They ruled out "The Masque of the Red Death"— due to perceived similarities to Ingmar Bergman's *Det Sjunde Inseglet* (The Seventh Seal, 1957), according to Corman, or to budgetary concerns, according to Arkoff; they then settled on "The Pit and the Pendulum," which surpassed its predecessor at the box office. It has been filmed several times, e.g., as a 1913 silent from the world's first female director, Alice Guy-Blaché, and as the alleged inspiration for the oft-retitled West German shocker *Die Schlangengrube und das Pendel* (The Snake Pit and the Pendulum, 1967). Despite its popularity with filmmakers, however, Poe's actual story does little more than enumerate its nameless narrator's physical and psychological travails at the hands of the Inquisition, from which he is saved at the last second when the French army enters Toledo.

"I kind of faked on the Poe things," Matheson told me in an interview for *Filmfax*. "I mean, *Pit and the Pendulum* was ridiculous, 'cause we took a little short story about a guy lying on a table with that razor thing going over him, and had to make a whole story out of it." He added in *Visions of Death*, "Other than that, it was a totally original plot. In fact, I had developed an outline for a novel I was starting to work on called *House of the Dead*. So ... I used [that] as the basis for my screenplay." Once again, the hero arrives at a remote and forbidding house to inquire after a beloved and apparently cataleptic female, and once again he is rebuffed by an agitated Price, who seems to have more than his share of secrets. Here, the house is a Spanish castle in 1546; the hero is Francis Barnard (John Kerr, previously the young lover in *South Pacific* [1958]); the object of the exercise is his sister, Elizabeth Barnard Medina (Barbara Steele); and Price plays her husband, the high-strung Don Nicholas Medina.

In flashbacks stylistically similar to *Usher*'s dream sequence, a young Nicholas (Larry Turner) secretly watches while his inquisitor father, Sebastian (also Price), disposes of his adulterous wife Isabella (Mary Menzies) and brother Bartolome (Charles Victor). Now Nicholas fears that his own wife, whose death Francis has come to investigate, might have shared Isabella's fate and been interred alive. But Elizabeth has colluded with her lover, Dr. Charles Leon (Antony Carbone), to fake her premature burial and drive Nicholas insane — a plan that succeeds only too well when Nicholas becomes convinced he is Sebastian and reenacts the scenario, placing a gagged Elizabeth in an iron maiden and preparing to put Charles under the pendulum. Unnoticed by Nicholas, Charles fatally stumbles into the pit while running away. Drafted as the new "Bartolome," Francis is rescued from the pendulum by Nicholas's sister, Catherine (Luana Anders), and a faithful servant, Maximillian (Patrick Westwood), who propels Nicholas into the pit during a struggle. The survivors lock the torture chamber forever ... without realizing that Elizabeth is still alive in the iron maiden, as revealed in an ending that still packs a considerable punch.

Matheson's published script provides the dying Nicholas with the final line, "Elizabeth. What have I done to you? [*beat*] *What have I done to you?*" as he lies in the pit, but according to Lucy Chase Williams in *The Complete Films of Vincent Price*, "Corman felt that the picture should be very visual at that point and dialogue would have destroyed the mood." In the finished film, however, the sequence segues from the now-mute Nicholas to Catherine's unscripted line, "No one will ever enter this room again." This is followed by a whip pan to Elizabeth — from whose plight the audience's attention has been cleverly distracted during Francis's ordeal under the pendulum. The image abruptly shrinks down to a small rectangle, surrounded by blackness, that just frames Barbara Steele's large and justifiably famous eyes, staring wide with the awful realization that she is now irrevocably imprisoned.

In his introduction to *Visions of Death*, Corman wrote that "adapting 'The Pit and the Pendulum' was one of Dick's most difficult assignments, because Poe's original story had almost no characterization at all.... [It] is simply about a man in a room who is being tortured during the Spanish Inquisition. Dick utilized that as the third act for an original story he wrote, by having our leading man, played by John Kerr, come to Vincent Price's castle in Spain, and putting him under the pendulum for the climax of the film. You could think of it as our creating a two-act prologue that leads up to the third act — which would be the actual Poe story. But in creating the first two acts, Dick attempted to use concepts

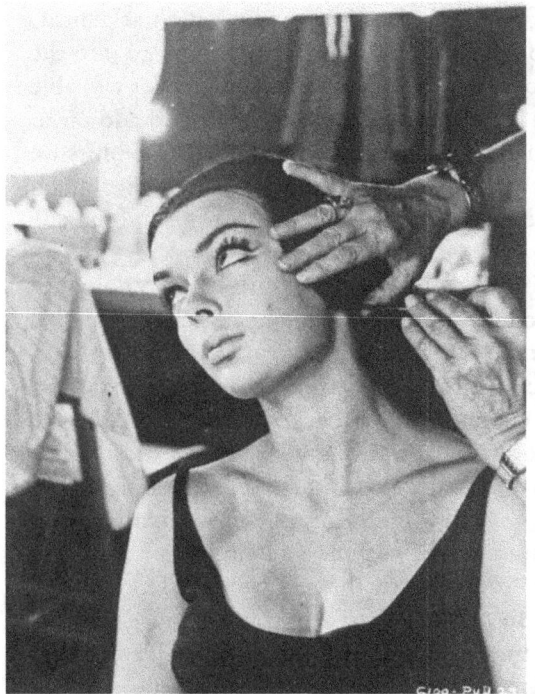

Left: Barbara Steele being made up for her role in *Pit and the Pendulum* (American International, 1961). *Right:* Steele in costume as the treacherous Elizabeth Barnard Medina, as she is seen in flashbacks in *Pit and the Pendulum* (American International, 1961).

and themes that Poe developed in his other stories. For example, the idea of Vincent Price walling up his unfaithful wife was [similar] to something Poe had used in several of his other stories, particularly in 'The Cask of Amontillado.' So although we were inventing a story of our own, we generally tried to maintain a consistency of thought towards Poe's work, by incorporating similar ideas we had taken from his other stories."

The director also told Lawrence French about creating the torture chamber scene for which *Pit and the Pendulum* is best known. "I remember we shot the whole pendulum sequence in less than a day, because after I finished principal photography, there was still an hour or so before we went into overtime. So I got on a Chapman crane with the camera operator and I said, 'Let's just move this crane all over the set.' I hadn't planned any of the shots; I just photographed anything that looked good to me: the moving shadows of the pendulum, or the magnificent murals Danny Haller had painted on the studio walls. Then, later on, I figured I'd be able to use all the different shots when I was cutting the scene together. In fact, we spent a fair amount of time cutting that scene — trying it many different ways — and using every technique I could think of to make it work." In an unusual move, Haller had removed the catwalks from the soundstage and built his sets all the way up to the ceiling, covering the black walls of the pendulum room with murals depicting hooded penitents. The illusion of the pit was convincingly created with a matte painting by that legendary master of the form, Albert Whitlock.

Never above cannibalizing itself, AIP borrowed footage from the *Pit* climax for Norman Taurog's genre spoof *Dr. Goldfoot and the Bikini Machine* (1965), with Price as a mad scientist who imprisons Frankie Avalon in a suspiciously familiar dungeon. Similarly, as Corman told Lawrence French, "We also had a habit of saving the sets from one picture to the next. That is, when you break a set down into its components and into flats, they all go into the scene docks at the studio. So when we came to do *Pit and the Pendulum* ... Haller was able to not only build new units, but also take the flats out from *House of Usher* and add on to them. We would repaint them, rearrange them and so on, but they were the same units we had used before. So each succeeding Poe film got a little bit bigger, without that much greater expense. It was as if a little boy had a set of blocks, and he was able to combine one set of blocks, with another set."

As in *House of Usher*, Corman was convinced that in keeping with his psychological approach to Poe's work, he should show the exterior reality beyond the castle's claustrophobic walls as little as possible. To that end, as he recalled in *The Complete Films of Vincent Price*, he cut out a scripted exterior sequence from the flashback scenes of happier days shared by Nicholas and Elizabeth, which showed them enjoying a horseback ride and a picnic. He told Lucy Chase Williams, "I had a lot of theories I was working with when I did the Poe films. Vincent commented to somebody ... 'I didn't necessarily believe everything Roger said, but it was really *interesting* to listen to [*laughs*]!' One of my theories was that these stories were created out of the unconscious mind of Poe and the unconscious mind never really sees reality, so until *Tomb of Ligeia*, we never showed the real world. Mark Damon rode through a burned-out landscape in *Usher*. In *Pit*, John Kerr arrived in a carriage against an ocean background, which I felt was more representative of the unconscious. That horseback interlude was thrown out because I didn't want to have a scene with people out in broad daylight."

Williams also notes that when *Pit* made its television debut in 1968, "it was deemed too short for the standard two-hour network time slot, and ten minutes of additional footage was shot by Corman assistant Tamara Asseyev [who later produced *Norma Rae* (1979) and others]. Of the original cast, only Luana Anders was available; the new scenes [running just under five minutes on the MGM Home Entertainment DVD] depicted Catherine Medina alone in a madhouse, telling her terrible tale in a flashback."

Her screen time necessarily limited, Steele appeared despite 20th Century–Fox's vow that she would never work in Hollywood again after walking out on both the Elvis Presley vehicle *Flaming Star* (1960)— in which she was replaced by Barbara Eden — and her contract, sold to Fox by the Rank Organisations. Ironically, the British-born Steele was dubbed by another actress (according to Williams, "the rushes had convinced Corman that her thick 'working-class' English accent 'didn't blend with the other actors'"), just as she was in most of the Italian genre films that made her the quintessential "scream queen," starting with Mario Bava's *La Maschera del Demonio* (Mask of the Demon, aka *Black Sunday*, 1960). "Vincent was just completely charming, so intelligent," she told *Filmfax*'s Mark A. Miller. "I think he was an extraordinary actor. I wish he'd done more classical parts away from the horror stuff that he was caught in all the time. I think he was very moving as an actor, someone who could do anything. I wish he'd done *Richard III*. He would have been fabulous." Price did play Richard III, albeit in Corman's *Tower of London* (1962).

In his awe-inspiring book *Mario Bava: All the Colors of the Dark*, Tim Lucas noted that Ernesto Gastaldi, the pseudonymous co-writer of Bava's *La Frusta e il Corpo* (The Whip and the Body, aka *What*, 1963), was "granted free rein with his scenario. His producers made only one provisional request: 'They showed me ... *Pit and the Pendulum* before I started writing it. "Give us something like this," they said.'... [In Italy, *Pit*] was an enormous hit — proving that there now existed an avid local market for the right kind of horror film...."

[I]ts influence on the Italian horror film, particularly in terms of linking deranged adult behavior to specific childhood traumas, would be profound....[and it] became the catalyst behind decades of similarly haunted characters in Italian horror, including ... Bava's *Il rosso segno della follia/Hatchet for the Honeymoon* (1970) and the killer of Dario Argento's *Profondo Rosso/Deep Red* (1975).... That the Italian horror film was so deeply influenced by Corman's movie is fascinating because, in some ways, *Pit and the Pendulum* was America's response to the Italian horror film: Barbara Steele was cast in the picture owing to AIP's great success with Bava's *Black Sunday*," which it released in the U.S.

Price, whose admirable restraint was one of *Usher*'s greatest strengths, pulls out all the stops here, and Crosby's flamboyant photography complements his performance perfectly. As quoted by McGee in *Faster and Furiouser*, the *Los Angeles Times* critic noted, "Kerr seemed to be trying to balance things by hacking out his lines so stiffly and disjointedly that he might have been a driller working on a block of concrete." Recalled Matheson in an interview with me for *Filmfax*, "[Ruth and I] were watching this program, a biography of Anthony Perkins, last night, and this fellow had been talking, and I said, 'Do you know who that is?' She said, 'No, I have no idea,' and I said, 'Well, he's the one who was in *Pit and the Pendulum*, John Kerr.' When you remember these people, you think they're never going to age. Then you see that they have aged, and it's a shock.... To this day, I wince every time I watch [the film]—not that I watch it that often, but whenever I happen to run across it—where he calls Vincent Price's character, Don Nicholas Medina, by his last name, 'Don Medina,' and you're supposed to call him 'Don Nicholas.' But who the hell knew it? Nobody knew."

Although *Pit and the Pendulum* was AIP's most profitable Poe film, its critical standing is more mixed. The *Time Out Film Guide* calls it "Corman at his intoxicating best, drawing a seductive mesh of sexual motifs from Poe's story through a fine Richard Matheson script. Vincent Price is superbly tormented ... and Barbara Steele ... embodies all the contradictions of Poe's quintessential female to perfection," but *Leonard Maltin's Movie Guide*, while praising it as "beautifully staged," advises viewers to "bear with [a] slow first half," and *Halliwell's Film and Video Guide* dismisses it as "lurid but mostly ineffective." Hardy's *Overlook Film Encyclopedia: Horror* epitomizes this ambivalence, calling it "marginally less successful [than *House of Usher*].... [A]lthough the plot is coherent enough, it doesn't quite cohere.... On the other hand, the sexual motif is again beautifully worked out.... From the great sequence in which Steele lures Price down into the crypt to the finale ... its action is terrific."

As with *Tales of Terror*, *The Raven*, and *The Comedy of Terrors* in later years, Lancer Books published the paperback novelization, authored in this case by Lee Sheridan. Writing in the first person allowed Sheridan to go off on various digressions about Francis's home in England and the characteristics of Spain and its people, although some auctorial adroitness was required to enable Francis to witness climactic events to which he was not privy in the film. The fact that Matheson's script is largely original lessens the essential absurdity of Sheridan's adapting a novel from a screenplay based on a short story (credited on the back cover to Edgar Allen Poe). The first four chapters of the movie's other literary antecedent, the unfinished *House of the Dead*, are scheduled to appear in Gauntlet's *Matheson Uncollected: Volume Two*. "I have no recollection why I didn't finish writing it," he told me in 2008. "I think the only thing I used [in the script] were the actual scare bits." There is clearly not a one-to-one correspondence between screenplay and novel; the latter concerns a writer for *People* magazine (which did not exist until 1974, suggesting that Matheson had revived the project at some point) who is assigned to profile a recently deceased artist, and encounters ominous undercurrents at the huge Connecticut estate where he meets the artist's widow and personal physician.

Night of the Eagle

(aka *Burn, Witch, Burn*; Independent Artists–Anglo Amalgamated–AIP [U.S./G.B.], released April 25, 1962) DIRECTOR: Sidney Hayers; PRODUCER: Albert Fennell; SCREEN-PLAY: Matheson, Charles Beaumont, George Baxt [uncredited in U.S.], based on Fritz Leiber's *Conjure Wife*; MUSIC: William Alwyn; MAKEUP: Basil Newall. Black and white, 87 minutes. CAST— Tansy Taylor: Janet Blair. Prof. Norman Taylor: Peter Wyngarde. Prof. Flora Carr: Margaret Johnston. Prof. Harvey Sawtelle: Anthony Nicholls. Prof. Lindsay Carr: Colin Gordon. Evelyn Sawtelle: Kathleen Byron. Dean Harold Gunnison: Reginald Beckwith. Hilda Gunnison: Jessica Dunning. Doctor: Norman Bird. Margaret Abbott: Judith Stott. Bill Jennings: Bill Mitchell. Cleaner's Man: George Roubicek. Truck Driver: Frank Singuineau. Trucker's Mate: Gary Woolf.

Night of the Eagle is one of several adaptations of *Conjure Wife*, a 1943 novel by Fritz Leiber, the award-winning author of the famed Fafhrd and Grey Mouser books. His father, Fritz Sr., was an accomplished screen actor, with genre credits that included *The Hunchback of Notre Dame* (1939) and *Phantom of the Opera* (1943). *Conjure Wife* had already been filmed by Universal as *Weird Woman* (1944), the second in a sextet of Inner Sanctum mysteries with Lon Chaney, Jr., whose frequent collaborator, Reginald LeBorg, also directed the first and third entries, *Calling Dr. Death* (1943) and *Dead Man's Eyes* (1944). Inspired by the popular line of novels published by Simon & Schuster, these low-budget films were whodunits with macabre elements and — unlike *Conjure Wife*— usually gave any apparently supernatural element a rational explanation in the end. Coincidentally, the elder Leiber later (1948) appeared in an unrelated mystery also titled *Inner Sanctum*.

Less than two years before this remake was released, Janice Rule and Larry Blyden starred in "Conjure Wife" (7/8/60), a live half-hour episode of NBC's short-lived color anthology series *Moment of Fear* that according to Alan Warren, author of *This is a* Thriller, was hailed by Leiber as the best version of his novel, appropriately marking the only time it has been dramatized under its original title. Somewhat confusingly, *Night of the Eagle* was released in the U.S. as *Burn, Witch, Burn*, which with a slightly different punctuation — as *Burn Witch, Burn!*— had also served as the title of an earlier novel by another well-known fantasist, Abraham Merritt (the author of *Seven Footprints to Satan*), filmed by *Dracula's* Tod Browning under yet another title, *The Devil-Doll* (1936). The laserdisc of *Burn, Witch, Burn* includes the two-and-a-half-minute U.S. theatrical prologue, a gimmick worthy of master showman William Castle, in which dubbing legend Paul Frees recites an incantation over a blank screen in order "to dispel all evil spirits that may radiate from the screen during this performance," so that lucky viewers might enjoy the film "with a free mind and a protected soul..."

In an interview with me for *Filmfax*, Matheson recounted how he and Charles Beaumont came to embark upon their only large-screen collaboration: "We just went to a bar one night, we were chatting, and we decided, 'Let's write a movie together.' We both loved *Conjure Wife*, and we knew that it had already been filmed, so we just ignored the fact and did it anyway. We were both working for American International at the time, and they liked the script very much, but since they had to buy the rights from Universal, who had made

Tansy Taylor (Janet Blair) with the "protections" she has been using on behalf of her husband Norman (Peter Wyngarde) in *Night of the Eagle* (Independent Artists–Anglo Amalgamated–American International, 1962). Photograph courtesy of the Paul M. Sammon Collection.

Weird Woman, the one with Lon Chaney, Jr., I think we split $10,000 between us for the script, that's all we ever made.... I wrote the first half, and he wrote the second half ... [and then] we just each looked at it and made suggestions on each other's half. Actually, it doesn't seem like it when you read our short stories, but when it came to scripts we wrote pretty similarly."

AIP bought their speculative script, acquired the rights to the novel from Universal, and arranged for it to be an Anglo-American co-production with the British studio Independent Artists, which had been founded in 1958 by the film's executive producers, Julian Wintle and Leslie Parkyn. *Night of the Eagle* was directed by Sidney Hayers and produced by Albert Fennell, who had been the production supervisor on *The Innocents* (1961), Jack Clayton's superb screen version of Henry James's "The Turn of the Screw." Because the film was shot in England, Matheson had no idea how it would turn out until he saw the finished product, and was pleasantly surprised by the results, particularly the score by Carol Reed's frequent collaborator, William Alwyn. Curiously, the credits for the British version, which are included as an extra on the Image Entertainment laserdisc, reveal that while Matheson was credited first in the U.S., Beaumont was first in England.

As the camera follows a car onto the campus of Hempnell Medical College and pans up to a huge stone eagle overlooking the grounds, Prof. Norman Taylor (Peter Wyngarde, a ghost in *The Innocents*) writes "I do *not* believe" on his classroom blackboard, telling his students they are "four words necessary to destroy the forces of the supernatural, witchcraft, superstition, the psychic, etc., etc." Relative newcomers to Hempnell who have spent time in Jamaica, Norman and his attractive wife Tansy (Janet Blair) are bitterly resented by some of the more deeply entrenched faculty members and their spouses, such as Evelyn Sawtelle

Norman carries the catatonic Tansy out of the cemetery after she almost drowns while trying to lift the curse on him in *Night of the Eagle* (Independent Artists–Anglo Amalgamated–American International, 1962). Photograph courtesy of the Paul M. Sammon Collection.

(Kathleen Byron), who is infuriated by the possibility that Norman might be promoted to the sociology chair ahead of her husband, Harvey (Anthony Nicholls). Lindsay Carr (Colin Gordon) observes during a faculty bridge party at the Taylor house that his host seems to lead a charmed life, unaware how close to the truth he is: After the party, Norman stumbles across a Jamaican good luck charm in the dresser. Meanwhile, Tansy frantically searches for, and then destroys, a more malevolent totem that was clearly concealed there by one of their guests.

Uncovering a multitude of other charms Tansy has secreted throughout the household, the skeptical Norman is shocked to find that she has been using spells she learned from a witch doctor back in Jamaica — not only to advance his career, but also to ward off the evil occult forces she is convinced are being used against him by his academic rivals. He burns all her paraphernalia in the fireplace. Now unprotected, Norman is, in quick succession, nearly run over by a truck; accused of rape by Margaret Abbott (Judith Stott), a student who had propositioned him in an obscene phone call; threatened at gunpoint by Margaret's frustrated suitor Bill Jennings (Bill Mitchell); and anonymously sent a package containing a recording of one of his lectures, overlaid with a strangely sinister whirring sound. While a violent thunderstorm rages outside, Tansy switches off the tape recorder and futilely begs Norman not to answer the phone, through which the whirring sound continues to emanate, or open the door, at which unseen forces screech and pound, ceasing only when she rips the phone cord out of the wall, as the door knocks Norman inward.

Tansy gets Norman drunk and persuades him to say, "All that I have is yours," thus completing a spell that will transfer his impending doom to her. When he awakens from a nightmare the next morning, he finds a farewell message left on the tape recorder in which Tansy reveals that she has gone away to protect Norman from this curse by dying in his place; "by midnight, it will be finished — over." After narrowly avoiding a collision with a truck, while following the bus that is taking Tansy to the seaside cottage where she spends much of her time, Norman himself resorts to a magic rite in the crypt of a nearby cemetery as she walks into the surf. The clock strikes twelve before he can finish and she appears in the doorway to the crypt, soaked with seawater and clutching the tape of his lecture. Refusing the aid of a doctor (Norman Bird), the robotic Tansy orders Norman to take her home, where she arises the following night to attack him with a knife while displaying the characteristic limp of Lindsay's wife, Flora Carr (Margaret Johnston). After subduing Tansy, who falls unconscious, Norman puts her to bed and heads for a final confrontation with Flora, exposed as his occult opponent.

The mocking Flora constructs a house of tarot cards and then sets fire to it, whereupon an accidental blaze breaks out in the Taylor home. Norman tries to race to Tansy's aid while Flora gloats, "Burn, witch, burn" (hence the alternate title), and plays the tape over the school's public address system, also sending the whirring sound — identified in the novel as an Australian bull-roarer — over the grounds. Suddenly, the stone eagle comes to life and chases Norman back inside, through the corridors, and into his classroom, where by cowering against the blackboard he partially erases the writing to omit the word "*not*" (leaving simply, "I do believe"). When Lindsay appears, Flora is forced to shut off the tape. As Norman finds Tansy is safe, the eagle, which has returned to stone, falls on and kills Flora. The screenplay simplifies Leiber's much more complicated climax, in which the wives of Professors Carr, Sawtelle, and Dean Gunnison are all revealed as practicing witches and Tansy's soul changes bodies several times. In the film, Flora is the sole antagonist and the Sawtelles are reduced to supporting characters, as are Harold (Reginald Beckwith) and Hilda Gunnison (Jessica Dunning).

In *Fearing the Dark: The Val Lewton Career*, Edmund G. Bansak argues, "*Burn, Witch, Burn* is the perfect companion piece to Jacques Tourneur's *Curse of the Demon*, and their parallels go much further than their similar sounding British titles.... Although Hayers' horror masterpiece, like *Curse of the Demon*, was largely ignored by American theatergoers, the critics were pleased and the film soon gained a cult audience when it began to play on television.... [His] dynamic direction and [the] moody, expressionistic photography [by early Hammer vet Reginald Wyer] add immeasurably to *Burn, Witch, Burn*'s exalted position among the multitude of films that have attempted to duplicate the dark magic of the Val Lewton productions." Bansak states that when Independent Artists became involved with the project, "producer Albert Fennell handed it over to George Baxt ... for a final revision and called in Sidney Hayers to direct," but Baxt is credited only on the British version. "That's one of those mysteries," Matheson pondered in an interview with me. "I don't know who George Baxt is. Obviously this happened in England. The picture that I look at, to my mind, is the script we wrote."

That Baxt was involved in some way is certainly plausible. His credits include two previous films for Hayers, *Circus of Horrors* (aka *Phantom of the Circus*, 1960) — also produced by Wintle and Parkyn — and *Payroll* (aka *I Promised to Pay*, 1961), as well as two other memorable British chillers of the '60s, John Moxey's *The City of the Dead* (aka *Horror Hotel*, 1960) and Hammer's Lewtonian *The Shadow of the Cat* (1961). Later a mystery novelist, Baxt asserted in an interview with me for *Filmfax*, "Charles Beaumont asked Arkoff, 'Please, don't put anybody's name on our credits, we've written everything alone.' And he said, 'I've got to give him credit, he wrote the whole script. It has no resemblance to what you wrote.' And it didn't. I wrote at least ninety percent of *Burn, Witch, Burn*, and I did that in four days. Sidney absolutely would not go on — at this point Sidney was now a star, so he would not go on the set with the script in the shape that they had.... I mean, their script was an embarrassment. Sidney was near tears when he got it.

"It was supposed to star June Allyson, who we did not know was ... a total alcoholic at the time. She really was falling down dead drunk. She was appearing in a show on Broadway called *Forty Carats*. She showed up like twice a week. The understudy, Iva Withers, played it more often than she did.... I read *Conjure Wife*. And I said, 'Sidney, I can give us a better story, but we've got to get rid of this fucking dialogue.' Let me give you a sample dialogue: Peter Wyngarde — we had trouble with him, he was stuffing toilet paper into his crotch; I mean, you don't see any shot of him below the waist, Sidney was shooting up.... Anyway, the line that Peter had, 'Tansy, you've got to give up this witchcraft.' She said, 'All at once?' He said, 'All at once, immediately.' She said, 'Well, can't I taper off?' [In the novel, Tansy does in fact say to Norman, "Not all at once ... couldn't I just quit by degrees?"] Well, you know, come on. We were hysterical. I said, 'Is this supposed to be a comedy?' Of course later it was done as a comedy, so-called, with Lana Turner and Teri Garr, *Witches' Brew* [1985]. Terrible movie."

There are differences between the film and the Matheson-Beaumont script (also titled *Conjure Wife*, and published in Conlon's *He Is Legend*), e.g., the expedient of giving Tansy a seaside cottage, which simplified Norman's involved efforts to trace her whereabouts. But most involve a simple polish of the dialogue — including the addition of the "Burn, witch, burn" line — and minor changes such as character names. Its substitution of a stone eagle

Opposite: Poster art for *Night of the Eagle* (Independent Artists–Anglo Amalgamated–American International, 1962) with its U.S. title (minus onscreen punctuation), *Burn, Witch, Burn*.

for the original gargoyle was presumably to economize on special effects, since many shots of the "giant" eagle appear to have been created using a live bird. Specific scenes that Baxt claimed to have added to the script were refuted, point by point, in a letter to the editors of *Filmfax* by contributor Christopher Koetting, who stated, "For Mr. Baxt to call anything written by two of the greatest fantasy writers of this century an 'embarrassment' is outrageous. The real embarrassment is the false credit Mr. Baxt wishes to give himself at their expense.... It is unfortunate that he feels the need to misrepresent the truth in order to make himself look disproportionately important." With many of the principals dead, the whole truth must remain elusive.

Regardless of its patrimony, the result is a minor masterpiece of supernatural horror, praised in *Leonard Maltin's Movie Guide* for its "shattering suspense [and] genuinely frightening climax" and in *Halliwell's Film and Video Guide* for the "solid production values in creepy sequences." In *Faster and Furiouser*, Mark Thomas McGee notes that *Night of the Eagle* "was the companion feature for [Matheson's *Tales of Terror*], which it easily eclipsed. It was one of the best films AIP ever had anything to do with.... The British Film Institute called the direction 'fresh and exciting, skillful in its reliance on suggestion, naggingly effective as a study of psychic attack.' Critic William [K.] Everson praised it, forgiving its somewhat erratic editing, which he explained was due in part to the hero's insistence on wearing ultratight pants. For modesty's sake, the director was forced to shoot him in close-ups or extreme long shots. A special screening of the film took place on October 28, 1962, at the Lytton Center Theatre for the members of the Writers Guild. Bill Everson assembled some horror film clips for the occasion and noted author Ray Bradbury made a speech, as he was often prone to do."

David Pirie raves in the *Time Out Film Guide*, "Hayers shoots the whole thing with an almost Wellesian flourish, and the script ... is structured with incredible tightness..." Bansak also quotes a favorable review by Howard Thompson of *The New York Times*:

> Don't miss *Burn, Witch, Burn*.... This low-budget British import is quite the most effective 'supernatural' thriller since *Village of the Damned* [1960]. For all we know it may be the best outright goose-pimpler dealing specifically with witchcraft since *I Walked with a Zombie*.... Simply as a suspense yarn, blending lurid conjecture and brisk reality, growing chillier by the minute and finally whipping up an ice-cold crescendo of fright, the result is admirable. Excellently photographed (not a single frame is wasted), and cunningly directed, the incidents gather a pounding, graphic drive that is diabolically teasing. The climax is a nightmarish hair-curler but, we maintain, entirely logical within the context.... For blueprinting a story that gallops toward occult darkness with feet touching the ground, the two scenarists rate credit for the blunt, steadying dialogue.... A good, unholy brew, seasoned by professional hands and rising to a boil.

According to Phil Hardy's *Overlook Film Encyclopedia: Horror*, "None of Hayers' other pictures before or after this one confirmed the talent shown here, which suggests that the particular chemistry at work in this collaboration with Matheson, Beaumont and Leiber could be responsible for the film's undoubted quality. In addition, the expertise of executive producers, Julian Wintle and Leslie Parkyn ... may have worked as the necessary congenial catalyst for the collaborative venture." More complimentary toward Hayers, Matheson noted in the author's interview for *Noir* that he had seen an article in which "they asked him about George Baxt, and he said, 'No, no, that's ridiculous. The script was all theirs, Beaumont and Matheson.'... Hayers's best picture was called *The Trap* [1966], with Oliver Reed and Rita Tushingham. It's about a French-Canadian trapper and this deaf-mute girl who comes to live with him. A marvelous piece of work." Hayers went on to direct several episodes of

The Avengers, the 1960s series on which Fennell and Wintle served as producer and executive producer, respectively.

Baxt noted that "we had a great supporting cast in that picture. Margaret Johnston, who played the one with the limp — her husband [Albert Parker] had been a silent film director in Hollywood; he was now an agent in London — a wonderful actress. Kathleen Byron from *Black Narcissus* [1947] was in it, and the men were wonderful. We had a terrific cast. Well, we didn't have June Allyson, and they called me up, they said, 'George, what do you think of Janet Blair?' I said, 'I just did a television [show] in New York with her called *Strawberry Blonde*.... She's a nice lady, Janet Blair, [but] is she a star? I mean, she hasn't really done a major movie in her life.' And they said, 'Well, what do you suggest?' I said, 'Why can't we get somebody here in England?' You know, there were lots of ladies that could have done it, but they wanted an American name. So Janet Blair arrived, very sweet ... [and it] was shot in five or six weeks."

Of the most recent adaptation of the novel to date, horror host and historian John Stanley notes in his *Creature Features Movie Guide Strikes Again* that the aforementioned *Witches' Brew* had a troubled history. "Originally shot in 1978 as *Which Witch Is Which?*, this failed to stir the cauldron and underwent reshooting before being sold to cable TV.... The jokes are thin, the production qualities cheap. Directed by Richard Shorr [who shared script credit with Syd Dutton] with new footage by Herbert L. Strock." Shorr's uncredited remake featured Turner, Garr, and Richard Benjamin in the Johnston, Blair, and Wyngarde roles, respectively. In a 1991 letter to me, Matheson reported an abortive attempt by Spike Lee's former cinematographer Ernest Dickerson to mount yet another version of *Conjure Wife* with black leads.

Tales of Terror

(AIP, released May 1962) DIRECTOR-PRODUCER: Roger Corman; SCREENPLAY: Matheson; MUSIC: Les Baxter; MAKEUP: Lou La Cava; SPECIAL EFFECTS: Butler-Glouner, Inc., Ray Mercer Co., Pat Dinga. Color, 89 minutes. "Morella" — based on Edgar Allan Poe's story. CAST — Locke: Vincent Price. Lenora: Maggie Pierce. Morella: Leona Gage. Coachman: Edmund Cobb. "The Black Cat" — based on Poe's story and "The Cask of Amontillado." CAST — Fortunato Luchresi: Vincent Price. Montresor Herringbone: Peter Lorre. Annabel Herringbone: Joyce Jameson. Wilkins: Wally Campo. Chairman: Alan DeWitt. Policeman: John Hackett. "The Case of M. Valdemar" — based on Poe's "The Facts in the Case of M. Valdemar." CAST — Ernest Valdemar: Vincent Price. Carmichael: Basil Rathbone. Helene Valdemar: Debra Paget. Dr. Elliot James: David Frankham. Servant: Scott Brown.

After a dispute with AIP over profits from *Pit and the Pendulum*, Corman decided to make his own (non–AIP) Poe film, *Premature Burial*. With Price under contract to AIP, he hired Ray Milland for the leading role. "I arranged financing though Pathé Lab, which helped back some AIP productions and did their print work," Corman wrote in his memoir. "On the first morning, Jim Nicholson and Sam Arkoff came on the set. I thought: 'They have *never* shown up like this before. And why are they smiling?' 'Roger,' Sam said, shaking my hand, 'we just wanted to wish you luck. We're partners again.' AIP, then the largest independent studio in town, had gone to Pathé, which did not have a distributor lined up yet, and *bought out* their position as producer. They had some leverage, as I had heard it:

'In case you don't want to play ball,' AIP told Pathé, 'we're pulling all our lab work with you.'"

He added in his introduction to *Visions of Death*, "For my third Poe film, *Premature Burial*, I was sorry at not being able to use [Matheson], because originally, the film was going to be made away from AIP.... Instead I picked a friend of Dick's, Charles Beaumont, to do the picture, because he had a similar writing style. However, I soon became aware

A TRILOGY of SHOCK
AND HORROR!
...A NEW CONCEPT IN
MOTION PICTURES!

"...and there was an oozing liquid putrescence ...all that remained of Mr. Valdemar." --POE

"I had walled the black monster up within the tomb!" --POE

AMERICAN INTERNATIONAL presents
EDGAR ALLAN POE'S
TALES of TERROR
in PANAVISION® and COLOR

VINCENT PRICE · PETER LORRE · BASIL RATHBONE ···· DEBRA PAGET
····ROGER CORMAN ·····RICHARD MATHESON ···· JAMES H. NICHOLSON · SAMUEL Z. ARKOFF

that the script for *Premature Burial* did not hold together quite as well as the previous two pictures that Dick had written. That was partly due to the fact that the Poe story wasn't really a story. It was more of an essay about premature burial. As a result, we had to go back and do more re-writing on that particular script than on any other film in the Poe series, eventually bringing in Ray Russell to collaborate with Chuck on the final re-writes. Happily, Dick returned to write my next two Poe films, *Tales of Terror* and *The Raven*..." *Premature Burial* features another unbalanced husband taking revenge on his adulterous wife and her lover, whose plot against him backfires; between that and the omnipresent themes of catalepsy and untimely interment, the movie came across as more than a little familiar.

So it was back to business for Corman, Matheson, and Price when they were reunited on *Tales of Terror*, which combined four of Poe's tales into three segments. It was Matheson's first experience with the feature-length anthology format that would soon prove so successful for Britain's Amicus Productions, founded by two expatriate American producers, Max J. Rosenberg and Milton Subotsky. Bloch adapted three Amicus films from his short stories, including *The House That Dripped Blood* (1970), one segment of which, "Sweets to the Sweet," is often misattributed to Matheson. "They never did well as motion pictures," Matheson said of anthology films in an interview with me for *Filmfax*. "They used to do that back in the '40s,

Poster art for *Tales of Terror* (American International, 1962).

they did *Tales of Manhattan* [1942] and things like that. [*Dead of Night* (1945)], that's a dandy.... But I don't think they were ever really big successes. People seem to prefer one story. I mean, both the [anthology TV-movies] I did with [Dan] Curtis [*Trilogy of Terror* and *Dead of Night*] were pilots for a series, and they didn't go." The need to engage the viewer's interest in a new story and characters every twenty to thirty minutes, and the concomitant inability to invest them with any degree of complexity, often resulted in a mere series of sketches, each little more than an excuse for a gory and/or ironic shock ending, usually with a revenge motif.

    Tales of Terror demonstrated that Poe, with his frequent focus on atmosphere over plotting and/or characterization, could be well served by this format, although according to Lucy Chase Williams, Corman attributed the slight dip in the box-office receipts for *Tales of Terror* to the anthology structure. "I combined a couple of stories, but the others were pretty much the way the stories were," said Matheson. He based the first segment on "Morella," which with "Berenice," "Eleonora," and "Ligeia" forms a quartet of variations on Poe's themes of necrophilia and reincarnation. Like "Ligeia"—filmed as *The Tomb of Ligeia*—it also concerns metempsychosis, the transference of a soul at the point of death. Yet another of Poe's anonymous narrators, given the name of Locke in Matheson's script (presumably after John Locke, the seventeenth-century English philosopher whose writings are alluded to in the story), weds his erudite and platonic friend Morella, but then becomes alienated by her obsession with "mystical writings," and as she wastes away he longs for her

Vengeful cuckold Montresor Herringbone (Peter Lorre) calmly walls up his rival, Fortunato Luchresi (Vincent Price), in "The Black Cat" from *Tales of Terror* (American International, 1962).

to die, which she does while giving birth to their daughter. "Her whom in life thou didst abhor, in death thou shalt adore," she had warned, and the nameless child grows into her image with unnatural speed while raised by her father in seclusion. As he impulsively speaks Morella's name at the baptismal font she answers, "I am here!" and expires, and when he places her body into the tomb, "I found no traces of the first, in the charnel where I laid the second, Morella."

In the film, Lenora (Maggie Pierce)—an obvious nod to Poe's "rare and radiant maiden," Lenore—returns to her home outside Boston 26 years after her father, Locke (Price), sent her away as an infant. She discovers that he has lived as an alcoholic recluse since the death of his beloved wife Morella (Leona Gage), who with her dying breath had blamed the baby for her imminent demise. When Locke learns that Lenora has consistently failed in her relationships with men and has only a few months left to live, the father and daughter are at last tearfully reconciled amid their cobweb-shrouded surroundings. Morella's mummified body, which Locke had disinterred and put in her bed, is mysteriously rejuvenated, and her vengeful shade makes its ghostly way upstairs to Lenora's room. Finding Lenora apparently dead, Locke covers her face, but when he sees movement beneath the sheet he pulls it back to reveal Morella instead. After discovering Lenora's own wizened figure lying in Morella's bed, the startled Locke drops a candle that sets the house ablaze as the ghost attacks him (and the infamous footage of the burning barn from *House of Usher* makes its second appearance).

Adopting a darkly comic tone, the second segment "The Black Cat" cleverly combines plot elements from both the title story and "The Cask of Amontillado," each of which involves a person being walled up (albeit one dead and one living). Peter Lorre is in fine form as Montresor Herringbone, a perpetual drunk who neglects and abuses his inoffensive young wife, Annabel (Joyce Jameson). Once attentive and romantic, Montresor is now a ne'er-do-well who has not worked for 17 years ("Has it been that long?" he sheepishly asks her). Annabel, whose beloved black cat he loathes, earns their meager subsistence by taking in sewing, but Montresor believes that she is selfishly hiding a vast fortune from him, and periodically searches the house for the elusive treasure. Finding himself with no money to buy alcohol, the omnivorous oenophile hilariously accosts a series of passersby in a vain effort to solicit a contribution ("Could you spare a coin for a moral cripple?"), and then literally stumbles into a wine merchants' convention where Fortunato Luchresi (Price), "without doubt the foremost wine-taster in the civilized world today," is preparing to demonstrate his expertise.

The indignant Montresor challenges him and, in the segment's most memorable sequence, matches Fortunato glass for glass in a comic drinking contest that is cited as a favorite by both viewers and the filmmakers themselves. Harry H. Waugh of John Harvey & Sons, Ltd., Bristol, England, advised the actors on their technique, and as the star recalled in *The Complete Films of Vincent Price*, "[He showed us] the whole thing about testing the wine and breathing it in, and doing all that stuff, then Peter and I just went a little further. I was trying to do it in an exaggerated fashion, which made it so funny.'" Corman and company brilliantly contrast the two contestants' wildly divergent methods, with Fortunato humorously sucking and swirling the wine in a broad execution of the "accredited procedure," and Montresor guzzling every glass he can get his hands on, yet flawlessly identifying each vintage and adding, his words increasingly slurred, "It's very good."

The spectacularly inebriated Montresor brings this "very good friend" home to meet his wife, and upon discovering such shared interests as an affection for felines, Fortunato and

Annabel are immediately smitten with each other. They then hit upon the simple expedient of keeping Montresor readily supplied with drinking money, so that they can carry on their adulterous affair behind his back. When bartender Wilkins (*Master of the World*'s Wally Campo) points out the correlation between their meeting and her newly cooperative attitude, Montresor kills Annabel, gives Fortunato some drugged amontillado, and walls him up in the cellar with her corpse. Montresor is now free to spend the fortune he finally finds and boasts that she will not need it "where she is," which Wilkins duly reports to the police. Montresor drunkenly and arrogantly agrees to accompany two policemen on a search of the premises, starting in the cellar, but the overconfident murderer is first tormented by the phantoms of the dead lovers, which only he can see, and then revealed by the yowling of Annabel's cat (identified as Pluto in Poe's original story, but not in the movie), which he has unwittingly walled up with them.

Debra Paget, who had known Corman since he was a 22-year-old story analyst and she a teenaged contract player at Fox a decade earlier, co-starred with Price in the last segment, "The Case of M. Valdemar," based on Poe's "The Facts in the Case of M. Valdemar." Incurably ill Ernest Valdemar (Price) selflessly wishes his young wife, Helene (Paget), to marry handsome Dr. Elliot James (*Master of the World*'s David Frankham) after his death. Valdemar shows his appreciation to Carmichael (Basil Rathbone), the mesmerist who alleviates his suffering but unnerves Helene, by consenting to become the subject of "a momentous experiment." Carmichael hypnotizes Valdemar *in articulo mortis* (at the point of death),

The ghostly Fortunato and Annabel Herringbone (Joyce Jameson) play with Montresor's severed head in a dream sequence from *Tales of Terror* (American International, 1962).

then refuses to release him from that state unless Helene agrees to marry the mesmerist instead. Having been kept in a kind of living death until long past his appointed time, Valdemar rises from his trance when Carmichael tries to molest Helene, attacking the mesmerist and covering him with "an oozing liquid putrescence."

Corman noted in *Cinefantastique*, "I shot [a sequence of Valdemar in Hades] and put it together, and for whatever reason I made the decision to take it out.... It may have been that these pictures really were rather low-budget films. We tried to make them look more expensive than they were, but they really were quite low-budget. I think when I looked at that Hades sequence for five minutes, I felt it really didn't look right." In the feature-length video interview *Vincent Price: The Sinister Image* (excerpted in the same article), the actor told Del Valle, "[Basil] was very disillusioned, very bitter, because he really had been a great star. People forget that because they think of him as Sherlock Holmes, or they think of him as a villain. But he had been a great Shakespearean actor, a great star in the theatre and in movies. And he suddenly found (as we all did when Jimmy Dean and Marlon Brando and those people came out, and there was a kind of speaking in the vernacular, and all of us spoke with trained accents and trained English, and theatrically we were different in our approach to acting) that if you wanted to stay in the business, you bloody well went into costume pictures. And Basil rather resented that."

It was with *Tales of Terror* that American International began using aging horror stars like Rathbone and Lorre, many of whose careers had fallen on hard times and whose services could thus be had cheaply. "Peter had an extraordinary personality, and it seemed to blend into a kind of strangeness about him," Price recalled of Lorre in *Round Up the Usual Suspects*, Aljean Harmetz's exhaustive book on the making of *Casablanca* (1942). "In ... *Tales of Terror*, in a dream sequence we cut off Peter's head and played basketball with it. And he could hardly stand to watch us kicking his rubber head around. I think Peter resented having to be in those pictures more than most of us did." Interestingly, another film released that same year, Robert Aldrich's seminal *What Ever Happened to Baby Jane?* (1962), kicked off a comparable distaff revival for its stars, Bette Davis and Joan Crawford, as they and many of their contemporaries who soon followed suit became the perpetrators and/or victims of dire doings in a variety of similarly themed and titled movies.

Matheson told *Fangoria*'s Tom Weaver and Michael Brunas that although the anthology idea was probably AIP's, he selected the stories himself. "In my script, ["Morella"] was a really great character relationship between the two of them: Vincent Price was up to it, and I was visualizing someone like Nina Foch playing the dying daughter. But this girl that they got [Maggie Pierce] was terrible, and they also cut a lot out of it, so it just didn't work.... I enjoyed that middle one. I thought Price was wonderful, and the wine-tasting sequence was just delightful. And the last one — except for the lousy special effect at the end — I thought it was very good...." Much kinder to what ended up on screen in "Morella," *The Overlook Film Encyclopedia: Horror* calls it "in many ways perfection.... Done with great delicacy as the triangular web of love and hatred conjures the dead woman's vengeful spirit."

In the Lancer Books novelization, the title page amusingly reads, "by EDGAR ALLAN POE.... Adapted by Eunice Sudak from the screenplay by Richard Matheson." In this book the sequence of stories is reversed, with "Valdemar" first and "Morella" last; the theatrical trailer suggests that the film had at one time also utilized the same sequence and, anticipating a Matheson hit from a decade hence, calls it "A triumphant trilogy of terror!" Although it unsurprisingly preserves Matheson's plotting and dialogue faithfully, the book provides Locke with a first name, Glanville, and Montresor with the more obvious last name of

Lushington, as well as offering an elaborate précis of Valdemar's past 42 years, a much more gruesome description of his putrefaction than anything found in the film, and a glimpse of the unused afterlife sequence. "There was a mass of swirling lights and forms; there was darkness abysmal. There were noxious vapors, grotesquely writhing shadows, distorted faces, male and female, bored, aimless, grinning hideously. All was chaos, chaos and confinement, meaningless torture.... [T]his was limbo, the abode of those who are barred from heaven, barred from hell."

The Raven

(AIP, released January 25, 1963) DIRECTOR-PRODUCER: Roger Corman; SCREENPLAY: Matheson, based on Edgar Allan Poe's poem; MUSIC: Les Baxter; MAKEUP: Ted Coodley; SPECIAL EFFECTS: Butler-Glouner, Inc., Pat Dinga. Color, 86 minutes. CAST—Dr. Erasmus Craven: Vincent Price. Dr. Adolphus Bedlo: Peter Lorre. Dr. Scarabus: Boris Karloff. Lenore Craven: Hazel Court. Estelle Craven: Olive Sturgess. Rexford Bedlo: Jack Nicholson. Maid: Connie Wallace. Grimes: William Baskin. Gort: Aaron Saxon. Raven: Jim Junior.

With its combination of humor and horror, Matheson's fourth and final entry in AIP's Poe cycle, *The Raven*, was an outgrowth of "The Black Cat," the second segment from *Tales of Terror*. Matheson, who once compared the churning out of the Poe films to making shoes, noted of the subsequent entries directed by Corman after he himself had left the series, "I think they turned out quite well. I know Chuck Beaumont did several. *The Masque of the Red Death* was quite artistic, I thought. Then there was [*The Tomb of Ligeia*], they got pretty arty and did quite a nice job of it. I could never have done it. After [*Tales of Terror*] I couldn't take them seriously; that's why I made one of the stories [in that film] a comedy with Peter Lorre in it, and after that, I couldn't take it seriously at all," as he told me in a *Filmfax* interview. The humor notwithstanding, there was some tension generated by the conflicting approaches of new addition Boris Karloff, whose stage training called for him to perform scenes exactly as written, and Peter Lorre, whose light-hearted ad-libs frustrated Karloff no end. Vincent Price, who had both classical and Method training, acted as a kind of balance between them.

After averaging a staggering five films per year during the 1930s (including Lew Landers' earlier version of *The Raven*) and a respectable two per year in the '40s, including many recognized classics in both decades, Karloff was finding film roles fewer and farther between by the time he joined AIP's stable of aging horror stars (he'd had fewer than a dozen largely undistinguished credits since 1949). For better or worse, Karloff lived to make the most of the AIP connection (Lorre died in 1964, and Rathbone in 1967), appearing in everything from *Bikini Beach* (1964) and *The Ghost in the Invisible Bikini* (1966) to Haller's *Monster of Terror* and another H.P. Lovecraft adaptation, *Curse of the Crimson Altar* (aka *The Crimson Cult*, 1968), which was co-produced in association with Tony Tenser's short-lived venture, Tigon British Film Productions.

Having marginally more to do with Poe's poem than its predecessor, Corman's *The Raven* opens circa 1506 (curiously, Sudak's novelization is set circa 1418 instead) as Dr. Erasmus Craven (Price), a magician mourning his second wife, Lenore, is visited by a colleague, Dr. Adolphus Bedlo (Lorre), who was transformed into the titular bird (Jim Junior) when he challenged Dr. Scarabus (Karloff) to a duel. Restoring Bedlo to human form, Craven

Foes Dr. Scarabus (Boris Karloff), Dr. Adolphus Bedlo (Peter Lorre), and Dr. Erasmus Craven (Vincent Price) in a deceptively collegial promotional shot for *The Raven* (American International, 1963).

learns that he has seen Lenore, or her imprisoned spirit, in the castle of Scarabus, a rival of Craven's father. With Craven's daughter Estelle (Olive Sturgess) and Bedlo's son Rexford (Jack Nicholson) in tow, they travel there, but not before "some diabolic mind control" forces first Craven's coachman, Grimes (William Baskin), and then Rexford to try to kill them. The travelers are perplexed by a warm welcome from Scarabus, who invites them to stay for dinner and claims everything has been a misunderstanding. When the drunken Bedlo becomes obstreperous and again challenges Scarabus, he is apparently reduced to a patch of raspberry jam, and it is revealed that the scheming Lenore (Hazel Court) actually left Craven for the more powerful Scarabus. Seeking the secret of Craven's hand manipulations, Scarabus imprisons the others and threatens to torture Estelle. The wily Bedlo, who has faked his own demise, begs Scarabus to turn him back into a raven instead of killing him, but after Bedlo pecks through his bonds, Rexford frees the others as Craven faces Scarabus in a sorcerous duel to the finish.

With a three-week shooting schedule, the film benefited from the cumulative collection of sets from the previous Poe pictures, but these handsome production values did not preclude another use of the burning barn footage from *House of Usher* (which made its swan song in *The Tomb of Ligeia*) as yet another castle goes up in flames. Although he is able to shield himself and Lenore from the blaze, Scarabus sadly states, "I'm afraid I just don't have it any more," after fruitlessly attempting to restore her ruined dress. This lighthearted denouement was absent from the novelization, in which Scarabus and Lenore are buried by a collapsing ceiling.

Adding to the film's farcical flavor was the unsubtle music of Les Baxter, who claimed much of the credit for the series' comic turn: "I introduced humor to horror scores," the composer claimed in *It Came from Weaver Five*. "After doing so many ... you're looking for different things to do in horror films. It was in *The Raven* that I first started doing this. Vincent Price did a little quick-step around the telescope, so I put in a little tap-dance motif. Most composers would be frightened. One way in which I was lucky was that I had carte blanche and I knew that I would be allowed to experiment. I did practically anything that I felt like doing, without fear. I used a lot of humor in that score. They liked it so well that they did a picture after that called *The Comedy of Terrors*, just because of the [use of humor in the music]. I used a lot of old themes in *The Raven*; for example, Vincent Price levitates himself and I played 'The Daring Young Man on the Flying Trapeze' in a symphonic style, more or less. Then there was a little flash somewhere and I played 'Shine, Little Glow Worm.'"

Looking back over their four-film association, Matheson told *Fangoria*'s Paul M. Sammon, "As a director, Corman was always very efficient and pleasant. We got along very well together. I don't think he was a film director in the sense that he dealt with actors, though. Actors would ask Roger questions and he would say something like, 'Do whatever you want,' which worked out all right when you had these old pros who would do what they wanted to do anyway. But there were a lot of young people in those films who couldn't act very well, and a different director might have helped them a bit more. Corman was a camera director, a visual director. He was very good at that." Asked if he still watched his older films, Price told Tom Weaver in *Attack of the Monster Movie Makers*, "Every once in a while, if it was one that I enjoyed making. The ones with Roger Corman I loved, because we had such a good time making 'em. We worked hard, really hard — oh, boy, he was a slavedriver! But it was wonderful fun, because he had it so carefully planned. He had Danny Haller doing the sets and Floyd Crosby on the camera, he got wonderful people around him and he just did a superb job. And, again, they were great fun. Roger did make pictures very quickly, but they were made thoroughly. They were brilliantly designed and brilliantly thought out. He was one of the best directors I ever worked with in my life."

However, in the same interview, Price also offered firsthand and amusing anecdotal evidence that contradicts the widely held impression of Lorre as an actor who, in Corman's characterization, simply "didn't spend much time learning his lines." Lorre "loved to rewrite the script. One time, in one of Roger's films, there was a scene where all Peter and I were doing was getting from one place to another, and there was some exposition there. I always know my lines and I was saying them, and Peter was sort of vaguely saying something else, I don't know what it was. And I said, 'Oh, for Christ's sake, Peter, *say the lines!!*' He said, 'You mean that, old boy? You don't like *my* lines better?' I said [*sharply*], 'No!' So he said all the lines — he knew every line in the script! But he didn't like to say them [*laughs*]!... [I]t's very annoying, it really is. Because no actor is funnier than a good writer."

British-born beauty Hazel Court was already a veteran of the cult classic *Devil Girl from Mars* (1954) and Hammer's *The Curse of Frankenstein* and *The Man Who Could Cheat Death* (1959) by the time she appeared in *Premature Burial*, and plays the spoiled and seductive Lenore with the same mix of sensuality and sinfulness she then brought to *The Masque of the Red Death*. The latter was her last major film role; after her 1963 marriage to former

Dr. Scarabus protests his innocence in *The Raven* (American International, 1963). Photograph courtesy of the Paul M. Sammon Collection.

actor Don Taylor (whom she had met five years earlier when he directed her in "The Croc-odile Case" on *Alfred Hitchcock Presents*), she confined herself largely to television, except for an unbilled cameo in *The Final Conflict* (1981), and died in 2008 shortly before the pub-lication of her autobiography *Hazel Court— Horror Queen*. Court wrote that making *The Raven* "was sheer joy. Working with Vincent Price, Boris Karloff, and Peter Lorre was quite a challenge, and it was a rare occasion for an actress to be working with those three giants at the same time. The teasing and laughter that went on was too much.... [Corman] did a wonderful job of controlling these three actors, all fighting to be the top dog."

Court also told Mark A. Miller in *Filmfax* that Lorre "had great sex appeal. Other actresses interviewed about him all agree that when Peter talked to you, it was as though you were the only person in the world. He would laugh and seem to be interested in whatever it was you were saying. He was very intelligent and had a fine mind.... [Nicholson] was very amusing, but I never had an inkling that he would become what he is now. It's funny. I always think of Jack Nicholson as a little boy."*

In "Corman's Comedy of Poe," an eight-minute making-of featurette on the MGM Home Entertainment DVD version of the film, the director related that Lorre "said what he thought would work is if Jack idealized him.... One of the things they came up with was Jack would always be tugging on Peter's robe to get his attention and his approval, and Peter'd always be sort of flinging him away, and that became sort of a running gag...." Nicholson added in Corman's autobiography, "Roger gave me one direction on that picture: 'Try to be as funny as Lorre, Karloff, and Price.' I loved those guys. I sat around with Peter all the time. I was mad about him. They were wonderful. It was a comedy, and Roger gave us a little more time to improvise on the set." According to Arkoff, Price and Karloff initially assumed that the actor must be James H. Nicholson's son, and frequently joked on the set about nepotism.

With its release of *De Sade*, MGM Home Entertainment began including a series of interview segments entitled "Richard Matheson — Storyteller" on the DVD versions of various Matheson films, with two episodes on the double-feature disc of *The Raven* and *The Comedy of Terrors*. Director of DVD production Greg Carson told *Video Store Magazine's* Enrique Rivero that Matheson was a favorite of his, "so when I saw titles like *De Sade* and *Master of the World*, I said 'Let's interview Matheson!'... He's an incredible writer. When you see his name on *Twilight Zone* and the Roger Corman movies, you see he is a storyteller and not just a horror writer." Conducted back to back ("It made for a nice day," Carson said), the interviews — some of which remain unreleased by MGM as of this writing — also covered *Master of the World*, *Burn, Witch, Burn* and *The Last Man on Earth*.

"I thought my tombstone should just say, 'Richard Matheson — Storyteller,'" he noted in the segment on *The Raven*. "Whatever area it's in, the story is offbeat. It's not, I hope, predictable. It's something different, and something interesting.... I made [*The Raven*] into a comedy, and they added Boris Karloff to Vincent Price and Peter Lorre, and he was wonderful.... [H]is legs were in such bad shape. I watched them shoot the scene of him coming down this long, very precipitous flight of steps, and it really made me uneasy because every step hurt him." In "Corman's Comedy of Poe," the director added that he devised an unusual use for the camera crane when shooting the climactic duel: "I said to Floyd [Crosby], 'What if we put Boris and Vincent, seated, on the edge of the crane, where the camera normally is, and put the camera halfway up the crane, so we see them seated there, but we don't see what they're seated *on*, and then we fly the crane all over the set and we show, *in reality*, them flying through the air?'"

One unexpected effect of Corman's customary economy in the making of *The Raven* was an entire second film, the cult favorite *The Terror* (1963), the bulk of which was filmed

---

*Nicholson and Robert Towne — who wrote four of his films, including *Chinatown* (1974) and its sequel *The Two Jakes* (1990) — met Corman in the late Jeff Corey's famed acting class. Corman had already served as the executive producer of *The Cry Baby Killer* (1958), which marked Nicholson's screen debut as well as his first leading role, and as the director of *The Little Shop of Horrors*, featuring the actor's memorable scene as a masochistic dental patient, Wilbur Force.

in two days to take advantage of the splendid sets assembled from all of the preceding Poe pictures, with a story concocted in a week and Karloff's additional services hastily secured when Price proved unavailable. Over the ensuing few months, exteriors and other additional scenes were directed, uncredited and tag-team style, by Corman protégés Francis Ford Coppola, Monte Hellman, Jack Hill, and leading man Jack Nicholson (with new assistant Dennis Jakob shooting some of the climactic flood footage). Each of them interpreted the incoherent screenplay somewhat differently. Not surprisingly, the resultant cinematic mishmash gives every indication that the cast and ever-changing crew essentially made it up as they went along. Coppola later cast Corman as a senator in *The Godfather Part II*, but contrary to recent Internet rumors that have metastasized to the IMDb, Wikipedia, and elsewhere, Matheson did not also make an uncredited appearance as a senator in the film.

Most of Matheson's entries in the Poe series were nominally remade in a wave of alleged adaptations appearing a quarter-century later. Corman himself produced Jim Wynorski's *The Haunting of Morella* (1989), which inexplicably borrowed several of its character names from *Premature Burial*, and Larry Brand's *Masque of the Red Death* (1989) for his own Concorde Pictures. In another omnibus film, *Due Occhi Diabolici* (Two Evil Eyes, 1990), two noteworthy genre writer-directors reunited the remaining segments that had joined "Morella" in *Tales of Terror*, with Dario Argento updating "The Black Cat" (filmed in Italy by goremaestros Lucio Fulci and Luigi Cozzi in 1981 and '89, respectively), and George A. Romero tackling "The Facts in the Case of Mr. [sic] Valdemar." Already remade for television with Martin Landau and by Spanish exploitation legend Jesus (aka Jess) Franco in 1982, *The House of Usher* (1988) was shot in South Africa by producer Harry Alan Towers, as were the *Premature Burial* update *Buried Alive* and another *Masque of the Red Death* (both 1990), while *The Pit and the Pendulum* (1990) was directed by Stuart Gordon, an adapter of H.P. Lovecraft.

Corman, too, bid adieu to the Poe series after *The Tomb of Ligeia*, which had a significantly different look and tone thanks to location shooting at an abbey in Norfolk, England, and a romantic script by Robert Towne, who later won a well-deserved Academy Award for *Chinatown*. In his last film for AIP, the ill-fated science fiction satire *Gas-s-s-s!... or It May Become Necessary to Destroy the World in Order to Save It* (1970), Corman included an homage to Poe in general and *The Raven* in particular, with a character named "Edgar Allan Poe" appearing periodically throughout the film to comment on the action, riding a Hell's Angels chopper with a raven perched upon his shoulder.

The Comedy of Terrors

(aka *Graveside Story*; AIP, released December 25, 1963) DIRECTOR: Jacques Tourneur; PRODUCER: James H. Nicholson, Samuel Z. Arkoff; SCREENPLAY: Matheson; MUSIC: Les Baxter; MAKEUP: Carlie Taylor; SPECIAL EFFECTS: Pat Dinga, Butler-Glouner. Color, 83 minutes. CAST—Waldo Trumbull: Vincent Price. Felix Gillie: Peter Lorre. Amos Hinchley: Boris Karloff. Amaryllis Trumbull: Joyce Jameson. Cemetery Keeper: Joe E. Brown. Mrs. Phipps: Beverly Hills. John F. Black: Basil Rathbone. Cleopatra: Rhubarb. Black's Servant: Alan DeWitt. Mr. Phipps: Buddy Mason. Doctor: Douglas Williams. Phipps's Maid: Linda Rogers. Girl: Luree Holmes. Riggs: Paul Barselow.

Uniting the stars of Matheson's last two Corman films, *The Comedy of Terrors* retained their blackly comic approach; Crosby, Haller, and Baxter stayed on in their usual capacities,

Amos Hinchley (Boris Karloff, left) gives his son-in-law Waldo Trumbull (Vincent Price) "a good dose of his own medicine" in *The Comedy of Terrors* (American International, 1963). Photograph courtesy of the Paul M. Sammon Collection.

but it was directed by Jacques Tourneur.* Matheson, who had successfully advanced Tourneur to helm his *Twilight Zone* episode "Night Call," suggested him for this film, and also served as its associate producer, but noted in his "Storyteller" segment, "I really did nothing as the associate producer.... Because *West Side Story* [1961] was [still] on the screen at that time, [Nicholson] wanted to call it *Graveside Story*. Unfortunately, it probably would have made more money with that title, he knew what he was doing, but my title was better."

In a wordless pre-credit sequence whose slapstick silent-film style is emphasized by speeded-up camerawork and a fast-paced piano score, unscrupulous undertakers Waldo Trumbull (Price) and Felix Gillie (Lorre) impatiently await the departure of the mourners from *Premature Burial*'s graveyard set before unceremoniously dumping the deceased from out of his expensive coffin and into the grave. All is not well at the Hinchley & Trumbull Funeral Parlor, where the alcoholic Trumbull haughtily belittles his long-suffering wife, Amaryllis (Joyce Jameson), whom he married only to gain control of the once-thriving

---

*The genre veteran succeeded Corman on the Poe series with his final feature, *City Under the Sea* (aka *War-Gods of the Deep*, 1965), whose tenuous legitimacy lies solely in its title, modified from a poem by Poe, with the ever-reliable Price as yet another Nemo-like leader, this time of a sunken city off the Cornish coast.

business. He also repeatedly threatens to kill her father Amos Hinchley (Karloff) with a ubiquitous bottle of poison, which the deaf and senile old man believes is his "medicine." With his rent an entire year in arrears, Trumbull is threatened with legal action in 24 hours by his sword-cane-wielding landlord John F. Black (Rathbone). In a nice reversal of the romantic triangle from "The Black Cat," enacted by the same three principals, the simple-minded and good-natured Gillie offers consolation to Amaryllis, an attractive but banshee-voiced would-be opera singer.

Not above forcing Gillie, a fugitive felon, to help him break into the homes of wealthy New Englanders and drum up a little business by creating customers the hard way, Trumbull smothers the elderly Mr. Phipps (Buddy Mason) in his sleep. But after being stiffed, as it were, by Phipps' young widow (Beverly Hills), who decamps to Boston, Trumbull finds himself still unable to produce the rent. He then decides to "kill two birds with one pillow" by doing in the increasingly insistent Black. After he and Gillie laboriously effect entry to his home in another protracted slapstick sequence, the Shakespeare-spouting landlord menaces Gillie with a sword before collapsing from the shock with an apparent heart attack. But, in an appropriately Poe-inspired touch, Black suffers from catalepsy and revives in his crypt, to the chagrin of the cemetery keeper (comedian Joe E. Brown). When Trumbull passes out following a frenetic finale in the funeral home, Hinchley helpfully administers the omnipresent "medicine" to his son-in-law while Gillie and Amaryllis happily run off together. (Lucy Chase Williams reports that only Hinchley survived the "climactic melee" in the original script.)

If Matheson's more bloodthirsty original intentions were frustrated, however, his lighter side is given full rein in depicting the delightfully dysfunctional Hinchley-Trumbull house-hold, introduced at breakfast under a sampler celebrating "Honor, Patience, Tranquility." Himself happily married for more than fifty years now, Matheson took obvious pleasure in providing Price with delicious dialogue in which he calls his wife's singing "the vocal emissions of a laryngitic crow." When asked by Amaryllis if he finds her repulsive, Trumbull takes an exquisitely timed beat before replying, "That's the word, yes." Black has his share of entertainingly florid verbiage, delivered with equally tongue-rolling satisfaction by Rathbone, to wit: "Much as I hate to dun, dear sir, it is unhappily incumbent upon me as owner of these premises to regard your monetary dereliction as, shall we say, inconvenient to my purposes. So vastly inconvenient, one might add, that should the debt remain outstanding for as much as 24 hours more, I fear that legal machinery must perforce be set in motion, and Messrs. Hinchley and Trumbull face the incommodious prospect of taking up residence in the street."

As Matheson noted in an interview with me for *Filmfax*, "I had a good relationship with James Nicholson ... and he responded to my ideas. I gave him the idea of a couple of rascally undertakers, and when business was slow they just went out and killed people, and provided their own customers. And he liked that, so I think that was all I had at the start. I knew I had Price, I knew I had Lorre, and I think I knew I had Rathbone. I didn't know that Karloff was going to be on it. Actually, [he and Rathbone] were supposed to play the opposite parts. Karloff was too ill to play the bigger part of the landlord ... so he himself suggested that they switch. What's amusing is, Rathbone was older than Karloff. He had so much energy, God, that man was full of energy.... I remember talking to him. We spent a whole fascinating day with him telling me about *The Adventures of Robin Hood* [1938], which is one of my favorite pictures, and how they spent three days filming the duel. Here we were doing a picture that we were shooting in ten days, and he was telling about doing

Poster art for *The Comedy of Terrors* (American International, 1963).

the duel in *Robin Hood* and taking three days just to do that. But he was just a lot of fun, that guy."

He noted in a subsequent letter, "Swashbucklers — notably in films — have always been a love of mine. I have the cassettes for *Adventures of Don Juan* [1949], *Scaramouche* [1952], *The Three Musketeers* [1948], *Robin Hood, The Mark of Zorro* [1940], *The Sea Hawk* [1940], and *The Prince and the Pauper* [1937]. The first two above are my favorites. I even have my own swashbuckler story I tried to interest [Gene] Kelly [star of the aforementioned version of *The Three Musketeers*] in, many years ago, then tried to start as a play, now have sitting on a shelf. Very clever story though. My one remaining dream in films now that I've done the Western [*Journal of the Gun Years*, an abortive adaptation of his novel, planned as a miniseries for Dan Curtis] and hope to sell it as a film one of these days." Given the conspicuous failure of films such as *The Pirate Movie* (1982), Roman Polanski's *Pirates* (1986), and especially Renny Harlin's *Cutthroat Island* (1995), the prospects for a revival of that particular genre seemed dim indeed until the success of Disney's Academy Award-nominated *Pirates of the Caribbean: The Curse of the Black Pearl* (2003).

According to *Faster and Furiouser* author Mark Thomas McGee,

I have a soft spot in my heart for [*The Comedy of Terrors*] because I got to visit the set one day. It was the first time I had ever been on a movie set. A friend of mine, Bill Ward, had phoned AIP's publicity department and told them we were doing an article for *Famous Monsters* magazine, which was a bald-faced lie. Even after we had gotten our passes from the guard at the gate I thought they would get wise to us and give us the shoe. They probably were wise to us and didn't care. My only regret is that Karloff wasn't there that day and I never did get the opportunity to meet him. I did however meet Jim Nicholson, who showed up in a white suit for about an hour, shortly after lunch, to see how things were going. The crew, which had been rather lethargic, suddenly got a burst of energy.... Lorre died shortly after the film was released. He had looked like a man who was dying. After every scene he would slump back into his chair and wheeze for several minutes. Whenever Tourneur could get away with it (and sometimes when he couldn't), he used [stuntman Harvey Parry] in a Peter Lorre mask."

The film marked a reunion for Price, Karloff, and Rathbone, who had appeared together in Universal's *Tower of London* (1939). In our *Filmfax* interview, Matheson said, "They were all just absolutely charming people, they couldn't have been nicer.... Lorre was so sweet and so funny. And the fact that he mangled all my dialogue, and just came out with some approximation of what I'd written — ordinarily that infuriates me, but with him, you just sort of let it go. He would tell me how [frequent co-star] Sydney Greenstreet used to go absolutely ape over it, because he [Greenstreet] had had stage training, and every line was exact."

He also related that he wrote an unproduced follow-up script, which was published with two other unfilmed screenplays in Gauntlet's *Unrealized Dreams* (2005). "They wanted to do a picture with those four plus Tallulah Bankhead. I wrote a movie called *Sweethearts and Horrors*, about the Sweetheart family, where Vincent Price was an alcoholic ventriloquist, and Peter Lorre was a magician with a great fire act who burned down every theater he ever performed in, Tallulah Bankhead was a terrible aging movie star with a drinking problem, Basil Rathbone was an old musical comedy star going to pot, and [eldest sibling] Karloff had a children's program called [*Funtime Frolics*], where he just hated children. And then they're all called home for the reading of the will of their father, who had one of these companies that made novelties and gags and everything, so the whole house is gimmicked up, and there are murders — it was a charming, very funny script, but they never did it."

Vampire Ben Cortman (Giacomo Rossi-Stuart) attacks his former best friend, Robert Morgan (Vincent Price), in *The Last Man on Earth* (Associated Producers–La Regina, 1964).

The accumulation of corpses, as the avaricious Sweethearts begin eliminating one another, recalls the scripted ending of *The Comedy of Terrors*, and Joyce Jameson was slated to return in the role of housekeeper Nola Bedworthy. Unfortunately, most of the proposed stars began to pass away, one by one: hard on the heels of Rathbone, Bankhead died in December of 1968 (followed by Karloff less than two months later), although she did survive long enough to appear in a Matheson film, and even enjoyed top billing when Hammer produced his script for *Fanatic*. In 1964, Lancer published Elsie Lee's *Comedy of Terrors* novelization, and according to Lucy Chase Williams in *The Complete Films of Vincent Price*, AIP reissued the film in March of 1965, pairing it with Ray Milland's *Panic in Year Zero!* (1962) and retitling them *Graveside Story* (reportedly its original working title) and *The End of the World*, respectively. In his "Storyteller" segment, Matheson added, "[Tourneur] was such a professional. He knew exactly what he was doing. He loved the script," although John McCarty noted in *The Fearmakers* that "Tourneur considered the studio's final cut ... dreadful and unfunny."

The Last Man on Earth

(*L'Ultimo Uomo della Terra*; Associated Producers–La Regina [U.S./Italy], released March 8, 1964) DIRECTOR: Sidney Salkow [U.S. version], Ubaldo B. Ragona [Italian version]; PRODUCER: Robert L. Lippert; SCREENPLAY: Logan Swanson [Matheson], William F.

Leicester, based on Matheson's *I Am Legend*; Music: Paul Sawtell, Bert Shefter; Makeup: Piero Mecacci. Black and white, 87 minutes. Cast—Robert Morgan: Vincent Price. Ruth Collins: Franca Bettoia. Virginia Morgan: Emma Danieli. Ben Cortman: Giacomo Rossi-Stuart. Dr. Mercer: Umberto Rau. Kathy Morgan: Christi Courtland. Governor: Tony [Antonio] Corevi. TV Reporter: Hector [Ettore] Ribotta. New People Leader: Giuseppe Mattei. With Rolando De Rossi.

Few works published in the twentieth century affected literary and cinematic horror as profoundly as Matheson's third novel, *I Am Legend*, issued as a Gold Medal paperback in 1954. "I realized [upon reading it] that horror didn't have to happen in a haunted castle; it could happen in the suburbs, on your street, maybe right next door," Stephen King — whose vampire town in *'Salem's Lot* is a microcosm of Matheson's global premise — told Douglas Winter in *Faces of Fear*.

"Stephen, I guess, has said that up till that time he thought you had to do crypts and graveyards and all that," Matheson told me in an interview for *Filmfax*, "and he found out that you could do a horror story in a supermarket, and that sort of altered his entire approach to what he was writing. I also got Steven Spielberg started out, too. *Duel* was his first [feature-length] film. So, I'm like their creative father. I have a big poster from *Duel*, and Steven Spielberg wrote on it, 'I feel like we grew up together.'" *I Am Legend* also inspired George A. Romero's *Night of the Living Dead* (1968), which revolutionized the genre with its graphic gore, nihilistic ending, and stunning commercial success for a micro-budget independent film.

Matheson had previously touched on vampirism in his early stories "Blood Son" (originally published as "'Drink My Red Blood...'" in *Imagination* in April 1951) and "Dress of White Silk" (*The Magazine of Fantasy and Science Fiction*, October 1951), the latter acknowledged by Anne Rice as an influence on her work. But, as noted earlier, the seed that ultimately grew into *I Am Legend* had been planted a decade earlier when the teenaged Matheson attended a showing of Tod Browning's *Dracula*. "The immediate thought was, 'Well, if one vampire is frightening, then a whole world full of vampires should be more frightening.'... That's not necessarily so," he conceded in an interview with me for the Gauntlet limited edition. "One well-done single vampire story can be a lot better than tons of 'em, but *I Am Legend* worked out anyway." Epitomizing his leitmotif of "the individual isolated in a threatening world, attempting to survive," the novel's premise is chillingly simple: What if a plague of unknown origin turned every human being on Earth into a vampire, save for one man who was presumably rendered immune by the bite of a Panamanian vampire bat years earlier?

As the novel opens in January of 1976, it is five months since the plague claimed its most recent victim; six since the protagonist, Robert Neville, has spoken to another human being; and seven since the death of his wife Virginia. Reflecting the Cold War anxiety of the period, the plague was spread by a germ borne on dust storms resulting from an apparent nuclear war. "That was in everybody's mind at that time," said Matheson. "That was always in our subconscious, and science fiction writers wrote endless amounts of stories about the nuclear catastrophe and what happened after; I did it myself in various short stories like "Tis the Season to Be Jelly' [*Fantasy and Science Fiction*, June 1963], 'Pattern for Survival' [*Fantasy and Science Fiction*, May 1955], 'When Day Is Dun' [*Fantastic Universe*, May 1954]." Like a Western hero besieged in his own private Alamo, Neville burns down the neighboring houses to prevent the vampires from jumping onto his. Forced to become completely self-sufficient, he maintains both his defenses (crosses, mirrors, garlic, boarded-up windows) and the means of his continued existence, like the workshop where he makes the all-important wooden stakes.

By day, Neville works his way systematically through the city of Los Angeles, a bag of stakes across his back and a mallet in a holster, disposing of the undead whenever he finds them in their hiding places and returning home by sunset. By night, he barricades himself inside his house in the suburb of Gardena (where Matheson lived in the 1950s and subsequently set several other works), and tries to drown out the cries of the vampires — especially the lewd provocations of the women, which underscore his necessarily unrequited desire for female companionship — at first with whisky and classical music, and then later on with soundproofing. The past haunts him continually, in the concrete form of his best friend and neighbor, Ben Cortman, who now leads the vampires and retains enough intelligence to elude Neville's search-and-destroy missions, and in his memories of Virginia and their daughter Kathy. After Kathy's body was consigned to the perennially burning pit that is the only safe method of disposal for plague victims — a bonfire a hundred yards square and a hundred feet deep — Neville defied the authorities by secretly burying Virginia, with predictably terrifying results.

"A man could get used to anything if he had to," Neville muses, yet he frequently wonders why he goes on instead of ending his nightmarish existence. Matheson simply and eloquently sums up its inescapable finality in his narration: "There was no waking up from this." In a devastating, bitterly ironic climax, he is hunted down and put to death by a

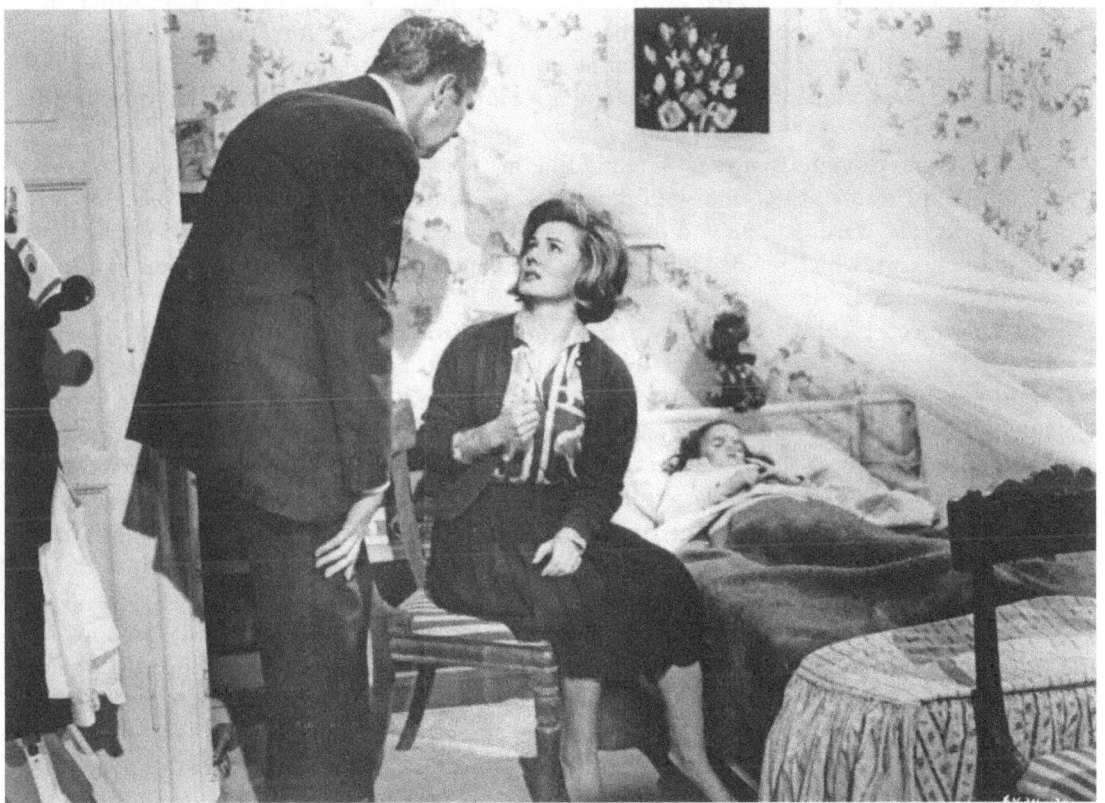

Morgan warns his wife Virginia (Emma Danieli) not to call a doctor for their plague-stricken daughter Kathy (Christi Courtland) in this flashback scene in *The Last Man on Earth* (Associated Producers–La Regina, 1964).

group of infected humans who have learned to control the plague by chemical means, and thus regard *him* as the aberration.

Romero, who has followed *Night of the Living Dead* with several sequels to date, said in George Hickenlooper's *Reel Conversations: Candid Interviews with Film's Foremost Directors and Critics* that the novel "dealt on an allegorical level with the idea of a new society stepping in and devouring the old." Responded Matheson in the interview for Gauntlet, "I don't know how allegorical it got. Obviously what I had in mind was that the only way the society could go on was to completely eliminate what had gone before and start all over. The mutations who were still afflicted with the *vampiris* bacillus realized that they could go on, they could contain it, but the older ones, the really bad ones would have to go.

"You don't ever write anything thinking it's going to be a classic.... It's just something you do. It's the idea I had, and I did the best I could. You never look ahead. *The Shrinking Man* is also... considered to be a classic, [but] only in that field. I have others. I'm hoping that one of my Westerns —*Journal of the Gun Years*, maybe — will end up as classic in [that] field, and I'm hoping *What Dreams May Come* [1978] will end up as a classic of some kind. *Bid Time Return* has, as a romantic fantasy; there aren't that many, so I don't have too much competition."

The seminal *Night of the Living Dead* notwithstanding, the novel has fared less well in its official screen versions, a saga that began in the late 1950s with Val Guest slated to direct the film, retitled *The Night Creatures*, for Hammer. "I went to England in [September of] 1957 ... to write the script," Matheson said in an interview for *Filmfax*. "I went over there, I lived there for about two months doing the screenplay on it. I went over on the *Queen Elizabeth*, and I lived in the Green Park Hotel, and I walked all over London. It was really nice.

"I always thought that they were kidding me when they said the censor wouldn't pass it, but then I read an interview with the guy who set up the whole *De Sade* project, [Louis M.] 'Deke' Heyward, and he said that that *was* the reason — that the censor wouldn't allow them to make it, which seemed kind of odd." Told by the censor's office just before shooting began to expect an outright ban on the movie in Britain, Hammer had no choice but to sell the project. Picking up the story in his *Midnight Graffiti* interview, Matheson told Sammon, "They resold it to [producer Robert L. Lippert, formerly Hammer's U.S. distributor, who] had a whole chain of theatres and an operation at 20th Century–Fox, a little filming operation that did things like *Alligator Women*. [*Laughs*] We later met, and he told me he was going to get Fritz Lang to direct it. And I was so excited! So I rewrote the script, and it was very good. This time it was really on the nose; it would have been *I Am Legend* right down to the teeth. Then he turned around and hired [television writer and actor William F. Leicester] ... for a rewrite, and this fellow just tore the hell out of it. I hated it so much I put my pen name, Logan Swanson, on it."

He was further disappointed when the project went to director Sidney Salkow, an undistinguished veteran of second features who had previously directed Vincent Price in *Twice-Told Tales* (1963), an anthology of horrific Nathaniel Hawthorne stories presumably inspired by the Poe pictures. (As Matheson dryly observed, Salkow was "a bit of a comedown from Fritz Lang.") The film's originally intended director, Val Guest, who had worked with Lippert on Hammer's *The Quatermass Experiment* (aka *The Creeping Unknown*, 1954), recalled in Tom Weaver's *Attack of the Monster Movie Makers*, "Robert Lippert was one of the — I don't want to say Poverty Row producers, but you know what I mean. He was one of the small independent producers working in Hollywood. Jimmy Carreras [who co-founded

Hammer Films] used to do quite a bit of work with Bob, and Bob used to give Jimmy [American] distribution of some kind in the early days of Hammer. Lippert was a nice enough guy and he had a girlfriend called Margia Dean who I was asked to put into [*Quatermass*]. She was a sweet girl, but she couldn't act [*laughs*]....

"Mike Carreras [the son of James, and later the head of Hammer himself] was a buddy of mine then, and just becoming a producer around that time. Mike was one of the best producers I have ever worked for, because you knew that if you were out there on a lonely moor, that everything you needed was going to be there. You could rely on the guy completely and utterly. He did his homework. Mike brought me the book *I Am Legend* one day and asked, 'Do you think we'll ever get away with a film like this?' I said, 'Let's try, let's see what we can do.' The British censor *absolutely* said no, under no condition whatsoever would it be allowed. They then tried it on the American censor, and, of course, *no* again. It was completely blocked on both sides [of the Atlantic], unless great alterations were made." Geoffrey M. Shurlock of the Motion Picture Association of America told Hammer's Anthony Hinds, "While this basic story seems to meet the requirements of the Production Code, this present script is in danger of resulting in a finished picture which could not be approved by this office because of its over-emphasis on gruesomeness." (This letter was printed in Matheson's 2006 collection *Bloodlines*.)

Poster art for *The Last Man on Earth* (Associated Producers–La Regina, 1964).

In the same book, Lippert colleague Harry Spalding offered his own version of the film's tortuous genesis to Weaver: "I went through the old cliché of finding a book in a second-hand bookstore, a paperback of *I Am Legend*.... I talked to Bob Lippert about it, and he liked the idea. (Last-man-on-Earth stories have very small casts, which makes 'em quite reasonable [*laughs*]!) So I got in touch with [Richard] Matheson, who is a very nice man, very talented. He had an idea which I love to this day: Make one of the major scenes the last man on Earth trying to make friends with the terrified last *dog* on Earth. It typified the whole story. Meanwhile, a deal was made to shoot it in Italy, so it got out of our hands altogether. I had to go back to Matheson and tell him that, which didn't make him too happy. Didn't make *me* too happy, either. American International made it as *The Last Man on Earth*, with Vincent Price, and they had their own approach. Matheson was talking along the lines of *Cat People*—using the audience's imagination. American International had the attitude of putting as many vampires at the window as they could afford!"

"Though there isn't any difference between them," noted *Video Watchdog*'s Tim Lucas, "the direction of the Italian version of this film —*L'ultimo uomo della terra*—is credited to Ubaldo Ragona ... while the American version is attributed to Sidney Salkow (the brother of Lester Salkow, Price's agent at the time), who was almost certainly the true director." Shot in 1963, it faithfully depicts the lonely existence of Robert Morgan (Price) in 1968, three years after the plague. In between the searches he conducts with a map grid, foraging for supplies and staking the vampires to keep their "body seal" from functioning, he dozes off while visiting his wife's coffin, fights his way through the vampires after sunset to reach his house and, safely barricaded behind garlic and mirrors, watches home movies of his family and Ben (Giacomo Rossi-Stuart). These prompt a flashback in which he seeks a cure for the plague that has ravaged Europe; sees Kathy (Christi Courtland) consigned to the pit when Virginia (Emma Danieli) disobeys his orders and calls the doctor; and must stake Virginia, after he buries her to avoid a similar fate and she rises from the grave.

Believing himself completely alone, Morgan is stunned to find the bodies of several vampires with iron spears in them and to encounter first a dog, which he befriends but later must stake when he learns it is infected, and then a woman, Ruth Collins (Franca Bettoia), who tells Morgan that she has been wandering around and hiding from the vampires, ever since she saw her husband torn to pieces. Caught injecting herself, Ruth reveals that she was sent to spy on him by a group of people who have learned to control the virus with defebrinated blood and vaccine, planning to "reorganize society, do away with all those wretched creatures who are neither alive nor dead, [and] start everything all over again." They regard Morgan as a monster because many of those he had destroyed were still alive. After he cures her with the antibodies in his blood—an idea not found in the novel but explored more fully in the remakes—the black-clad, Gestapo-like group (led by Giuseppe Mattei) destroys Cortman and the others. Despite Ruth's frantic attempts to intervene, they pursue Morgan into a church, where he is wounded with gunfire, cornered, and killed with a spear while gasping, "You're freaks—I'm a man!"

"Price was totally wrong for it," Matheson lamented in an interview with me for *Filmfax*. "I mean, he was marvelous in many of the pictures I wrote, but that really wasn't his kind of thing.... It doesn't look like the United States, there's something about the architecture of the buildings." As Price himself acknowledged in Weaver's *Attack of the Monster Movie Makers*, "The problem doing *The Last Man on Earth* was that it was supposed to be set in Los Angeles, and if there's a city in the world that doesn't look like Los Angeles, it's Rome [*laughs*]! We would get up and drive out at five o'clock in the morning, to beat the police, and try to find something that didn't look like Rome. Rome has flat trees, ancient buildings — we had a terrible time! And I never was so cold in my life as I was in that picture. I had a driver and I used to tip him a big sum to keep the car running, so I could change my clothes in the back seat." The only notable member of the supporting cast, Rossi-Stuart (aka Jack Stuart) appeared in several Italian genre films of the 1960s, e.g., Mario Bava's *Operazione Paura* (Operation Fear, aka *Kill, Baby ... Kill!*, 1966) and two Antonio Margheriti space operas.

Its *faux*–American setting aside, the film benefits from the moody, monochromatic photography of Franco Delli Colli (who went on to work with Sergio Leone), which along with its impoverished production values and the appearance of its slow-moving, almost robotic vampires would be echoed in *Night of the Living Dead*. Widely considered to be closer in spirit to the novel than any of its feature-film adaptations, Romero's classic originated with an untitled and unpublished story he had written several years earlier, inspired by *I Am Legend*, that depicted a group of people similarly barricaded against an undead horde seeking to feed on them. The first version to use Matheson's title, albeit in Spanish, was *Soy Leyenda* (1967), a fifteen-minute black-and-white film — apparently unavailable in English — written by Alfonso Núñez Flores and its director, Mario Gómez Martín. The novel was also adapted almost verbatim by Steve Niles and artist Elman Brown as a graphic novel from Eclipse Books in 1991. In author Michael Slade's *Bed of Nails*, three characters travel to the World Horror Convention in Nashville to have Matheson, the guest of honor, autograph their "well-thumbed copies" of *I Am Legend*.

Bloodlines offers the opportunity to compare the novel with Matheson's *Night Creatures* script, which retained the novel's flashback structure, relocated the story to northern Canada and introduced such elements as a birthday party for Kathy during happier times, an electrified fence around Neville's house, and the pistol he carries to kill himself if needed. The version that Matheson rewrote for Lippert, and was in turn rewritten by Leicester, has not been published, but it was presumably Leicester who made the character of Morgan a scientist rather than a layman with an unspecified job at "the plant," as in the novel. In some ways, however — most notably the ending — *The Last Man on Earth* hews more closely to *I Am Legend* than does *The Night Creatures*. The latter ends with Neville led away to the headquarters of the "new society" while Ruth tells him, "You're too valuable to kill [because of your] immunity to the germ," but according to Matheson (in *Bloodlines*), "I hadn't written that many movies at the time that I tried adapting *I Am Legend* for Hammer, and I was much more vulnerable to suggestions. I was more willing to make changes."

Fanatic

(aka *Die! Die! My Darling!*; Hammer [G.B.], released March 21, 1965) DIRECTOR: Silvio Narizzano; PRODUCER: Anthony Hinds; SCREENPLAY: Matheson, based on Anne Blaisdell's *Nightmare*; MUSIC: Wilfred Josephs; MAKEUP: Roy Ashton, Richard Mills; SPECIAL EFFECTS: Syd Pearson. Color, 96 minutes [several sources list the U.S. running time as 105 minutes, but home video prints bearing the U.S. title run 96 minutes]. CAST — Mrs. Trefoile: Tallulah Bankhead. Pat Carroll: Stefanie Powers. Harry: Peter Vaughan. Alan Glentower: Maurice Kaufmann. Anna: Yootha Joyce. Joseph: Donald Sutherland. Gloria: Gwendolyn Watts. Ormsby: Robert Dorning. Oscar: Philip Gilbert. Shopkeeper: Winifred Dennis. Woman Shopper: Diana King. Vicar: Henry McGee.

Based on Anne Blaisdell's novel *Nightmare*, *Fanatic* was one of Hammer's entries in the "dotty old lady" subgenre initiated by *What Ever Happened to Baby Jane?* Its American title, *Die! Die! My Darling!* (which, like *Burn, Witch, Burn*, is at least legitimized by being an actual line of dialogue from the film), is evidently meant to evoke Aldrich's follow-up, *Hush ... Hush, Sweet Charlotte* (1964). Its British title also places the film squarely within the studio's cycle of psychological thrillers made in the wake of *Psycho*, including Michael Carreras's *Maniac* (1963) and Freddie Francis's *Paranoiac* (1963), *Nightmare* (1964)—which presumably necessitated the alteration to *Fanatic* from Blaisdell's original title—and *Hysteria* (1965), all the work of Hammer's seminal screenwriter, Jimmy Sangster. Seth Holt's *The Nanny* (1965) and Roy Ward Baker's *The Anniversary* (1968) were also written by Sangster and featured Bette Davis, a veteran of both *Baby Jane* and *Sweet Charlotte*. Joan Fontaine (whose older sister, Olivia de Havilland, had supplanted Joan Crawford opposite Davis in the latter) joined Hammer's distaff revival with Cyril Frankel's *The Witches* (aka *The Devil's Own*, 1966).

A young American woman, Pat Carroll (Stefanie Powers), arrives in England planning to marry television journalist Alan Glentower (Maurice Kaufmann), and decides to close the book on her past life once and for all by paying a brief courtesy call on Mrs. Trefoile (Tallulah Bankhead, in the final onscreen role of her film career), the widowed mother of her deceased former fiancé, Stephen. When Pat makes the mistake of revealing that she had intended to break off their engagement, she is held at gunpoint by the elderly ex-actress, who is a religious fanatic as the title suggests. Deciding that Pat has "fallen into error," Mrs. Trefoile imprisons her in the Spartan and secluded house, "for the good of her soul," with the reluctant aid of her married servants, Harry (Peter Vaughan) and Anna (Yootha Joyce). A relative of Mrs. Trefoile's late husband, Harry fears arrest on a forgery rap, and has labored there thanklessly with the long-suffering Anna for 16 years, expecting a hefty inheritance, but is fired for his lecherous advances to Pat instead. After brandishing a knife, he is shot by his former employer, who explains Harry's absence by telling Anna that he has been sent out to London on an errand in Pat's car.

Following a failed attempt to smuggle out a message to the police via the retarded handyman Joseph (Donald Sutherland), Pat enrages Mrs. Trefoile by informing her that Stephen actually killed himself in a self-inflicted car crash. The most effective aspect of Matheson's script (arguably one of his very best) is its gradual revelation of Mrs. Trefoile as a dangerous psychopath rather than a harmless eccentric, one who wants to keep Pat faithful to Stephen's memory yet obviously harbored more than motherly feelings for her son. After assuring an inquiring Alan that Pat has come and gone, Mrs. Trefoile tells Pat, "You must die, die, my darling." Fortunately, Alan spots Harry's girlfriend Gloria (Gwendolyn Watts) sporting a brooch that he had given to Pat, and returns just as Mrs. Trefoile is about to sacrifice Pat in front of Stephen's portrait in an effort to reunite them. Anna learns from Joseph that the car is still in the garage, finds her husband's body, and metes out to Mrs. Trefoile the very fate intended for Pat.

"I got to meet [producer] Tony Hinds [while adapting *I Am Legend*]," Matheson said in an interview with me for *Filmfax*. "Of course, they didn't make that, but then because I knew him and he liked my work, later on he gave me *Fanatic*.... It was quite well done, I thought, though it got a little heavy on the melodramatics toward the end. I didn't know Tallulah Bankhead was going to be in it, I had no idea. In the book she's a dumpy little lady with pulled-back gray hair and everything, and then it ended up as this flamboyant ex-actress with a drinking problem.... [*Nightmare* was] a pretty good book. And actually, the picture wasn't bad. I thought Stefanie Powers was quite good, although [John Brosnan] told me that, in an interview, she said that it had been a terrible script, and she'd managed to 'save' it, and I thought, 'Here we go again, another one of these egomaniacal people.'" Matheson also wrote an episode of her series *The Girl from U.N.C.L.E.* the following year, during which *Fanatic*'s Canadian director, Silvio Narizzano, a veteran of British television in the 1950s, made the most celebrated of his few features, *Georgy Girl*, which earned a BAFTA Award nomination for Best British Film.

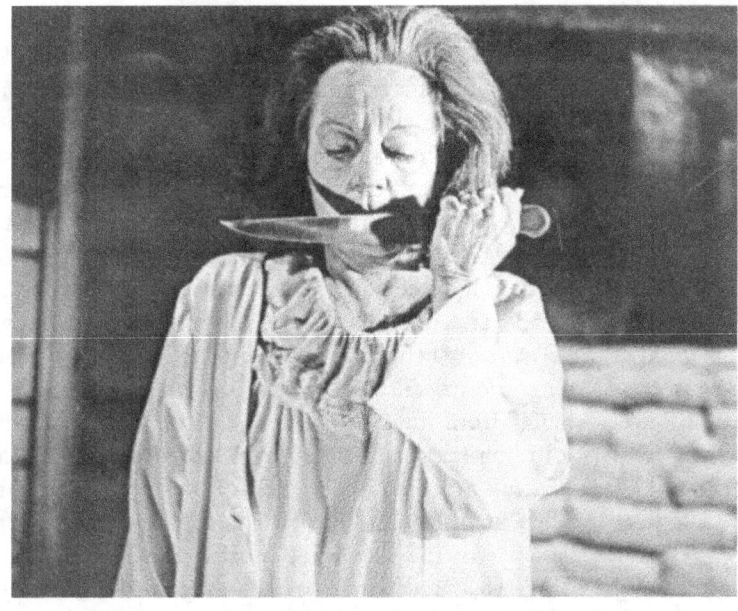

Mrs. Trefoile (Tallulah Bankhead) quotes *Genesis* 9:6 after killing a servant in *Fanatic* (Hammer, 1965). Photograph courtesy of the Paul M. Sammon Collection.

Lee Israel relates in *Miss Tallulah Bankhead* that during a 1964 visit to British Columbia fan and friend Dola Cavendish, the actress was sent by agent Joyce Selznick (niece of David) "the script of a chilling horror story called *Fanatic*.... Since *Baby Jane*, a big commercial success which was filmed finally with Bette Davis and Joan Crawford [after Bankhead had been offered and declined the latter's role], there had been a rash of similar pictures in which other glamourous ladies, including Olivia de Havilland and Barbara Stanwyck, had agreed to look their worst amid murder and mayhem. A precedent had been established for Tallulah, who had not been prepared at that earlier date to be so heinously deglamorized. Now, with some final coaxing from Dola, Tallulah agreed to do what was unquestionably a character role." Then in her sixties and beset with sometimes inexplicable ailments, Bankhead was very nearly replaced when an insurance investigator advised his company against indemnifying U.S. distributor Columbia in the event of her inability to finish the film.

Continued Israel, "Tallulah's relationship with ... Narizzano has been described as a 'love-hate' amalgam. She truly enjoyed him as a man. The little bit of socializing she did in England involved him, his wife, a deck of cards, and a poker table. He had intelligence, talent, and, most important, he could make Tallulah laugh. But though they joked about it, she bitterly resented what he, as a director, compelled her to do. There were no compromises with the filmic aging process. The bone structure of her face, in which she took such great pride, was compromised with a mound of putty. Her face was furrowed like new-plowed farmland. Her hair grayed so that it wasn't even interesting and twisted up into a severe, New England knot. And then he zoomed his cameras in for a series of merciless close-ups. To Stefanie Powers, the ingénue whom she did not want in the first place, she was civil but cool." By now sick of being associated with her signature expression "dahling," Bankhead objected to the film's retitling in the States, but upon consulting her contract found that she had no legal recourse.

In *The House That Hammer Built*, continuity person Renée Glynne told Wayne Kinsey that Bankhead "was wonderful.... The runner, Nigel Wooll ... was chosen as the special assistant to escort Tallulah from her dressing room down the iron staircase and onto the set. On this occasion he knocked on her dressing room door, was told to enter and when confronted with her nakedness, she said, 'Don't worry, you'll only see that I'm a natural blonde.'... [Powers] was like a breath of fresh air, and I seem to remember Tony Hinds really liking her. She was lovely. And Donald Sutherland, another breath of fresh air."

The stage legend, whose best-known film was Hitchcock's *Lifeboat* (1944), had not been seen on the big screen since her cameo in Tay Garnett's backstage tale *Main Street to Broadway* (1953), and passed away in 1968 after lending her voice to Jules Bass's partly animated *The Daydreamer* (1966). Powers enjoyed her biggest success opposite Robert Wagner in the TV series *Hart to Hart*. According to Phil Hardy's *Overlook Film Encyclopedia: Horror*, "Powers' change from mild amusement to sheer terror and Bankhead's development from eccentricity to homicidal mania are handled with consummate skill by the two actresses." The *Time Out Film Guide*'s David Pirie calls *Fanatic* "one of the best of Hammer's psychological thrillers, mainly thanks to Richard Matheson's ingenious and terrifying script.... Bankhead is great in the title role, and for once the basis of the plot seems disturbingly credible." In 2010, Bonkhead's performance in the film was the subject of a short-lived Broadway play, *Looped*.

Matheson skillfully streamlined the novel, eliminating a virtual travelogue of the English countryside before Pat reaches Llandudno, Mrs. Trefoile's house in the remote little Welsh village of Abervy (neither of which is named in the film). He also simplifies Pat's relationship with Alan, who instead meets her en route and falls in love with her on just six hours' acquaintance. Blaisdell — one of several pseudonyms for Elizabeth Linington, a prolific American author of police procedurals — also paints a much more detailed picture of Stephen and his father, whom the villagers believe Mrs. Trefoile murdered for impregnating a local lass, and concocts a somewhat far-fetched subplot in which Pat includes a coded cry for help on the postcard that she is forced to send off to Alan. The greatest changes involved Harry and Anna; in the novel, Mrs. Trefoile blackmails them into staying because she knows that Harry, who is more sympathetic than in the film, is an escaped convict. Anna enjoys tormenting Pat because she envies her privileged lifestyle, only to be killed with an axe by Mrs. Trefoile before Alan at last comes to the rescue and beats Mrs. Trefoile senseless.

"Dress of White Silk" was not Matheson's only work to have influenced Anne Rice, although such influence has sometimes taken unusual forms. As the bestselling author of the Vampire Chronicles explained in Christopher Golden's *Cut! Horror Writers on Horror Film*,

I wrote a story once, called "Die, Die My Darling," in which I tried to describe my sense of [being profoundly affected by horror throughout her life]. It was about a bunch of hippies watching TV, smoking grass. One of the hippie women complains about how her intensity puts everybody off. So they're watching this hokey movie called *Die! Die! My Darling!* with Tallulah Bankhead, and there's this scene where Tallulah Bankhead pauses on this gothic staircase and is about to try to murder her daughter-in-law [sic]. The hippie freaks out and says, "That's me. I am that woman and I am on that staircase forever and I am always trying, and I am the daughter being killed. I am all those people. That's it! That's it!" There have been many times when I have tried to write something that expresses that feeling of, "There I am, that's it!" At moments like that, I know exactly what it's about and I know why I feel that I'm in it."

The Young Warriors

(aka *Eagle Warriors*; Universal, released February 7, 1968) DIRECTOR: John Peyser; PRODUCER: Gordon Kay; SCREENPLAY: Matheson, based on his *The Beardless Warriors*; Music: Milton Rosen; MAKEUP: Bud Westmore. Color, 93 minutes. CAST— Sgt. Horatio Cooley: James Drury. Pvt. Everett H. "Hack" Hacker: Steve Carlson. Guthrie: Jonathan Daly. John Foley: Robert Pine. Cpl. Dave Lippincott: Jeff Scott. Bill Riley: Michael Stanwood. Harris: Johnny Alladin ["Aladdin" in opening credits]. Loren Fairchild: Hank Jones. Tremont: Tom Nolan. Sgt. Wadley: Norman Fell. Schumacher: L.E. "Buck" Young. The Lieutenant: Kent McWhirter [aka McCord]. Soldier: Robert Angelo [aka Fuca]. Also with George Sawaya, Morgan Jones, Noam Pitlik, Jon Drury, Buck Kartalian.

During World War II, Matheson saw action in Germany with the 87th Division of the U.S. Infantry, and later received a medical discharge after sustaining a combat-related injury. Of his seventh published novel, based on his wartime experiences, he told Rathbun in *He Is Legend*, "The reviews I have on *The Beardless Warriors* said the combat sections were so vividly described that it was almost painful to read. But you cannot overdescribe the horrors of war. It's not just like describing violence in a crime story where you can say, 'Well, that's not necessary — that's gratuitous.' Nothing in war is gratuitous. I was part of every one of the characters in *The Beardless Warriors*.... I liked the book, and I think it's pretty well done. It's one of the few things that I can re-read and think, 'Well, gee, that's not bad.' Of course, they made a terrible movie out of it, and that's a shame." Adapted by Matheson, the now-rare film version, *The Young Warriors*, was dismissed in *Leonard Maltin's TV Movies* as a "clichéd World War 2 yarn filled with Universal Pictures contract players."

As actor and singer Hank Jones, who is also an accomplished genealogist, recalled in a series of e-mails sent to me in the summer of 2005,

Hank Jones as the ill-fated Loren Fairchild in *The Young Warriors* (Universal, 1968). Photograph courtesy of Hank Jones.

We shot it in 1966, the original title being *The Beardless Warriors*. I found a notation in a journal of mine dated June 3, 1966 (my 26th birthday), which noted, "We just completed shooting *Young Warriors* two months ago." I know that 1966 is the correct year of shooting also because Walt Disney personally cast me in his *Blackbeard's Ghost* [1968] starring Peter Ustinov by seeing my footage in *Young Warriors*. *Blackbeard* started production in December of 1966 (Walt died in the middle of production), so this shows again that *Young Warriors* had to be shot

Pvt. Everett H. "Hack" Hacker (Steve Carlson) and Fairchild at chow time in *The Young Warriors* (Universal, 1968). Photograph courtesy of Hank Jones.

before that date. I remember the making of the film well. The entire cast went through a sort of basic training (taking apart our rifles, actually eating the terrible KP rations, marching, etc.) for about a week prior to initial shooting. It was a good experience, with a real bond developing among the cast. Lots of laughs! Richard was on the set a lot, giving his input to John Peyser, our director, and Gordon Kay, the producer. Gordon just died a few months ago.

They saved money by using footage from *To Hell and Back*; the rest of the new footage was shot on Universal soundstages or on the backlot overlooking the freeway. Most all the cast members were Universal contractees except me and were sort of thrown in the film as a showcase. Richard, I remember, was a soft-spoken man, modest, very kind, and easy to talk with. Only ... years later did I really get a handle on what an important and wonderful writer he was! As I recall, the brass at Universal thought that it needed a little "lightening" upon seeing the dailies, so Jonathan Daly, who was in the picture too and quite a good writer himself, was asked to augment Richard's script and added the scene where we chased a duck through a minefield. I remember we shot a scene where the wounded soldiers were in a hospital. They were all under blankets and dressed in army-issue garb. Just before the camera rolled, one of the soldiers jumped up, shook off the blanket and took off the uniform-hospital garb. The "soldier" turned out to be a very well-endowed female model who did kind of a joke mini-striptease to loosen up the set. Everybody broke up.

"This is a story of young men in war," an opening title after the credit sequence of *The Young Warriors* informs the viewer somewhat portentously, while the camera follows a truck containing members of an infantry squad through the smoldering aftermath of an unspecified battle. "It takes place in Europe during World War II. It could be any army ... any place ... any time..." Unfolding primarily — and economically — on the battlefield, with no interiors save for a war-torn farmhouse and a makeshift field hospital, the episodic story dramatizes the war's effects on a newcomer, Private Everett H. Hacker (Steve Carlson), who later replaces the wounded Corporal Dave Lippincott (Jeff Scott) as the assistant squad-leader to veteran Sergeant Horatio Cooley (James Drury). The battle scenes are competently staged, albeit bolstered by *To Hell and Back*, in which Audie Murphy reenacted his heroic wartime exploits. But the film otherwise offers little to belie Maltin's assessment; a seemingly endless parade of interchangeable and short-lived supporting characters marches through the story, and Hacker, in a familiar finale, supplants the seriously wounded Cooley after saving his life.

Drury had worked with Sam Peckinpah on *The Rifleman* and *Ride the High Country* (1962) and was then starring in Universal's *The Virginian* on NBC. In addition to Daly (a regular on the final season of *Petticoat Junction*), the supporting cast included soap opera star Carlson; Robert Pine, later the commanding officer on *CHiPs*; and Kent McWhirter, soon to star — under the name Kent McCord — in *Adam-12*. Best known as landlord Stanley Roper on ABC's hit sitcom *Three's Company* and its short-lived spin-off *The Ropers*, tenth-billed character actor Norman Fell pops up periodically as the cynical and sarcastic Sgt. Wadley to deliver replacement troops to Cooley's squad. Peyser, whose television work included episodes of *The Rifleman, The Virginian, CHiPs* and the World War II series *Combat!* and *The Rat Patrol*, headed an equally undistinguished lineup behind the camera. One noteworthy exception: cinematographer Loyal Griggs, who had won an Oscar for *Shane* (1953) and been nominated for another wartime story, *In Harm's Way* (1965).

As Matheson wrote in a 1992 letter to me, "I guess you could say it was

Poster art for *The Young Warriors* (Universal, 1968).

loosely derived [from *The Beardless Warriors*]. By the time I had done a final rewrite to incorporate major battle scenes from *To Hell and Back* (if you look carefully you can see Audie Murphy in some of them), there wasn't that much left of the book. Originally, Richard Zanuck [a producer and the son of 20th Century–Fox mogul Darryl F. Zanuck] was going to do it. Fred Zinnemann [who had directed another celebrated World War II film, *From Here to Eternity* (1953)] liked the book and asked me to wait 'til he could do it. Like an idiot I said no; didn't want to wait that long. So it ended up the way it did. Using all the contract players at Universal. The footage from *To Hell and Back*. Not exactly a masterpiece. Except if you compare it to *The Beat Generation*." Matheson later theorized to me that Zanuck decided against the project when his father, who had been the head of production at Fox and was then acting as an independent producer (with Richard as his vice-president), embarked upon perhaps the greatest World War II epic of all, *The Longest Day* (1962).

The Beardless Warriors was praised in *The Detroit News*: "Not just another war novel; it is one of the finest books that has come out of World War II or any other," and described by *The New York Times* as "ten grim and terrible days of bloodshed and carnage.... The sounds, sights and smells of war in their most intimate and appalling forms. An individual and memorable picture of battle." While much of its action and dialogue reached the screen intact (although with the latter suitably sanitized for civilian ears), the film failed to capture Matheson's first-hand insights into the mindset, maturation, and internal conflicts of its protagonist, whose name was shortened from Hackermeyer to Hacker in the script and who, like his creator, was raised in Brooklyn and sent to Germany at the age of 18. The novel, which Matheson dedicated to his sons with the hope that "the reading of this story [may] be the closest they ever come to war," explored in great psychological detail Hackermeyer's strained relationships with his widowed father and the uncle who raised him, and presented a chilling portrait of a young man who comes perilously close to being transformed by battle into a soulless killing machine.

One scene from the novel was condensed considerably for the film version: Cooley tells Hackermeyer, who has killed a German soldier trying to surrender, "We all know killing can be fun. Hell, it's exciting. But the excitement goes fast, Hack — real fast. And, if you get too wrapped up in it, it'll wind up making you sick. It can turn you into so much an animal you'll never get back from it. I know; believe me, I know. I've seen it happen. I don't know what your ... background is, really. I guess, from what you told me the other day, it was pretty rough. But don't let it carry over into what we're doing here. Don't let this war become part of ... whatever war's going on inside of you." Hacker blames Cooley after he freezes up during another German ambush, causing the death of Loren Fairchild (Jones). But in the finale, when Cooley is wounded, Hacker drags him to safety, shielding him with his body as a shell hits the farmhouse. Perhaps now, with the horrors of World War II combat having been depicted both viscerally in Steven Spielberg's Oscar-winning *Saving Private Ryan* and philosophically in Terrence Malick's woefully underrated *The Thin Red Line* (both 1998), the time is ripe for a remake.

The Devil Rides Out

(aka *The Devil's Bride*; Seven Arts–Hammer [G.B.], released July 20, 1968) DIRECTOR: Terence Fisher; PRODUCER: Anthony Nelson Keys. SCREENPLAY: Matheson, based on Dennis Wheatley's novel; MUSIC: James Bernard; MAKEUP: Eddie Knight; MASKS: Roy

Ashton [uncredited]. SPECIAL EFFECTS: Michael Stainer-Hutchins. Color, 95 minutes. CAST—Nicholas, Duc de Richleau: Christopher Lee. Mocata: Charles Gray. Tanith Carlisle: Niké Arrighi. Rex Van Ryn: Leon Greene [dubbed by Patrick Allen]. Simon Aron: Patrick Mower. Countess D'Urfé: Gwen Ffrangcon-Davies. Marie Eaton: Sarah Lawson. Richard Eaton: Paul Eddington. Peggy Eaton: Rosalyn Landor. Malin: Russell Waters. African: Yemi Ajibade. Receptionist: John Bown. Indian: Ahmed Khalil. Servant (First Apparition): Willie Payne. Goat of Mendes: Eddie Powell. Max: Keith Pyott. Mocata's Servant: Mohan Singh. Indian Girl: Zoe Starr. Financier: Richard Huggett. Teuton: Peter Swanwick. Satanists: Liane Aukin, John Falconer, Anne Godley, Richard Scott, Bert Vivian.

Shot in 1967, Matheson's second script to be produced by Hammer remains one of the finest efforts by all concerned, combining his tight, fast-paced work with tense direction by Terence Fisher and powerful performances by Christopher Lee and Charles Gray, both of whom later played Mycroft Holmes (in *The Private Life of Sherlock Holmes* [1970] and *The Seven-Per-Cent Solution* [1976], respectively). Making the most of an unusually large amount of screen time, in addition to a rare heroic role, Lee complements the film's exciting episodes with his trademark intensity. His commanding presence has rarely been used to such great effect outside Hammer's Dracula films, in which he was often given painfully little to do. Gray is well matched against him as the literally mesmerizing villain, Mocata. Known in the U.S. as *The Devil's Bride*, this was Hammer's first attempt to film the work of Britain's

Rex Van Ryn (Leon Greene) confronts Nicholas, Duc de Richleau (Christopher Lee), with the body of Tanith Carlisle (Niké Arrighi) in *The Devil Rides Out* (Seven Arts–Hammer, 1968).

leading occult author, Dennis Wheatley, whose more than fifty books have reportedly sold as many millions of copies in 27 languages. The novel featured a cast of characters used in his debut, *The Forbidden Territory* (filmed in 1934), as well as such sequels as *Strange Conflict* and *Gateway to Hell.*

Set in an unspecified period between the wars (the novel was published in 1934), the film opens with Rex Van Ryn (Leon Greene) and Nicholas, the Duc de Richleau (Lee), puzzled by the absence from their reunion of Simon Aron (Patrick Mower), with whose father they had served in the Escadrille Lafayette. After they forcibly remove Simon from his London house filled with devil worshippers, he escapes. His friends face an apparition (Willie Payne) while searching the house, and later save Simon and Mocata's medium, Tanith Carlisle (Niké Arrighi), from their Satanic rebaptism on Walpurgis Nacht, when the Devil appears as the Goat of Mendes (Eddie Powell, Lee's regular stunt double). Simon and Tanith are taken to the home of the Duc's niece, Marie (Sarah Lawson), and her husband, Richard Eaton (Paul Eddington). In one of the most powerful sequences, the outwardly charming Mocata gains entry to their home under false pretenses and hypnotizes Marie, only to have his concentration broken by the sudden appearance of the Eatons' daughter Peggy (Rosalyn Landor). The enthralled Simon and Tanith try to slay Richard and the sleeping Rex, respectively.

In this scene, Fisher's direction and the cinematography of Hammer mainstay Arthur Grant visualize Matheson's script perfectly, cross-cutting between Marie and Mocata as she falls gradually under his influence, while the camera moves closer and closer to each of them. Mocata utilizes only the sound of his voice and the intensity of his penetrating gaze to lull Marie into a false sense of complacency. As described by Simon in the novel, Mocata "possesses extraordinary force of character, and he can be the most charming person when he likes. He's clever of course — amazingly so, and seems to have read pretty well every book that one can think of. It's extraordinary, too, what a fascination he can exercise over women. I know half a dozen who are simply 'bats' about him." Best known to some viewers for *The Rocky Horror Picture Show* (1975), Gray appeared in the James Bond films *You Only Live Twice* (1967) and *Diamonds Are Forever* (1971), embodying Bond's evil nemesis, Ernst Stavro Blofeld, in the latter. Among his other genre credits are the Amicus werewolf film *The Beast Must Die* (1974) and Richard Marquand's *The Legacy* (1978).

Realizing that her presence constitutes a danger to Rex and his friends, Tanith flees the Eatons' country home and is apprehended by the lovestruck Rex, who ties her up in the stable to try to prevent Mocata from gaining control of her. De Richleau, Simon, and the Eatons spend a night of terror inside the protection of a pentacle, besieged by an oversized tarantula and the skeletal Angel of Death. The desperate De Richleau uses the last two lines of the dread Sussamma Ritual, which can alter time and space, to turn the Angel of Death back against the one who had invoked him. When Mocata's unwilling catspaw, Tanith, perishes instead, De Richleau must conjure up her spirit to ascertain the whereabouts of the Satanist, who has abducted young Peggy to use as a sacrifice in his Black Mass. Simon offers himself to Mocata in a vain attempt to effect her release, while the others arrive during the ritual. As Tanith's soul inhabits Marie and has Peggy recite the Ritual, the coven is destroyed by fire and time reverses itself to before Tanith's death. Yet as Nicholas explains, the Angel of Death, once being summoned, cannot return empty-handed, and with Tanith restored to life, Mocata replaces her in death.

"I think that this is an invention of Dennis Wheatley's, the Sussamma Ritual, because I couldn't find it anywhere," Lee noted of his own research on the audio commentary of Anchor Bay's laserdisc version of the film. "I did eventually find a sort of incantation or prayer against evil" — and that prayer, according to Lee, was not in Matheson's script. Sharing the commentary mike was Sarah Lawson, who — like her onscreen spouse, Paul Eddington — had appeared on such seminal spy series as *Danger Man* (aka *Secret Agent*) and *The Avengers*. She added that Fisher "was so gentle, so kind, and he gave us such a lot of freedom. I mean, he never said, 'You stand there, do this.'... [I]f you went the wrong way, he would pull you back onto track. But you never felt you were doing anything simply because you had been told to, never."

In *More Classics of the Horror Film*, pioneering genre historian William K. Everson called *The Devil Rides Out* Fisher's masterpiece, and opined that it provided Lee and Gray with the roles of their respective careers. He particularly praised Fisher's pacing (making no mention of Matheson's contribution in that area), pointing out that, like Robert Wise, Fisher was a former editor. "There are a surprising number of incidents and highlights ... yet there aren't *too* many to clutter up a logical procession.... The dynamic pacing of the film tends to make the audience feel physically tired too, and it shares that weariness with the protagonists of the film who must fight off sleep until the job is done." Everson also enumerated the indignities to which the film was subjected when it was released in the U.S. in December 1968, five months after its domestic debut:

> First of all, 20th Century–Fox which bought this particular Hammer film for U.S. release, promptly retitled it *The Devil's Bride*, thus removing it from any association with the very highly regarded Dennis Wheatley novel on which it was based. Second, the lurid advertising made it look like merely a rip-off of the then successful and increasingly prolific Devil Worship thrillers, which had included *Rosemary's Baby* and *The Devil's Own*. Third, Fox declined to seek out a first-run, but threw it into a saturation release in the key cities, with many theaters playing it simultaneously — usually (though not here) a tip-off that the film isn't very good and must reap its rewards quickly before the word gets around. Finally, it had the bad timing (in most cities) to get its release immediately after *Night of the Living Dead* (which may now be regarded as a cult classic but at the time reaped universally awful reviews which particularly stressed its amateurish qualities) and a Columbia schlock double-bill headed by Peter Cushing's *Corruption* [1967], which likewise got the thumbs-down from the critics. Small wonder that audiences had little chance (or inclination) to see *The Devil Rides Out*.

The film also benefits greatly from the work of Hammer's house composer James Bernard, who wrote some two dozen scores for the company over 20 years, and is best known for the theme introduced in *Dracula* (aka *Horror of Dracula*, 1958). In *Cinefantastique*, Randall Larson praised *The Devil Rides Out* as "another of Bernard's best non-series scores ... dark and dismal, devoid of themes except for a single recurring motif which reinforces the hero's struggles against devil worship. Not until very near the end does a theme emerge for the heroes, as they finally begin to thwart the demonic influence of the satanists. Bernard's penchant for cohesive dissonance is well displayed during the satanists' ceremony, heralded by a slowly thundering, ominously doom-sounding low, low tuba or trombone chords over pounded drums and rapidly dancing xylophone notes and shimmering cymbal."

According to the unsigned liner notes on Anchor Bay's VHS version, Anthony Hinds expressed reservations about the production to Bernard, who recalled, "I went down to the set and it all looked quite splendid. The book had been a favorite of mine since I was a boy, along with *Dracula* and *She*, all of which I ended up scoring for Hammer. At any rate, Tony turned out to be quite wrong in his judgment, didn't he?" Lee, a close friend of Wheatley's, was praised for his portrayal of De Richleau; Lee recalled, "There were censorship problems, because rather than fantasy, these books dealt with the absolute reality of Black Magic.

Nicholas (center) watches with the horrified Marie (Sarah Lawson) and Richard Eaton (Paul Eddington) as Peggy (not pictured) is about to be sacrificed in *The Devil Rides Out* (Seven Arts–Hammer, 1968).

There are such cults and such people even today, at every level of society." Johnson and Del Vecchio note, "Hammer would produce over thirty more films after this, but only *Frankenstein Must Be Destroyed* [1969] equalled its quality.... This would be [Lee's] last non–Dracula part for Hammer until [their penultimate feature, Peter Sykes's] *To the Devil—A Daughter*," the most recent (1976) feature-film adaptation of Wheatley's work.

The Devil Rides Out* and Michael Carreras's vastly inferior *The Lost Continent* (1968), based on the novel *Uncharted Seas*, were intended to begin a series of Wheatley films, but the plan was abandoned due to disappointing box-office returns for both films. (The former did well domestically despite its comparative failure in the U.S.) Matheson was later approached to adapt another of Wheatley's novels, *The Haunting of Toby Jugg*, for the company. "I think I even read it, and I guess I said, 'Yeah, sure, I'll do it,' and then nothing came of it," he recalled in an interview with me. "Who knows what happens with these things? One day they're full of enthusiasm, and everything's a go, and then you don't hear anything for a year, and you finally ask, 'Whatever happened to that?,' and they just sort of shrug and look embarrassed or something."

Johnson and Del Vecchio note in *Hammer Films: An Exhaustive Filmography*, "Although the film is considered one of Terence Fisher's best, he had some doubts. 'The love angle,' he told Harry Ringel, 'was very superficial. I don't know why, probably my fault. The relationship between Niké Arrighi and Leon Greene never develops as it should have. The film would have been much stronger if it had.'... Fisher might have felt better about the film if it had not indirectly led to the end of his career. He was hit by a car while crossing a road after a post-production session. His broken right leg kept him from directing *Dracula Has Risen from the Grave* [1968] (taken over by Freddie Francis), and he would only direct two more films [*Frankenstein Must Be Destroyed* and *Frankenstein and the Monster from Hell*, not released until 1974] before his retirement in 1972." In *The Men Who Made the Monsters*, an excellent in-depth study of Fisher, Francis, and other noteworthy genre filmmakers, author Paul M. Jensen added, "Although Fisher later spoke of possibly directing ... *The Haunting of Toby Jugg*, there would, for him, be no more opportunities to continue his work. He died in 1980."

An initially disappointed Matheson later reconsidered the film's many merits in a letter to me: "I recorded it recently from TV and — as usual — found it not as bad as I remembered. My main pique was with the [supporting] cast — except for Charles Gray — but they really aren't that bad. I still found fault with some of the — unavoidable, I guess — flaws. The attack on them in the circle was much more involved and exciting, I thought, in my screenplay. Also giant spiders are definitely passé. [According to Jensen, Matheson's script actually describes a "Thing" that "begins to laugh, [in] a distorted parody of Mocata's laughter."] And I thought the black guy in the attic of the house in the early section of the film just didn't look scary at all and could have very easily. But it had a nice flavor to it and Lee was excellent as always. I thought it was a very good adaptation and so did Dennis Wheatley who wrote me and said so." The novel "had a lot of material, so that you had to cut it down a little. But I caught his right on the nose, he was very happy.... It's got a great plot, and it never slows down — that's what Dennis Wheatley liked about what I did, I kept the thing rolling along," Matheson added in an interview.

In an author's note that precedes *The Devil Rides Out*, Wheatley wrote, "The literature of occultism is so immense that any conscientious writer can obtain from it abundant material for the background of a romance such as this. In the present case I have spared no pains to secure accuracy of detail from existing accounts when describing magical rites or formulas for protection against evil, and these have been verified in conversation with certain persons, sought out for that purpose who are actual practitioners of the Art. All the characters and situations in this book are entirely imaginary* but, in the inquiry necessary to the writing of it, I found ample evidence that Black Magic is still practised in London, and other cities, at the present day." In adapting the novel for the screen, Matheson wisely excised Wheatley's frequent (and often long-winded) digressions into alchemy, astrology, Egyptian mythology, lycanthropy, numerology, palmistry, Stonehenge, the Tarot, Voodoo, and other arcana. He also simplified the ending, and omitted a lengthy pursuit of Mocata to Paris and a ruined monastery in northern Greece following the abduction of the Eatons' daughter, which considerably slowed the pace.

Supplanting a rejected draft by John Hunter, who had written Hammer's unjustly obscure *Never Take Sweets from a Stranger* (1960), the adaptation is otherwise extremely faithful, excepting certain character traits altered as much by casting as by the script, with Rex — described in the novel as a young American — embodied by an Australian and dubbed by an Englishman, Hammer veteran Patrick Allen. The very British Lee is Wheatley's "elderly French exile," the Duc, while the novel's Princess Marie Lou, a ravishing Russian expatriate, is now a model middle-aged English wife, well played by Lawson (Allen's real-life wife and co-star, with Lee, in Fisher's *Night of the Big Heat* [1967]). Most changed was Mocata,

---

*Wheatley based Mocata on the notorious English Satanist Aleister Crowley.

described by Wheatley as obese, pale, bald, and lisping. Anthony Hinds wanted Gert Frobe, best known for his title role as the villain in *Goldfinger* (1964), but Fisher insisted on Gray, whose debonair characterization is more in line with his Hitchcockian use of suave, handsome villains in such Hammer films as *The Curse of Frankenstein* and *The Two Faces of Dr. Jekyll* (aka *House of Fright*, 1960), a trait that found its zenith in Lee's portrayal of Count Dracula.

Hammer's frequent makeup artist, Roy Ashton, made an uncredited contribution to the film. He recalled in an interview with Jan Van Genechten and Gilbert Verschooten, published posthumously in *Little Shoppe of Horrors* magazine:

> I didn't do any makeup in that film [Eddie Knight is the credited makeup artist] but made two masks for it. I think it was [producer] Tony Keys who contacted me to do them. The first one was the Angel of Death who was supposed to come galloping in on a horse. I got a skull at home and modelled the mask as near correct as anatomically possible, in such a way it could be fitted over a man's face. The other one was basically goat-like in accordance with the traditional image of the Devil. At that time I was working on *Oliver!* [1968] at Shepperton, with a colleague called George Frost. We had to move over to some other place one day and I suddenly saw a goat in a yard there. 'Good heavens, that is what I want,' I said. As soon as I had finished my commitment with George, I modelled and cast in plaster a full-sized goat's head out of plasticine again. Into the female mold I pressed some laminated paper, which I next overlaid with actual fleece.
>
> I formed the ears out of cloth and that was funny, because in England we have an expression which we used when a chap doesn't take much notice or doesn't hear you: "To have cloth ears".... Yet I couldn't think of anything to give them rigidity. Ultimately, I took the cylinders out of two lavatory rolls and shaped the ears with them in a wonderful way, the tips of them hanging down. Then I made eyes as usual and fabricated horns in paper with a similar process: I would wrap pieces of string around them right up to the top and covered them in, to match this curious spiral effect on the goat's horns. The final outcome resembled the natural structure of the animal pretty well. The mask had to come right down over the shoulders, and that was sufficient as far as my share was concerned. They put Eddie Powell, who was covered with large bits of skin, behind a sort of dais and got some artificial legs stuck out in front of him. These were arranged in a joined position, so nobody had to worry about the man's real legs as you never saw them at all. It was the same Eddie Powell I suggested years ago as a double for Chris Lee, since he had the most fantastic likeness to him."

According to Phil Hardy's *Overlook Film Encyclopedia: Horror*, "Fisher builds his atmosphere with uncannily precise editing, a marvelously controlled camera style and, above all, through an astonishingly sophisticated use of color schemes, summarized in the image of the dazed Arrighi standing motionless in the swirl of a sabbath, dressed in a white robe splattered with intensely red blood. Set around 1925, the attention to period detail, which extends to objects, dress and cars, evokes a world in which Fantomas might still be active..." Praised by Christopher Lee in his audio commentary as "the true star of Hammer," production designer Bernard Robinson shared with AIP's Daniel Haller the ability to give his films a lavish look that belied their relatively modest budgets.

With insufficient space at Hammer's traditional studio, Bray, the interiors were shot at Elstree, where Wheatley himself visited the set on September 15, 1967, according to Johnson and Del Vecchio. As Lee opined to Johnson and Mark A. Miller in *The Christopher Lee Filmography: All Theatrical Releases, 1948–2003*, "[T]here is justification for a remake after over 30 years. The advances in special effects, the use of computers, digital images.... What they could do with the Satanic manifestations *now*. The Angel of Death, as described by Wheatley —'Do not look upon his face'— well, there we are in the pentacle, and here comes the horse, with a stunt man riding it on a slippery floor. How can they make an effective scene like that? Well, they can't. The visor on the rider opens and you see the skull-face and we should have all dropped dead. Just think what they could do with this scene today. They could make it *really* terrifying. But the film was a good one for its time ... a good period sense, a good story — the age-old but always effective story of good vs. evil — a good cast, Charles Gray especially. I'm pleased with my performance, and so was the author, but I was a bit young. I'm the right age now!"

Added Johnson and Miller, "Originally offered the part of Mocata, Lee insisted on the Duc de Richleau instead and handily demonstrates his versatility. His character is allowed a complexity of emotions, and the subtle refinement of Lee's acting is given full opportunity at last.... Lee delivers explanations of supernatural powers in a confident tone and manner that render them instantly believable. Of course, this is possible because Richard Matheson's script supplies such sharp, smart dialogue, the likes of which Lee had not spoken in a long time, and Lee takes appreciative advantage of every word.... The crack Hammer team had not been this good since the late 1950s at Bray, when the company produced their best classic horror films. Beautiful photography, a musical score that sets the pulse to thumping, and rich sets evoke the supernatural atmosphere memorably. Terence Fisher's direction is flawless, and so are most of the performances.... Luckily, the film does not hinge on [the effects] but instead on the otherwise outstanding craftsmanship on both sides of the camera that even the low budget could not undermine."

A sometime champion of Matheson's work on page and screen, groundbreaking British horror historian David Pirie hailed him as "one of America's most talented screenwriters" in *The Vampire Cinema*. Pirie also joined the chorus of critical praise for *The Devil Rides Out*, calling it "the best film that Fisher and Hammer ever made, an almost perfect example of the kind of thing that can happen when melodrama is achieved so completely and so imaginatively that it ceases to be melodrama at all and becomes a full-scale allegorical vision. Christopher Lee has never been better than as the grim opponent of Satanism," an admiring Pirie enthused in his *Time Out Film Guide* review.

"It's Alive!"

(Azalea, 1969 [released directly to television]) DIRECTOR-PRODUCER-SCREENPLAY-EDITOR: Larry Buchanan, based on Matheson's "Being" [uncredited]; SPECIAL EFFECTS: Jack Bennett. Color, 80 minutes. CAST— Wayne Thomas: Tommy Kirk. Leslen Sterns: Shirley Bonne. Greevie, Creature: Billy Thurman. Bella Pitman: Annabelle Macadams. Norman Sterns: Corveth Ousterhouse.

Moving from the sublime to the ridiculous, this is an uncredited bastardization of Matheson's "Being" by director-producer-writer-editor Larry Buchanan, an *auteur* of awfulness who remade several 1950s AIP films under the Azalea Pictures banner, mostly in his hometown of Dallas, to beef up two packages of films for American International Television. *Zontar, the Thing from Venus* (1966) and *In the Year 2889* (1967) served to make even Corman's cut-price originals (*It Conquered the World* and *Day the World Ended*, respectively) look like A pictures, while Edward L. Cahn's *Invasion of the Saucer Men* (1957), *The She-Creature*, and *Suicide Battalion* (1958) became *The Eye Creatures* (1965), *Creature of Destruction* (1967), and *Hell Raiders* (1968). Because they went directly to television, where they became late-night staples in the pre-cable era, these micro-budgeted turkeys are difficult to date. *"It's Alive!"*— which bears no relation to writer-director Larry Cohen's hit *It's Alive* (1974)— is listed as 1968 in several sources (including Buchanan's book *It Came from Hunger!: Tales of a Cinema Schlockmeister*), but bears a 1969 copyright.

Paul Blaisdell, the ill-fated and long-unsung makeup and special effects artist who had often worked miracles on a mere shoestring for AIP, contributed to all five of the 1950s SF films that were eventually remade by Buchanan. In his exemplary biography *Paul Blaisdell, Monster Maker*, Randy Palmer writes,

> In the 1950s, Buchanan had worked in front of and behind the camera in several legitimate Hollywood productions ... But after almost ten years kicking around tinseltown without lucking into the big time as either an actor, producer, or director (he didn't care which), Buchanan drifted back to Dallas and settled into the exploitation niche. Buchanan made a film called *Free, White, and 21* [1963] which caught the attention of American International. AIP distributed the film, and it made enough of a profit that Arkoff and Nicholson decided to bankroll a series of super-low-budget films for their television subsidiary [produced to round out its "Chiller" and "The World Beyond" packages]. By making the films in Texas, production costs could be minimized.
>
> With Larry Buchanan directing, AIP knew they wouldn't be getting any Oscar-caliber work; but at least they were assured of receiving exposed film with images on it. When it came to making film sales to television, sometimes that was all that mattered. AIP sent Buchanan four [science fiction] screenplays ... with instructions to make new versions under alternate titles. Because they would be going directly to television, Buchanan's films were made in 16mm at an average cost of $22,000 per picture.... [He also made] *It's Alive!* ... a title that had already been registered by AIP for a planned horror-comedy to star Boris Karloff, Vincent Price, Basil Rathbone, and Peter Lorre. Lorre died before the film went into production, so AIP used the title on Buchanan's picture.

Palmer's account suggests that the abortive project was Matheson's *Sweethearts and Horrors*, yet according to the IMDb, AIP gave Buchanan the script for an unfilmed adaptation of "Being" that was to star Lorre and Elsa Lanchester.

"It's Alive!" opens as New Yorkers Leslen Sterns (Shirley Bonne) and her acrid husband Norman (Corveth Ousterhouse) leave the highway for some sightseeing in the Ozarks — filling in for the story's Arizona desert setting. Making a wrong turn lands them in the proverbial middle of nowhere. In search of gas, they meet paleontologist Wayne Thomas (Tommy Kirk), who directs them to an isolated farmhouse that belongs to the burly and sinister Greevie (Billy Thurman). Greevie keeps his housekeeper Bella Pitman (Annabelle Macadams) in line with intimidation and violence, and smilingly assures the ever-bickering New Yorkers that the fuel truck will arrive "any minute." Leslen is nervous and Bella terrified — both with good reason, as it turns out, for Greevie plans to feed the couple to the pet monster he keeps as a potential tourist attraction. Leading them into Onyx Cave, which is connected to the house, he imprisons them behind bars with Wayne, whom Greevie had knocked unconscious when he came to inquire after the couple's welfare.

Later, Greevie confronts the prisoners at gunpoint as they are about to explore a misty, bubbling pool in the tunnel leading from the cave to the cellar. ("Perhaps you know of my creature," he boasts to Wayne. "It's great and powerful, my greatest discovery!") After Leslen refuses his offer to spare her, Greevie is disarmed by Wayne. Jealous of the mutual attraction between his wife and Wayne, Norman retrieves the pistol and tries to lure the latter down to the pool by saying that he has found a way out. Norman's plan to kill Wayne backfires as a laughable *Creature from the Black Lagoon* knockoff (also played by Thurman) emerges, shrugs off three gunshots, and disposes of him instead. "It's impossible! There's been nothing like that for millions of years," cries Wayne, who states that the creature looks like a

Masasaurus. (It is unlikely that anything even remotely resembling Greevie's anthropomorphic amphibian has ever existed outside a Buchanan film; amusingly, this one credits Skip Frazee, his sound man from *The Other Side of Bonnie and Clyde* [1968], for its dubious paleontology.)

Greevie had befriended his "magnificent creature" after digging through to the cavern while he was prospecting for gold. He has since begun selecting human victims who cannot be traced, and continually threatens Bella that if she does not help him, she will become the next victim herself. Bella relates to the prisoners that as a vacationing schoolteacher she fell into his clutches in a similar fashion two years earlier, with Greevie slowly breaking her spirit by starving her, depriving her of sleep, and beating her. She agrees to help the couple flee by surreptitiously bringing Wayne his canvas bag, which contains dynamite caps. But Greevie has drugged their coffee. As he takes Leslen to the pool, offering her a final chance to save her life by giving herself to him, Bella revives Wayne, lights the dynamite, and tosses it at her tormentor, who shoots her. The result of the blast is that Greevie is buried alive with his creature. The Sternses stagger out of the cave as a closing credit reads, "The end?"

"We shot '*It's Alive!*' ... in a Tennessee cave in seven days," Buchanan told Greg Goodsell in a career overview for *Filmfax*. "It looks it," adds Goodsell. "Running for the most part without sound, '*It's Alive!*' is Buchanan at his most minimal.... Filming a chase through the woods, Buchanan could not afford slow motion cameras and opted to have his actors *perform* in slow motion instead. The sight of Thurman whipping [Macadams] with a thin leather belt, in stylized slow motion, is a truly surreal sequence." Buchanan, who died in 2004 before he could complete a projected trilogy about Marilyn Monroe, remembered that AIP told him, "'Give us color in 80 minutes, and here's your check!' They never talked about aesthetics.... [T]hat hasn't changed about Hollywood."

Providing what little star power "*It's Alive!*" has to offer, Tommy Kirk had played opposite Annette Funicello in Disney's *The Misadventures of Merlin Jones* (1963) and its sequel *The Monkey's Uncle* (1964). After being fired by the studio because of his homosexuality, Kirk "graduated," just as Funicello did, to AIP's *Beach Party* series, starring in two genre-oriented entries directed by Don Weis. Portraying a Martian visitor to Earth, Kirk was Annette's leading man in *Pajama Party*, and then joined veteran horror stars Boris Karloff and Basil Rathbone, this time *sans* Frankie and Annette, in Weis's *The Ghost in the Invisible Bikini*, which mercifully brought this fading series of juvenile quickies to an end. A Buchanan regular, Thurman had previously appeared in his *Mars Needs Women* (1966), a rehash of *Pajama Party* in which Kirk virtually repeated his Martian role, as well as *In the Year 2889* and *Curse of the Swamp Creature* (1966), a remake of Cahn's *Voodoo Woman* (1957).

In a *Filmfax* interview by Kevin Minton, Kirk was penitent about making the film. After Disney fired him, "I did some of the worst movies ever made and I got involved with a manager who said it didn't matter *what* you did as long as you kept working.... What I was doing in [Buchanan's] pictures, I don't know. The only thing I can say is that I had a drug problem then, and I didn't know what I was doing, or what I was getting into.... *But,* I'd also like to add that *personally,* Larry Buchanan was one of the nicest, most gracious men I ever worked for."

Originally published in the August 1954 issue of *If* magazine, Matheson's "Being" also concerns a married couple who find themselves lost and low on gas during a cross-country drive, and are earmarked as the latest victims of a monster by a rural heavy who lives in a remote house with a "zoo." Buchanan, who wisely took no screen credit as scriptwriter, made a number of alterations: He expanded the story in some ways, adding the character of the housekeeper and turning one of the other victims, previously no more than nameless cannon fodder, into the film's hero. The husband in Matheson's sourcework is a completely sympathetic character, and both he and the wife survive to escape from the monster's climactic destruction with a hand grenade by their former captor. The most significant changes lay in the nature of the monster, originally a gelatinous alien "being," and its relationship with the human villain; far from being its friend, he is instead a pathetic stalking-horse and, like Bella in the film, is forced under the threat of his own absorption to provide food to the alien, which has implanted a subcutaneous "location cone" to monitor his movements and enforce its control.

In his *Collected Stories* commentary, Matheson told Stanley Wiater, "I actually turned that one into a script for American International Pictures. And I think later on John Tomerlin did a rewrite on it, and they ... actually made a motion picture from it — but one completely different from my story. I followed the original storyline in my version, but they chose not to use it.... I got the original idea when my wife and I were driving back East on our honeymoon [a trip that also inspired "Dying Room Only"]. We stopped at a place just like that — and saw all these poor, bedraggled-looking animals in their cages behind this gas station. And the writer in me thought, 'What if a man were lying in one of those cages...?'" He added in his interview with James H. Burns, "It's the story where the monster is sort of like Jell-O. For my version of it I suggested, 'Why don't we call it *G.O.O.*? Those initials would stand for Galactic Octopoidal Ooze.' I was making a joke, which you shouldn't do at certain meetings, because Jim Nicholson *loved* the idea of calling it *G.O.O.* and made it the working title of the picture [which was announced in *Variety*]. If they had shot it, that's what it would have been called!"

If the hilariously cheesy amphibious monster suit featured in *"It's Alive!"*— reportedly a modified wet suit with scissor-cut fins — looks familiar to the film's insomniac viewers, it's because the ultra-economical Buchanan had used the same suit previously in *Creature of Destruction*. According to Randy Palmer's *Paul Blaisdell, Monster Maker*:

> Jack Bennett, a Dallas advertising executive who taught himself the rudiments of theatrical makeup and film technique ... supplied creature costumes for all of the Azalea films. In at least one instance, a Bennett monster was used in two different pictures, recalling Blaisdell's experience with the She-Creature [recycled in 1959's *Ghost of Dragstrip Hollow*]. The big difference, of course, was that Paul's monster costumes looked a hundred times better than the best thing Bennett ever did.... The monster in *Creature of Destruction* might possibly have been the worst piece of work Jack Bennett ever contrived. With eyes made from ping-pong balls and rubber-tipped claws that bent every time there was a strong breeze, it looked like nothing so much as an assembly-line Halloween costume for undiscriminating trick-or-treaters.

Matheson might reasonably have been furious with AIP for ripping off "Being" so shamelessly in *"It's Alive!,"* since neither he nor Tomerlin was recognized for either the original story or the screenplay that was ultimately filmed. But given the embarrassing caliber of the results, it is perhaps just as well. He would presumably have gotten a minimal fee at best for the film rights to his story.

Buchanan's book is oddly reticent regarding the genre films for which he is best known, usually offering only a few lines on each before excerpting articles by "brilliant young minds who understand the nuances of the subtext that flows from all of my AIP pictures.... They realized that I had no choice but to deliver the banality, crude structure, rough editing and in many instances bad acting to satisfy my contract. With the pathetic monies given me, I could do no better. They saw that with persistent determination, I defined a theme that only now is being appreciated and vivisected at home and abroad." Typical of these curious critiques, at once adulatory and harsh, is Goodsell's "Tape Loop of the Unconscious: Plumbing Buchanan's '*It's Alive!*'" : "The film connects with the subconscious mind unlike any avant-garde effort I have seen. It strikes a responsive chord to those who can recall dreams that occur midway between slumber and consciousness.... Buchanan is similar to [cult director Edgar G.] Ulmer in his ability to create within the viewer anxiety, despair, hopelessness, and the feeling of a genuine raging bummer" (quoted by Buchanan from *Zontar, the Magazine from Venus*, Vol. 4, No. 2).

De Sade

(aka *The Marquis de Sade, Das Ausschweifende Leben des Marquis de Sade, Die Liebesabenteuer des Marquis S*; AIP–CCC Film–Trans Continental [U.S.–West Germany], released August 27, 1969) DIRECTOR: Cy Endfield, Roger Corman [uncredited]; PRODUCER: Samuel Z. Arkoff, James H. Nicholson; SCREENPLAY: Matheson, based on the life and writings of the Marquis de Sade; MUSIC: Billy Strange; MAKEUP: Freddy Arnold. Color, 104 minutes. CAST— Marquis de Sade (Louis Alphonse Donatien de Sade): Keir Dullea. Lady Anne-Prospère de Launay: Senta Berger. Mme. de Montreuil: Lilli Palmer. Lady Renée Cordier de Launay: Anna Massey. La Beauvoisin: Sonja Ziemann. Marquis' Mistress: Christiane Krueger. Rose Keller: Uta Levka. M. de Montreuil: Herbert Weissbach. Abbé François de Sade: John Huston. Marquis as a Boy: Max Kiebach. Also with Barbara Stanek, Susanne von Almassy, Friedrich Schoenfelder, Heinz Spitzner, Tilly Lauenstein, Ortrud Gross.

During the 1960s, American International Pictures increasingly lived up to its middle name with a growing involvement with foreign filmmakers, first by acquiring their films for U.S. distribution and then through inexpensive co-production arrangements that eventually encompassed Australia, Czechoslovakia, Denmark, England, Germany, Hong Kong, Ireland, Italy, Japan, the Philippines, Spain, Sweden, and Yugoslavia. Nicholson and Arkoff were most active in Italy, where they worked extensively with producer Fulvio Lucisano, and in England, where the production of the Poe films was shifted beginning with *The Masque of the Red Death* and AIP's "third man," Louis M. "Deke" Heyward, presided in London as the studio's "Director of European Production." One such international hybrid was *De Sade,* made in conjunction with producer Artur Brauner and his German company, CCC Filmkunst.

The film was shot in Berlin, with access to a heavily guarded Charlottenburg Palace and to Saint Nikolai's Cathedral. *The Marquis de Sade*, as it was originally known, was envisioned as the flagship production of Heyward's European division, the first in an ambitious slate of high-profile pictures intended to usher in a new era of critical and commercial respectability for AIP. Matheson wrote screenplays for several of these proposed productions, but only *De Sade* reached the screen. In a *Filmfax* interview he told me:

> The last couple of years with American International, they had me doing some really high-toned projects they were going to make in England [including a version of H.G. Wells's novel *When the Sleeper Wakes*]. And whereas in the earlier [cases], the ink was barely dry on the paper and they were shooting them, these, nothing ever came of.
> One of them was very good. It was called *Implosion*, based on a book [by D.F. Jones] about something getting in the water, I don't know whether it's put there by an enemy or not, but all the women in England except for a small handful become barren, and they can't have children.

So in order for civilization not to disappear, they create these breeding camps. And the protagonist, this guy who's high in the government, his wife is one of them. It's a very strong story, and it turned out to be a very good script. Again, the British wouldn't allow it to be shot, because it reflected badly on their government. And then I did another one which I kept turning down, it was called *Private Parts in Public Places* [based on Robin Cook's novel, first published in England as *Public Parts and Private Places*], about the pornographic business in England — just an insane, dark, savage humor type of thing. It's very serious for a movie, and I turned it into an out-and-out bizarre comedy, and they never made that, either. I took my story "Being," and made a long script [*G.O.O.*] about that — although they had made one earlier [the aforementioned "*It's Alive!*"], this was a different version of it — and saw nothing.

I read all about De Sade. As a matter of fact, it was the only script I ever did for them where I didn't have to change a word. And then Arkoff called me and said, "Don't forget, you owe us a rewrite."

The eponym of sadism, or at least his denuded cranium, had already been the subject of one of the best Amicus films, *The Skull* (1965), directed by Freddie Francis and adapted by Subotsky from Bloch's "The Skull of the Marquis de Sade." In his "Storyteller" segment, Matheson said De Sade "was totally unlike the way most people think of him. He was a pudgy little guy who ... physically did very little. It was ... what he wrote about that made him outrageous. I mean, during the Revolution he was a judge, and he was so kind-hearted he could never condemn anybody to the guillotine so they fired him.... [I had] one basic theme running through it, his search for the sister of the woman he actually did marry, who he did love and never could manage to have any consummation with." He added to Christopher Koetting in *Filmfax*, "It was a real challenge to take someone that people associate with whips and chains and turn him into a believable, acceptable person."

The fugitive De Sade is welcomed at his ancestral chateau, La Coste, by his uncle, the Abbé François de Sade (John Huston). The Abbé stages a performance recounting his nephew's life, depicted in the film with a series of disjointed flashbacks punctuated by

appearances of Anne (Senta Berger), the daughter of the arriviste Madame de Montreuil (Lilli Palmer) and the elusive object of his obsessions. Fresh from starring in Kubrick's *2001: A Space Odyssey* (1968), Keir Dullea portrays Louis Alphonse Donatien de Sade (1740–1814), who is forced into an arranged marriage with Anne's sister Renée (Anna Massey). When he is imprisoned in the Fortress of Vincennes for "vile excesses" after finding scandalous solace in the arms of a profusion of prostitutes, his mother-in-law effects his release. For his uncle's amusement, Louis arranges his own

The imprisoned Marquis (Keir Dullea) vows to change his ways in this lobby card from *De Sade* (American International–CCC Film–Trans Continental, 1969).

autobiographical performance in which he recalls being whipped with a riding crop by the Abbé as a boy (Max Kiebach). Then Louis is incarcerated once again in Miolans Prison when he tries to run off with Anne, and the play transforms into a trial at which he is accused of killing her. He protests to the court that she actually died of the plague.

As Dullea recalled in an interview with me for *Filmfax*, "The funny thing is that *Space Odyssey* didn't lead to a lot of offers suddenly. It's peculiar, but it didn't. I filmed *Space Odyssey* in '66, and filmed *De Sade* at the end of '68, and I did some television but I didn't do a feature in between that whole period. I wanted to do another film, so I think I perhaps did it for less pure reasons than I like to think that I do most of my projects with. I don't like the film, but if I had to pick a favorite scene, it's where I'm putting on a show for my uncle, the Abbé.... I loved working with Lilli Palmer and Anna Massey [with whom he had appeared in Otto Preminger's *Bunny Lake Is Missing* (1965)]....we all got along very well. There was nothing dramatic on the set, no real stories to tell except that John Huston was an incredible raconteur. I sat around him at his knee, you know, to hear him hold forth about all his experiences. Imagine all the people he'd worked with ... and he had this wonderful way of speaking that sounded like Captain Ahab.... [I]t was a real honor to encounter him."

What wound up as a classic example of the so-called "troubled production" had actually begun life as a carefully researched screenplay that not only pleased Arkoff, but also created a sensation at the 1968 Cannes film festival. "It was the best script I ever had," as Heyward told Koetting. "That year in Cannes, I could've made 20 deals — I could've had *anybody* as a partner. I had meetings in Prague about producing *Marquis de Sade* with the Czechs, but the Russian invasion killed that. I also had meetings with Fulvio [Lucisano] about coming in on it, but he backed out because he didn't have the money." Yet Arkoff related in *Flying Through Hollywood By the Seat of My Pants* that despite its subject's obvious commercial possibilities, the film was both problematic from the beginning and — after a disastrous premiere at the Rivoli Theater, during which it was virtually laughed off the screen — a disappointment at the box office.

According to Koetting, *De Sade* was originally to have been produced by Heyward's friend, Berlin-born Gordon Hessler, and directed by British *wunderkind* Michael Reeves. When Heyward and German partner Artur Brauner were made its executive producers, and Reeves bowed out due to mental health problems, the two men were reassigned to AIP's next Poe film, *The Oblong Box* (1969). Tragically, after backing out once again just before filming was due to start, Reeves himself was dead by February of 1969, forcing Hessler to direct a script that had been substantially rewritten by Christopher Wicking. Like James Dean, Reeves became a cult figure on the basis of an early death (from an overdose at the age of 25) and three films: *La Sorella di Satana* (Satan's Sister, aka *The She Beast*, 1965), *The Sorcerers* (1967) and *Witchfinder General* (1968), which AIP then retitled *Conqueror Worm* in the U.S. to link it with Poe.

De Sade was then assigned to Cy Endfield, the blacklisted American expatriate best known for such films as Ray Harryhausen's *Mysterious Island* and the historical epic *Zulu* (1963). In his hands it wound up as a commercial and critical failure that was disowned by AIP and, significantly, became Matheson's last produced script for the company. Matheson told me in an interview for *Noir* that he was initially pleased with the choice of Endfield: "Although it had some flaws in it, the best suspense picture I ever saw was Andrew L. Stone's *The Last Voyage* [1960]. It just started out behind the titles and went right through to the very end, never flagging, and that to me is really good suspense. In *Zulu*, the time span was a little longer, but still it progressed and progressed. A wonderful movie. I was so happy that [Endfield] was going to direct *De Sade*, and then I found out he was having a mental breakdown. You know, last night, or early in the morning, we were watching some old Our Gang comedies, and one of them was directed by 'Cyril' Endfield. We all started somewhere." Endfield contributed the entries *Radio Bugs*, *Tale of a Dog*, and *Dancing Romeo* in 1944.

Roger Corman lent Endfield an uncredited directorial hand on *De Sade*, as Matheson told me in *Filmfax*: "Roger went [to Germany] because Cy Endfield was having a mental breakdown, they told me. He shot the picture as though it were a straight story and not a fantasy, which I found bizarre, because my idea was like that film *Jacob's Ladder* [1990]. It was a strange, fantastic horror story that jumped time and jumped place and everything, and it turned out [as a surprise that was revealed only] at the end it was all going through De Sade's mind as he was dying in prison. But Endfield took out the fact that it was a dying hallucination in his brain, so that actually it made no sense whatever. And then Roger told me that [Endfield] would put red Xs through the pages which indicated they were shot, and they weren't shot, so [Corman] had to go over there and shoot these things. He went over to shoot a lot of orgy scenes, which did nothing for the picture. I didn't write [those scenes], but the dialogue is mine. And then what killed me was that [James] Nicholson said that [John] Huston, who was in it, said, 'Why didn't you ask me to direct it?' That made my day."

"Not long after the shooting began," Arkoff elaborated in his autobiography, "we started getting reports of serious problems on the set. Deke ... sent us an urgent memo that said, 'Endfield had [*sic*] been hospitalized. But even when he's on the set, he's having difficulty filming the sex scenes.'" After flying to Berlin, Arkoff learned that Keir Dullea's contract gave him director approval, and he was initially unwilling to consider replacing Endfield; Arkoff approached Huston, who declined to

Poster art for *De Sade* (American International–CCC Film–Trans Continental, 1969). Note the original X rating.

supplant Endfield after having worked for him as an actor, and then at last was able to convince Corman to step in. "When Roger arrived in Berlin, he met with Dullea for an hour. Keir was impressed, gave Roger the thumbs up, and the picture went back into production. Roger shot for ten days, the movie was wrapped up, and all of us flew home, still clinging to great hopes for *De Sade*. As *De Sade* was being edited, however, my anxiety resurfaced. The picture just didn't have the spirit and the passion it needed. Roger tends to be a hands-off-the-actor type of director, and he did an admirable job under difficult circumstances. But *De Sade* needed someone with a licentious soul."

According to *Faster and Furiouser*, however, Corman had been involved at the outset. Corman told McGee,

> I got together with [Richard] Matheson with whom I'd worked a number of times. We worked out a rather intricate flashback structure. And I stayed with it through the first draft. I went to lunch with Jim and told him that I wanted to step off the project. I was supposed to get some development money but I said I would walk away and give him the benefit of the work I'd done. I thought the picture was a trap. If we tried to show what De Sade did, or as ... Matheson and I did, some of his fantasies, or more specifically what De Sade did in his fantasies, we'd be arrested. And if we *didn't* show it, the audience was going to be cheated. They were going to be cheated because of the title and because of the way I knew American International would sell the picture [e.g., the Signet novelization by Henry Clement, which was much more sexually explicit]. So I stepped away and Jim got a first draft from me for nothing. Matheson went on to do a second draft.... They needed somebody to go to Berlin [later on] for just a few days to finish it and I was the only person who knew the script.

Dullea offered a somewhat different account of the situation with Endfield in his interview with me for *Filmfax*:

> I don't remember any other director being attached to it, and in fact I don't even remember having director approval. They had approached me to do this film, and Cy Endfield was the director, and so he came and saw me while I was doing a play in summer stock. We had a conversation, and I liked him enormously, and it was based on that meeting that I decided to do the film. Cy Endfield got very sick and couldn't continue, and they brought in another director, which was Roger Corman, and he seemed to have a different style of working. I think [the cast] had a certain allegiance to Cy, and I liked working with him so much. So it was like suddenly a different style, and it just colored everything. The morale of the film suffered from this change, and it certainly wasn't Roger Corman's fault *per se*, you know, he's coming in to do them a favor. The bad guys from my point of view were [Arkoff and Nicholson], insomuch as most of their films were pretty exploitative, all these kind of grade B films to a great extent, and I [had at first] thought this was going to be an unusual film.
>
> I began to see the writing on the wall and I thought that it was going to be less than the kind of artistic endeavor it might be able to be, even though I began all this by saying perhaps I did it for less pure reasons. But given the fact that I did it, I certainly wanted it to be the best film it could possibly be, and I thought we did have a chance with Cy Endfield directing it.... Cy couldn't have continued [because of his hospitalization], so they needed to bring someone in. I didn't have any problem with their having to do that, but I also had a feeling that they weren't going to really respect Cy Endfield's notes. You know, a director has a certain thrust, and they were going to re-edit his stuff so that it would appear in a different way than his intention, and not use stuff or put it together in a different kind of way, and I thought, "A director has a vision, and suddenly if you lose that vision, it becomes somebody else's vision, or it becomes a vision done with too many cooks. I think it's going to be a thing of too many cooks putting it together, making an exploitation film out of it," and that's what I think it ended up being.

Endfield did direct one final film, *Universal Soldier* (1971), and eventually died in 1995. While categorically denying that Endfield had a "mental breakdown," Dullea agreed with

Matheson about the film's erotic content, which originally earned *De Sade* an X rating (despite being almost laughably tame by today's standards); it was later re-edited to receive an R. Dullea said:

> I think all those orgy scenes were really corny. It was a lot of putting Vaseline over [the lens] and red [tinting], and it was just not interesting.... [Endfield] was under a lot of stress, because of disagreements about the thrust of the film. He wanted to do a more artistic film.... I can't imagine that Cy would have been reticent about filming [those scenes], it might have been the way he wanted to film them. Maybe they weren't, from [AIP's] point of view, raw enough, maybe he wanted to do it more artfully. Just knowing Cy I would guess that would be it.... Again, things go on behind the scenes that you're not aware of, and in that sense I was a journeyman, arriving to do my job, and some of the aspects of it were pleasant, but I got all involved — I was very much on Cy's side throughout the whole thing. I was sad for him, and I just sensed that the soul of the film was going to be wrong, and I think I was right.

De Sade marked a sad end to a professional relationship that had spawned some of Matheson's most successful films; it was rivaled in its productivity only by his television work with Dan Curtis during the 1970s. Looking back on his association with AIP, he recalled in his *Hell House* interview with me, "After I wrote the first two Poe pictures, [Nicholson] of his own free will gave me a bonus on them [of $2,500 each], because what I was paid for them [$5,000 apiece] was ridiculous. Even with the bonus it was ridiculous, but at least it was a very nice thought on his part." He added in his audio commentary for the laserdisc version of *Burn, Witch, Burn,* "The Writers Guild was on strike, so I was one of the few writers around who was able to work, since they weren't striking American International.... I think by [the time of *De Sade*] I was getting $20,000 for a script, so for American International I was getting high pay!"

In an amusing postscript, Dullea told me that he selected as well as dubbed the person who portrayed the aged De Sade seen at the end of the film in the Charenton asylum, where he spent the last of his 74 years: "It was my father! We have exactly the same color eyes.... So I had this idea, I said, 'Why don't you have my father do it?' It didn't require much shooting. He didn't have many lines.... My father was always young-looking for his age, so they actually added a little bit — well, [De Sade was] hairy and unkempt. But I looked, at that point, [32] and I've always looked young for my age, and I said, rather than put on a lot of [makeup on me, "Use my father." He] came to Berlin, and then in post-production, after I was back in New York, they needed to do a retake or something, so they flew my father out to Hollywood and put him up at the Beverly Wilshire Hotel, and [then] he came in for a day of shooting."

Cold Sweat

(aka *De la Part des Copains* [From the Boys], *L'Uomo dalle Due Ombre* [The Man with Two Shadows]; Films Corona–Comacico–Fair Film [France-Italy-Belgium], released December 18, 1970) DIRECTOR: Terence Young; PRODUCER: Robert Dorfmann; SCREENPLAY: Shimon Wincelberg, Albert Simonin [uncredited], Jo Eisinger, Dorothea Bennett, based on Matheson's *Ride the Nightmare*; MUSIC: Michel Magne; MAKEUP: Marie-Madeleine Paris, Anatole Paris. Color, 94 minutes. CAST — Martin (aka Moran): Charles Bronson. Fabienne Martin: Liv Ullmann. Capt. Ross: James Mason. Moira: Jill Ireland. Katanga: Jean Topart. Fausto Gelardi: Luigi Pistilli. Michele Martin: Yannick de Lulle. Vermont (aka Whitey): Michel Constantin. Doctor: Paul Bonifas. Nurse: Sabine Sun.

Joe's Assistant: Nathalie Varallo. Poker Player: Roger Mailles. Marius: Remo Mosconi. Also with Dominique Crosland.

Two of Matheson's *noir* novels, *Someone Is Bleeding* and *Ride the Nightmare*, were filmed as French-Italian co-productions during the 1970s; he observed to *Starburst's* James E. Brooks that in France, "I'm a great artist; [in the U.S.,] I'm just a nut who writes for television. I was having dinner ... at a convention in France. We were talking about wine and I mentioned that I had done a brief scene in [*Tales of Terror* with] a wine tasting contest. I thought they would be surprised, but they knew it and knew every damned piece of dialogue...!" Now prohibitively expensive and extremely hard to come by in their original paperback editions, both were published in hardcover for the first time by G&G Books, along with *Fury on Sunday*, in the omnibus edition *Noir: Three Novels of Suspense* (1997).

It is not widely known that *Ride the Nightmare* was expanded from Matheson's short story "Now Die in It," which was originally published in the December 1958 issue of *Mystery Tales* and, perhaps understandably, has never been reprinted to date. (It is currently scheduled to appear in *Matheson Uncollected: Volume Two* in 2010.) While details such as most of the character names differ, the events in the story otherwise mirror those of the first few chapters in the novel until the point at which the wife considers calling the police to report the death of the intruder; it is as if Matheson, having completed and sold the story, asked himself, "What if she *didn't* call them?" which in the story she does, yet despite being urged by her husband to tell the truth, she claims that their assailant was a stranger. Shorter versions of *Someone Is Bleeding* also saw magazine publication — as "The Frigid Flame" (*Justice*, October 1955; later included in the 1997 anthology *American Pulp*) and "The Untouchable Divorcee" (*Stag*, May 1956). But these were actual abridgements, as was "The Frenzied Weekend" (*For Men Only*, June 1956), a truncation of Matheson's other *noir* novel, *Fury on Sunday*.

Discussing *Ride the Nightmare*, Matheson told Mark Rathbun in *He Is Legend*, "I adapted it [for *The Alfred Hitchcock Hour*], and it was a good show.... Then they made it into a picture years later called *Cold Sweat* with Charles Bronson, James Mason and Liv Ullmann — which sounds great, but it was terrible. It was made by the man who did the early James Bond pictures, Terence Young. He bought the rights to it, and it had a hell of a cast, but it didn't work out too well." The film was known in France as *De la Part des Copains* (From the Boys), the title under which Bruno Martin's translation of the novel was published there, and in Italy as *L'Uomo dalle Due Ombre* (The Man with Two Shadows). Bronson, who had appeared in Matheson's *Master of the World* nine years earlier, rose to fame among the outstanding ensemble casts of *The Magnificent Seven*, *The Great Escape* (1963), and *The Dirty Dozen*. His earlier work with Robert Aldrich included the Westerns *Apache*, *Vera Cruz* (both 1954), and *4 for Texas* (1963), and he had recently starred in one of Sergio Leone's revisionist takes on that by-now-formulaic genre, *C'era una Volta il West* (Once Upon a Time in the West, 1969).

Relocated to the south of France, where it was shot in the port of Beaulieu-sur-Mer and Studios la Victorine in Nice, *Cold Sweat* — a phrase that appears in the novel — typified the polyglot productions in which Terence Young, a former screenwriter, specialized after directing three out of the first four Bond pictures: *Dr. No* (1962), *From Russia with Love* (1963), and *Thunderball* (1965). It featured an American leading man, Bronson, who starred in Young's next two films, *Red Sun* (1971) and *The Valachi Papers* (1972); a British villain, Mason, who had appeared in the director's *Mayerling* (1968); and a Norwegian leading lady, Ullmann, acclaimed for her frequent work with Swedish *auteur* Ingmar Bergman. Among the film's French personnel were Robert Dorfmann, the producer of *Red Sun*, and composer Marcel Magne, an Academy Award nominee for Gene Kelly's *Gigot* (1962). Italian actor Luigi Pistilli was known for his roles in Leone's earlier spaghetti Westerns *Per Qualche Dollari in Più* (For a Few Dollars More, 1965) and *Il Buono, il Brutto, il Cattivo* (The Good, the Bad and the Ugly, 1966).

Amusingly, one of the few film adaptations of Matheson's work outside the fantasy genre was co-scripted by Shimon Wincelberg, a prolific television writer in that very genre, with Jo Eisinger and Dorothea Bennett; some sources attribute the script to Wincelberg and French screenwriter and author Albert Simonin, but the latter's name does not appear in the credits of the English-language version. Under his own byline or his frequent pseudonym of S. Bar David, Wincelberg worked on such SF series as *Star Trek*, *The Immortal*, *Logan's Run*, *The Man from Atlantis*, *Planet of the Apes*, *The Starlost*, and Irwin Allen's *Voyage to the Bottom of the Sea*, also helping to develop Allen's *Lost in Space* and *The Time Tunnel* for television, and shared an Emmy Award for an episode of *Law & Order*. A veteran of such *noir* classics as *Gilda* (1946) and *Night and the City* (1950), American screenwriter Eisinger was an appropriate collaborator to adapt the novel, and had worked with Young previously on *The Poppy Is Also a Flower* (1966), a United Nations anti-drug TV-movie from a story by James Bond's creator, Ian Fleming.

In his book on Bronson, Michael R. Pitts notes that, like the actor's previous starring vehicle *Città Violenta* (Violent City, aka *The Family*, 1970), *De la Part des Copains* was popular in Europe and around the world but did not see a U.S. release (as *Cold Sweat*) until 1974 (presumably to cash in on Bronson's success that same year with Michael Winner's *Death Wish*). Stunt coordinator Rémy Julienne, who provided the superb car sequences with his team and later worked on every Bond film from *For Your Eyes Only* (1981) to *GoldenEye* (1995), was a fellow veteran of *Città Violenta*, as were cast members Jill Ireland and Michel Constantin. Credited as "Whitey" in some sources, the latter's character is called "Vermont" in the U.S. version. According to the IMDb, his voice in U.S. prints was provided by David Hess, who had starred in Wes Craven's notorious *The Last House on the Left* (1972), and was then engaged in a multilingual dubbing career.

Like the *Hitchcock Hour* version, the film begins fairly faithfully as Joe Martin (Bronson), an American expatriate and Korean War veteran now running a fast fishing boat and sharing a somewhat strained relationship with wife Fabienne (Ullmann), receives a threatening phone call and a nocturnal visit from his "army buddy," Vermont, and then is forced to dispose of him. (The killing is effectively shot through a swinging door that gradually loses momentum and shuts, so that the audience and Fabienne only *hear* Vermont's neck being broken.) Joe reveals that seven years ago, as Sgt. Joe Moran, he abandoned his four companions when they killed a policeman during an escape from a German stockade; the others were sentenced to 20 years apiece. Now, aspiring Mafioso Fausto Gelardi (Pistilli), ex–Foreign Legionnaire Katanga (Jean Topart), and Capt. Ross (Mason, affecting a jaw-droppingly broad Southern accent), Joe's former commanding officer turned black marketeer, are on the run after breaking out of prison along with Vermont. They demand the use of Joe's fishing boat, the *Leinad II*, to pick up a shipment of Turkish heroin offshore.

The three escaped convicts take Fabienne and Joe's stepdaughter, Michele (Yannick de Lulle), hostage in order to ensure his cooperation. He neatly turns the tables by intercepting Ross's girlfriend Moira (Ireland), who arrives at the airport with a briefcase full of money to be exchanged for the heroin. Joe agrees to trade them Moira, the money, and a free boat ride to safety for his family. When both factions converge near the old shack where Joe has hidden Moira, Ross orders Katanga to shoot the tires of the car in which Fabienne and Michele are leaving. As Joe grabs him, his wildly firing *Schmeisser* kills Fausto and wounds Ross, who is brought to the shack and holds the mutinous Katanga at gunpoint while sending Joe and Moira down into Grasse to fetch a doctor (Paul Bonifas). Their high-speed return trip through busy Bastille Day traffic over winding mountain roads marks the film's highlight, as Fabienne tries to keep Ross — who has been shot in the stomach — from succumbing to loss of blood. After finally killing him, Katanga escapes the forest fire set by Michele and forces Joe to take him away on the *Leinad II*, where he is ignited with a flare pistol and plunges over the side.

Although the film restores the standoff in the shack (albeit interchanging the villains equivalent to Ross and Katanga in the novel) and the character of the daughter, Matheson lamented in his interview for *Noir* that once again, his story was changed. "They tried to open it up and make it big, he's got a boat, and it's in the Riviera. I mean, it should have been great, with James Mason as the villain [a role that, according to Michael R. Pitts, was originally intended for Jason Robards] and Liv Ullmann playing his wife, my Lord. It should have turned out better. I haven't seen that, again, in a long time. But most of my stuff is small-scale. Whenever they try to open it up and make it big-scale, it takes away from it. You take it and put it in the Riviera instead of Latigo Canyon in Los Angeles, you know, it puts too much of a weight on it." The primary departure from the novel is the addition of Moira, a guitar-toting, pot-smoking, free-loving hippie, presumably as a vehicle for British actress Ireland, Bronson's frequent co-star and real-life wife from 1968 until her death of cancer in 1990. She reportedly once said, "I'm in so many Charles Bronson films because no other actress will work with him."

The Omega Man

(Warner Bros., released August 1, 1971) DIRECTOR: Boris Sagal; PRODUCER: Walter Seltzer; SCREENPLAY: John William Corrington, Joyce H. Corrington, based on Matheson's *I Am Legend*; MUSIC: Ron Grainer; MAKEUP: Gordon Bau. Color, 98 minutes. CAST— Col. Robert Neville: Charlton Heston. Brother Matthias: Anthony Zerbe. Lisa: Rosalind Cash. Dutch: Paul Koslo. Richie: Eric Laneuville. Zachary: Lincoln Kilpatrick. Little Girl: Jill Giraldi. Woman in Cemetery Crypt: Anna Aries. Tommy: Brian Tochi. Family Members: DeVeren Bookwalter, John Dierkes, Monika Henreid, Linda Redfearn, Forrest Wood.

An even bigger disappointment to admirers of *I Am Legend* than *The Last Man on Earth*, Warner Bros.' remake *The Omega Man* wound up as an action vehicle for a machine-gun-toting Charlton Heston, complete with a jazzy score by Ron Grainer and a trendy interracial romance with Rosalind Cash. An Academy Award winner for *Ben-Hur* (1959), Heston was no stranger to apocalyptic, issue-oriented science fiction; after tackling animal rights, evolution, and nuclear war in *Planet of the Apes* (1968) and its first sequel, plus pollution, overpopulation, and euthanasia in *Soylent Green* (1973), he seemed as ubiquitous in that subgenre as he soon became in disaster movies like *Earthquake* and *Airport 1975*. Among Heston's other fantasy credits are *The Awakening* (1980), the soporific second version of Bram Stoker's *Jewel of the Seven Stars*, and *Solar Crisis* (1990), for which director Richard C. Sarafian, a veteran of Matheson's *Lawman* episode "The Actor," hid behind the Directors Guild of America's generic pseudonym of Alan Smithee.

The Omega Man was written by the husband-and-wife team of John William and Joyce Hooper Corrington, whose scripts range from Scorsese's *Boxcar Bertha* (1972) to *Battle for the Planet of the Apes* (1973); producer Walter Seltzer and cinematographer Russell Metty both worked with Heston on *The War Lord* (1965) and others films, and it was Seltzer who produced *Soylent Green*. With only a handful of feature films to his credit, director Boris Sagal made more than a dozen TV-movies before his untimely death in 1981, including one segment of the aforementioned *Night Gallery* pilot and *Hauser's Memory* (1970), based on Curt Siodmak's sequel to his SF novel *Donovan's Brain*. He also produced the adventure series *T.H.E. Cat*, directed the highly rated miniseries *Masada* (1981), and fathered a virtual dynasty of television actors that includes Katey Sagal, who starred in the Fox network comedies *Married ... with Children* and *Futurama*; Joe Sagal, who made his debut in *Masada*; and twin sisters Jean and Liz Sagal, who had the title roles in NBC's short-lived series *Double Trouble*.

Set in 1977, the Corringtons' script restores the protagonist's original name, but Heston's character, Col. Robert Neville, has once again received an intellectual upgrade, this time from a working man to a military scientist. After surviving a helicopter crash, he injects himself with a test vaccine he helped develop to counter bacilli spread during a Sino-Russian War in 1975. Otherwise, the film is a far cry from the novel, supplanting its vampires with a "Family" of light-hating albino mutants that is led by ex-newscaster John Matthias (Anthony Zerbe) — now known as Brother Matthias — and tries to use fire to "purify" Neville, who leads a solitary existence in L.A. watching *Woodstock* (1970) at a local cinema between hunting expeditions, and returning home to repel them as night falls. Neville encounters Lisa (Cash) while he is scavenging in a department store; she immediately flees before he can talk to her. But after he is caught in a wine cellar by the Family, interrogated by Matthias, and taken to a football stadium for purification, Lisa and former medical student Dutch (Paul

CHARLTON HESTON
LE SURVIVANT
Un film de BORIS SAGAL

The relationship between Col. Robert Neville (Charlton Heston) and Lisa (Rosalind Cash) gets off to a rocky start in this French lobby card for *The Omega Man* (Warner Bros., 1971).

Koslo) temporarily blind the mutants with the stadium's night-game lights and escape with Neville by motorcycle.

Interestingly, while no mention is made of his ever having had a wife or daughter, Neville now becomes a kind of surrogate father to a group of infected youngsters led by Lisa and Dutch. After using a serum made from his blood to save Lisa's brother Richie (Eric Laneuville), who is deteriorating the fastest, Neville announces that, given sufficient time, his antibodies can do the same for the others. Following another battle in which Neville kills Matthias's henchman Zachary (Lincoln Kilpatrick), he, Lisa, Dutch and the rest plan to leave for greener pastures, enabling Neville to give more blood. But Richie naively goes to Matthias with an offer to share his good fortune, little dreaming that the Family does not wish to return to "normal," and is soon found dead by Neville. Returning to discover that Lisa has "turned" while obtaining supplies and let the Family into his home, the horrified Neville must watch it destroyed, and then is impaled with a spear by Matthias while trying to lead Lisa away. Leaning against an abstract sculpture in a Christ-like pose, he dies after giving Dutch a bottle of his blood from which they can make more serum, in a parallel with Christ's "blood of life."

The Last Man on Earth ends with Robert Morgan struck down while standing at an altar; *The Omega Man* expands the religious symbolism with the "crucifixion" of Heston, known for roles such as John the Baptist in *The Greatest Story Ever Told* (1965), and other allusions to Christ, who said, "I am the Alpha and the Omega" (*Revelation* 21:6, 22:13). Appropriately, an uncredited rewrite on the Corringtons' script was done by William Peter Blatty, the author, screenwriter, and producer of *The Exorcist*, who recalled in an interview with me and Gilbert Colon, "*The Omega Man* had been shelved when Chuck Heston's producer asked me if I would rewrite it. I was starving [this was prior to the publication of *The Exorcist*], and I was very happy to have any kind of a rewrite gig. I recall doing a great deal of restructuring. I didn't change the story at all; the story was exactly as I had found it. I don't have a copy of that, and I don't remember whether or not that crucifixion scene was there already. I have a feeling that it was.... I've always wanted to do [more work as a "script doctor"] but I've never been asked except on *The Omega Man*."

Seltzer told *Filmfax*'s Robert Coyle, Jr., and Mark Phillips, "Warners wanted insurance that we had the best screenplay possible, and before we started production, they wanted me to hire somebody to do a polish on the screenplay. We got Blatty. I didn't think much of whatever few changes he suggested." Agreed Mrs. Corrington in the same article, "Blatty re-wrote some of the dialogue, mostly trying for humor. He applied for a 'written by' credit but the matter was arbitrated by the Writers Guild, and his contribution was judged not significant enough to force Bill and me to share credit." In *Focus on the Science Fiction Film*, Matheson related a brush of his own with "script doctoring": "I was called in to do a rewrite on *Fantastic Voyage* [1966]. After reading David Duncan's script, I told them they were crazy to want a big rewrite. It only needed a little polishing here and there. They chose to differ, I didn't get a job, and they rewrote it into a comic strip."

In an interview with Don Shay for *Vampires and Slayers*, Heston called his death scene "a personal indulgence.... [Since] Neville's blood becomes the basis for a serum that will save mankind, then the Christ analogy becomes almost inescapable.... I thought it worked, but it seemed to annoy some people." (In another sequence, a little girl [Jill Giraldi] actually asks Neville, "Are you God?") Heston called the novel "just marvelous," but despite Matheson's scientific approach toward vampirism, he said, "When you're doing a last man on Earth story that involves all kinds of scientific plausibility, it seemed that vampires would not fit very well and would really get you into another kind of story. Instead, we tried to render the spooks in scientific terms, with a blood disease and albinoism and photophobia and all." Thus the drastic revisions made by the Corringtons at the behest of Heston and Seltzer (who praised them in *Filmfax* as "a very inventive couple, pleasant to work with, and very business-like, despite the fact that they were not experienced screenwriters").

Hooded and robed, the members of the pasty-faced Family are reminiscent of the witches in *The City of the Dead* and the atomically disfigured mutants Heston faced in

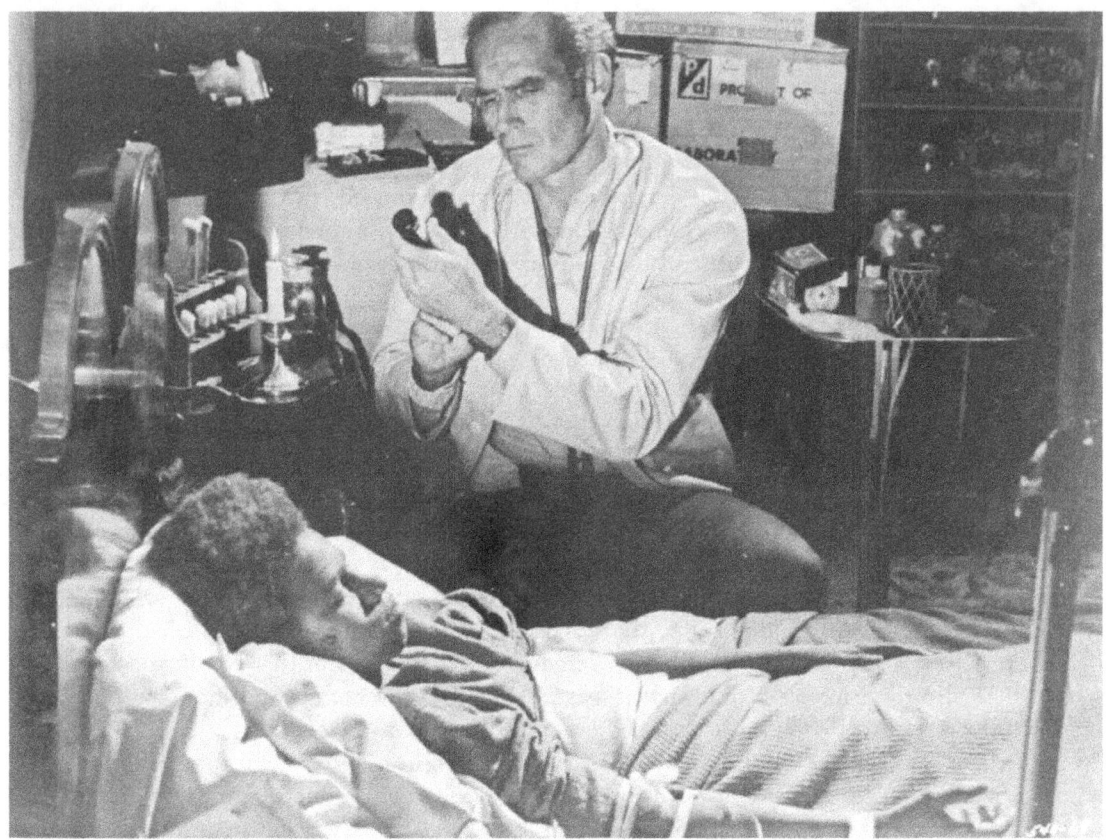

Neville prepares to inject Richie (Eric Laneuville) with the serum that will effect a short-lived cure in *The Omega Man* (Warner Bros., 1971).

Beneath the Planet of the Apes, with sunglasses covering their colorless eyes. Zerbe, who had appeared as a villain opposite Heston in producer Seltzer's *Will Penny* (1968), is suitably sinister as their leader. In her second screen role (after debuting in Alan J. Pakula's *Klute* earlier that same year), 32-year-old Cash gives a strong performance, peppered with the profanity and brief nudity that had then become acceptable. Her other credits range from *Cornbread, Earl and Me* (1975) to W.D. Richter's *The Adventures of Buckaroo Banzai Across the Eighth Dimension* (1984). While Metty's cinematography is hardly the equal of his work on *Touch of Evil*, in which Heston had co-starred with writer-director Orson Welles, or *Spartacus* (1960), for which Metty won an Academy Award, it strikingly captures the scope of the desolate and depopulated Los Angeles. The crew shot on Sunday mornings and holidays to capture the appearance of an abandoned city.

According to Jeff Bond's admirable retrospective in *CFQ* (formerly *Cinefantastique*), Welles himself had suggested *I Am Legend* as a possible project for Heston, who then mentioned it to Seltzer. As Seltzer told Bond, "I said, 'We could probably do something with it.' We proceeded to poke around with ideas, and we decided to get the rights to the book, and we talked to the author's agent, and we got far enough along that I assumed we had everything free and clear — we had the rights to the book. But after we made a deal with Warner Bros. for distribution, I found that there had been a previous movie version [*The Last Man on Earth*] made by American International Pictures, which was run by a tough

Poster art for *The Omega Man* (Warner Bros., 1971).

cookie named Sam Arkoff.... Here I was, faced with the dilemma of having made a deal with Warner Bros. and commissioned a screenplay, and I really didn't have the right to do it. The Arkoff people had the film rights. So I was in a very difficult position of having to proceed at one end and spend money, and on the other end, of not knowing whether I could shake it loose or not. Eventually, we did."

In an introduction to the Warner Home Video DVD of the film, Joyce Corrington noted that as an engineer with a Ph.D. in chemistry, she felt more comfortable writing about germ warfare as the cause of an apocalypse than about vampires; her husband, who died in 1988, had been a poet with a Ph.D. in English literature. "Our two sides made up Neville's character: the cold scientist, the killer, and yet the compassionate person who is willing to sacrifice himself, and through his blood save humanity.... Rosalind Cash did a great job. I thought she was really fun as Lisa. She had that Black Power panache, you know. I must say it was my idea to make her black. I was teaching at a black university at the time [Xavier, in New Orleans], and this was the '70s, and Black Power was very big."

She told Coyle and Phillips in *Filmfax* that the couple was shown the original version but may not have read the novel:

> The project was generated by Charlton Heston's interest in being "the last man on Earth," and we worked directly with him and his producer, Walter Seltzer. Heston was always gracious but, even though we once met in his home, there was always that "pane of glass" in place that famous people develop to protect themselves when interacting with the public.... My husband and I worked as a writing team. I usually did most of the plotting, and he wrote most of the dialogue. When Seltzer wanted to introduce some Warner executive to his new writer, he told me that while I had been a lot of help, I should stay in his office while he took Bill to meet the executive. At the time, Bill was the published writer, and since his was the only name on the contract, this was not quite as sexist on Seltzer's part as it seems. But it did generate a big fight between my husband and me, and almost led to a divorce. Bill finally conceded that we should share equal credit on the screenplays we did. He even had Roger Corman change the credit on the first movie we wrote [*Von Richthofen and Brown*] that had not come out yet....
>
> There was never any thought to a sequel at the time we wrote the script. Afterward, I thought that a natural sequel would have been *Alpha Children*, a chronicle of the efforts of the kids, who escaped with Neville's serum, trying to re-establish civilization but having to make dangerous periodic forays into the city to scavenge stuff they needed.... The Christ-like allegory of Neville was a deliberate literary symbol. The kids — and thus humanity — were to be saved by Neville's blood. However, we should never have told Charlton Heston about this. We were dismayed when we saw the movie to find how obviously they presented this. Heston died and died and died. We figured that he just enjoyed symbolically playing Christ. With the exception of the end scene, we liked Heston's performance.... Our own criticism with the film had to do with Anthony Zerbe's over-acting. He did not especially please us, since he played the role pretty broadly. And we objected to the producer adding the catapult scene. If the followers [of Brother Matthias] were anti-technology, in our opinion, they would not have used a catapult.

Corrington's criticism aside, Zerbe is a respected actor who won an Emmy for the series *Harry O*. As Seltzer told *CFQ*, "I knew Zerbe from *Will Penny*. We picked him out after a reading: He came in and just pickled the part. I had seen him do the best Iago I had ever seen at the Globe Theater in San Diego. I thought he was marvelous, and he was a natural for *The Omega Man*." Zerbe discussed the theatricality of his role in the same article: "If you stand outside of it, it can have an almost comic-book ideal to it. I've done a lot of stage, and my background is really the theater. Shakespeare had his own science fiction. Look at *The Tempest*— it's fantastic. That was the first *Star Trek*, wasn't it?... [Matthias is] misunderstood. Most villains are. There are a lot of people who feel that what Matthias had to say is where things are going. Even then there were groups of people that were all for us." He told Jeff Bond of the infamously uncomfortable contact lenses developed for the Family by Hollywood optometrist Dr. Morton K. Greenspoon: "It was odd to wear them, but it was worth it because I felt they worked. They didn't have all the technical things they have now — that would be a wild film to make today."

The Omega Man was another Matheson-based work to be spoofed on *The Simpsons* ("I love 'em, that's great," he says of their parodies). In "Treehouse of Horror VIII" (10/26/97), "The Homega Man" opens with France threatening "swift and massive retaliation" for Mayor Quimby's "now-famous frog's legs joke," while the Springfield leader stands equally adamantly by his "ethnic slur." Shopping for a fallout shelter as a precaution, Homer emerges from "The Withstandinator" to find that the French have launched "le bombe neutron" (conspicuously labeled "intel inside") on Springfield. As the last man alive he can finally do everything he's always wanted, like watching Chris Farley and David Spade in a cinema full of corpses and dancing naked to rock music inside the church. Pursued by a mutated brotherhood of cloaked, cannibalistic freaks who are trying to create "a new perfect society in which the mistakes of the past will be eliminated," Homer flees back to his home and is overjoyed to find that all of the layers of lead paint in the house have protected Marge and the children, who abruptly cut short the brotherhood's plea for harmony by blasting them with shotguns. And, in 2010, Matheson's "The Splendid Source" *(Playboy*, May 1956) was parodied on the Fox series *Family Guy*.

Duel

(ABC-TV, November 13, 1971) DIRECTOR: Steven Spielberg; PRODUCER: George Eckstein; TELEPLAY: Matheson, based on his story; MUSIC: Billy Goldenberg. Color, 74 minutes (broadcast version); 90 minutes (theatrical and home video version). CAST— David Mann: Dennis Weaver. Mrs. Mann: Jacqueline Scott. Café Owner: Eddie Firestone. Bus Driver: Lou Frizzell. Man in Café: Gene Dynarski. Lady at Snakerama: Lucille Benson. Gas Station Attendant: Tim Herbert. Old Man: Charles Seel. Waitress: Shirley O'Hara. Old Man in Car: Alexander Lockwood. Old Woman in Car: Amy Douglass. Radio Interviewer: Dick Whittington. The Truck Driver: Carey Loftin. Car Driver: Dale Van Sickel. Girl on School Bus: Shawn Steinman.

Matheson's tale of a truck terrorizing a man marked a turning point in his career, just as the day it was born — November 22, 1963 — was a watershed in history. "I was playing golf with Jerry Sohl when we found out that Kennedy had been assassinated," he told Burns. "We broke off our game and headed for home. As we were driving, muttering and moaning about the assassination, a truck started tailgating us on the narrow pass that we were driving through [Grimes Canyon]. This went on for miles and miles with us screaming infuriatedly, until finally we pulled over to the side of the road and let the son of a bitch pass us. When we were stopped, I wrote the idea for 'Duel' down on a piece of mail that Jerry had in the car. I didn't write the story, though, until years later." Recounting its history in the Rathbun-Flanagan *He Is Legend*, Sohl wrote, "I'll never forget Matheson. He took out [some mail] and started scribbling [on] it. I asked him what he was doing. He said he was going to write a story about what was happening to us and sell it to *Playboy*, a story about a truck that unrelentingly follows a car, as if the truck were being driven by a mad alien (which it seemed to us our truck was)."

In a tribute from the posthumously published collection *Filet of Sohl*, Matheson added,

"If I had been with anyone else, what I did would have undoubtedly repelled them. They would likely have said, 'How can you *think* that way? What the hell is *wrong* with you? President Kennedy has just been killed by an assassin. A crazy truck driver has just come damn close to killing *you*. And you can do *this*?'... [But] first and foremost, Jerry was a writer. He knew exactly how my writer's mind was functioning — because he had the same sort of mind — in spades. So, despite the double trauma we had just undergone, Jerry understood perfectly the bizarre machinations of a writer's psyche. And it amused us both simultaneously.... Such is the writers' mentality we shared."

After unsuccessfully pitching the idea to various television series that found it too limited, Matheson gave up and wrote it as a short story. It was with "Duel" — which he considered the ultimate embodiment of his leitmotif, "the individual isolated in a threatening world, attempting to survive" — that he bid *adieu* to that form after twenty years. Hitherto unpublished stories have since appeared in various chapbooks, collections, and tribute anthologies, but the magazines for which he once wrote have largely ceased to exist. Just a few years after "Duel" first appeared in 1971, he said in an interview with John Brosnan for *The Horror People*, "There's really no market now, outside of *Playboy* magazine. There's no point in writing them for the science fiction and fantasy magazines. To spend a lot of time writing something that will sell for just $50 is hardly worth the effort."

Matheson wrote the first draft of "Duel" in a single sitting, using the ingenious method of driving from his home to Ventura and back, dictating everything he saw along the way into a tape recorder, in order to provide his protagonist with a realistic route. In "Richard Matheson: The Writing of *Duel*," a documentary written, directed and produced by Laurent Bouzereau for the Universal Studios Home Video DVD, he added, "I named the main character 'Mann' with some sort of foolish idea that I was making a metaphor for mankind, which didn't last." Published in *Playboy* in April 1971, "Duel" became an *ABC Movie of the Week* seven months later, airing on November 13. It received an Emmy for best sound editing and a nomination for Jack A. Marta's cinematography. Also nominated for a Golden Globe as the Best Movie Made for TV, *Duel* was hailed by Cecil Smith of *The Los Angeles Times* as the "best TV movie of 1971 ... a classic of pure cinema."

If "Duel" ended one phase in Matheson's career, then *Duel* began another, for after more than a decade of writing feature films, this was his first TV-movie — a relatively new form with which he would enjoy some of his greatest successes of the 1970s. It was also a first for 24-year-old Steven Spielberg, who had directed "Eyes," Joan Crawford's segment of the 1969 *Night Gallery* pilot. He continued to work for Universal

Beleaguered motorist David Mann (Dennis Weaver) and his automotive attacker from *Duel* (ABC-TV, 1971).

on episodes of *Marcus Welby, M.D.*, *The Name of the Game*, *The Psychiatrist*, and *Columbo*, in addition to *Night Gallery*. When his secretary stumbled across "Duel" in *Playboy* and learned that Matheson was already adapting the short story into a teleplay, longtime *Twilight Zone* fan Spielberg approached George Eckstein, formerly a writer and co-producer on *The Fugitive*. Spielberg felt that "Duel" might be the perfect property for a feature-length debut to help cement his Hollywood reputation.

The fledgling filmmaker's success often overshadows Matheson's own role as the creator of this classic tale; he wrote in "An Open Letter to Robert Bloch" (published in the Gauntlet thirty-fifth anniversary edition of Bloch's seminal 1959 novel *Psycho*), "Alfred Hitchcock was *not* the *auteur* of *Psycho*. He directed it brilliantly. End of story. To be fair to the late gentleman, he *did* say that the film all came from your book. That was very decent of him; not at all typical of Hollywood. But how many people are aware of it? Very few. Too few. The disparity remains. I know how you feel. I had the same experience with the film *Duel*; Steven Spielberg's first. Like Hitchcock, Spielberg has given me due credit. But, to this day, the film is known as *Steven Spielberg's Duel*.... Everyone involved in the film [version of *Psycho*] did consummate work. But the film was *your story*, Robert. Totally." Matheson added an ironic postscript in our interview for *Filmfax*: "I saw [*Twilight Zone* producer William] Froug on a talk show once — he had a talk show on cable or something, and he was talking

Mann reflects on his plight in this lobby card for the theatrical release of *Duel* (ABC-TV, 1971).

to George Eckstein, and [Eckstein] was saying, 'You know, it's really not fair that this thing be called "Steven Spielberg's *Duel*."' And I thought, 'Gee, is he actually going to mention my name?' And he said, 'It should be called "George Eckstein's *Duel*."' So I said, 'Well, you know, that figures.'"

In TCM's documentary *Spielberg on Spielberg* (2007), the director graciously addressed the situation, telling filmmaker Richard Schickel, "I get a lot of credit for figuring out how to make *Duel* a very suspenseful, Hitchcockian story, but Matheson's script was already Hitchcockian and suspenseful, and I think that was the first time I realized, 'Hey, if I have a good script and I'm a good director, I can make a pretty terrific movie.'" He also noted that after reading the advance proofs of Peter Benchley's *Jaws* he said, "I really want to make this, because this is *Duel* in the sea.... [And then later on] when I read [Michael Crichton's] *Jurassic Park* ... [I said] this is kind of like *Duel* and *Jaws* combined, and this is right up my alley."

Duel begins with David Mann (Dennis Weaver) heading for a sales call on a sparsely populated California highway where he overtakes a grimy, smoke-belching gasoline tanker truck. The driver (played by stunt coordinator Carey Loftin, whose face, as stipulated in the script, is never shown) then passes Mann, who in turn passes him again before stopping for gas. Ignoring a warning by the attendant (Tim Herbert) that his red Plymouth Valiant needs a new radiator hose, he phones home and spars with Mrs. Mann (Jacqueline Scott)—identified in the story but not the script as Ruth—emphasizing the importance of his appointment, before hitting the road again, only to find the trucker, who had also pulled into the same gas station, mercilessly tailgating him. Mann receives his first indication that the truck driver is taking this all a bit too personally when, after he has waved the truck around him, the driver slows down, blocking the road, then deliberately signals for Mann to pass him on a blind curve. Another car is coming in the opposite direction, nearly causing a head-on collision, with Weaver registering a believable blend of frustration, fright, and shock. "What was interesting is that when I went to watch them shooting, several people came up to me and said the same thing had happened to them," Matheson told Bouzereau.

Mann finally passes the truck again by cutting around it on a dirt side road, but the driver continues to tailgate him at almost 100 miles per hour, blasting his horn, until the desperate Mann pulls over across from Chuck's Café. After collecting himself in the men's room, he discovers in horror that the truck is outside in the parking lot. Having seen nothing of the driver but his boots back at the gas station, Mann is uncertain which of the café's patrons he is. This sequence appears in the story, but was expanded in the film. According to Matheson, "That was where I first met Steven, and I went in the café, and it was so realistic I thought, 'Well, the café is open for the day, and they're just shooting around their real customers.' I didn't realize that they were all actors, because they looked so good and so real."

Summoning up his courage, Mann decides to confront his tormentor, only to get into a scuffle with the wrong patron (Gene Dynarski), during which the driver leaves the café. As Mann attempts to aid the operator of a stranded school bus (Lou Frizzell), the truck pulls behind him at a railroad crossing and almost pushes his car into a passing freight train. When Mann stops at a combination gas station and snake farm to call the police, the truck demolishes the phone booth (a sharp-eyed viewer can spot Spielberg's reflection in the glass) and the Snakerama, nearly killing Mann and the owner (Lucille Benson, who later spoofed the scene in Spielberg's comic flop *1941* [1979]). Matheson told Bouzereau that this sequence was inspired partly by the unusual roadside attractions he and his wife saw during their cross-country honeymoon drive, and praised Spielberg for adding such details as the tarantula that clings to Mann's leg after its cage is smashed.

Deciding that the account is not worth dying for, Mann pulls over to take a nap until the truck has gone but awakens to find it waiting for him. Mann hopes to outdistance it on another upgrade, but the radiator hose at last gives out. After barely making it over the summit of the slope, he coasts downhill in neutral until the car cools down sufficiently for him to pull off the highway onto a side road. There he restarts his overheated engine, drives toward a cliff that overlooks the canyon, jams his monogrammed briefcase onto the gas pedal, and jumps out of the Valiant. The truck driver rams it and, blinded by smoke and flames, plunges spectacularly over the cliff. The triumphantly capering Mann experiences "a primeval tumult in his mind: the cry of some ancestral beast above the body of its vanquished foe," as described in the story's last line. (The truck, conspicuously marked "flammable," does not blow up in the film as it had in both the story and script.)

Matheson noted in a letter to me, "I'm sure they didn't have the truck explode because it would have made the last scene impossible, in that you'd see only flames and smoke. I kind of liked what Spielberg did. It was like the death throes of an animal, some great beast [befitting a 'leviathan' motif in the script]. As a matter of fact, they actually used elephant sounds for part of the noise. I suppose one could rationalize by saying that the driver had already delivered his load of fuel and was on his way home and that's why the truck could go so fast, because it was empty. It wasn't my idea though." In "*Duel*: A Conversation with Steven Spielberg," the director told Bouzereau that he equated the truck with Godzilla and added a dinosaur roar to its death throes; it was later used in the last scene of *Jaws* (1975). "I put the sound at the same point that the fin of the shark comes out of the cloud of blood, like the truck came out of the cloud of dirt, and it was a little bit of a self-congratulatory pat on the back, but it was also kind of like saying, 'Gee, thank you, *Duel*, for putting me on the map.'"

An excellent example of Matheson's literary style in its brevity and specificity ("At 11:32 A.M., Mann passed the truck," reads the first paragraph *in toto*), "Duel" inevitably required some expansion to fill a 74-minute running time. The bulk of his teleplay follows the story quite faithfully, with many descriptions transposed practically verbatim. He considered having Mann accompanied on the road by his spouse, so that they could exchange dialogue, but was eventually dissuaded. (While the teleplay eliminates her almost inevitable first name of Ruth, it also adds one for Mann — David — that is not found in the story.) Also original to the script are the visits to the gas station and Snakerama (the former dramatizing Mann's pivotal need for a new radiator hose, only alluded to in the story), his plea for help from an elderly couple, and a slightly different ending. The existing scene in Chuck's was augmented by Mann's encounters with an old man outside, and with the other driver whom he mistakes for his nemesis inside.

Instead of using storyboards, Spielberg developed an unusual method of visualizing *Duel*, plotting the entire film on an overhead mural that covered the walls of his motel room during location shooting; it depicted the highways north of L.A. in Pearblossom, Soledad Canyon, and Sand Canyon near Palmdale. He credited unit production manager Wallace Worsley, Jr. — whose father had directed Lon Chaney in *The Hunchback of Notre Dame* (1923) — with helping him complete the difficult location shooting only two or three days over his ten-day schedule, and related how art director Robert S. Smith arranged an "audition" with several possible trucks: "The Peterbilt that I chose was a little more retro, it was an older truck. It had a face: The windows were the eyes, and it has a huge, protruding snout, and the grille and the bumper are the mouth.... It had to have a personality [so] it couldn't just be a sparkling new, freshly minted truck..."

Weaver had won a 1959 Best Supporting Actor Emmy for *Gunsmoke*, and garnered two more nominations as Lead Actor for *McCloud*, in which he was then starring for Universal on NBC. (*Duel* was shot during a *McCloud* hiatus.) But Spielberg cast him because of a much smaller character role as the anxious motel caretaker in *Touch of Evil*. In addition to anchoring *Duel* firmly in reality with his Everyman quality, Weaver also increased the tension of the climactic scenes with the impressive panic he had achieved for Welles. In an interview for Matheson's *Duel & The Distributor* (2004), Weaver told me, "I hadn't read [the story], but my son Rob had read it, and he got very excited when he heard that I'd been offered it.... I hadn't seen *any* of [Spielberg's] work. The heads of the studio at the 'Black Tower' called me, and asked me if I would accept this young director that they'd just put under contract. They hyped him pretty good. They said he was very exciting, very creative, very enthusiastic, and had a lot of energy. They said, would it be okay to go with this director?, and I said sure. He was absolutely everything they said that he was, and even more."

"When it was absolutely so dangerous in the eyes of the studio that it would have been silly to have me do a particular stunt, then [stuntman] Dale [Van Sickel] did it, but I think 90 percent of the driving I did, and I did some pretty hairy stunts in it also. I couldn't wait to get up in the morning and go to work, because I'm a frustrated stuntman anyway, and the idea of doing stunts in an automobile, which I hadn't done before, was very exciting to me. I had some good instruction on certain stunts from Dale and from others, so it was fun." He added of the phone booth scene, in which he jumps out of the booth seconds before it is demolished, "That was pretty stupid of me, actually, but I was young and full of whatever, and I just told Steven, 'Let me do this, because I think it would be more effective.' And I think it was. I just made sure that the door of the telephone booth operated very easily. I tested that several times, because if it had hung up for some reason, I'd have been ground burger." *Duel & The Distributor* includes both the original short story and the script.

Matheson told me in an interview for *Filmfax*, "I was flabbergasted at how good [the film] was. Actually, when I first saw it, they had a huge screening party at Universal. They showed it to all these critics in about six or seven screening rooms, and when it started out I didn't realize that what they had done was [to] buy a recent broadcast from some well-known guy on the radio [Dick Whittington]. When I heard that, I thought, 'Oh, my God, they've rewritten my entire script!' And then as soon as that was over, there was the script, intact. I don't think I indicated that he was listening to a radio broadcast. I think probably in the script I just had him driving along, and then he has that thing with the truck. But it was a good way to start it off.... [Spielberg] took my script — and it *is* my script — and added his own incredible touch to it, but they didn't make big changes. All they did was cut some of my narration."

Quoted in the liner notes from the MCA Home Video laserdisc version of *Duel*, Spielberg said, "I actually wanted to make a feature-length silent movie. No dialogue at all ... but finally, I had to come to terms with the network executives.... I promised to shoot some dialogue. There's maybe 35 to 40 lines in it. That's unusual for television." A comparison with the finished film reveals that he did eliminate some dialogue and voiceovers, such as Mann's reactions in transit to graffiti and signs advertising night crawlers and a mortuary, as well as several small sequences left either unfilmed or on the cutting room floor, including a phone call to tell Mr. Forbes, the account with whom he has his appointment, that he is running late due to "car trouble." But by and large, Spielberg stuck as closely to the script as Matheson did to the story when adapting it. The latter acknowledged in interviews for *Filmfax* that "Steven did marvelous a job with *Duel*.... [Later on], he made a speech at the Writers Guild when they gave him a big award, in which he personally read off the names of every writer who had helped create his career, and my name was certainly in it."

This minimalist tale underwent one last expansion when Universal decided to release *Duel* theatrically in Europe; it was an award-winning commercial smash in 1973. (It was not shown in U.S. theaters until 1983.) Spielberg wrote and directed three new scenes to bring it to the requisite running time of 90 minutes. Weaver told this writer, "When they saw what they had, they said, 'Look, let's put this on the big screen and release it worldwide.'... They came to me and made sure that I was available, and we shot three more days, so the final film was shot in 16 days. It was 13 days that we shot on the original script.... If somebody watches the final cut of the movie version, they would be terribly hard pressed to figure out which scenes were added."

The scenes depicted Mann's conversation with his wife, his encounter with the bus and the truck trying to push him into the train. In 1994, Matheson wrote me, "I didn't care for them since I felt that the original version ... was really tight. I didn't like Mann [being] berated by his wife. I hated the bus incident which went on interminably. The truck pushing Mann's car was okay but my intent was that there would be no contact whatever between the two vehicles until the very end. On the other hand, Spielberg had to come up with *something* or Universal wouldn't have released it as a film in theaters. If they had asked me to write additional scenes, I don't know if I would have come up with anything at all."

Like many a then-recent film in the Universal library, *Duel* was shamelessly cannibalized by *The Incredible Hulk* with "Never Give a Trucker an Even Break" (4/28/78), a first-season episode written by executive producer Kenneth Johnson and directed by Kenneth Gilbert. It begins with Dr. David Banner (Bill Bixby) on the road in Nevada, hitchhiking from Las Vegas to Carson City. Picked up by trucker Joanie (Jennifer Darling), Banner becomes embroiled in an attempt to reclaim her tanker truck — painted and suitably begrimed so that the new scenes shot by Gilbert would match the *Duel* sequences — from a gang of hijackers led by Ted (Frank R. Christi), who are using it to smuggle stolen computer components (and pursue her in, naturally, a red Plymouth Valiant). Banner inevitably settles the hijackers' hash after turning into his eponymous emerald alter ego (Lou Ferrigno). While the use of Spielberg's footage is an obvious cost-cutting measure, one wonders if the challenge of shooting and writing around it might not be prohibitive, with Johnson contriving to make the principals switch vehicles so that the truck would be chasing the Valiant instead of vice versa.

Duel's influence is apparent in works ranging from George Miller's *Mad Max* trilogy and John Dahl's *Joy Ride* (2001) to Stephen King's short story "Trucks," adapted by King himself as *Maximum Overdrive* in 1986 and for cable TV under its own title in 1997. King and his son Joe Hill also contributed "Throttle," a story overtly inspired by "Duel," to Conlon's *He Is Legend* tribute anthology.

Shown daily as the October 1997 Movie of the Month at New York's Museum of Television & Radio, *Duel* was chosen in 1999 as one of *Entertainment Weekly*'s "100 Greatest Moments in TV." As an addendum to the "Storyteller" series, MGM included an "Easter egg" with Matheson explaining the origins of "Duel" on their DVD of *Jeepers Creepers* (2001), which visually quotes from the film. To access the one-minute Matheson portion of the egg, go to the scene selection screen, highlight scenes 1–4, press the up arrow button (which will highlight one of the stitches on the screen), and press enter. Other portions produce writer-director Victor Salva's cameo as a corpse and an effect of the film's fearsome Creeper looking at you, as revealed on the invaluable dvdeasterggs.com website.

As Weaver concluded in his interview with me, "When you're talking about movies, if in your career you have one classic that is going to be around forever, and talked about forever, and shown forever, you're pretty lucky, and I happen to have two of them. One is *Touch of Evil* with Orson Welles — that was the most exciting relationship that I ever had, and to this date have ever had, with a director. Orson Welles was an absolute genius. His creativity just never ceased — and the other is *Duel* with Steven Spielberg. I've made a lot of good films, too. I'm not trying to belittle anything; it's just the way I feel about those two efforts." Asked if he'd had hopes of another Emmy for his virtual one-man show in *Duel*, he laughed and answered, "Well, you always have a hope! But I really didn't even give that much thought at the time, because the odds of getting a nomination for an acting job on a movie for television — there's so many movies made, so many great parts, and so many good performances — are very much against you. So I really didn't have any high hopes of doing that. In retrospect, I think that Steven should have gotten at least a nomination."

The Night Stalker

(ABC-TV, January 11, 1972) DIRECTOR: John Llewellyn Moxey; PRODUCER: Dan Curtis; TELEPLAY: Matheson, based on Jeff Rice's *The Kolchak Papers* (aka *The Night Stalker*); MUSIC: Robert Cobert; MAKEUP: Jerry Cash. Color, 74 minutes. CAST — Carl Kolchak: Darren McGavin. Gail Foster: Carol Lynley. Tony Vincenzo: Simon Oakland. Bernie Jenks: Ralph Meeker. Sheriff Warren A. Butcher: Claude Akins. Police Chief Edward Masterson: Charles McGraw. D.A. Thomas Paine: Kent Smith. Mickey Crawford: Elisha Cook, Jr. Fred Hurley: Stanley Adams. Dr. Robert Mokurji [spelled "Makurji" in credits]: Larry Linville. Dr. John O'Brien: Jordan Rhodes. Janos Skorzeny: Barry Atwater. Shelley Forbes: Irene Forrest. Helen O'Brien: Peggy Rea. Olive Bowman: Virginia Gregg. Cheryl Hughes: Patti Elder. First Officer: Edward Faulkner. Second Officer: Jim Hodge. Arnold Bishop: Victor Masi. Nurse Alberta Harris: Marilyn Moe. Dr. Regenhaus: William Long, Jr. Dr. John McManus: Ron Doyle. Barney: Bob Golden. Second Cop: Larry Watson. Watchman: Al Ward.

The Night Stalker initiated a productive relationship between Matheson and writer-producer-director Dan Curtis, who had already pioneered the contemporary small-screen vampire with the character of Barnabas Collins (Jonathan Frid) on the phenomenally popular *Dark Shadows* (1966–71), the world's first Gothic soap opera, which still has a faithful fan following after more than four decades. But while the moody and secluded rural New England settings of that show's fictional Collinsport could easily have stood in for those of an earlier era (indeed, many of the characters traveled back in time to meet their ancestors in later years), *The Night Stalker* cleverly placed its vampire amid the all-night hustle of Las Vegas, where he is pursued by an intrepid reporter, Carl Kolchak (Darren McGavin). Based on Jeff Rice's then-unpublished *The Kolchak Papers*, it set a record with 75 million viewers in 1972 and, according to *TV Guide*, remained among the top ten telefilms into the twenty-first century; won Matheson the Writers Guild of America Award and the Mystery Writers of America's Edgar Allan Poe Award; and spawned a sequel, two series, comic books, and several volumes of fiction and non-fiction.

Reporter Carl Kolchak (Darren McGavin) wards off evil in this promotional shot for *The Night Stalker* (ABC-TV, 1972).

While ample humor was provided by the feisty, fast-talking character of Kolchak — a role McGavin seemed born to play — and his tempestuous relationship with his boss, Tony Vincenzo (Simon Oakland), much of the film's power derives from the absolutely serious approach of both Matheson and John Llewellyn Moxey, the director of George Baxt's aforementioned *The City of the Dead*. The splendidly feral vampire, Janos Skorzeny (Barry Atwater), is wisely little shown, and the film never descends into camp or pokes fun at the idea of his being on the loose in modern-day Las Vegas. Matheson was a particularly appropriate choice for screenwriter as this simple but supernatural premise is developed with characteristically rigorous realism and logic. "It was pretty astonishing," he noted in an interview with me for *Filmfax.* "It was awfully well done. It had a great character to it, it was very fast, and sharp, and Moxey did a great job. That was the only one I ever did with Dan where he didn't direct it." Moxey also directed "The New House," Matheson's pilot script for the *Ghost Story* anthology series.

The notoriously temperamental Curtis, who refused repeated requests from me for an interview, told Mark Dawidziak in *Night Stalking: A 20th Anniversary Kolchak Companion* (subsequently expanded into *The Night Stalker Companion*),

> People don't realize that it's far more difficult to do a horror picture well than a straight drama. That's why most supernatural pictures stink. It attracts a lot of people who have no talent and don't know what the hell they're doing. Now, I'm telling you from experience. I know that the supernatural pictures I made were really good, and they were really good because I knew what the hell I was doing. It was very, very difficult. Anybody can make a gory, slasher type of horror. That's easy, and it's not really horror. Those things are abominations as far as I'm concerned. *Dark Shadows* was never a gory, slasher type of horror. Anybody can make a horror movie if you don't have to end it or make it clever. It's an enormously tough thing to do right, and that's why you see really terrible things all the time. I got into the field because I love it. This sprang from a deep childhood fascination with the genre.

The film opens as Vincenzo assigns Kolchak to cover the murders of a series of young women for the Las Vegas *Daily News.* One of the victims, who were drained of blood, was a friend of the reporter's sometime inamorata, Gail Foster (Carol Lynley), and another was found in the sand with no footprints nearby, suggesting that her body had been hurled some 22 feet. Even after a hospital is robbed of its blood supply and the coroner, Dr. Robert Mokurji (Larry Linville, best known as Major Frank Burns on *M*A*S*H*), says that human saliva was found in the victims' neck wounds, District Attorney Thomas Paine (Kent Smith) squelches Kolchak's memorably expressed hypothesis that "this nut thinks he's a vampire," for fear of inciting a panic. A fourth woman is killed and a fifth disappears and is presumed dead. The killer displays superhuman strength and invulnerability to bullets during a skirmish with the police before being identified as Skorzeny, who incredibly was born in Rumania in 1899.

Kolchak has gambler Mickey Crawford (Elisha Cook, Jr.) canvass local realtors, while the police — more receptive to outside advice after another run-in with Skorzeny, atmospherically set in and around a swimming pool — arm themselves with crosses and stakes. (This echoes Curtis's theatrical debut *House of Dark Shadows* [1970], a feature-film version of the serial.) Locating Skorzeny's house just before dawn, Kolchak finds the missing Shelley Forbes (Irene Forrest) being used as "his own private blood bank" and is attacked by the vampire. Kolchak's friend, FBI agent Bernie Jenks (Ralph Meeker), arrives, and they tear down the curtains and fling open the door, the sunlight holding Skorzeny at bay just long enough for Kolchak to pound a stake into him. The triumphant reporter writes his exclusive and proposes to Gail, yet in an ending that would form the template for most of Kolchak's subsequent dealings with various law-enforcement agencies, he finds the story spiked and himself charged with first-degree murder by Sheriff Warren A. Butcher (Claude Akins). He is forced to leave town, as are Gail, whom Kolchak never sees again, and Vincenzo.

While Matheson's teleplay conflates and shuffles some of Rice's supporting characters

(Bernie Jenks, for example, is a composite of FBI Special Agent Bernie Fain and Sheriff's Lieutenant Bill Jenks), it follows the narrative of the novel quite closely, at times almost verbatim. Where the two works differ dramatically is in the characterization of Carl Kolchak; Matheson makes him much more sympathetic. Matheson told me that in the original book, "he's sort of a heavy-set Hungarian who believes in vampires right from the start, at least that's what he was in the manuscript that I saw, and I just turned him into something out of *The Front Page*; you know, a wisecracking reporter with a love-hate relationship with his editor." Although Rice's Kolchak does not immediately accept that Skorzeny is a real vampire in the published version of the novel, he is a second-generation American steeped by his grandfather, "a cabinetmaker from Rumania with a penchant for telling his young grandson endless folktales in the dark of night," in supernatural lore and the historical facts surrounding the real Count Dracula.

Rice is an award-winning former Las Vegas newsman who presents the novel as a straightforward transcript of a factual account, interspersing periodic editorial comments to add to the documentary effect. Rice's Kolchak is a stout, lazy drunk and "an irascible second-rate journalist," while in the film even Tony Vincenzo grudgingly admits, "Kolchak, you're one hell of a reporter." McGavin, who turned 49 just a few months before shooting began, was a year older than the literary Kolchak but in much better shape, as demonstrated by one sequence in which he is seen shirtless with Gail, and as befits an actor whose many television roles include Mickey Spillane's legendary tough guy, Mike Hammer. The more

Kolchak and the undead subject of his greatest story, Janos Skorzeny (Barry Atwater), in *The Night Stalker* (ABC-TV, 1972).

sprightly McGavin also acts as his own photographer, unlike Rice's Kolchak, and bravely enters Skorzeny's house alone. In the novel, Kolchak is accompanied by 14 deputies and must be forced by Jenks, who calls the reluctant reporter a "gutless sonofabitch," to stake Skorzeny.

In his exhaustive *The Transylvanian Library: A Consumer's Guide to Vampire Fiction*, Greg Cox observes, "This is a thin book, padded out by frequent digressions on local history and famous mass murderers. There's even a bibliography and appendix on Jack the Ripper. The plot bears a strong resemblance to *Progeny of the Adder* ... which Rice has denied reading..." A novel by Leslie H. Whitten, *Progeny* depicts Washington, D.C., homicide detective Harry Picard's search for a serial killer who turns out to be a vampire; there *are* striking parallels, including similar backgrounds for Janos Skorzeny and Whitten's bloodthirsty Sebastian Paulier. Comparable scenes from each book depict a shady used-car dealer relating a Friday-night visit from an ominous accented man with bad breath, dark clothes, a hat, a large wallet full of hundred-dollar bills, and no driver's license; in another pair of scenes, the police find broken mirrors, burned shirts, health and beauty aids to conceal his breath and pallor, and a coffin or steamer trunk full of soil in his fetid lair. Dawidziak recounts in *Night Stalking*:

> Shortly before *The Night Stalker* was to begin filming, American International Pictures (AIP) informed ABC that a lawsuit was imminent. AIP owned the rights to *Progeny of the Adder*, a 1965 horror novel by Leslie H. Whitten (*The Alchemist*). With a film version of *Progeny of the Adder* in the planning stages, AIP was claiming that Jeff Rice had plagiarized Whitten's book for *The Night Stalker*. Rice calmly insisted that he hadn't read Whitten's novel. AIP replied that, since the book had been out for five years, he had "implied access." Because someone wasn't with him for every minute of those five years, Rice asked, how could he prove that he hadn't purchased or read *Progeny of the Adder*? Finally, Rice pointed out that the characters in *The Night Stalker* were based on real people, and he'd "subpoena half of Las Vegas" to prove it. That was enough. AIP dropped the lawsuit. But charges of literary theft tend to linger.... Yes, there are some remarkable similarities. But remarkable similarities are not uncommon in fantasy literature.

Coincidentally, Matheson has had his own brush with Whitten's novel, possibly in connection with AIP's proposed version. He told Sammon in *Midnight Graffiti*, "I was supposed to do a screenplay on it. I actually did finish a complete outline.... Thank God I didn't own the rights, hadn't done it before, because it is tremendously close. It would have made a fantastic movie." Of Rice's own lawsuit against ABC and Universal over the specifics of his contract and the rights to *The Kolchak Papers*, Matheson added, "I had to go to a deposition. I had to go downtown to the courthouse, and I wasn't even one of the people being sued. Rice did not feel I was culpable in any way. I had also helped him in the publication of [the novel and its sequel, *The Night Strangler*]. But, finally, the suit was [settled].... I don't think anyone in the business will touch him now.... [H]e spent too much time on that. He should have gone on to some other project."

In a 1990 interview excerpted in *Vampires and Slayers* magazine, Matheson told Dawidziak, "I liked [Rice's *The Kolchak Papers*] very much, obviously. It was quite a complete novel. Don't make any mistake about that. The story was all there, the structure was there, and that's what got everybody excited. It was sort of a *cinema verite* vampire story. It seemed so realistic. You're reading this story, and it sounds like something that really happened. That's what makes it so remarkable, and that feel did come from the book. If you watch the movie and read the book, you see that all the basic story steps are in the novel." But, he added in Dawidziak's *Night Stalking*, "I didn't think [the literary Kolchak's predisposition to believing in vampires] was going to work at all. If he starts out like that, where do you have to go? Jeff Rice made him a smart-ass reporter, so I made him more of a smart-ass reporter who finally has to believe it. The other major change I made was to pick up on the *Front Page* humor in the book and emphasize it even more. The realistic approach and the smart-alecky sense of humor are what give the story an edge..."

Although disgruntled over alleged double-dealing in the acquisition of the rights to his work, and disappointed at not being able to play the pathologist, Rice expressed equal satisfaction with Matheson's adaptation in *Night Stalking*: "I wrote my novel because I had some things I wanted to say about Las Vegas and I also wanted to write a vampire story in a modern setting. Matheson, on the other hand, was writing on assignment ... to fill a time slot, so things had to be tightened quite a bit; many of my more pithy observations on Las Vegas and the whole milieu had to be eliminated or toned down.... Still, he managed to keep a good deal of the flavor of my approach and much of the style of my own work intact, and in so doing got in a few shots at the 'Don't let the public know, it's bad for business' attitude of the authorities that was so much a part of Las Vegas at that time.... In keeping with the story I had written, he also contributed some excellent dialogue almost wholly original with him.... I think Matheson did a fine job and, in the main, realized at least 75 percent of my novel. I have no complaint in regard to his scripting at all."

Matheson recounted in an interview with me for *Filmfax* that he was unfamiliar with *Dark Shadows* at that time. "The only thing I knew about Dan Curtis was that some editor had given him a galley of [one of Matheson's novels] before it was published, which he wasn't supposed to have, and they were trying to buy it from me for $10,000, all rights to it. So when I met him, I hated him before I even knew him. I found out later it was like taking my life in my hands, 'cause he had a violent temper, and I treated him rudely and impolitely, I'm surprised he didn't rip my throat out. Just a tremendous temper. But once I got to know him, he's a lot of fun. The guy's got a marvelous sense of humor, which helps to balance it out.... I saw one [episode of the 1991 prime-time *Dark Shadows* revival] one night, but I thought to myself, 'Jeez, Dan, you did [the miniseries based on Herman Wouk's] *The Winds of War* [1983] and [the Emmy Award-winning follow-up] *War and Remembrance* [1988–89], you've done the definitive picture of the Holocaust, and now you're back to this? I mean, how can you *do* it?'"

According to *TV Guide*'s Ted Johnson and Tim Williams, "[D]etermined to concentrate on feature films, Curtis was reluctant to take on the [*Night Stalker*] project — until he read the script.... He had no one but McGavin in mind for the lead.... Shot on location over just 12 days and on a budget of $450,000, the movie drew enough buzz to convince ABC to give it a large promotional push." Curtis related to Johnson and Williams that after hearing the enthusiastic audience reaction at a screening shortly before the film premiered, ABC executive Barry Diller told him, "We should have released this is as a feature."

Another factor affected Curtis's decision to tackle *The Night Stalker*, as he told Dawidziak in *Richard Matheson's Kolchak Scripts* (2003): "Barry told me he had [Richard] Matheson working on the script. Now I thought Matheson was a bloody genius. I always wanted to work with him. So how could you not be sold by [that] combination...? He's just a sensational writer, but I knew he didn't like me because of an offer I made on one of his books.... so I told Diller, 'Matheson hates me,' and I tell him why. And Diller just says, 'I don't care.'" When they met, "Here's this bookish, reserved guy. So I figure I'll break the ice, and I tell him I think he's just the best writer in the whole world. And he just looks at me — nothing. He hardly talks to me. But as we go over notes for the script, he gradually loosens up. I think he liked some of my ideas and saw that I knew what I was talking about. And we went on to do a bunch of other things after that. I have nothing but respect for [Matheson]. He's a wonderful writer with a wonderful creative imagination — an imagination that worked beautifully with the kind of crazy stuff I was doing back then."

In my *Filmfax* interview with Matheson, he called Curtis "very talented. He's a very good writer, he's great on story, and ... he did some wonderful things with stuff that I wrote." He also praised McGavin despite an unfortunate misunderstanding: "When I went to the shooting ... I saw all these colored pages, the change pages, and I thought, 'Oh, my God, there's nothing left of my script,' and I got so infuriated. I was there with my wife and my kids, we were passing through Las Vegas, and I left in a rage, and I didn't express it to anybody, but I guess he heard about it, and thought there was something wrong with me. Then, when I saw the picture, I saw that they hadn't changed it that much.... So there was this thing through the years, and I kept telling people that. Finally he and I were talking on the phone, and we sort of made peace when I explained it to him." According to *Richard Matheson's Kolchak Scripts*, uncredited revisions were made by Rice himself. A comparison between the published script and finished film does reveal the rearrangement of several scenes, plus a significant amount of additional dialogue, much of it between Kolchak and Jenks.

McGavin told Mark Dawidziak in *Night Stalking*, "In the first draft of the script, Kolchak was wearing Bermuda shorts, socks and brown shoes, a Hawaiian shirt and a golf cap. Apparently, somebody thought that was the uniform for a newspaperman in Las Vegas. But there was a line in there about him wanting to get back to New York, so I got this image of a New York newspaperman who had been fired in the summer of 1962 when he was wearing a seersucker suit, his straw hat, button-down Brooks Brothers shirt and reporter's tie, and he hasn't bought any clothes since. Well, I knew that was the summer uniform of reporters in New York of that time, so that's how the wardrobe came about. I added the white tennis shoes, and that was Kolchak. It might have been totally at odds with what everybody else was wearing in Las Vegas, but he hasn't bought any clothes since then. You need goals for characters, and Kolchak's goal is to get back to the big time. He always wanted to get back to New York and work on the *Daily News*."

Certainly, Kolchak remains McGavin's most recognizable role, even after more than 30 years, and for many viewers the two are almost interchangeable. His wife, actress Kathie Browne, said in *Night Stalking*, "He's very, very close to Kolchak. The people who really love *The Night Stalker* love Kolchak because he never gives up. He's fighting, always fighting. You can take the monsters and take them to be anything you want — the government, big business, corrupt officials. Their hero comes out at the end beaten up but ready to go on fighting another day. I think Darren has a lot of that in his own personality." Added Jeff Rice in the same source, "Basically, he was perfect. He didn't have the face of the Kolchak I imagined, but he so quickly merged himself with the character, bringing his own personality to Kolchak's similar one, that he very quickly *became* Kolchak. To create Kolchak for the novel, I'd started with what I imagined I'd look like ten-to-twenty years older and having no beard, only a moustache, and being McGavin's size.... Just watching McGavin work ... was seeing my creation come to life, in the flesh."

The stellar cast of seasoned character actors included legendary tough guy Charles McGraw, the star of Richard Fleischer's *film noir* classic *The Narrow Margin* (1952), as Chief Masterson, and Stanley Adams, a veteran of Matheson's *Twilight Zone* episode "Once Upon a Time." Akins and Atwater had appeared together in Serling's *TZ* entry "The Monsters Are Due on Maple Street" (3/4/60). Many in the cast had previous experience in the genre, most notably Elisha Cook, Jr., a fellow *noir* mainstay from the vintage Humphrey Bogart films *The Maltese Falcon* (1941) and *The Big Sleep* (1946). Cook's half-century in Hollywood encompassed Castle's *House on Haunted Hill*, Corman's *The Haunted Palace*, and Polanski's *Rosemary's Baby* among his hundred-odd feature films. Simon Oakland was widely seen as the psychiatrist at the conclusion of *Psycho*, and Kent Smith had starred in Lewton's *Cat People* and *The Curse of the Cat People*. Ralph Meeker, in a curious coincidence, had enjoyed what was probably the juiciest role of his career as another screen incarnation of Mike Hammer in Robert Aldrich's apocalyptic, genre-bending SF parable *Kiss Me Deadly* (1955).

Guiding this enviable assemblage of talent through Matheson's script was Moxey, who had just worked with McGavin on *The Death of Me Yet* (1971), another well-received telefilm that aired less than three months before *The Night Stalker*. As Moxey told Dawidziak in *Night Stalking*, "I was going to work with Dan [Curtis] on something else. One day, this story was there and we were all excited about it. I read the Jeff Rice book on the beach, and I was pleased. I read Richard Matheson's screenplay, and I was more pleased. I always thought it was going to be a very special piece.... It was one of the better experiences of my career. Everybody just sort of came together in a very happy working team. I believed from the start that we had something very special on our hands. I don't know how much that view was shared by others. I do know we enjoyed making the movie. It was fun — outrageous fun, great joy, and a happy collaboration.... Darren is an actor of immense talent. He brought a spark to that part. He's a very funny man. He has a wry sense of humor, and that's what made the part work. Everybody remembers Darren, but there also was this splendid ensemble of great actors."

Barry Atwater's Skorzeny was one of the screen's most memorable vampires (with green, bloodshot eyes, courtesy of scleral lenses created by Hollywood optometrist Dr. Morton K. Greenspoon). He offered his thoughts on their continued appeal in Donald F. Glut's *The Dracula Book*: "Let's assume the first reason is a desire to root for the underdog. We seem to feel that the vampire is getting a bum shake, getting ganged up on by the intellectuals like Van Helsing; whereas the vampire is not an intellectual, he's working on an emotional basis.... Maybe there's another reason, though, that the vampire is really an evil person. He lives off other people. And I think we would like to live off other people. But we can't because that's considered to be wrong. There are a lot of people living off us, the tax collectors certainly, and the merchants and everybody making a big profit off what we do. And we'd certainly like to have this freedom to go out into the world and feed on other people. It satisfies our fantasies to do that. And yet we know that this is all going to be okay because the vampire is going to be destroyed in the end, good shall prevail and the evil in us is propitiated."

The Night Strangler

(ABC-TV, January 16, 1973) DIRECTOR-PRODUCER: Dan Curtis; TELEPLAY: Matheson, based on some characters created by Jeff Rice; MUSIC: Robert Cobert; MAKEUP: William Tuttle; SPECIAL EFFECTS: Ira Anderson. Color, 74 minutes [broadcast], 90 minutes [syndication, home video and overseas theatrical release]. CAST — Carl Kolchak: Darren McGavin. Louise Harper: Jo Ann Pflug. Tony Vincenzo: Simon Oakland. Dr. Richard Malcolm: Richard Anderson. Capt. Roscoe Schubert: Scott Brady. Titus Berry: Wally Cox. Prof. Hester Crabwell: Margaret Hamilton. Llewellyn Crossbinder: John Carradine.

Tramp: Al Lewis. Gladys Weems (aka Charisma Beauty): Nina Wayne. Wilma Krankheimer: Virginia Peters. Janie Watkins: Kate Murtagh. Dr. Christopher Webb: Ivor Francis. Joyce Gabriel: Diane Shalet. Policewoman Sheila: Anne Randall. Restaurant Woman: Françoise Birnheim. Ethel Parker (aka Merissa): Regina Parton. James Stackhaus (aka Jimmy Stacks): George Tobias [does not appear in televised or home video versions]. Underground Tour Guide: George DiCenzo. Bartender: Bill McLean. Nurse: Dee Carroll. Artist: John Calvin Johnson. Musician: Eddie Quillan. Intern: Bill Michaels. Policemen: Rick Richards, Robert Palmer. Burly Officer: Chuck Hicks. Club Emcee: Roger Shantry. Club Storyteller: William C. Speidel. Club Singer: Joseph Roberts.

The tremendous success of *The Night Stalker* dictated an immediate sequel, with Curtis taking the director's chair himself this time. In creating his original teleplay, Matheson faced a problem that would become even more acute for the writers of the subsequent series. The necessity of finding new antagonists for Kolchak resulted in a restrictive "monster-of-the-week" format, and the series quickly ran through the obvious candidates (e.g., vampire, werewolf, zombie, U.F.O., robot, missing link, witch) in its 20-episode lifespan. "It was trouble enough for me to think up an idea for the second movie, much less an idea every week," Matheson admitted in an interview with me for *Filmfax*. "I remember sitting up at ABC with Jim Greene — he and Allen Epstein [who produced Matheson's *Dying Room Only*] have their own production company now — and Dan Curtis and several other executives, and we were just talking about it: 'Well, what'll we do, shall we make it a werewolf? Shall we make it a vampire?' And I remember saying, 'This is insane, we're a bunch of grown men sitting up here talking about this nonsense!'"

Rehired by Vincenzo and Llewellyn Crossbinder (John Carradine), publisher of the Seattle *Daily Chronicle*, Kolchak covers the death of Merissa (Regina Parton), *née* Ethel Parker, a belly dancer at Omar's Tent, and interviews her colleagues: Charisma Beauty (Nina Wayne), who lives with a butch "husband," Wilma Krankheimer (Virginia Peters), and Louise Harper (Jo Ann Pflug). After a second murder, he learns that each victim lost a small amount of blood through a puncture mark and bore a residue of rotted flesh. Aided by the paper's researcher Titus Berry (Wally Cox, who died weeks after the film premiered), Kolchak discovers that a series of six similar murders has occurred in Pioneer Square, over a period of 18 days, every 21 years since 1889. The culprit is described as a rotting man by Joyce Gabriel (Diane Shalet), who witnessed the third murder. The maniac routs the police after a fourth killing in one of many scenes reminiscent of the original. Prof. Hester Crabwell (Margaret Hamilton) tells Kolchak of the alchemists said to use human blood in their elixir of life, and Charisma (aka Gladys Weems) becomes the strangler's fifth victim.

Kolchak realizes that a photo of Union Army surgeon Richard Malcolm, whose arrival in 1868 followed a similar string of New York killings, matches a portrait of Dr. Malcolm Richards, the founder of a local clinic, but he fails to prevent the sixth murder. He discovers an entrance in the clinic to the Underground City — a trip to which had inspired Matheson's setting — where he finds the body of a tramp (Al Lewis of *The Munsters*) he had met during the Underground Tour, and arrives as Malcolm (Richard Anderson, best known as Oscar Goldman on *The Six Million Dollar Man* and *The Bionic Woman*) is brewing the final dosage of his elixir of life. Kolchak smashes the vial, and the 144-year-old alchemist begins crumbling with age in an expert makeup effect by fellow *Twilight Zone* veteran William Tuttle, then jumps to his death. The luckless reporter is once again silenced and driven from town, along with Louise and the apoplectic Vincenzo, by yet another representative of the local constabulary, Capt. Roscoe Schubert (Scott Brady).

"Actually," adds Matheson, "I wanted to make the guy in the second one Jack the Ripper, who was still alive and had come over to this country, but I'm a friend of Robert Bloch's, and I called him and asked him if it would disturb him if I did that [because of his story "Yours Truly, Jack the Ripper"], and I could sense that he felt that it would, so I didn't do it. Then of course right afterward, on *The Sixth Sense*, they did the same thing anyway ["With Affection, Jack the Ripper" (10/14/72)], but at least I didn't do it." The very first episode of the *Night Stalker* series, "The Ripper" (9/13/74), did feature the notorious Saucy Jack, who is still plying his gruesome trade in the modern-day era, and as noted, Rice also devotes an appendix to him in *The Kolchak Papers*. Rice explains, "Next to Janos Skorzeny, I think Jack the Ripper is one of history's most fascinating villains. Kolchak appears to have been particularly fascinated by the stories of this killer. The material he amassed was far too lengthy to include in a book this size, and he indicated he had hopes, some day, of doing such a book from the viewpoint of a Victorian-era reporter 'on the scene.'"*

"Dan did a marvelous job with [the sequel]," Matheson told Dawidziak in *Night Stalking*. "The whole thing had a great feel to it. A lot of people who do sequels just don't want to be bothered. We were still keyed up and in tune with the characters, and we had fun doing it. And it was Dan's first directing job in a TV film, so he really poured himself into it to show what he could do. I added even more humor to it than we had in the first one.... Richard Anderson was just wonderful as Malcolm. He had a wonderful way of suggesting a quiet power. There was a tremendous dignity to his portrayal. He made the monster very human." Added Curtis, "In most of my horror films, I try to find an additional dimension to the monster. Sometimes you actually end up feeling sorry for him. We certainly did that with Barnabas [who became *Dark Shadows'* de facto hero].... Now that really wasn't possible for Janos Skorzeny, mostly because he doesn't talk and he's not on camera that much. And he's not the central character in *The Night Stalker*. Kolchak is. But that was more of a possibility with Richard Anderson's character. Let's see what makes him tick."

In an interview with Jonathan Etter for *Filmfax*, Anderson enthused, "Liked that. A guy that ... resuscitates himself.... *Night Strangler* was a great opportunity to do some heavy makeup. We shot it in a house on Pacific Coast Highway that still sits there. It's a huge mansion. It's eerie. That was a good, good part. Worked with McGavin. Bill Tuttle, as a matter of fact, was the makeup artist on that, and I worked with Bill six years at Metro-Goldwyn-Mayer. It took them hours to apply this makeup [*sounding exhausted*]. Hours! Felt like I was back doing a Universal horror picture." Anderson also played the lead in *Curse of the Faceless Man* (1958) and appeared in such acclaimed films as Stanley Kubrick's *Paths of Glory* (1957) and John Frankenheimer's *Seven Days in May* (1964) and *Seconds* (1966), as well as on the genre series *Thriller*, *The Alfred Hitchcock Hour*, and *Darkroom*.

The sequel's inevitable similarity to *The Night Stalker* was heightened by airing it within days of that film's anniversary, changing its working title of *Time Killer*, and recycling

---

*Originally published in the July 1943 issue of Lovecraft's longtime outlet *Weird Tales*, Bloch's story was one of several adapted into episodes of *Thriller* before he himself began contributing scripts to the series. Directed by Ray Milland and written by Barré Lyndon, "Yours Truly, Jack the Ripper" (4/11/61) starred distinguished British thespian John Williams. While the villain in *The Night Strangler* is not the Ripper, the two teleplays do bear several similarities: Both invoke the ageless alchemist, the Comte de St. Germain, and involve regularly recurring series of six identical murders, dating back to the 19th century, by killers who retain their youth with their victims' blood (in the Ripper's case as sacrifices to "the dark gods"). Lyndon also scripted *The Lodger* with Laird Cregar—fresh from starring in a CBS radio version of Bloch's story on *The Kate Smith Hour*—as the Ripper. *The Man in Half Moon Street* (1944) filmed that same year and based on Lyndon's play, was about a physician kept youthful with periodic glandular transplants. It was remade by Hammer as *The Man Who Could Cheat Death* (1959).

much of the original's effectively eerie score by Curtis's longtime collaborator, Robert Cobert. Interestingly, the customarily colorful supporting cast includes characters with obvious antecedents in Rice's novel. Vincenzo's immediate superior in *The Kolchak Papers*, for example, is the newspaper's fearsome managing editor Llewellyn Cairncross, who tells Kolchak, "For years I have suspected you were mentally deranged and now I have confirmation of that suspicion," which would sound perfectly at home coming from John Carradine, playing Llewellyn Crossbinder in his third Matheson teleplay. Likewise, Rice's Kolchak obtains his research materials from Dr. Kirsten Helms, who heads the humanities department at the University of Nevada at Las Vegas, and whose feisty, acid-tongued character is perfectly personified as *The Night Strangler*'s Prof. Hester Crabwell by Margaret Hamilton, iconic as Miss Gulch and the Wicked Witch of the West from *The Wizard of Oz* (1939).

This literary cross-pollination reached its *ne plus ultra* when Pocket Books published not only a revised and reworked version of *The Kolchak Papers* (suitably retitled *The Night Stalker*), but also a novelization of *The Night Strangler* by none other than Jeff Rice, which at a mere 150 pages is even thinner than the original. "I don't think they're as big as they

used to be," Matheson said of novelizations in general, in an interview with me for *Filmfax*. "It's kind of silly, it's like merchandising, like making a toy of a Ninja Turtle, that's all. You're making a book, and you hope you make a few extra bucks out of it. I would think it would be pretty easy, because you have the whole script there, you would just sort of put yourself on automatic and turn it into past tense and get the novel. But most writers, they want to do more, they really want to turn it into a novel, which to me is a waste of time. You might as well just do the script in past tense." Rice understandably makes little attempt to embellish upon Matheson's script, apart from a characteristically lengthy digression on the subject of alchemy, and an appendix into which he playfully inserts a work written by "Kirsten Helms."

An uneasy Carl Kolchak (Darren McGavin, left) is welcomed by ageless alchemist Dr. Richard Malcolm (Richard Anderson) in *The Night Strangler* (ABC-TV, 1973).

In *Richard Matheson's Kolchak Scripts*, Dawidziak

notes, "When the twelve-day shoot was completed, Curtis realized he had filmed enough footage for a two-hour movie — without commercials. He had hoped for a two-hour time slot, so the editing process wouldn't be too brutal. The network wouldn't budge past 90 minutes. The *Night Strangler* that premiered in January 1973, therefore, was an incredibly abbreviated version. All of the scenes with the tramp ... including the one where Kolchak discovers his body, were dropped. The rundown on alchemy ... was reduced to a few lines. And the tour of the Seattle underground led by young George DiCenzo was cut to almost nothing." These and additional scenes with labor reporter Janie Watkins (Kate Murtagh), who originated in *The Kolchak Papers* as Janie Carlson, were restored in a 90-minute version for syndication, home video, and overseas theatrical release. Included in some cast lists is James Stackhaus (George Tobias), aka "Jimmy Stacks," a reporter alluded to in Kolchak's dialogue with Berry. According to Dawidziak, the footage of his interview with Kolchak about the '30s killings appears to be irretrievably lost.

Rice said in *Richard Matheson's Kolchak Scripts* that *The Night Strangler* is "basically a rehash of the first Kolchak film," and this was echoed by McGavin: "When ABC wanted to do another *Night Stalker*, Dan literally redid the first one in another town. You know what the problem with a sequel is? They don't know how to make a sequel with the character, so what they do is take the formula and redo it. That's why I didn't like *Night Strangler* that much. If you run the two movies consecutively, you say to yourself, 'Wait a minute, I just saw that?' And that's why I didn't want to do a third one at the time. I suppose, as TV movies go, it's all very good, but it was ... like we'd done it before." In fact, a third Kolchak telefilm was scripted but never shot, as Matheson told Dawidziak in his *Vampires and Slayers* interview: "I was a little surprised to get the call. McGavin and Curtis had had a falling out [during the shooting of *The Night Strangler* in Seattle], and I wasn't sure they'd work together again. But ABC wanted a third Kolchak movie and Dan wanted to do it. I really had a lot on my plate at the time, so I asked a friend of mine to work on it with me.

"William F. Nolan and I wrote a third script called *The Night Killers*. It was set in Hawaii, and it was dandy, real dandy. I don't know why they didn't go ahead with it. It was a neat premise for the time. Key politicians were being killed off and replaced by lookalike androids. That was the basic idea. It was very fresh in 1973, but it has been used interminably since. It was a very funny, very fast script, and I tried to talk Dan into making it a number of times." He was also offered the job of story editor on the series, as he had been with *Night Gallery*, but declined in both cases. "I didn't have much interest in that. If Dan had done the series, I would have done the series. When I learned that he didn't have involvement in it, I decided not to have involvement in it. Frankly, I was sort of relieved. We'd had so much trouble coming up with a story for *The Night Strangler*. But that was so tough that I couldn't imagine how they could come up with a new monster every week. They did come up with some interesting ones, I thought, but egocentric though it may sound, since Dan and I weren't involved in the series, I'll say that it missed two of the key building blocks."

The Night Killers was one of several unrealized collaborations with Nolan, including *Ali Baba and the Seven Marvels of the World*, written for AIP. "We worked out the 7,000-word story treatment in July of 1961," Nolan wrote in a 2005 letter to me. Next, "we were hired as a team by Columbia studios [in 1962] to adapt Jack Finney's novel *Assault on a Queen* for filming. We found it so incredible that we turned it into a 13,000-word screen comedy, delivering the treatment [*Under the Bounding Main*] to Columbia in the spring of '62. They didn't agree on the comic approach — and it was later turned over to Rod Serling who [in 1966] did a 'serious' version (which *bombed* at the box office)." Ironically, Serling biographer Gordon F. Sander notes that among his abortive film projects of the 1960s was "*Gresham's People*, later retitled *The 'R' Project*, a *Frankenstein*-like story about a military man who invents a race of robots in an attempt to end war, [which] was eventually assigned to Richard Matheson, to Serling's dismay." In 1968, Matheson also rewrote *The Last Revolution*, a script adapted by Serling from Lord Dunsany's novel, for producer George Pal; neither project was produced.

Nolan relates that their next effort "started in January of '62 when Matheson drove down to my motel in Palm Springs (where I was working on another project) to plot out *Double, Double*. The plot was based on some real-life experiences of mine in which I had used the name 'Frank Anmar.' (Don't recall exactly what they were!) When we finished the screenplay [written between July and December of 1962], our agent took it to Abbey Greshler ... who was then repping Tony Randall. We felt it would be a perfect screen vehicle for Randall (in the *Pillow Talk* [1959] mode). Greshler seemed to like it, but it never went anywhere. We were never sure that Randall ever *saw* the script. Matheson tried to re-sell it to Hollywood, via another agent, many years later — but no dice." As Nolan lamented in *Richard Matheson's Kolchak Scripts*, "You never get accustomed to things falling apart. It's emotionally and financially devastating. It's a knife to the heart every time it happens. It's always a terrible blow when it happens, and it does happen plenty of times. TV and film writing just drives you crazy. It's a maddening life. The books and stories are what keep you sane."

Matheson later turned the *Ali Baba* treatment into an award-winning children's book, *Abu and the 7 Marvels* (2001). He noted in a joint interview with famed fantasy artist William Stout (who illustrated both *Abu* and Matheson's *Collected Stories*), conducted by Lisa DuMond for scifi.com's *Science Fiction Weekly*, "It was 40 years ago when the idea of writing a children's novel came to me. Actually, it was intended to be a full-length cartoon, and the story was prepared by me and William F. Nolan.... Nothing has been changed. It's exactly the way it was when I wrote it." Unfortunately, Nolan's shared credit for the original story was accidentally omitted from the published book. Added Stout, "*Abu* is a natural for the big screen. It's got monsters, heroes, exoticism, humor, fantasy, thrills, adventure, spectacle, a quest and a true-love romance.... I think that with today's cinematic technology being what it is that *Abu* could work superbly as either a full-length live-action or animated feature film."

Nolan noted in his *Filmfax* interview with me that his own association with Curtis had begun through Matheson: "[He] told me in 1971 that I should contact Dan. Curtis had just come out to California from New York after his vampire soap opera, *Dark Shadows*, finally wound down. We hit it off right away; he asked me to write a movie of the week for him, *The Norliss Tapes* ... [which] was my first major credit and launched my scripting career." Following a successful telecast, however, NBC's proposed series was scuttled by a writers' strike. "He's wild," added Nolan of Curtis, with whom he later collaborated on *The Turn of the Screw* (1974), *Melvin Purvis, G-Man* (1974) and its sequel *The Kansas City Massacre* (1975), and one of Curtis's few features, *Burnt Offerings* (1976). "I once described him in an article as 'a tall, curly-haired, fierce-eyed man with a toothy wolf's smile who thrives on crisis.' Most of what Dan says is delivered in a shout. He bellows over the phone, yells down the hall to his secretary, shouts at his production crew. We work well together because I refuse to be cowed by him; when he yells at me, I yell back. So we get along."

The Norliss Tapes (1973) — to which Nolan wrote an unproduced sequel, *The Return* — featured Roy Thinnes, who had starred in the 1960s cult SF series *The Invaders* and would later appear on Curtis's short-lived prime-time *Dark Shadows* revival, plus such familiar faces from Kolchak's world as Claude Akins (once again playing a skeptical sheriff), George DiCenzo, and Stanley Adams. Thinnes played a writer investigating the supernatural, and the Kolchak similarities don't stop there, because according to Dawidziak, one of *The Night Stalker*'s working titles was *The Kolchak Tapes*. (It was changed by ABC to avoid any possible confusion with Sidney Lumet's recent feature *The Anderson Tapes* [1971].) Curtis once again directed and produced, as he was to have done on *The Night Killers*; the latter saw the light of day at last, on the printed page if not on the screen, when it was finally published after thirty years in *Richard Matheson's Kolchak Scripts*.

"Here we go again," Kolchak aptly mutters as he rejoins Tony Vincenzo and Llewellyn Crossbinder at the *Honolulu Daily Tribune* and is assigned to a career feature on the late Lieutenant Governor Ronald Tawakami, one of six people killed in a freak explosion attributed to a "random spark," said to have ignited a leaking oxygen canister in the emergency room of Kuakini Hospital. The death or disappearance, in quick succession, of an anesthetics technician who survived the blast, the nurse in charge of his room, the ambulance attendants who picked up Tawakami the night of his car crash, and Tawakami's widow, who insists that he had changed radically over the past month, put the dogged reporter onto the trail of an impassive, white-uniformed killer in a red truck. Kolchak is reassigned to a flying saucer story by Crossbinder after running afoul of local Police Chief Mac McFarlin; he soon realizes that both stories are one and the same when he discovers a plot by alien invaders to establish a beachhead on Earth, by replacing the leadership of Hawaii with nuclear-powered android duplicates that — like the ersatz Tawakami — explode whenever they are damaged.

Nolan included *The Night Killers* in his collection *Night Shapes* (1995), but was then forced to drop it from the published book in the proof stage because Rice controls the print rights to the character of Kolchak. In his unpublished preface to the script, Nolan wrote, "Late in 1973 I drafted a 100-page version of the script in seven days. Matheson then took over, writing the final, network-approved draft. Everyone loved our teleplay, and it received a 'green light' for production — to be shot entirely on location in Hawaii. I was set to go along in order to handle any scenes that might need revision.... With everything in place for the shoot, we were within a week of leaving for Hawaii when, as the saying goes, the roof caved in. Our movie of the week had been cancelled in favor of a new weekly series, *Kolchak: The Night Stalker*. And Dan Curtis, Nolan, and Matheson were suddenly out of the Kolchak business. After this, although we retained our close friendship, Rich and I decided to go our separate ways as writers. There would be no further collaborations." Nolan did, however, adapt Matheson's "Slaughter House" (first published in *Weird Tales* in July of 1953) into an unproduced teleplay in 1975.

In *Richard Matheson's Kolchak Scripts*, Curtis contradicts any notion that his production team was on the verge of departing for Hawaii: "Absolutely not, no way. We never had a go. We never got that far. The script was finished, but getting McGavin on board would have been a real problem, anyway, because he and I ended up not even speaking to each other after *Night Strangler*." Dawidziak also suggests that McGavin, already bothered by the similarity between the first two teleplays, was unhappy with *The Night Killers*. "I'd never heard that McGavin didn't like the script," Nolan told Dawidziak. "I also hadn't heard about any fight between Darren and Dan. Not that it surprises me. Dan will tell you he's not in it to win any popularity contests. But Richard and I got along with him because we always shared a lot of laughter. To say we never had an angry word would be untrue, but 95 percent of the time, we got along fine." According to Dawidziak, parallel negotiations had been underway for either a third telefilm (and possible pilot) or an ABC weekly series, produced by Universal, and studio president Sid Sheinberg prevailed with the latter.

While McGavin and Oakland were as entertaining as ever, the series lasted for only a single season (1974–75) of 20 episodes, four of which were later cobbled together into the *faux* telefilms *Crackle of Death* and *Demon and the Mummy* (both 1976). As a characteristically blunt Curtis told Mark Dawidziak in *Night Stalking*, "You can't do that each week. It was a disaster. It was a terrible show. It deserved to be quickly off the air." The title — given simply as *The Night Stalker* for the first four episodes, and then expanded to *Kolchak: The Night Stalker* — presented a problem of identification akin to that of William Powell's character of Nick Charles in *The Thin Man* (1934) and its sequels, with the title of *The Night Strangler* only reinforcing the notion of Skorzeny, and not Kolchak, as the original's eponymous stalker. The only direct link with the original film came in the fourth episode, "The Vampire" (10/4/74), in the form of a beautiful bloodsucker, presumably a previously unknown victim of Skorzeny's, who carves a bloody path from Las Vegas to Los Angeles before Kolchak stakes her.

The series featured an interesting assemblage of creative talent, ranging from genre veterans Gordon Hessler and Jimmy Sangster to up-and-coming writers such as Robert Zemeckis and Bob Gale, Oscar nominees for *Back to the Future* (1985); Michael Kozoll, the Emmy-winning co-creator of *Hill Street Blues*; and story editor David Chase, who created the HBO Mafia phenomenon *The Sopranos*. Killed by a combination of low ratings, an arduous production schedule, and a frustrated star who aspired to produce, it upheld the strong casting tradition of the telefilms, with Larry Linville and Stanley Adams in new roles and a steady stream of police plaguing Kolchak: Charles Aidman, James Gregory, William Daniels, Philip Carey, Keenan Wynn, John Marley, John Dehner, and even Kathie Browne. The keeper of the Kolchak flame, Dawidziak has penned the Kolchak novel *Grave Secrets* (1994) and served as a creative consultant for the Moonstone comic-book series *Kolchak: The Night Stalker*, which featured adaptations of the original TV-movie (by Rice himself) and of Don Mullally's "The Get of Belial," one of two teleplays in development when ABC reduced its order from 22 episodes to 20.

Kolchak's long-range impact includes the acknowledged inspiration for the Fox series *The X-Files*, which more successfully leavened the original monster-of-the-week format with an intricate web of governmental conspiracies, and even gave FBI special agent Fox Mulder (David Duchovny) a Congressional contact in the person of "Senator Richard Matheson." Soon after the senator (Raymond J. Barry) was introduced in the second-season premiere "Little Green Men" (9/16/94), the writer had a transport ship named after him in a second-season episode of another SF series, J. Michael Straczynski's *Babylon 5* ("A Spider in the Web" [12/7/94]), and later a regular character, Lt. John Matheson (Daniel Dae Kim), on its short-lived spin-off, *Crusade*. While a Kolchak cameo never materialized, McGavin did appear on *The X-Files* as the recurring character of Arthur Dales, a retired FBI agent from the McCarthy era, and on its sister show, *Millennium*, as the estranged father of Frank Black (Lance Henriksen) in "Midnight of the Century" (12/19/97). *X-Files* veteran Frank Spotnitz later developed a *Night Stalker* revival that was quickly cancelled by ABC.

An earlier, albeit short-lived, Fox series, *Werewolf*, had borrowed the name of Janos Skorzeny for an eponymous lycanthrope, played by Chuck Connors; *The Night Stalker* likewise inspired the founders of a second upstart broadcast network, the WB, to create one of its own biggest hits, Joss Whedon's *Buffy the Vampire Slayer*, which also spawned a spin-off, *Angel*, and relocated to yet another young and hungry network, UPN, in its final seasons.

As *X-Files* creator Chris Carter (who also provided an affectionate afterword to *Richard Matheson's Kolchak Scripts*) told *TV Guide*'s Johnson and Williams, "That character of Kolchak as the hysterical outsider left an impression on me. I carried it with me, knowing I wanted to do something in that vein, ever since I was a kid."

The Legend of Hell House

(Academy Pictures–20th Century–Fox [U.S./G.B.], released June 15, 1973) DIRECTOR: John Hough; PRODUCER: Albert Fennell, Norman T. Herman; SCREENPLAY: Matheson, based on his *Hell House*; MUSIC: Brian Hodgson, Delia Derbyshire; MAKEUP: Linda Devetta; SPECIAL EFFECTS: Roy Whybrow. Color, 94 minutes. CAST— Florence Tanner: Pamela Franklin. Benjamin Fischer: Roddy McDowall. Dr. Lionel Barrett: Clive Revill. Ann Barrett: Gayle Hunnicutt. Rolf Rudolph Deutsch: Roland Culver. Hanley: Peter Bowles. Emeric Belasco: Michael Gough.

Matheson adapted *The Legend of Hell House* from his eighth published novel, his first in the decade since *The Beardless Warriors*. "It took me ten years to finish *Hell House* [1971]," he told James H. Burns in the interview quoted in *He Is Legend*. "Ray Russell told me that *Hell House* read like it was written by three different writers. It probably was, considering how long I took to complete it." He elaborated on its background in Stanley Wiater's book *Dark Dreamers*: "I had so much other work to do out here [in Hollywood] that I would put it aside, then go back to it. It doesn't sound like much money, compared to what they're paying for books now, but at the time I had gotten a $5,000 advance, and I was too cheap to give it back [*laughs*]. Even though I just wanted to drop the whole project — so I just kept laboring at it through the years. The first version of *Hell House* that I submitted was told in the first person — each of the characters writing their own story. Which is kind of interesting, but it's very difficult — if not impossible — to get suspense that way.... You know that no matter what they go through, they already got through it, because they're writing the book!"

Its lengthy gestation period aside, *Hell House* remains one of Matheson's most commercially and critically successful works. Rod Serling raved in a jacket blurb, "I thoroughly enjoyed *Hell House*. The class, flair and style of Matheson shine through every page, and it's unquestionably the best of anything that he's done to date." Contemporary critics concurred, calling the novel "a fine horror story ... a walloping good book of its kind" (*The New York Times Book Review*) and "a shocking book, totally absorbing in its progression, brutally compelling in its conclusion" (*Best Sellers*). Its reputation has not suffered over the years: According to Stephen King, "*Hell House* may be the scariest haunted house novel ever written — it looms over the rest the way a mountain looms over foothills.... If you're planning to read it at night, lock the doors before you start." Peter Straub, the bestselling author of *Ghost Story, Floating Dragon, Koko* and others, who also collaborated with King on *The Talisman* and its sequel, *Black House*, notes, "*Hell House* is one of the absolute best contemporary horror novels, and has been one of my own favorites since I first read it. It's jumpy and scary and full of invention."

As its title suggests, *Hell House* evokes Shirley Jackson's *The Haunting of Hill House* and Robert Wise's film version, *The Haunting* (1963); each concerns an assault on an infamous haunted house by a quartet of psychic investigators, including a scientist and two sensitives. *The Haunting* displays Val Lewton's influence, Wise rigorously eschewing any visual manifestations — demonstrating his mentor's principle that what is unseen is most terrifying.

Benjamin Fischer (Roddy McDowall), Dr. Lionel Barrett (Clive Revill), Ann Barrett (Gayle Hunnicutt), and Florence Tanner (Pamela Franklin) arrive at the Belasco House in *The Legend of Hell House* (Academy Pictures–20th Century–Fox, 1973).

Conversely, the horrors of *Hell House* were not only overt but also extremely graphic for the time. "My intention was to write a haunted house novel," Matheson told Douglas E. Winter, "and once I had set the premise that this was the most horrible haunted house in existence, I couldn't very well do otherwise than make it as horrific as I could. I had to let out all the stops. To say that this is the most evil house in the world, and then to have leprechauns running around, would have been silly."

As in Henry James's "The Turn of the Screw," Jackson's *The Haunting of Hill House* leaves open the question of whether the "haunting" was truly supernatural or sprang from the mind of her sexually repressed female protagonist, who is portrayed in the film by Julie Harris. "There certainly was a connection between my book and Shirley Jackson's," Matheson confirmed in a letter to me. "I think I did it deliberately. I always wanted to write a haunted house novel and I ultimately found myself dissatisfied with the 'maybe it was, maybe it wasn't' explanation in *The Haunting of Hill House* although [*The Haunting*] was a very scary film indeed; one of the three scariest (most shocking anyway) moments in my film memory came in that one when the wife's face suddenly appeared in the ceiling trapdoor. The other two, if you're curious, are in *Jaws* when, while Brody is throwing chum into the water and kvetching to Quint, the shark suddenly leaps out of the water; the third is when the husband's dead body sits up in the bathtub in the French *Diabolique* [1955]. In all three cases, I felt myself lurch backward in my movie theater seat. However, I did find the idea that everything was, maybe, caused by the Julie Harris character not satisfying to me and I decided that, in my haunted house novel, I would have it *really* haunted by really-truly ghosts — at least one anyway."

Like *The Shrinking Man*, *Hell House* made a quick transition from page to screen. It opens with a testimonial from Tom Corbett, "Clairvoyant and Psychic Consultant to European Royalty," who also served as its technical advisor; he asserted that "the events depicted involving psychic phenomena are not only very much within the bounds of possibility, but could well be true." Like the novel, the film utilizes the documentary-style device of periodically noting the date and time: In a pre-credit sequence set on Friday, December 17 (the year is not specified, although it is given as 1970 in the novel), physicist Lionel Barrett (Clive Revill) is offered £100,000 by newspaper and magazine publisher Rolf Rudolph Deutsch (Roland Culver) "to establish the facts [regarding] survival after death" by investigating the notorious Belasco House. Sealed up for 20 years, "Hell House" has been sold by the cash-poor Belasco family to Deutsch, who imposes a one-week deadline and has also hired a mental medium, Florence Tanner (Pamela Franklin), and the only survivor from the prior attempt, Benjamin Fischer (Roddy McDowall).

"It's the Mount Everest of haunted houses," Barrett tells his wife and assistant Ann (Gayle Hunnicutt), noting that eight people were killed during the two previous investigations, and that "when [Fischer] crawled out he was a mental wreck." (Nancy A. Collins chronicled Fischer's earlier visit in "Return to Hell House," an ambitious prequel written for *He Is Legend*.) Considered one of the five best in his field, Barrett has spent 20 years studying parapsychology and arranges for Deutsch's secretary, Hanley (Peter Bowles), to hire enough electronics experts for the hasty completion of the Reversor, a machine that will represent his crowning achievement, proving the theory that ghostly manifestations are really caused by an energy field that can be measured and reversed. Heard over the opening titles and sparingly used thereafter, the evocative electronic score by Brian Hodgson and Delia Derbyshire of Electrophon Ltd. helps set the proper mood, as do the atmospheric shots by Alan Hume — a Hammer and Amicus veteran who later photographed several Bond films — of the team entering the fog-enshrouded Hell House, its windows bricked up, on the morning of the 20th.

Over dinner, Fischer relates the unsavory history of multi-millionaire Emeric Belasco, born the illegitimate son of an American munitions maker in 1879; he built the house in 1919 and disappeared after a decade of debauchery and depravity such as "drug addiction, alcoholism, sadism, bestiality, mutilation, murder, vampirism, necrophilia, cannibalism — not to mention a gamut of sexual goodies." Believing that the haunting force is not the house itself but multiple surviving personalities, Florence tries a sitting that night. She manifests physical phenomena (e.g., pounding noises), despite being a mental rather than a physical medium like Fischer, and speaks in the voice of a young man, who begs them to get out of the house, saying, "I don't want to hurt you, but I must." The next morning, Florence tells Barrett that the unseen young man, who has begun visiting her in her bedroom, is Belasco's frightened and angry son Daniel, and that persuading him to move on will eliminate much of the haunting force. After a violent poltergeist attack during which Barrett is slightly injured, Fischer warns her that she is being used, and should leave Hell House.

Florence seeks proof of Daniel's existence, which she finds in the form of a skeleton walled up in chains inside the wine cellar. Under the house's influence, Ann tries to seduce Fischer, and in a scene prefiguring Frank De Felitta's novel and 1981 film *The Entity*, Florence is apparently raped by the spirit of Daniel, which she believes Belasco is manipulating. "It preceded *The Exorcist*," Matheson said of his novel in an interview with me for the Gauntlet limited edition, "which had a lot of sex in it.... My other ghost story [*Earthbound* (1982)] had some eroticism in it, too, but it was just a matter of necessity. I don't usually write that stuff in my novels.... Once you've set the concept, the premise, you've got to stay with it, even if it means you're gonna end up writing stuff you never wrote before. Or will write again." Written shortly before *Hell House* was completed but unsold for more than a decade (and first published under the Swanson pen name), *Earthbound* concerns a married couple menaced by a succubus-like "earthbound spirit" that first seduces the husband, then possesses the wife. "There again," said Matheson, "it was a story that had largely to do with sex, so I had to be honest about it."

Intending to take the money and run, Fischer has deliberately blocked himself off from Hell House's emanations, and advises Florence to do the same if she values her life and sanity. But by Friday, Christmas Eve, Barrett is ready to dissipate the destructive mental and physical residual energy with a massive counter-charge of electromagnetic radiation (EMR) from the Reversor. Florence makes an attempt to wreck the Reversor and then is crushed by a crucifix when she goes to the chapel to warn Daniel, drawing a "B" in a circle with her own blood to indicate that it was only one entity — Belasco — all along. Barrett is found dead under a chandelier beside her after what at first seems to be a successful "exorcism." This leaves Fischer and Ann to solve the riddle of Hell House. Finding the perfectly preserved body of the so-called "Roaring Giant" inside a lead-sheathed vault that shielded it from the EMR, Fischer discovers "that which Belasco's giant ego could not face: He so despised his own shortness that he had both his legs cut off and wore [prostheses] instead to give himself height." With his secret revealed, the house is cleared with another burst from the Reversor.

In his essay on the film in *Cinematic Hauntings*, Robert Alan Crick points out that when their bodies are found, both Barrett and a cat that had attacked Florence (possessed, she says, by Daniel) have been blinded in one eye, tying in with the "if thine eye offend thee, pluck it out" motif. This detail is not specified in Matheson's published script, included in Richard Chizmar's collection *Screamplays*. There are several significant differences between this script and the finished film, such as a number of elements from the novel that appear in the screenplay but not the film and vice versa. Among the former is the character of William Reinhardt Deutsch, who considers Barrett a fraud and, at the climax of the story, makes good on his threat to withhold the promised payment when his elderly father abruptly dies. In all three versions, Barrett is astounded when evidence of renewed EMR activity in the apparently cleared house begins to register on his instruments, one of which explodes and showers him with metal splinters. But both novel and screenplay then depict him being attacked by an unseen force that breaks his legs and drags him down to the steam room rather than in the chapel.

A still reproduced on the laserdisc jacket apparently shows the Barretts in the steam room, suggesting that an earlier scene from the novel in which Ann — once again under the house's influence — tries to initiate sex with Lionel, and then mocks him for the impotence he suffers from due to polio, was shot but discarded. The unsigned liner notes offer an eerie epilogue: "Hough ... asked Corbett to find him an actual haunted

Barrett conducts a sitting with Florence as Ann observes in *The Legend of Hell House* (Academy Pictures–20th Century–Fox, 1973).

house, and was pointed to Wykehurst Park, [which was also] built by a wealthy industrialist. But the similarities went further. Corbett claimed that the walk leading up to the front door was haunted by the ghost of a man in a frock coat. 'Who or what he is I do not know,' the psychic reported, 'but I see him walking agitatedly up to the door and then vanishing.'"

Given the novel's commercial success and Matheson's parallel screenwriting career, it was only natural that he should adapt *Hell House* for the screen, but he was forced to sell the project after an abortive attempt to set up his own production. He explained in a letter to me, "Actually, I was in the process of planning a film on the novel with Stanley Chase but nothing came of it. I recall talking to Richard Sarafian about directing it. Could have been great. Not that it wasn't well done, of course." Chase had previously produced Matheson's episode of *Bob Hope Presents the Chrysler Theatre*, "Time of Flight," as well as one of his personal favorite genre films, the aforementioned *Colossus: The Forbin Project* (based on the novel *Colossus* by D.F. Jones), both of which were directed by Joseph Sargent. As fate would have it, the screen version of *Hell House* ultimately reunited Matheson with his long-time advocate at American International, James H. Nicholson, who was then ending his almost 20-year relationship with Samuel Z. Arkoff to set up a new company in England, Academy Pictures, and wound up as the film's executive producer.

Nicholson's widow Susan Hart (who appeared in Tourneur's *City Under the Sea*) explained in *Attack of the Monster Movie Makers*: "He left AIP because his hands were tied in many respects. He had become an executive more than a filmmaker. He was very creative, he was always a hands-on type of guy as far as production was concerned. He knew what to make, how to make it, how to sell it, and had original ideas for what came next.... [But] *other parties* got involved in his bailiwick. When that happened, I believe he lost his enthusiasm for working with those people who attempted to take away his expertise. Mr. Arkoff began hiring many people at [AIP] at very large salaries, to do the very things that Jim Nicholson could do with his eyes closed. He was able to do this because, when Jim Nicholson got his divorce from Sylvia Nicholson to marry [me], he also gave up a lot of his stock, which put Sam Arkoff in the driver's seat in so far as the amount of stock held was concerned. So he allowed Sam Arkoff to do the driving, and I don't know how long AIP lasted after he left.... He made a five-picture deal with [Fox]; I think he was one of the first producers that they allowed complete autonomy."

In *Flying Through Hollywood By the Seat of My Pants*, Arkoff offered his own version of events: "Jim told me he was leaving AIP, with plans to become an independent producer. 'I figure I'll produce a couple pictures a year, and have more leisure time,' he said. 'I've worked since I was a kid. It's time to slow down a bit.' I tried to talk Jim into staying. 'Why don't you make the pictures you want to produce here at AIP?' I told him. But he felt it was time for a change of scenery.... Even after Jim left American International, he and I still met frequently. We remained general partners in a trust over a large number of pictures that we had produced." Nicholson's first feature (which according to Arkoff had previously been in development at AIP) would also be his last; he died of a malignant brain tumor at the age of 56 on December 10, 1972, six months before its release.

The Legend of Hell House was produced by Albert Fennell and Norman T. Herman. In the decade since the former had made Matheson's *Night of the Eagle*, a veritable generation of his *Avengers* colleagues had graduated from that stylishly influential, genre-blending British series to make their marks as fantasy filmmakers (e.g., Peter Duffell, Peter Sykes), often working with Fennell. Examples include Robert Fuest and Roy Ward Baker, who directed *And Soon the Darkness* (1970) and Hammer's *Dr. Jekyll and Sister Hyde* (1971), respectively; writer-producer Brian Clemens, who worked on both, as well as Hammer's *Kronos* (aka *Captain Kronos: Vampire Hunter*, 1974); and *Hell House* director John Hough, whose first feature was *Wolfshead: The Legend of Robin Hood* (1969). Hough made his genre debut with the conclusion of Hammer's Karnstein trilogy, *Twins of Evil* (1971), also directing an undistinguished international production of *Treasure Island* (1972), Academy's *Dirty Mary, Crazy Larry* (which Hart stated "was Fox's biggest grosser in 1974 and it helped finance *Star Wars*"), and the Disney films *Escape to Witch Mountain* (1975) and *The Watcher in the Woods* (1980).

Pamela Franklin hardly fit the novel's description of a tall, Junoesque woman almost twice her age (in the film, Barrett objects to her participation because "she's practically a child"). But her genre credentials were impeccable, having made her debut opposite Martin Stephens as the haunted children in *The Innocents*. She had previously appeared in Hammer's *The Nanny* and Clayton's *Our Mother's House* (1967), and bracketed her role in *Hell House* with two more for the infamous Bert I. Gordon in *Necromancy* (1972) and *The Food of the Gods* (1976). "On *Hell House*," she told Ted Newsom in *Femme Fatales*, "I was already here in California, and married. I was 21 or 22 at that time. The film itself was shot in England, so I went back over there to do it. That was wonderful, because I had worked with [Fennell] on *The Innocents* and he'd also done ... *And Soon the Darkness*. I always called it *Two Dykes on a Bike*. So *Hell House* was the third thing I did for him. It was a good experience. I enjoyed that, especially having worked in America for a while, it was refreshing to go back over there."

Franklin, who had earned a BAFTA Film Award nomination as Best Supporting Actress in *The Prime of Miss Jean Brodie* (1969), discussed her brief nudity with Newsom. "It wasn't embarrassing, because I was too young to know any better. And second of all, it was done in such a nice way. There, again, is the difference between English and American pictures. Everybody did nudity in England. It was just one of those things. And it was done very nicely. They closed the set off, there were no visitors running around. Mostly, you'd look up and see people reading a newspaper, you know. If other people aren't uncomfortable with it, then you're not uncomfortable with it. It was the same with *Brodie*.... Roddy

McDowall was fine. I didn't socialize with him too much. He got sick at one point; we all caught colds on that picture. The four of us sort of paired off, appropriately, I think, in a funny sort of way. I don't mean this in a sexual way. I socialized with Clive more than Roddy and Gayle. They liked to go to parties and socialize and stuff. Clive was more down to Earth, more like me, more quite happy to be at home. We were quite connected in that way."

McDowall had been acting onscreen since the late 1930s in classics like *Lassie Come Home* (1943) and John Ford's *How Green Was My Valley* (1941), and gave a strong performance as Fischer. Uncharacteristically grim as Barrett, New Zealander Clive Revill was better known for comedies such as Billy Wilder's *Avanti!* (1972), which earned him a Golden Globe nomination. Token American Gayle Hunnicutt debuted in Corman's biker movie *The Wild Angels*, and was also seen in the genre film *Eye of the Cat* (aka *Wylie*, 1969) and Sarafian's *Fragment of Fear* (aka *Freelance*, 1970). The three remaining cast members were also *Avengers* alumni (as was cinematographer Alan Hume): Roland Culver, who had appeared in the original *Dead of Night* and with Hunnicutt in *Fragment of Fear*; Peter Bowles, a veteran of Hough's *Eyewitness* (aka *Sudden Terror*, 1970); and Michael Gough, the sinister star of numerous horror films, in an unbilled and unusual cameo as Belasco's corpse.

The script faithfully follows the novel for the most part, retaining much of the dialogue almost verbatim, although the sex, violence, and profanity were toned down to maintain a PG rating, reportedly at Nicholson's insistence. "If I'd had my choice, I probably would have just put everything in it," Matheson recalled in the Gauntlet interview. "I guess it was pretty racy for 1973. Now it's probably a children's picture." His casting ideas would have made for a very different film, and would have been more realistic in the wake of the subsequent success of *The Exorcist*, as he added in a separate interview with me for *Filmfax*. "Later on, my dream casting at the time might have been feasible. Right after this film was made, *The Exorcist* was made, and all of a sudden the horror film became an 'A' product, I think, which would have reflected well on *Hell House*.... I would have liked to have seen Elizabeth Taylor and her husband, Richard Burton, as the two psychics, and Claire Bloom and her husband, Rod Steiger, as the parapsychologist and his wife." Bloom also appeared in *The Haunting*, and starred with Steiger in the disappointing 1969 film of Bradbury's *The Illustrated Man*.

The screen version was well received by critics such as Judith Crist ("one of the most absorbing, goose-fleshing and mind-pleasing ghost breaker yarns on film") and Leslie Halliwell ("Harrowing thriller, a less solemn but more frightening version of *The Haunting*"). "Not the usual ghost story, and certain to curl a few hairs," said *Leonard Maltin's Movie Guide*; horror connoisseur Leonard Wolf added, "It is a film that leaves a viewer with an uneasy sense that even more horror is implicit in it than has managed to reach the eye." According to Roger Ebert, it "manages to be several things at once. It's a supernatural thriller; it's a shocker, with things leaping out of corners and hurling chandeliers; and it's an almost-convincing pseudoscientific study of psychic events. The last was the trademark of the movie's author ... who also wrote the book *Hell House* (which I liked more than *The Exorcist*).... [His] novels of the 1950s and early 1960s anticipated pseudorealistic fantasy novels like *Rosemary's Baby* and *The Exorcist*. And now here he is again with a tightly wound and really scary story, which has been directed by John Hough with a great deal of sympathy for the novel's spirit."

Among its harsher critics was Matheson himself, who is often disappointed when he initially sees his scripts rendered onscreen, only later becoming more receptive to the efforts of others involved. "When I first saw it I disliked it intensely," he told John Brosnan in *The Horror People*. "Then people told me how good it was so I went to see it again with a more tolerant view. It's not bad really. People have expressed disappointment that it doesn't hew strictly to the book, which would have made it like *The Exorcist*, and I don't think I would have cared to have it *that* graphic.... I thought the special effects [by Roy Whybrow, an Emmy nominee for *All Quiet on the Western Front* (1979)] were marvelous, and so were the performances, though I didn't care too much for Clive Revill.... They had to simplify the whole puzzle which was much more complicated in the book. If you thought about it when you saw the picture you would wonder why it took them so long to work out the mystery of Hell House because it all looked so simple the way the film presented it. And I thought the ending was absurd..."

Years later, Matheson wrote in a letter to me, "*The Legend of Hell House*—why they had to tack 'The Legend of' onto my title, I have no idea; like tacking 'Incredible' onto *The Shrinking Man* as though shrinking wasn't incredible without the audience being informed of the fact—I like better now. As I usually do after a number of viewings when my original vision has faded and I can look more carefully at what was actually done.... I *do* miss the shower scene from the novel [reduced to a ghostly silhouette and a none-too-convincing dead cat in the film] and the actual sight of the Belasco ghost who raped the woman psychic. However, I respect the intent of the producer and director to show *nothing* overtly, suggesting everything. Quite sophisticated." Its doubly derivative title aside, writer-director Mitch Marcus's *The Haunting of Hell House* (1999) owes nothing to Jackson or Matheson, but is instead a Roger Corman-produced adaptation of Henry James's "The Ghostly Rental" (under which title it is also known), with Michael York as a metaphysician plagued by dark secrets in his past.

Hell House was also adapted by Ian Edginton and artist Simon Fraser into a four-part graphic novel, released in 2004–2005 by IDW Publishing. As with the Niles-Brown *I Am Legend* (which IDW reissued in a one-volume hardcover in 2003), the story was somewhat condensed but virtually verbatim. *The Legend of Hell House* was the subject of an offbeat homage in *Grindhouse* (2007), a mock double-feature that combined Robert Rodriguez's *Planet Terror* and Quentin Tarantino's *Death Proof,* both of which were also released separately, with trailers for nonexistent 1970s-style exploitation films by the likes of Rodriguez (*Machete*), Eli Roth (*Thanksgiving*), and Rob Zombie (*Werewolf Women of the S.S.*). Edgar Wright, director of the cult favorite *Shaun of the Dead* (2004), contributed a trailer for the *faux* film *Don't*, which not only spoofed the various genre entries whose titles begin with that word (e.g., *Don't Answer the Phone, Don't Go in the House* [both 1980]), but also recreated the overall look of Hough's film and several specific shots of Barrett's team approaching and entering the Belasco House.

Matheson added a sad postscript in our Gauntlet interview: "One reason I regretted writing this book, and ... 'The Distributor,' which was in *Playboy* [March 1958], was that there was a backfire. ['The Distributor'] was going to be made into a movie but never did. It's just about a man who moves into a neighborhood and totally decimates it by detail; I just detailed it all out. And then later on, some nut in Los Angeles started doing the same things, and they wrote a column about it in the newspaper, and it made me feel terrible, that I had contributed to this. And then with *Hell House*, two things happened. One, a teacher put it on the reading list for her students and got fired, because of what they thought was the graphic sex and everything. And even worse than that, in some Central American or South American country, I never found out which, I was told there was a dictator. The leader of the country was named Belasco, and the publisher was put in jail because they thought he was making a comment, that he'd turned the whole country into a haunted house or something. Those things disturb me terribly."

Dying Room Only

(ABC-TV, September 18, 1973) DIRECTOR: Philip Leacock; PRODUCER: Allen S. Epstein; TELEPLAY: Matheson, based on his story; MUSIC: Charles Fox; MAKEUP: Mel Berns, Jr. Color, 74 minutes. CAST—Jean Mitchell: Cloris Leachman. Jim Cutler: Ross Martin. Tom King: Ned Beatty. Sheriff: Dana Elcar. Vi: Louise Latham. Bob Mitchell: Dabney Coleman. Lou McDermott: Ron Feinberg.

Driving back from a vacation through the Arizona desert, Jean Mitchell (Cloris Leachman) and her abrasive husband Bob (Dabney Coleman) stop at the seedy and isolated Arroyo Motel and Café, where he spars with the surly chef, Jim Cutler (Ross Martin, who had made such a memorable appearance in Matheson's *Twilight Zone* episode "Death Ship"). Bob is gone from the table when Jean returns from the rest room. The café's only other customer, the equally antisocial Tom King (Ned Beatty), tells her that he is also not in the men's room, whereupon she walks outside and sees that Bob is not in their car. In a highly effective shot, she calls his name as the camera pulls steadily back to show Jean and the Arroyo dwarfed by a vast desert wasteland.

Vi (Louise Latham), the desk clerk at the adjacent motel, is just as unhelpful. As Jean returns to the café, the viewer sees—but does not hear—a telephone conversation between Vi and Jim, who locks the men's room, claiming that it is out of order. When Jean insists on being allowed to enter, she finds another locked door inside, which according to Tom leads only to a long-disused shed filled with trash.

After Jean has placed a call to the sheriff's office, Tom says that he has seen Bob leaving. By the time she dashes outside, she is able to see their car racing away into the twilight but not who is in it. After forcing Jim to show them the empty shed, the sheriff (Dana Elcar) leaves Jean at the motel, where Vi's refusal to put through a call to the FBI or their home raises her suspicions. Snooping around outside that night, Jean flees into the desert when hulking ex-con Lou McDermott (Ron Feinberg) pulls up in their car. She watches helplessly while the captive Bob is driven off. Upon the sheriff's return, he deduces that the locals, who previously preyed on unaccompanied men for their money and cars by spiriting them out of the men's room and through the shed, grabbed Bob by mistake. Trailing them to an old pump house, the sheriff radios for help, kills Lou, and is killed by Tom in a shootout. Jean crashes the patrol car in an attempt to run down Tom. The thieves fall out as they plan to kill the Mitchells in a faked auto accident; after Vi has shot Tom, Jean disarms her with an emergency flare and frees Bob, who holds Jim and Vi at gunpoint until the deputies arrive.

Among the final films of British director Philip Leacock, who spent the last decade of his career in U.S. television before retiring in 1980, *Dying Room Only* plays like a modern-day American version of Hitchcock's *The Lady Vanishes* (1938) or, more appropriately, an expanded episode of *The Twilight Zone*, minus the fantasy element. Matheson faithfully adapted the script from his story, published in *Fifteen Detective Stories* in October 1953, although adding such elements as the tension between the couple (as Buchanan did in *"It's Alive!"*), the character of Vi, and the climactic shootout. As he told Sammon in *Midnight Graffiti*, "That's the one script I've done where I've told people it got a better treatment than it deserved. It was just a little Mickey Mouse suspense story, and Allen Epstein, who produced it, treated it as if it were great literature. It also had all these marvelous actors, it was just super.... [Ross Martin] and Ned Beatty [were] great and the director ... was too. Everything about it was so fantastic." Echoed *Leonard Maltin's TV Movies*: "Excellent mood thanks to Richard Matheson's surprise-ending script, thoughtful direction, and small ensemble cast. Above average."

Matheson noted in the introduction to his *Collected Stories* that in some of the earliest, written while he was still single, "I felt uncertain and fearful about [marriage]. In the stories published here — as well as others unpublished from the same period — I revealed myself as highly apprehensive that marriage would entrap me and destroy my creative freedom. I saw, in marriage, little but acrimony and bitterness which ... leads, in one ('Disappearing Act') to literal extinction of people from the protagonist's existence.... Later on, after I discovered that marriage was not the total threat I had assumed it to be, my attitude toward it eased somewhat ('Return,' 'Trespass,' 'Dying Room Only,' 'Being'). The circumstances in which these now more successful marriages existed remained, as ever, paranoiac. But, at least, within the confines of the terrifying situations, husbands and wives got along." He added in his "Dying Room Only" commentary, "This happened when I was driving across country with my wife on our honeymoon.... I went into the rest room, and something happened which delayed me for several minutes, and my wife naturally became very concerned. It could still happen to anyone."

Cloris Leachman's performance as the increasingly distraught Jean Mitchell is clearly the centerpiece of *Dying Room Only*. Her intensity befits the actress who made a memorable early impression as an ill-fated asylum escapee in *Kiss Me Deadly*, and won an Oscar as Best Supporting Actress — as well as several other awards — for Peter Bogdanovich's *The Last Picture Show* (1971). But she is probably best known for the television work that has earned her a record eight prime-time Emmy Awards and many additional nominations for such characters as Mary's acerbic landlady on *The Mary Tyler Moore Show* and its eponymous spin-off, *Phyllis*, and Grandma Ida on another sitcom, *Malcolm in the Middle*, for which she received six consecutive nominations (with two wins). Leachman and Dabney Coleman were reunited in the feature-film version of *The Beverly Hillbillies* (1993).

Matheson later told Arnett, "Recently people asked me, 'Have you seen this movie, *Breakdown* [1997]? It's like *Duel* and *Dying Room Only* combined.'" Written and directed by Jonathan Mostow, the film does indeed echo the former, with several shots of the hero menaced by high-speed trucks, and the latter, with both its premise and its Southwestern desert setting. "Actually, there were elements of [both of my stories in] it, but it was so well done. I don't mind when somebody uses some of my ideas if they do it extremely well, it's when they take the idea and screw it up, then I don't like it." Stranded en route to San Diego, Jeff Taylor (Kurt Russell) stays with his Jeep as trucker Red Barr (J.T. Walsh) offers Mrs. Taylor (Kathleen Quinlan) a lift to a nearby diner. When Jeff gets to the diner later, the proprietor and patrons deny any knowledge of her existence, as does Red — who ultimately turns out to be in league with several unsavory locals in a scheme to extort a $90,000 ransom from Jeff. Again, the sheriff shoots and is shot by one of the villains, who have concealed Amy and preyed upon other couples in the past.

Dracula

(aka *Bram Stoker's Dracula*; CBS-TV, February 8, 1974 [postponed from 10/12/73])
DIRECTOR-PRODUCER: Dan Curtis; TELEPLAY: Matheson, based on Bram Stoker's novel; MUSIC: Robert Cobert; MAKEUP: Paul Rabiger; SPECIAL EFFECTS: Kit West. Color, 98 minutes. CAST — Count Dracula, Vlad Tepes: Jack Palance. Arthur Holmwood: Simon

Ward. Dr. Abraham Van Helsing: Nigel Davenport. Mrs. Westenra: Pamela Brown. Lucy Westenra, Maria: Fiona Lewis. Mina Murray: Penelope Horner. Jonathan Harker: Murray Brown. Dracula's Wives: Virginia Wetherell, Barbara Lindley, Sarah Douglas. Innkeeper: George Pravda. Innkeeper's Wife: Hanna-Maria Pravda. Zookeeper: Reg Lye. Priest: Fred Stone. Whitby Inn Clerk: Roy Spencer. Stockton-on-Tees Clerk: John Challis. Midvale Shipping Clerk: Nigel Gregory. Richmond Shipping Clerk: John Pennington. Coastguard: Martin Read. Madam Kristoff: Gita Denise. Whitby Inn Maid: Sandra Caron.

With *I Am Legend* and *The Night Stalker* already among his credits, Matheson next adapted the most famous vampire story of all, Bram Stoker's *Dracula*, for a version produced and directed by Dan Curtis and shot in England and Yugoslavia by British cinematographer Oswald Morris, an Oscar winner for *Fiddler on the Roof* (1971). Anticipating some of the devices used by Francis Ford Coppola and screenwriter James V. Hart in *Bram Stoker's Dracula* (1992), which is how Curtis's title actually appears on the screen, their version was the first to link the character with his historical antecedent, Vlad Tepes. Scheduled to air on October 12, 1973, it became a victim of history in the making when it was pre-empted by President Richard M. Nixon's announcement of Vice-President Spiro T. Agnew's resignation. Matheson told Paul Sammon in his *Midnight Graffiti* interview, "It would have had a fantastic rating. Everyone was going to watch it. Then Nixon gave a speech that night.... In fact, when they finally did show it, they'd had so much publicity on it that someone later remarked that everyone thought they had already seen it! So no one tuned in, and it didn't do well."

Dracula was one of several literary classics Curtis adapted for television (when he wasn't strip-mining their plots for *Dark Shadows*), starting with Jack Palance in the Emmy-nominated *The Strange Case of Dr. Jekyll and Mr. Hyde* (1968), directed on videotape in Toronto by Charles Jarrott. The first half of 1973 was a prolific period that — in addition to *The Norliss Tapes*— included two-part versions of *Frankenstein* and *The Picture of Dorian Gray* for ABC's late-night *Wide World of Entertainment*. The former debuted just hours after *The Night Strangler*, but was overshadowed later that year by NBC's star-studded, albeit mistitled, *Frankenstein: The True Story*. *Dorian Gray* was scripted by Group member John Tomerlin, who ghost-wrote Beaumont's *Twilight Zone* episode "Number Twelve Looks Just Like You" (and, like Matheson, also contributed to *Wanted: Dead or Alive, Lawman,* and *Thriller*). Nolan tackled yet another two-parter, *The Turn of the Screw*, which was shot primarily on videotape in London, with Curtis himself directing Lynn Redgrave.

As noted, Matheson first saw Bela Lugosi in *Dracula* in 1943. Not long afterward, as he related in *Bloodlines*, "I read the book when I was in basic training. Even though I should have been in bed sleeping, I sat in the latrine at night, bone tired, reading *Dracula*. Obviously, I was impressed by it. I've always liked stories where many first-person accounts are put together to form a story." His adaptation is rivaled in its fidelity by several others, including *Bram Stoker's Dracula* and Jess Franco's threadbare but underrated *El Conde Dracula* (Count Dracula, 1970); both correctly portray the count as an old man who grows younger as he feeds, a device that is stipulated in Matheson's treatment and script, but not incorporated into the film. He said in our *Filmfax* interview:

> I think my script was closer to the book than anybody's had ever been, which I found kind of amazing after all the number of times the story was filmed. *Dracula* started out based on the Broadway play [by Hamilton Deane and John L. Balderston, also with Lugosi], which was kind of a remove from the novel, and I don't think anyone had ever just started out the way the book did.

I guess they finally figured, "Well, we've done everything else, let's try to be faithful to the book."... I never had seen one that I thought was worthy of the book, really, and I still haven't.... [R]ecently when they said that Coppola was going to make it and Anthony Hopkins was going to play Van Helsing, I thought, "Oh, wow," and then I read the script, and [it was like] a porno version of *Dracula*. It's unbelievable! It's just nothing but sex. Dracula walks around in the daytime [which he does in the novel], it's all young people, and all they're doing is screwing all the time. When Jonathan Harker goes to the castle, it's just one orgy scene after another, with him and Dracula's wives. I was stunned.... I remembered that when [the BBC] did it [in 1977] with Louis Jourdan, I was thinking, "Well, that's great casting, Dracula should be attractive, he should be extremely attractive." But then I saw it; it was not good at all ... it just wasn't that well done. I mean, why don't they give up on vampires? I think they've done it to death. You would think they'd come up with something new — they have Dracula, they have Frankenstein, they have the mummy, the wolf man, and that's it."

His reaction to Coppola's finished film was kinder. "Much to my surprise, I rather enjoyed it. Very flashy and vivid," he wrote me in 1992. "Amusingly, the people behind [it] telephoned Dan Curtis and told him he couldn't call his movie *Bram Stoker's Dracula* when he put out a new videocassette of same. That did it. Curtis was already pissed that they stole our idea about Lucy (Mina in the movie) looking like Drac's long-dead, beloved wife. We decided, 'To hell with it.' But when they did the title bit, he blew his cork and called his lawyer. Also talked Jeff Sagansky into buying his *Dracula* and showing it during the Thanksgiving week [but] sadly, the run of our *Dracula* was its eleventh and they only pay residuals for ten runs. So I only got the pleasure of seeing it play on TV. A lot of people seem to like it very much. Except for Palance's popcorn-big teeth, I like it too. Originally, we intended it to be three hours long but that was not allowed. I asked Curtis if there wasn't enough footage for a three-hour movie. 'Hell, I have enough footage for a *six*-hour movie!' he said. That might be interesting. It *is* a *long* story. Ninety-six minutes wasn't quite enough in which to tell it."

The publication of Matheson's 24-page screen treatment and three-hour teleplay in *Bloodlines* offers a unique opportunity to trace the evolution of the project. In his introduction to the treatment he noted, "Except for those areas of the novel which, literally, 'do not work' because of faulty logic or Victorian overstatement or excess length, the film transcription of the book should reflect the same intelligent fidelity to its source as that of *The Godfather* [1972]." For example, as Matheson wrote me, "I took out all that turning into bats, rats, smoke, *et al*. I never did buy that. Physiologically, it seems absurd. Also, why are vampire stories always sexual? They're corpses, for Chrissake. They just want blood, they don't want to get laid. But Hollywood has always associated it with sex. Maybe there's a sensual under-current in the novel too but not to the degree that it's become today." Curiously, he also states in the treatment, when describing Dracula's first visit to Lucy to be depicted onscreen, "This scene should not be hurried but present, in lingering detail, what other vampire films have only touched upon, the obvious sexuality involved in the vampire-victim relationship."

Joining the long line of screen Draculas in Curtis's film was Jack Palance, whose inter-pretation of Jekyll and Hyde — in makeup by *Dark Shadows* veteran Dick Smith — was one of the best in that story's century-long cinematic history. Prolific genre historian Donald F. Glut noted in *The Dracula Book*, "Hurd Hatfield was considered to star as the Count but the role finally went to an actor I had been touting as the perfect Dracula ever since the publication of the Dell Publishing Company edition of the book in 1965. The cover artwork depicted the Count as Stoker described him and also bore a resemblance to Jack Palance as the actor looked during the early 1950s, with high cheek bones accenting an almost skeletal

A flashback to happier days with Maria (Fiona Lewis), the long-lost love of Vlad Tepes — better known as Count Dracula (Jack Palance) — in *Dracula* (CBS-TV, 1974).

countenance. The actor's portrayal of Attila in *Sign of the Pagan* in 1954 suggested the fine Vlad the Impaler he would have made in those days." Coincidentally, as Matheson later told Mark Dawidziak in their interview for *Vampires and Slayers*, "When I first had sold *The Shrinking Man* to the movies, I kept thinking about a movie version of *I Am Legend*, and I kept seeing Jack Palance as Robert Neville."

Finally broadcast on CBS on February 8, 1974 (and, like *Duel*, released theatrically overseas), Matheson's version does indeed "[start] out the way the book did," opening in May of 1897 — the year of the novel's publication, although it is set seven years earlier — as English solicitor Jonathan Harker (Murray Brown) arrives in Bistritz, Hungary, and then travels to the castle of his client, Count Dracula. While searching through a number of available properties, Dracula sees a framed photograph of Harker with Arthur Holmwood (Simon Ward) and their respective fiancées, best friends Mina Murray (Penelope Horner) and Lucy Westenra (Fiona Lewis). Upon learning that Lucy lives quite near one of the properties, a dilapidated estate called Carfax, the count immediately makes plans to purchase it. Imprisoned in the castle, Harker comes across a newspaper clipping of the same photo with Lucy's face circled, and is stunned to see that Vlad Tepes, prince of Wallachia, and the woman with him in a 1475 portrait are the exact image of the count and Lucy.

This plot device, which was in keeping with Curtis's m.o. of adding a sympathetic "additional dimension" to his monsters, does not appear in Matheson's published script. In an interview on the MPI Home Video DVD of the film, Curtis admits borrowing it from his own *Dark Shadows*. "In the novel, Dracula leaves Transylvania and goes to England for no reason at all. Stoker says he's virtually sucked everybody dry down there, and he had to find new blood.... I always felt that was ridiculous, and we came up with the central love story to *Dracula* that never existed in the novel.... [H]e saw a picture of a girl in the newspaper, and we established that she is the reincarnation of this woman that he was in love with in the 1400s, and she is in England, and he goes to England to get her back." Both *Dark Shadows* and *Dracula* even feature romantic music-box themes by frequent Curtis collaborator Robert Cobert.

Dracula saves Harker from an attack by his wives (Virginia Wetherell, Barbara Lindley, and Sarah Douglas), and then orders him to write to his employer, Mr. Hawkins, and Mina to say that he will be remaining in Europe for some time, perhaps even inaugurating his own business on the Continent. In a brief and lyrical flashback sequence, the count recalls his lost love, Maria (Lewis). The next day, Harker escapes from his locked room by climbing a vine onto the roof and gains access to the rest of the castle. He discovers Dracula in his coffin, but as he attempts to attack him with a shovel he is knocked out by one of the count's gypsy minions, who have been transporting wagonloads of coffin-shaped crates full of earth away from the castle, and left at the hands of his wives. Five weeks later, a Russian vessel, the *Demeter*, mysteriously beaches itself in Whitby, England, "with only one man on board, a dead seaman who'd apparently lashed himself to the wheel," as Mina later learns from Lucy's mother, Mrs. Westenra (Pamela Brown), when she comes to their nearby home of Hillingham to see her friend, who has been suffering from an unknown illness and walking in her sleep. To treat his ailing fiancée, Arthur calls in an old family friend, Dr. Abraham Van Helsing (an apparent Englishman played by *Dorian Gray* veteran Nigel Davenport, rather than Stoker's eccentric Dutch professor). As the two men doze, Dracula lures Lucy outside to feed on her, necessitating a hasty transfusion. He later frees a wolf from the Scarborough Zoo; it kills the zookeeper (Reg Lye), then bursts through a window at Hillingham and terrifies Mrs. Westenra before being shot by Arthur. During this diversion, Dracula makes a final, fatal visit to Lucy, who succumbs to his predation and is soon interred. When she returns to try to seduce an astonished Arthur, Van Helsing drives her off with a cross and stakes her inside her tomb. The devastated Dracula finds Lucy's mutilated body and wrecks the tomb in his rage over losing his love a second time. Van Helsing confides in Mina, who recalls that the *Demeter* carried a cargo of boxes partly filled with earth. He and Arthur trace the boxes to Carfax, where they find and burn all but one. They then race back to Hillingham, only to discover Dracula crouching over Mina.

Threatening to strangle Mina, the vengeful vampire orders Van Helsing to throw away his cross and opens a vein in his own chest, forcing Mina to drink from it and gloating, "Now, she will be blood of my blood, kin of my kin, later my companion in the night, now my slave and helper." But upon returning to Carfax he finds his refuge violated, and sails for home with his last remaining box of earth. Traveling overland to reach Varna before the *Czarina Catherine*, Van Helsing and Arthur learn that Dracula has already disembarked, so they trail him to Transylvania via his psychic link with the hypnotized Mina — whose increasing thralldom is demonstrated when a cross worn by a servant, Madam Kristoff (Gita Denise), burns her hand. The vampire hunters stake his wives once they reach the castle. In a major departure from the novel that does not appear in Matheson's published script, but had been used previously in Hammer's version of *Dracula*, Harker is found to have been vampirized. After attacking Van Helsing and Arthur, he is dispatched by being pushed into a convenient pit full of spikes. The Count is finally impaled with a medieval pike by Van Helsing as the morning sun streams in.

Harker's varying fates exemplify the different versions of this adaptation: In the treatment, as in the novel, he survives to rejoin the heroes and participates in Dracula's destruction, whereas in the published version of the script, he escapes and is taken to a hospital in Buda-Pesth, only to die before Mina can reach him. Handwritten changes to the script reveal this elimination to be a late development. In compressing Stoker's lengthy novel, Matheson also removed major characters like Lucy's other suitors, Texan gentleman Quincey P. Morris and psychiatrist John Seward, whose asylum is next door to Carfax, as well as the latter's zoöphagous patient, R.M. Renfield. As usual, much of the dialogue comes straight from Stoker, and Palance is properly powerful as Count Dracula (who in the novel aptly claims Attila as his ancestor). "That is the best *Dracula* that was ever made," Curtis told Mark Dawidziak (in *Night Stalking*) with characteristic immodesty. "In all my horror films, my monster usually is more than something there to kill people. Dracula was an interesting monster because he was an interesting person. You were interested in the code and great past of this noble warrior."

Sarah Douglas, who played the villainous Ursa in *Superman* and *Superman II* (1980), and Virginia Wetherell (misspelled "Wetherall" in the credits), a sometime horror actress and the widow of Hammer star Ralph Bates, recalled their roles as Dracula's wives in *Femme Fatales*. Douglas told Steve Biodrowski, "[T]hat was when I knew I was doomed never to be serious.... I remember they got so furious. Every time I went to bite Simon Ward's neck, I left the fangs in his shoulder. They said, 'You have to spit them out!' So I would snarl and spit them over his shoulder." Wetherell had less fond memories of the shoot, telling Bruce G. Hallenbeck, "Curtis was a bit cold, a bit scary. I wouldn't be happy working with him again. I can't say it was an enjoyable time.... [Palance] was a pain. An arrogant show-off, very violent. We had a scene where we were in this huge room and, for some reason, he had to push me around a bit. In rehearsals, he didn't know it, I was actually five and a half months pregnant and was desperately trying to conceal it. But he pushed me right across the room, and this was just in rehearsal."

Palance provided an interesting counterpoint to her statement in a separate interview on the DVD (amusingly sold as "Dan Curtis' *Dracula*"): "I had a feeling of, perhaps on occasion, becoming ... too much the character, and I used to walk away from the set hoping that the entire production would end as soon as possible, because I didn't really want to become Dracula.... Since then, I've been offered Dracula several more times ... [but] I think once was enough. It's good to see what somebody else does with it, how they approach it, what they accomplish, and of course I've seen a lot of Draculas. I've never seen mine. Perhaps someday I will get the courage to look at it, and see how mean and cruel I was."

Already replete with misinformation, John L. Flynn's *Cinematic Vampires: The Living Dead on Film and Television, from* The Devil's Castle *(1896) to* Bram Stoker's Dracula *(1992)* perpetuates a hoary myth in its appendix on "Proposed Films Never Made." According to Flynn, "During my extensive research, I discovered three vampire film projects that for one reason or another were never made. On all three, the script had been finished, an announcement of casting and production had appeared in *Variety*, and filming was set to commense [sic] on a particular date, but they were simply not made." *Dracula Walks the Night* was allegedly to have reunited Terence Fisher and Jimmy Sangster (scripting with Matheson, who has disavowed any knowledge of the project) with a cast of Hammer veterans headed by Christopher Lee, Peter Cushing, and Barbara Shelley in yet another version of Stoker's novel, with the surprising addition of Sherlock Holmes and Dr. Watson — plus Palance as Dracula's servant! "What sounded like Hammer's most ambitious Dracula effort, however, was finally exposed as a hoax," Don Glut had already noted in *The Dracula Book*.

Scream of the Wolf

(ABC-TV, January 16, 1974) PRODUCER-DIRECTOR: Dan Curtis; TELEPLAY: Matheson, based on David Case's "The Hunter"; MUSIC: Robert Cobert; MAKEUP: Mike Westmore; SPECIAL EFFECTS: Roger George. Color, 74 minutes. CAST — John Wetherby: Peter Graves. Byron Douglas: Clint Walker. Sandy Miller: Jo Ann Pflug. Sheriff Vernon Bell: Philip Carey. Grant: Don Megowan. Deputy Charlie Crane: Brian Richards. Student: Lee Paul. Boy: James Storm. Lake: Dean Smith. Brian Hammond: Randy Kirby. Newsman: Vernon Weddle. Reporter: William Baldwin. Coroner: Orville Sherman. Girl: Bonnie Van Dyke. Deputy Bill: Grant Owens. First Deputy: Douglas Bungert. Second Deputy: Kenneth Stimson. Stretcher Bearer: Tom Dever. Handler: Chuck Hayward. Man: Russ Grieve.

Monterey County Sheriff Vernon Bell (Philip Carey) asks author and ex-hunter John Wetherby (Peter Graves) to help investigate the death of Brian Hammond (Randy Kirby), a Los Angeles salesman who was apparently mangled by an animal after he made a wrong turn and ran out of gas. They find evidence suggesting a lupine creature that can alter its scent. Seeing tracks at the scene of a second murder that change from quadrupedal to bipedal and then vanish, the baffled John consults his friend and fellow hunter, Byron Douglas (Clint Walker). Byron predicts that the animal will kill again, and refuses to become involved in the ongoing investigation, claiming that he must prepare for his upcoming trip to South America. John dismisses both the werewolf rumors that follow the slaughter of a young couple and the suspicions of his girlfriend Sandy Miller (Jo Ann Pflug, who had appeared in *The Night Strangler* one year earlier to the day) when Byron, once badly bitten by a wolf while hunting in Canada with John, opines that "the life of a predator is superior to that of its victim."

"Only in mortal danger are we alive, John. Only by risking our lives can we truly appreciate them," Byron says upon meeting the two of them at a restaurant. "I give life as well as take it. The animals I kill are never more alive than in that instant before my bullet strikes them ... and I'm never more alive than in that instant when they could kill me just as easily." Soon, Sandy is nearly the victim of another attack, and a deputy is killed while searching Byron's house. Byron cites the salutary effects of fear on the local populace and tells John, "I was hoping that letting you work on the problem unaided might help you to regain some portion of your once-consummate skill as a hunter." Byron fakes his own death by planting his clothes on the body of his servant, Grant (Don Megowan), who had threatened to expose him. He reveals that he was perpetuating the werewolf myth with a ferocious dog, which John kills. When Byron forces a final showdown, John produces a concealed handgun and reluctantly shoots his old friend.

Matheson adapted this derivative Dan Curtis production from David Case's story "The Hunter" (also the film's working title). While he and Curtis may have felt that a TV-movie about an apparent lycanthrope that turns out *not* to be supernatural would provide a nice inversion of *The Night Stalker*, the threadbare results could appropriately have been entitled *The Most Dangerous Wolf of the Baskervilles*. Graves, who later worked with Curtis again in

Sandy Miller (Jo Ann Pflug) and John Wetherby (Peter Graves) debate the identity of the killer in *Scream of the Wolf* (ABC-TV, 1974).

The Winds of War, headed the cast of seasoned television veterans. While best known as Jim Phelps on *Mission: Impossible*, he had enjoyed early leading roles as scientists in such SF films as *Red Planet Mars* (1952), *Killers from Space* (1954), Corman's *It Conquered the World*, and Bert I. Gordon's *Beginning of the End*. Interestingly, both of his male co-stars had embodied the title roles in series to which Matheson contributed teleplays: Walker was featured in the long-running Western show *Cheyenne* before becoming a member of *The Dirty Dozen*, while Carey played Philip Marlowe in the eponymous program on which Matheson had collaborated with Beaumont, as well as appearing in *Laredo*.

The author of several hundred mostly pseudonymous novels in a variety of genres, David Case had also written *Fengriffen*, which was adapted into the oft-retitled Amicus film —*And Now the Screaming Starts!* (1973). The primary changes wrought by Matheson on "The Hunter," which appeared in Case's first collection *The Cell: Three Tales of Horror*, were to relocate it from Dartmoor to Monterey, and to provide a more commercially palatable alternative to its unresolved ending, as Wetherby prepares for his final showdown with Byron and his animal accomplice, in this case a wolverine. Case actually gives the literary Byron the last word regarding his unorthodox theories: "Wetherby was afraid. But it was a healthy fear.... He wanted very much to live, and he understood Byron at last. In that much, at least, Byron had known. He wanted to live because he was alive, and because the wind was blowing across the moors, and because he had two bullets in his rifle."

In Jim Pierson's *Produced and Directed by Dan Curtis*, Dawidziak noted, "For the first time, the magic seemed to be missing from the Curtis-Matheson connection." Matheson told me in 2008, "It could have been one of the best if they'd had two good actors. I was very disappointed when I found out that [Walker] was going to do it. All I remember is him talking to me when I wrote a *Cheyenne*, and he came up to me in his deep, rumbling voice and said, 'Cheyenne wouldn't do that.' Why Cheyenne had such a deep significance in his life, I don't know. Peter Graves did a better job, but not enough. There was a sort of a homosexual underpinning to the whole story that Dan Curtis, I guess, decided to cut out. It was something I had in the script. It was a relationship between them that was much more intense than it turned out to be in the movie. I imagine that that whole element of the attraction between the two men was in the [story, which] was sent to me by Dan Curtis; I don't think I made it up. I've probably had failings at times where I'm *too* faithful to the original source, but my attitude is, if it's good enough to buy in the first place, it should be good enough to make into a movie."

The film does offer a wealth of verbal and visual cues emphasizing Byron's relationship with John, whom he tries to "arouse" out of a complacent life writing stories, "emasculated by society and safety." There is also an obvious antipathy — or rivalry — between Byron and Sandy, who tells John, "I may go to my grave not understanding how the two of you could be so close for so many years." A motif is established with Byron's very first scene, as Curtis zooms in to a close-up of the two men shaking hands, then cuts to John's expression of discomfort as Byron evidently holds the handshake for too long. John later explains to Bell that Byron hired the burly Grant after meeting him in a bar and being impressed that it took him ten minutes to defeat Grant at arm-wrestling for their drinks. This motif reaches its, shall we say, climax when Byron challenges John to arm-wrestle him and agrees to help with the investigation if John can hold his arm for one minute. But Walker's dramatic deficiencies make the scene, replete with suggestive dialogue ("Can you still last seven minutes?" and "Can't you even hold me for a minute now?") and close-ups of clasped hands, somewhat risible.

The Morning After

(ABC-TV, February 13, 1974) DIRECTOR: Richard T. Heffron; PRODUCER: Stan Margulies; TELEPLAY: Matheson, based on Jack B. Weiner's novel; MUSIC: Mike Post, Pete Carpenter; MAKEUP: Bob Westmoreland. Color, 73 minutes. CAST—Charlie Lester: Dick Van Dyke. Fran Lester: Lynn Carlin. Rudy King: Don Porter. Toni: Linda Lavin. Karen Lester: Jewel Blanch. Fisherman: Sam Gilman. Dr. Paul Emmett: Joshua Bryant. Dr. Tillman: Richard Derr. Frank Lester: Robert Hover. Carol Lester: Carolyn Ames. Stewart: Doug Johnson. Danny Lester: Dermott Downs. Jim Doherty: Jim B. Raymond. Kathy Doherty: Penny Kunard. Telly Curran: Sandy Ward. Rita: Joyce Easton. Girl in Bar: Rebecca Ray.

Comedian Dick Van Dyke made his television dramatic debut as a public relations writer whose drinking costs him his self-respect, his career, his family, and almost his life in this seldom re-broadcast film. His powerful performance earned him an Emmy nomination as Best Actor in a Drama Special.

Van Dyke, who subsequently went public regarding his own alcoholism, later recalled on A&E's *Biography* that he was still privately battling the problem when he made the film.

"That I thought was moving," Matheson told me regarding this significant departure from his better-known work in the fantasy field. "I've had more success in television than I've had in films by far.... You can do things that *say* something on television; the 'message' film in theatricals today is almost unheard of ... unless you get a star to do *Silkwood* [1983] or something like that." He also told Mark Rathbun, "[T]here's no getting away from the fact that television is the medium of our times. You can reach one hundred million people in one night, like *The Day After* [1983] did."

Airing only five days after *Dracula*, Matheson's third telefilm broadcast during the first two months of 1974 included in its cast Lynn Carlin, an Academy Award nominee as Best Supporting Actress for John Cassavetes's *Faces* (1968); Richard Derr, a veteran of George Pal's SF epic *When Worlds Collide* (1951); and Linda Lavin, two years away from stardom in the hit sitcom *Alice*. Prolific director Richard T. Heffron's many other TV-movies include the 1974 pilot film for the successful series *The Rockford Files* and the historical drama *I Will Fight No More Forever* (1975); among his few theatrical features are the genre film *Futureworld* (1976), the sequel to writer-director Michael Crichton's *Westworld* (1973), and a 1982 remake of the Mike Hammer film *I, the Jury* (1953).

Faithfully adapted from the first novel by Jack B. Weiner, Matheson's teleplay is in the tradition of such classic, hard-hitting theatrical films as *The Lost Weekend* (1945), *Come Fill the Cup* (1951), and *Days of Wine and Roses* (1962) as it depicts the grim downward spiral of Charlie Lester's personal and professional life, from unacknowledged alcoholism to the DTs and ultimately the hospital psycho ward.

A business journalist like Weiner himself, Charlie lives in Los Angeles with his long-suffering spouse Fran (Carlin) and their children Karen (Jewel Blanch) and Danny (Dermott Downs). He makes his living by ghostwriting annual reports, speeches, and slogans such as "conservation isn't fearing, my friends; conservation is caring" for Rudy King (Don Porter), pompous president of King Petroleum. Adding further verisimilitude to the role, Van Dyke had worked in an advertising agency in his native Danville, Illinois, and played a similarly self-destructive character (modeled after several silent film stars) in *The Comic* (1969), directed by Carl Reiner, creator of the Emmy-winning *Dick Van Dyke Show*. While excising the explicit sex, infidelity, and profuse profanity in the novel, Matheson is unsparing in chronicling Charlie's crumbling relationships with his friends and family — including his younger brother, Frank (Robert Hover), and sister-in-law, Carol (Carolyn Ames). He retains much of Weiner's dialogue, albeit rearranging and compressing many of his scenes to fit a 90-minute format.

When Fran threatens to leave him (Van Dyke was himself separated in 1978), Charlie consults his physician, Dr. Tillman (Derr), who refers him to Beverly Hills psychoanalyst Paul Emmett (Joshua Bryant). Dr. Emmett uncovers some underlying problems, such as a family history of alcoholism and childhood feelings of inadequacy and guilt, but Charlie refuses to continue the treatment. With a Joey Scarbury cover of John Lennon and Paul McCartney's "Yesterday" as a musical motif, he backslides further following each new resolve until he passes out on a beach embankment, wrapped in a blanket. When he wakes up from his bender, screaming that crabs are crawling all over him, it takes three men to hold him down. Coming to his senses four days later, he learns that Fran and Tillman have had him committed to the city hospital. Charlie escapes from the psychiatric ward, tearfully tells Fran from a pay phone that "it's just no good," and is last seen guzzling booze back at the beach in an ending that is little more hopeful than the novel's overt suicide attempt.

Matheson himself had many alcoholic men in his family, most notably his father. Nolan, writing in *Firsts*, says the father "served in the Norwegian Merchant Marine. He met Richard's mother at a dance in Brooklyn. They both felt alienated and insecure in the Unit-ed States ['What better background for the breeding of a paranoiac point of view?' Mathe-son asked in the introduction to his *Collected Stories*], and that sense of insecurity formed a bond between them. Their marriage was strained at the outset, however, by the elder Matheson's dependence on alcohol which, as Richard has pointed out, 'served to numb his fears and anxieties.' Living in New Jersey, the Mathesons had two more children — a daughter, Gladys, and another son, Robert. When Richard was three, they all moved back to Brooklyn, where his father separated from the family. Young Richard, stunned by the loss, retreated deep into himself. 'My mother joined the Christian Science Church,' he says. 'Religion became her escape. *My* escape was fantasy, fairy tales, stories of giants and ogres and maidens in distress. I lived inside these imaginary worlds where I could be safe and protected.'"

"I didn't know when I adapted the novel that Van Dyke would be starring in it," Matheson told me, "nor did I know that he himself had been an alcoholic, although I think it came out around that time, probably because of the film. However, he did tell me that he was pretty startled when he got the script, because he said he felt like somebody had been looking in through his window. I had to make the character more sympathetic than in the book, where he's a pretty unpleasant guy who cheats on his wife, because I knew that otherwise the story would never work on TV. But his performance really rips your heart out. Thank God they didn't have him say at the end, 'It's okay, I'm over it now,' like with Ray Milland in *The Lost Weekend*. As always, you have to stay true to the premise right through to the end. I've been told that they actually used it as an educational film in some medical schools, which made me very proud. It's too bad that this and some of my other TV films aren't more readily available, like *The Dreamer of Oz*, with John Ritter as L. Frank Baum. Maybe now with Ritter's sad and sudden death [in 2003], that will get some attention."

Matheson added in his 1978 *Midnight Graffiti* interview with Paul Sammon,

[Executive producer] Larry Turman told me that the two-hour version of *The Morning After* was even stronger and infinitely better than the 90 minutes they ultimately showed, but they had to cut it down to an hour and a half. I was sorry they couldn't present it in its original length.... It was a beautiful piece of work. I loved that. I'll always be grateful to [producer] Deanne Barkley at NBC, bless her. She was with ABC at the time, and she called my agent and asked, "Does Dick always want to do fantasy and horror stories, or does he want to do other stuff?" Because she liked my writing. And they told her, "My God, he's forever on our necks trying to get out of this rut!" And anyway, I have been trying to get out of it. Not that I dislike it, or that it hasn't been fun, but I want to do other things as well. So [Barkley] offered him this book, and I jumped. The background I came from [*laughs*] ... well, I was ideally suited to do it, and it turned out fantastically.... [Van Dyke] was marvelous. Well, you know, it was like a personal cry from himself [even though] it was just sheer coincidence that [this project] was sent to him....

I remember, I guess it was the director telling me, that he, Van Dyke, was unable to show anger. [Heffron] had spoken to Van Dyke's secretary and she'd said that she had never seen him angry in 25 years. And that he couldn't cry. I think Jeff Corey was trying to help him with that, and when Van Dyke finally started, it was like it was all bottled up. When he cried during the shooting it just tore your heart out.... [But] just to show you about categorization ... I think it was Cecil Smith who wrote a review of *The Morning After* and said, "This is a real horror story. And who better to do the screenplay than the King of Horror?" I mean, how far afield can you go to tie things together and keep someone stuck in his pigeonhole?... [Then], for instance, this project I'm doing now, this adaptation of the book concerning the search for King Tut's tomb [most likely Thomas Hoving's *Tutankhamun: The Untold Story*], all about [Howard] Carter and [Lord] Carnarvon. When it comes out they'll say, "Oh, here's another horror story. It's the mummy. And who better to do a story about the mummy of King Tut?" It'll be the same damned thing all over again.

The miniseries was never shot.

Icy Breasts

(*Les Seins de Glace*; Lira-Belstar-Capitolina [France-Italy], released August 28, 1974) DIRECTOR-SCREENPLAY: Georges Lautner, based on Matheson's *Someone Is Bleeding*; PRODUCER: Ralph Baum; MUSIC: Philippe Sarde. Color, 101 minutes. CAST— Marc Rilson: Alain Delon. Peggy Lister: Mireille Darc. François Rollin: Claude Brasseur. Commissaire Eric Garnier: André Falcon. Mrs. Rilson: Nicoletta Machiavelli. Denis Rilson: Fiore Altoviti. Steig: Emilio Messina. Albert: Michel Peyrelon. Also with Philippe Castelli, Jean-Pierre Lorrain, Jean Luisi, Mario Darsac.

Since the French coined the term *film noir*, it was aptly left to a Frenchman, writer-director Georges Lautner, to film Matheson's first novel, *Someone Is Bleeding* (dedicated to "Bill Gault, a guy you can call your friend without crossing your fingers"), under its French title, *Les Seins de Glace* (Icy Breasts). "I saw it some time ago," Matheson said in our *Noir* interview. "My recollection is it doesn't follow the book all that closely, and of course it takes place in France, so it has a different environment. I'd like to get the film rights back because I think in today's market it might do well out here.... I don't even recall it all that well. I know Alain Delon played the lawyer. The hero was some guy I never heard of, or the woman I'd never heard of. That was the right thing—Alain Delon looked too sophisticated to play this sort of naive writer.... Now that we're talking about it, I seem to have a vague recollection that someone sent me a copy, but if they did, I still don't remember it. It must be a very memorable film if I've seen it in the last few years and I still don't remember it!" His noir novel *Fury on Sunday* was published in France as *Jour de Fureur* (Day of Fury).

Claude Brasseur, whose credits range from Emile Zola's *Germinal* (1963) to the romantic comedy *Pardon Mon Affaire* (1976), stars as François Rollin, a self-described "TV hack" who writes serial crime dramas. Appropriately, while the novel's protagonist David Newton was an aspiring author like his creator, Matheson was by this time a successful writer for television as well. Like *Cold Sweat*, the film begins fairly faithfully as François meets Peggy Lister (Mireille Darc) while walking alone on a beach in Nice in the winter and soon becomes obsessed with the attractive blonde. She tells him that she was married long ago and that her divorce was handled by Marc Rilson (Delon), a debonair lawyer who soon summons François to a meeting. Marc warns François to stay away from Peggy, whom he says is a mentally disturbed former addict with an aversion to men and in fact killed her husband. But Marc's brother Denis (Fiore Altoviti) reveals an ulterior motive: Marc is in love with Peggy and wishes to marry her, a situation complicated by the presence of the current Mrs. Rilson (Nicoletta Machiavelli).

Peggy denies killing her husband and asks François to help her find an apartment because she fears the unwelcome attentions of Albert (Michel Peyrelon), the gardener at the house where she has been placed by Marc. Marc uses his influence to hamper their search for new lodgings and has them followed by his burly, menacing chauffeur, Steig (Emilio

Messina). In the darkened parking garage of an apartment building, François is knocked unconscious and Peggy terrified by an unseen assailant. She is at first convinced that Steig is the culprit, whose face she says she scratched in the struggle, but Marc shows her that the chauffeur's face is unmarked, knowing full well that it was Albert who tried to scare François off at his behest. Returning home, Peggy deliberately scratches the face of the sleeping Albert, who approaches her ominously as she screams. She is next shown phoning Marc and screaming that Albert is outside her door. When he and Steig arrive to find Albert with a pair of scissors protruding from his neck, the implication is clear that he was already dead when she made the call.

Marc and Steig dump the body in the sea, where it is found after an anonymous phone call (apparently from Denis) tips off the police. While Peggy is being interrogated by Commissaire Eric Garnier (André Falcon), Marc tells François to corroborate her manufactured alibi of having spent the night together, observing that Albert's death confirms his account of her husband's fate. Mrs. Rilson visits François's apartment in Antibes, warning him that Peggy is "a violent animal" with whom no man can sleep and that she severely lacerated Denis's arm when he tried to do so. Their conversation is rudely interrupted by the arrival of Steig, who brutally beats François when he tries to prevent Steig from transferring Peggy's belongings to Marc's house. On her way to explain things to François, Peggy is followed by a vengeful Denis, who in turn is followed by Marc and Steig, and they pass François going the opposite way. He commiserates with Mrs. Rilson over drinks in Peggy's absence, but upon returning home finds Garnier waiting for him with the body of Denis, who has been fatally stabbed with François's letter opener.

François is jailed when Mrs. Rilson denies that she was with him at the time of Denis's murder. But after summoning Marc to his cell ostensibly to represent him, he threatens to implicate Peggy if he is not cleared of the crime, whereupon Mrs. Rilson suddenly changes her statement in order to corroborate his alibi and François is released by Inspector Garnier. Attempting to shield Peggy, Marc confesses to both murders. When his old friend Garnier tells him that the evidence against Peggy is insurmountable, that she must be committed to an asylum permanently, and that the killings are his fault for arranging her release in the first place, Marc asks for 24 hours to sort things out. Meanwhile, Steig has followed Peggy and François to the Turini Pass, where they check into a hotel as husband and wife. As the naked Peggy slashes his chest with a razor, François realizes she truly is insane. After arriving just in time to save his life, Marc takes Peggy to an observation point overlooking the pass and shoots her as a heartbroken François watches. (John Maclay's *He Is Legend* sequel "The Case of Peggy Ann Lister" offers an unusual take on the character.)

Delon incarnated Patricia Highsmith's Tom Ripley in *Plein Soleil* (aka *Purple Noon*, 1960), and also appeared in Luchino Visconti's *Rocco e i Suoi Fratelli* (Rocco and His Brothers, 1960) and *Il Gattopardo* (The Leopard, 1963), Michelangelo Antonioni's *L'Eclisse* (The Eclipse, 1962), and the Poe anthology film *Histoires Extraordinaires* (Extraordinary Stories, aka *Spirits of the Dead*, 1968). He came to epitomize the cool, cynical, laconic tough guy in crime films such as Henri Verneuil's *Mélodie en Sous-sol* (aka *The Big Grab, Any Number Can Win*, 1963) and *Le Clan des Siciliens* (The Sicilian Clan, 1969), Ralph Nelson's *Once a Thief* (1965), and Jean-Pierre Melville's *Le Samouraï* (The Samurai, aka *The Godson*, 1967), *Le Cercle Rouge* (The Red Circle, 1970), and *Un Flic* (A Cop, 1972). These included two other collaborations with Lautner, *Il Était Une Fois un Flic* (There Was Once a Cop, 1971) and *Mort d'un Pourri* (Death of a Corrupt Man, 1977); Delon was cast in both those films and many others — including one of his biggest hits, *Borsalino* (1970), and its sequel, *Borsalino and Co.* (1974) — along with none other than Darc, with whom he was then involved in a long-term relationship.

Not surprisingly, Rilson is portrayed as more sympathetic, and even noble, than Matheson's Jim Vaughan, a former friend and romantic rival of David's from college who actually does have his brother eliminated — presumably by Steig, a Chicago gunman killed in self-defense by David during the novel's climactic chase through Will Rogers State Park — for threatening to reveal his links to organized crime. David's encounter with Peggy on the beach is modeled after Matheson's first meeting with Ruth, and the couples have other similarities: David is also a World War II veteran who has come to California from New York just a few years after graduating from the University of Missouri Journalism School, while Peggy and Ruth share brothers named Phil, naval captains for fathers, and the middle name Ann. Lautner's denouement is decidedly different from that of the novel, in which Jim follows the couple to Tijuana, where they actually wed. But after Peggy (who did kill Albert, albeit not Dennis Vaughan) wounds David with her weapon of choice, an icepick, for trying to insist on "wedding night pleasures," Jim takes her away. She is later found in a Kansas City hotel room with his severed head in her lap.

Matheson told me in our *Noir* interview that *Someone Is Bleeding* was his first novel only in terms of publication:

> My first novel was written when I was 16 years old. It was called *The [Years] Stood Still.* It was a true story that Mary Baker Eddy mentioned in *Science and Health* or one of her books, about a teenaged girl who had fallen down a flight of stairs and never aged, until when she was in her fifties she still looked like she was 17. And so I wrote a terrible, terrible novel [eventually published in *The Richard Matheson Companion*]. ... And then actually I started writing another one, which was sort of like a variation on *The Island of Dr. Moreau* called *Island of the Animals*, and wrote quite a bit of that. And then, long before I wrote *Someone Is Bleeding*, I wrote this novel in New York with the pretentious title of *Hunger and Thirst*, like a great Russian epic, a young man's pretentious attempt to be really arty. It was about a young guy who's down and out and robs a pawn shop and the [proprietor] shoots him in the back. He manages to get back to his furnished room, and then when he falls on the bed, something snaps in his back, and he's paralyzed.

The Stranger Within

(ABC-TV, October 1, 1974) DIRECTOR: Lee Philips; PRODUCER: Neil T. Maffeo; TELEPLAY: Matheson, based on his "Trespass" (aka "Mother by Protest"); MUSIC: Charles Fox; MAKEUP: Karl Herlinger. Color, 74 minutes. CAST — Ann Collins: Barbara Eden. David Collins: George Grizzard. Phyllis: Joyce Van Patten. Bob: David Doyle. Dr. Edward Klein: Nehemiah Persoff.

Matheson adapted this TV-movie from his story "Trespass" (which was also reportedly the film's working title), originally published as "Mother by Protest" in the September-October 1953 issue of *Fantastic* magazine. He told Stanley Wiater in his *Collected Stories* commentary, "'Mother by Protest' was the editor's crappy title. (Though the new title for the television movie was okay.) Although it's apparently a common concept now — UFO abductions and implanted babies — at the time I wrote the story it apparently had never been done, which I found incredible: The idea that aliens would invade the Earth by impregnating a human being, and then having their child be the beginning of their invasion. I've always been surprised that nobody had ever used that idea before — it seemed so obvious to me." Indeed, Matheson's tale of an attempted "invasion by flesh" predates the best-known treatment of that theme, the classic 1957 SF novel *The Midwich Cuckoos* by John Wyndham, which to date has spawned two adaptations, both entitled *Village of the Damned* (1960 and 1995), and one semi-sequel, *Children of the Damned* (1963).

Tests confirm that Ann Collins (Barbara Eden) is two months pregnant, and that her husband David (George Grizzard) was successfully rendered infertile by the vasectomy he had three years earlier, after a miscarriage endangered her life. Ann assures him she has not been unfaithful, but despite desperately wanting a baby, she is advised to terminate the pregnancy because of the health risk. Her marriage understandably strained by the fact that she carries a child of which her husband is not the father — an aspect echoing *The Beat Generation* that is focused on more heavily in the story — Ann asks their friend Bob (David Doyle, best known as Bosley on *Charlie's Angels*) to prove her fidelity by hypnotizing her. Yet even then, she is unable to explain how the fetus inside her womb was conceived. Although it is winter, Ann has begun turning down the thermostat and opening the windows, as well as drastically oversalting her food. After twice becoming suddenly and violently unwell while en route to the hospital for the purpose of aborting the fetus, which is developing with extraordinary speed, Ann announces that she intends to keep it regardless of the risk.

Ann's blood type changes, while her behavior grows increasingly erratic and bizarre: She becomes hypersensitive to sound (shades of Roderick Usher!), omnivorously absorbs information from science texts and records by touch, guzzles pots of scalding black coffee, and disappears on mysterious walks; some strange scratches on her face heal in less than a minute. As in *Rosemary's Baby*, her unborn child not only influences her actions, but also effects an uncanny recovery whenever they threaten her well-being, curing her of pneumonia. Now given to violent mood swings and speaking in an unearthly tongue, she undergoes another session with Bob which reveals that Ann, an amateur artist, was impregnated by a ray from a spaceship above her while painting in the hills. Under hypnosis, she cries out, "Now am I alien, forgotten, lost.... I cry, sickened of this hot, heavy land.... Send me not to make the way.... Return me, fathers, take me back." After trying to kill the fetus — which, as revealed by her x-rays, has two hearts — with a straight razor, Ann briefly becomes catatonic, then decamps with some volumes on childbirth that she had taken from her doctor's office earlier.

The Stranger Within marks a rare case in which Matheson changed his work substantially while adapting it for the screen, most notably in the resolution of this "miscegenation from space," as Bob's literary antecedent calls it in the story, which ends with the child stillborn and David wondering if the aliens (explicitly identified as Martians) will try again in a less accessible area, perhaps Africa or Asia. In the film, after delivering the interplanetary baby by herself, Ann joins a contingent of other "mothers by protest" and is spirited away, while her painting of the Earth as seen from another world, presumably the father's, inexplicably catches fire. "Frankly," Matheson wrote me, "I don't know what that painting running and smoldering meant either; I never wrote it in my script. The director's fancy — as were the interminable clock shots." Said shots were included in a montage under the opening credits that foreshadows many of the story elements, alternating scenes of David driving home with a pot of coffee, a calendar, an overturned saltshaker, textbooks, the pendant used to hypnotize Ann, a sphygmomanometer, a thermostat, and curtains blowing at an open window.

In our interview for *Noir*, Matheson noted that this was to have reunited him with Allen Epstein, the producer of *Dying Room Only*, "and then he had a misunderstanding, I guess, at Lorimar and he left and they gave it to [*Dying Room Only*'s associate producer, Neil T. Maffeo], and I wasn't too happy with the way it turned out." Both films were scored by two-time Oscar nominee Charles Fox. Director Lee Philips had previously acted in two *Twilight Zone* episodes credited to Beaumont, "Queen of the Nile" (ghosted by Sohl) and "Passage on the *Lady Anne*." Joyce Van Patten, who plays Bob's wife Phyllis, appeared opposite Philips in the latter, and Grizzard had starred in Beaumont's "In His Image." Although best known for the title role on *I Dream of Jeannie*, Eden displays an impressive dramatic range here. Her additional genre credits include Irwin Allen's *Voyage to the Bottom of the Sea* (1961) and *Five Weeks in a Balloon* (1962), as well as George Pal's Beaumont-scripted *The Wonderful World of the Brothers Grimm* (1962) and *7 Faces of Dr. Lao* (1964).

While its location is unspecified in the film, "Trespass" is one of several stories set at Indiana's fictional Fort College, named for Charles Fort, whose writings had inspired "Witch War" (*Startling Stories*, July 1951). As Matheson told Wiater, "I had a series of stories in mind that I called the Fort College stories.... I didn't do enough for a collection, and people later said they weren't aware that I was consciously trying to do a number of science fiction stories in this particular setting.... I didn't call it the University of Missouri, but I thought of [them] as taking place at the University I went to..." Most share only that physical setting, although "Return" (*Thrilling Wonder Stories*, October 1951), "F —" (aka "The Foodlegger"; *Thrilling Wonder Stories*, April 1952), and "The Traveller" (*Born of Man and Woman*) all depict the faculty's rather mixed success with time travel. The others include "Mountains of the Mind" (*Marvel Science Fiction*, November 1951), "SRL Ad" (*Fantasy and Science Fiction*, April 1952), "Mad House," "Lazarus II" (*Fantastic Story Magazine*, July 1953), and the previously unpublished "An Element Never Forgets" (*Matheson Uncollected: Volume Two*).

Trilogy of Terror

(ABC-TV, March 4, 1975) DIRECTOR-PRODUCER: Dan Curtis; MUSIC: Robert Cobert; MAKEUP: Mike Westmore; SPECIAL EFFECTS: Richard Albaine; PUPPET MASTER: Erik M. Von Buelow. Color, 72 minutes. "Julie"—TELEPLAY: William F. Nolan, based on Matheson's "The Likeness of Julie." CAST— Julie Eldridge: Karen Black. Chad Foster: Robert Burton. Eddie Nells: James Storm. Anne Richards: Kathryn Reynolds. Motel Manager: Orin Cannon. Arthur Moore: Gregory Harrison. Drive-In Clerk: Redmond Gleeson. "Millicent and Therese"—TELEPLAY: Nolan, based on Matheson's "Therese" (aka "Needle in the Heart"). CAST— Millicent Larimore, Therese Larimore: Karen Black. Dr. Chester Ramsay: George Gaynes. Thomas Anmar: John Karlen ["Karlin" in credits]. Tracy Stephenson: Tracy Curtis. Therese as a Girl: Blithe Egan. Ambulance Attendant: Grant Owens. "Amelia"—TELEPLAY: Matheson, based on his "Prey." CAST—Amelia: Karen Black.

Originally entitled *Trilogy in Terror*, and written in 1973 before the ill-fated *Night Killers* teleplay, Matheson's fifth film with Curtis at last marked a collaboration with William F. Nolan that actually came to fruition. Nolan wrote me in 2007, "Until we finally got *Trilogy* off the ground, we used to joke with each other about the fact that when Matheson and Nolan write *together* they never get produced! *Trilogy* broke that dark pattern."

One of the best-known adaptations of Matheson's work, *Trilogy* was also a return to the anthology format of *Tales of Terror*, and both titles echo his preference for the term "terror" over "horror" to describe his work. As he told Sammon in his *Midnight Graffiti* interview, "To me, horror is blood and guts ... grotesque stuff. Eyeballs popping out, blood spouting—

An autographed behind-the-scenes shot (note crew member in lower left-hand corner) of Karen Black regarding her relentless pursuer from "Amelia" in *Trilogy of Terror* (ABC-TV, 1975).

that's horror. Terror is a much more subtle thing. You don't have to have one drop of blood to have your hair standing on end.... I would rather scalpel at the mind, a little bit more and more until, finally, the audience goes crazy.... That's my favorite kind of story. It's not easy to do for most writers; I don't know why. But it is always the most satisfying."

Each segment was based on a Matheson story and named after its protagonist(s), all played by Karen Black, who also starred in Curtis's *Burnt Offerings*. A critically acclaimed stage actress who had an early film role in Francis Ford Coppola's *You're a Big Boy Now* (1966), Black previously co-starred with Jack Nicholson in two counter-culture classics, Dennis Hopper's *Easy Rider* (1969) and Bob Rafelson's *Five Easy Pieces* (1970), earning a

Best Supporting Actress Oscar nomination for the latter. Black was then in her heyday, working regularly with respected A-list directors such as Jack Clayton (*The Great Gatsby* [1974]), John Schlesinger (*The Day of the Locust* [1975]), Robert Altman (*Nashville* [1975], *Come Back to the Five and Dime, Jimmy Dean, Jimmy Dean* [1982]), and Alfred Hitchcock (*Family Plot* [1976]). Many of her later vehicles degenerated into substandard fare.

Adapting Matheson's "The Likeness of Julie" into the opening segment, "Julie," Nolan wisely allowed for the fact that Black was then in her thirties by changing the title character, Julie Eldridge, from a mousy coed into a frumpy English teacher. As she walks by, student Chad Foster (Robert Burton) suddenly, inexplicably muses, "I wonder what she looks like under all those clothes." He soon finds himself peeping through her window as she undresses; after luring her to a French vampire film at the drive-in (slyly represented by Curtis with monochromatized clips from *The Night Stalker*) and drugging her root beer, he takes the unconscious Julie to a motel. There he registers as "Jonathan Harker," shoots compromising photos, and then rapes and blackmails her into sexual slavery. But Julie eventually reveals that she has been mentally controlling and corrupting him for her own amusement. Now having grown bored with Chad, she poisons him, torches his darkroom chemicals, and starts in on her next victim, Arthur Moore (Gregory Harrison, soon to star in the short-lived series *Logan's Run*, which was based upon the novel by none other than Nolan and George Clayton Johnson).

Matheson told Sammon, "I didn't want to adapt ['The Likeness of Julie'] myself. I could have adapted it. But I didn't think it would translate well into film. So Bill Nolan did it, and he adapted it as well as you could. But I still don't think it worked. There was sexuality in that story that you couldn't show on television, and it was a part and parcel of the whole story.... As I recall, I couldn't sell that [story] anywhere. Don Congdon ... put it in one of his anthologies [*Alone by Night*]." Once again, Matheson had two stories in the same publication, and Congdon did not want his byline to appear twice, so it debuted under the Swanson pen name. "I guess Logan has had one good thing [to his credit]. On his deathbed, he'll remember Julie." In his *Collected Stories* commentary he added, "I liked this idea of a plain-looking girl — I didn't even know the term 'succubus' at the time I wrote it — managing to lure men into this situation and finally destroy them. And then she would go on — just like 'The Distributor' — to the next location." F. Paul Wilson, who selected "The Distributor" for *My Favorite Horror Story*, later speculated on that character's fate in "Recalled," a sequel written for *He Is Legend*.

Matheson's short story "Therese" comprises three diary entries by a woman planning to kill her libertine sister Therese with a voodoo doll, and a note in which Dr. Ramsay reveals that Millicent Therese Marlowe, "the most advanced case of multiple personality it has ever been my misfortune to observe," has been found dead of an apparent heart attack with the doll lying beside her. In expanding the tale — which aptly appeared as "Needle in the Heart" in *Ellery Queen's Mystery Magazine* in October 1969 — into "Millicent and Therese," Nolan gave Therese's love interest Thomas Anmar (John Karlen) the surname of his sometime pseudonym, Frank Anmar. Spinsterish Millicent Larimore tells the shocked Anmar that Therese is a Satan-worshiping matricide who seduced their late father. When Ramsay (George Gaynes, who had a small role in Matheson's "Ride the Nightmare") comes in answer to Millie's call, the peroxide-blonde Therese throws him out after he proves impervious to her trashy charms. At this point, Millicent decides, "Therese must die."

Discussing the writing of the film with me for *Filmfax*, Matheson noted, "I was kind of cruel to Bill Nolan and gave him the two other stories, because I didn't want to do them.

I was amazed that he was able to make anything out of them. One of them, with the girl who had a double personality, was a *page-and-a-half* short story, and he did a remarkable job with them. But I kept the good one for myself." He later added that Nolan, adapting "Therese," "made it a whole half-hour thing with Karen Black. I couldn't do it. I wouldn't even try it, because if the story's a page and a half, that's the length it demands, but Bill did a very good job. I don't know how he did it. It was an excellent adaptation. It kept the flavor of the piece, and it's easier, I think, to do that with somebody else's short story. I could never do it with one of my own. I would just say, 'Now what am I going to do? How can I make this a half-hour?' I mean, I had to do it in *Duel*, as a matter of fact. I had to make it longer, you know, extend it, but not too often, I think, because my short stories that I sold to *The Twilight Zone* were adaptable to a half-hour."

Matheson himself adapted the last and by far the best-known segment, "Amelia," from his short story "Prey," which was originally published in *Playboy* in April 1969. It concerns a woman forced by her possessive mother to cancel a date with her anthropologist boyfriend, Arthur, for whom she has just purchased a fearsome-looking Zuni hunting fetish doll known as "He Who Kills" as a birthday present. Equipped with a sharp spear, the foot-high wooden doll has a golden chain wrapped around its waist to keep the Zuni hunter's spirit inside from making it come to life. When the chain slips off, it does just that (courtesy of puppet master Erik M. Von Buelow), chasing her through the apartment with a steak knife while shrieking maniacally like the Tasmanian Devil of Warner Bros. cartoon fame. Amelia unsuc-

cessfully traps the doll in a suitcase, and then at last imprisons it under the broiler and incinerates it — but as she opens the oven door to confirm its destruction, she is engulfed by black smoke. After calling her mother back to invite her over to the apartment, she squats on the floor with a butcher knife, now (in Mike Westmore's eerie makeup) resembling the doll, patiently awaiting her prey.

Matheson told Sammon, "I used to like to write what they call *tour de forces*, because it pleased my ego to write a *tour de force*. And that's what 'Prey' was. Just sheer description. I like the filmization. For the difficulties inherent in that, I thought Dan Curtis did a marvelous job with it. I'm very rarely impressed with anything, and I found myself pressing back into the sofa on that one, it was so shocking. This doll, it was such a horrible looking thing.... There were three of them." (According to Sammon, one is on display at the Universal Studio Museum.) Nolan told me in *Filmfax*

He Who Kills gives anything but a "wooden" performance in *Trilogy of Terror* (ABC-TV, 1975).

that *Trilogy of Terror* "was the high point of my work with Matheson.... Dick and I have often chuckled about this, since everyone recalls the devil doll segment he scripted, yet no one remembers the two that I wrote! Dan Curtis had asked us to adapt these three printed Matheson stories, and, quite naturally, Dick selected the strongest one. I really don't think the *quality* of our scripts differed, but Dick knew he had the gem of the lot. That sharp-fanged little devil doll made a deep psychic impact on everyone."

Calling *Trilogy of Terror* "above average," *Leonard Maltin's TV Movies* stated of "Amelia" that "this segment alone is worth your time." It has even been released separately on video as *Devil Doll* and *Terror of the Doll*; Nolan realized his long-standing desire to have a crack at the doll himself 20 years later when he and Curtis co-wrote the sequel *Trilogy of Terror II* after Matheson declined to do a follow-up. In his *Collected Stories* commentary for "Prey," Matheson said, "Dan once showed me a slightly longer version of the television adaptation, and it was even more scary than what was broadcast. And this was before digital effects. Dan was able to get so much sense of total movement from that doll when that's all it was. The sound effects were fairly effective, but to me it sounded like Snoopy having a nervous breakdown. But I think I'm the only one who ever felt that way." According to Jeff Thompson, the author of *The Television Horrors of Dan Curtis: Dark Shadows, The Night Stalker and Other Productions, 1966–2006*, the doll's uncredited screeches were provided by veteran voice actor Walker Edmiston, whom Curtis later cast as Gen. Douglas MacArthur in *War and Remembrance*.

Black related that the longer version was considered too intense for television: "I think what was not used were scenes where I'm trying to get out through a window and then a door. I don't know why those sequences were so scary, but they were cut," she told *Filmfax*'s Harvey F. Chartrand. In an interview with Scott Michael Bosco for the Anchor Bay Collector's Edition videotape, she added, "I made up some of the things I was saying when I was frightened. I also thought in order to look more like the doll at the end, I should have these little sharp teeth. [Curtis] said that would look really silly and overdone. But he said, 'We'll make them and see how they look.' So the teeth were my idea.... The doll itself was quite goofy...."

Curtis told Dawidziak in *Produced and Directed by Dan Curtis*, "I was scared out of my wits because I didn't know what we were going to do. How was I going to make this thing work? All we had was a hand puppet and a little model with hands and legs that could move. So what we did was to build the apartment set on risers, and the plan was to have a shag carpet and a puppeteer underneath the floor, moving the Zuni doll by means of a rod stuck up the puppet's ass. Well, forget it. It absolutely didn't work. It was the most awful thing you've ever seen. So I got the idea of chasing Karen Black with a hand-held camera about two inches off the ground. So that was very effective, but I still didn't have anything with the doll. When it was over, everybody was going home, and I was sitting there in total depression. I didn't know what to do. Then I got one last thought, which saved the picture. I got hold of the puppeteer, and we hung a piece of black velvet. And I just shot a ton of close-ups on the doll: opening its mouth, thrashing around, exiting frame. I sent it to the lab and had it skip-framed, and before you knew it, it was zipping around. I edited those into the scene, and it was very effective."

Leonard Wolf, whose scholarly annotations have enhanced editions of such classics as *Dracula* and *Frankenstein*, praised the story on page and screen in *Horror: A Connoisseur's Guide to Literature and Film*: "'Prey' is a seamless, fully realized and absolutely stunning tale. Unquestionably one of the finest horror fictions ever written in English.... Matheson, who has spent years writing for the movies, has an extraordinary gift for colloquial speech whose rhythms he captures in an absolutely unadorned prose. When he is at his best, as he is here, it is a prose capable of considerable revelation. In a story that is essentially a playlet with a single character, Matheson has with a few deft strokes managed to imply Amelia's entire lifetime as a victim of the tyrant love. But just as deftly, he does more. The tragic irony of the story is that the raging spirit of the Zuni fetish is as much a manifestation of Amelia's self-hatred as it is an accidental force of the universe. In the final moment of the tale, we see that she and the fetish share a subtle if Pyrrhic victory." He calls their onscreen encounter "sheer genius ... one of the great achievements in the history of the horror film.... Karen Black surpasses herself in the role..."

Interestingly, Black told Bosco, "I didn't want to do [the film]. But what happened was, the guy that portrayed the student to my teacher was really my husband [at the time]. So I said that I would do it if he would play that part." She added in an interview with Al Ryan and Dan Cziraky for *Imagi-Movies*, "These days, you have monsters over seven feet tall, paint all over them with boils and bubbles, and they look a little bit like pterodactyls, and that's pretty awful to look at! Now, you know you can't overcome these pterodactyl-monsters, but you certainly can overcome a little doll ... or so you think!... You know, the last thing in the world you think is going to get you — do you in — is something small.... Why can't this small thing be defeated? The continued inability to overcome this little doll touches on something true ... and deep."

Stephen Holden of *The New York Times* noted that the compilation of gay-oriented short films *Boys in Love 2* (1998) featured "David Briggs's leering horror spoof, *Karen Black Like Me*, [which] finds a young man chased around his apartment by an extremely determined sex toy." Other homages include a collectible Zuni doll figure released by Majestic Studios in 2004, complete with spear and charmed waist chain; a cameo in "Battleground" (7/12/06), adapted by R.C. Matheson for the Stephen King series *Nightmares and Dreamscapes*; and "Quarry," a sequel written by Joe R. Lansdale for *He Is Legend*. In her collection *Last Summer at Mars Hill*, Elizabeth Hand relates that she once purchased a "demonic puppet" during her lunch hour while working at the Smithsonian, and then incorporated it into her first published story "Prince of Flowers." Employed in the Anthropology Department, Hand's protagonist discovers the eponymous wooden doll — which also has "spindly arms [and] needle teeth," in addition to a slip of paper bearing its name — and brings it home to her apartment, where it attacks her and again transforms her into an inhuman monster.

He Who Kills also became the first Matheson creation to be accorded what many would consider pop culture's highest honor when it was spoofed on *The Simpsons* in the cleverly titled "Clown Without Pity" from the fourth season's "Treehouse of Horror III" (10/29/92). Homer buys a cursed Talking Krusty Doll at a shop named the House of Evil as a belated birthday gift for Bart. The segment is primarily a parody of the lethal "Talky Tina" toy in the most celebrated of Sohl's three ghostwritten *Twilight Zone* episodes, "Living Doll" (11/1/63), as Krusty's diminutive double publicly professes his love for Homer and then, when they are alone, announces, "I'm Krusty the Clown, and I'm going to kill you." Yet the relentless doll also bears the distinctive pointed teeth of He Who Kills, brandishes a knife, and is unsuccessfully imprisoned by Homer in a suitcase. "Everybody around our age was flipped out by the doll that chased Karen Black around with a knife," the episode's creators noted in their DVD audio commentary. "[The segment was] a basic smashing together of several things that we all watched [in childhood] ... the kind of common language of television and movie references."

The Strange Possession of Mrs. Oliver

(NBC-TV, February 28, 1977) DIRECTOR: Gordon Hessler; PRODUCER: Stan Shpetner; TELEPLAY: Matheson; MUSIC: Morton Stevens; MAKEUP: Stephen B. Gautier. Color, 78 minutes. CAST— Miriam Oliver, Sandy: Karen Black. Greg Oliver: George Hamilton. Mark: Robert F. Lyons. Mrs. Dempsey's Housekeeper: Lucille Benson. Mrs. Dempsey: Jean Allison. Bartender: Burke Byrnes. Saleslady: Gloria LeRoy. Young Man in Bar: Asher Brauner. Mr. Logan: Charles Cooper. Mrs. Logan: Danna Hansen. Old Man: William Irwin. Rose: Nancy Hahn Leonard. Minister: Macon McCalman. Man Working: Bob Palmer. Flowerman: Delos V. Smith. Real Miriam: Sunny Woods.

After dodging a bullet with the *De Sade* debacle, director Gordon Hessler succeeded Michael Reeves on *The Oblong Box*, which teamed Vincent Price and Christopher Lee for the first time, and also led to an AIP contract that encompassed three further collaborations between Hessler and screenwriter Christopher Wicking. *Scream and Scream Again* (1970) added Peter Cushing to the mix, putting all three modern-day horror icons in their first film together; *Cry of the Banshee* (1970) invoked Edgar Allan Poe in its ads but owed more to *Witchfinder General*, with Price as another evil witch-hunter; and *Murders in the Rue Morgue* (1971), AIP's final Poe entry —*sans* Price — was subjected to extensive studio pre-release tampering. His relationship with AIP thus soured, Hessler made only occasional theatrical films such as the Ray Harryhausen fantasy *The Golden Voyage of Sinbad* (1974) while spending most of the 1970s working in American television, where he had been the associate producer of *The Alfred Hitchcock Hour* when Matheson was a contributor. Now their paths crossed once again with this telefilm made for NBC.

One of Matheson's less distinguished efforts, *The Strange Possession of Mrs. Oliver* bears more than a passing similarity to the second segment from *Trilogy of Terror*; this is heightened by the casting of Karen Black as the bespectacled Miriam Oliver, who resembles Millicent Larimore. Hessler told Christopher Koetting in *Filmfax* that Black "was [then] married to a young pop composer and they had a very erratic lifestyle. She's a wonderful actress, though; a real pro. She'd just given birth before doing the picture and one of the conditions for her taking the role was that she could breast-feed her child [actor Hunter Carson, her son by her second husband, screenwriter L.M. Kit Carson] on the set. Then the producer [Stan Shpetner] got upset because she was taking too much time. So to appease him, when we had a closeup to do, we'd roll in the camera and get the shot while she breast-fed her baby!" Adding unintentional hilarity to the film, Miriam states at one point, "I'm 26 years old, not 40," when in fact Black was in her late thirties (per the IMDb) and looked it, presumably due to the rigors of her recent childbirth.

Plagued by nightmares in which she encounters a mysterious stranger and sees herself in a coffin, as well as by an abhorrence of fire, Miriam also feels smothered by the insistence of her husband Greg (George Hamilton), an arrogant attorney, that she stay home and have a baby. She purchases a red blouse, blonde wig, and earrings (which make her look suspiciously like the *other* Larimore sister). Drawn to Crystal Beach, she rents a house there and, spotting a restaurant called Sand & Shore, impulsively rechristens herself Sandy. Soon, she is addressed as Sandy by various locals, including Mark (Robert F. Lyons)— the stranger from her nightmares — and Mrs. Dempsey (Jean Allison), who accuses a wigless Miriam of impersonating her late daughter, Sandy's best friend, also named Miriam. Greg drives off Mark while the latter is trying to kill Miriam, which releases repressed memories of how Mark had set fire to a car after Sandy refused to marry him. The resulting blast killed the real Miriam

(Sunny Woods) and Sandy's parents, so the grief-stricken Sandy made Miriam live again by adopting her identity, *à la* Norman Bates in *Psycho*, and her "strange possession" is merely the Sandy persona reasserting itself.

Matheson, who also served as the film's associate producer, recalled in our *Noir* interview that producer Shpetner "was a friend of mine who was into titles. He felt that you had to have a really catchy title. He did television movies, and he always came up with some catchy title which would tell the whole story and get people into watching it. The one I did for him he called *The Strange Possession of Mrs. Oliver*." Among his other credits are *The Bonnie Parker Story* (1958) and *Paratroop Command* (1959), both directed by *Master of the World*'s William Witney for AIP, and the television series *The Sixth Sense*. Hessler had already directed Hamilton and his then-wife Alana in the obscure vanity project *Medusa* (aka *Twisted*, 1974), while Lucille Benson, previously seen in *Duel*, appears as Mrs. Dempsey's housekeeper. Composer Morton Stevens had contributed the score for "The Return of Andrew Bentley," Matheson's sole episode of *Thriller* on the same network.

Opinions differ as to the quality of the results. *Leonard Maltin's TV Movies* calls the film a "pretentious split-personality study by Richard Matheson of a bored housewife who assumes a seductive blonde's identity, unaware that the girl she pretends to be really exists. Black chews the scenery, all kept in dreamy soft focus by director Hessler. Below average." In his *Creature Features Movie Guide Strikes Again*, however, John Stanley calls this an "intriguing tale of dual personality [with] Karen Black as a bored housewife [who] gets the yen to wear a low-cut red blouse, blonde wig and slinky skirt. She is also compelled to buy a house in a beach community, where it would appear a woman who looks just like her once resided — before her tragic demise. Director Gordon Hessler builds the mystery with a deft camera, creating ambiguities to intrigue us: Is Black undergoing possession, reincarnation or what? Supernatural mood blends with psychological thrills." If nothing else, the similarity to the earlier Black-Matheson effort gives it an air of familiarity.

"That wasn't a horror movie," Black told *Filmfax*'s Harvey F. Chartrand. "It was a mystery story about a woman obsessed with a painting that resembles her, finding out the history of the deceased lady who posed for it, and taking on her personality. I protest when people categorize me as a horror actress."

This was the only one of several scripts Matheson wrote for Shpetner that came to fruition; among the ones that *didn't* was a teleplay adapted from *Bid Time Return*. Another was a marked departure for Matheson: *Skedaddle*, a comedic Western. "The number-one stuntman, Hal Needham, was going to [direct it and] orchestrate all the stunts. He wanted to do a Western that used all the stunts he never got to use in all his work. It was a great script. I may have [Gauntlet] publish that sometime."

Matheson was on more familiar ground with another original script, *The French Villa* (aka *Nicole*). "[We (i.e. He and Shpetner)] did that for Sir Lew Grade. It seems to me it was going to be a miniseries at first, because it was quite a long, long story. It was about a pop singer, like a Whitney Houston or something, who has a breakdown and goes to France to recover in this house that belongs to a deceased rock singer, and she has scary experiences there." They also attempted to film Matheson's ill-fated *Earthbound*. "That would make, I think, a fascinating, almost an X-rated horror picture," Matheson said in our *Filmfax* interview. "But, at this moment, I don't know whether anything's going to happen with that. Actually, they ripped me off, there was a television film [*The Haunting Passion* (1983), directed by Emmy-winner John Korty] with, of all people, Jane Seymour [who had previously starred in *Somewhere in Time*], where she was being assaulted sexually by a male ghost.

But I still hope something comes of *Earthbound*— or as my good friend Stan Shpetner ... insists on calling it, *The Cold and Alien Kiss of Death.* Try to squeeze that onto a 12-inch screen!"

He discussed both novel and script in a separate interview for *Noir*. "[Shpetner] was going to make it, but we never got around to it, and then what I did was, I novelized it.... The manuscript was [originally] like a hundred pages longer, and I could never sell it. My agent suggested a radical cutting job [but] they didn't cut it, they just rewrote it, because I 'didn't know how to write.'" Published as a paperback original by Playboy Press under the Swanson pseudonym, the novel did not appear in the U.S. under his own name in its intended form until 1994. Matheson told me, "And then we were going to do the movie and then it didn't work out, and then I revised the novel so that it would sound like me instead of them, and so I have the motion picture rights. I think it would make a very intriguing film. Roger Corman [has] got a whole set-up over in Ireland, they built a studio for him over there — and he said he was going to make it there as one of his early productions, but I never heard from him." An unrelated feature film version of *Earthbound* is in development.

Dead of Night

(NBC-TV, March 29, 1977) DIRECTOR: Dan Curtis; PRODUCER: Robert Singer; MUSIC: Robert Cobert; MAKEUP: Frank Westmore; SPECIAL EFFECTS: Cliff Wenger. Color, 73 minutes. NARRATOR: John Dehner. "Second Chance"—TELEPLAY: Matheson, based on Jack Finney's story. CAST— Frank Cantrell: Ed Begley, Jr. Mrs. McCauley: Ann Doran. Helen McCauley: Christine Hart. Old Farmer: Orin Cannon. Mrs. Cantrell: Jean LeVouvier. Mr. Dorset: Dick McGarvin. Mrs. Dorset: Karen Hurley. Young Man: Jeff Reese. Vinnie McCauley: E.J. Andre. Young Vince: Michael Talbott. "No Such Thing as a Vampire"—TELEPLAY: Matheson, based on his story. CAST— Dr. Petre Gheria: Patrick Macnee. Alexis Gheria: Anjanette Comer. Karel: Elisha Cook, Jr. Dr. Michael Vares: Horst Buchholz [misspelled "Bucholz" in credits]. Maria: Gail Bowman. Eva: Joan Lemmo. "Bobby"—TELEPLAY: Matheson. CAST— Alma: Joan Hackett. Bobby: Lee H. Montgomery. Dwarf: Larry Green.

This TV-movie's complex history dates back to attempts by Matheson and Curtis to create an eponymous anthology series — originally called *Inner Sanctum*— in the fall of 1973, for which Matheson adapted Jack Finney's "The Love Letter" and his own "Prey" (as "He Who Kills") and "No Such Thing as a Vampire." Nolan adapted "Therese." In his *Collected Stories* commentary on "The Children of Noah," Matheson recalled, "I did adapt it, I believe, into a script for Dan Curtis, but it was never produced," and that script may also have been written for the series; "He Who Kills" and "Therese" were, of course, filmed as "Amelia" and "Millicent and Therese," respectively, in *Trilogy of Terror.* "No Such Thing as a Vampire," notes Jim Pierson in *Produced and Directed by Dan Curtis*, "was produced by Dan Curtis Productions with Metromedia Producers Corporation in 1973 as a stand-alone, unaired *Dead of Night* pilot for ABC-TV. Not to be confused with Curtis' 1969 pilot of the same name," which was thus released on home video under its episode title *A Darkness at Blaisedon.*

After the success of *Trilogy of Terror*, Curtis combined the unaired ABC pilot with two new segments written by Matheson and sold them to NBC. Matheson told me in *Filmfax*, "*Trilogy of Terror* was such a [hit]. We tried to use [it] as a pilot for a series, and that didn't work, and then we decided together to create this other thing, and we prepared an opening for the [series], which was very similar to what they did later in *Tales from the Crypt*, you know, moving toward this old house and going into it [as unbilled narrator John Dehner intones, "The dead of night is a state of mind, that dark, unfathomed region of the human consciousness from which all the unknown terrors of our lives emerge"], and then using these three stories. I guess [NBC] just didn't like the idea. At that time, I think anthologies were sort of *persona non grata*. They preferred just one story, and [Curtis] couldn't sell that, either. So there were two pilots, for two series like that, and neither one of them sold." The script for "No Such Thing as a Vampire" was published in the lettered edition of *Matheson Uncollected: Volume One*; the story had been acquired for *Playboy* by Ray Russell.

When Russell died at the age of 74 in 1999, Matheson said in an obituary item for *Filmfax*, "My relationship with Ray Russell was mostly that of writer to editor. Ray was outstanding as a *Playboy* editor for many years and most helpful to me with regard to the stories I was able to sell him. I did see Ray socially now and then, mostly in the company of Chuck Beaumont and William F. Nolan, who were very close to him. He possessed a highly droll sense of humor and was good company always. As a writer, Ray was tremendously skilled. His novel *The Case Against Satan* [1963] was a splendid precursor to *The Exorcist* and his novelette 'Sardonicus' [1960] is one of the great horror stories written in the classical style." For director William Castle, Russell scripted the latter as *Mr. Sardonicus* (1961) and adapted *Zotz!* (1962) from Walter Karig's novel; in addition to his work on *Premature Burial*, he also collaborated with Robert Dillon on Corman's *X— The Man with the X-Ray Eyes* and wrote Terence Fisher's spoof *The Horror of It All* (both 1963), while John Hough of *The Legend of Hell House* fame filmed his novel *Incubus* in 1981.

As Matheson stated in his *Collected Stories* commentary for "A Flourish of Strumpets" (his second sale to *Playboy*, published in November 1956), "There were certain stories that I could sell to Ray Russell at *Playboy*. If you wrote about sex ... or did something really dark like 'The Distributor,' or 'By Appointment Only' [April 1970]. Chuck Beaumont was selling to them well before I did, but I decided I wanted to try them. They were the highest paying market back then — you could sell them a story for a thousand dollars, or you could sell it to a fantasy or science fiction magazine and get $75. I imagine it may still be that way today." He added in our *Duel & the Distributor* interviewer, "I was supporting a wife and four children, and if I could sell a story to them — you have to realize, there is no great psychological depth to a lot of this.... [Russell] seemed to prefer stories like 'No Such Thing as a Vampire,' where there's the revenge of a man who had been cuckolded, that sort of thing." According to Scott Skelton and Jim Benson, the story was also suggested to Serling by producer Jack Laird for an adaptation on *Night Gallery*, but ultimately rejected.

Rarely rebroadcast, *Dead of Night* was ignominiously relegated to the "Thriller Video" series hosted by Elvira, Mistress of the Dark (aka comedienne Cassandra Peterson), although later released by MPI Home Video in an unadulterated version. Lacking the unifying link or even the sheer novelty value provided by the "stunt casting" in *Trilogy of Terror*, it strove to evoke that film in its own final segment "Bobby," an original teleplay in which the eponymous boy terrorizing his mother is played by Lee Harcourt Montgomery, who had appeared in *Ben* (1972) and Curtis's *Burnt Offerings*. "We tried to recapture the same pace and mood of the one with the doll chasing Karen Black. It's the same type of thing," Matheson said in our *Filmfax* interview. Missing and presumed drowned, Bobby is conjured up with an occult ritual by Alma (Joan Hackett), who is finally forced to shoot him when his taunts and defiance escalate into violence. But then the diminutive figure reveals that Bobby had drowned himself in order to escape her and sent it back in his place. Reverting to its true appearance as a hideous dwarf (Larry Green), it attacks Alma.

The opening segment, "Second Chance," was based on another story by Finney (author of the oft-filmed SF classic *The Body Snatchers*) from his first collection, *The Third Level.* Matheson utilized time travel in many of his *Twilight Zone* teleplays; he told me: "It's a fascinating theme — not time travel *per se*. I don't know how many time-travel stories have gone into the future, I know the H.G. Wells one [*The Time Machine*]. That I find doesn't interest me. It's going into the past that is interesting. I don't know why, it just seems more romantic, the idea of going back in time.... Jack was the master of the time-travel story." Other Finney adaptations include *5 Against the House* (1955), *House of Numbers* (1957), *Good Neighbor Sam* (1965), *Maxie* (aka *Free Spirit*, 1985), and episodes of *Science Fiction Theater* ("Time Is Just a Place"), *Alcoa-Goodyear Theatre* ("Points Beyond"), and *Amazing Stories* ("Such Interesting Neighbors"). "Freshness of thought is Matheson's hallmark," Finney wrote in a tribute for the Rathbun-Flanagan *He Is Legend.* "Over and over it shows itself in single sentences, paragraphs, entire new concepts, and in oblique delightful ways of seeing old ones."

A senior at Poynt College in his home town of Hylesburg, Illinois, Frank Cantrell (Ed Begley, Jr., in his pre–*St. Elsewhere* days) buys a vintage Jordan Playboy from an old farmer (*Trilogy of Terror*'s motel manager Orin Cannon) and painstakingly restores the wrecked car, in which a young couple had died racing a train in 1926, to its former condition, right down to the original license plates. One summer night, on the old county road where it was wrecked, Frank drives the Jordan back into 1926. Vincent (Michael Talbott) — a reckless youth who is apparently the car's original owner — drives it away while Frank futilely tries to stop him.

Cantrell encounters Mr. and Mrs. Dorset (Dick McGarvin, Karen Hurley), the future grandparents of a boyhood friend, and eventually dozes off. Reawakening in the present, Frank meets and falls in love with Helen McCauley (Christine Hart). When he learns that her grandfather Vinnie (E.J. Andre) and grandmother (Ann Doran) own the same Jordan, in which they narrowly escaped death while racing a train on that road, he realizes that by momentary delaying the young Vince, he gave them a second chance at life, allowing Helen to be born.

Previously adapted as an episode of the BBC series *Late Night Horror*, "No Such Thing as a Vampire" is set in Solta, the 19th-century Rumanian village to which Dr. Petre Gheria (Patrick Macnee) summons Dr. Michael Vares (Horst Buchholz) to help him deal with the apparently undead attacks upon his wife. As a fellow man of science, the handsome young Michael scoffs at the idea that a vampire is draining Alexis (Anjanette Comer), but Gheria assures him that he is convinced of the legendary creatures' existence, and that his sole remaining servant, Karel (Elisha Cook, Jr.), has even put one of them to rest himself. Michael passes out after drinking a cup of drugged coffee, whereupon Gheria removes some blood from the sleeping Alexis with a syringe, squirts a small quantity of it onto Michael's lips, and places him in a coffin in the attic. He then excitedly summons the terrified Karel, who uses his hammer and stake to dispose — unwittingly — of Alexis's apparent lover. Dawidziak noted that when it was included in *Dead of Night*, Curtis's pilot, which had been intended for a half-hour series, was "trimmed to about 20 minutes."

Deleted footage from "No Such Thing as a Vampire" is among the bonus material on the Dark Sky Films DVD of *Dead of Night*, as are several variant versions of the title sequence with the opening narration delivered by Dehner and others, including Dan Curtis himself (in obvious imitation of Rod Serling) and, apparently, character actor Edward Binns. The extra footage, some of which is silent and subtitled, features such scenes as Dr. Gheria reassuring

Alexis, discussing her condition with Karel, and lamenting the failure of bolted windows, garlic and the cross to protect her. There are also amusing outtakes of Elisha Cook, Jr., hitting his thumb as Karel attempts to stake Michael. "I very much liked what Dan did with [the segment]," Matheson told Dawidziak in *Bloodlines*. "I thought Patrick Macnee was very good in that. He turned in a very fine performance. He played it just right, and you needed that for the story to work." Also on the DVD is the earlier *Dead of Night* pilot episode *A Darkness at Blaisedon*, a haunted-house story that starred genre mainstay Kerwin Mathews and reunited *Dark Shadows* alumni Cobert, prolific director Lela Swift, scenarist Sam Hall and actors Thayer David and Louis Edmonds.

The Martian Chronicles

(NBC-TV, January 27–29, 1980) DIRECTOR: Michael Anderson; PRODUCER: Andrew Donally, Milton Subotsky; TELEPLAY: Matheson, based on Ray Bradbury's book and Bradbury's story "The Fire Balloons" from *The Illustrated Man*; MUSIC: Stanley Myers; MAKEUP: George Frost, Mark Reedall, Colin Arthur; SPECIAL EFFECTS: John Stears. Color, 289 minutes. CAST— Col. John Wilder: Rock Hudson. Ruth Wilder: Gayle Hunnicutt. Maj. Jeff Spender: Bernie Casey. Ben Driscoll: Christopher Connelly. Capt. Arthur Black: Nicholas Hammond. Father Stone: Roddy McDowall. Sam Parkhill: Darren McGavin. Genevieve Selsor: Bernadette Peters. Anna Lustig: Maria Schell. Elma Parkhill: Joyce Van Patten. Father Peregrine: Fritz Weaver. Marilyn Becker: Linda Lou Allen. David Lustig: Michael Anderson, Jr. Gen. Malcolm Halstead: Robert Beatty. Mr. K: James Faulkner. Christ: Jon Finch. Wise Martian: Terence Longdon. Peter Hathaway: Barry Morse. Alice Hathaway: Nyree Dawn Porter. Lafe Lustig: Wolfgang Reichmann. Ylla: Maggie Wright. Briggs: John Cassady. Lavinia Spaulding: Alison Elliott. Sam Hinkston: Vadim Glowna. Capt. Conover: Richard Heffer. Sandship Martian: Derek Lamden. McClure: Peter Marinker. Capt. Nathaniel York: Richard Oldfield. Edward Black: Anthony Pullen-Shaw. Bill Wilder: Burnell Tucker. Mr. Black, Narrator: Phil Brown. Mrs. Black: Estelle Brody. Marie Wilder: Laurie Holden.

One of many SF projects set in motion by the box-office behemoth *Star Wars*, *The Martian Chronicles* was based on the 1950 book by Ray Bradbury, who told me in an interview for *Outré* that it "looks like a novel but isn't. I'm not a novelist, only occasionally in my life have I written a few novels. But some of my major books are books of short stories. *The Martian Chronicles* was written over a period of five years as a series of short stories that I'd published in the pulp magazines for a penny a word or two cents a word. *Dandelion Wine* is a collection of short stories which looks like a novel.... Everything is a surprise, everything in my life is a surprise, and I surprise myself every day, every week, every month, I never know what I'm going to be doing. And these novels write themselves intuitively, behind my back, as it were, behind my ears. And then I look around one day and I say, 'My God, look at all these short stories about Illinois, there's a novel here if you can tie them together, sew them together, make a tapestry.' The same way with *The Martian Chronicles*—you take all the short stories, and you write little pieces of material to tie them together."

Averaging only seven pages, the 26 stories in Bradbury's "tapestry" present a challenge to the adapter, with no single protagonist or narrative line beside the gradual colonization of Mars by humans and its subsequent depopulation when Earth is ravaged by an atomic war. Matheson reportedly met with Bradbury to discuss the ways in which he might dramatize this sprawling saga, and ended up integrating the stories partly by recombining various characters and themes, making Wilder (Rock Hudson) a central figure in more of the stories than he is in the book. Bradbury expressed satisfaction with Matheson's adaptation, noting that "it looked fine at the time, but see, screenplays are hard to judge. They lie there on the paper, and unless you have a very active imagination, you can't get them up on their feet and walk them around. You have to depend on a director and a cinematographer and an editor and the actors to make it all work. And the same way with stageplays. I can't judge anyone else's stageplays, or my own, until I get the actors in and get them up on stage and walk them around and say, 'Hey, this works, or it needs cutting,' whatever. So Matheson's screenplay looked fine."

The project had long been mooted in Hollywood without success. Of his own earlier attempts to bring it to the screen, Bradbury relates that before he was called in at the last moment to rewrite the ending of Nicholas Ray's *King of Kings* (1961), "they finished the film mainly over in Spain, and they came back to MGM studios. I was

A concerned Col. John Wilder (Rock Hudson), perhaps pondering the fate of the planet's indigenous population, in *The Martian Chronicles* (NBC-TV, 1980).

working on *The Martian Chronicles* then for Julian Blaustein [who produced Robert Wise's *The Day the Earth Stood Still* (1951)], doing the screenplay. I predicted when I turned it in they'd fire me, of course, because this was, God, 32 years ago, and there were no science fiction films around at the time. Nothing had been done, *2001: A Space Odyssey* [1968] hadn't come out yet. And sure enough, when I turned in the script, they got rid of me. So I've done four or five scripts on *The Martian Chronicles* over the years.... Everything of mine takes lots of time. It took 30 years before *The Martian Chronicles* got made into a TV film, and roughly 20 years for *The Illustrated Man* to get turned into a film. Everything of mine takes a lot of time for people to discover. I still have a lot of good books that haven't been touched by films yet."

"The Expeditions," the first part of this six-hour NBC miniseries produced by the BBC's Andrew Donally (with Amicus co-founder Milton Subotsky sharing nominal credit), opens with a 1976 unmanned probe and an adaptation of Bradbury's "Ylla," as Captains Conover (Richard Heffer) and Nathaniel York (Richard Oldfield) lead the NATO Alliance's first Martian expedition in January 1999. Just as the production apparently drew on actual news footage and aspects of NASA's equipment and mission control center, the advantage of hindsight enabled Matheson to invest the preparations for the flight with the kind of "internal politics" that characterized our own space program, as Major Jeff Spender (Bernie Casey) gets bumped at the last minute by the project's director, Colonel John Wilder. As

Zeus I approaches Mars, the indigenous Mr. K (James Faulkner) is perturbed by the evident ecstasy with which his wife Ylla (Maggie Wright) anticipates its arrival in precognitive dreams of York, the tall stranger who says telepathically that he will take her away in his ship and perhaps even kill for her. The jealous husband slays both the astronauts with a bellows-shaped weapon that fires golden bees.

Eliminating "The Earth Men," Bradbury's tale of an equally ill-fated Second Expedition locked up as lunatics and subjected to euthanasia by the Martians, the miniseries jumps ahead to April 2000 as Captain Arthur Black (Nicholas Hammond, fresh from starring as *The Amazing Spider-Man* on CBS) arrives with his crew, David Lustig (Michael Anderson, Jr.) and Sam Hinkston (Vadim Glowna). Astonished to find the *Zeus II* landing outside a replica of his hometown of Green Bluff, Illinois, in 1979 and his dead younger brother Edward (Anthony Pullen-Shaw) welcoming him, Black gasps, "Mars is Heaven," the title under which Bradbury later adapted this story, "The Third Expedition," for his cable anthology series *The Ray Bradbury Theater*, on which he also dramatized "The Earth Men." Lustig

A masked Martian bearing gifts in *The Martian Chronicles* (NBC-TV, 1980).

and Hinkston also encounter deceased loved ones, while Black meets his long-lost sweet-heart Marilyn Becker (Linda Lou Allen) but realizes too late that, as in Stanislaw Lem's twice-filmed novel *Solaris* and Matheson's own "Death Ship," the Martians have telepathically tapped their memories, disguising themselves as humans to "divide and overcome [the] invaders," all three of whom are killed.

Wilder had been forbidden by General Malcolm Halstead (Robert Beatty) to lead the previous expeditions, but both he and Spender realize their interplanetary ambitions in June 2001, although Spender is dubious about the morality of colonization. In a variation on H.G. Wells's *The War of the Worlds*, Spender finds as he begins to explore the planet in "— And the Moon Be Still as Bright" that while four out of five cities have been empty for a thousand years or more, the remainder were wiped out no more than ten days ago, most likely by chicken pox brought by the previous expeditions. A handful of surviving Martians have escaped into the hills and are now in hiding. Horrified by their inadvertent genocide and the irreverence of the *Zeus III*'s crew, Spender disappears, steeps himself in the local culture and, claiming to be "the last Martian," returns a week later to shoot Briggs (John Cassady)—who had tossed garbage into a canal—and two others with a Martian weapon. Sam Parkhill (Darren McGavin) and the reluctant Wilder are compelled to track down and kill Spender.

Part Two, "The Settlers," begins in February 2004 with narration derived by Matheson from Bradbury's story of the same title, as well as from "The Locusts" and "The Naming of Names." Wilder, now the chief coordinator of the planet, is inspired by Spender's final request to try to preserve whatever he can of the old Martian civilization from the encroachment of the human colonists. By September 2006, settlers Lafe (Wolfgang Reichmann) and Anna Lustig (Maria Schell) are living on Lustig Creek, named for their murdered son David. (Bradbury, not bound to tie their story into a larger narrative when he remade it on his show, restored the family name to LaFarge.) They encounter "The Martian," who appears in David's likeness to the grateful old couple. Like those who killed David, he manifests himself as people's lost loved ones. When Anna insists that he come to town with them, he is unable to control his abilities and appears first as Christ (Jon Finch) and then as the drowned Lavinia Spaulding (Alison Elliott) before dying, overwhelmed by the conflicting desires of the crowd surrounding him, while his protean features swiftly shift back and forth.

Published the following year in Bradbury's *The Illustrated Man*, "The Fire Balloons" is a Martian mythos story that was not collected in *The Martian Chronicles*, although its protagonist, Father Peregrine (played by Fritz Weaver) appears in the latter in a brief, unfilmed segment, "The Luggage Store." He asks Wilder, who has brought his wife (the inevitable Ruth, played by Gayle Hunnicutt) and children to Mars, about unsubstantiated rumors that spheres of light had rescued an injured prospector in the hills. Despite the skepticism of his fellow missionary Father Stone (Roddy McDowall), Peregrine clings to the hope and belief that the spheres might represent a surviving Martian intelligence. As the Fathers wander in the wilderness, the spheres save them from an avalanche and deliver Peregrine when he steps off a cliff to test his faith. But after he proposes building a church with a blue sphere instead of a cross to represent the Martian Christ, a disembodied voice explains that it is not needed, since the "Old Ones," in freeing themselves from their corporeal forms, "have left sin behind."

With Earth an armed camp and the widely predicted "final war" inevitable, Wilder must race back in the hope of rescuing his brother Bill (Burnell Tucker). He first warns the settlers of the coming evacuation, discovering that Sam Parkhill has married Elma (Joyce Van Patten) and realized his long-standing dream of opening a Western-style café. Confident that there will be no war, and that subsequent rockets will make him rich by bringing "100,000 hungry mouths," Sam is so startled to see a Martian appear that when the latter brandishes an unknown object, saying, "This is for you," the terrified Sam shoots him down *à la* Klaatu in *The Day the Earth Stood Still*. Fearing retribution, he then flees with Elma in an antique Martian sand ship. Surrounded by sand ships, the Parkhills are confronted with a Martian (Derek Lamden) who reveals to the relieved Sam that they were merely trying to present him with a grant for territory encompassing roughly half of Mars. But after the couple watches through a telescope as atomic fire envelops the Earth, Elma sarcastically observes that, for Sam's Café, it will truly be "The Off Season."

Part Three, "The Martians," opens in November 2006 with what Matheson had intended as an adaptation of Bradbury's "There Shall Come Soft Rains" (which depicted the last hours of a mechanized house, whose owners have been reduced to silhouettes burned onto the wall by an atomic blast). Instead the show has Wilder reaching the space center and seeing a videotape of Bill being vaporized. The miniseries also gives the name of Benjamin Driscoll, the Johnny Appleseed of Mars in Bradbury's "The Green Morning," to Walter Gripp, the protagonist of "The Silent Towns." Left behind during the exodus, Ben (Christopher Connelly) thinks he is the last man on Mars until he hears a phone ringing somewhere in New Texas City. Making contact with Genevieve Selsor (Bernadette Peters) and flying 1,500 miles to meet her, he finds that although gorgeous (unlike the obese grotesquerie in the story and script), she is so vain and shallow he prefers to return to the wilderness.

Also left behind is Peter Hathaway (Barry Morse), who has spent "The Long Years" with his wife Alice (Nyree Dawn Porter) and daughter Marguerite (named for Bradbury's wife), desperately hoping for someone to make a last attempt to rescue the remaining colonists, which seems at hand as Wilder and Father Stone arrive. Wilder is surprised to see that while Hathaway has aged since they last met years ago, his family has not. Wilder's suspicions are confirmed when he finds the graves of Alice and Marguerite, both of whom died from an unknown virus in July 2000. A member of Wilder's original crew in Bradbury's book, Hathaway has created android duplicates of his deceased family to keep him company. When his aged heart gives out at last, Father Stone convinces Wilder to leave the androids, who were never programmed to know sadness, in the home they loved — a home at which a wandering Ben Driscoll soon arrives, to give them a new *raison d'être*.

In March 2007, Wilder learns from Parkhill that the Martians had known about the impending war on Earth, and speculates that perhaps they are permitting the humans to begin again, with the remnants of both civilizations coexisting on Mars. Fulfilling his greatest wish, he then comes in contact with a ghostly Wise Martian (Terence Longdon), a figment from either the distant future or the distant past. When asked about the secret of living, the Martian speaks of observing and existing in harmony with nature, in eloquent dialogue derived partly from Spender's conversation with Wilder earlier in the book:

> Life is its own answer. Accept it and enjoy it, day by day. Live as well as possible. Expect no more. Destroy nothing, humble nothing, look for fault in nothing, leave unsullied and untouched all that is beautiful. Hold that which lives in all reverence, for life is given by the sovereign of our universe, given to be savored, to be luxuriated in, to be respected.

Just as Wilder replaces the original character of Tomàs Gomez in this adaptation of Bradbury's "Night Meeting," he and his family supplant that of William Thomas in the concluding segment, based on "The Million-Year Picnic": John and Ruth pack up their belongings and leave their prefabricated, Earth-manufactured dwelling for an ostensible camping trip with their children Marie and Robert. As their boat travels down one of the planet's legendary canals, Wilder invites the children to pick a place to stop, promising them that they will see Martians. While they explore a long-deserted city, he announces that they will remain and make their home there, learning the Martian language and way of life. Symbolically burning a stack of papers to represent the greed and warfare that destroyed life on Earth, Wilder indicates their reflection in the waters of the canal (which, in a glaring gaffe by the effects department, is not a mirror image). Stating, "Those are the Martians," he detonates a bomb he had planted aboard the *Zeus III* by remote control, thus ensuring that they can never go back to Earth.

The most ambitious of Matheson's produced scripts, *The Martian Chronicles* was filmed in Britain, Malta, and on Lanzarote in the Canary Islands, and featured such familiar faces from the Matheson *oeuvre* as Hunnicutt, McDowall, Van Patten, and McGavin. It marked the television debut of British director Michael Anderson, whose hugely successful adaptation of Jules Verne's *Around the World in Eighty Days* had won several Academy Awards, including Best Picture. But Anderson had more recently been responsible for such critically reviled genre films as *1984* (1956), *Doc Savage—The Man of Bronze* (1975), and *Orca* (1977). Even his 1976 screen version of Nolan and Johnson's classic SF novel *Logan's Run*, which won an Academy Award for its special effects, is widely acknowledged as a visually impressive but otherwise unsatisfying effort. Anderson included in the cast not only his son and namesake but also, as Marie Wilder, his stepdaughter Laurie Holden, later a regular on *The X-Files*.

Bradbury and Matheson singled out Anderson as the project's weakest link. "I haven't really discussed it with Ray," Matheson said in our *Filmfax* interview. "I know we were both unhappy with the final product. I tried to be faithful. They actually wrote one in there themselves ["The Long Years"], about the guy who's got a robot wife, and he's out in the desert or something, I didn't write that one. I had done 'Usher II,' one of the [other] stories, rather than that, and it turned out quite well, actually. I had [set] 'There Shall Come Soft Rains' back on Earth, where the Rock Hudson character goes to his brother's house after the atomic war, and sees this house in operation, so that it's more or less identical to the story, except that he's there observing it, which Ray liked a lot. But then, because they'd put so much money in the space center [set], they stuck the story in that. Lost it entirely. I saw 'Usher II' on Ray's own anthology show. It was wonderfully done [by director Lee Tamahori and Patrick Macnee]."

According to Christopher Landry's liner notes for the soundtrack CD, released on the Airstrip One label in 2002,

> At the time he was selected to score *The Martian Chronicles*, composer Stanley Myers was at the height of his popularity, having received international acclaim for *The Deer Hunter* [1978], released the same year the miniseries went into production. Myers had previously worked for director Michael Anderson [on *Conduct Unbecoming* (1975)], as well as virtually all of the various producers at one time or another. All endorsed Myers wholeheartedly. "Stanley added greatly to what I had done," says Anderson today. The music ... spans a wide range of styles. While predominantly an orchestral score, Myers augments the strings and woodwinds with electronic keyboards and guitar [with] pan pipes and a variety of wood flutes to represent the aliens and their culture. These instruments were all played by Myers' assistant and frequent collaborator, Richard Harvey."

Matheson told Landry that "Myers was a great, great composer. He wrote such beautiful music for *The Martian Chronicles*."

In his overview of the production, Landry states that Bradbury rewrote some scenes uncredited, objected vocally when certain story points were later altered to accommodate the actors or the Standards and Practices department, and requested reshoots. "With the film already over-budget and as NBC and other distributors had approved the final cut, the producers declined.... Critical response to the miniseries was mixed, with most of the negative reviews arguing that the much-loved book had not been adapted faithfully. Still, it bears remembering that Bradbury himself was in favor of Matheson's restructuring, and numerous passages of screen dialogue and narration were taken directly from the original text. All three nights had an impressive share of the viewing audience — seen in more than 20 million homes according to Nielsen Media Research — and [it] was generally considered a success, despite its not recouping its production cost for many years." It shared the 1981 Hugo nomination for Best Dramatic Presentation with *The Lathe of Heaven* (1980).

"Everything seems to get done over in my life," Bradbury told me.

On my TV series I did over [the ill-fated screen version of] *The Illustrated Man*, I did over *The Martian Chronicles*, most of the stories there, because the original was a bore. It wasn't bad, it was just boring. A lot of people liked that miniseries with Rock Hudson.... [The problem was] mainly the director.... Okay, he did *Around the World in Eighty Days*. Well, even that has its *longueurs*. I admired the film when it came out, and I went to see it two or three times and took my kids, because it had a great score and widescreen and a lot of actors that you enjoyed seeing. It was a trick film, and mainly to be seen in theaters. You can't watch it on TV; it's much too slow, and it's not fresh and original enough. But I've seen others of Michael Anderson's films since, and when he can take people like John Gielgud and Ralph Richardson, people like that, and put them in a film and bore the hell out of you, you've got a real problem.

So I went to a press meeting of 150, 200 press reporters from all over the United States and Canada when *The Martian Chronicles* was finished, and I was the only one there that represented the film. My director wasn't there, my producers weren't there, none of the stars were there. How come I was invited, hunh? Because I had nothing to do with the film! I didn't write the script, I didn't edit it, I gave them suggestions and they pretended to listen, the same old story. Same old story, time and again, time and again, on *Something Wicked This Way Comes* [on which he clashed with director Jack Clayton when it reached the screen in 1983] and *The Illustrated Man*. So here I was at a press conference with Muhammad Ali, of all people, sitting next to me, in his decline, God bless his dear soul. Finally during the press conference, one of the reporters in the back of the room said, "Mr. Bradbury, have you seen *The Martian Chronicles*?" I said, "Yes." He said, "What did you think of it?" I said, "Boring, *boring*." Well, they'd never heard that comment at a press conference. You're supposed to pump up the film, aren't you, and say, "Oh, wow, it's terrific...."

Later that evening there was a cocktail reception and Fred Silverman, the head of the network, was there. I'd never met him before, and he came up to me and introduced himself and said, "I heard about your press conference today. Is the film as boring as you say?" And I said, "Haven't you seen it?" He said, "No." I said, "You'd better go look at it, you've got problems." He said, "I will, I will." So, by God, two or three days later there was a story on the front page of *Variety* saying, "*The Martian Chronicles* has been shelved by NBC," a big headline. The phone started ringing, people calling me and saying, "Poor Ray, poor Ray." I said, "No, no, no, no, no. Maybe we can make some changes, do some cutting." The special effects are dreadful. I mean, all the little sand ships look like toy boats being pulled through a sandbox, and that's what they were.*

In January [of 1980], three months after it was supposed to be on, *The Martian Chronicles* appeared on the network three nights running. And I invited my friends over, naive Ray here, just like with *The Twilight Zone*, trusting Ray. All my closest friends were over — Bill Nolan and George Clayton Johnson, and a lot of other nice people, and my God, you know, by the end of the evening I had drunk a case of beer, the same old thing again. I was very depressed by the whole thing. It wasn't bad, it was just slow, and I discovered in others of Michael Anderson's films that was the problem, constantly. He didn't know how to pace. I mean, if you examine really good films like *Patriot Games* [1992] and *In the Line of Fire* [1993], the Clint Eastwood film, and then compare it to another Harrison Ford film ... *Clear and Present Danger* [1994] just doesn't work. The pacing's off, there's no economy to the scenes, there's no economy to the editing. It's a tricky business of learning how to pace a motion picture so it's just the right speed. And so, later on in my life, when I had a chance, I did over almost all the sequences in *The Martian Chronicles*, and this time did them right.

---

*As executive producer Charles Fries later told Landry, "We tried to shoot [them] in so many different ways: full-scale, quarter-scale, table-top miniatures. At one point we tied the big one on the back of a truck and drove it around the studio parking lot while shooting up into the sky, day-for-night. In the end, they all looked terrible."

Equally uninspired by the results was Johnson, who told me:

I suggested to Ray that if given the choice of a scriptwriter for *The Martian Chronicles*, now that it had been bought and a deal had been struck for it to be filmed, why didn't he bring up Matheson's name? Because Richard loved him, was his fan, understood these kinds of stories, was a dramatist, could deliver the script, and would listen to and consult with Ray about it. "Wouldn't that be wonderful? Then your *Martian Chronicles* could come out with you liking it. How great!" He said, "Hey, that's a good idea." So he mentioned Matheson and Matheson got the job. [Landry states that NBC vice-president Deanne Barkley, who had worked with Matheson several times while at ABC, suggested him.] I don't know what went on behind the scenes there, except that when I saw *The Martian Chronicles*, I didn't think it inspired on any level. I didn't think the writing was altogether that indicative of what tender depths and power those stories have, and what went wrong here? I didn't know who to blame — Dick Berg, the [executive] producer [with Fries]; Michael Anderson, the director; or Matheson. These various actors were really trying.

There's a few striking scenes in it, but it's very dark, and lacks any of the majesty or fluorescence or detailed decoration, because Bradbury's stories are rich with decoration. The civilizations glitter, they have spires and strange projections and alcoves. These are not little boxes that these people live in in a Bradbury story. [According to Landry, the budget forced production designer Assheton Gorton to substitute "geodesic designs ... partially inspired by megalithic stone circles."] They have access into other realms.

The miniseries marked an inauspicious reunion for two talented craftsmen: South African cinematographer Ted Moore, the winner of an Academy Award for *A Man for All Seasons* (1965), and his frequent collaborator on the James Bond films, John Stears, an Oscar winner for the special visual effects in *Thunderball* and *Star Wars*, who also served as the second unit director. Adding to its uninspired look was the extremely amateurish miniatures.

Matheson's carefully constructed teleplay was eventually subjected to a final network-inflicted indignity when, on subsequent airings, *The Martian Chronicles* was shorn by fully a third of its original running time and shown in a two-part, four-hour form. (The miniseries has been released in its entirety — just under five hours, *sans* commercials — in a variety of home-video formats.) "For the first time in nearly twenty years, Ray Bradbury's classic saga returns to network television," the Sci-Fi Channel announced in touting a rebroadcast as one of its "scini series events," sidestepping the awkward fact that while "The Expeditions" remained unchanged, "The Settlers" and "The Martians" were drastically truncated, with the two parts conflated into one under the former title. Because of the episodic nature of the miniseries, "The Fire Balloons," the vestigial "There Shall Come Soft Rains," "The Silent Towns," and "The Long Years" were easily excised in their entirety, as were the characters played by Roddy McDowall, Christopher Connelly, Bernadette Peters, Barry Morse, and Nyree Dawn Porter, whose names were likewise expunged from the shorter form's revised credits.

Somewhere in Time

(Rastar-Universal, released October 3, 1980) DIRECTOR: Jeannot Szwarc; PRODUCER: Stephen Deutsch; SCREENPLAY: Matheson, based on his *Bid Time Return*; MUSIC: John Barry; MAKEUP: Jack Wilson, Paul Sanchez; SPECIAL EFFECTS: Jack Faggard. Color, 103 minutes. CAST— Richard Collier: Christopher Reeve. Elise McKenna: Jane Seymour. William Fawcett Robinson: Christopher Plummer. Laura Roberts: Teresa Wright. Arthur: Bill Erwin. Dr. Gerald Finney: George Voskovec. Older Elise: Susan French. Arthur's

Father: John Alvin. Genevieve: Eddra Gale. Young Arthur: Sean Hayden. Astonished Man: Matheson. Richard's Date: Audrey Bennett. Critics: W.H. Macy, Laurence Coven. Penelope: Susan Bugg. Beverly: Christy Michaels. Students: Ali Matheson, George Wendt. Hippie: Steve Boomer. Professor: Patrick Billingsley. Agent: Ted Liss. Desk Clerk: Francis X. Keefe. Maitre D's: Taylor Williams, Jerry Kaufherr. Librarian: Noreen Walker. Coin Shop Proprietor: Evans Ghiselli. Tourists in Hall of History: Barbara Giovannini, Don Franklin. Hotel Manager: David Hull. Doctor: Paul M. Cook. Maude: Victoria Michaels. Rollo: William P. O'Hagan. Marie: Maud Strand. Man in Elevator: Bo Clausen. Second Man in Elevator: James P. Dunnigan. Stage Manager: Hal Frank. Man with Stage Manager: Hayden Jones. Director: Val Bettin. Bones: Bruce Jarchow. Fisher: Ed Meekin. Miss Hammond: Erin Tomcheff. Prompter: J.J. Butler. Bearded Stagehand: Chukuma. Dinner Guest: Michael Woods. Diamond Jim: Don Melvoin. Teacher: Ann K. Irish. Second Day Desk Clerk: Jo Be Cerny. Maid in Play: Audrey Neenan. Photographer: Tim Kazurinsky. Stagehand With Note: Bob Swan.

Matheson's adaptation of his novel *Bid Time Return* (from Shakespeare's *Richard II*, Act III, Sc. 2: "O call back yesterdays, bid time return") has the distinction of inspiring one of only three fan clubs devoted to a single motion picture, the International Network of *Somewhere in Time* Enthusiasts (INSITE), founded in 1990 by Bill Shepard. Matheson told me in *Filmfax*, "In October, they have a *Somewhere in Time* Weekend at ... Grand Hotel [the film's setting], which is totally sold out. People are going back there and bringing all their own costumes and everything." Shepard later passed the reins to Jo Addie, an extra in several scenes of the movie, who since 1999 has run the society and edited its journal. Also called *INSITE*, the elegant quarterly boasts more than a thousand subscribers, and has published an almost unprecedented 1,700 pages on one film. She also authored the extensive website (www.somewhereintime.tv) with her husband Jim, and has redesigned, updated and expanded Shepard's comprehensive *The* Somewhere in Time *Story: Behind the Scenes of the Making of the Cult Romantic Fantasy Motion Picture* for the twenty-fifth anniversary of the film's release in 2005.

Richard Collier (Christopher Reeve) comforts young Arthur (Sean Hayden) after his father scolds him for playing in the lobby in *Somewhere in Time* (Rastar-Universal, 1980).

Discussing the novel's origins in Laurent Bouzereau's DVD documentary "Back to *Somewhere in Time*," Matheson recounted that during a camping trip with his family he visited the opera house in Virginia City, Nevada, and saw a photograph of actress Maude Adams, best known for J.M. Barrie's *Peter Pan*. Its effect on him was so profound that he began to wonder what would happen if its pull were strong enough to draw a man back in time to her. While writing the first section of the book in 1971, he stayed in its setting, the Hotel del Coronado in San Diego, and placed himself in the persona of his protagonist. When the novel was completed, he sold it to Viking, but it was not a financial success. As he told Mark Rathbun in *He Is Legend*, it "got some very nice reviews, and some reviews [that] were really downright nasty.... I've had more mail, though, from *Bid Time Return* and *What Dreams May Come* than any other book..." The film reunited him with former *Night Gallery* director Jeannot Szwarc, whose features include *Jaws 2* (1978) and William Castle's *Bug* (1975).

This also marked the beginning of Matheson's warm personal and professional association with Stephen Deutsch, who — as Stephen Simon — went on to co-produce the screen version of *What Dreams May Come*. Matheson told me in an interview for the Gauntlet limited edition of *What Dreams May Come*, "His blood father was S. Sylvan Simon, who directed all the old Red Skelton 'Fox' pictures [beginning with *Whistling in the Dark* (1941), and] was preparing to do *From Here to Eternity* when he had a heart attack and died [in 1951]. When his mother remarried, Steve was adopted by his stepfather, Armand Deutsch, and then later on decided he wanted to go back to his blood father's name." Simon wrote movingly of their relationship in *The Richard Matheson Companion*, and recounted his experiences producing both Matheson films in his book *The Force Is With You: Mystical Movie Messages That Inspire Our Lives*. He has also co-founded a DVD subscription service called the Spiritual Cinema Circle (www.spiritualcinemacircle.com).

Matheson added in our *Filmfax* interview, "I think on *Somewhere in Time*, because I had a closer relationship with the producer, it was the only time I had ever been *asked* to come on the shooting and stay there, and have transportation provided, a room provided, and my presence [actually] *desired*. They just don't do that. There's nothing more of a pariah in this business than the writer after the script is written, they just want [the writer] out of the picture. They don't want to see him, they don't want to be reminded of how beholden they are to him. So they'd just as soon he disappeared, and then they can act like it's theirs entirely. Which they usually do. Actors and actresses talk about how they 'saved' the picture. And the directors, of course, have this monstrous ego that they have done it all themselves — you know, the *auteur* theory, which started in France, but has reached absurd [proportions] in this country."

In his afterword to *What Dreams May Come*, Simon noted, "In January 1976, I was twenty-nine years old and looking for a job in the movie business. A friend recommended I read a book named *Bid Time Return*, by Richard Matheson. As soon as I finished the book, I knew I *had* to get in the movie business right away so I could produce the film version of the book. A month later, I managed to get myself hired by a film producer named Ray Stark as his assistant. My very first phone call on my very first day of work was to Richard's agent to arrange to meet Richard. The next week, we met for lunch at an old restaurant in Burbank named Sorrentino's. We became instant friends and, in a handshake, he promised we could work out a deal..." Szwarc told Bouzereau that he responded just as immediately to the novel, which was deemed noncommercial by Universal, but Ned Tanen — then the studio's creative head — agreed that Szwarc was owed a favor after replacing John D. Hancock and salvaging *Jaws 2*, so he greenlit the project while sharply reducing its budget.

British-born leading lady Jane Seymour, who had made an early splash in the James Bond film *Live and Let Die* (1973), felt an equally strong affinity for the story. She had already appeared in such genre entries as the miniseries *Frankenstein: The True Story*, Ray Harryhausen's *Sinbad and the Eye of the Tiger* (1977), and the 1978 pilot for *Battlestar Galactica*. Co-star Christopher Plummer, best known as Captain Von Trapp in *The Sound of Music* (1965), told Bouzereau that he welcomed the opportunity to play a role based on a historical figure, theatrical entrepreneur Charles Frohman, who had cast Maude Adams as Peter Pan. Szwarc related that the Coronado itself, seen in *Some Like It Hot* (1959), was deemed unsuitable for filming because it looked too modern. When associate producer Steve Bickel found a photo of Grand Hotel in a book, it was selected as a replacement. With cast and crew staying in dormitories — traveling by foot, horse and buggy, or bicycle because of a prohibition on automobiles — the location enhanced an egalitarian "summer stock" feeling required by the reduced budget, which according to Matheson was just over five million dollars.

The film opens in May of 1972 at the Millfield College Workshop, as aspiring playwright Richard Collier (Christopher Reeve) celebrates the premiere of *Too Much Spring*, which an agent in attendance has said might be good enough for Broadway, and is suddenly approached by an elderly stranger (played by Susan French, a *Jaws 2* alumna who, according to Szwarc, actually resembled Seymour in photos from her younger days). She presses an antique watch into his hand and says, "Come back to me," before departing as mysteriously as she appeared. In a chauffeur-driven car she rides to Grand Hotel, where she tearfully and lovingly embraces the program for *Too Much Spring*.

The scene shifts ahead to 1980 Chicago as Richard, now a successful playwright having trouble completing his latest opus, takes a drive with no particular destination, and impulsively stops for the night at Grand Hotel (which is located on Mackinac Island, Michigan). He is asked by bellman Arthur (Bill Erwin), who has been at the hotel since he was a boy of five in 1910, if they have ever met before. While waiting for the dining room to open, Richard strolls through the hotel's "Hall of History," where he is drawn to, and quickly becomes obsessed with, the photograph of a beautiful young woman. He learns from Arthur that she is Elise McKenna (the luminescent Seymour), a famous actress who had starred in a play at the hotel theater in 1912. Because Seymour's first actual scene does not occur for almost 45 minutes — nearly halfway through the film — Szwarc knew how critical the photograph was. At Reeve's request, he (Reeve) did not see it beforehand, so his reaction is real. Richard decides to stay on at the hotel and begins doing research at the local library on Elise's life and career, learning that she was guided by her manager, William Fawcett Robinson; after retiring, she was "never seen in public in her later years, apparently without an offstage life the absolute quintessence of seclusion." The real-life Adams also retired unexpectedly at the height of her career, not long after Frohman, her friend and mentor, was killed when the *Lusitania* was sunk by a German U-boat in 1915.

Discovering the last photograph ever taken of Elise, Richard recognizes her as the woman from the cast party and continues his quest for knowledge with a visit to her longtime acquaintance, theatrical historian Laura Roberts (Teresa Wright).* After learning that the antique watch never left Elise's possession, and was thought to have disappeared the night she died — the same night she had visited him — Richard notices a copy of *Travels Through Time*, a book by his Millfield philosophy teacher, Dr. Gerald Finney, which Laura says Elise read repeatedly. Richard then visits Finney (George Voskovec), a character not found in the novel. Finney tells him that through a form of self-hypnosis, it might be possible for a person to surround himself with the sights and sounds of a bygone era and literally "think" himself back to an earlier time, provided there were no objects present to remind him of the modern-day period.

*Celebrated stage actress Wright appeared in Alfred Hitchcock's *Shadow of a Doubt* (1943), and was nominated for Oscars as Best Supporting Actress and Best Actress in *Mrs. Miniver* and *The Pride of the Yankees* (both 1942), respectively, receiving one for the former.

Dressing and coiffing himself in period style, Richard lies down on his hotel bed and tries to project himself back to June 27, 1912, but his efforts are unsuccessful until Arthur helps him locate the registration book from that year, which proves that he actually did check in on the 28th; his next attempt bears fruit as he awakens in the past. Szwarc and cinematographer Isidore Mankofsky did not want to use special effects to show the transition, so the noise of a horse-drawn carriage on the soundtrack and a simple change of light within the scene, showing that it was a different time of day, did the job subtly but effectively. Mankofsky told Bouzereau that he had hit upon the idea of using two separate film stocks to differentiate the two time periods: the sharper Kodak stock for the modern-day scenes set in Chicago and a softer Fuji stock, which had a more pastel look, for the scenes set in 1912.

Richard meets a young Arthur (Sean Hayden), whose father is the desk clerk (John Alvin, a friend of Matheson's also seen briefly in "One for the Books"), watches the preparations for the play at the hotel theater, and finally finds Elise walking by the lake, where he approaches and responds in the affirmative when she cryptically asks, "Is it you?" Their meeting is cut short by the fanatically possessive W.F. Robinson (Plummer), who has long predicted that meeting a man will change her life. Despite Robinson's efforts to separate them, Richard manages to steal a few hours with Elise, during which their love quickly blossoms; in the first scene of the play, Elise ad-libs a romantic speech about "the man of my dreams" that is obviously directed at Richard in the audience. Seymour told Bouzereau that when shooting her close-up, she addressed the speech to Matheson in an empty theater; further cementing his identification with Collier, Matheson used the same method he had with "Duel" in writing the first part of the novel, recording his impressions in character on cassette tapes (copies of which were published by INSITE in 1993) while driving from Los Angeles to the Coronado.

Robinson summons Richard to the gazebo behind the theater with an urgent note citing "a matter of life and death"; there he is beaten, bound and gagged by two thugs who

Elise McKenna (Jane Seymour) and Richard reunited at last in the afterlife in *Somewhere in Time* (Rastar-Universal, 1980). Photograph courtesy of the Paul M. Sammon Collection.

hide him in the stable. By the time Richard frees himself, the theatrical company has left, yet Elise has stayed behind in the hope of seeing him again. They enjoy an idyllic day and night together until the next morning when, despite all of his careful planning, Richard accidentally stumbles upon a 1979 penny in the coin compartment of his vintage suit, and on seeing it is wrenched abruptly back to the present day. Devastated, he tries desperately to return to 1912 but is unable to do so. After sitting by an open window for days wasting away in a grief-stricken vigil, during which he becomes catatonic and effectively dies of a broken heart, Richard sees himself rising above his own body and into a blinding white light, where he finds Elise waiting for him. The two lovers join hands, reunited for all eternity.

In "Back to *Somewhere in Time*," Reeve revealed that a near-fatal drug reaction caused him to undergo a similar out-of-body experience some two months after his riding accident that paralyzed the actor on May 27, 1995. Mankofsky told Shepard that this elaborate final scene was originally a single camera move:

> It was an amazing shot. It was all done on the soundstage.... We started filming on the ceiling, and tilted down past the windows to Reeve's stand-in on the bed. We then had a dimmer change, where we switched from one set of lights to another. We started dollying toward the window. At this point, the ceiling piece had to roll back, the curtains had to part, and the set divided for us to go through.... The background was a white cyclorama, the floors were painted white, and Jane Seymour was standing there. And Reeve was ready to walk into the shot in his period costume. We had everybody working in that shot — pulling walls, rolling back the ceiling, pushing the dolly, changing the lights — it was all done in one continuous shot. But in the course of editing, the studio executives thought it was too long and they put in an optical dissolve to shorten the shot."

In the novel, Richard is a television scriptwriter instead of a playwright. His encounter with the older Elise is merely alluded to rather than described in detail, and his aimless wandering is motivated not by writer's block but by the knowledge that he has an inoperable brain tumor, which has resulted in the decision to write a book about his last four to six months of life while he is traveling. Matheson's screenplay eliminated the minor character of Elise's mother, but introduced those of Dr. Finney; Arthur, who links the scenes of the past (more plausibly updated from 1896 to 1912) and the present; and Laura Roberts, who provides much of the exposition regarding Elise's life and career, which Richard previously gleaned from the local library. Elise's unscripted speech to "the man of my dreams" during her performance was also added, as was the overt depiction of the lovers reunited in the hereafter, presumably to make the ending less downbeat. Their parting was made more affecting by having Richard torn almost literally from the screaming Elise's arms when he sees the coin, rather than returning to the present while she sleeps, as in the book.

As Finney wrote in "Second Chance," adapted by Matheson for *Dead of Night*, "I wonder if we aren't barred from the past by a thousand invisible chains. You can't drive into the past in a 1957 Buick because there are no 1957 Buicks in 1923; so how could you be there in one? You can't drive into 1923 in a Jordan Playboy, along a four-lane superhighway; there are no superhighways in 1923. You couldn't even, I'm certain, drive with a pack of modern filter-tip cigarettes in your pocket — into a night when no such thing existed. Or with so much as *a coin bearing a modern date* [emphasis mine], or wearing a charcoal-gray and pink shirt on your back. All those things, small and large, are chains keeping you out of a time when they could not exist." In my interview with Matheson, he praised Finney's "many wonderful stories. His novel *Time and Again* is just marvelous.... [W]hen I was going to do *Bid Time Return*[,] I asked Jack if he minded if I wrote a time-travel novel, and of course he didn't. That's why there's a 'Professor Finney' in [the film]." *From Time to Time*, Finney's sequel to his 1970 time-travel romance, was published shortly before his death in 1995.

Victoria Michaels and Maud Strand — then married to Deutsch and Szwarc, respectively — had minor roles, while Matheson made his first appearance in his own work with a cameo as an "astonished man" who sees Richard emerge from the bathroom, his face dotted with toilet paper after shaving with an unaccustomed straight razor. "As a matter of fact," he told me, "I remember Chris Reeve telling me, they had a scene which I had written, it was in the book and in the [script], where this guy is talking to Chris Reeve in the elevator while he's coming downstairs to the lobby, and everything he says is totally incomprehensible to him, because of the [period] language and what he's talking about, and the guy did it so badly that they cut it out. And Chris said, 'They should've let you do it.' Anyway, hell, *one word*, how could they go wrong? You get all dressed up to say one word. I tried to up it to two words, but the director wouldn't let me." In fact, he *does* say two words, although only one on camera: Upon encountering Richard, Matheson's character returns his sheepish greeting of "Morning" offscreen and then, after Richard has left, he looks after him, shakes his head, and says, "Astonishing."

Matheson had previously appeared in the NBC miniseries *Captains and the Kings* (1976), scripted and co-directed by his *Twilight Zone* colleague Douglas Heyes. "I was in a drama group [the Hidden Hills Players] out here where I live," he told me, "and I did a lot of plays, and this producer we knew [Jo Swerling, Jr.] saw me in it, and had me do a part in ... the miniseries. I played President Garfield. There's a funny story about me finding out I was going to do a scene with Henry Fonda, which chilled my blood. But then another guy [Bernie Willits] saw me act out here and he had me a do a whole educational film [*Jefferson and Hamilton*] where I play this sort of diabolical master of ceremonies who brings Alexander Hamilton and Thomas Jefferson back from the grave to debate — and not only their period and the Industrial Revolution, but the Civil War and Vietnam. It was quite imaginative."

Of the "astonished man" cameo, Szwarc said in his DVD commentary, "Both Matheson and I felt that one of the pitfalls of the film was that it was going to get heavy.... So whenever possible, we injected lightness into it, and I must say that Matheson did an extraordinary job of putting humor into the film, and right at the right moments." Keeping it all in the family, Matheson's daughter Ali appeared with William H. Macy and a pre–*Cheers* George Wendt in the opening scene. He told me, "She got excised [as did Wendt, who was credited nonetheless, per Screen Actors Guild rules, because he had a scripted line]. She had a lot more footage. She was going to be Chris Reeve's girlfriend in it, and then they edited it down so much that she had very little — as a matter of fact, I don't know whether you can even see her. She had no lines left.... We did create the whole college sequence and the old lady coming up to him. None of that's in the book." This was the first of Reeve's attempts to avoid being typecast as Superman, a role he reprised in three sequels.

A real-life hero who fought tirelessly for spinal-cord research until his death, Reeve discussed the film's reception in his memoir *Still Me*: "When [*Somewhere in Time*] was completed and test screenings were held a year later, audiences loved it. Early reviews were extremely favorable, especially one in *Daily Variety* that praised everyone involved. But when the film opened in October, it bombed. Later I often joked that it left a crater on the street." It was hampered by an actors' strike that prevented the stars from promoting it, and Universal insisted on opening it in 800 theaters rather than allowing word-of-mouth to build slowly. According to Reeve, "Audiences stayed away in droves, and the film disappeared within a few weeks. Needless to say, this was a huge blow. I had never failed so visibly before. Of course, I blamed myself entirely. In retrospect, I think that because I had worked on *Superman* for so long, my characterization of Clark Kent may have crept into Richard Collier. We had such a wonderful time filming [it], but maybe we lost our objectivity. In any case, we were devastated by the public's rejection of our work."

"Cast and crew alike moved quickly into other projects. Over the years, however, a miraculous transformation took place. Cable television spread across the country, and people began to discover our little movie. Charles Champlin, a critic for the *Los Angeles Times*, hosted a film series on a local station, and soon people began talking about *Somewhere in Time*. We became the most popular and requested offering on Z Channel and soon developed a cult following.... [My wife] Dana and I attended [INSITE's annual *Somewhere in Time* weekend] in the fall of 1994 and enjoyed an overwhelming reception." Reeve also credited INSITE with helping him receive a star on Hollywood's Walk of Fame in 1997. Matheson was one of 19 members of the film's cast and crew who were reunited for a fifteenth-anniversary celebration with Jane Seymour, held in May of 1995 at Universal City. His participation was extensively documented in one of INSITE's two-hour "event videos," including a panel discussion with Stephen Deutsch and a bus trip to the Hotel del Coronado, with Matheson acting as a kind of tour guide.

Approached by Universal to write a sequel in 1999, Matheson declined. Szwarc told Bouzereau that he had wanted "to start ... with the scene of the penny, and then to stay with Elise and be with her as she tries to understand what happened, how this man she loves suddenly vanished, as she little by little becomes familiar with the concept of what he did and comes to terms with it: how she becomes a recluse, how she moves out, how she becomes very private, how she ages. And then suddenly one day she sees an ad with his name on it, and she goes to Chicago and she sees this play with the young author there, and it's the love of her life, and she recognizes him, and then how she gives him the watch and then goes to the hotel and dies." In "Two Shots from Fly's Photo Gallery," a sequel by John Shirley written for Conlon's *He Is Legend*, a man uses Collier's time-travel method to alter history by intervening in the gunfight at the OK Corral.

Of the friends and fellow artists who paid tribute to Reeve when he was paralyzed, biographer Adrian Havill notes that Seymour "offered perhaps the most generous gesture of all. Three months pregnant at the time of the accident, she would name one of her twin sons after Chris when she gave birth on November 30 [of 1995]. John Barry's musical score from their film was played in the delivery room as the two children came into the world." Seymour persuaded Barry, a personal friend who also scored almost a dozen James Bond films, to write the music, despite being outside their price range. Added Matheson in his *Burn, Witch, Burn* commentary, "I think *The Rocky Horror [Picture] Show* [1975] is about the only one that's ahead of it now as a cult film.... It was not a box-office success when it first came out, but through the years it has become very profitable. The video sold a lot; John Barry's score has sold tremendously. It was the most popular score he ever wrote, and it's one of those things. You can't predict how it's going to happen, what pictures will last."

An Academy Award winner for *Born Free* (1966), *The Lion in Winter* (1968), *Out of Africa* (1985), and *Dances With Wolves* (1990), Barry crafted a suitably romantic score that incorporated Rachmaninoff's *Rhapsody on a Theme of Paganini* (Op. 43, Variation XVIII), but dropped the novel's use of Matheson's favorite composer, Gustav Mahler. In the earlier *He Is Legend*, Matheson told Mark Rathbun, "I had wanted to use Mahler in *Somewhere in Time*....Szwarc was all ready to do it. He had cassettes [of his music] that he was playing while we were shooting the film. And John Barry ... *loves* Mahler. He loves Mahler so much that he was willing to just take all of Mahler's music and adapt it to the picture. And then they decided not to, and he wrote his own score. It's too bad, but he did write a lovely score."

Himself a sometime composer and lyricist, Matheson added in a 1986 interview with Michael Blaine for *Rod Serling's The Twilight Zone Magazine*, "I've been working on a symphony, in the style of Mahler, for years.... At one time I was going to go entirely into songwriting and composition. I gradually realized that was putting a great deal of pressure on me ... to make a living that way." As a student at the University of Missouri, Matheson wrote the musical numbers for two of the journalism school's annual "J-Shows," *When Nights Were Bold* (1947), which he also directed, and *The Eyes Have It* (1948), for which he wrote the script with Norman Kennelly. In the 1980s, he wrote the lyrics for two songs recorded by Perry Como and composed by Como's music director Nick Perito: the title track to Como's 1982 album *I Wish It Could Be Christmas Forever* and "Do You Remember Me."

Matheson and Szwarc cleverly use the Rachmaninoff theme in various ways as a musical "bridge across time," such as the transition from 1972 to 1980, wherein the elderly Elise is shown putting on a record of the *Rhapsody*, which continues seamlessly on the soundtrack over a title card reading "Chicago — Eight Years Later," until Richard is seen shutting off a record player playing the same music. In a subsequent scene, Laura Roberts shows him a variety of theatrical memorabilia from her collection, including a scale model of Grand Hotel that had been commissioned by Elise. When she opens the top to reveal that it is actually an oversized music box, which plays the *Rhapsody*, the stunned Richard says in awe, "That's my favorite music in the whole world. I don't understand what's happening." Finally, after Elise hears him humming the piece while rowing on the lake during their day together, she asks what it is and, when told, says, "I saw [Rachmaninoff] with the Philharmonic once. I love his music, but I've never heard this piece," to which the smiling Richard wryly responds, "Really? Well, I'll introduce you to it sometime." (The piece was not composed until 22 years later, in 1934.)

According to *The* Somewhere in Time *Story*, this use of the *Rhapsody* was part of an overall effect that the producer, writer, and director dubbed "circles within circles," which Szwarc defined as "the delicate blending of past and present which would give the audience a permanent feeling of 'déjà vu.'" Shepard notes, "Matheson suggested a unique visual device to connect Richard Collier with the old and the young Elise McKenna. His idea was to have the old Elise present an ornate pocket watch to Richard, which he would give back to the young Elise in 1912. But then Matheson suddenly realized the time paradox inherent in the idea. 'As soon as I said it, I realized it was impossible — the watch would have no beginning in time.' It was too late, they loved it. After discussing it over and over, the three finally decided to include the device, reasoning that it would not interfere with the appreciation of the picture."

One of Matheson's most cherished dreams is a musical version of *Somewhere in Time*, which along with *Magician's Choice* has come close to fruition.* According to an update by Jo Addie in a recent *INSITE*, Matheson and Broadway producer Ken Davenport "are very close to 'zeroing in' on an all-important member of the production, the composer.... 'We've

---

*Matheson's other proposed stage projects include an adaptation of his novel *A Stir of Echoes* (1958); an unfinished play about an alcoholic poet inspired by Dylan Thomas, *Do Not Go Gentle*, written in the early '60s with Beaumont; and *Wild Bill and His Lady*, a one-man show based on his *Memoirs of Wild Bill Hickok*.

been in the selection process for the right composer for a long time, and I hope my favorite one will be signing a contract soon.'... Davenport initially approached Matheson to ask for the rights to produce it years back, but he declined at the time, favoring his own script version [for which the songs had also been written by *Duel* composer Billy Goldenberg and lyricist Harry Shannon]. But Davenport persisted and tried again. This time, Matheson felt his approach was a good one, and gave permission to this longtime fan of his story."

Many remarked upon the similarity between *Somewhere in Time* and Dan Curtis's TV-movie *The Love Letter* (1998), in which an antique writing desk becomes the vehicle for an epistolary romance between Scotty Corrigan (Campbell Scott), who purchases it in the present, and Elizabeth Whitcomb (Jennifer Jason Leigh), its original owner during the Civil War era. Scott told *TV Guide*'s Annabel Vered, "People equate it with a movie I've never seen called *Somewhere in Time*." Susan Stewart's review in the magazine's "Hits & Misses" column notes that this Hallmark Hall of Fame presentation "steals from *Somewhere in Time* and even *Backdraft* [1991]." Aptly, the film was based on a Finney tale. Matheson told me in *Filmfax*, "I adapted [the same story in 1973] for an old anthology pilot film that Curtis and I were doing [for the abortive *Dead of Night* series], but it never got made, and it was really enlarged upon [in James Henerson's teleplay].... I couldn't take a story that to me is perfection at its length and then try to stretch it out to fit a time period." Another CBS telemovie, *The Two Worlds of Jennie Logan* (1979), and the feature *Happy Accidents* (2000) also had similar premises.

The Incredible Shrinking Woman

(Universal, released January 30, 1981) DIRECTOR: Joel Schumacher; PRODUCER: Hank Moonjean; SCREENPLAY: Jane Wagner, suggested by Matheson's *The Shrinking Man*; MUSIC: Suzanne Ciani; MAKEUP: Ve Neill; SPECIAL EFFECTS: Bruce Logan, Roy Arbogast, Guy Faria, David Kelsey. Color, 88 minutes. CAST— Patricia Kramer, Judith Beasley: Lily Tomlin. Vance Kramer: Charles Grodin. Dan Beame: Ned Beatty. Dr. Eugene Nortz: Henry Gibson. Dr. Ruth Ruth: Elizabeth Wilson. Rob: Mark Blankfield. Concepcion: Maria Smith. Sandra Dyson: Pamela Bellwood. Tom Keller: John Glover. Logan Carver: Nicholas Hormann. Lyle Parks: James McMullan. Beth Kramer: Shelby Balik. Jeff Kramer: Justin Dana. Sidney: Richard A. Baker. Mike Douglas: Himself. Neighbors: Karen Knapp, David Marsh, Mary McCusker, Betty McGuire, Maria O'Brien, Julie Payne, Randolph Powell, David Rupprecht, Donovan Scott, Charles Woolf. Guards: John Achorn, Martin Ferrero, Ron House, Will Knox, Mitch Kreindel, Nancy Lenehan, Holly McCarver, Mimi Seton, Alan Sherman, Joe Spano, Ron Vernan, Diz White, Grace Woodard. Jacki King: Herself. Dr. Atkins: Macon McCalman. Store Manager: Dick Wilson. Store Cashier: Sally Kirkland. Customers: Pat Ast, Dorothy Andrews, June Sanders. Bag Boy: Jonathan Prince. Cheese Demonstrator: Terry McGovern. Woman Executive: Betty Beaird. Spanish Soap Opera Actress: Irene De Bari. Spanish Soap Opera Actor: Dante D'André. Policemen: Todd Everett, Joseph Hardin. Newscasters: Gary Goetzman, M.E. Loree, Robert Phelps, Glenn Robards. Interviewers: James Beach, Dick McGarvin. TV Commercial Actresses: Julie Brown, Janice Carroll. Kitchen Worker: Annie Knight. Neighborhood Children: Kevin Brando, Randy Morton, Ari Zeltzer. Vance's Secretary: Mitzi Hoag. Toys: Albert Marotta, Tommy McLoughlin, Jan Stuart Schwartz, Richmond Shepard, Mitchel Young-Evans.

Although it has its partisans, this is widely considered both an exceedingly unfunny comedy and a complete bastardization of Matheson's novel. It was reconfigured as a vehicle for Lily Tomlin by her personal and professional partner, Jane Wagner, who had shared three Emmy Awards with Tomlin as a writer and/or executive producer on her network specials, and acted in the same capacities on this film. Designed and photographed with an aggressively pastel palette that prefigures Tim Burton's *Edward Scissorhands* (1990), it jettisons the anti-nuclear ambience of the original novel and film to take broad, unsubtle strokes at such contemporary concerns as consumerism, corporate greed, advertising, environmental incorrectness, processed food, and industrial espionage. Tomlin essays a dual role as the

Hamster-sized captive Patricia Kramer (Lily Tomlin) in *The Incredible Shrinking Woman* (Universal, 1981).

eponymous suburban housewife, Patricia Kramer, and her neighbor, Judith Beasley. Rick Baker, an Academy Award winner for *An American Werewolf in London* (1981), *Harry and the Hendersons* (1987), and *Ed Wood* (1994), donned his own ape makeup (as he had in producer Dino De Laurentiis's disastrous 1976 remake of *King Kong*) as Sidney, billed as "Richard A. Baker."

Pat's husband, Vance (Charles Grodin) is an advertising executive whose job involves finding names for products like Sexpot perfume and Galaxy Glue, and the home they share with their children, Beth (Shelby Balik) and Jeff (Justin Dana), in the California community of Tasty Meadows is full of various chemical concoctions. Tomlin's fellow *Laugh-In* alumnus, Henry Gibson, is Dr. Eugene Nortz of the Kleinman Institute for the Study of Unexplained Phenomena, who attributes Pat's shrinkage to a combination of tap water, a flu shot, birth control pills, smog, and a myriad of products — half of which she and Vance helped name — all set off by an imbalance already present in her system. Pat appears on television with Mike Douglas, intending to warn the public about the products' potential dangers, but changes her mind at the last minute out of deference to Vance and his boss, Dan Beame (*Dying Room Only*'s Ned Beatty), who fears "a crisis in confidence in American consumerism" and reports to a shadowy consortium of industry leaders, presumably in a nod to Beatty's role in *Network* (1976). Known as the Organization for World Management and headed by Tom Keller (John Glover), the cabal aims to "be the trailblazers of tomorrow and be assured our place as the power elite forever," and plots with Nortz and his colleague, Dr. Ruth Ruth (Elizabeth Wilson), to develop a "shrink serum" from Pat's blood with which they can reduce entire populations.

Like Scott Carey, Pat moves into a dollhouse (also losing her parental authority, unlike the childless cinematic Carey), begins working on her memoirs, and is believed dead after the horrified maid, Concepcion (Maria Smith), finds a tiny yellow sneaker beside the garbage disposal unit. (In Pat's case the culprit is not a cat but Keller, who has abducted her.) Escaping from Nortz and Ruth with the aid of the super-intelligent Sidney, a fellow test subject, and Rob (Mark Blankfield), a disaffected employee, Pat uses the public address system at her nearby supermarket to reveal her continued existence to the world before shrinking out of sight and falling into a chemical soup of spilled products, which restores her to her original size.

The Incredible Shrinking Woman marked the feature-film directorial debut of Joel Schumacher, a self-described "hardcore drug addict" in the 1960s who — as he told *Cinefantastique*'s Craig Reid — then turned his life around, working his way up through the ranks of the film industry as a costume designer, production designer, and the writer of *Car Wash* (1976) and *The Wiz* (1978). After helping to establish the Hollywood "Brat Pack" with *St. Elmo's Fire* (1985), which starred Emilio Estevez, Rob Lowe, Andrew McCarthy, Demi Moore, Judd Nelson, Ally Sheedy, and Mare Winningham, Schumacher further bolstered the ranks of contemporary stars with similar ensemble casts in *The Lost Boys* (1987) and *Flatliners* (1990), both of which featured Donald Sutherland's son, Kiefer. Schumacher also enjoyed spectacular box-office success as one of the foremost interpreters of John Grisham's bestselling legal thrillers with *The Client* (1994) and *A Time to Kill* (1995). His stock slipped badly when he inherited from Tim Burton — and subsequently mishandled — Warner Bros.' cherished cash cow, the Batman franchise, with *Batman Forever* (1996) and *Batman and Robin* (1997).

Shrinking Woman "was originally planned in 1976 as a comedy remake of the original tailored for Chevy Chase by scripter Ron Clark," Richard Meyers noted in *S-F 2*. "Director John Landis was already deeply into pre-production when the studio rejected his budget of fifteen million dollars. In August 1977, [the new team] took over." *Shrinking Man* director Jack Arnold told *Filmfax*'s David J. Schow, "They never approached me [or] Matheson, and then they complained to me that they were having trouble getting a good script! Then, I was brought up to the people at Universal, but it's not the same Universal, and the people who are running it don't know anything about me. Many of them are not even movie *fans*; they're just business people. Management has changed." Matheson told me in *Filmfax*, "If they had made [it] into a really funny picture, you know, like the Zuckers [did] with *Airplane!* [1980], I wouldn't have said a word. It would have been great. Not that I said a word anyway, but I would have enjoyed it. I just didn't think they did a good job on it.... I would have been happy to turn it into a comedy myself, and I think it would have been funnier. It turned out pretty poorly."

Baker was brought aboard the *Shrinking* project by Landis, for whom he had already created the gorilla suits in *Schlock* (1971) and *The Kentucky Fried Movie* (1977), and then carried over into the new team. "I got to do a lot of things I hoped to do on *King Kong*," he said of Sidney's innovative design in the book *Men, Makeup, and Monsters: Hollywood's Masters of Illusion and FX* by Anthony Timpone. "The suit had different densities of foam. I wanted the bony part to be hard, while the fatty part should be soft and mushy and the muscle part should be something else — so we made these different density things. The rib cage, for instance, was a hard section, so that when I moved to the side, you would see the definition of the ribs — not just a bunch of buckling kapok stuff. It had rigid shoulder blades, the stomach was softer — without the hair on it, it looked like a skinned gorilla. It was a fairly decent suit, much better looking — in person, especially — than Kong."

Paying dubious tribute to Arnold, Jeff Kramer at one point appears outside Pat's window dressed in a *Creature from the Black Lagoon* costume. When asked about the remake, the director of the original echoed Matheson's own sentiments in Reemes's *Directed by Jack Arnold*: "I hated it. There was no point of view and the special effects weren't even that good. But the major fault is that it's not comedy even though they tried so hard to make it funny.... I saw a recent revival of the original film a few months ago. I could hardly get a seat, there were so many young people trying to get in. It played to full capacity. The audience enjoyed the film even more than when it was made. They got all the nuances that I put in. It was a joy to me, just to watch their reaction to the film. And they were mostly too young to have seen it when it was first released.... I like all kinds of stories. There isn't a kind of story I don't like. I like science fiction, I love comedy. I love *The Mouse That Roared*— it's my favorite picture, and it's a comedy — I think almost as much of *The Incredible Shrinking Man*, which is science fiction. I don't have a favorite subject. The only preference I have is a good script."

Both the remake and Matheson's unproduced sequel, published in *Unrealized Dreams*, have the kind of conventional ending U-I had wanted, with the heroine restored to, or at least approaching, her proper size, although *The Fantastic Little Girl* is a misnomer, for the "girl" is Carey's wife Louise. (According to collector Brian Kirby, the first draft — dated June 28, 1956, several months before the first film's release — is entitled *The Fantastic Shrinking Girl*, and attributes the original story to Zugsmith.) As Matheson told Sammon in *Midnight Graffiti*, "It took the wife down. Somehow, she had gotten the same effect [while] down in the galley, so it took longer to affect her [*laughs*]. So she went down there [to the cellar] and searched for him, and [had] all kinds of adventures, and then rejoined him. At which point, they both began regaining size. You know. It incorporated everything but the kitchen sink." Shrinking faster than Scott, Louise somehow locates him in his microscopic backyard world when they reach the same size, and then both begin fortuitously growing at the same rate. Thomas F. Monteleone also focused on Louise in a variation entitled "The Diary of Louise Carey" in *He Is Legend*.

Phil Hardy's *Overlook Film Encyclopedia: Science Fiction* dissects how the remake's own kitchen-sink approach "transforms the terror of [the original] into a would-be satire on the world of big business and the media.... Wagner and director Schumacher spend far too much time explaining why Tomlin starts shrinking.... The Arnold film was made from the point of view of Grant Williams, this from the point of view of a detached observer. In the course of this radical shift of emphasis any paranoia implicit in the central situation is lost." In James Gunn's *New Encyclopedia of Science Fiction*, Barry Keith Grant observed that its intention "was to make the story a more contemporary feminist statement about sexual inequality.... And the film succeeds in creating some wonderful images to express this theme: the tiny Tomlin housed in a hamster cage, for example, or buried by table scraps in the kitchen sink and forced down the drain with all the gunk. Finally, though, this film relies too heavily on Tomlin's presence and not enough on the inherent drama of the physical transformation her character experiences ... so the familiar never really becomes strange but merely amusing."

Twilight Zone —The Movie

(Warner Bros., released June 24, 1983) PRODUCER: Steven Spielberg, John Landis; inspired by *The Twilight Zone*, created by Rod Serling; MUSIC: Jerry Goldsmith; PROJECT CONSULTANT: Carol Serling; NARRATOR: Burgess Meredith. Color, 101 minutes. Prologue— DIRECTOR-SCREENPLAY: Landis. CAST— Passenger: Dan Aykroyd. Driver: Albert Brooks. "Time Out"— DIRECTOR/SCREENPLAY: Landis; MAKEUP: Robert Westmoreland, Melanie E. Levitt; SPECIAL MAKEUP EFFECTS: Craig Reardon; SPECIAL EFFECTS: Paul

Stewart. CAST— Bill Conner: Vic Morrow. Larry: Doug McGrath. Ray: Charles Halla-han. German Officers: Remus Peets, Kai Wulff. Waitress No. 1: Sue Dugan. Waitress No. 2: Debby Porter. Bar Patron: Steven Williams. French Mother: Annette Claudier. Vietnamese: Joseph Hieu, Albert Leong. Charming G.I.: Stephen Bishop. G.I.s: Thomas Byrd, Vincent J. Isaac, William B. Taylor, Domingo Ambriz. K.K.K.: Eddie Donno, Michael Milgram, John Larroquette. Soldier No. 1: Norbert Weisser. "Kick the Can"— DIRECTOR: Spielberg. SCREENPLAY: George Clayton Johnson, Matheson, Josh Rogan [Melissa Mathison]; STORY: Johnson; MAKEUP: John Elliott. CAST— Mr. Bloom: Scatman Crothers. Leo Conroy: Bill Quinn. Mr. Weinstein: Martin Garner. Mrs. Weinstein: Selma Diamond. Mrs. Dempsey: Helen Shaw. Mr. Agee: Murray Matheson. Mr. Mute: Peter Brocco. Miss Cox: Priscilla Pointer. Young Mr. Weinstein: Scott Nemes. Young Mrs. Weinstein: Tanya Fenmore. Young Mr. Agee: Evan Richards. Young Mrs. Dempsey: Laura Mooney. Young Mr. Mute: Christopher Eisenmann. Mr. Gray Panther: Richard Swingler. Mr. Conroy's Son: Alan Haufrect. Mr. Conroy's Daughter-in-Law: Cheryl Socher. Nurse No. 2: Elsa Raven. "It's a Good Life"—DIRECTOR: Joe Dante; SCREENPLAY: Matheson, based on Jerome Bixby's story; MAKEUP: Elliott; SPECIAL MAKEUP EFFECTS/MONSTER EFFECTS: Rob Bottin. CAST— Helen Foley: Kathleen Quinlan. Anthony Fremont: Jeremy Licht. Uncle Walt: Kevin McCarthy. Mother: Patricia Barry. Father: William Schallert. Ethel: Nancy Cartwright. Walter Paisley: Dick Miller. Sara: Cherie Currie. Tim: Bill Mumy. Charlie: Jeffrey Bannister. "Nightmare at 20,000 Feet"— DIRECTOR: George Miller; SCREENPLAY: Matheson, based on his story; MAKEUP: Elliott; SPECIAL MAKEUP EFFECTS: Reardon, Michael McCracken; VISUAL EFFECTS: Peter Kuran (V.C.E.), Jim Danforth (Effects Associates), David Allan; MONSTER CONCEPTUAL DESIGN: Ed Verreaux. CAST— John Valentine: John Lithgow. Senior Stewardess Dionne: Abbe Lane. Junior Stewardess Shelly: Donna Dixon. Co-Pilot: John Dennis Johnston. Creature: Larry Cedar. Sky Marshal: Charles Knapp. Little Girl: Christina Nigra. Mother: Lonna Schwab. Old Woman: Margaret Wheeler. Old Man: Eduard Franz. Young Girl: Margaret Fitzgerald. Young Man: Jeffrey Weissman. Mechanic No. 1: Jeffrey Lampert. Mechanic No. 2: Frank Toth. Passenger: Carol Serling. Pilot Announcement: Byron McFarland.

Any merits of this ill-advised attempt to recreate the classic anthology series in a large-screen format were inevitably overshadowed by the helicopter crash during filming that killed Vic Morrow and two Vietnamese children working illegally. "It was horrible," Matheson told me in an interview for *Filmfax.* "I remember when I had lunch with Steven [Spielberg] and Joe Dante and John Landis [who produced with Spielberg], that Steven was kind of horrified by the script [for Morrow's segment]. I mean, it had nothing to do with the accident, but it was so dark and foul and ... profane. Especially if you compared it to the second story, 'Kick the Can,' about the old folks' home. I did the script on that ... but Steven had Melissa Mathison [the writer of his *E.T. The Extra-Terrestrial* (1982)] ... redo it and they made it kind of mushy; mine was a lot harder-edged, I thought." The project reunited Matheson with Spielberg for the first time since *Duel,* although there had been near-misses in between.*

Other returning veterans of the original series included composer Jerry Goldsmith and actors Kevin McCarthy and Burgess Meredith (the latter filling in for the late Rod Serling to handle the opening narrations). What struck many — including Matheson — as unwise was the decision to remake some of the best-loved episodes instead of creating new stories.

---

*According to Matheson, "I remember one time [producers] Julia Phillips and her husband Michael had me in, and asked me if I wanted to write a movie about flying saucers, and I said no. And I gather that's what turned into *Close Encounters* [*of the Third Kind* (1977)].... And it seems to me that I was even asked to do a rewrite on *Jaws,* though I'm not positive of that, and if I was, I turned that down, too. I've got great judgment."

Matheson updated Johnson's "Kick the Can," Serling's "It's a Good Life," and his own "Nightmare at 20,000 Feet" for segments directed by Spielberg, Dante, and George Miller, respectively, while Landis, hot off the success of such comedies as *National Lampoon's Animal House* (1978), *The Blues Brothers* (1980), and *An American Werewolf in London*, wrote and directed the first segment, as well as an eight-minute prologue.

After driver Albert Brooks plays "TV Theme Songs" with passenger Dan Aykroyd, who turns into a monster and kills him, the film segues into a variation on "A Quality of Mercy" (12/29/61), a third-season *Zone* episode in which a G.I. in the Philippines is forced to see things through the eyes of the enemy when suddenly transformed into his Japanese counterpart. "Time Out" begins as bigoted Bill Conner (Morrow) meets his friends for a drink and bemoans the fact that he has been passed over for a promotion in favor of a Jew. This escalates into a tirade of racial epithets that upsets a black patron (Steven Williams, who later had a recurring role as the aptly named Mr. X on *The X-Files*) and Bill's angry exit from the bar. Outside, he inexplicably finds himself in, successively, occupied France, where he is pursued as a Jew by German officers; the South, where he is nearly lynched as a "nigger" by Klansmen (including comedian John Larroquette); Vietnam, where he is shot at as a "gook" by Americans and rescues two children in the fatal sequence (later excised); and, finally, a railway car bound for a concentration camp.

As Anne Francis, who starred in Morrow's film debut *Blackboard Jungle* (1955), said in our *Filmfax* interview, "[Morrow] had a career that could have continued on if he hadn't had his head chopped off [by a helicopter blade]. I mean really, it was a terrible blunder, with a group of serious mistakes made, for which no one would take responsibility after. I'm sorry about that, too, because I think that people could have taken responsibility for what happened and had a lot more respect from folks because of it.... You know, nobody intentionally killed Vic Morrow, but I do feel that it was too bad that nobody would even stand up and say, 'It's terrible what happened and we feel awful about it, and mistakes were made.' I don't know, it was just sad to me that Vic should just die that way." Almost five years after the out-of-control camera helicopter killed Morrow, Renée Shinn Chen, and Myca Dinh Le on July 23, 1982, Landis and his colleagues were acquitted of involuntary manslaughter.

Hollywood reporters Stephen Farber and Marc Green covered the crash, the ensuing trial and its aftermath in their book *Outrageous Conduct: Art, Ego, and the* Twilight Zone *Case*, noting, "Originally Spielberg had considered remaking one of the most memorable episodes from the original series, 'The Monsters Are Due on Maple Street.' It focused on the panic that envelops a placid suburban community infiltrated by aliens.... The central character was a young boy, and most of the story took place at night. What originally attracted Spielberg were the opportunities for suspense and imaginative special effects in the scenes of the bemused aliens watching the behavior of the earthlings. But after the accident at Indian Dunes [California], Spielberg decided that the combination of children, night shooting, and terrifying special effects was an inflammatory mix ... and hurriedly settled on one of the most sweet-tempered episodes he could find..." Matheson, who was involved in all three of the non–Landis segments of the film, told me he was unaware that a remake of "The Monsters Are Due on Maple Street" had ever been considered.

However, in Jean-Marc and Randy Lofficier's *Into The Twilight Zone: The Rod Serling Programme Guide*, he recounted, "Spielberg wanted me to write something for him, a Halloween story about a not-nice young man who went out and tormented these kids while they were trick-or-treating. Then all the things that were make-believe began to become real and turn against him as a sort of cosmic punishment. It ended up like a painting by Hieronymus Bosch. I don't know whether they didn't like it or what, I think it was a very good script. I think one thing that they did say is that it would cost too much money, and I can see the truth in that. Beyond that, I don't know. That was replaced by 'Kick the Can'.... I worked very closely with Joe Dante on the Jerome Bixby story ["It's a Good Life"]. We worked together on the script, he, his associates and I, all through it. With Spielberg I worked less closely, although I did work with him on the script. We had a good relationship.... With Miller, I didn't work with him much at all, although I did go in one day when he was preparing to shoot, and sat with him. I admired how he worked with the performers and I admired his visual sense of what he wanted."

Landis, who as mentioned earlier had also developed *The Incredible Shrinking Woman* but not been able to bring it to fruition, was later preempted by Spielberg from collaborating with Matheson on a subsequent project. According to an article by Frank Barron and Jay Stevenson (aka Steve Biodrowski) in *Cinefantastique*, before co-executive producing another remake of Sir Arthur Conan Doyle's oft-filmed novel *The Lost World* as a two-hour pilot for a syndicated action-adventure series, which debuted in 1999, Landis "had hoped to film a big screen version ... at Universal Studios, but his plans came to an end when the studio opted instead to film another dino-opus. 'We actually had a great script by Richard Matheson to do *The Lost World*, with Sean Connery as Professor Challenger,' said Landis. 'We were going to do a very traditional, old-fashioned adaptation of Wells' [sic] book. Unfortunately, it was in development at Universal, and they bought *Jurassic Park* [filmed in 1993]. They said, 'We don't want to do *The Lost World*; we want to do the rip-off of *The Lost World*!'" Crichton borrowed Conan Doyle's title for his sequel, filmed (also by Spielberg) in 1997 as *The Lost World: Jurassic Park*.

"A shame indeed that *The Lost World* will not be made," Matheson wrote me in 1993. "John Landis said it was a 'brilliant script' at the Ackerman Famous Monsters Con in Washington, D.C. Of course, he knew I was sitting in the audience too. But it *is* a good script and would have made a delightful film. One more misfire. *One Cut to Paradise* is now kaput too.... Landis and I have bad karma, I think." In a follow-up letter, he explained, "*One Cut to Paradise* was a screenplay re-write I did for John Landis. About a retired L.A. bomb squad member who is drawn back into the squad by a mad bomber. Sound familiar? They are shooting it at this moment. Entitled *Blown Away* [1994]. How major studios can allow a project to go on without having the least idea that the same project is going on at two (!) other studios is beyond me.... At least it was only a rewrite on my part. Original by Crash Leyland, son of motor car builders in England. Odd name to pick for their son." The film was finally made as *The Final Cut* (1995), directed by Roger Christian from a screenplay by Raul Inglis, with no credit going to Matheson, whose material was presumably not used.

Spielberg's saccharine, golden-hued "Kick the Can" is set at the Sunnyvale Rest Home, where over the skeptical objections of Leo Conroy (Bill Quinn), pixieish new arrival Mr. Bloom (Scatman Crothers) persuades the Weinsteins (Martin Garner, Selma Diamond), Mr. Mute (Peter Brocco), and the other residents to feel — and then miraculously become — young again by playing the titular game. In a marked departure from the original ending, where the rejuvenated seniors vanished laughing into the night, all but one of them, Mr. Agee (Murray Matheson, no relation to Richard), decide to return to their "old, nice bodies, but with fresh, young minds," and even Conroy is seen playfully kicking the can in the front yard as the beaming Bloom departs, preparing to bring his magic to the next nursing home. As Marc Scott Zicree explained in *The Twilight Zone Companion*, the new ending originated with Johnson, who had long contemplated what would next become of the children and explored one possible answer in an outline he submitted to the producers, some of which was incorporated into the feature version, but unfortunately, neither he nor Matheson was pleased with Mathison's rewrite.

"It's one thing to get a remake," Johnson told me in *Filmfax*, "but it's another to have *the* Steven Spielberg as the guy who's chosen to direct your work, with me sort of hanging back and saying, 'I'm not so sure, I'd love to have a meeting with Steven,' and Steven through his representative saying, 'No, I do not audition any more,' a 'take it or leave it' sort of attitude. Ultimately I ended up taking their deal, watching the way they put it all together, and feeling somewhat dismayed when I actually saw it. Although I was touched quite a bit by that lady [Mrs. Dempsey, played by Helen Shaw and, as a young girl, Laura Mooney] whose husband was Jack Dempsey, not the boxer but Jack Dempsey, and she lost her ring — right at the end, this ring has become too big and has fallen off of her [as in Matheson's *The Incredible Shrinking Man*] — that was all very moving to me, but basically I sat there sort of depressed by what they had done with it. I was blessed, though, I ended up making large amounts of money from it. They screwed up the credits, got punished by the Writers Guild [of America], and had to pay everybody some kind of a penalty for that.

"I was fortunate enough to think of an ending for 'Kick the Can' that would make sense, so I typed it up on three pages and took it with me to my little meeting with the producers. Before I signed the deal, I gave them these three pages, so later on when I saw that they had used some of the information from the three pages, I called it to the attention of the business affairs department and they ended up giving me yet more money. So all in all I came away from the experience really satisfied, except for my real disappointment that Spielberg didn't have a clearer idea of stories [which echoes Matheson's similar sentiments regarding Spielberg's work on *Amazing Stories*].... For example, in *Twilight Zone— The Movie*, Steven did not have a story editor. He had Matheson to help him, and brought in some other writer, 'Josh Rogan,' who is Melissa Mathison, who wrote *The Black Stallion* [1979]. She must have been very unhappy because she changed her name on it. When the Writers Guild wanted to know how to credit it, I said, 'Credit everybody, don't let anybody off the hook.' So [everybody is] on there, but it was still a very strange situation..."

According to Farber and Green, "Spielberg wanted to walk away from *Twilight Zone* after the accident. When Warner Bros. informed him that he would have to meet his contractual obligations and direct one segment of the film, he resolved to finish it off as quickly as possible.... Spielberg's was the shortest shooting schedule of all four segments — a mere six days. The director did not even attend the preproduction meeting ... [and] asked the script supervisor, Katherine Wooten, and his friend Melissa Mathison ... to block out the action with the performers and work with them on their line readings. Filming was scheduled to start November 26, which was the day after Thanksgiving. The crew was unhappy about having to work that Friday, but Spielberg needed to finish by the end of the following week so that he and his entourage could leave for London to attend the royal command performance of *E.T.* ... Spielberg finished promptly on schedule." Neither Spielberg nor his executive producer, Frank Marshall, offered so much as a deposition in the *Twilight Zone* case.

"It's a Good Life" was eminently suited to the ghoulishly comic sensibilities of Joe Dante, a fan turned filmmaker who had collaborated with up-and-coming screenwriter John Sayles when they cut their teeth (as it were) on *Piranha* (1978) and *The Howling* (1981), and went on to bigger-budgeted films such as *Gremlins* and *Innerspace* (1987). Airing on November 3, 1961, the original episode was directed by James Sheldon and faithfully based by Serling (minus the emphasis from its title, "It's a *Good* Life") on a story by Jerome Bixby, whose genre credits include *The Lost Missile, It! The Terror from Beyond Space* (both 1958), *Curse of the Faceless Man, Fantastic Voyage,* and memorable episodes of the original *Star Trek.* Bixby's unsettling tale (included in the Matheson-edited *The Twilight Zone: The Original Stories*) concerns Anthony Fremont, a purple-eyed mutant boy who has cut off the Ohio village of Peaksville and its terrified residents from the rest of the world, controlling them with his ability to read minds and alter reality at his whim, and "thinking" those who displease him into an ominous cornfield. The story's greatest strength is its almost Lovecraftian evocation of the indescribable horrors visited upon the people of Peaksville, as Bixby repeatedly alludes to Anthony's having done *something* terrible to someone without specifying exactly what it is, leaving readers to fill in the blanks with their own imagination — the most effective tool in any tale of terror. Television being of necessity a more literal medium, and one with perennial budgetary constraints as well, the original *Twilight Zone* version includes the single *outré* image of a character who is turned into a human jack-in-the-box during the dreaded weekly ritual of "television night," and ends as the story does with no resolution, leaving the vengeful young mutant's self-imposed status quo maintained.

Matheson's update is restricted primarily to the house where Anthony (Jeremy Licht), who has no longer cut off contact with the outside world, holds his parents (Patricia Barry, William Schallert), his Uncle Walt (Kevin McCarthy), and his sisters Ethel (Nancy Cartwright, the voice of Bart Simpson) and Sara (Cherie Currie) as obsequious, terrified prisoners. It abounds with *Twilight Zone* references. Schoolteacher Helen Foley (Kathleen Quinlan) stops for directions at a café whose patrons include the small-screen incarnation of Anthony, Bill Mumy; the dialogue alludes to Serling's fictional towns of Cliffordville, Homewood, and Willoughby (as well as "Beaumont"); and Helen is the namesake of the protagonist in his "Nightmare as a Child" (4/29/60). Bumping into Anthony on his bike in the parking lot, she drives him home, where Rob Bottin's special makeup and monster effects embody the cruelly cartoonish torments inflicted on the "family" he forced to replace his real one. But after Ethel is banished to Cartoonland for incurring his wrath, and the others are wished out of existence, Helen voluntarily remains with Anthony to help him master his special gift.

Dante told *Cinema Retro*'s Dean Brierly that Jerry Goldsmith, who had scored Matheson's "The Invaders,"

Helen Foley (Kathleen Quinlan) and Anthony Fremont (Jeremy Licht) in an atmospheric shot from "It's a Good Life" in *Twilight Zone—The Movie* (Warner Bros., 1983).

was "a brilliant composer who understood the emotions of a scene without it having to be explained to him.... [H]e had to write a lot of cartoon music because the episode I directed had all these vintage cartoons in it. I had gotten hold of some of the original tracks, but many of them needed to be in stereo, so they had to be redone. Modern studio musicians found it extremely difficult to play as fast as [Warner Bros. mainstay] Carl Stalling's orchestra played. Some of the musicians would just get lost. We also made a lot of changes in

The co-pilot (John Dennis Johnston) tries to calm terrified passenger John Valentine (John Lithgow) in "Nightmare at 20,000 Feet" from *Twilight Zone—The Movie* (Warner Bros., 1983).

the score on the spur of the moment. Jerry handled it all with such great humor. And it became collaborative in the sense that I never felt funny about saying, 'This doesn't work,' or 'Could you give me more of this?' or 'Could you take the strings out?' He would just get together with his orchestrator and they would redo it right on the scoring stage. Working with Jerry was the one stage in the process that you always looked forward to. Even if you were having a lousy time making the movie, you knew that the scoring was going to be fun."

Known for his unhappy — or at least grimly ironic — endings, Matheson had attempted, by introducing the character of Helen and altering Bixby's somber conclusion, to make the film something more than merely a rote retelling. But as he revealed to Stanley Wiater in *Richard Matheson's* The Twilight Zone *Scripts*, this attempt backfired in the eyes of certain viewers. "I was called to task in *Twilight Zone—The Movie* for putting a happy ending on Jerome Bixby's 'It's a *Good* Life.' But my reasoning was, it's too *easy* to have a downbeat ending. It's the easiest thing in the world! And I think writers in these genres who keep doing it are taking the easy way out. I thought, 'Well, can I maintain the integrity of the story, yet still give it a better ending?' And I tried. But the outcome was predictable: A lot of people said, 'Oh, you ruined a great ending!' Which was so downbeat, bleak, hopeless. Now, this worked great in the original short story, and it worked fine in the first *Twilight Zone* adaptation. But I just didn't want to do it again."

Interestingly, Anthony's story was given a different but comparatively upbeat conclusion when the character was revisited after another 20-year interval on the most recent revival of *The Twilight Zone*, airing on the UPN Network. In the follow-up episode "It's Still a Good Life" (2/19/03), scripted by executive producer Ira Steven Behr and directed by Allan Kroeker, 40 years later Anthony (Mumy) is still holding his mother Agnes (Cloris Leachman, repeating her role from the original episode) and the rest of the residents of Peaksville in his arbitrary and deadly grip. He has a daughter, Audrey (Mumy's real-life daughter Liliana), who is immune to his mind-reading powers and also — unknown to Anthony — shares his ability to "make things go away." Learning of this, Agnes hopes she has found the means to "finally get rid of that monster I gave birth to," only to be banished by Audrey along with all the "bad, sneaky people" of Peaksville who wanted to hurt him, yet her power has a twist: Unlike Anthony, she can bring things back into existence, so she recreates the outside world that he had wished away long ago, and they prepare to explore its wonders.

Genre icon Kevin McCarthy starred in the original *Invasion of the Body Snatchers* (1956) and Beaumont's *Twilight Zone* episode "Long Live Walter Jameson" (3/18/60), as well as appearing in Dante's *Piranha* and *The Howling*. In *"They're Here...": Invasion of the Body Snatchers: A Tribute*, he told John McCarty,

> Joe sent me the script. It was all very hush-hush. Steven Spielberg was producing and he exerts a lot of control over who gets to play what. [Joe] said, "Do you want to play the father?" I said, "No, I want to play the uncle, the guy who pulls the rabbits out of the hat." So he said okay, and William Schallert, another Joe Dante regular, was cast as the father.... Uncle Walt had special qualities. He was kind of a bum, a down-and-out hanger-on. I found a lot of things to do with him.
>
> A big part of the pleasure I get in creating a character is trying to find stuff that's interesting, amusing — some piece of business.... When it was my turn to vanish, Joe said, "Go over and throw yourself down in that big old armchair surrounded by all those magazines and comic books you've been reading over the years, and we'll zap you there." I suggested having a flask hidden under the cushion, which I would take a swig from just as the end comes, and Joe said okay. Right before I get the kibosh, before the boom gets lowered, before I get this atomic swat out of existence by the kid, I turned to the camera, raised the flask to my lips, and ad-libbed, "This really is the last of Walter Jameson!" Joe cracked up.

A technical snafu prevented the line from being used in the film.

Australian director George Miller was also coming off a tremendous hit (*The Road Warrior* [1981]) when he was tapped to direct "Nightmare at 20,000 Feet." Here, the white-knuckle flyer is John Valentine (John Lithgow), who as in Matheson's original short story is traveling alone. Despite there being no mention of a preexisting mental condition, he is portrayed as hysterical to the point of madness even before the gremlin (Larry Cedar) first appears, with Valentine's eyes literally bugging out of his head in one practically subliminal special-effects shot. As before, he seizes a pistol from a sky marshal (Charles Knapp), and is nearly sucked from the plane as he blasts away at the gremlin. After the plane safely lands, the mechanics discover the damage; the film ends with a forcibly restrained Valentine taken away in an ambulance driven by the sinister Aykroyd.

In *Richard Matheson's* The Twilight Zone *Scripts*, he related to Wiater,

> Originally I was told [the big-screen version of "Nightmare at 20,000 Feet"] was going to be a ten-minute filler, and I tried to work on it from that aspect. Then they said, "No, it's going to be more full-length — we need a half-hour. And Gregory Peck is going to play the main role." You know — like the role he played in *Twelve O'Clock High* [1949] — so it could have been very effective. Then they gave the segment to George Miller, who is a very talented director, but he "revised" it. He took out the idea of the guy recovering from a mental breakdown; it became just a nervous guy who nobody would believe. John Lithgow is a wonderful actor, but I thought he was a little over-the-top in his performance. He was already up to the level of ten from the outset — so where could he go? But I loved the thing on the wing — I wish we had that in the original episode. Though the guy who was in that furry suit in my original *Twilight Zone* [actor and acrobat Nick Cravat] was just the way I described the gremlin in my script.

Carol Serling has a quick cameo as a concerned passenger outside the lavatory where Valentine is cowering.

As with several of the Poe films, *Twilight Zone—The Movie* resulted in a curious phenomenon whereby stories were adapted for the screen, and then back into prose via a novelization—this time by none other than Robert Bloch, whose work on *Thriller*, the Hitchcock series, and various features had kept him from joining Serling's team. In his autobiography, he wrote, "[O]nly two of [the] segments were screened for me. Nobody bothered to mention there was also a wraparound for the anthology format, any more than they revealed the fact that one of the leading characters in the film was the black performer Scatman Crothers. They merely stipulated that I take the four unrelated episodes, originally dramatized from individual short stories possibly totaling twenty thousand words in length, and expand them into a sixty thousand-word novel without adding any new characters or plot developments. Needless to say, it would be wise if the result in no way resembled any of the original sources, but I could work out this and other problems as I went along. After all, they didn't need the finished novel for six weeks."

Jaws 3-D

(aka *Jaws III*; Universal, released July 22, 1983) DIRECTOR: Joe Alves; PRODUCER: Rupert Hitzig; SCREENPLAY: Matheson, Carl Gottlieb, suggested by Peter Benchley's *Jaws*; STORY: Guerdon Trueblood; MUSIC: Alan Parker; SHARK THEME: John Williams; MAKEUP: Kathryn Bihr; SPECIAL EFFECTS: Praxis Film Works, Inc., Robert Blalack (photographic and optical effects), Private Stock Effects, Inc. (miniatures and electronic composites). Color, 99 minutes. CAST—Mike Brody: Dennis Quaid. Dr. Kathryn Morgan: Bess Armstrong. Philip FitzRoyce: Simon MacCorkindale. Calvin Bouchard: Louis Gossett, Jr. Sean Brody: John Putch. Kelly Ann Bukowski: Lea Thompson. Jack Tate: P.H. Moriarty. Dan: Dan Blasko. Liz: Liz Morris. Ethel: Lisa Maurer. Shelby Overman: Harry Grant. Silver Bullet: Andy Hansen. Tunnel Guide: P.T. Horn. Bob Woodbury: John Edson, Jr. Mrs. Kallender: Kaye Stevens. Leonard Glass: Archie Valliere. Fred: Alonzo Ward. Sherrie: Cathy Cervenka. Suzie: Jane Horner. Sheila: Kathy Jenkins. Announcer: Steve Mellor. Paramedic: Ray Meunnich. Reporters: Les Alford, Gary Anstaett. Workmen: Scott Christoffel, John Floren. Screaming Skier: Debbie Connoyer. Reporter at Party: Mary Davis Duncan. Anxious Tunnel People: Barbara Eden, Barbara Quinn. Rick: John Gaffey. Mr. Brit: Joe Gilbert. Man in Crowd: Will Knickerbocker. Skiers: Jackie Kuntarich, Patrice Wallace. Tourist Dad: Edward Laurie. Girls in Tunnel: Holly Lisker, Laura Tracy. Pirate Girl: M.J. Lloyd. Stand-off Player: Carl Mazzocone. Red: Ken Olson. Clyde: Ronnie Parks. Mr. Bluster: Al Pipkin. Stunt Double: Betty Raymond. Reporter: Irene Schubert. Ted: August Schwartz. Concessionaire: Sandy Scott. Beer Belly on Beach: Tony Shepherd. Charlene Tutt: Dolores Starling. Candy: Tamie Steinke. Ed: Danny Stewart. Mermaid: Roxie Stice. Shark Tour Guide: Laurie Thomas. Tourist Mom: Carol Tracy. Mrs. Brit: Doreen Weese. Randy: Jim Wilhelm.

In our 2008 interview, Matheson disavowed any knowledge of reports on the IMDb and elsewhere that the third installment in the *Jaws* tetralogy was originally proposed as a spoof entitled *National Lampoon's Jaws 3, People 0*, with Joe Dante as the director. Universal abandoned plans for a big-budget remake of *Creature from the Black Lagoon* (to be directed by Jack Arnold and written by genre giant Nigel Kneale) in favor of this ill-fated venture, which was drastically rewritten by Carl Gottlieb, who shared script credit on the original *Jaws* with author Peter Benchley. Matheson observed on an earlier occasion, "Actually, the 3-D was my idea. We went down looking for locations, and we saw this wonderful thing ... called 'Sea Dreams,' which is just incredible, the effects of it. You're surrounded by the noises of underwater, you really feel like you're underwater. And it was so eerie, and I thought, 'Boy, if we could get this effect in the film, and do it in 3-D.' And then Joe Alves put them together and called it *Jaws 3-D*, but what they did with the 3-D was ludicrous. It added nothing, no effect whatever. And it just made the film darker. So that was really bad."

Matheson told me in *Filmfax*,

They gave the story credit to some guy who I never met [Guerdon Trueblood, the scenarist of several 1970s TV-movies about killer ants, bees, and tarantulas], who I didn't know was involved with the story. As far as I knew, I had made up the story myself. Carl Gottlieb got the co-credit on the screenplay. But this other guy, they gave him credit for the story [the three writers shared a "Razzie Award" nomination for worst screenplay]. I never saw it, I never met him, I didn't know he was working on it, I don't know who he is to this day. It was just one of those little rulings that the Writers Guild makes. I always say this, I sound paranoiac, but I came up with a really good idea, which is what made it so odd that this other guy got the story credit, because I came up with the idea of setting it in a marine park, like a Sea World, and I had a really excellent story. And my script was very good. It's just that this guy who had been the art director [on the first two films], Joe Alves, directed it, and as you notice he's never directed since. He's a wonderful art director, but he just simply is not cut out to be a director.

The brainchild of entrepreneur Calvin Bouchard (Louis Gossett, Jr.), the Undersea Kingdom is the newest addition to Sea World, incorporating four pressurized viewing tunnels radiating from a central control hub in its 40-foot man-made lagoon, connected to the open ocean by a deep-water channel. Arriving in time for the opening are Calvin's friend, famed showman Philip FitzRoyce (Simon MacCorkindale); Sean Brody (John Putch), the son of Sheriff Martin Brody (played in the first two films by Roy Scheider), whose older brother Mike (Dennis Quaid) built the park and is in love with its senior biologist, Dr. Kathryn Morgan (Bess Armstrong); and a great white shark. Searching the lagoon in a submersible for a missing employee, Shelby Overman (Harry Grant), Mike and Kay are rescued by a pair of dolphins from the unwelcome aquatic visitor. When FitzRoyce suggests killing it on-camera for the media coverage, Kay convinces Calvin to let her preserve it as the only great white in captivity, with Mike's understandably reluctant assistance.

A great white is captured and, in the grand tradition of *King Kong* (1933), *Revenge of the Creature*, and *Gorgo* (1961), put prematurely on display by Calvin, whereupon it promptly dies from his mishandling. When Shelby's body is recovered, the bite radius of his wounds reveals that the baby shark's 35-foot mother is responsible — and at large inside the park. The mother injures Sean's new inamorata, water skier Kelly Ann Bukowski (Lea Thompson), during a mass attack in the lagoon and then cracks the wall of one of the underwater tunnels as Calvin tries to evacuate the park, trapping a group of terrified tourists between watertight doors. Mike and his staff frantically attempt to effect repairs and FitzRoyce goes shark hunting at last. In the frenzied finale, FitzRoyce is swallowed whole, Mike and Kay rescue the tourists after being saved by the dolphins once more, Calvin nearly dies when the shark crashes into the control hub, and Mike destroys the shark by reaching into its mouth with a makeshift hook to pull the pin on an underwater grenade, which is still clutched in the hand of the lifeless FitzRoyce.

The bemused screenwriter said in our *Filmfax* interview,

It was just awful, and then Gottlieb did a terrible rewrite on it, and it just turned miserable. It was a pitiful piece of work. It could have been very good. Actually, although Jeannot [Szwarc] did a very good job with the second one, [*Jaws 3-D*] could have been better in that [Alves] didn't have to have a carryover from the prior film. *Jaws 2 had* to be a continuation of *Jaws*, in

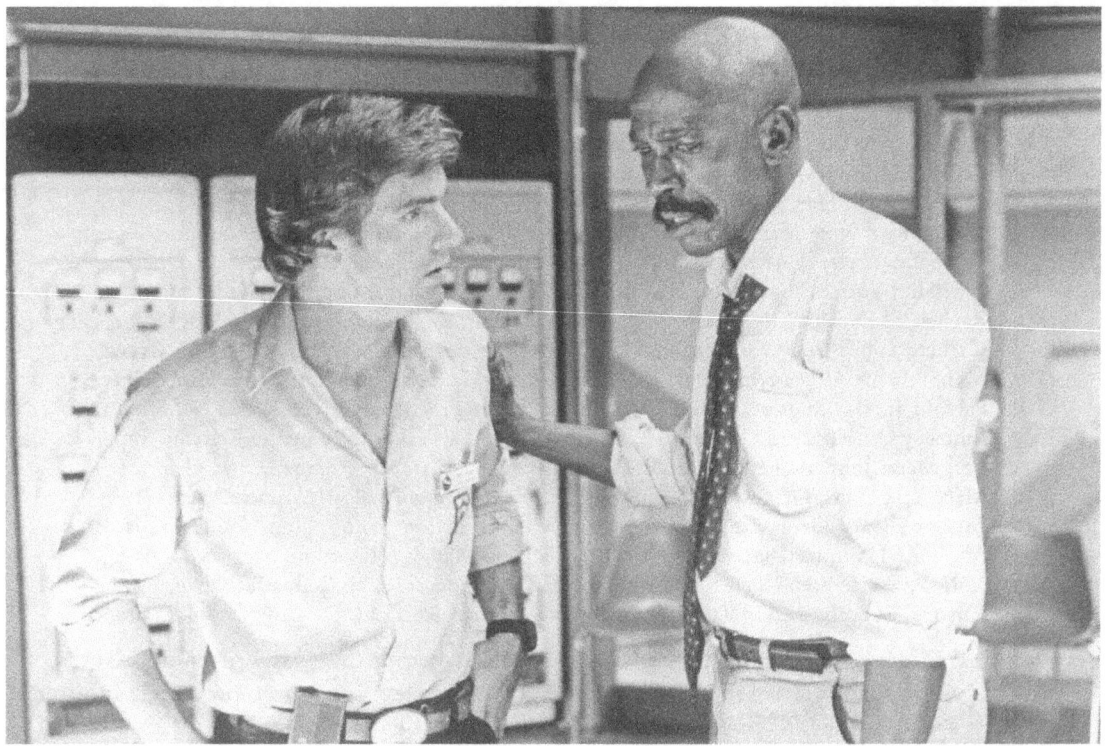

Mike Brody (Dennis Quaid) and Calvin Bouchard (Louis Gossett, Jr.) discuss their shark problem in *Jaws 3-D* (Universal, 1983).

the same location, with the same people, and everything. [With] *Jaws 3-D*, you could have completely jumped away from that, which I did. It was [Sidney] Sheinberg, of Universal, who insisted that it be the two sons of Sheriff Brody.... I mean, it's ludicrous. The two sons of the sheriff go all the way down to Florida and have troubles with a great white? And he wanted it to be the same damn shark that had been burned in *Jaws 2*! In the last one [*Jaws the Revenge* (1987)], they had Brody's wife being chased — it's like these sharks have been to Oxford or something, they know exactly how to get around, they know where to find people, and they've got terrible, vengeful personalities.

Adding insult to injury, Matheson was asked to create a role specifically for Mickey Rooney, which was then summarily eliminated when the actor proved to be unavailable. "They wanted me to make the girl's father, who's in the [original] script, an expert on fish and all that's involved with fish," he said in 2008. "I don't know how they wanted me to turn it into Mickey Rooney; just say the guy was short. The father in my script runs a small, run-down Sea World nearby, and she goes to ask him what he thinks about the shark and everything. I re-read my script and I thought, 'My God, why didn't they use my script? It would've made a great movie.' But I've thought that a lot. I don't think there was the younger brother coming to see him. The hero was the guy who was in charge of the construction at this Sea World-type place. Basically, the idea [was that] the first shark, the eight-footer or ten-footer, turns out to be the baby, and the real nemesis is in the water circulation outfit, where it can get aeration in its system [and thus remain concealed without having to stay in constant motion to survive]. It turned out to be like 25 feet long. I took it seriously. I wrote a very good outline, and a very good script."

Loose Cannons

(TriStar, released February 9, 1990) DIRECTOR: Bob Clark; PRODUCER: Aaron Spelling, Alan Greisman; SCREENPLAY: Richard Christian Matheson, Matheson, Clark; MUSIC: Paul Zaza; MAKEUP: Michael R. Thomas; SPECIAL EFFECTS SUPERVISOR: Roy Arbogast. Color, 94 minutes. CAST— Det. MacArthur "Mac" Stern: Gene Hackman. Ellis Fielding: Dan Aykroyd. Harry Gutterman: Dom DeLuise. Bob Smiley: Ronny Cox. Riva: Nancy Travis. Kurt Von Metz: Robert Prosky. Joseph Grimmer: Paul Koslo. Captain: Dick O'Neill. Steckler: Jan Triska. Weskit: Leon Rippy. Monseigneur: Robert Elliott. Cheshire Cat: Herb Armstrong. White Rabbit: Robert Dickman. Drummond: David Alan Grier. Rachel: S. Epatha Merkerson. Willie: Reg E. Cathey. Moderator: Alex Hyde-White. Gerber: Tobin Bell. TV Station Man: Thomas Kopache. Lady Tenant: Susan Peretz. Man Tenant: Al Mancini. Oaf: Kevin McClarnon. Oaf's Sweetie: Debbee Hinchcliffe. Patrolman: Jay Ingram. Bus Driver: Arthur French. Train Driver: Clem Moorman. Embassy Officer: Brad Greenquist. Hitler: Ira Lewis. Eva Braun: Margaret Klenck. Young Von Metz: John Bolger. Giant: Bill Fagerbakke. Guy at Bar: Robert Pentz. Grimmer's Men: Erik Cord, George P. Wilbur, Gene LeBell, Danny Aiello III. Israeli Agents: Billy Anagnos, Gary Tacon. Guy in Baths: Dean Mumford. Cop: John J. Finn. Security Guard: Adrienne Hampton. Jacuzzi Guy: Dutch Miller. Marsh Policeman: Gregory Goossen. Military Policeman: Chris S. MacGregor. Train Engineer: Ralph Redpath. Nurse: Nancy Parsons. Orderly: David Correia. Little Girl: Jennifer Roach. Little Boy: Philip Shafran.

Loose Cannons began life as *Face Off*, a speculative script that was written by Matheson and his son Richard Christian (R.C.), then a successful television writer-producer, and sold by their agents at the Creative Artists Agency to TriStar as a planned sequel to *Cobra* (1986). When star Sylvester Stallone dropped out, the project was reconfigured for CAA clients Gene Hackman and Dan Aykroyd as a variation on the *Lethal Weapon* franchise and extensively rewritten — with a working title of *The Von Metz Incident*— by its director Bob Clark, creator of the raunchy comedies *Porky's* (1981) and *Porky's II: The Next Day* (1983). "It's reached a point now where the director will be hired, and part of his contract is that he gets to rewrite the script, whether he's a good writer or not," Matheson told me in *Filmfax*. *Leonard Maltin's Movie Guide* dubbed the result a "below-rock-bottom car-chase excuse about two D.C. cops caught between ex–Nazis and Israeli adversaries scuffling over a mysterious Hitler home movie. Unfunny and offensive, film stagnated on the shelf while the studio figured out what to do with it. [A] career nadir for most of its participants."

Reassigned back to homicide from the vice squad, maverick D.C. cop MacArthur Stern (Gene Hackman) is reluctantly partnered with Ellis Fielding (Dan Aykroyd), a forensics expert with a brilliant analytical mind and a multiple personality disorder triggered by violence. Investigating a series of murders culminating in a waterfront massacre, they learn from one of the two survivors, S&M club owner "Harry the Hippo" Gutterman (Dom DeLuise), that all of the victims were porno dealers who were shown an amateur film starring Adolf Hitler. The other survivor, Steckler (Jan Triska), stole the film from his former employer, Kurt Von Metz (Robert Prosky), intending to sell it to the highest bidder. A candidate for chancellor of Germany, Von Metz steadfastly denies any association with Hitler and has sent Joseph Grimmer (*The Omega Man's* Paul Koslo) to recover the film. But Grimmer, a psychotic neo–Nazi fanatic, has exceeded his mandate and is now systematically killing off anyone who has seen the film, much to the dismay of Von Metz's underlings.

As Ellis's multiple personalities manifest themselves in a series of ostensibly amusing "fragmentary episodes," he and Mac escort Gutterman to New York, where Steckler plans to complete the sale. They are pursued by not only Grimmer but also Bob Smiley (Ronny

Cox), an assistant deputy director of the FBI, and Riva (Nancy Travis), a Mossad agent, who want Harry for their own agendas. Irreverent and often abrasive, Mac owes more than a little to Hackman's *French Connection* (1971) character Detective Jimmy "Popeye" Doyle, and thus it is no surprise that the climax, set in and under Grand Central Station, plays like an extended homage to that film. Trapped *à la* Doyle by the closing doors of a departing subway train as Grimmer wounds Ellis, Mac races through traffic back to Grand Central in a commandeered bus to rescue him. After Ellis dispatches Grimmer, the Israelis project the film at an international conference during a speech by Von Metz, who is revealed therein delivering the *coup de grace* to Hitler (Ira Lewis).

In our interview in *Mystery Scene*, Clark was refreshingly candid about the shortcomings of *Loose Cannons*, saying of Matheson *pére et fils*,

Ellis Fielding (Dan Aykroyd) and MacArthur "Mac" Stern (Gene Hackman) endure a brush with bureaucracy, FBI-style, in *Loose Cannons* (TriStar, 1990).

> My apologies to them. I didn't meet with them. I admire them a great deal, but I didn't know them. It was just given to me to come up with a totally new idea, so the screenplay that we evolved, they are not responsible for, I am. They shouldn't take any of the blame. Theirs was a darker piece.... There's not really much comparison between the screenplay I started with and the screenplay we ended up with, which in terms of high concept wasn't a bad idea, it's just that the elements weren't there because I didn't make it work. It's as simple as that, and they are not responsible. As best I remember, their script was about a psychotic hockey player [hence the original title]. The multiple personality idea is theirs, that was the thrust. The co-cop who had been through a terrible experience which gave him the multiple personality, and then the older, grizzled cop, that's what the two scripts shared. The story, the whole thrust of it became an entirely different approach...
>
> I'm not being pretentious or snobbish — anything for me with Gene Hackman and Dan Aykroyd in it can't be that bad, it's just I felt my work was poor. I had asked Dan to create the multiple personalities, because I wasn't happy with what I was doing. I thought he came up with some extraordinary ones, and the studio would not let us use them. They forced us to use the ones that they had requested of me, the more cartoonish ones that I created.... It was difficult to reconcile the style of that broad a comedy with the utter reality that Hackman brings to everything he does, even if he's playing farce, like *Young Frankenstein* [1974]. So there are many failures in the film, and I sort of felt I let my actors down, but I don't say it's not an entertaining film. It actually is, it just gets silly often..... [The reference to *The French Connection*] fit our

milieu anyway. Gene certainly wouldn't want to be, I think, a part of any of that, but just a del-icate touch I don't think he minded.... We were having a little bit of fun, but it was inherently part of the story element, too. The chase across town had to be, so why not?

Clark attributes TriStar's delay in releasing the finished film to studio changes in manage-ment:

> They missed the one slot, the first one, when they were going to open it, so I don't think it was actually shelved as much as they were just waiting for a slot until [studio executive] Dawn [Steel] came in. The film tested, really, pretty well. She looked at it, and they thought they could definitely go somewhere with it, but a year went by from the time we were ready. We went back and did some reshooting. We shot a new ending the following spring [1989].... We stopped, and figured there were some problems we wanted to solve. In fact, we reshot twice. We redid the bar scene the first time, and then we came up with a new ending for the final reshoot. Originally, it ended at the monastery with just Gene and Dan walking, a little *denouement*. A very simple ending, talking about how [Aykroyd] was on the mend again, and then we reshot in the hospital with the Mossad and the idea that Dom DeLuise had been recruited. That comedy bit that we did at the end took the place of the monastery scene.

Of *Face Off* and *Red Sleep*, an unproduced script that he wrote with Mick Garris and sold to producer Joel Silver, which stalled after being completely rewritten by John Landis, R.C. told Stanley Wiater in a joint interview with his father for *Cemetery Dance*,

> There's a mythology about directing. Everyone that you meet thinks they can write. They may not be convinced they can write brilliantly, but they're convinced they can *write*. Not everyone is convinced they can direct. Directing seems to bring out a lot more anxiety because there are technical aspects to it: knowing what lenses do, knowing how to light a scene. When you talk to people about this, it brings up a certain amount of apprehension. So the director has an incredible amount of mythological power, and that is why the system in Hollywood is set up this way — and why it's so out of whack. The director is the last person to come in to perceive and render the material. But it's crazy to bring in somebody literally a month before a produc-tion begins, who has nothing to do with it, and then have the power to wreck your screenplay, simply because that's the position of power that they're in. But that's the system.

As early as 1972, the Mathesons had joined forces for *PSI*, a one-hour pilot story and script about the work of the UCLA Parapsychology lab bought by Lorimar Television and ABC. But *Loose Cannons* is their only collaboration to have been produced. They followed *Face Off* with *Shifter*, a horror comedy about a shape-shifter who is having a nervous break-down, which they sold to "Nightmare at 20,000 Feet" director Richard Donner. The senior Matheson told Wiater, "Then we started having meetings, and one day we walked in — Richard Donner's wife's production company was going to make it — and she handed out a little outline which indicated she wanted to do another picture entirely. And this was after we had been working weeks on the script, getting down to the nitty-gritty of details. Neither of us cared to do it again, and after that point she became less interested in our collaboration. It's amazing. In Hollywood, it's like the crest of a wave when a project has its most interest, and if it's made then, then it will get produced. If the interest fades, or the project takes time to develop, then the project somehow becomes an 'old' property to them. Even if it's still good."

In a 1996 letter, Matheson told me that their next effort, *Midvale*, was "a sort of life-after-death story but entirely different from *What Dreams*..." Sought by several prospective buyers, it became the first speculative script purchased by powerhouse producer-director Ivan Reitman in the 20-year history of his production company, Northern Lights Enter-tainment. Reportedly moved to tears by the script, Reitman so enjoyed working with the

Mathesons on minor rewrites that after starting a new company, Montecito, he asked them to pen a second screenplay for an "A" horror film in the tradition of *The Haunting* and Donner's *The Omen*, while he pursued casting ideas for *Midvale*. The Mathesons responded with *The Nature of Evil*, a story about supernatural horror on a college campus, but neither has gone before the cameras in the decade since. With no time for further screenplay collaborations, father and son have since turned down multiple offers from studios and producers with whom they felt less simpatico, although their Gauntlet collection *Pride* (2002) does contain a unique collaborative script.

Publisher Barry Hoffman wrote in *The Richard Matheson Companion*, "I suggested to Richard Christian that he and his father collaborate on a short story. Each would write his own version, centered around a theme they both agreed upon, then combine them into a single story. They wrote their stories, and then the project almost fell apart. They simply couldn't combine each other's stories into one. Over the years their styles had become incompatible (they had collaborated on the short story 'Where There's a Will' [for Kirby McCauley's anthology *Dark Forces*] in 1980). While Richard was a minimalist, like his son, his story was still two to three times longer than Richard Christian's. R.C. had become adept at what is called the short-short. In two to four pages, he could craft an emotionally wrenching tale of horror. Not wanting to give up on the project, I suggested they use their short stories as the basis for a teleplay collaboration. Richard Christian had told me that he and his father had recently collaborated on a number of screenplays.... Thus *Pride* saw publication with short stories by father and son and a teleplay collaboration."

The Dreamer of Oz

(aka *The Dreamer of Oz: The L. Frank Baum Story*; NBC-TV, December 10, 1990) DIRECTOR: Jack Bender; PRODUCER: Ervin Zavada; TELEPLAY: Matheson; STORY: David Kirschner, Matheson, suggested in part by a book by Michael Patrick Hearn; MUSIC: Lee Holdridge; MAKEUP, OZ CHARACTERS: Craig Reardon; VISUAL EFFECTS: Stargate Films. Color, 93 minutes. CAST — Lyman Frank Baum: John Ritter. Maud Gage Baum: Annette O'Toole. Matilda Electra Joslyn Gage: Rue McClanahan. Al Badham, Cowardly Lion: Charles Haid. William Wallace Denslow, Jr.: David Schramm. Harriet Alvena Baum Neal: Nancy Lenehan. Dorothy Leslie Gage, Dorothy Gale: Courtney Barilla. Helen Leslie Gage Gage: Nancy Morgan. Charlie H. Gage: Pat Skipper. Ned Brown, Farmer: Ed Gale. Frank Joslyn Baum (5–9 years): Tim Eyster. Frank Joslyn Baum (3 years): Joshua Boyd. Salesman: Roger Steffans. Albert the Reporter: John Cameron Mitchell. Sullivan: Frank Hamilton. George M. Hill: Steven Gilborn. Mr. Munchkin: Jerry Maren. Mrs. Munchkin: Elizabeth Barrington. Photographer: Terry Wills. Actress: Laura Owens. Stage Manager: Richard Marion. Carpenter: Rod Gist. Publisher: Bill DeLand. Scarecrow: David Ellzey. Tin Man: Derek Loughram. Announcer: Dale Tarter. Teenage Frank, Jr.: Christopher Pettiet. Robert Stanton Baum: Ryan Todd. "Tweety Robbins": Alexis Kirschner. Harry Neal Baum: Jason Ritter. Opie Read: Paul Linke. Aberdeen Townspeople: Dr. Robert A. Baum, Jr., Carolyn Baum, Christine Baum, Clare Baum.

Originally aired by NBC as a holiday special in December of 1990, Matheson's second biopic makes for an unlikely pairing with *De Sade*. It stars John Ritter as Lyman Frank Baum (1856–1919), who wrote *The Wonderful Wizard of Oz* and 13 sequels. In a 1994 letter, Matheson told me he was satisfied with the results of his last feature-length script produced to date: "I'm very fond of it. I think they did a nice job of it and followed my script religiously — which (he said humbly) usually makes the project work out." The film reunited Ritter with Annette O'Toole, his co-star in the ABC miniseries of Stephen King's *It* (1990). She enthused in an interview with Dan Scapperotti for *Femme Fatales*, "It's a wonderful made-for-TV film. It's a love story about two people and how *The Wizard of Oz* came to be. It clarifies that the Oz books wouldn't have been written without the support of Frank's wife, Maud [Gage]. She really pushed him into sitting down and writing this thing. It goes back and forth with Frank telling the story of *The Wonderful Wizard of Oz*, and his book is very different from the MGM movie. Jack Bender did a wonderful job of directing."*

The Dreamer of Oz is bookended with scenes of Baum's widow (O'Toole) attending the premiere of Victor Fleming's classic *The Wizard of Oz* at Grauman's Chinese Theatre; like that film, this one begins in monochrome before shifting into color, as one lone reporter in attendance recognizes the elderly Maud Gage Baum, asking her to reflect on her husband's life and creation of *The Wonderful Wizard of Oz*. She recalls that when they met, Baum was an actor with a touring Shakespearean company. He is introduced by his sister Harriet Alvena Baum Neal (Nancy Lenehan) to Maud, the daughter of suffragette Matilda Electra Joslyn Gage (Rue McClanahan). In the first of Matheson's many fantasy interpolations, Baum immediately envisions Maud as the future Glinda, the Good Witch of the North.

Over Matilda's objections, Maud gives up Columbia Law School to marry Baum and tours with him until 1883, when Frank Joslyn Baum is born. Later, in a gripping incident, Baum — now running a retail outlet store in Syracuse — must rescue three-year-old Frank, Jr. (Joshua Boyd), from the attic window where he is playing, heedless of the danger. In an effort to distract the boy, nicknamed Bunny, and prevent him from falling, Baum begins spinning the tale of a faraway "magic land" to which a cyclone could carry a person's house. As the years go by and the family grows to include Robert Stanton Baum (Ryan Todd) in 1886, he expands his creation, not surprisingly imagining the visiting Grandmother Gage as the Wicked Witch of the West. Baum persuades Maud to move west to Aberdeen (several residents are played by present-day Baum family members) in the Dakota Territory, where they stay with Maud's sister Helen Leslie Gage Gage (Nancy Morgan), brother-in-law Charlie H. Gage (Pat Skipper), and young niece Dorothy Leslie Gage (Courtney Barilla), later the inspiration for Baum's young heroine, Dorothy Gale.

Although the stories Frank shares with the children about the Scarecrow (David Ellzey) and others are a resounding success, his store Baum's Bazaar is not, due to a drought. As Maud observes in her narration, "Our bank account kept getting smaller, while our family kept getting bigger. Harry Neal Baum [Ritter's own son, Jason, in his screen debut] was born on December 17th, 1889." That same year, Dorothy lies ill, albeit enthralled by the tales of the Tin Woodsman (Derek Loughram), and dies soon afterward. The saddened Baum buys a local newspaper, *The Dakota Pioneer*, in an effort to pay his creditors and is challenged to a duel by Al Badham (Charles Haid), a reader who is disgruntled over a harmless typo. By backing out of it, Badham inspires the character of the Cowardly Lion. In 1891, Baum loses the paper and relocates to Chicago, where Maud encourages him to begin committing *The Magic Land* to paper. While working as a traveling salesman for Pitkin and

*David Kirschner, who executive produced the film for Ritter's Adam Productions and shared the story credit with Matheson, is best known for the lurid horror film *Child's Play* (1988) and its sequels; Bender later directed *Child's Play 3* (1991), while Kirschner gave Ritter a small role as one of the victims in the fourth entry, Ronny Yu's *Bride of Chucky* (1998).

Brooks, he encounters Sullivan (Frank Hamilton)—later immortalized as the Wizard himself—a cigar-smoking "total humbug who manages to sell himself to almost everyone," in the words of a colleague.

In the person of the Wizard, and the journey of Dorothy and her friends along the Yellow Brick Road to find him, Baum finally finds the spine to hold together the disparate parts of his story. When one member of his rapt, youthful audience asks the name of the magic land, he desperately draws immediate inspiration from the lower drawer of a nearby filing cabinet, which is labeled "O-Z." At the Chicago Press Club, his writer friend Opie Read (Paul Linke) introduces him to a junior partner in the firm that will eventually publish his first book, *Mother Goose in Prose* (1897). After a heart condition prevents Baum from going back on the road as a salesman, he and artist William Wallace Denslow, Jr. (David Schramm), begin a successful collaboration with *Father Goose, His Book* (1899). The Oz book, however, is rejected until Baum takes a final, desperate gamble by financing it himself, signing away all future royalties on the still-selling *Father Goose* until he can cover the costs of *The Emerald City*, which publisher George M. Hill (Steven Gilborn) insists be retitled. The gamble pays off spectacularly when *The Wonderful Wizard of Oz* at last appears to widespread praise in 1900.

Usually associated with comedies like *Problem Child* (1990) and *Problem Child 2* (1991), Ritter (the son of singing cowboy star Tex Ritter) won Emmy and Golden Globe Awards for the long-running comedy series *Three's Company* (1977–84). He gives a good account of himself in the unusually serious (for him) and multifaceted role of Baum. McClanahan and O'Toole offer strong supporting performances as the only other substantial characters. Much of the film's effectiveness is created by the colorful fantasy sequences dramatizing the tales told by Baum. Craig Reardon's makeup design for the Oz characters and the visual effects by Stargate Films (which had previously been involved with Disney's groundbreaking computer graphics epic *Tron*) paint simple but boldly colored scenes of the Scarecrow, Cowardly Lion, Tin Woodsman, Dorothy, and Toto, including an impressive tracking shot running all the way from the farmhouse door to the legendary Emerald City.

Matheson told me in 2008, "I remember talking to Frank Baum's grandson [presumably Baum's great-grandson Dr. Robert A. Baum, Jr., who played one of the Aberdeen townspeople]. He liked [the film] very much. They were just shooting a scene where the Tin Man goes out to chop some wood in the rain. The whole thing was done extraordinarily well. And I thought [Rue McClanahan] did a very good job. I wrote her a letter, praising her work.... [During the *Oz* shoot] I saw John Ritter. He was really hugging and kissing this woman [Nancy Morgan], who played his sister-in-law when he went out to [Aberdeen] to open that store, and I thought, wow, is he a womanizer, or what? He may have been, but this turned out to be his wife [from whom Ritter was divorced in 1996]. She was very pretty, and she was quite good.

"We went to a wrap party, and an announcer was up on the stand praising all the people involved who were responsible for this wonderful show, and they never mentioned my name once. So I said to Ruth, 'Let's get out of here.' As I started to get up, John Ritter obviously saw my reaction, and he went right up to the stage and told the people through the microphone that they had to give me credit, too. He was a very pleasant and thoughtful young man. It was a pity he died so young. They did a very good job on that. It was one of the few [films] that I'm really pleased with [but] I had trouble with [Kirschner] about credits, because he wanted me to sign a paper saying that I had collaborated with him extensively, which of course I hadn't done. He may have [contributed] a few brief story elements. He's a very nice young man and he's been very generous in many ways. That's the one little fallibility he has shown in the past." Around that time, Matheson wrote an unproduced musical teleplay, *Through the Golden Horn*, for Kirschner. "I was going to work with Danny Elfman [but] they never got that far. I wrote an entire script, and then they decided not to make it. It was a good script, too — 'as usual,' I say."

Twilight Zone: Rod Serling's Lost Classics

(CBS-TV, May 19, 1994) DIRECTOR: Robert Markowitz; PRODUCER: S. Bryan Hickox; MUSIC: Patrick Williams; SPECIAL MAKEUP EFFECTS: Alterian Studios, Jim Beinke. Color, 92 minutes. HOST: James Earl Jones. "The Theatre"—TELEPLAY: Matheson; STORY: Rod Serling. CAST— Melissa Sanders: Amy Irving. Dr. Jim McCain: Gary Cole. Joanie: Heidi Swedberg. Moviegoers: Priscilla Pointer, Scott Burkholder, Don Bloomfield, Michael Burgess, Grey Silbley. Big Man: Alex Van. Nurse: Deborah Winstead. Ticket Lady: Joan Pankow. "Where the Dead Are"—TELEPLAY: Serling. CAST— Dr. Benjamin Ramsey: Patrick Bergin. Jeremy Wheaton: Jack Palance. Susan Wheaton: Jenna Stern. Maureen Flannagan: Julia Campbell. Dr. Ames: Peter McRobbie. Ezekiel Perkins: Bill Bolender. Flannagan: Malachy McCourt. Workmen: J. Michael Hunter, Mark Joy. Billy O'Neil: Stan Kelly. Attendant: Tony Pender. Medical Student: Hank Troscianiec. Magistrate: Richard K. Olsen. Bainbridge: Chris O'Neill.

Years after Serling's 1975 death, his widow Carol discovered a 90-minute script entitled "Where the Dead Are," which was clearly too long to have been a *Twilight Zone* episode from even the fourth season, thus making the title of this telefilm a bit of a misnomer. As Matheson told Tom Weaver in *Starlog*, "Before all this happened, through some other company and *with* Carol, I had made an outline of what was going to be a two-hour movie which would incorporate three of Rod's [five or six] stories that ... had never been made into scripts. That didn't work out; CBS was not interested. Then, later on, Carol found this complete shooting script." He took Serling's ten-page outline "The Theatre," one of the stories selected for the aborted three-part film, and turned it into a half-hour teleplay to round out this TV-movie. "There was enough there [to expand the story faithfully into script form]. As a matter of fact, there were certain changes I *wanted* to make, but they wanted me to stick to the story he had written."

An Academy Award nominee for *Yentl* (1983) and the former wife of Steven Spielberg, Amy Irving portrays sculptress Melissa Sanders, the protagonist of "The Theatre." Indecisive about every aspect of her life, including the decision to wed Dr. Jim McCain (Gary Cole), she enters the Twilight Zone when she attends a revival of Howard Hawks's classic *His Girl Friday* (1940). Sitting in the movie house, Melissa sees scenes from her own life interpolated into the film, which none of the other audience members seems to notice. Although Jim is a known prankster, he denies having arranged this as a joke. Returning for another screening, she sees a shooting outside the theater depicted up on the screen; when she leaves that night it actually happens, exactly as she had witnessed it. Against Jim's advice, Melissa goes back and sees herself hit by a bus just after a billboard car dated "March 20th" drives by. Jim assures her the next day that it is now the 21st, so she seems to have altered her own future. When he realizes that he mistook the date and it is really the 20th, he races to try to warn her, only to see her killed, enter the theater himself, and watch her death occur once again.

"Where the Dead Are" opens in Boston in 1868 as surgeon Benjamin Ramsey (Patrick

Bergin) finds an old wound that should have been fatal on the body of a patient from Yarmouth Village. He travels there in search of Jeremy Wheaton (Jack Palance), who is said to have experimented with tissue regeneration. He learns that the former apothecary is now a crippled resident of nearby Shadow Island; villager Ezekiel Perkins (Bill Bolender) takes him there. After Wheaton rebuffs him, Ramsey is shocked to see Wheaton's niece and ward Susan (Jenna Stern) giving an injection to a longshoreman who was crushed by a crate. Ramsey confronts Wheaton and is bludgeoned by one of the locals. Ramsey awakens to find Perkins murdered; the acting magistrate refuses to investigate. He is summoned by Susan to the dying Wheaton, who reveals that he had stumbled upon a formula to restore life. The islanders, who are dead yet animated by the formula, crippled Wheaton to keep him there. But he has been substituting water for their maintenance doses and they start to decay—as does Susan.

Introducing these disparate segments, which differ markedly in length, setting, and tone, was the distinguished actor James Earl Jones, best known to genre fans as the voice of Darth Vader in the original *Star Wars* trilogy. Director Robert Markowitz was a veteran of such telemovies as *Decoration Day* (1990), based on a novella by *The Omega Man*'s John William Corrington, and *Afterburn* (1992). A few weeks after the film aired, Matheson wrote me, "My reaction to the *Twilight Zone* episode ["The Theatre"] is limited. I think the story needed some more explanation. I don't like it when things happen to people for no apparent reason. But it was done nicely." He was even less complimentary in a *Filmfax* interview years later: "The long one was [filmed] exactly as Serling had written it. I did the other one, and I really wasn't crazy about it. It was difficult to do properly, and I don't think what they did was all that good anyway." Jean-Marc and Randy Lofficier, the authors of *Into The Twilight Zone: The Rod Serling Programme Guide*, noted that "in the original Serling treatment, Melissa was a secretary in love with a co-worker."

Trilogy of Terror II

(USA Network, October 30, 1996) DIRECTOR: Dan Curtis; PRODUCER: Julian Marks; MUSIC: Bob Cobert; MAKEUP: Marie Nardella; SPECIAL MAKEUP EFFECTS: Tom Irvin; SPECIAL EFFECTS: Frank C. Carere; CREATURE EFFECTS: Eric Allard; PROSTHETICS: Rick Stratton. Color, 91 minutes. "The Graveyard Rats"—TELEPLAY: William F. Nolan, Curtis, based on Henry Kuttner's story. CAST—Laura Ansford: Lysette Anthony. Ben Garrick: Geraint Wyn Davies. Roger Ansford: Matt Clark. Arly Stubbs: Geoffrey Lewis. Akers: Gerry Quigley. Brig: Dennis O'Connor. Taylor: John McMahon. Minister: Alan Bridle. Waitress: Brittaney Edgell. Officers: Norm Spencer, Bruce McFee. "Bobby"—TELEPLAY: Matheson. CAST—Alma: Lysette Anthony. Bobby: Blake Heron. Dwarf Bobby: Joe Geib. "He Who Kills"—Teleplay: Nolan, Curtis, based on the Zuni doll from Matheson's "Prey." CAST—Dr. Simpson: Lysette Anthony. Lt. Jerry O'Farrell: Richard Fitzpatrick. Lew: Thomas Mitchell. Arthur Breslow: Alex Carter. Pete: Philip Williams. Sgt. Rothstein: Tom Melissis. Steve: Aron Tager. Leonard Spaulding: Durward Allen. Dennis Winslow: Peter Keleghan.

Hoping to duplicate the success of the original *Trilogy of Terror*, Dan Curtis reassembled his screenwriting "dream team" two decades later for a made-for-cable sequel shot in Toronto. It premiered on Halloween Eve of 1996.

Curtis co-wrote two of the episodes with Nolan, also serving as the film's executive producer. Matheson's participation was nominal at best, for the second segment, "Bobby," is merely a remake of the concluding episode from *Dead of Night*, with no additional work on his part; as he told me in 2008, "They weren't even going to give me a credit until I called Dan Curtis. I said, 'You know, if you're going to [redo] it, you've gotta give me credit and give me some money.'" His other connection to *Trilogy II* is that its final episode, "He Who Kills," features the Zuni fetish doll from the original, and picks up almost exactly where it left off.*

While the film was still in the planning stages, Nolan told me in our *Filmfax* interview that the project had an unusually long gestation period. "I adapted Henry Kuttner's 'The Graveyard Rats' and Philip K. Dick's 'The Father Thing'— both were originally written by me as pilot segments for an aborted series, *House of Terror*, in 1979 — along with an original story by Curtis, 'He Who Kills,' which was based on the Matheson devil doll. So I'm finally getting my shot at this fiendish little creature. I think this new segment will have the same jolting effect on viewers as the original did. It'll give them nightmares!... It was originally written as *Trilogy of Terror II*, a Movie of the Week for ABC, but Dan was so high on the script that he withdrew it from the network. He wants to do it is a major feature film called *Trilogy of Terror — The Movie*, as in *Twilight Zone — The Movie*." After Curtis's unsuccessful attempt to secure a theatrical release, the project landed at the USA network, with Matheson's "Bobby" supplanting Dick's story.

Inheriting the mantle of multiple leading roles was British actress Lysette Anthony, who had made her debut in Peter Yates's *Krull* (1983) and appeared as Angelique in the *Dark Shadows* revival. She told Alan Jones in *Femme Fatales*, "I hadn't seen or spoken to Dan for six years, and have no idea at all why he wanted me for the project. I'd heard he was trying to get hold of me, but I thought it must have something to do with a *Dark Shadows* convention. Dan fought with the network as they wanted a heavyweight star name in *Trilogy of Terror II*. I could see why. Playing three different women in one movie is a real challenge for any actress. I styled one of the women after an Hitchcockian blonde heroine. It was a dream come true for me, and I felt like Bette Davis on acid!... We shot for a month ... in Toronto, and I froze my butt off. It was a relentless schedule and the hardest thing I've ever done. We were working 17-hour days...

"Dan Curtis directed [the sequel] which was nice for me, because I never worked for him on *Dark Shadows* as he only directed the pilot I wasn't in. He shouts and swears rather a lot, and is surprised to learn people are terrified of him as a result. He finds that funny. I'm very fond of him, he's been my saviour, and he's incredibly dear to me." When asked by Jones if she had watched the original *Trilogy*, Anthony replied, "There was no point. I wanted our version to be unique and not a copy of what's gone before. I didn't want her dark shadow, so to speak, over me. [*Smiling*] But watch closely — I won't tell you in which episode — for my homage to Karen Black. There's a moment where I pick up a telephone receiver, bring it close to my face — and cross my eyes! Dan hadn't caught it until I pointed it out during looping, and he thought it was hilarious. I get away with it because it's in a moment of sheer terror. Dan thinks Part II is scarier than the first one, but I can't tell, to be honest. Audiences have become much more sophisticated since the original aired. We'll see. I went to the extreme with the emotions I conveyed, and I know I've done good work in it."

"The Graveyard Rats" opens with wealthy invalid Roger Ansford (Matt Clark) planning to fire Ben Garrick (Geraint Wyn Davies, the vampire cop of *Forever Knight*), his wife

---

*The first segment, "The Graveyard Rats," was based on a story by Henry Kuttner, to whom Matheson dedicated *I Am Legend*. Kuttner frequently collaborated with his wife C.L. Moore, and is perhaps best remembered for "The Twonky," written under the pseudonym of Lewis Padgett.

Laura's cousin and lover. Ben plots with her to scare Roger to death but gets carried away and emulates his favorite film, *Kiss of Death* (1947), by pushing Roger down the stairs in his wheelchair. Before the funeral, Ben rudely dismisses a warning from caretaker Arly Stubbs (Geoffrey Lewis) that the family plot is in a section of the Salem cemetery eaten away by huge rats. Laura learns that Roger's fortune is stashed away in Swiss bank accounts accessible only with microfilmed codes, which she deduces are buried with him in the secret compartment of his antique watch. Ben finds Stubbs robbing the grave and kills him with a crowbar. He locates the watch, only to be shot by Laura, who follows Roger's body when the rats drag it through the side of his open coffin, grabs the watch, and meets a fitting end after losing her way in the tunnels and entering the closed, empty coffin in the adjacent grave, where she is trapped and devoured.

"The Graveyard Rats" was Kuttner's first published story, originally appearing in *Weird Tales* in March 1936. Adapters Nolan and Curtis used a method identical to that of Matheson in *Pit and the Pendulum*, grafting the gruesome set piece as a climax onto an entirely original scenario about a wife and her lover who conspire to dispose of the husband with unexpected and deadly results. Masson, the greedy caretaker, is the only human character in Kuttner's eight-page original. He is trapped and devoured in an empty coffin by his four-legged fellow grave robbers — whispered of in local legends — after pursuing a cadaver into their burrows in search of valuables. Kuttner's brief but gripping account of his claustrophobic fate is nightmarish in the extreme. Interestingly, although they expanded the story considerably, Nolan and Curtis eliminated an equally unpleasant element in which the rats are joined by another legendary horror, "a brown and shriveled mummy.... It was the passionless, death's-head skull of a long-dead corpse, instinct with hellish life; and the glazed eyes swollen and bulbous betrayed the thing's blindness."

As before, "Bobby" begins with Alma returning to her clifftop home and performing an occult ritual that conjures up her son (Blake Heron), who was presumed drowned accidentally. The son relates being found on the beach with no memory and sheltered by another family before he starts to taunt and defy Alma, angrily demanding that they play hide-and-seek together. During the game, Bobby's behavior becomes increasingly violent as he chases her through the house and garage with a carving knife and a sledgehammer, even imitating the voice of her husband John on a phone whose cord is cut. At last the terrified Alma is forced to shoot the boy, who is propelled by the impact through an upstairs window and onto the rocks below. But when Alma attempts to leave he returns, pushes her downstairs, and says mockingly, "You lied, Mommy. Bobby didn't drown by accident. You knew that. Bobby drowned himself to get away from you. Bobby didn't want to come back, Mommy. Bobby hates you, Mommy. So he sent me instead," then turns into a hideous dwarf (Joe Geib) and lunges toward her.

"He Who Kills" starts amid the aftermath of Amelia's ordeal as Arthur Breslow (Alex Carter) — invoked but unseen in the original — tells Lt. Jerry O'Farrell (Richard Fitzpatrick) that when he learned that Amelia's phone was off the hook, he had the manager let him into the apartment where he found the bloody bodies of Amelia, whose throat was slashed, and her mother. Suspecting a ritual cult killing, O'Farrell takes the doll to ethnologist Dr. Simpson (Anthony), who postpones a date with Dennis Winslow (Peter Keleghan) to try to identify it. When they find the doll almost perfect beneath its burned surface, her assistant Leonard Spaulding (Durward Allen) drily suggests that it is restoring itself. (Never above a bit of self-promotion, Curtis then shows one of the museum's security guards, Lew [Thomas Mitchell], reading a comic book adaptation of the *Dark Shadows* revival and telling his colleague Steve [Aron Tager], "I love this stuff. Every day I used to race home from school to see this thing.")

Dr. Simpson calls O'Farrell to explain that the Zuni were a particularly fierce tribe of African warriors, extinct for at least five centuries and possibly cannibals. The doll later disappears from her workbench, along with the knife with which she was scraping it clean. While Lew investigates its apparent theft, presumably by the murderer O'Farrell is seeking, the doll kills him by releasing the arrow from a bow held by a mannequin in a tribal exhibit. When a worried Dr. Simpson comes looking for him, she finds both Steve and the switchboard brutally slashed and the museum doors locked, forcing her to return to the lab to get her keys. As with *The Night Strangler*, the sequel is in some ways a virtual remake of the original, with the harried heroine alternately fleeing and battling the knife-wielding doll, unsuccessfully trapping it in a case, and being overcome by the spirit after she burns it, this time with sulfuric acid. The transformed ethnologist kills Dennis with a fire axe when he arrives to pick her up.

As Curtis observed in Mark Dawdziak's introduction to *Produced and Directed by Dan Curtis*,

> It's murder having to compete with yourself. That's the scary part. It gave me a little pause to consider that I was competing against a Dan Curtis who was 20 years younger and maybe smarter. Believe me, I didn't like the competition. Horror stories are the most difficult type of things to do because you need imagination and humor, and you can never make a mistake. The first screwup, you lose all credibility and you're dead with the audience. Most people say, "Well, it's a ghost, so we can do whatever we want with it." They're the people who are dead before they start. A logic lapse or the wrong kind of laugh can sink you. Every single word is a death-trap. That's the worst part of it. Every single line in a horror picture becomes dangerous. A simple "hello" at the wrong place can bring an unwanted laugh. You don't want any unwanted laughs. You want chuckles in the right places. You want people smiling with you when you do certain things. So if you can do these kinds of pictures, you can do anything. Most people think just the opposite — that if you can do these kinds of pictures, you can't do anything else. Well, I've proven them wrong.

What Dreams May Come

(PolyGram, released September 28, 1998 [premiere], October 2, 1998 [general]) DIRECTOR: Vincent Ward; PRODUCER: Stephen Simon (aka Stephen Deutsch), Barnet Bain; SCREENPLAY: Ron Bass, based on Matheson's novel; MUSIC: Michael Kamen; SPECIAL MAKEUP EFFECTS: Todd Masters; SPECIAL VISUAL EFFECTS: Mass Illusions, POP Film & Animation, Digital Domain. Color, 114 minutes. CAST — Chris Nielsen: Robin Williams. Albert: Cuba Gooding, Jr. Annie Nielsen: Annabella Sciorra. The Tracker: Max Von Sydow. Marie Nielsen: Jessica Brooks Grant. Ian Nielsen: Josh Paddock. Leona: Rosalind Chao. Mrs. Jacobs: Lucinda Jenney. Stacey Jacobs: Maggie McCarthy. Angie: Wilma Bonet. Rev. Hanley: Matt Salinger. Best Friend Cindy: Carin Sprague. Woman in Car Accident: June Lomena. Paramedic: Paul P. Card IV. Face: Werner Herzog. Little Girl at Lake: Clara Thomas. Little Boy at Lake: Benjamin Brock. Funeral Guest: Scott Trimble.

Few writers have pondered the fate of the human spirit after death as eloquently as Shakespeare did through the mouth of the melancholy Dane in Act III, Sc. 1, of *Hamlet*: "For in that sleep of death what dreams may come,/When we have shuffled off this mortal coil,/Must give us pause." In the introduction to his *Collected Stories*, Matheson described *What Dreams May Come* as "the ultimate application of my leitmotif—a survival attempt against what is referred to, in the Bible, as 'the last enemy to be destroyed.'" Even more than such previous novels as *A Stir of Echoes* and *Hell House*, it grew out of his lifelong interest in the "supernormal." As he added in our interview for the Gauntlet edition, "There were so many nonfiction books written about [the afterlife], and I thought maybe I could put the sub-

The Tracker (Max Von Sydow) tells Chris Nielsen (Robin Williams) that they must leave "Albert" (Cuba Gooding, Jr.) behind on their trip through Hell in *What Dreams May Come* (PolyGram, 1998).

ject across to more people more interestingly if I wrote it in the form of a novel." The result is an unusual literary form in which the characters and their relationships, although based to a large degree on Matheson's family, are fictional, while, "*with few exceptions, every other detail is derived exclusively from research*," as he emphasized in a 1977 introductory note to the reader.

Many of Matheson's novels have drawn upon the details of his past, and in *What Dreams May Come* there are many similarities between protagonist Chris Nielsen's life, career, and marriage and Matheson's own, including his first meeting with Ruth on a beach in Santa Monica in 1952, shortly after he came to California from Brooklyn. (This had also formed the opening scene of *Someone Is Bleeding*.) "It was more a study of how a man reacts after life," he told me, "and the easiest thing for me to do was to put as much of my family in as I could so I didn't have to make up a family. But of course beyond that I had to make up the basics of the plot, the wife committing suicide and all that stuff. It's not autobiographical in the sense that it follows events of my life, it just incorporates my wife and my children. It was a hook to hang the story on, not the story itself." The parallels between the families extend even to their similar names: The former Ruth Ann Woodson is rendered as Ann, while Bettina Louise, Richard Christian, Alison Marie, and Christian Logan Matheson become Louise, Richard (who aspires to follow in his father's literary footsteps), Marie, and Ian Nielsen, respectively.

What Dreams May Come is in many ways a companion piece to *Bid Time Return*, which was reissued as *Somewhere in Time* in an omnibus edition subtitled "Two Novels of Love and Fantasy." In his introduction to that edition, Matheson noted, "*Somewhere in Time* is the story of a love which transcends time, *What Dreams May Come* the story of a love which transcends death. I never planned that they should be so joined at the psychic hip but I think they are.... Some of my readers were disappointed in these two novels. Accustomed to reading my work in the other genres, they found these two stories 'soft.' I did, however, acquire a new group of readers. For the first time in my career, there was a shift from predominantly younger people to grown men, women and couples." He told me that producer Stephen Simon "was now into my work and read it and fell in love with it and again wanted to do it. We actually tried to do it together. I did a script on it, and then he could never get the backing to make it. My original script was, of all places, for the Lucille Ball company [Desilu].... [We] flew to Munich several times to consult with Wolfgang Petersen, who was interested in doing it, but it didn't work out."

As Simon added in his afterword to the novel, "Just before we commenced pre-production of *Somewhere in Time* (late 1978), Richard asked me if I wanted to read the galleys of a new book he had written. Of course, I was thrilled. Early that evening ... I read it in one sitting and cried—no, sobbed—all the way through. When I finished, I felt like I had gone through an initiation into mysteries of love and life that I had been looking for forever ... [and] became a conscious metaphysician and a man determined to find a way to bring the most unique love story ever written to the screen; hence, the second time Richard and his work changed my life. The next morning, I rushed to Richard's house to hug him, thank him, and beg him to 'let me run' with *What Dreams May Come*; that is, pursue it as a film. Richard had been very pleased with *Somewhere in Time* so that, combined with his recognition of and his bemusement with my obsessive passion to do it, convinced Richard to make another handshake deal with me. And, I assured him, it 'wouldn't take three years this time.' Well, I was kind of right..." Simon eventually wound up nurturing the project through a 20-year transition from page to screen.

What Dreams May Come was instead directed by Vincent Ward, who had made *Vigil* (1984) and *The Navigator: A Medieval Odyssey* (1988) in his native New Zealand, and retained story credit on *Alien³* (1992), despite being supplanted as its director by David Fincher. The script was by Ron Bass, who had shared an Academy Award with Barry Morrow for *Rain Man* (1988), and whose diverse body of work ranges from *Black Widow* and *Gardens of Stone* (both 1987) to *The Joy Luck Club* (1993) and *Waiting to Exhale* (1995). Matheson told me, "It's been suggested to me a number of times that I should arbitrate for a credit on the screenplay and I can't do it, because his screenplay is so different, and whatever similarities there are are in the source material. He claims he has never read my script, and I have no reason to doubt his word." Matheson told James E. Brooks in *Starburst* that Petersen "wanted my script redone radically and Steve wouldn't agree to it. Finally, though, he reached the point where he had to get a writer that had some sort of clout."

According to *Movieline*'s Stephen Farber, "The novel was first optioned in the '70s, but studios, which don't generally share Bass's view [that women are more interesting people in life and in drama], kept getting cold feet about the subject matter. 'It's an extremely romantic piece, and thank God Hollywood has discovered the young female audience that will go to romantic movies over and over again,' says Bass." The editors added in the same issue (October 1998), "Michelle Pfeiffer, Meryl Streep and *many* others all passed on this project." Annabella Sciorra did not; a veteran of Spike Lee's *Jungle Fever* (1991) and Abel Ferrara's *The Addiction* (1995) and *The Funeral* (1996), she co-starred with Cuba Gooding, Jr., and Robin Williams. Matheson told me that Simon had considered another title change: "He said the public would think it was *Wet Dreams May Come*. That's the way they think out here [in Hollywood]. I'm going to be on *The Jerry Springer Show*. It's so stupid that your eyes glaze over."

Dispensing with the similarities between Chris Nielsen and Matheson, like his literary alter ego a successful television writer at that time, the film portrays Chris (Williams) as a doctor—perhaps not coincidentally the profession for which he is destined at the end of the novel, when his reincarnated soul is finally reunited with Ann's in India. It depicts their courtship and marriage in the credit sequence. Their children, Marie (Jessica Brooks Grant) and Ian (Josh Paddock), are killed when a truck collides with the van driven by their nanny, Angie (Wilma Bonet). Because Marie had asked her to drive that day, Annie believes that her "maternal instinct" might have enabled her to save them. Four years later, Chris dies in another car crash while doing a favor for Annie, who blames herself once again. As in the novel, Chris rises to look down at his body lying in a hospital bed, attends his own funeral, and struggles with intangibility while trying to tell Annie, "I still exist," all the while accompanied by the initially blurry figure of Albert (Gooding), who assures him that this painful transitional state "ends when you want it to." After Chris has visited his own grave beside the grief-stricken Annie, it does.

"That which you believe becomes your world," Albert says in the novel when Chris finds himself in the afterlife, and in the film's central visual conceit, Chris's self-created Heaven is a three-dimensional version of the picture that Annie — a restorer of fine art whose literary counterpart was not so employed — painted of the place where they met and had hoped to retire. Bass may have been inspired by a brief passage in which Matheson explains, via Chris, "Every work of art here is alive. Colors glow with reality. Each painting seems almost — not a good description but the closest I can come — three-dimensional, possessing all the qualities of relief. From a short distance, they look like real scenes rather than flat representations." Now seen clearly for the first time, Albert is revealed as a younger version of Chris's medical mentor, rather than his cousin in the novel. As Chris slips around in the wet paint (courtesy of the complex special effects that necessitated a seven-and-a-half-minute credit crawl at the end of the film), Albert tells him, "You're making all of this.... We all paint our own surroundings, Chris."

The later scenes set in Hell were shot on unusually large sets, built around a 300,000-gallon pool in a converted airplane hangar on San Francisco's Treasure Island. Other location shooting for the "painted world" sequences took place at Glacier National Park in Montana. Himself a painter, Ward explained in his DVD audio commentary, "It was live-action cinematography, filmed in the same way as you'd film anything else ... and it was in the ten months of post-production that we enhanced the footage and turned it into a series of paintings. Long after the art directors and the film crew had departed, the three visual effects companies [Mass Illusions, POP Film & Animation, and Digital Domain] worked on the various shots..." The

Chris braves the sea of faces in *What Dreams May Come* (PolyGram, 1998).

filmmakers used Biblical engravings and other images ranging from the medieval period to the nineteenth century for inspiration, including the work of artists Francis Bacon, Hieronymus Bosch, Gustav Doré, Caspar David Friedrich, Edouard Manet, Homer Martin, Claude Monet, and Vincent Van Gogh.

Chris has already been reunited with his longtime canine companion Katie, whom he and Annie had been forced to put to sleep. He later realizes that another of his spiritual guides, a colleague of Albert's named Leona (Rosalind Chao, known to genre fans as Keiko O'Brien on *Star Trek: Deep Space Nine*), is the soul of Marie in the form of a flight attendant from a trip they once took together. His delight in his beautiful new surroundings is marred only by his concern for his soulmate, which soon proves justified: As flashbacks reveal, Annie has a history of mental instability that included a period of institutionalization following the children's death, and finally, overwhelmed with grief and guilt, she takes her own life with an overdose of sleeping pills. Chris is overjoyed at the prospect of seeing her again until Albert reveals that suicides go to a Hell in which people don't know they're dead, and explains, "It's not all fire and pain. The real Hell is your life gone wrong." According to Albert, she must spend all eternity there for violating the natural order, but Chris is convinced that as Annie's soulmate he can locate her and bring her back from Hell.

"My screenplay literally followed the book," Matheson told *Starlog*'s Marc Shapiro. "I think a big problem MGM had with [my] script was that in my novel, the children did not die but the mother commits suicide, leaving the children behind. The studio felt it would be hard for audiences to feel sympathy for this character if she chose to leave her children by committing suicide.... In the novel, the dead father tries to communicate with the daughter. Obviously, the movie is much more effective if he tries to get through to his wife." As of this writing, his unfilmed screenplay for *What Dreams May Come* is scheduled to be published in 2010 in Gauntlet's *Matheson Uncollected: Volume Two*.

In the novel, Albert also leads Chris on his search for Annie's soul, but the film introduces a new character who fulfills the same function, known as the Tracker. He is played by Max Von Sydow, best known for the films he made with writer-director Ingmar Bergman in his native Sweden, as Jesus in *The Greatest Story Ever Told*, and for the title role in *The Exorcist*. Chris realizes that like Leona, "Albert" is really Ian, who modeled himself after "the only guy you ever listened to," and stays behind so as not to distract Chris from Annie's "signals" as the Tracker takes him on a stunning voyage through apocalyptic vistas and across a sea of upturned faces, one of them marking a bizarre cameo by Ward's friend, German director Werner Herzog. The Tracker, in turn, is revealed as a manifestation of Albert's soul. He brings Chris to a grim mockery of their home, where his willingness to stay with Annie and "choose Hell over Heaven just to hang around you" opens her eyes to the truth at last. After being reunited with her family in Heaven, she agrees to be reborn with Chris so they can find each other all over again.

Steve Biodrowski's *Cinefantastique* review noted that the film "translated the intent [of the novel] into visual terms that register with viewers. It's not just pretty or effects-laden; it's beautiful, because the imagery of the afterlife reveals the characters, whose inner visions create their own personal heavens. Even if you think there's something wrong with the film, it deserves respect for what it did right. The visual effects may seem to outshine the story and characterization — but only initially." He also enumerated such last-minute changes as the replacement of Ennio Morricone's score with a new one by Michael Kamen "and the extra scenes added after the preview (a family reunion in the afterlife, followed by reincarnation on Earth)..." In the original ending, which is truer to the novel, Annie is told that suicides are required to return and be reborn; when Chris volunteers to go back as well, he learns that they will be reunited in Sri Lanka, where she will die in his arms and he will live alone for 40 years mourning her. This finale is an extra on the DVD.

The same year Ward's film was released, a deceased man trying to remain in contact with his grieving young widow (Marg Helgenberger) was the subject of Lifetime's comedy *Giving Up the Ghost* (1998). Several critics noted the similarities between *What Dreams May Come* and *Ghost* (1990), whose script (by Bruce Joel Rubin) was on Oscar winner. In a bitter irony, unwitting viewers might have assumed that the makers of *What Dreams May Come* had ripped off the far more financially successful *Ghost*, whereas if anything the latter borrowed from Matheson's tale of "a love which transcends death," published a dozen years earlier. In fact, *Ghost* echoes certain sequences in the novel that were, perhaps understandably, omitted from the film. For example, Oda Mae Brown (Oscar winner Whoopi Goldberg) is a medium via whom the late Sam Wheat (Patrick Swayze) hopes to contact his despondent but skeptical lover, Molly Jensen (Demi Moore), after his untimely death in an apparent mugging puts an abrupt end to their idyllic romance, just as a psychic named Perry — eliminated from the film — tries unsuccessfully to reassure Ann Nielsen.

Although *What Dreams May Come* was considered a critical and commercial disappointment, Nicholas Brooks, Joel Hynek, Kevin Scott Mack, and Stuart Robertson justifiably shared an Oscar for its stunning visual effects. Cindy Carr and Eugenio Zanetti were nominated for Best Art Direction — Set Decoration, but they lost to that year's Best Picture, *Shakespeare in Love*. Philosophical as always, Matheson told me that he still remains gratified by the effect that the novel, which became a national bestseller in its movie tie-in edition, has had on his readers. "I got a lovely letter from somebody whose mother was dying and had read this book and had found great comfort in it. I remember thinking then, and I think now, that no writer can have a greater tribute to what he does than that they bring comfort in such a situation." The film has had its own afterlife on home video — as well as on the syllabus of at least one college philosophy course — and was endorsed by many New Age writers, so perhaps Simon's labor of love will one day be appreciated not only as a technical *tour de force*, but also for the honest emotion of its characters, and for its hopeful message on a subject that many find terrifying and painful.

Stir of Echoes

(Artisan, released September 10, 1999) DIRECTOR-SCREENPLAY: David Koepp, based on Matheson's *A Stir of Echoes*; PRODUCER: Gavin Polone, Judy Hofflund; MUSIC: James Newton Howard; SPECIAL MAKEUP EFFECTS: Tony Gardner, Jim Beinke; SPECIAL EFFECTS: Banned from the Ranch Entertainment. Color, 99 minutes. Cast — Tom Witzky: Kevin Bacon. Maggie Witzky: Kathryn Erbe. Lisa: Illeana Douglas. Jake Witzky: Zachary David Cope. Frank McCarthy: Kevin Dunn. Harry Damon: Conor O'Farrell. Debbie Kozak: Liza Weil. Sheila McCarthy: Lusia Strus. Bobby: Stephen Eugene Walker. Vanessa: Mary Kay Cook. Lenny: Larry Neumann, Jr. Samantha Kozak: Jenny Morrison. Neighborhood Man: Richard Cotovsky. Kurt Damon: Steve Rifkin. Adam McCarthy: Chalon Williams. Security Guard: George Ivey. Debbie's Mother: Lisa Lewis. Train Station Cops: Mike Bacarella, Christian Stolte. Neil the Cop: Eddie Bo Smith, Jr. Korean Woman: Hyowon K. Yoo. Elderly Man: Jim Andelin. Upset Woman: Karen Vaccaro. Homey: Antonio Polk. Clarita: Rosario Varela. Polish Priest: Duane Sharp. Angry Man: Gavin Polone. Gothic Street Punk: Louie Meza.

A Stir of Echoes was Matheson's first novel concerning "what psi investigators choose to call the *supernormal*— as distinguished from the old hackneyed term, *supernatural*. It's a lot easier to deal with proceedings which fit into the natural scheme of things than it is to deal with beyond-the-pale marvels. Miracles are out of fashion," as one character, a psychiatrist, puts it. Matheson dedicated the book "for Chuck and Helen [Beaumont] with affection" (altered to "in loving remembrance" in a 1979 Berkley reprint), and took its memorable and highly appropriate title from "Chambers of Imagery," written by American poet Archibald MacLeish. After more than 40 years, during which Matheson himself had adapted it into a stage play and a screenplay, both unproduced, the novel was finally filmed by writer-director David Koepp, whose special thanks in the end titles to Andrew Kevin Walker, the scenarist of *Seven* (1995) and *Sleepy Hollow* (1999), are reportedly for uncredited script-doctoring.

In the decade since his first screen credit, *Apartment Zero* (1989), Koepp had cowritten the blockbusters *Jurassic Park* and *The Lost World*; worked with Brian DePalma on *Carlito's Way* (1993), *Mission: Impossible* (1996), and *Snake Eyes* (1998); and made his debut as a writer-director with *The Trigger Effect* (1995). Koepp told *Cinefantastique's* Peter Sobczynski, "The [adaptive] process is always the same. I read the books two or three times and highlight the stuff that I love and see if I'm highlighting the same stuff every time. Then I scene-card every thing in the book and start throwing out everything that I know won't fit. When I feel I have the bare bones version, I come up with those few transition scenes that I might need to make a script and then I start writing.... When I'm working with a director like Spielberg or DePalma, a really heavyweight guy who has been doing it for a long time, they are going to impose their visual ideas on the script, which they should. When I do it myself, I stick a little closer to the initial visual ideas, which is not always good. A director has to reinterpret the writer's work, because that's what makes it come alive. If you shoot it exactly, it's usually dull."

Kevin Bacon plays Tom Witzky, "pretty much an ordinary guy," as Bacon told Sobczynski. "He used to play music, but he had to give up that dream when his wife got pregnant. I liked the guy's story and the story of his family. If you took out all the ghosts and mystery and the horror, it was still an interesting character. [The musical aspect] wasn't even my idea. It was Dave's idea. I think he had me being, I don't know, an engineer or something originally. He called me up one day and said, 'Maybe we should take advantage of this other side.' It's good because it gave me more to relate to and a little more focus about who he was.... I'm not much of a reader, frankly. For *Apollo 13* [1995], I read Jim Lovell's [*Lost Moon*]. You can sometimes get some interesting stuff [that way] but this time I just stuck to the script."

A telephone linesman who lives in a working-class Chicago neighborhood, the skeptical Tom is hypnotized at a party by his New Age-oriented sister-in-law Lisa (the marvelous Illeana Douglas), who reports that he is unusually susceptible. Later that night, while making love with his newly pregnant wife Maggie (Kathryn Erbe), Tom begins to be assailed by a series of disjointed psychic flashes. Upon seeing a ghostly vision of a teenage girl, Tom is told by his five-year-old son Jake (Zachary David Cope) not to be afraid of it. Lisa, asked if she can explain this unnerving new ability, admits to giving him a post-hypnotic suggestion: "After you wake up, your mind will be completely open, like an open door, open to receive everything around you." Planning to attend a football game with their friends Frank (Kevin Dunn) and Sheila McCarthy (Lusia Strus), Tom has a presentiment of danger from the moment he meets Debbie Kozak (Liza Weil), the new babysitter hired by Maggie. When Jake tells Debbie — who is shown reading a copy of *The Shrinking Man*— that he has talked to someone named Samantha, she kidnaps him.

Tom's newfound power enables him and Maggie to trail Debbie to the Logan Square train station, where in a tense confrontation with the police it is revealed that her sister Samantha (Jenny Morrison) vanished six months ago, and that when Jake claimed to have spoken to Samantha in the Witzkys' own house, Debbie took the boy to show him to her mother (Lisa Lewis), a ticket seller. Tom conceals the fact that he recognized a photo of Samantha as his ghostly vision, and declines to press charges. Becoming obsessed with the missing girl, who speaks briefly through the obviously psychic Jake, he learns that she was believed to have run away and is told by his landlord, Harry Damon (Conor O'Farrell), that he and Maggie are the house's original tenants. In another vision, Frank says that someone is going to kill Maggie and Tom, who goes in search of Sheila but arrives just before their son Adam (Chalon Williams) shoots himself in front of Tom. When Tom races up the steps of the McCarthy home after returning to reality, he hears a gunshot and breaks in to find that Adam has indeed attempted suicide.

Jake wanders into a police funeral while out walking with Maggie and they meet Neil (Eddie Bo Smith, Jr.), a black cop reminiscent of Scatman Crothers in *The Shining* (1980). Neil later tells her, "He's a receiver now. Everything's coming in. He can't stop it, he can't slow it down, he can't even figure it out. It's like he's in a tunnel with a flashlight, but the light only comes on every once in a while. He gets a glimpse of something, but not enough to know what it is.... [Samantha has] asked for something, and now she's waiting, getting more and more pissed off that he's not doing it." But after giving Maggie this information — similar to the psychiatrist's explanation in the novel (which includes the flashlight metaphor) — Neil and a group of other psychics are dropped. In his DVD audio commentary, Koepp revealed that he had cut a scene in which Tom visited Neil's group and received some explanation for what he was undergoing, because he did not want the audience to be too reassured.

Bacon effectively portrays Tom's mental and physical deterioration, especially after he has Lisa hypnotize him again in an effort to close whatever door she has opened in his mind. He instead receives the psychic command, "Dig," which makes him turn the backyard into a mud pit. Utterly neglectful of Maggie and their marriage, he then takes a jackhammer to the cellar, where he finally finds Samantha walled up and wrapped in a plastic sheet while Maggie is away attending her grandmother's funeral. He senses that Harry's son Kurt (Steve Rifkin) and Adam had accidentally smothered the girl when trying to rape her on the construction site, a crime Frank and Harry concealed. The guilt-ridden Frank apparently kills himself in the cellar. When Maggie arrives just in time to distract Harry and Kurt from silencing Tom, Frank emerges

Tom Witzky (Kevin Bacon) is terrified by the ghostly presence of Samantha Kozak (Jenny Morrison) in *Stir of Echoes* (Artisan, 1999).

to shoot both Damons. The head wound that Tom suffers in the scuffle apparently removes his powers (as in the novel), although Jake's remain, as shown in an ominous final fadeout that replaced Koepp's original ending of the baby's birth.

"I've always liked Matheson," Koepp told Sobczynski. "I was in Vagabond Books in L.A., a great science fiction and fantasy bookstore. I was in there looking around and saw this little book of his that I hadn't heard of before. The guy at the store said, 'Oh, you've gotta read *Stir of Echoes*.' I read it and I loved it.... I will proudly say that it is a horror movie. However, it is not a slasher movie.... I've always been more attracted to the kinds of movies that get under your skin a little more. What to me is the scariest is not that the monster will catch me and kill me, because if it kills me, it's over. What scares me is that the monster will chase me, catch me and disappear and then I'll start to turn into him. That's the thing that freaks me out; that I'm changing or that someone I love is changing and there is nothing I can do about it. I'm trying to do something a little more disturbing." The film was released by newcomer Artisan Entertainment, as was that summer's surprise hit *The Blair Witch Project* (1999), and was hailed as part of a resurgence of genre entries more mature than *Scream* (1996) and *I Know What You Did Last Summer* (1997).

Other than relocating the story to Chicago from the suburbs of Los Angeles, where the literary Tom worked in publications at an aircraft plant, Koepp is generally faithful to the spirit if not always the letter of the novel, streamlining the plot and linking the hitherto unrelated incident involving the babysitter to the telepathic whodunit that lies at the center of the story. Depicting the dark underbelly of 1950s suburbia, Matheson's tale involves the murder of Helen Driscoll, the previous tenant of the Wallaces' home whose brother-in-law, landlord, and lover, Harry Sentas, is set up as a red herring until the killer is finally unmasked as Elizabeth Wanamaker, the wife of yet another in Helen's seemingly unending parade of paramours. While the spirit of the murder victim in the novel also speaks briefly through young Richard Wallace, Jake Witzky is much more of a major character in the film and his own psychic abilities more overt. This was an unfortunate coincidental similarity to *The Sixth Sense* (1999), which was released the month before *Stir of Echoes* and completely overshadowed it at the box office.

Koepp told Bernard Weinraub in *The New York Times*, "The kinds of stuff I do as a writer tend to be much bigger, a lot of summer-type movies. They're a lot of fun. The characters tend to be larger than life. But you don't develop a very intimate relationship with them. And I wanted that.... It's a young couple with a family, like me." Then recently relocated from Los Angeles to New York's Upper West Side with his wife Rosario Varela (who has a small role in *Stir of Echoes* and also appeared in *Apartment Zero*) and two sons, Koepp might almost have been speaking for Matheson himself when he told Weinraub, "I've worked with some brilliant directors: Spielberg, Zemeckis, DePalma. But even when I saw them doing it far better than I ever could, it's still different from what's in my head. Therefore it's wrong."

The filmmakers created the fictional blue-collar Chicago community by weaving together actual locations shot in the Wicker Park, Polish Village, and Brighton Park areas. In his commentary, Koepp said, "Matheson was telling me that the house in [the novel] *Stir of Echoes* was exactly the house that he was living in at the time, and I put in a lot of details that were [from] the house that I was living in at the time, and I think it's still a pretty happy marriage of our two points of view. He was very happy with the film, which gave me a great deal of pleasure." Once again, he echoed Matheson's own thoughts regarding the depiction of Samantha's attempted rape and murder: "I knew I would be criticized by some people for being exploitative. I certainly tried not to be.... You must see what happened to her, and it must be horrible. It must be shocking. The movie demands it, and I don't think I could let my personal squeamishness get in the way of that..." In a note he wrote me shortly before the film was released, Matheson called this "really a marvelous film. I am very happy with it; a rare situation for me. David Koepp did a great job on the updated adaptation and the direction. Kevin Bacon is excellent."

Janet Maslin of *The New York Times* singled out Bacon's "taut, grippingly intense performance," and several critics praised the film's effectively understated horror. Steve Biodrowski wrote in *Cinefantastique*, "Koepp has crafted a screenplay that diverges from its source but retains the essential premise and set-up, resulting in a solid storyline set in a believably realistic world where the sudden intrusion of the supernatural is that much more uncanny.... Aided by solid performances all around, and augmented with a judicious use of special effects that are actually creepy rather than just technically impressive,* he has managed to generate some genuine scares in the course of telling an interesting story peopled with engaging characters."

In his introduction to the Gauntlet edition of *A Stir of Echoes* (also containing his unproduced 1959 script, which follows it virtually verbatim), Matheson recalled, "When I wrote this novel, I wanted to do my share in upending the genre phenomenon. So I wrote a murder mystery combined with a ghost story and a study of involuntary psychic possession.... It was nicely reviewed and, presently, purchased by Universal for a specific producer [William Sackheim]. I wrote the screenplay which, because of the producer's intercession, was altered more and more until it became — to me — unrecognizable. (For example, a tract house in Gardena became an ocean-view mansion in Carmel.) I soon left the project — or was put off it, I forget which. It doesn't matter. It was one more example (typical) of a very good story twisted out of shape and, finally, discarded completely.... Interestingly enough, although [Koepp] altered the story in location and updated it to the present, he retained the basic story so well that I was (and am) extremely happy with how the film turned out.... It was a happy — and not a typical turn of events in movie making."

Koepp opined in an afterword to the same edition, "One of the reasons Richard Matheson is such a brilliant writer is because of the effortless way he achieves the most difficult thing in storytelling — simplicity. Complicated is easy, anybody can do complicated, but the clarity with which Matheson's ideas jump off the page is unique and arresting. True horror hides behind the truly mundane ... and its awfulness is magnified by the quality of his observation, the detail and rightness with which Matheson sketches the house, the marriage, the neighborhood, all in the first two or three pages. This was my guiding principle while making the film I adapted from his book; like the novel, the more real the movie seemed, the more horrifying it would be."

In the Sci-Fi Channel's nominal sequel *Stir of Echoes: The Homecoming* (2007), Ted Cogan (Rob Lowe), a wounded National Guard vet, returns from Iraq haunted by visions of the dead. They eventually reveal that his son and two friends — one of whom just lost her father in the war — have immolated a young Arab-American man inside a Dumpster as a warped way of avenging the soldiers. A blind Jake Witzky appears in a single scene (inexplicably played by adult actor Zachary Bennett) and tells Cogan, "When I was a kid, they just talked to me, y'know? But the older I got, the harder it was for them to come through. They got more annoyed — mean as hell — drove me a little nuts, and one day I kinda lost

---

*According to the film's press kit, the ghost's unnervingly jerky movements were created by having the ballet-trained Morrison move at one-quarter speed while being photographed at six frames per second.

it and ... [*indicates his disfigured eye sockets*]. Needless to say, puberty sucked." According to reports on upcominghorrormovies.com, an earlier version of the script, written by Harris Wilkinson and rewritten by Adam Green, focused on Jake's frightening visions as a high-school senior, although the film (formerly subtitled *The Dead Speak*), written and directed by Ernie Barbarash and shot in Toronto for Lionsgate, does not credit Matheson as the creator of the character.

Blood Son

(Buffalonickel Films, released April 2, 2006) DIRECTOR/SCREENPLAY: Michael McGruther, based on Matheson's story (aka "'Drink My Red Blood...'" and "Drink My Blood"); PRODUCER: Tom MacDonald, Michele Santos; MUSIC: Matt Heider; MAKEUP: Ingrid Okola. Color, 15 minutes. CAST—Jules: Lucas Wotkowski. Antique Shopkeeper: Robert Hancock. Teacher: Julie M. Finch. Mother Christianson: Mandi Bedbury. Jim Christianson: Joseph Michael Somma. Principal: Cash Tilton. Dracula: Paul Coughlan. Rico: Alan Tavarez. Manny: Aldous Davidson. Tony: Richard Giambalvo. Classroom Students: Lauren Barbara, Angelica Catalini, Kaitlyn Clark, Dylan Coonrad, Ryan Gilpatrick, Alex Hestvik, Alexis Malafatopolous, Melina McQuillan, Rachel Patti, Leslie Pillepich, Amanda Pollak, Joe Rosatao, Erica Russell, Patrick Scheid, Katie Stevens, Kathy Taylor, Ali Terzini, Elizabeth Trum, Jamie Vernon.

My Ambition

(k2 Productions, released May 14, 2006) DIRECTOR/SCREENPLAY: Keith Dinielli, based on Matheson's "Blood Son"; PRODUCER: Robert Myrtle; MAKEUP/SPECIAL MAKEUP EFFECTS: Karen Stein. Color, 8 minutes. CAST—Jules Walters: Johnny Simmons. Teacher: Brooke Morgan. Zookeeper: Bernard Zilinskas. Mother: Elena Finney. Principal: Christopher John Fetherolf. Class: Alice Berkan, Ashley Brady, Sara Brassfield, Gunnar Douroux, Brittany Hanner, Ellen Huggett, Sarah Kay, Kevin Stark, Schaun Stevens, Stephanie Stutzel, Kyle Warstler, Rachel Wess. The Count: Jonas Barnes.

Three adaptations of Matheson's classic "Blood Son" have appeared in recent years, including a comic-book version by Chris Ryall and artist Ashley Wood in the first issue of the short-lived IDW publication *Doomed*. (*Doomed* subsequently tackled his short stories "Crickets" [*Shock*, May 1960], "The Children of Noah," and "Legion of Plotters" [*Detective Story Magazine*, July 1953].) IDW editor-in-chief Ryall told me, "When I got a chance to adapt his short story 'Blood Son' into comic form, and then got my first Eisner [Award] nomination for that adaptation, it was not only a pleasure to be able to have done justice to his work, but doing so was also a hyperbolic-free culmination of my years of studying and admiring his works. Knowing that Richard trusted IDW enough to tackle many of his projects as graphic novels was a joy, and having conversations with him about the works was an honor. And it was all done in an effort to spread his work to an even wider audience, and hopefully set some other impressionable kid on the path to knowing just what he's always been so capable of doing — telling a great story."

Matheson's oft-anthologized tale tells of the misfit Jules, a frail, blank-eyed, pale-skinned 12-year-old whose life is changed when he sees the movie *Dracula* and then steals a copy of the novel from the library. It inspires him to write a composition ("My Ambition by Jules Dracula") that horrifies his teacher and classmates by describing, in vivid and unsettling detail, how he wants to grow up and be a vampire. A year later, he sees a vampire bat in the zoo and dubs it "the Count"; gradually loosening the wire covering its cage, Jules removes the Count and takes it to a deserted shack, where he hacks at his own throat with a pen knife and tells the bat, "Drink my red blood!" As it does so, the dying boy realizes his mistake and tries to run for help, whereupon a "tall dark man whose eyes shone like rubies" lifts him up and says, "My son." Matheson stated in his *Collected Stories* commentary, "[O]riginally it was just going to be a straight character story, and the main character was going to die at the end, and that would simply be the end of it [with no supernatural element whatsoever]. Then I realized that nobody was going to buy that, so I just threw those little extra lines at the end so that it would sell."

The first of two independent shorts based on the story to appear in 2006, *Blood Son* marked the directorial debut of Michael McGruther, who had co-scripted Joel Schumacher's *Tigerland* (2000). McGruther also served as the screenwriter, co-editor and executive producer of this 15-minute film, which was shot in Matheson's home state of New Jersey and won a Director's Award at the Trenton Film Festival. Obviating the need for an expensive rental of zoo facilities, McGruther retooled the story to introduce the character of a sympathetic antique shopkeeper (Robert Hancock) who offers Jules (portrayed as a teenager in the film by Lucas Wotkowski) refuge from the harassment of three hoods, provides him with the copy of *Dracula* and also owns the bat (which Jules later steals). The script is otherwise quite faithful, especially in the classroom sequence that constitutes its highlight, with a powerful performance by Wotkowski that discomfits the teacher (Julie M. Finch) and class. McGruther even dramatizes a scene that is only presented as an example of town gossip in the story, as the infant Jules draws blood from Mother Christianson (Mandi Bedbury) while she breast-feeds him.

"I called the agent and asked for the rights to make the short story into a short film," McGruther related in an e-mail interview with me. "I only asked for permission to do a film as my first step into directing. In other words, I in no way intended to try and profit from it [through commercial distribution]. I think if I did, the agent would have given me a more difficult time. I could not find a zoo that I could afford to shoot in, and didn't realize in my naïveté that I could 'cheat' a location to look like a zoo. So I changed the location to what I could find, and that became an old antique store. I feel that the short film suffered because of that. It lost some of the magic that is in the written story. It was first shown at the Garden State Film Festival and also won a nice award for the composer [Matt Heider] and myself at the Park City Film Music Festival. My goal was never to change my career, but to start down a new path with interesting material, and *Blood Son* was a great first step that has taught me quite a bit. My desire is to turn [it] into a TV series called *Jules Dracula*, about a teenager who is not yet a vampire, but works for an all-powerful one."

Soon after, an eight-minute adaptation entitled *My Ambition* was written and directed by Keith Dinielli, a longtime fan of Matheson's work who had been the director, executive producer, co-writer and costar of *Changeover* (1998). The classroom confrontation between Jules Walters (Johnny Simmons) and his teacher (Brooke Morgan) formed the opening scene. Dinielli told me, "When I started thinking about directing another film, I decided to make it short in order to maximize my money, unlike my first film, in which we stretched every resource we had to make a feature. I immediately thought of 'Blood Son' as the perfect story. Mr. Matheson's agents granted us permission to make the film for festivals and non-commercial showings." Evoking the disaffected teens of the Columbine era, Dinielli's film cuts from the classroom to a shot of Jules reacting to an offscreen conversation in which his mother (Elena Finney) tells the principal (Christopher John Fetherolf), "I disconnected the Internet, I sold our television — I don't know what else to do," and then to an altercation between the black-trenchcoat-clad Jules and the zookeeper (Bernard Zilinskas).

"About a month before we were to start shooting, I placed an ad in *Back Stage West* looking for actors over 18 that could play 14-year-old Jules," Dinielli related. "Shortly after the ad ran, I was bombarded with headshots from teenaged girls! *Back Stage* had misprinted the ad, saying I was looking for a female lead! They apologized, but unfortunately, had already printed the new edition, so the misprint would run for one more week. With two weeks to go before shooting, I started calling everyone I knew, scrambling to find a lead to play Jules, when I received an e-mail from Johnny. It said, 'I know you are looking for a lead actress, but if you have any roles for a guy, I'd love to try out.' And he attached his headshot. The moment I saw it, I realized this could be Jules. I had originally been looking for someone dark and brooding, but Johnny had such a fresh-faced innocence about him that I realized it would make Jules even creepier. He came to my office and read for the part. It was a no-brainer. We cast him in the room and never read another actor." Simmons later appeared in *Evan Almighty* (2007) and as the young Denny Colt in *The Spirit* (2008).

Said McGruther, "My first reaction was disappointment that Matheson's agent would allow two filmmakers to work on the material at the same time. However, upon seeing Mr. Dinielli's version, I was very impressed. He went with a more terrifying on the surface *Nosferatu*-type Dracula. It worked well in his version. I wish there were a way to combine them so the short could be fully realized between the two of us in the closest version to the story." Added Dinielli, "A few months after we wrapped, a friend of mine, who was working for a producer, had received Michael's film and told me I should take a look. I liked his very much. It was interesting to see how similar we envisioned the classroom scene. But Michael chose to cover some of the backstory, which gives his a very different feel. I think both stand alone and certainly as companion pieces as an example of how two filmmakers can realize a piece of material. The positive reaction at festivals always included the question, 'What happens to Jules?' I realized there could be more to his story." Dinielli is now developing the story as a feature with producer Michael Phillips, who has acquired the rights.

Among YouTube's amateur videos based on Matheson tales are multiple adaptations of "The Near Departed" (the story of a man making funeral arrangements for the young and beautiful wife whose time of death is "as soon as I get home," first published in *Masques II* in 1987, but written c. 1971); one of them is a distaff version retitled *The Last Rites of Richard Keene*. There are also music videos, tributes to *Trilogy of Terror*, a stop-motion animation of "No Such Thing as a Vampire," adaptations of "Button, Button," and many films inspired by *I Am Legend*. There's even "a video response to [the] *I Am Legend* teaser trailer" based on "Person to Person" (*Rod Serling's The Twilight Zone Magazine*, April 1989), in which a man receives an unsettling "phone call" from a voice inside his head. Hunter Lurie directed and starred in an adaptation of Matheson's "Through Channels" (*Fantasy and Science Fiction*, April 1951) — set to an excerpt from Ennio Morricone's score for *The Thing* (1982) — in which a boy recounts to a detective voiced by Lurie's own father, writer-director Rod Lurie, how his parents were horribly killed by the television set that displayed the letters "F-E-E-D," and then "F-E-D."

I Am Legend

(Warner Bros., released December 14, 2007) DIRECTOR: Francis Lawrence; PRODUCER: Akiva Goldsman, James Lassiter, David Heyman, Neal Moritz; SCREENPLAY: Mark Protosevich, Goldsman, based on John William & Joyce H. Corrington's screenplay [*The Omega Man*] and Matheson's novel; MUSIC: James Newton Howard; VISUAL EFFECTS SUPERVISOR: Janek Sirrs; CREATURE DESIGN: Patrick Tatopoulos; VISUAL EFFECTS: Sony Pictures Imageworks-CIS-Hollywood. Color, 100 minutes [original release], 104 minutes [alternate theatrical and DVD version]. CAST— Dr. Robert Neville: Will Smith. Anna: Alice Braga. Ethan: Charlie Tahan. Zoe: Salli Richardson. Marley: Willow Smith. Mike (Military Escort): Darrell Foster. TV Personality: April Grace. Alpha Male: Dash Mihok. Alpha Female: Joanna Numata. Sam: Abbey, Kona. Jay (Military Driver): Samuel Glen. Male Evacuees: James McCauley, Alexander DiPersia, Abraham Sparrow. Woman Evacuee: Marin Ireland. Sergeant: Pedro Mojica. Evacuation Cops: Anthony Mazza, Tyree Simpson. Military Police: Steve Cirbus. Little Girl Evacuees: Calista Hill, Gabriella Hill, Madeline Hill. Military Scanning Tech: Adhi Sharma. Coast Guard Ground Crew: Blake Lange. Voice of President: Patrick Fraley. Special Blond Model: Caitlin McHugh. Civilian: Deborah Collins. Creature Vocals: Mike Patton. Infected: Exo, Katherine Brook, Vince Cupone, Lynná Davis, Anika Ellis, John Grady, Moses Harris, Jr., Kennis Hawkins, Marc Inniss, Eric Jenkins, Reed Kelly, Grasan Kingsberry, Heather Lang, Drew Leary, Asa Liebmann, Deborah Lohse, Jon-Paul Mateo, Ian McLaughlin, Luke Miller, Courtney Munch, Kimberly Shannon Murphy, Okwui Okpokwasili, Erin Owen, Victor Paguia, Paradox Pollack, Will Rawls, William Schultz, Hollie K. Seidel, Hannah Sim, Eric Spear, Mark Steger, Charlie Sutton, David Hamilton Thomson, Anthony Vincent, Greg Wattkis. Dr. Alice Krippin: Emma Thompson.

As Matheson himself told John Brosnan, *The Last Man on Earth* "was very poorly done, but it did follow the book. *The Omega Man* bore no resemblance at all to my book, so I can't comment on it. I had absolutely nothing to do with the screenplay but they did pay me a very small remake fee." He added to Sammon in *Midnight Graffiti*, "Dan Curtis tried to get the rights to it, he wanted to do it as it was written, but Warners wouldn't give it up." While those rights languished in a legal tangle, the possibility of a definitive film version — which, in his opinion, would have reunited Andrew Davis and Harrison Ford, the director and star of *The Fugitive* (1993) — seemed increasingly remote. The studio announced a remake with Ridley Scott directing Arnold Schwarzenegger, but then scaled back its plans due to budgetary concerns. *CFQ*'s Stanley Manders summarized subsequent efforts by a revolving door of actors (Kurt Russell, Will Smith), directors (*The X-Files*'s Rob Bowman, Michael Bay), and screenwriters (Mark Protosevich, John Logan, Neal Jimenez).

In our 1998 interview for Gauntlet's limited edition of *What Dreams May Come*, Matheson discussed an early version of the *I Am Legend* screenplay, presumably one of on-again, off-again scenarist Protosevich's many drafts, which were eventually revised by screenwriter-producer Akiva Goldsman (the film credits both the novel and the Corringtons' *Omega Man* script as its source material). "They are not vampires any more.... Now they're hemophobes or hemomorphs or something like that. Some plague has caused them to take on vampiric qualities. Ultraviolet rays are bad for them, so they have to go out at night and need constant revitalization of blood to replenish the cells that keep dying. It's not a bad script at all, but it's not mine. I have very little interest in the outcome of the project simply because it's neither my book nor my screenplay, it's just my title. When they made *The Omega Man*, I think I got the munificent sum of $2,500 for the remake, so losing that amount of money is not going to put me into penury, but they're not going to pay me anything for *I Am Legend*. In those days, they bought the rights to novels until the end of time. I'm sure I won't get a penny."

Regarding the first draft of his abortive attempt at filming the novel, Bowman told Edward Gross in *Vampires and Slayers*, "I didn't have Cortman ... speaking at all. He went from waxing poetic to nothing.... The idea sort of comes from how viruses are building up immunities to our antibiotics and making super-viruses.... [T]here's a world plague and somebody comes up with an antidote for it, except the antidote has side effects which is that they basically create super-viruses and make these people into vampires.... The spirit of the novel is very much the core of the movie. As a matter of fact, in the previous draft nothing from the novel was there."

I Am Legend became the second feature directed by music-video veteran Francis Lawrence, who had filmed the DC/Vertigo *Hellblazer* comics as *Constantine* (2005). Matheson received nothing for the rights, but the $584 million global box-office blockbuster propelled the tie-in editions of his 53-year-old novel to his biggest sales ever, peaking at #2 on the *New York Times* bestseller list. Wisecracking superstar Smith, ultimately cast as Neville, and writer Goldsman, an Oscar winner for *A Beautiful Mind* (2001), had collaborated on the disappointing 2004 adaptation of Isaac Asimov's *I, Robot*, but here, fresh from a well-deserved nomination for *The Pursuit of Happyness* (2006), Smith delivers a strong and serious performance that captures much of the military scientist's existential pain. Some of the ideas from Bowman's version survived, e.g., the plague is caused by a mutation of the measles virus, which Dr. Alice Krippin (an unbilled Emma Thompson) had genetically retrofitted to cure cancer. Yet Cortman was eliminated, and the fact that "the infected" are

Canine companion Sam (Abbey) protects Dr. Robert Neville (Will Smith) after he is injured while escaping from a trap set by the Dark Seekers in *I Am Legend* **(Warner Bros., 2007)**

no longer led by Neville's former best friend is one of several changes that rob Matheson's story of considerable dramatic power.

For instance, the pathetic and ill-fated mutt in the novel has been elevated to a German shepherd named Sam (played by four-legged thespians Abbey and Kona). Sam not only provides Neville with a life-saving ally in his war with the infected, but also sharply reduces his epic loneliness, notably in a poignant shot showing the two of them curled up in a bathtub as the infected howl outside. Unlike the mournful demise of Matheson's nameless pooch, Sam's death is given a heroic dimension when she helps Neville escape from a trap set by his nemeses and is herself infected by their canine counterparts; only then does he refer to the family pet by its full name, Samantha, thereby informing the audience that it is female. After his experimental vaccine fails, he is obliged to strangle her. Interestingly, in Matheson's *Night Creatures* script, Neville dubs the dog Friday (in a nod to Daniel Defoe's *Robinson Crusoe*), allows it to ride shotgun in his station wagon, watches in agony as it is killed by the vengeful Cortman, and says, "For a while there was hope. With Friday to share my life there was some meaning to existence," elements that are not in the novel but anticipate the 2007 film.

Similarly, the loss of Neville's family occurs in a heartbeat as his wife Zoe (Salli Richardson) and daughter Marley (played by Smith's own daughter, Willow) perish in a helicopter crash, seen in flashbacks to the quarantine of the story's new setting in New York City, thus sparing him the slow and painful ordeal of witnessing both their successive dissolution and Virginia's horrific resurrection. Surrounded when he goes out at night in a suicidal rage after Sam's death, Neville is rescued and brought back to his fortified Washington Square townhouse by Anna (Alice Braga), who — far from representing a new society that fears and kills him — is on her way from Maryland to a colony of uninfected survivors in the Vermont mountains, where the Krippin virus could not endure the cold. Like Neville, whose daily radio broadcasts to any other survivors summoned her there, Anna and her young companion, Ethan (Charlie Tahan), are among the one percent of the populace immune to the virus, which killed 90 percent outright and turned the rest into what she calls "Dark Seekers." But this convenient device eliminates Neville's unique status and gives hope for eventual repopulation by normal people.

Just as the house is overrun by the infected, who have followed Anna, Neville discovers that drastically lowering the body temperature of his captured test subject, their Alpha Female (Joanna Numata), has made his vaccine effective. After concealing Anna and Ethan with a sample of her blood containing the cure, Neville dies to protect them by blowing up himself and the Dark Seekers. The two-disc special-edition DVD includes an "alternate theatrical version" in which it is theorized that the infected are evolving to develop higher-brain functions (already implicit in their copying his trap) and emotions, with a "controversial" ending allowing for a possible sequel, as Neville returns the female to her male counterpart (Dash Mihok) and is allowed to depart unmolested for Vermont. A prequel has been announced. DC/Vertigo's online comic-book tie-in *I Am Legend: Awakening* also featured tales set during the plague by such writers as Protosevich, R.C. Matheson (adapting his story "Vampire"), and Steve Niles, who — after adapting *I Am Legend*— wrote the 2002 graphic novel *30 Days of Night*. Mick Garris contributed his own prequel, "I Am Legend, Too," to *He Is Legend*.

Location shooting enhanced the evacuation in the 2009 flashbacks and the desolate concrete canyons of the main story, set in 2012, where lions hunt deer in the overgrown streets. In *The New York Times*, Lewis Beale enumerated such shooting locales as TriBeCa and the aircraft carrier *Intrepid.* Interiors were constructed at the Marcy Avenue Armory in Williamsburg and the Kingsbridge Armory in the Bronx. "In a particularly brazen piece of logistics, the production company cleared the area around St. Patrick's Cathedral for a ghostly New York-without-humans sequence. 'It's hard to make Los Angeles feel empty,' Mr. Goldsman said. 'Here, you just have to look down Fifth Avenue empty, and you understand something. There's a conveyance of information and fantasy that is wonderful and amazing.... [Matheson] is like H.G. Wells and William Gibson, people who do a little leapfrogging imaginatively. And you wait around long enough, and ... you're in one of their books.'"

Like the AIDS parallel provided by the virus, the shots of the plague's "ground zero" in New York inevitably offered topical echoes (in this case of the September 11, 2001 attacks), and their visual verisimilitude was beefed up by CGI, as were the infected themselves. David M. Halbfinger, also writing in *The New York Times,* noted that after a week of shooting, "actors portraying victims of the rabieslike virus romped around on camera, but looked too much like romping actors wearing prosthetics. Mr. Lawrence, with the studio's blessing, decided to enhance the actors [35 of whom are credited among the rank-and-file infected] with computer-generated effects, adding millions to the movie's cost and weeks to its post-production timetable. 'We just weren't able to get out of people what we really wanted,' he said. 'They needed to have an abandon in their performance that you just can't get out of people in the middle of the night when they're barefoot.'"

An Oscar-winner for *The Matrix* (1999), visual effects supervisor Janek Sirrs aided the work of cinematographer Andrew Lesnie — himself a winner for *The Lord of the Rings: The Fellowship of the Ring* (2001) — by erasing telltale signs of life and adding such details as the flora and fauna reclaiming the city. Unfortunately the creatures, designed by Patrick Tatopoulos, are one of the weakest links. Cartoony and characterless, they are fast-moving like the viral victims — also called "the Infected" — from Danny Boyle's *28 Days Later* (2002), a hit whose similar storyline prolonged *I Am Legend*'s decade-plus in development hell. The department-store mannequins Neville sets up and talks to in a video store recall the scene from *The Omega Man* in which Rosalind Cash poses as one to hide in plain sight from Heston. ("There's a mannequin with a big Afro in the background of one scene," Lawrence told *Entertainment Weekly*'s Tom Russo. "It's my one very specific homage.") The filmmakers have also widely acknowledged the influence of *Cast Away* (2000).

A *Los Angeles Times* review by Carina Chocano noted that "it was precisely the helpless plebe factor of the main characters in *28 Days Later* and the sequel that made those films so easy to identify with, and scary in a visceral, it-could-happen-to-you way," underlining the contrast between Matheson's layman and Smith's decorated virologist. "Despair proceeds agreeably apace until a couple of fellow immunes show up on the scene, dangling a crucifix from their rearview mirror and spouting moony-eyed homilies about faith [Anna says that God told her about the survivors' colony, which they do find]. This alone, one would think, would be enough to send the brilliant scientist diving off a pier..." Despite such changes, Matheson told me in 2008, "I think it's very well made. As usual, it's not my book. When I'm 100, maybe they'll make it. It'll be like a Jane Austen movie, a period [piece. The movie's storyline] works, but on its own terms; it ignores the value I have in the book. Fortunately, people keep telling me the book is better than any movie they've made. It's selling very well.

"I spoke to producer Akiva Goldsman about the sequel — they're having something written right now — and I said, 'Well, I hope you're using some of my book at last,' and he said, 'No, no.' If they actually make it, I'll get a nice piece of money. What they're going to do is continue it from the point where his wife and child die in that crash, and then go on from there. People are all still alive. I was hoping in the sequel they would go back to the beginning, where he was still a doctor in the army or whatever, and he was living in the house with his wife and child, and you went through the whole thing. But I can't worry about it." The studio's multimedia marketing blitz also included a soundtrack album and an online role-playing game. A direct-to-DVD ripoff, *I Am Omega*, was released one month earlier.

Raising its creator's profile and bankability within the industry, *I Am Legend*'s stunning success proves that after more than half a century, Richard Matheson is still a viable cinematic commodity and, with several other adaptations in the works, is likely to remain so for quite some time.

Other Unproduced Projects

In addition to those already mentioned, Matheson has written many scripts that were never produced. "I could have written prose all that time," he lamented in our *Filmfax* interview. "I was paid for them, but they were never filmed. It [is] the unfulfillment I [regret]. But then, as ... my wife always points out, I was supporting four children at that time, so I really didn't have much choice. But it's too bad.... A lot of novels lost." Matheson has not kept complete records of his unproduced work; I compiled the most comprehensive list to date for *The Richard Matheson Companion*, aided by collectors Don Cannon and Brian Kirby, who own copies of many of his scripts, outlines, and treatments, both produced and unproduced, and have generously shared details regarding them. Information can be elusive or unreliable: *Forbidden Land* is listed among Matheson's unfilmed screenplays in Susan Avallone's *Film Writers Guide*— which, among other errors, attributes Richard Christian Matheson's unproduced *Red Sleep*, *Dedman*, and *Novum* to his father instead. But Matheson has no recollection of the project whatever.

Some of these projects are difficult to date, such as *Ossian's Ride*, an outline adapted from the novel by Fred Hoyle for producer Sydell Albert and director Daniel Petrie, and *Shadowed Places*, a projected four-hour miniseries. Matheson's earliest unproduced credits predate the release of *The Incredible Shrinking Man*, and shortly afterward, he adapted Roger Manvell's novel *The Dreamers* for Burt Lancaster's production company, Hecht-Hill-Lancaster. Based on the novel by Michael Barrett, whose work also inspired *The Reward* (1965) and *The Invincible Six* (aka *The Heroes*, 1968), *Appointment in Zahrain* would have been another star vehicle. Introducing the script in *Unrealized Dreams*, Matheson noted that it "was to have been Clark Gable's next film. I worked on the screenplay with Edward Dmytryk who was to have directed the film. Unhappily, Gable's over-exertions on *The Misfits* [1961] resulted in his premature heart failure and death." The novel was adapted the following year with another title (*Escape from Zahrain*), director (Ronald Neame), screenwriter (Robin Estridge), and actor (Jack Warden, co-starring with Yul Brynner and Sal Mineo).

Matheson discussed his "unknown material" in our *Noir* interview. "There was that second Western published [in 1993] that I'd forgotten I wrote, *The Gun Fight*.... I'd written it completely, and then nothing happened. I don't even know whether it was submitted [to a publisher at that time]. It must have been. But then I showed it to William R. Cox, who was one of the Fictioneers, and he said, 'This would make a great movie.' So we made a movie script out of it, and we spent so much time on it that I thought of that story in terms of the script, so much so that I forgot there was a novel preceding it. It was just in a cabinet, then after I sold the first one [*Journal of the Gun Years*] to Gary Goldstein at Berkley, I was looking for something else and I ran across this and thought, 'Oh, my Lord, I completely forgot.' I went through it and corrected it, and fortunately he liked it. And on the screenplays, my *oeuvre* would be double what it is now if they'd made every one I wrote." (This is a conservative estimate, to say the least; triple is probably more accurate.) He and Cox wrote another unproduced script, around the 1960s, about a baseball team that heads west.

"The Distributor" was adapted into two speculative scripts, one written by Matheson around 1965, and one written by Paul Schrader decades later. In our interview for *Duel & The Distributor*, which includes Matheson's story and script, he said, "I just wanted to indicate how banal evil can be. You know, people think of Satan and black magic and witches and all that, and I just wanted to show how, on the simplest of banal neighborhood levels, evil could function.... [T]he character was a visualization of the one-man stage performer Theodore [Gottlieb, aka Brother Theodore].... He was a friend of the family, and I thought I would do a story about it. He seemed the ideal person, and I even used his name.... I visualized [casting] Kirk Douglas, because [several characters] had to be attracted to him.... He couldn't be just a squirrelly little guy." Other projects from that period included *Cybernia*, adapted from Lou Cameron's novel for producer John Cutts (Matheson may also have written *The Rogue* for Cutts, based on Jay Williams's *The Good Yeoman*), and *The Raft*, adapted from Robert Trumbull's 1942 nonfiction bestseller for Paramount Television and Emmet Lavery, Jr., in 1974.

The most ambitious of Matheson's screenwriting projects, either produced or unproduced, was *The Link*, which began life as a 557-page narrative outline written for ABC (like "The Distributor," it had a character based on Gottlieb). When this was published by Gauntlet in 2006, Matheson noted in his introduction that he and Stephen Deutsch had planned a miniseries "which would incorporate spiritualism, parapsychology, the occult and metaphysics all told through three major stories. Since Stephen had just produced my script for *Somewhere in Time*, I felt confidence in his ability to produce this story." Matheson devoted a year and a half to the outline, but when Deutsch submitted it, the network asked that it be reduced from a projected 20 hours to seven. They parted ways after Matheson scripted the first three hours; he then spent *another* year and a half writing the first 800 pages of a novelization, but was told by his literary agent that the result would probably be too lengthy to sell. Some of the historical material from *The Link* wound up in *Mediums Rare*, Matheson's "brief account of psychic beginnings." Gauntlet has also published excerpts from his abortive teleplay and novel.

In his 1986 interview with Michael Blaine for *Rod Serling's The Twilight Zone Magazine*, Matheson discussed *Arrow M.E.E.* (Mystery Evaluation and Explanation), an ABC/Lorimar pilot he was then writing for David Goldsmith and Linda Yellen, and even planned to produce himself. Based on Alfred Lewis's nonfiction book *The Evidence Never Lies*, the teleplay concerned the work of criminologist Professor Leon MacDonald. "He's worked on all the major cases, the Jean Harris case, the Robert Kennedy assassination. He is really unbelievable.... No writer could make up the intricacies of these [cases]. I used one from the book, and maybe there are a couple of others that could be dramatized."

Also in the 1980s, Matheson adapted Patrick Tilley's novel *Fade-Out* for producer Tony Bill and director Ulu Grosbard, and around 1990 he wrote *Power and Light*, a script about Nikola Tesla, for Lucasfilm and director Walter Murch. Among his more recent efforts are *The Disappearance*, a six-hour miniseries adapted from the novel by Philip Wylie for actor-producer Peter Strauss; *Needle in a Timestack,* based on the story by Robert Silverberg; and adaptations of several of his own novels. In our *Noir* interview, Matheson noted that he and Allen Epstein tried to bring *Fury on Sunday* to the screen in the 1990s: "We were ready. He had a director [James Sadwith], the guy who directed this two-part Frank Sinatra story on television [in 1992]. He was going to direct it, and I had [written] the script, and we were going to HBO, and they didn't say yes." Others that he based on his work during this period include *7 Steps to Midnight* and *To Live,* the latter restoring his preferred title for *Hunted Past Reason.* Matheson has also transformed unproduced screenplays and stage plays into such novels as *Shadow on the Sun, The Memoirs of Wild Bill Hickok* (from his script *Wild Bill*), and *Woman* (2005).

In our 1991 *Filmfax* interview, Matheson said, "I recently did a John Saul novel [*Creature*], and it was pretty difficult, because it's quite long, and it's kind of rambling, and to try to cut it down so that's it going to be maybe a hundred minutes long is difficult. There are some writers who are very visual, and it's easy to adapt them to a screenplay form; others are not—some writers do a lot of introspection, interior monologues and everything, and that's difficult, too." Several months later, he wrote in a follow-up letter, "I have about given up on it. I wrote a script which the producer loved, the Universal executive in charge of the project loved and even John Saul loved, telling me that some of my ideas were so good, he wished he'd had them to use in the book. Then Universal hired this director [Frank LaLoggia] who, as far as I know, is *still* rewriting. God knows what the script will look like when he's through. He [wrote and] directed *Lady in White* [1988] which was okay but not enough to let him completely re-do a script. But that's the way this town is. So, as I say, I have about given up on it. I will be amazed if they film it and even more amazed if it resembles my script at all."

When Matheson's version was published in his collection *Darker Places* (2004), he called the novel "a story which combined modern technology with tried and true 'scare elements'…. To my surprise—and distaste—the director rewrote my script turning it into, of all things, a *Gothic* story—an approach which was completely out of sync with John Saul's novel. I was told that Universal didn't like this approach, but, instead of using common sense and going back to my script, they canceled the entire production. Hollywood mentality at work."

Circa 1992, he told me about another project: "I just started working on adapting L. Ron Hubbard's *Fear* for NBC. Kirstie Alley [a member of the Church of Scientology founded by Hubbard] is going to produce it and, I hope, appear in it. Definitely set are her husband Parker Jamieson and Kelsey Grammer from *Cheers.* The book is terribly dated but I think it can be worked out…. Actually *Fear* is a rather awful book. I took the job mostly for money. I hate altering authors' work when I do this but Hubbard's novel is pretty badly done. A nice jolt at the end which I hope will push it over the top on TV."

Bibliography

Addie, Jo. "Richard Matheson Updates, Exciting Developments." *INSITE* 19:1 (First Quarter 2008), pp. 10–12.

_____. "A Tribute to Christopher Reeve." *INSITE* 15:3 (Third Quarter 2004), pp. 3–24.

_____, and Sue Uram. "Christopher Reeve." *Cinefantastique* 28:2 (September 1996), pp. 56–57.

Albarella, Tony. "Jack Klugman's Twilight Times." *Filmfaxplus* #113 (January-March 2007), pp. 83–87, and #114 (April-June 2007), pp. 62–65, 108–09.

Alexander, Chris. "Classic Cut Presents *I Am Legend.*" *Rue Morgue* #32 (March-April 2003), p. 72.

_____. "Richard Matheson: He Is Legend." *Rue Morgue* #35 (September-October 2003), pp. 14–20.

Arkoff, Samuel Z., with Richard Trubo, *Flying Through Hollywood by the Seat of My Pants* (New York: Birch Lane Press, 1992).

Avallone, Susan. *Film Writers Guide*, sixth edition (Los Angeles: Lone Eagle, 1996).

Baker, Mike, and Martin H. Greenberg, editors. *My Favorite Horror Story* (New York: DAW, 2000).

Bansak, Edmund G. *Fearing the Dark: The Val Lewton Career* (Jefferson, NC: McFarland, 1995).

Barron, Frank, and Jay Stevenson (aka Steve Biodrowski). "*Lost World* Rediscovered." *Cinefantastique* 29:10 (February 1998), p. 6.

Barson, Michael. *The Illustrated Who's Who of Hollywood Directors, Volume I: The Studio System in the Sound Era* (New York: Farrar, Straus and Giroux, 1995).

Baxter, John. *Science Fiction in the Cinema: 1895–1970* (New York: A.S. Barnes, 1970).

Beale, Lewis. "A Variation on Vampire Lore That Won't Die." *The New York Times*, January 14, 2007, p. AR 18.

Beaumont, Charles. *The Howling Man*, edited by Roger Anker (New York: Tor, 1992).

_____. *The Twilight Zone Scripts of Charles Beaumont, Volume One*, edited by Roger Anker (Colorado Springs, CO: Gauntlet, 2004).

Beck, Calvin Thomas. *Heroes of the Horrors* (New York: Collier, 1975).

_____. *Scream Queens: Heroines of the Horrors* (New York: Collier, 1978).

Berger, Christian K. (bibliographical essay), and Robert Arnett (interview). "The Macabre Cinema of Richard Matheson." *Creative Screenwriting*, September-October 1998, pp. 56–63.

Biodrowski, Steve. "Classic Horror." *Cinefantastique* 31:8 (October 1999), p. 61.

_____. "Mega Bad!" *Femme Fatales* 2:1 (Summer 1993), pp. 10–13, 61.

_____. "1998 in Review," *Cinefantastique* 31:4 (April 1999), pp. 47–49.

_____. "Over the Rainbow," *Cinefantastique* 31:1/2 (February 1999), p. 113.

Blaine, Michael. "A Richard Matheson Update." *Rod Serling's The Twilight Zone Magazine*, June 1986, pp. 22–23, 94.

Blaisdell, Anne. *Nightmare* (New York: Crest, 1962).

Blish, James. *Star Trek 8* (New York: Bantam, 1972).

Bloch, Robert. *Once Around the Bloch: An Unauthorized Autobiography* (New York: Tor, 1993).

_____. *Psycho* (Springfield, PA: Gauntlet, 1994).

_____. *Twilight Zone—The Movie* (New York: Warner Books, 1983).

Boisson, Steve. "The Prime of Miss Ida Lupino: Glamour Girl of the '30s, Femme Fatale of the '40s, Filmmaker of the '50s, & TV Director of the '60s! (Part Two)." *Filmfax* #86 (August-September 2001), pp. 68ff.

Bojarski, Richard, and Kenneth Beals. *The Films of Boris Karloff* (Secaucus, NJ: Citadel, 1974).

Bond, Jeff. "It Is Legend." *Cinefantastique* 35:1 (February-March 2003), pp. 54–67.

Bosco, Scott Michael, liner notes for *Trilogy of Terror* VHS Special Edition (Troy, MI: Anchor Bay Entertainment, 1999).

Bradbury, Ray. "The Fire Balloons," in *The Illustrated Man* (New York: Bantam, 1967), pp. 75–90.

_____. *The Martian Chronicles* (New York: Bantam, 1954).

Bradley, Matthew R. "Altair Ego: An Out-of-This-World Interview with Anne Francis." *Filmfax* #78 (April-May 2000), pp. 50–59.

_____. "And in the Beginning Was the Word…: An

Interview with Screenwriter Richard Matheson." *Filmfax* #42 (December 1993-January 1994), pp. 40–44, 78–82, 98.

_____. "Baxt Stabs Back." *Filmfax* #50 (May-June 1995), pp. 58–62.

_____. "A *Black Christmas* Story: An Interview with Bob Clark," *Mystery Scene* #67 (2000), pp. 66–75.

_____. "Enter *The Twilight Zone* with Richard Matheson." *Filmfax* #75–76 (October 1999-January 2000), pp. 78–84, 125.

_____. "The Future Is Now: An Interview with *2001* Star Keir Dullea." *Filmfax* #86 (August-September 2001), pp. 44–9, 90, and #87–88 (October 2001-January 2002), pp. 110–15, 130.

_____. "The Illustrative Man: An Interview with SF Legend Ray Bradbury." *Outré* Vol. 1 #4 (Fall 1995), pp. 26–32, 70–4, 86.

_____. Introduction to *Hell House* by Richard Matheson (Springfield, PA: Gauntlet, 1996), pp. 17–32.

_____. Introduction to *I Am Legend* by Richard Matheson (Springfield, PA: Gauntlet, 1995), pp. 31–41.

_____. Introduction to *Noir: Three Novels of Suspense* by Richard Matheson (q.v.), pp. 7–17.

_____. Introduction to *What Dreams May Come* by Richard Matheson (Springfield, PA: Gauntlet, 1998), pp. 9–15.

_____. "The Last Men on Earth." *Fangoria* #268 (November 2007), pp. 68–69.

_____. "Nolan's Run: The Screenwriting Career of Logan's Papa." *Filmfax* #48 (January-February 1995), pp. 42–48, 98.

_____. "Ray Russell Tribute," *Filmfax* #73 (June-July 1999), p. 6.

_____. Reading Group Guide to *Somewhere in Time* by Richard Matheson (New York: Tor, 1999), pp. 317–20.

_____. "The 'Richard Matheson Storyteller' Series." *The New York Review of Science Fiction* #169 (15:1; September 2002), pp. 17–18.

_____. "Sohl Man: An Interview with Jerry Sohl." *Filmfax* #75–76 (October 1999-January 2000), pp. 90–93, 138.

_____. "The Third Gremlin: An Interview with George Clayton Johnson." *Filmfax* #75–76 (October 1999-January 2000), pp. 85–89, 126–29, #77 (February-March 2000), pp. 67–71, and #78 (April-May 2000), pp. 75–80, 86–87, 89.

_____, and Gilbert Colon. "Devil May Care: An Interview with William Peter Blatty." *Filmfax* #69–70 (October 1998–January 1999), pp. 104–08, 118.

_____, and Gilbert Colon. "Invasion of the Scene Stealers: My Second Career as a Genre Icon," in *Invasion of the Body Snatchers: A Tribute*, edited by Kevin McCarthy and Ed Gorman (Eureka, CA: Stark House Press, 2006), pp. 203–31.

Brierly, Dean. "Joe Dante: Hollywood Maverick, Part 2." *Cinema Retro* 4:12 (Autumn 2008), pp. 44–47.

Brooks, James E. "Richard Matheson." *Starburst* #268 (December 2000), pp. 54–57.

Brooks, Tim, and Earle Marsh. *The Complete Directory to Prime Time Network TV Shows, 1946-Present*, third edition (New York: Ballantine, 1985).

Brosnan, John. *Future Tense: The Cinema of Science Fiction* (New York: St. Martin's, 1978).

_____. *The Horror People* (New York: Plume, 1977).

Brownfield, Paul. "Finding Hope in Dystopia." *The Los Angeles Times*, December 13, 2007, pp. E1 and E4.

Brunas, Michael, John Brunas, and Tom Weaver, *Universal Horrors: The Studio's Classic Films, 1931–1946* (Jefferson, NC: McFarland, 1990).

Buchanan, Larry. *It Came from Hunger! Tales of a Cinema Schlockmeister* (Jefferson, NC: McFarland, 1996).

Case, David. "The Hunter," in *The Cell: Three Tales of Horror* (New York: Hill and Wang, 1969), pp. 69–148.

Chartrand, Harvey F. "Out of the Shadows with Karen Black: A Tenacious Tigress Surviving in the Hollywood Jungle." *Filmfax* #88 (February-March 2002), pp. 52–57, 84–85.

"Cheers and Jeers." *TV Guide*, June 19, 1999, p. 12; August 7, 1999, p. 6.

Chocano, Carina. "The Last Man Is a 'Legend.'" *The Los Angeles Times*, December 14, 2007, p. E5.

Clark, Al. *Raymond Chandler in Hollywood* (New York: Proteus, 1982).

Clement, Henry. *De Sade* (New York: Signet, 1969).

Conlon, Christopher. "Group Dynamics." *Filmfax* #97 (June-July 2003), p. 44.

_____, editor. *He Is Legend: An Anthology Celebrating Richard Matheson* (Colorado Springs, CO: Gauntlet, 2009).

Corman, Roger, with Jim Jerome. *How I Made a Hundred Movies in Hollywood and Never Lost a Dime* (New York: Random House, 1990).

Court, Hazel. *Hazel Court—Horror Queen: An Autobiography* (Sheffield, England: Tomahawk Press, 2008).

Coville, Gary, and Patrick Lucanio. *Jack the Ripper: His Life and Crimes in Popular Entertainment* (Jefferson, NC: McFarland, 1999).

Cox, Greg. *The Transylvanian Library: A Consumer's Guide to Vampire Fiction* (Borgo Literary Guides #8; San Bernardino, CA: Borgo Press, 1993).

Coyle, Robert, Jr., and Mark Phillips. "Alpha Male Omega Man! Behind-the-Scenes on the Making of *The Omega Man*." *Filmfax* #93–94 (October-November 2002), pp. 52–56.

Crick, Robert Alan. "*The Legend of Hell House*," in

Cinematic Hauntings, edited by Gary J. and Susan Svehla (Baltimore: Midnight Marquee, 1996), pp. 166–89.

Cutler, Colin. "*Late Night Horror*: No Such Thing as a Vampire." *The Illustrated Gazette* (http://www.the-mausoleum-club.org.uk/, 2004).

Davis, Richard, editor. *The Encyclopedia of Horror* (London: Octopus, 1981).

Dawidziak, Mark. "He Is Legend: Richard Matheson on His Vampire Creations." *Vampires and Slayers* 1:1 (c. 1999), pp. 19–29.

_____. *Night Stalking: A 20th Anniversary Kolchak Companion* (New York: Image Publishing, 1991).

Decker, Sean. "*I Am Legend*." *Fangoria* #268 (November 2007), pp. 64–69.

Derleth, August, and Mark Schorer. *Colonel Markesan and Less Pleasant People* (Sauk City, WI: Arkham House, 1966).

The Devil Rides Out, unsigned VHS liner notes (Troy, MI: Anchor Bay Entertainment, 1998).

Di Fate, Vincent. *Infinite Worlds: The Fantastic Visions of Science Fiction Art* (New York: Penguin Studio, 1997).

Downes, Edward, *The New York Philharmonic Guide to the Symphony* (New York: Walker, 1976).

Duel, unsigned laserdisc liner notes (Universal City, CA: MCA Home Video, 1993).

Dumars, Denise. "Sex and Horror Films: The Career of Karen Black." *Femme Fatales* 10:4 (September-October 2001), pp. 20–23.

DuMond, Lisa. "Richard Matheson and William Stout Collaborate on a Children's Fantasy." *Science Fiction Weekly* #254 (www.scifi.com), March 2002.

Dziemianowicz, Stefan. "The Matheson Zone." *Publishers Weekly*, June 17, 2002, pp. 31–35.

Edginton, Ian, and Simon Fraser. *Richard Matheson's Hell House* (four volumes; San Diego: IDW Publishing, 2004–05).

"Editors' Choice: The Love Letter." *TV Guide*, January 31, 1998, p. 94.

Etter, Jonathan. "*Forbidden Planet*'s Richard Anderson: How Gary Cooper Got Him Into the Movies." *Filmfax* #88 (February-March 2002), pp. 58–65, 90–92.

Everson, William K. *Classics of the Horror Film* (Secaucus, NJ: Citadel, 1974).

_____. *More Classics of the Horror Film* (Secaucus, NJ: Citadel, 1986).

Eyles, Allen, Robert Adkinson and Nicholas Fry, editors. *The House of Horror: The Story of Hammer Films* (New York: Third Press, 1974).

Fagen, Herb. "Sheena, Queen of the Jungle and Beyond! An Interview with Irish McCalla." *Filmfax* #66 (April-May 1998), pp. 74–78.

Farber, Stephen. "The Collaborator." *Movieline*, October 1998, pp. 74–101.

_____, and Marc Green. *Outrageous Conduct: Art,*

Ego, and the Twilight Zone *Case* (New York: Arbor House/Morrow, 1988).

Finney, Jack. "The Love Letter," in *I Love Galesburg in the Springtime* (New York: Simon & Schuster, 1963), pp. 205–24.

_____. "Second Chance," in *The Third Level* (New York: Rinehart, 1957), pp. 151–69.

Fischer, Dennis. *Horror Film Directors, 1931–1990* (Jefferson, NC: McFarland, 1991).

Flynn, John L., *Cinematic Vampires: The Living Dead on Film and Television, from* The Devil's Castle *(1896) to* Bram Stoker's Dracula *(1992)* (Jefferson, NC: McFarland, 1992).

Foundas, Scott. "Infectious." *L.A. Weekly*, December 14–20, 2007, pp. 82 and 86.

Gagne, Paul R. *The Zombies That Ate Pittsburgh: The Films of George A. Romero* (New York: Dodd, Mead, 1987).

Garcia, Frank. "*Outer Limits* Episode Guide." *Cinefantastique* 30:5/6 (September 1998), pp. 26ff.

Gifford, Denis. *Karloff: The Man, the Monster, the Movies* (New York: Curtis, 1973).

_____. *A Pictorial History of Horror Movies* (London: Hamlyn, 1973).

Glut, Donald F. *The Dracula Book* (Metuchen, NJ: Scarecrow, 1975).

Golden, Christopher, editor. *Cut! Horror Writers on Horror Film* (New York: Berkley, 1992).

Goodsell, Greg. "The Weird & Wacky World of Larry Buchanan." *Filmfax* #38 (April-May 1993), pp. 60–66.

Gorman, Ed. "About Richard Matheson: The Art of Heart and Brain." *Filmfax* #103 (July-September 2004), pp. 115–18, 146.

Grams, Martin, Jr. *The Twilight Zone: Unlocking the Door to a Television Classic* (Churchville, MD: OTR Publishing, 2008).

_____, and Les Rayburn. *The Have Gun—Will Travel Companion* (Arlington, VA: OTR Publishing, 2000).

Graydon, Danny. "Richard Matheson." *SFX Magazine*, June 2005, pp. 113–15.

Greenberg, Martin Harry, Richard Matheson and Charles G. Waugh, editors. *The Twilight Zone: The Original Stories* (New York: MJF Books, 1985).

Gross, Edward. "Directing *Legend*: An Interview with Rob Bowman." *Vampires and Slayers* 1:1 (c. 1999), pp. 15–18.

_____. "Jerry Sohl: The Broken Promise of the Green Hand." *Starlog* #136 (November 1988), pp. 68–72.

Gunn, James, editor. *The New Encyclopedia of Science Fiction* (New York: Viking, 1988).

Halbfinger, David M. "The City That Never Sleeps, Comatose." *The New York Times*, November 4, 2007.

Hallenbeck, Bruce G. "Karloff, Kubrick & *Clock-*

work Orange." *Femme Fatales* 3:4 (Spring 1995), pp. 50–55.

Halliwell, Leslie. *Halliwell's Film and Video Guide 1998*, edited by John Walker (New York: HarperPerennial, 1997).

_____. *Halliwell's Who's Who in the Movies*, thirteenth edition, edited by John Walker (New York: HarperPerennial, 1997).

Hand, Elizabeth. "Prince of Flowers," in *Last Summer at Mars Hill* (New York: HarperPrism, 1998), pp. 309–24.

Hardy, Phil, editor. *The Overlook Film Encyclopedia: Horror* (Woodstock, NY: Overlook, 1995).

_____. *The Overlook Film Encyclopedia: Science Fiction* (Woodstock, NY: Overlook, 1995).

Harmetz, Aljean. *Round Up the Usual Suspects: The Making of* Casablanca— *Bogart, Bergman, and World War II* (New York: Hyperion, 1992).

Havill, Adrian. *Man of Steel: The Career and Courage of Christopher Reeve* (New York: Signet, 1996).

Henderson, Jan Alan. "William Campbell." *Filmfax* #74 (August-September 1999), pp. 62–69.

Hickenlooper, George. *Reel Conversations: Candid Interviews with Film's Foremost Directors and Critics* (New York: Citadel, 1991).

Holden, Stephen. "The Other Love Story of the Trojan War." *The New York Times*, July 17, 1998, p. E12.

Israel, Lee. *Miss Tallulah Bankhead* (New York: Putnam, 1972).

Jensen, Jeff. "*I Am Legend.*" *Entertainment Weekly* #949–950 (August 24, 2007), pp. 90–93.

Jensen, Paul M. *The Men Who Made the Monsters* (New York: Twayne, 1996).

Johnson, George Clayton. *Twilight Zone Scripts and Stories* (Santa Monica, CA: Streamline Pictures, 1996).

Johnson, Ted, and Tim Williams. "The Stalk Market." *TV Guide*, November 4, 2000, pp. 23–25.

Johnson, Tom, and Deborah Del Vecchio. *Hammer Films: An Exhaustive Filmography* (Jefferson, NC: McFarland, 1996).

_____, and Mark A. Miller. *The Christopher Lee Filmography: All Theatrical Releases, 1948–2003* (Jefferson, NC: McFarland, 2004).

Johnson, William, editor. *Focus on the Science Fiction Film* (Englewood Cliffs, NJ: Prentice-Hall, 1972).

Jones, Alan. "Lysette Anthony." *Femme Fatales* 5:10 (April 1997), pp. 28–31, 60.

Katz, Ephraim. *The Film Encyclopedia*, third edition, revised by Fred Klein and Ronald Dean Nolen (New York: HarperPerennial, 1998).

King, Stephen. *Danse Macabre* (New York: Berkley, 1983).

King, Susan. "*I Am Legend* and Other Chilly Matheson Progeny." *The Los Angeles Times*, December 13, 2007, p. E4.

Kinsey, Wayne. "Interview with James Bernard." *The House That Hammer Built* #13 (Vol. 2:5, March 2000), p. 256.

_____. "Interview with Renée Glynne." *The House That Hammer Built* #13 (Vol. 2:5, March 2000), p. 263.

Kirsch, Jonathan. "When Mystery Comes Knocking." *The Los Angeles Times Book Review*, July 31, 2005, p. R2.

Klein, Andy. "Mr. Smith Goes to Zombietown." *CityBeat*, December 13–19, 2007, p. 18.

Koetting, Christopher. "AIP's Third Man: The Other Guy: Deke Heyward's Untold Story." *Filmfax* #60 (April-May 1997), pp. 36–41, 64–65, and #62 (August-September 1997), pp. 62–66, 123.

_____. "Baxt to the Wall." *Filmfax* #54 (January-February 1996), p. 79.

_____. "The Golden Voyage of Gordon Hessler." *Filmfax* #62 (August-September 1997), pp. 48–54.

_____, with Denis Meikle. "The AIP X-Files: Mysteriously Missed Opportunities Encountered by American International Pictures." *Filmfax* #56 (May-June 1996), pp. 59–62, 68–72.

Konow, David. *Schlock-O-Rama: The Films of Al Adamson* (Los Angeles: Lone Eagle, 1998).

Kuttner, Henry. "The Graveyard Rats," in *The Graveyard Reader*, edited by Groff Conklin (New York: Ballantine, 1961), pp. 38–45.

Labbe, Rod. "Hammer Goes Hollywood, Part Three: *She, One Million Years B.C.* & *Journey to the Unknown* Take Hammer into the Future!," *Filmfaxplus* #107 (July-September, 2005), pp. 52–57, 131.

Landry, Christopher, liner notes for *The Martian Chronicles* soundtrack CD (Los Angeles: Airstrip One, 2002).

Larson, Randall. "The Horror of James Bernard." *Cinefantastique* 30:7/8 (October 1998), pp. 94–98.

Lee, Christopher. *Tall, Dark and Gruesome* (Baltimore: Midnight Marquee, 1999).

Lee, Patrick. "*Donnie Darko* Director Richard Kelly Reveals Just What's in *The Box.*" *SCI FI Wire* (www.scifi.com), June 19, 2009.

Lee, Walt. *Reference Guide to Fantastic Films: Science Fiction, Fantasy, & Horror* (three volumes; Los Angeles: Chelsea-Lee Books, 1972–74).

The Legend of Hell House, unsigned laserdisc liner notes (Beverly Hills, CA: Twentieth Century–Fox Home Entertainment, 1996).

Leiber, Fritz. *Conjure Wife* (New York: Award Books, 1970).

Lentz, Harris M. III. *Science Fiction, Horror & Fantasy Film and Television Credits* (two volumes; Jefferson, NC: McFarland, 1983).

_____. *Television Westerns Episode Guide* (Jefferson, NC: McFarland, 1997).

Lochte, Dick. "Living Legend: A Talk with Richard

Matheson." *Mystery Scene* #95 (Summer 2006), pp. 44–47.

_____. "Mr. Paranoia." *The Los Angeles Times Magazine*, September 18, 2005, pp. 16–17.

Lofficier, Jean-Marc, and Randy Lofficier. *Into The Twilight Zone: The Rod Serling Programme Guide* (New York: Mystery Writers of America Presents, 2003).

Lucas, Tim. "*Apocalyptic Nightmares: The Last Man on Earth-Panic in Year Zero*," *Video Watchdog* #55 (January 2000), pp. 48–50.

_____. *Mario Bava: All the Colors of the Dark* (Cincinnati: Video Watchdog, 2007).

Lundstrom, Jim. "Richard Matheson Reflects on *Somewhere in Time*." *INSITE* 14:2 (Second Quarter 2003), pp. 10–11.

Maltin, Leonard, editor. *Leonard Maltin's Movie Encyclopedia* (New York: Dutton, 1994).

_____, editor. *Leonard Maltin's Movie Guide*, 2008 edition (New York: Plume, 2007).

_____, editor. *Leonard Maltin's TV Movies*, 1985–86 edition (New York: Signet, 1984).

Manders, Stanley. "Taking Their Shots." *CFQ* 35:1 (February-March 2003), pp. 60–61, 67.

Marill, Alvin H. *Movies Made for Television: The Telefeature and the Mini-Series, 1964–1986* (New York: New York Zoetrope, 1987).

Maslin, Janet. "With a Party Trick, Supernatural Forces Enter Into an Ordinary Man's Life." *The New York Times*, September 10, 1999, p. E18.

Matheson, Richard. *The Beardless Warriors* (New York: Bantam, 1961).

_____. *Bid Time Return* (published as *Somewhere in Time*), in *Somewhere in Time* and *What Dreams May Come: Two Novels of Love and Fantasy* (Los Angeles: Dream/Press, 1991).

_____. *Bloodlines: Richard Matheson's* Dracula, I Am Legend, *and Other Vampire Stories*, edited by Mark Dawidziak (Colorado Springs, CO: Gauntlet, 2006).

_____. *By the Gun* (New York: Evans, 1993).

_____. *Collected Stories* (Los Angeles: Dream/Press, 1989).

_____. "Crossover Books: *Journal of the Gun Years*." *Mystery Scene* #32 (December 1991-January 1992), pp. 51–52.

_____. *Darker Places* (Colorado Springs, CO: Gauntlet, 2004).

_____. *Duel & The Distributor*, edited by Matthew R. Bradley (Colorado Springs, CO: Gauntlet, 2004).

_____. *Earthbound* (New York: Tor, 1994).

_____. *The Funeral* (Colorado Springs, CO: Gauntlet, 2006).

_____. *Hell House* (New York: Warner, 1985).

_____. *Hunger and Thirst* (Springfield, PA: Gauntlet, 2000).

_____. *I Am Legend* (New York: Berkley, 1971).

_____. *The Legend of Hell House*, in *Screamplays*, edited by Richard Chizmar (New York: Del Rey, 1997), pp. 41–183.

_____. *The Link* (Colorado Springs, CO: Gauntlet, 2006).

_____. *Matheson Uncollected: Volume One* (Colorado Springs, CO: Gauntlet, 2008).

_____. *Mediums Rare* (Baltimore: Cemetery Dance, 2000).

_____. *Noir: Three Novels of Suspense* (Delavan, WI: G&G Books, 1997).

_____. *Off Beat: Uncollected Stories*, edited by William F. Nolan (Burton, MI: Subterranean Press, 2000).

_____. *Richard Matheson: Collected Stories*, edited by Stanley Wiater (three volumes; Colorado Springs, CO: Edge Books, 2003–05).

_____. *Richard Matheson's Kolchak Scripts*, edited by Mark Dawidziak (Colorado Springs, CO: Gauntlet, 2003).

_____. "Richard Matheson's Other Cameo Role." *INSITE* 12:4 (Fourth Quarter 2001), pp. 22–26.

_____. *Richard Matheson's* The Twilight Zone *Scripts*, edited by Stanley Wiater (Abingdon, MD: Cemetery Dance, 1998).

_____. *The Shrinking Man* (New York: Berkley, 1979).

_____. *A Stir of Echoes* (Springfield, PA: Gauntlet, 2002).

_____. *Unrealized Dreams: Three Scripts* (Colorado Springs, CO: Gauntlet, 2005).

_____. *Visions of Death: Richard Matheson's Edgar Allan Poe Scripts, Volume One*, edited by Lawrence French (Colorado Springs, CO: Gauntlet, 2007).

_____. *What Dreams May Come* (New York: Tor, 1998).

_____, and Ricia Mainhardt, editors, *Robert Bloch: Appreciations of the Master* (New York: Tor, 1995).

McCarty, John, editor. *The Fearmakers: The Screen's Directorial Masters of Suspense and Terror* (New York: St. Martin's, 1994).

_____. "An Interview with Kevin McCarthy," in "*They're Here...*": Invasion of the Body Snatchers: A Tribute, edited by Kevin McCarthy and Ed Gorman (New York: Berkley Boulevard, 1999), pp. 187–273.

_____, and Brian Kelleher. *Alfred Hitchcock Presents: An Illustrated Guide to the Ten-Year Television Career of the Master of Suspense* (New York: St. Martin's, 1985).

McCarty, Michael. "A Talk with Richard Matheson"/"Matheson's Movies: A Critical Overview," *H.P. Lovecraft's Magazine of Horror*, Vol. 1, No. 2 (Spring 2005), pp. 24–27, 31–32.

McGee, Mark Thomas. *Faster and Furiouser: The Revised and Fattened Fable of American International Pictures* (Jefferson, NC: McFarland, 1996).

_____. *Roger Corman: The Best of the Cheap Acts* (Jefferson, NC: McFarland, 1988).

McGilligan, Pat. "Richard Matheson: Storyteller," in *Backstory 3: Interviews with Screenwriters of the 1960s* (Berkeley: University of California Press, 1997), pp. 229–56.

McNeil, Alex, *Total Television: The Comprehensive Guide to Programming from 1948 to the Present*, fourth edition (New York: Penguin, 1996).

Meikle, Denis, with Christopher T. Koetting. *A History of Horrors: The Rise and Fall of the House of Hammer* (Lanham, MD: Scarecrow, 1996).

_____. "The Lost Horrors of Hammer! Misplaced Projects from the British House of Horror." *Filmfax* #58 (October 1996-January 1997), pp. 112–16, 132–33.

Meyers, Richard. *S-F 2: A Pictorial History of Science Fiction Films from* Rollerball *to* Return of the Jedi (Secaucus, NJ: Citadel, 1984).

Miller, Mark A. "An Interview with Barbara Steele, Diva of Dark Drama." *Filmfax* #51 (July-August 1995), pp. 37–44, 80.

_____. "Terror in the Isles: Hazel Court, Britain's Duchess of Dark Drama." *Filmfax* #51 (July-August 1995), pp. 73–76.

Minton, Kevin. "Sex, Lies and Disney Tape: Walt's Fallen Star." *Filmfax* #38 (April-May 1993), pp. 67–71.

Mr. Beaks. "Richard Kelly Cracks Open *The Box* for Mr. Beaks." Ain't It Cool News (www.aintitcool.com), June 18, 2009.

Mitchell, Charles P. "Peter Lorre on Television." *Filmfax* #74 (August-September 1999), pp. 70–90.

Modler, Harriet. "*Somewhere in Time*." *Cinefantastique* 28:2 (September 1996), pp. 54–56.

Naha, Ed. *The Films of Roger Corman: Brilliance on a Budget* (New York: Arco, 1982).

Nelson, Resa. "Edgar Allan Poe Plumbs the Depths of the Subconscious Mind." *Realms of Fantasy* 8:1 (October 2001), pp. 22–27.

Newman, Kim, editor. *The BFI Companion to Horror* (London: Cassell, 1996).

Newsom, Ted. "The Legend of Pamela Franklin." *Femme Fatales* 5:2 (August 1996), pp. 50–55, 61.

Niles, Steve, and Elman Brown. *Richard Matheson's* I Am Legend (four volumes; Forestville, CA: Eclipse Books, 1991–92).

Nolan, William F. "Collecting Richard Matheson." *Firsts The Book Collector's Magazine* 11:8 (October 2001), pp. 38–45.

_____, and William Schafer, editors. *California Sorcery: A Group Celebration* (Abingdon, MD: Cemetery Dance, 1999).

"The 100 Greatest Moments in TV." *Entertainment Weekly* #472–473 (February 19–26, 1999), p. 65.

"Oscar Bait 1998." *Movieline*, October 1998, pp. 68–106.

"Oscar Winners." *Cinefantastique* 31:6 (June 1999), p. 6.

Palmer, Randy. *Paul Blaisdell, Monster Maker: A Biography of the B Movie Makeup and Special Effects Artist* (Jefferson, NC: McFarland, 1997).

_____, David Del Valle and Steve Biodrowski. "Invasion of the Monster Movie Moguls, Part One." *Cinefantastique* 30:7/8 (October 1998), pp. 78–89.

Passen, Lisa. *The Incredible Shrinking Teacher* (New York: Henry Holt, 2002).

Phillips, Mark, and Frank Garcia. *Science Fiction Television Series* (Jefferson, NC: McFarland, 1996).

Pierson, Jim. *Produced and Directed by Dan Curtis* (Los Angeles: Pomegranate Press, 2004).

Pirie, David. *The Vampire Cinema* (London: Galley Press, 1977).

Pitts, Michael R. *Charles Bronson: The 95 Films and the 156 Television Appearances* (Jefferson, NC: McFarland, 1999).

The Playboy Book of Science Fiction and Fantasy (Chicago: Playboy Press, 1966).

Poe, Edgar Allan. *The Annotated Tales of Edgar Allan Poe*, edited by Stephen Peithman (New York: Avenel, 1986).

_____. *Collected Tales and Poems* (New York: Vintage, 1975).

Presnell, Don, and Marty McGee. *A Critical History of Television's* The Twilight Zone, *1959–1964* (Jefferson, NC: McFarland, 1998).

Pym, John, editor. *Time Out Film Guide*, seventh edition (New York: Penguin, 1999).

Rathbun, Mark, and Graeme Flanagan. *Richard Matheson: He Is Legend* (Chico, CA: Mark Rathbun, 1984).

Reemes, Dana M. *Directed by Jack Arnold* (Jefferson, NC: McFarland, 1988).

Reeve, Christopher. *Still Me* (New York: Random House, 1998).

Reid, Craig. "Joel Schumacher, Director." *Cinefantastique* 29:1 (July 1997), pp. 46–47.

Rice, Jeff. *The Night Stalker* (New York: Pocket, 1973).

_____. *The Night Strangler* (New York: Pocket, 1974).

Rigby, Jonathan. *Christopher Lee: The Authorised Screen History* (London: Reynolds & Hearn, 2001).

_____. *English Gothic: A Century of Horror Cinema* (London: Reynolds & Hearn, 2000).

Rivero, Enrique. "Writer Gets Spotlight in MGM Series." *Video Store Magazine*, December 9–15, 2001, p. 12.

Rochon, Lela. "Roger & Me: Hollywood's Greatest Maverick Chronicles the Past and Future of B's." *Femme Fatales* 2:3 (Winter 1994), p. 62.

Rudolph, Ileane. "Insider Q&A: Lily Tomlin." *TV Guide*, November 22, 2003, p. 14.

Russo, John. *The Complete Night of the Living Dead Filmbook* (New York: Harmony, 1985).

Russo, Tom. "Apocalypse Now and Then." *Entertainment Weekly* #969 (December 14, 2007).

Ryan, Al, and Dan Cziraky. "Prey of the Devil Doll." *Imagi-Movies* 2:4 (Summer 1995), pp. 42–45.

Sammon, Paul M. "An Interview with Richard Matheson." *Midnight Graffiti*, Fall 1992, pp. 20–49, and *Midnight Graffiti Special*, Winter 1994–95, pp. 44–71.

_____. "Richard Matheson: Master of Fantasy, Part One — The Films of Richard Matheson." *Fangoria* #2 (October 1979), pp. 26–29, 52.

Sander, Gordon F. *Serling: The Rise and Twilight of Television's Last Angry Man* (New York: Plume, 1994).

Scapperotti, Dan. "Annette O'Toole." *Femme Fatales* 4:7 (April 1996), pp. 24–31.

_____. "Mamie Van Doren: '50s Blonde Bombshell." *Femme Fatales* 5:8 (February 1997), pp. 12–23, 60.

Schindler, Rick, and Stephanie Williams. "The Genealogy of *Medusa's Child*." *TV Guide*, November 15, 1997.

Schnakenberg, Robert E. *The Encyclopedia Shatnerica* (Los Angeles: Renaissance Books, 1998).

Schow, David J. *The Outer Limits Companion* (Hollywood: GNP/Crescendo, 1998).

_____. "Revenge of the Return of the Remake of *Creature from the Black Lagoon*." *Filmfax* #73 (June-July 1999), pp. 62–87.

"The Sci-Fi 100." *Entertainment Weekly*, October 16, 1998, pp. 28–53.

Seabrook, John. "Taking Dover Street." *The New Yorker*, February 5, 2007, pp. 26–27.

Serling, Rod. *As Timeless as Infinity: The Complete* Twilight Zone *Scripts of Rod Serling, Volume One*, edited by Tony Albarella (Colorado Springs, CO: Gauntlet, 2004).

_____. Letter to Charles Beaumont, December 5, 1960 (courtesy of Martin Grams, Jr.).

_____. Letter to Ray Bradbury, December 5, 1960 (courtesy of Martin Grams, Jr.).

_____. Letter to Ray Bradbury, September 13, 1962 (courtesy of Martin Grams, Jr.).

Shapiro, Marc. "He Is Legend." *Starlog* #256 (November 1998), pp. 60–61.

_____. "Mamie Van Doren." *Femme Fatales* 10:4 (September-October 2001), pp. 25–30.

Shatner, William, with Chris Kreski. *Star Trek Memories* (New York: HarperPaperbacks, 1994).

Shay, Don. "Heston: Omega Man." *Vampires and Slayers* 1:1 (c. 1999), pp. 30–32.

Shepard, Bill. "Richard Matheson: He Is Legend." *INSITE* 12:3 (Third Quarter 2001), pp. 10–11.

_____. *The* Somewhere in Time *Story: Behind the Scenes of the Making of the Cult Romantic Fantasy Motion Picture*, fifth edition, edited by Jo Addie (La Grange Park, IL: The Somewhere in Time Gallery, 2004).

Sheridan, Lee. *The Pit and the Pendulum* (New York: Lancer, 1961).

Sherman, Fraser A. *Cyborgs, Santa Claus and Satan: Science Fiction, Fantasy and Horror Films Made for Television* (Jefferson, NC: McFarland, 2000).

Simmons, William P. "Reflections of a Storyteller: A Conversation with Richard Matheson." www.rodserling.com (originally published in *Cemetery Dance* #49 in 2004).

Singer, Mark. "What Are You Afraid Of?" *The New Yorker*, September 7, 1998, pp. 56–67.

Skelton, Scott, and Jim Benson. *Rod Serling's Night Gallery: An After-Hours Tour* (Syracuse: Syracuse University Press, 1999).

Skotak, Robert. "Famous Fantastic Factoids from Fantasy Films!" *Filmfax* #63–64 (October 1997-January 1998), pp. 70–73, 140.

_____. "More Fantastic Factoids." *Filmfax* #72 (April-May 1999), pp. 62–65, 90.

Slade, Michael. *Bed of Nails* (New York: Onyx, 2003).

Sobczynski, Peter. "David Koepp." *Cinefantastique* 31:4 (April 1999), p. 45.

_____. "Stir of Echoes." *Cinefantastique* 31:8 (October 1999), pp. 60–61.

Sohl, Jerry. *Filet of Sohl: The Classic Scripts and Stories of Jerry Sohl*, edited by Christopher Conlon (Boalsburg, PA: BearManor Media, 2003).

_____. *The Twilight Zone Scripts of Jerry Sohl*, edited by Christopher Conlon (Boalsburg, PA: Bear-Manor Media, 2004).

Spielberg, Steven. "An Introduction to Richard Matheson's *Duel*." *Zoetrope: All-Story* 8:1 (Spring 2004), pp. 86–89.

Spignesi, Stephen J. *The Lost Work of Stephen King: A Guide to Unpublished Manuscripts, Story Fragments, Alternative Versions, and Oddities* (New York: Birch Lane/Carol, 1999).

Stanley, John. *Creature Features Movie Guide Strikes Again* (Pacifica, CA: Creatures at Large Press, 1994).

Stewart, Susan. "Hits & Misses." *TV Guide*, January 31, 1998, p. 39.

Stoker, Bram. *The Essential Dracula*, edited by Leonard Wolf (New York: Plume, 1993).

Stout, Ed. "Richard Matheson Tribute: 'The "Twilight" of His Career.'" *INSITE* 12:3 (Third Quarter 2001), pp. 11–13.

Sudak, Eunice. *The Raven* (New York: Lancer, 1963).

_____. *Tales of Terror* (New York: Lancer, 1962).

Symons, Julian. *The 31st of February* (New York: Harper & Brothers, 1950).

Taylor, Al, and Sue Roy. *Making a Monster: The Creation of Screen Characters by the Great Makeup Artists* (New York: Crown, 1980).

Thompson, Jeff. *The Television Horrors of Dan Curtis: Dark Shadows, The Night Stalker and Other Productions, 1966–2006* (Jefferson, NC: McFarland, 2009).

Timpone, Anthony. *Men, Makeup, and Monsters: Hollywood's Masters of Illusion and FX* (New York: St. Martin's Griffin, 1996).

Uram, Sue. "*Star Trek*: The 30th Anniversary," *Cinefantastique* 27:11–12 (July 1996), pp. 24–111.

Van Genechten, Jan, and Gilbert Verschooten. "Roy's Nightmares: The Life of Hammer's Make Up Master Roy Ashton (1909–1995)," *Little Shoppe of Horrors* #14 (December 1999), pp. 61ff.

Vered, Annabel. "Period of Adjustment." *TV Guide*, January 31, 1998, p. 6.

Verne, Jules. *Master of the World* and *Robur the Conqueror* (New York: Ace, 1961).

Walter, Elizabeth. "The New House," in *Snowfall and Other Chilling Events* (New York: Stein and Day, 1985), pp. 73–119.

"Warner Readies *Legend* Prequel." *SCI FI Wire* (www.scifi.com), September 25, 2008.

Warren, Alan. *This Is a Thriller: An Episode Guide, History and Analysis of the Classic 1960s Television Series* (Jefferson, NC: McFarland, 1996).

Warren, Bill. *Keep Watching the Skies! American Science Fiction Movies of the Fifties* (two volumes; Jefferson, NC: McFarland, 1982–86).

Weaver, Tom. *Attack of the Monster Movie Makers: Interviews with 20 Genre Giants* (Jefferson, NC: McFarland, 1994).

_____. *Interviews with B Science Fiction and Horror Movie Makers: Writers, Producers, Directors, Actors, Moguls and Makeup* (Jefferson, NC: McFarland, 1988).

_____. *It Came from Weaver Five: Interviews with 20 Zany, Glib and Earnest Moviemakers in the SF and Horror Traditions of the Thirties, Forties, Fifties and Sixties* (Jefferson, NC: McFarland, 1996).

_____. "Twilight Testaments." *Starlog* #203 (June 1994), p. 32.

_____, and Michael Brunas. "Quoth Matheson, 'Nevermore!,' Part Two," *Fangoria* #90 (February 1990), pp. 14–18.

Weinberg, Robert. *Horror of the 20th Century: An Illustrated History* (Portland, OR: Collectors Press, 2000).

Weiner, Jack B. *The Morning After* (New York: Delacorte, 1973).

Weinraub, Bernard. "At the Movies," *The New York Times*, August 27, 1999, p. E14.

Weldon, Michael. *The Psychotronic Encyclopedia of Film* (New York: Ballantine, 1983).

Wheatley, Dennis. *The Devil Rides Out* (London: Mandarin, 1991).

Whitten, Leslie H. *Moon of the Wolf* and *Progeny of the Adder* (New York: Leisure, 1992).

Wiater, Stanley. "A Conversation with Richard Matheson and R.C. Matheson." *Cemetery Dance* 4:2 (Spring 1992), pp. 52–57.

_____. *Dark Dreamers: Conversations with the Masters of Horror* (New York: Avon, 1990).

_____. *Dark Visions: Conversations with the Masters of the Horror Film* (New York: Avon, 1992).

_____, Matthew R. Bradley, and Paul Stuve, editors. *The Richard Matheson Companion* (Colorado Springs, CO: Gauntlet, 2008).

_____, Matthew R. Bradley, and Paul Stuve, editors. *The Twilight and Other Zones: The Dark Worlds of Richard Matheson* (New York: Citadel, 2009).

Williams, Lucy Chase. *The Complete Films of Vincent Price* (Secaucus, NJ: Carol, 1995).

Williamson, J.N., editor. *Masques* (Baltimore: Maclay & Associates, 1984).

Willis, Donald C. *Horror and Science Fiction Films II* (Metuchen, NJ: Scarecrow, 1982).

Winter, Douglas E. *Faces of Fear: Encounters with the Creators of Modern Horror* (New York: Berkley, 1985).

Wolf, Leonard. *Horror: A Connoisseur's Guide to Literature and Film* (New York: Facts on File, 1989).

Wright, Bruce Lanier. *Nightwalkers: Gothic Horror Movies: The Modern Era* (Dallas: Taylor, 1995).

Zicree, Marc Scott. *The Twilight Zone Companion*, second edition (New York: Bantam, 1989).

Zugsmith, Albert. *The Beat Generation* (New York: Bantam, 1959).

Index

*Numbers in **bold italics** indicate pages with photographs.*

A&E Network 194
Abbey (dog) 265, *266*, 267
ABC Movie of the Week 156, 250
ABC-TV 28, 51, 54–6, 58–9, 61,
  67–8, 76, 129, 155–7, 162–3,
  165–7, 169–70, 172–3, 175–6,
  185, 187, 192–4, 196, 199, 201–2,
  204, 209, 219, 244, 246, 270
Aberdeen, South Dakota 246–7
Abu and the 7 Marvels 174
Academy Award 34, 73, 112, 116,
  148–9, 152, 195, 216–7, 219, 226,
  229, 248, 254; *see also* Oscar
Academy of Motion Picture Arts
  and Sciences 87
Academy Pictures 177–8, 181–2
"O Acidente" 29
Ackerman, Forrest J ("Forry") 60
Ackerman Famous Monsters Con
  234
"Act of Faith" 53
"The Actor" (episode) 57, 149
Adam and Eve (screenplay) 21
Adam Productions 246
Adam-12 (1968 series) 129
Adams, Maude 220, 222
Adams, Stanley 37, 162, 168, 175–
  6
Adams, Ray, and Rosenberg
  (agency) 49
Adamson, Al 21
Addelson, Lenny 85
The Addiction 254
Addie, Jim 220
Addie, Jo 220, 227
*The Adventures of Buckaroo Banzai
  Across the Eighth Dimension* 152
Adventures of Don Juan 116
The Adventures of Robin Hood 114,
  116
Afterburn (1992) 249
"The Aftermath" *see* "And When
  the Sky Was Opened"
Agnew, Spiro T. 187
Aickman, Robert 67
Aidman, Charles 27–8, 38–9, 176
AIDS 268
Ain't It Cool News 73–4
AIP *see* American International Pic-
  tures

Airplane! 230
Airport 1975 70, 149
Airstrip One (music label) 217
Ajibade, Yemi 131
Akins, Claude 162, 164, 168, 175
Alaska 75
Albaine, Richard 201
Albarella, Tony 29, 31, 42–3
Albert, Sydell 269
The Alchemist 166
Alcoa-Goodyear Theatre 211
Aldrich, Robert 45, 106, 124, 147,
  169
Alexander, Denise 29–31
The Alfred Hitchcock Hour 7, 62–4,
  147–8, 171, 207
Alfred Hitchcock Presents 53, 68,
  110, 239
Alfred Hitchcock's Mystery Magazine
  61
Ali, Muhammad 218
*Ali Baba and the Seven Marvels of
  the World* 173–4
Alice (series) 195
Alien³ 254
All Quiet on the Western Front (1979
  film) 184
All Together Now 26
Alladin, Johnny 127
Allan, David 232
Alland, William 10–1, 17
Allard, Eric 249
Allen, Durward 251
Allen, Elizabeth 63
Allen, Irwin 148, 201
Allen, Linda Lou 212, 214
Allen, Patrick 131, 135
Allendale, New Jersey 4
Alley, Kirstie 271
Allison, Jean 207
Allyson, June 98, 101
Almodóvar, Pedro 17
Alone by Night 47, 203
Alpha Children 154
Alterian Studios 248
Altman, Robert 33, 61, 203
Altoviti, Fiore 197
Alves, Joe 239–40
Alvin, John 220, 223
Alwyn, William 94, 96

Alzheimer's Disease 25
Amante Menguante (Shrinking Lover)
  17
The Amazing Colossal Man 79, 81
The Amazing Spider-Man (series)
  214
Amazing Stories (magazine) 39
Amazing Stories (series) 22, 39, 43,
  74–7, 211, 235
Amazing Stories: The Movie II 74
Amblin Entertainment 75
AMC (American Movie Classics)
  39
"Amelia" 201, *202*, 204–6, *204*,
  209, 250–2
American International Pictures
  (AIP) 78–82, 84–9, 91, 93–6,
  98, 100–3, 105–8, 110, 112–3,
  115–7, 122, 136–46, 152, 166, 173,
  181–2, 207–8
American International Television
  137
American Movie Classics *see* AMC
American Pulp 147
American Releasing Corporation
  78
An American Werewolf in London
  229, 233
Ames, Carolyn 194–5
Ames, Jimmy 44
Amicus Productions 102, 132, 142,
  179, 193, 213
The Amityville Horror (1979 film) 41
"Amok Time" 50
Anatomy of the Syndicate see *The
  Big Operator*
Anchor Bay Entertainment 132–3,
  205
"And Now I'm Waiting" 32–3
—And Now the Screaming Starts!
  193
And Soon the Darkness 182
"—And the Moon Be Still as
  Bright" 214
"And When the Sky Was Opened"
  24, 27–8, 39
Anders, Luana 89–90, 92
Anderson, Beau 37
Anderson, Ira 169
Anderson, John 62

Anderson, Mary 57
Anderson, Michael 212, 217–9
Anderson, Michael, Jr. 212, 214
Anderson, Richard 169–71, *172*
The Anderson Tapes (film) 175
Andre, E.J. 209, 211
Andrews, Edward 29–30
Angel (series) 176
Angelo, Robert (aka Fuca) 127
"Angels of Vengeance" 22
Anglo-Amalgamated 94–6, 98
Anker, Roger 23, 25, 50
Anmar, Frank (pseudonym) 174, 203
The Anniversary (1968 film) 124
Anthony, Lysette 249–50
Anthony, Ray 9, 18, 20
Antibes, France 198
Any Number Can Win see *Mélodie en Sous-sol*
Apache (film) 147
Apache Woman 81
Apartment Zero 258, 260
Apollo 13 (film) 258
Appointment in Zahrain 269
Arbogast, Roy 228, 242
Argento, Dario 93, 112
Aries, Anna 149
Arizona 138, 185
Arkoff, Samuel Z. ("Sam") 78, 80–2, 89, 98, 101, 111–2, 138, 141, 143–5, 154, 181–2
Arlington Cemetery 56
Armstrong, Bess 239–40
Armstrong, Dave 37, 47
Armstrong, Herb 242
Armstrong, Louis 18
Arnett, Robert 4, 16, 46, 53, 66, 76–7, 186
Arnold, Freddy 141
Arnold, Jack 4, 9–11, *11*, 13–8, 62, 230–1, 239
Around the World in 80 Days (1956 film) 21, 217
Around the World in 80 Days (novel) 217
Arrighi, Niké 131–2, *131*, 134, 136
Arrow M.E.E. 270
"The Art of Richard Matheson" 7
Arthur, Colin 212
Artisan Entertainment 257, 259–60
Arts & Entertainment Network see A&E Network
As Timeless as Infinity: The Twilight Zone Scripts of Rod Serling, Volume One 29–30, 34
Asher, William 45
Ashton, Roy 123, 130–1, 136
Asimov, Isaac 12, 50, 266
Assault on a Queen 173
Asseyev, Tamara 92
Associated Producers 117, 119, 121
Asylum (1972) 72
Atlantis 67, 84
"The Atlantis Affair" *66*, 67
Attack 45
Attack of the Monster Movie Makers 109, 120, 122–3, 181–2
Attila 189, 191
Atwater, Barry 162–3, *165*, 168–9
Aukin, Liane 131

Das Ausschweifende Leben des Marquis de Sade see *De Sade* (film)
Austen, Jane 268
Australia 141
Avallone, Susan 269
Avalon, Frankie 91
Avanti! 183
The Avengers (series) 101, 133, 182–3
The Awakening 149
Away All Boats 15
The Awful Truth 10
Aykroyd, Dan 231, 233, 238, 242–3, *243*
Azalea Pictures 137, 140

Baar, Tim (aka Barr) 85, 87
Babylon 5 176
Bachelor in Paradise 17
Bachman, Richard (pseudonym) 5
Back Stage West 264
"Back to *Somewhere in Time*" 220, 224
Back to the Future (film) 176
Backdraft 228
Bacon, Francis 256
Bacon, Kevin 257–9, *259*, 261
Badham, John 70
BAFTA Film Award 125, 182
Bailey, Raymond 9, 12
Bain, Barnet 252
Baker, Pip and Jane 89
Baker, Rick ("Richard A.") 228–30
Baker, Roy Ward 124, 182
Balderston, John L. 187
Baldwin, William 192
Balik, Shelby 228–9
Ball, Lucille 254
Balsam, Martin 74
Bankhead, Tallulah 116–7, 123–4, *125*, 126
Banned from the Ranch Entertainment (effects company) 257
Bannister, Jeffrey 232
Bansak, Edmund G. 98, 100
Bar David, S. (pseudonym) 148
Barbarash, Ernie 262
Barbary Coast (series) 28
Bare, Richard L. 29–30, 33–4, 38–9
Barilla, Courtney 245–6
Barkley, Deanne 196, 219
Barnes, Jonas 262
Barr, Tim see Baar, Tim
Barrett, Michael 269
Barrie, J.M. 220
Barron, Frank 234
Barry, John 219, 226–7
Barry, Patricia 232, 236
Barry, Raymond J. 176
Barselow, Paul 112
"Bart Simpson's Dracula" 48
Bartlett, Martine 45
Barton, Larry 44
Baskin, William 107–8
Bass, Jules 126
Bass, Ron 252, 254–5
Bassett, Joe 27
Bates, Ralph 191
Batman and Robin 230
Batman Forever 230
Battle for the Planet of the Apes 150

"Battleground" (episode) 206
Battlestar Galactica (1978–79) 221
Bau, Gordon 149
Baum, L. Frank 7, 196, 245–7
Baum, Maude Gage 246
Baum, Ralph 197
Baum, Dr. Robert A., Jr. 245, 247
Bava, Mario 92–3, 123
Baxley, Barbara 41
Baxley, Paul 26
Baxt, George 94, 98, 100–1, 163
Baxter, John 10, 12, 14
Baxter, Les 78, 84–5, 88–9, 101, 107, 109, 112
Bay, Michael 265
BBC-TV 67, 188, 211, 213
Beach Blanket Bingo 37
Beach Party (film series) 139
Beale, Lewis 267
The Beardless Warriors 7, 23, 127, 130, 177
The Beast Must Die 132
The Beat Generation (film) 12, 17–21, *19*, 130, 200
The Beat Generation (novelization) 18
Beatty, Ned 185, 228–9
Beatty, Robert 212, 214
Beau Geste (1966 film) 28
Beaulieu-sur-Mer, France 147
Beaumont, Cathy 25
Beaumont, Charles ("Chuck") 3, 21–7, 32, 41, 46, 49–50, 53–4, 59–60, 68, 72, 76, 79, 84, 89, 94–6, 98, 100, 102, 107, 187, 193, 201, 210, 227, 238, 258
Beaumont, Chris 25–6
Beaumont, Elizabeth 25
Beaumont, Greg 25
Beaumont, Helen 25, 258
A Beautiful Mind (film) 266
Beckwith, Reginald 94, 97
Bed of Nails 123
Bedbury, Mandi 262–3
Beginning of the End 64, 193
Begley, Ed, Jr. 209, 211
Behr, Ira Steven 237
"Being" 137–40, 142, 185
Beinke, Jim 248, 257
Beir, Frederick 42
Belgium 146
Believe It or Not see *O Impossível Acontece*
Bell, Tobin 242
"The Bells of Hell" 67
Belstar (production company) 197
Ben 210
Ben-Hur (1959 film) 149
Benchley, Peter 158, 239
Bender, Jack 245–6
Beneath the Planet of the Apes 31, 152
Benjamin, Richard 101
Bennett, Dorothea 146, 148
Bennett, Harvey 52
Bennett, Jack 137, 140
Bennett, Zachary 261
Benson, Jim 70–1, 210
Benson, Lucille 155, 158, 207–8
Benton, Douglas ("Doug") 60, 67
Beregi, Oscar 41, 59
"Berenice" 103

Berg, Richard ("Dick") 219
Berger, Christian K. 4
Berger, Howard 78
Berger, Senta 141–2
Bergin, Patrick 248–9
Bergman, Ingmar 89, 147, 256
Bergman, Slim 44, 47
Berkley Books 258, 270
Berlin, Germany 141, 143–6
Berlin Express 45
Bernard, James 130, 133
Bernay, Lynne 89
The Bernie Mac Show 49
Berns, Mel, Jr. 185
Besbas, Peter 85
Best Sellers 177
Bettoia, Franca 118, 122
Bevans, Philippa 62
The Beverly Hillbillies (film) 186
Beverly Hills, California 51, 79, 195
Beverly Hills High 79
Beverly Wilshire Hotel 146
Beyond Fantasy Fiction 26, 76
BFI *see* British Film Institute
The BFI Companion to Horror 67
Bickel, Steve 222
Bickford, Charles 52
Bid Time Return (novel) 4, 72, 120, 208, 219–21, 224–5, 253
Bierce, Ambrose 69
The Big Grab see *Mélodie en Sous-sol*
The Big Heat (film) 45
The Big Operator 18
The Big Sleep (1946 film) 169
"Big Surprise" 68–71
Bihr, Kathryn 239
Bikini Beach 107
Bill, Tony 270
Bill & Ted's Bogus Journey 5
Bill & Ted's Excellent Adventure 5
Binns, Edward 211
Biodrowski, Steve 81, 191, 234, 256, 261
Biography (series) 194
The Bionic Woman (1976) 170
Bird, Michael J. 68
Bird, Norman 94, 97
The Birds (film) 28, 63, 70
"The Birds" (story) 64
Birney, David 72
Birnheim, Françoise 170
Bistritz, Hungary 189
Bixby, Bill 161
Bixby, Jerome 10, 232, 234, 236–7
Black, John D.F. 65
Black, Karen 201–7, *202*, 210, 250
"The Black Cat" (1962 film segment) 101, *103*, 104–7, *105*, 114
"The Black Cat" (1990 film segment) 112
"The Black Cat" (story) 101, 104–5
Black Eye 17
Black Heat 21
Black House 177
Black Narcissus (1947 film) 101
The Black Scorpion 62
The Black Stallion (film) 235
Black Sunday (aka *La Maschera del Demonio* [Mask of the Demon], 1960) 92–3

Black Widow (1987) 254
Blackbeard's Ghost (film) 127
Blackboard Jungle (film) 233
Blackmer, Sidney 67
Blackwood, Algernon 70
Blaine, Michael 227, 270
Blair, Janet 94, *95*, 96, *96*, 101
The Blair Witch Project 260
Blaisdell, Anne (aka Elizabeth Linington) 123–4, 126
Blaisdell, Paul 138, 140
Blalack, Robert 239
Blame It on Rio 77
Blanch, Jewel 194–5
Blankfield, Mark 228–9
Blasetti, Alessandro 72
Blasko, Dan 239
Blatty, William Peter 151
Blaustein, Julian 213
Blazing Stewardesses 21
Blees, Robert 62
Blish, James 65
Bloch, Robert 3, 7, 13, 50, 59, 61, 68, 102, 142, 157, 171, 239
Blood from the Mummy's Tomb 67
Blood of Ghastly Horror 21
Blood Son (film) 262–4
"Blood Son" (story) 118, 262–4
Bloodlines 121, 123, 187–8, 212
Bloom, Claire 183
Blown Away 234
Bluebook 57
The Blues Brothers 233
Blyden, Larry 94
Blythe, Peter 67
Bob Hope Presents the Chrysler Theatre 64, 181
"Bobby" (1977 film segment) 209–10, 251
"Bobby" (1996 film segment) 249–51
The Body Snatcher (film) 47
The Body Snatchers (novel) 211
Bogart, Humphrey 169
Bogdanovich, Peter 79, 186
Bohn, Merritt 44–5
Bolender, Bill 248–9
Bonanza 9, 62
Bond, Jeff 152, 155
Bonet, Wilma 252, 255
Bonifas, Paul 146, 149
Bonne, Shirley 137–8
The Bonnie Parker Story 208
Bookwalter, DeVeren 149
Boon, Robert 41
Boone, Richard 54, *55*
Boorman, John 45
Born Free (1966 film) 226
Born of Man and Woman (collection) 6–7, 23, 201
"Born of Man and Woman" (story) 3, 6
Borsalino 198
Borsalino and Co. 198–9
Bosch, Hieronymus 234, 256
Bosco, Scott Michael 205–6
Boss Nigger 17
Boston, Massachusetts 83, 104, 114, 248
Bottin, Rob 232, 236
Boucher, Anthony ("Tony") 72
Bourbon Street Beat 55–6

Bourneuf, Philip 59
Bouzereau, Laurent 156, 158–9, 220–1, 223, 226
Bower, Antoinette 59
Bowles, Peter 177, 179, 183
Bowman, Gail 209
Bowman, Rob 265–6
Bown, John 131
The Box (2009 film) 73–4
Boxcar Bertha 150
Boyd, Joshua 245–6
Boyle, Danny 268
Boys in Love 2 206
Bradbury, Marguerite 216
Bradbury, Ray 1, 3–4, 10, 23–4, 38, 42, 50, 60, 72, 100, 183, 212–3, 217–9
Brady, Scott 169–70
The Brady Bunch 17
Braga, Alice 265, 267
Brahm, John 35–6, 38
The Brain Eaters 84
Brain of Blood 21
Bram Stoker Award 4
Bram Stoker's Dracula (1974 film) see *Dracula* (1974 film)
Bram Stoker's Dracula (1992 film) 187–8
Brand, Joshua 75
Brand, Larry 112
Brand, Max 4
Brandenburg, Chester 31
Brando, Marlon 106
Brasseur, Claude 197
Brat Pack 73, 230
Braunbeck, Gary A. 73
Brauner, Artur 141, 143
Brauner, Asher 207
Bray Studios 136–7
Breakdown (1997 film) 186
Brennert, Alan 26
Breslin, Patricia 33–4
Bride of Chucky 246
The Bridge on the River Kwai (film) 66
Brierly, Dean 236–7
Briggs, David 206
Brighton Park (Chicago) 260
Bristol, England 104
British Columbia, Canada 78, 125
British Film Institute (BFI) 100
Brocco, Peter 232, 234
Brody, Estelle 212
Broken Arrow (series) 9
Bronson, Charles 85–7, *86*, *88*, 146–9
Bronson, Lillian 55
Bronx, New York 268
Brooklyn, New York 4–5, 10, 27, 30, 52, 130, 196, 253, 268
The Brooklyn Eagle 5
Brooklyn Technical High School 6
Brooks, Albert 231, 233
Brooks, James E. 147, 254
Brooks, Nicholas 257
Brooks, Richard 45
Brophy, Sallie 53
Brosnan, John 125, 156, 183, 265
Brother Theodore *see* Gottlieb, Theodore

Broussard, Everett H. 9, 13
Brown, Elman 123, 184
Brown, Helen 35–6
Brown, Joe E. 112, 114
Brown, Murray 187, 189
Brown, Pamela 187, 190
Brown, Peter 56, **58**
Brown, Phil 212
Brown, Scott 101
Browne, Kathie 168, 176
Browning, Tod 94, 118
Brubaker 41
Brunas, Michael 106
Bryant, Joshua 194–5
Bryar, Claudia 41
Bryar, Paul 27, 52
Brynner, Yul 269
Buchanan, Larry 137–41, 185
Buchholz, Horst 209, 211
Buck Rogers in the 25th Century (TV
    series) 26
A Bucket of Blood 80
Buckskin (series) 53
Buda-Pesth, Hungary 190
Buffy the Vampire Slayer (series) 176
Bug (1975) 221
Bulldog Drummond (film series) 60
Bungert, Douglas 192
Bunny Lake Is Missing (film) 143
Il Buono, il Brutto, il Cattivo (The
    Good, the Bad and the Ugly) 148
Burbank, California 221
Buried Alive (1990 film) 112
Burn, Witch, Burn (film) 50, 94,
    98, **99**, 100, 111, 124, 146, 226; *see
    also Night of the Eagle*
Burn Witch, Burn! (novel) 94
Burns, James H. 4, 10, 140, 155, 177
Burnt Offerings (film) 174, 202, 210
Burton, Richard 183
Burton, Robert 201, 203, 206
Burton, Tim 229–30
Bus Stop (series) 61–2
Butler-Glouner, Inc. 85, 89, 101,
    107, 112
"Button, Button" 73
"By Appointment Only" 210
By the Gun 57
Byrnes, Burke 207
Byron, Kathleen 94, 97, 101
CAA *see* Creative Artists Agency
    (CAA)
Cabaret (film) 78
Cabot, Sebastian **71**, 72
Cahn, Edward L. 137, 139
Cain, James M. 4
California 4, 7, 10–1, 20, 25, 34,
    39, 51, 54, 72, 79, 83, 89, 146,
    154–5, 158, 171, 174, 182, 186,
    193, 199, 221, 226, 229, 233,
    253, 255, 261; *see also* Los Ange-
    les, California
California Sorcerers 3; *see also* The
    Group
Call for Small 21
Callan, Michael 68
Calling Dr. Death 94
Cámara, Javier 17
Cameron, James 12, 79
Cameron, Lou 270

Camp Pleasant 7
Campbell, Julia 248
Campbell, R. Wright 79–80, 89
Campbell, William 80
Campo, Wally 85, 101, 105
Canada 78, 123, 125, 187, 192, 218,
    249, 262
Canary Islands 216
Cannes film festival 143
Cannon, Don 269
Cannon, Orin 201, 209, 211
Cantinflas 21
Capitolina (production company)
    197
*Captain Kronos: Vampire Hunter see
    Kronos* (1974 film)
Captain Nemo and the Floating City
    89
*Captain Nemo and the Underwater
    City* 89
Captains and the Kings (miniseries)
    225
Car Wash 230
Carbone, Antony 89–90
Carere, Frank C. 249
Carey, Philip 54, 176, 192–3
Carlin, Lynn 194–5
Carlito's Way (film) 258
Carlson, Steve 127, **128**, 129
Carmel, California 261
Carnarvon, Lord 196
Caron, Sandra 187
Carpenter, Pete 194
Carr, Cindy 257
Carradine, John 57, 68, 71, 169–70,
    172
Carreras, James ("Jimmy") 120–1
Carreras, Michael ("Mike") 121,
    124, 134
Carribean 67, 116
Carrol, Regina (aka Gelfan) 18, 21
Carroll, Dee 33–4, 170
Carroll, Leo G. 66
Carson, Greg 111
Carson, Hunter 207
Carson, L.M. Kit 207
Carson City, Nevada 161
Carter, Alex 249, 251
Carter, Chris 77
Carter, Howard 197
Cartwright, Nancy 232, 236
Casablanca 106
Case, David 192–3
The Case Against Satan 210
The Case of Charles Dexter Ward 79
"The Case of M. Valdemar" (1962
    film segment) 101, 105–6
"The Case of Peggy Ann Lister" 198
Casey, Bernie 212–3
Cash, Jerry 162
Cash, Rosalind 149–50, **150**, 152,
    154, 268
"The Cask of Amontillado" 91, 101,
    104
Cassady, John 212, 215
Cassavetes, John 62, 195
Cast Away 268
Castle, Peggie 57, **58**
Castle, William 72, 94, 169, 210,
    221
Cat Ballou 44–5

Cat People (1942) 45–6, 122, 169
Cathey, Reg E. 242
Catholic Church 21
Catron, Jerry 26
Cavalier, Lou 44
Cavendish, Dola 125
CBS Radio 171
CBS-TV 17, 22, 24, 40, 43, 52–5,
    62, 73, 186, 189, 214, 228, 248
CCC Film 141–2, 144
Cedar, Larry 232, 238
Cell (novel) 5
The Cell: Three Tales of Horror 193
Cemetery Dance (magazine) 17, 244
C'era una Volta il West (Once Upon
    a Time in the West) 147
Le Cercle Rouge (The Red Circle)
    198
Cerf, Bennett 60
CFQ 152, 154, 265; *see also Cine-
    fantastique*
Chadler, C. Adolpho (aka Cícero
    Adolpho Vitório da Costa Cha-
    dler) 29
Challee, William 41
Challis, John 187
Chamberlain, Richard 56
"Chambers of Imagery" 258
Champlin, Charles 226
Chandler, Jeff 18
Chandler, Raymond 54
Chaney, Lon, Jr. 94–5
Chaney, Lon, Sr. 159
Chang, Wah 85, 87
Changeover 263
"Changing of the Guard" 26
Chao, Rosalind 252, 256
Chaplin, Charles, Jr. 18
Charenton (asylum) 146
*Charles Bronson: The 95 Films and
    the 156 Television Appearances* 148
Charlie's Angels (series) 200
Charlottenburg Palace 141
Charly 32
Chartrand, Harvey F. 205, 208
Chase, Chevy 230
Chase, David 176
Chase, Eric 68
Chase, Stanley 181
Cheers (series) 225, 271
Chen, Renée Shinn 233
Chetwynd-Hayes, R. 70
Cheyenne (1955–63 series) 56, 193–
    4
Chicago, Illinois 199, 222–3, 226–
    7, 246–7, 258–60
Chicago Press Club 247
"The Children of Noah" 61, 209,
    262
Children of the Damned 200
Child's Play (1988 film) 246
Child's Play 3 246
Chiller (TV package) 138
Chinatown 111–2
CHiPs 129
Chizmar, Richard 180
Chocano, Carina 268
Christi, Frank R. 161
Christian, Roger 234
Christian Science Church 196
Christian symbolism 151, 154, 215

Christopher Award 4
The Christopher Lee Filmography: All Theatrical Releases, 1948–2003 136
Church of Scientology 271
Ciani, Suzanne 228
Cinefantastique 65, 77, 81, 106, 133, 230, 234, 256, 258, 261; *see also* CFQ
Cinema Retro 236–7
CinemaScope 79, 81–2
Cinematic Hauntings 180
Cinematic Vampires: The Living Dead on Film and Television, from The Devil's Castle (1896) to Bram Stoker's Dracula (1992) 191
Circle of Fear 72
Circus of Horrors (aka *Phantom of the Circus*) 98
CIS-Hollywood (effects company) 265
Citizen Kane 34, 38
Città Violenta (Violent City, aka *The Family*) 148
"The City in the Sea" (poem) 113
City of the Dead (aka *Horror Hotel*) 98, 151, 163
City Under the Sea (film) 113, 181
Civil War 225, 228
Le Clan des Siciliens (The Sicilian Clan) 198
Clanton, Ralph 55
Clark, Al 54
Clark, Bob 242–4
Clark, Matt 249–50
Clark, Ron 230
Clarke, Arthur C. 50, 65
Clarke, John 57
Classic TV Archive 53
Clatworthy, Robert 14
Clavell, James 18
Claxton, William 26
Clayton, Jack 96, 182, 201, 218
Clear and Present Danger (film) 218
Clemens, Brian 182
Clemens, George T. 28–9
Clement, Henry 145
The Client (film) 230
Clinton, Jack 37
The Clipper of the Clouds see *Robur le Conquérant*
A Clockwork Orange (film) 78
Close Encounters of the Third Kind (film) 232
"Clown Without Pity" 206
Cobb, Edmund 101
Cobert, Robert ("Bob") 162, 169, 172, 186, 190, 192, 201, 209, 212, 249
Cobra 242
Coburn, James 56
Cochran, Steve 17, 20–1
Cohen, Larry 138
The Cold and Alien Kiss of Death see *Earthbound*
Cold Sweat (aka *De la Part des Copains* [From the Boys], *L'Uomo dalle Due Ombre* [The Man with Two Shadows]; 1970 film) 63, 146–9, 197
Cold War 29, 118

Cole, Gary 248
Coleman, Dabney 185–6
Collected Stories (Matheson) 4, 6, 27, 30–1, 35, 45, 52, 65, 68, 72, 74, 76, 78, 140, 174, 186, 196, 199, 203, 205, 209–10, 253, 263
"Collecting Richard Matheson" 6
Collier, John (actor) 54
Collier, John (writer) 24
Collins, Nancy A. 179
Colon, Gilbert 151
Colonel Markesan and Less Pleasant People 59–60
Colossus (novel) 181
Colossus: The Forbin Project 64, 181
"The Colour Out of Space" 79
Columbia Law School 246
Columbia Pictures 125, 133, 173
Columbia Presbyterian Medical Center 12
Columbine, Colorado 264
Columbo 16, 157
Comacico (production company) 146
Combat! 7, 61–2, 129
Come Back to the Five and Dime, Jimmy Dean, Jimmy Dean (film) 203
Come Back to the Five and Dime, Jimmy Dean, Jimmy Dean (play) 33
Come Fill the Cup (film) 195
The Comedy of Terrors (film) 45, 70, 88, 93, 109, 111–7, *113*, *115*
The Comedy of Terrors (novelization) 93, 117
Comer, Anjanette 209, 211
The Comic (1969) 185
The Complete Films of Vincent Price 90, 92, 104, 117
Compton, John 53
Comte de St. Germain 171
Conan Doyle, Sir Arthur 67, 234
Concorde-New Horizons 79, 112
El Conde Dracula (Count Dracula, 1970) 187
Conduct Unbecoming 217
Congdon, Don 47, 203, 270
Congdon, Michael 47
"Conjure Wife" (episode) 94
Conjure Wife (novel) 94, 97–8, 101
Conjure Wife (published screenplay) 98–9
Conlon, Christopher 29, 58, 98, 161, 226
Connecticut 94
Connelly, Christopher 212, 216, 219
Connery, Sean 234
Connors, Chuck 176
"The Conqueror" (story) 57
Conqueror Worm (film) see *Witchfinder General* (film)
Conrad, William 63
Constantin, Michel 146, 148
Constantine 266
Contino, Dick 18
Conway, Tom 60
Coodley, Ted 89, 107
Coogan, Jackie 18, 20
Cook, Elisha, Jr. 162, 164, 169, 209, 211–2
Cook, Robin 142

Cooksey, Jon 5, 76–7
Cool Hand Luke (film) 41
Cooper, Charles 207
Cooper, Gladys 45
Cooper, Maxine 27–8
Cooper, Wyllis 27
Coopersmith, Jerome 61
A Cop (1972) see *Un Flic* (1972)
Cope, Zachary David 257–8
Coppola, Francis Ford 14, 79–80, 112, 187–8, 202
Corbett, Tom 179, 181
"The Corbomite Maneuver" 50
Corday, Mara 16–7
Corevi, Tony [Antonio] 118
Corey, Jeff 111, 196
Corman, Gene 80
Corman, Roger 4, 78–85, 87, 89–93, 101–7, 109, 111–3, 137, 141, 144–5, 154, 169, 183–4, 193, 209–10
"Corman's Comedy of Poe" 111
Cornbread, Earl and Me (film) 152
"Cornered" 57
Coronado Hotel 72, 221–3, 226
Corrington, John William 149–51, 154, 249, 265
Corrington, Joyce Hooper 149–51, 154, 265
Corruption (1967 film) 133
Cosby 48
Cosmopolitan 20
Cotsworth, Staats 63
The Couch 13
Coughlan, Paul 262
Count Dracula (1970) see *El Conde Dracula*
Count Dracula (1977 TV production) 188
Court, Hazel 107–11
Courtland, Christi 118, *119*, 122
Cox, Greg 166
Cox, Ronny 242–3
Cox, Wally 169–70
Cox, William R. 9, 37, 269–70
Coyle, Robert, Jr. 151, 154
Cozzi, Luigi 112
Crackle of Death 176
The Crash of Flight 401 48
Cravat, Nick 47–8, 238
Craven, Wes 148
Crawford, Joan 42, 106, 124–5, 156
Creative Artists Agency (CAA) 242
Creative Screenwriting 4, 16, 46, 66, 76
Creature 271
Creature Features Movie Guide Strikes Again 101, 207
Creature from the Black Lagoon 10, 138, 230, 239
Creature of Destruction 137, 140
The Creature Walks Among Us 13
The Creeping Unknown see *The Quatermass Xperiment* (film)
Cregar, Laird 36, 171
Crevoy, Jim 37
Crichton, Michael 158, 195
Crick, Robert Alan 180
"Crickets" 262
The Crimson Cult see *Curse of the Crimson Altar*

Crist, Judith 183
A Critical History of Television's The Twilight Zone, *1959–1964* 49
"The Crocodile Case" 110
Crosby, Cathy 18
Crosby, Floyd 79, 89, 93, 109, 111–2
Crosland, Dominique 147
Crothers, Scatman 232, 234, 239, 259
Crowley, Aleister 135
Crusade 176
The Cry Baby Killer 111
Cry of the Banshee 207
Culp, Robert 52
Culver, Roland 177, 179, 183
Cunha, Richard E. 18
Currie, Cherie 232, 236
The Curse of Frankenstein 3, 109, 136
Curse of the Black Widow 62
The Curse of the Cat People 47, 169
Curse of the Crimson Altar (aka *The Crimson Cult*) 107
Curse of the Demon see *Night of the Demon* (1958)
Curse of the Faceless Man 171, 236
Curse of the Swamp Creature 139
Curtis, Billy 9
Curtis, Dan 4, 23, 62, 103, 146, 162, 164, 167–76, 186–92, 194, 201–4, 209–12, 228, 249–52, 265
Curtis, Tracy 201
Cushing, Peter 133, 191, 207
Cut! Horror Writers on Horror Film 126
Cutler, Colin 67
Cutthroat Island 116
Cutts, John 270
Cybernia 270
Czechoslovakia 141, 143
Cziraky, Dan 206

Dahl, John 161
Dahl, Roald 24, 67
Dailey, Irene 41
Daily Variety 225
The Dakota Pioneer 246
Dakota Territory 246
The Dakotas 56
Dallas, Texas 137–8, 140
Daly, Jonathan 127–9
Damon, Mark 78, **80**, 82, **82**, 92
Dan Curtis Productions 209
Dana, Justin 228–9
"Dance of the Dead" 77–8
Dances with Wolves (film) 226
Dancing Romeo 144
Dandelion Wine 212
Danforth, Jim 232
Danger Man (aka *Secret Agent*) 133
Danieli, Emma 118, *119*, 122
Daniels, Billy 18
Daniels, William 176
Danse Macabre (book) 31, 61
Dante, Joe 4, 79, 232–6, 238–9
Danton, Ray 17–8, 39, 57
Danville, Illinois 195
Darc, Mireille 197, 199
"The Daring Young Man on the Flying Trapeze" 109

Dark Dreamers (book) 177
Dark Forces (anthology) 245
The Dark Half 61
Dark Shadows (1966–71) 162, 164, 167, 171, 174, 187–8, 190, 212
Dark Shadows (1991) 167, 174, 250–1
Dark Sky Films 211
Darker Places 271
A Darkness at Blaisedon 209, 212
Darkroom 171
Darling, Jennifer 161
Darrin, Diana 9
Dartmoor, England 193
The D.A.'s Man 53
Davenport, Ken 227–8
Davenport, Nigel 187, 190
David, Thayer 212
Davidson, Aldous 262
Davies, Geraint Wyn 249–50
Davis, Andrew 265
Davis, Bette 106, 124–5, 250
Davis, Brad 73
Davis, Dee Dee 49
Davis, Roger 43
Dawidziak, Mark 164, 166–9, 171–3, 175–6, 189, 191, 194, 205, 211–2, 252
Dawson, Anthony M. *see* Margheriti, Antonio
The Day After (1983) 195
A Day in the Death of Joe Egg (1972 film) 73
Day of Fury see *Fury on Sunday*
The Day of the Locust (film) 203
The Day the Earth Stood Still (1951) 12, 213, 215
Day the World Ended (1956) 80, 137
The Daydreamer 126
Days of Wine and Roses (film) 195
DC/Vertigo Comics 266–7
De la Part des Copains see *Cold Sweat* (1970 film)
Dead Man's Eyes 94
Dead of Night (1945 film) 103, 183
Dead of Night (1977 film) 67, 103, 209–12, 224, 249, 251
Dead of Night (proposed series) 209, 212, 228
The Deadly Powder of Thomas Roch 89
Dean, James ("Jimmy") 106, 143
Dean, Margia 121
Deane, Hamilton 187
Death of a Corrupt Man see *Mort d'un Pourri*
The Death of Me Yet 169
"Death on a Barge" 70
Death Proof 184
"Death Ship" 24, 42–3, 185, 214
Death Wish (film) 148
De Carlo, Yvonne 9
Decoration Day (film) 249
Dedman 269
Deep Red see *Profondo Rosso*
The Deer Hunter 217
De Felitta, Frank 180
Defoe, Daniel 267
De Havilland, Olivia 124–5
Dehner, John 176, 210–11
DeKova, Frank 57
De Laurentiis, Dino 229

Dell Publishing Company 188
Delli Colli, Franco 123
Delon, Alain 197
DeLuise, Dom 242, 244
De Lulle, Yannick 146, 148
Del Valle, David 81, 106
Del Vecchio, Deborah 67–8, 134, 136
De Marney, Terence 59
Dementia 13 80
Demme, Jonathan 79
Demon and the Mummy 176
Denise, Gita 187, 190
Denmark 141
Dennis, Winifred 123
DePalma, Brian 258, 260
Derbyshire, Delia 177, 179
Derleth, August 59–60, 70
De Rossi, Rolando 118
DeRoy, Richard 22
Derr, Richard 194–5
De Sade (film) 111, 120, 141–6, *142*, *144*, 207, 245
De Sade (novelization) 145
De Sade, Louis Alphonse Donatien (Marquis de Sade) 7, 141–2, 145
Desilu Productions 254
Detective Story Magazine 262
The Detroit News 130
Deutsch, Armand 221
Deutsch, Stephen 219, 221, 225–6, 252, 270; *see also* Simon, Stephen
Dever, Tom 192
Devetta, Linda 177
"The Devil and Homer Simpson" 48
"Devil Doll" (Matheson submission) 35
The Devil-Doll (1936 film) 94
Devil Doll (videotape) *see* "Amelia"
Devil Girl from Mars 109
The Devil Rides Out 130–7, *131*, *134*
Devil's Angels 80
The Devil's Bride see *The Devil Rides Out*
The Devil's Own see *The Witches* (1966 film)
DeWitt, Alan 101, 112
Dhiegh, Khigh 67
Diabolique (1955 film) 179
Diamond, Selma 232, 234
Diamonds Are Forever (film) 132
"The Diary of Louise Carey" 231
DiCenzo, George 170, 173, 175
Dick, Philip K. 250
The Dick Powell Theatre 16
Dick Powell's Zane Grey Theater 9
The Dick Van Dyke Show 195
Dickerson, Ernest 101
Dickman, Robert 242
"Dick's Big Giant Headache" 48
Die! Die! My Darling! (film) see *Fanatic*
"Die, Die My Darling" (story) 126
Die, Monster, Die see *Monster of Terror*
Dierkes, John 149
Digital Domain (effects company) 252, 255
Diller, Barry 167
Dillon, Robert 210

Dinga, Pat 78, 85, 89, 101, 107, 112
Dinielli, Keith 262–4
Directed by Jack Arnold 14–5, 230
Directors Guild of America 149
The Dirty Dozen (film) 45, 147, 193
Dirty Mary, Crazy Larry 182
The Disappearance 270
"Disappearing Act" (script) *see*
    "And When the Sky Was
    Opened"
"Disappearing Act" (story) 24, 27–
    9, 33, 186
Disney (company) 77, 85, 116, 139,
    182, 247
Disney, Walt 127
Disney Channel 5
Disney Imagineering 75
"The Distributor" 184, 203, 209,
    270
Dixon, Donna 232
Dmytryk, Edward 269
Do Not Go Gentle 227
"Do You Remember Me" 227
Doc Savage—The Man of Bronze 217
Dr. Goldfoot and the Bikini Machine
    91
Dr. Jekyll and Mr. Hyde (1931 film) 29
Dr. Jekyll and Sister Hyde 182
Dr. No (film) 147
Dr. Phibes Rises Again 62
Dr. Strangelove 33
Doctor Who (series) 67
"The Doll" 22, 43, 73–4, 76
Donally, Andrew 212–3
Donner, Richard 47, 244–5
Donovan's Brain (novel) 150
Don't 184
Don't Answer the Phone 184
Don't Be Afraid of the Dark 60
Don't Go in the House 184
Doohan, James 64
Dooley, Paul 33
Doomed (magazine) 262
Doran, Ann 209, 211
Doré, Gustav 256
Dorfmann, Robert 146, 148
Dorn, Susan 31
Dorning, Robert 123
Double, Double 174
Double Trouble (1984 series) 150
Douglas, Illeana 257–8
Douglas, Kirk 270
Douglas, Mike 228–9
Douglas, Sarah 187, 190–1
Douglas Aircraft 6–7, 18
Douglass, Amy 155
Downs, Dermott 194–5
Doyle, Sir Arthur Conan *see*
    Conan Doyle, Sir Arthur
Doyle, David 199–200
Doyle, Ron 162
Dracula (aka *Bram Stoker's Dracula*;
    1974 film) 186–92, **189**, 195
Dracula (aka *Horror of Dracula*;
    1958 film) 133, 190
Dracula (Dean & Balderston play)
    187
Dracula (1931 film) 10, 94, 118, 187,
    262
Dracula (novel) 133, 186–92, 205,
    263

The Dracula Book 169, 188–9, 192
Dracula Has Risen from the Grave
    135
Dracula—Prince of Darkness 67
Dracula vs. Frankenstein (1971) 21
Dracula Walks the Night 191
Dragnet (1951–59 TV series) 53
Drake, Ken 45
Drasnin, Robert 63
The Dreamer of Oz 196, 245–8
*The Dreamer of Oz: The L. Frank
    Baum Story* see *The Dreamer of
    Oz*
The Dreamers (novel) 269
"Dress of White Silk" 118, 126
"Drink My Blood" *see* "Blood Son"
    (story)
"'Drink My Red Blood…'" *see*
    "Blood Son" (story)
The Drowning Pool (film) 41
Drury, James 127, 129
Drury, Jon 127
Duarte, Anselmo 29
Duchovny, David 176
Due Occhi Diabolici (Two Evil Eyes)
    112
Duel (film) 27, 70, 118, 155–62,
    156–7, 189, 204, 208, 228, 232
"Duel" (story) 155–9, 161, 223
"*Duel*: A Conversation with Steven
    Spielberg" 159
Duel & the Distributor 1, 7, 160,
    210, 270
Duff, Howard 31–2, 75
Duffell, Peter 182
Duggan, Andrew 56
Dullea, Keir 141–6, **142**
Du Maurier, Daphne 64
DuMond, Lisa 174
DuMont network 51
Duncan, David 10, 151
Dunn, Kevin 257–8
Dunning, Jessica 94, 97
Dunsany, Lord *see* Lord Dunsany
The Dunwich Horror (film) 79
Dusseldorf, Germany 41
Dutton, Syd 101
Dying Room Only (film) 170, 185–6,
    200–1, 229
"Dying Room Only" (story) 140,
    185–6
Dynarski, Gene 155, 158

Eagle Warriors see *The Young War-
    riors*
"The Earth Men" 214
Earthbound 180, 208–9
Earthquake 70, 149
"Earthquakes Happen" 70
East Rutherford, New Jersey 48
Eastmancolor 79
Easton, Joyce 194
Eastwood, Clint 31, 74, 218
Easy Rider 202
Ebert, Roger 183
Eckstein, George 155, 157–8
The Eclipse (1962) see *L'Eclisse*
    (1962)
Eclipse Books 123
L'Eclisse (The Eclipse, 1962) 198
Ed Wood 229

Eddington, Paul 131–3, **134**
Eddy, Mary Baker 199
Eden, Barbara 92, 199–200
Edgar Allan Poe Award 4, 162
Edge Books 27
Edginton, Ian 184
Edmiston, Walker 205
Edmonds, Louis 212
Edward Scissorhands 229
Edwards, Saundra 56
Eerie, Indiana 32
Effects Associates 232
Egan, Blithe 201
87th Division, U.S. Infantry 127
Eisinger, Jo 146, 148
Eisner, Michael 51
Eisner Award 262
Eitner, Don 64
Elam, Jack 57
Elcar, Dana 185
Elder, Patti 162
Electrophon Ltd. 179
"An Element Never Forgets" 201
"Eleonora" 103
Elfman, Danny 248
Ellerbe, Harry 78, **82**, 83
Ellery Queen's Mystery Magazine
    68–9, 203
Elliott, Alison 212, 215
Elliott, John 232
Elliott, Robert 242
Elliott, Ross 42
Ellison, Harlan 3, 73, 76
Ellzey, David 246
Elstree Studios 68, 136
Elvira, Mistress of the Dark (aka
    Cassandra Peterson) 210
The Emerald City see *The Wonder-
    ful Wizard of Oz*
Emmy Award 16–7, 22, 28, 32, 41,
    48, 52, 70, 74, 148, 154, 156, 160,
    162, 167, 176, 184, 186–7, 194–5,
    208, 229, 247
Emperor of the North 45
The Empire Strikes Back 52
The End of the World see *Panic in
    Year Zero!*
Endfield, Cy 141, 143–6
"The Enemy Within" 47, 50, 64–
    66, 74
England 58, 93, 96, 98, 104, 112,
    125–6, 136, 142, 182, 190, 193, 216,
    234; *see also* London, England
English, John 87
Englund, Robert 78
Entertainment Weekly 17, 161, 268
The Entity 180
Epcot Center 75
Epstein, Allen S. 170, 185, 200, 271
Erbe, Kathryn 257–8
Erwin, Bill 219, 222
"*L'Esame*" (The Test) 72
Escadrille Lafayette 132
Escape from Zahrain 269
Escape to Witch Mountain (1975
    film) 182
Estevez, Emilio 230
Estridge, Robin 269
E.T. (proposed series) 51
E.T.: The Extra-Terrestrial 51, 232,
    235

Etchison, Dennis 49
Etter, Jonathan 171
Etterre, Estelle 47
"*Eu, Ela e o Outro*" 29
Evan Almighty 264
Evans, Jeanne 29–30
Everson, William K. ("Bill") 100, 133
"Everything of Beauty Taken from You in This Life Remains Forever" 73
The Evidence Never Lies 270
The Exorcist (film) 151, 183–4, 256
The Exorcist (novel) 151, 180, 183, 210
"The Expeditions" 213, 219
Extraordinary Stories see *Histoires Extraordinaires* (1968 film)
The Eye Creatures 137
"Eye of the Beholder" 26
Eye of the Cat (aka *Wylie*) 183
"Eye, Tooth" 34
"Eyes" 156
The Eyes Have It 227
Eyewitness (aka *Sudden Terror*; 1970 film) 183

"F —–" (aka "The Foodlegger") 201
F Troop 57
Face Off (Matheson script) 242–4
Faces (1968) 195
Faces of Fear 6, 118
Facing the Flag 89
"The Facts in the Case of Mr. Valdemar" (1990 film segment) 112
"The Facts in the Case of M. Valdemar" (story) 101, 105
Fade-Out 270
Fagen, Herb 18
Fagerbakke, Bill 242
Faggard, Jack 219
Fahey, Myrna 78, **82**, 83
Fair Film (production company) 146
Falcon, André 197–8
Falconer, John 131
The Fall of the House of Usher (1960 film) see *House of Usher* (1960 film)
"The Fall of the House of Usher" (story) 78–9, 82–3
Falsey, John 75
The Family see *Città Violenta*
Family Guy 155
Family Plot 203
Famous Ghost Stories 60
Famous Monsters of Filmland 116
Fanatic (aka *Die! Die! My Darling!*) 117, 123–6, **125**
Fangoria 5, 7, 9, 106, 109
Fantastic (magazine) 77, 199
The Fantastic Little Girl 16, 21, 231
The Fantastic Shrinking Girl see *The Fantastic Little Girl*
Fantastic Story Magazine 42, 201
Fantastic Universe 118
Fantastic Voyage (film) 151, 236
Farber, Stephen 233, 235, 254
Faria, Guy 228
Farley, Chris 155
Farrington, Floyd 14

Faster and Furiouser: The Revised and Fattened Fable of American International Pictures 80, 87, 93, 100, 116, 145
Father Goose, His Book 247
"The Father Thing" 250
Faulkner, Edward 162
Faulkner, James 212–3
Faver, Hank 37
FBI 176, 185, 243
Fear (Hubbard novel) 271
Fearing the Dark: The Val Lewton Career 98
The Fearmakers (book) 117
Feinberg, Ron 185
Fell, Norman 127, 129
Femme Fatales 21, 182, 191, 246, 250
Fengriffen 193
Fennell, Albert 94, 96, 98, 101, 177, 182
Ferrara, Abel 254
Ferrigno, Lou 161
Fetherolf, Christopher John 262, 264
Ffrangcon-Davies, Gwen 131
Fictioneers 6, 9, 269
Fiddler on the Roof (film) 187
Field, Logan 27
Fielding, Elizabeth 27
Fields, W.C. 37, 54
The Fiend in You 41
Fifteen Detective Stories 185
Fifteen Western Tales 57
Filet of Sohl 155–6
Filho, Daniel 29
Film Writers Guide 269
Filmfax 7, 9, 18, 22–3, 27, 29, 33, 35–6, 39, 42–5, 47, 49, 51, 58–9, 61, 64, 67, 69, 72–3, 75, 77, 81, 83, 89–90, 92–4, 98, 100, 102, 107, 111, 114, 116, 118, 120, 122, 124, 139, 141–5, 151, 154, 157, 160–1, 164, 167–8, 170–2, 174, 183, 187, 203, 205, 207–10, 217, 220–1, 228, 230, 232–3, 235, 240, 242, 249–50, 269, 271
Films Corona 146
The Final Conflict 110
The Final Cut (film) 234
Finch, Jon 212, 215
Finch, Julie M. 262–3
Fincher, David 254
Finney, Elena 262, 264
Finney, Jack 173, 209, 211, 224–5, 228
Finochio, Madeline 47
"The Fire Balloons" 212, 215, 219
Firestone, Eddie 155
"First Anniversary" 76–7
Firsts: The Book Collector's Magazine 6, 196
Fisher, Terence 4, 130–1, 133–7, 191, 209
Fitzpatrick, Richard 249, 251
5 Against the House (film) 211
Five Easy Pieces (1970) 202
Five Gates to Hell 18
Five Guns West 80
Five Million Years to Earth see *Quatermass and the Pit*

Five Weeks in a Balloon (film) 201
The Flame and the Arrow 48
Flaming Star 92
Flanagan, Graeme 4, 50, 52, 54, 64, 155, 211
Flatliners 230
Flavin, James 37
Flaxy Martin 30
Fleet, Harry 37
Fleischer, Richard 168
Fleming, Ian 148
Fleming, Victor 246
Flesh and Flame see *Night of the Quarter Moon*
Flesh and the Spur 80
Un Flic (A Cop, 1972) 198
"Flight" 26–7; see also "The Last Flight"
Floating Dragon 177
Flores, Rosario 17
Florida 241
"A Flourish of Strumpets" 210
Flying Dutchman 42
Flying Through Hollywood By the Seat of My Pants 80, 143–5, 182
Flynn, Joe 69
Flynn, John L. 191
Foch, Nina 106
Focus on the Science Fiction Film 16, 151
Fonda, Henry 225
Fontaine, Joan 124
Food of the Gods (film) 182
"The Foodlegger" see "F —–"
For a Few Dollars More see *Per Qualche Dollari in Più*
For Men Only (magazine) 147
For Your Eyes Only (film) 148
Forbidden Land 269
Forbidden Planet 34, 42
The Forbidden Territory 132
The Force Is with You: Mystical Movie Messages That Inspire Our Lives 221
Ford, Harrison 218, 265
Ford, John 183
Forever Knight 250
"Forgotten Front" 61–2
Forrest, Irene 162, 164
Fort, Charles 201
Fort College 201
Fortress of Vincennes 142
Forty Carats (play) 98
Four Feathers (1939 film) 87
4 for Texas 147
Four Star Productions 52; see also Four Star Television
Four Star Television 54; see also Four Star Productions
Fox, Charles 185, 199, 201
Fox Network 5, 49, 150, 155, 176
Fragment of Fear (aka *Freelance*) 183
France 26, 61, 143, 146–7, 149, 197–8, 208, 221
Francis, Anne 233
Francis, Freddie 124, 135, 142
Francis, Ivor 170
Franco, Jesus (aka Jess) 112, 187
Frankel, Cyril 124
Frankenheimer, John 67, 171
Frankenstein (1973 film) 187

Frankenstein (novel) 174, 205
Frankenstein and the Monster from Hell 135
Frankenstein Must Be Destroyed 134–5
Frankenstein: The True Story 187, 221
Frankham, David 85, *86*, 87, **88**, 101, 105
Franklin, Pamela 177, *178*, 179, **181**, 182–3
Franz, Eduard 232
Fraser, Simon 184
Frazee, Skip 139
Free Spirit see *Maxie*
Free, White and 21 138
Free Willy 48
Freelance see *Fragment of Fear*
Frees, Paul 94
French, Lawrence 84–5, 91–2
French, Susan 219, 222
The French Connection (film) 243
French Revolution 142
The French Villa (aka *Nicole*) 208
"The Frenzied Weekend" 147
The Fresh Prince of Bel-Air 34
Freud, Sigmund 84
Frewer, Matt 77
Frid, Jonathan 162
Friedrich, Caspar David 256
Fries, Charles 218–9
"The Frigid Flame" 147
Frizzell, Lou 155, 158
Frobe, Gert 136
Frogs (film) 62
Frohman, Charles 222
From Here to Eternity (film) 130, 221
From Russia with Love (film) 147
From the Boys see *Cold Sweat* (1970 film)
From the Earth to the Moon (film) 62
From Time to Time 225
The Front Page (play) 165, 167
Frost, George 136, 212
Froug, William 22, 43, 54, 69, 74, 157
La Frusta e il Corpo (The Whip and the Body, aka *What*) 92
Frye, William ("Bill") 60
Fuca, Robert see Angelo, Robert
Fuest, Robert 182
The Fugitive (1993 film) 265
The Fugitive (series) 157
Fulci, Lucio 112
"The Funeral" (episode and story) 69–70
The Funeral (film) 254
Funicello, Annette 139
Fury on Sunday 6, 147, 197, 271
Futurama 49, 150
Futureworld 195

G&G Books 147
Gable, Clark 269
Gage, Leona 101, 104
Galaxy (pilot script) 50
Galaxy Science Fiction (magazine) 28–9, 50
Gale, Bob 76, 176
Gallagher, Thomas 67

Garcia, David 52
Garcia, Frank 39, 64, 69–70, 76–7
Garden State Film Festival 263
Gardena, California 119, 261
Gardens of Stone 254
Gardner, Tony 257
Garfield, James A. 225
Garner, Martin 232, 234
Garnett, Tay 126
Garr, Teri 98, 101
Garriguenc, Rene 43
Garris, Mick 74, 76, 244, 267
Gas-s-s-s!...or It May Become Necessary to Destroy the World in Order to Save It 112
Gastaldi, Ernesto 92
Gateway to Hell 132
Il Gattopardo (The Leopard; film) 198
Gault, William Campbell ("Bill") 6–7, 75, 197
Gauntlet Press 5, 29, 78, 93, 116, 118, 120, 157, 180, 183–4, 208, 221, 245, 253, 256, 261, 265, 270
Gausman, Russell A. 14
Gautier, Stephen B. 207
Gaynes, George 201, 203
Geib, Joe 249, 251
Gelfan, Regina see Carrol, Regina
General Electric Theater 29, 60
Genesis (Old Testament book) 125
George, Roger 192
Georgia (1994) 73
Georgy Girl 125
Gerber, David 50
German Corners, Pennsylvania 41
Germany 41, 127, 130, 141, 143–6, 148, 242, 254
Germinal (1963 film) 197
Gernsback, Hugo 9
Gershenson, Joseph 9, 17
Gertz, Irving 9
Gestalt Team 51
"The Get of Belial" 176
Ghost (1990) 257
The Ghost in the Invisible Bikini 107, 139
Ghost of Dragstrip Hollow 140
Ghost Story (1972–73 series) 71–2, *71*, 164
Ghost Story (novel) 177
The Ghostly Rental see *The Haunting of Hell House*
Giambalvo, Richard 262
Gibson, Henry 228–9
Gibson, William 268
Gielgud, John 218
Gigot 148
Gilbert, Kenneth 161
Gilbert, Philip 123
Gilborn, Steven 245, 247
Gilda 148
Gilligan's Island 17
Gilman, Sam 194
Giraldi, Jill 149, 151
Girard, Bernard 62
The Girl from U.N.C.L.E. 66–7, *66*, 125
"Girl of My Dreams" 68
Girls in Prison (1956) 80

Girls in the Night 10
Girls Town 18
Giving Up the Ghost 257
Glacier National Park, Montana 255
The Glass Web 10, 62
Glasser, Albert 17
Glatter, Lesli Linka 74
Gleeson, Redmond 201
A Global Affair 17
Globe Theatre (London) 87
Globe Theater (San Diego) 154
"The Glorious Gift of Molly Malloy" 28–9
Glover, John 228–9
Glowna, Vladim 212, 214
Glut, Donald F. 169, 188, 192
Glynne, Renée 126
The Godfather (film) 188
The Godfather Part II 14, 112
Godley, Anne 131
The Godson (1967) see *Le Samouraï*
Gold, Horace 50, 52
Gold Medal (publisher) 10, 118
Goldberg, Whoopi 257
Golden, Bob 162
Golden, Christopher 126
The Golden Blade 9
Golden Globe Award 156, 183, 247
Golden Spur Award 4
The Golden Voyage of Sinbad 207
Goldenberg, Billy 155, 228
GoldenEye 148
Goldfinger (film) 136
Goldsman, Akiva 265–6, 268
Goldsmith, David 270
Goldsmith, Jerry 34–5, 231–2, 236–7
Goldstein, Gary 270
Golitzen, Alexander 14
Gómez Martín, Mario 123
G.O.O. 140, 142
Good Neighbor Sam (film) 211
The Good, the Bad and the Ugly see *Il Buono, il Brutto, il Cattivo*
The Good Yeoman 257
Gooding, Cuba, Jr. 252, *253*, 254–5
Goodsell, Greg 139, 141
Goodson, Mark 54
Goodwins, Les 37
A Goofy Movie 5
Gordon, Bert I. 81, 182, 193
Gordon, Colin 94, 97
Gordon, Stuart 112
Gorgo 240
Gorton, Assheton 219
Gossett, Louis, Jr. 239–41, **241**
Gottlieb, Carl 239–40
Gottlieb, Theodore (aka Brother Theodore) 270
Gough, Michael 177, 183
Grabowski, Norman "Woo Woo" 18
Grade, Sir Lew 208
Grainer, Ron 149
Grammer, Kelsey 271
Grams, Martin, Jr. 26–7, 32, 34–5, 37, 39, 45, 74
Grand Central Station (New York) 243

Grand Hotel (Mackinac Island, Michigan) 220, 222, 227
"The Grandfather Clock" 22
Grandinetti, Darío 17
Granet, Bert 22, 42–5, 47, 74
Grant, Arthur 132
Grant, Barry Keith 231
Grant, Harry 239–40
Grant, Jessica Brooks 252, 255
The Grapes of Wrath (film) 71
Grasse, France 149
Grauman's Chinese Theatre (Los Angeles) 246
"The Grave" 44
Grave Secrets (1994 novel) 176
Graves, Peter 192–4, *193*
Graveside Story see *The Comedy of Terrors* (film)
"The Graveyard Rats" 249–51
Gray, Charles 131, 133, 135–7
The Great Escape (film) 147
Great Eyrie 87
The Great Gatsby (1974 film) 203
The Greatest Story Ever Told 151, 256
Greece 135
Green, Adam 262
Green, Larry 209–10
Green, Marc 233, 235
Green Hand (corporation) 51
Green Hand (literary circle) 3; *see also* The Group
"The Green Morning" 216
Green Park Hotel 120
Greenberg, Martin H. 26
Greene, Jim 170
Greene, Leon 131–2, *131*, 134–5
Greenspoon, Dr. Morton K. 155, 169
Greenstreet, Sydney 116
Gregg, Virginia 54, 162
Gregory, James 176
Gregory, Nigel 187
Greisman, Alan 242
Gremlins 235
Gresham's People 174
Greshler, Abbey 174
Grey, Joel 78
Grier, David Alan 242
Grieve, Russ 192
Griffith, Charles B. 80–1
Griggs, Loyal 129
Grimes Canyon, California 155
Grindhouse 184
Grisham, John 230
Grizzard, George 199–201
Grodin, Charles 228–9
Groening, Matt 49
Grosbard, Ulu 270
Gross, Edward 51, 266
The Group 22–3, 49–50, 58, 187; *see also* California Sorcerers; Green Hand (literary circle); Matheson Mafia; Southern California School of Writers
Growing Pains 5
Guest, Lucie 78
Guest, Val 120–1
"The Guests" 76
Gulliver's Travels (novel) 21
The Gun Fight 7, 269

The Gunfighter (1950) 57
Gunn, James 231
Gunslinger (1956 film) 80
Gunsmoke (series) 160
Guy-Blaché, Alice 89
Gypsy Wildcat 56

Haas, Charles 17–8, 21
Hable con Ella (Talk to Her) 17
Hackett, Joan 209–10
Hackett, John 101
Hackman, Gene 242–4, *243*
Hague, Albert 74
Haid, Charles 245–6
Haigh, Kenneth 26
Halbfinger, David M. 268
Hale, Barbara 52
Hale, Bernadette 63
Hall, Sam 212
Hallahan, Charles 232
Hallenbeck, Bruce G. 191
Hallenbeck, E. Darrell 67
Haller, Daniel ("Danny") 79, 89, 91–2, 109, 112, 136
Halliwell, Leslie 183
Halliwell's Film and Video Guide 20, 85, 89, 93, 100
Hallmark Hall of Fame productions 228
Halloween 39, 48, 140, 233, 249
Halloweentown 5
Halloweentown II: Kalabar's Revenge 5
Hamilton, Alana 208
Hamilton, Alexander 225
Hamilton, Frank 245, 247
Hamilton, George 207–8
Hamilton, Margaret 169–70, 172
Hamlet (play) 252–3
Hammer Films 3, 67–8, 72, 79, 98, 109, 117, 120–1, 123–6, 130–2, 134–7, 171, 179, 182, 190–2
Hammer Films: An Exhaustive Filmography 68, 134
Hammond, Nicholas 212, 214
Hancock, John D. 221
Hancock, Robert 262–3
Hand, Elizabeth 206
Hands of a Stranger 18
The Hands of Orlac (novel) 18
Hang 'Em High 31
Hangover Square (film) 36
Hansen, Danna 207
Happy Accidents 228
Hardy, Phil 85, 93, 100, 126, 136, 231
Harmetz, Aljean 106
Harmony, New York 37
Harris, Jean 270
Harris, Julie 179
Harris, Stacy 63
Harrison, Gregory 201, 203
Harrison, Joan 68
Harrison, Noel 66
Harrison, Richard 85
Harry and the Hendersons 229
Harry O 154
Harryhausen, Ray 143, 207, 221
Hart, Christine 209, 211
Hart, James V. 187
Hart, Susan 80, 181–2

Hart to Hart 126
Harvey, Richard 217
Haskett, Ed 47
Hatchet for the Honeymoon (aka *Il Rosso Segno della Follia*) 93
Hatfield, Hurd 188
The Haunted Palace 59, 79, 169
The Haunting (1963) 177, 179, 183, 245
The Haunting of Hell House 184
The Haunting of Hill House 177–8
The Haunting of Morella 112
The Haunting of Toby Jugg 134–5
The Haunting Passion 208
Hauser, Robert B. 61
Hauser's Memory (film) 150
Have Gun—Will Travel 49, 54–5, *55*
Havill, Adrian 226
Hawaii 173, 175
Hawaii Five-O 67
Hawks, Howard 248
Hawthorne, Nathaniel 120
Hayden, Sean 220, *220*, 223
Hayers, Sidney 94, 96, 98, 100
Hayes, Maggie 18
Hays Office 21
Hayward, Chuck 192
Hazel Court—Horror Queen 110
HBO 176, 271
He Is Legend (Rathbun & Flanagan) 6, 10, 61, 127, 147, 155, 161, 177, 211, 221, 226; *see also Richard Matheson: He Is Legend*
He Is Legend: An Anthology Celebrating Richard Matheson 29, 73, 98, 179, 198, 203, 206, 226, 231, 267
"He Who Kills" (film segment) 249–51
"He Who Kills" (1973 script) *see* "Amelia"
"The Healing Woman" 54
Hearn, Michael Patrick 245
Hecht-Hill-Lancaster 269
Hee Haw 20
Heffer, Richard 212–3
Heffron, Richard T. 194–6
Heider, Matt 262–3
Heisler, Stuart 57
Helgenberger, Marg 257
Hell House (graphic novel) *see Richard Matheson's Hell House*
Hell House (novel) 7, 78, 146, 177–81, 183–4, 253
Hell in the Pacific 45
Hell Raiders 137
Hellblazer (comic-book series) 266
Hellman, Monte 112
Helm, Annie 74
Helmore, Tom 10
Helton, Percy 41
Hemingway, Ernest 45
Henerson, James 228
Hennesy, Tom 59
Henreid, Monika 149
Henriksen, Lance 176
Henry V (1944 film) 87
Herbert, Tim 155, 158
"Here There Be Tygers" (story) 24
Herlinger, Karl 199

Herman, Norman T. 177, 182
The Heroes (1968) see *The Invincible Six*
Heron, Blake 249, 251
Herrmann, Bernard 26, 38–9
Herzog, Werner 256
Hess, David 148
Hessler, Gordon 143, 176, 207–8
Heston, Charlton 149–52, **150**, **152**, 154, 268
Heyes, Douglas 27–8, 34–5, 38, 70, 225
Heyman, David 265
Heyward, Louis M. ("Deke") 120, 141, 143–4
Hickenlooper, George 120
Hickok, Wild Bill 7, 56, 227
Hickox, S. Bryan 248
Hicks, Chuck 44, 170
Hidden Hills Players 225
Hiestand, John 9
High Noon 57
High School Confidential! 18, 21, 62
Highsmith, Patricia 198
Hill, Arthur 54
Hill, Jack 112
Hill, James 89
Hill, Joe 161
Hill, Robert 21
Hill Street Blues 176
Hills, Beverly 112, 114
Hinds, Anthony ("Tony") 121, 123–4, 126, 133, 136
Hirschman, Herbert ("Herb") 22, 41–3
His Girl Friday 248
Histoires Extraordinaires (Extraordinary Stories, aka *Spirits of the Dead*; 1968 film) 198
Hitchcock, Alfred 38, 62–4, 72, 76, 126, 157–8, 185, 201, 222, 250
Hitler, Adolf 242–3
"Hits & Misses" (*TV Guide* column) 228
Hitzig, Rupert 239
Hodge, Jim 162
Hodgson, Brian 177, 179
Hofflund, Judy 257
Hoffman, Barry 29, 245
Hoffman, Basil 73
Hoffman, Roswell A. 9, 13
Hogan, Jack 52, 61
Hogan, Robert 43
Holden, Jan 68
Holden, Laurie 212, 217
Holden, Stephen 206
Holdridge, Lee 245
"The Holiday Man" 50
Holocaust 167
Hollywood Hills, California 83
Hollywood Walk of Fame 226
Holmes, Luree 112
Holt, Seth 124
"Home Is the Brave" 56–7
"Homecoming" (episode) 57
"The Homega Man" 155
"Homer³⁼ⁱⁿ⁼" 39
Hong Kong 141
Honolulu, Hawaii 175
Hooper, Tobe 75, 77–8

"Hop-Frog" 79
Hope, Bob 17
Hopkins, Anthony 188
Hopper, Dennis 64, 79, 202
Horger, Emory 56
Horner, Penelope 187, 189
Horror: A Connoisseur's Guide to Literature and Film 205–6
The Horror at 37,000 Feet 48
Horror Hotel see *The City of the Dead*
Horror of Dracula see *Dracula* (1958 film)
The Horror of It All 210
The Horror People 156, 183–4
Horse Feathers 37
Hotel del Coronado see Coronado Hotel
Hough, John 177, 181–3, 210
Houghton, Buck 22, 26–9, 31–9, 42–3
"The House" see "Young Man's Fancy"
House of Dark Shadows 164
House of Fright see *The Two Faces of Dr. Jekyll*
House of Numbers (film) 211
House of Terror 250
House of the Dead (unfinished novel) 90, 93–4
House of Usher (1960 film) 78–85, **80**, **82**, 89–90, 92–3, 104, 108, 146
The House of Usher (1988 film) 112
House of Wax (1953) 79
House on Haunted Hill (1958) 79, 169
The House That Hammer Built 126
The House That Dripped Blood 102
Houston, Whitney 208
Hover, Robert 194–5
How Green Was My Valley (film) 183
How I Made a Hundred Movies in Hollywood and Never Lost a Dime 79, 83, 111
How to Stuff a Wild Bikini 37
How to Write Tales of Horror, Fantasy and Science Fiction 5
Howard, Clint 77
Howard, Hath 47
Howard, James Newton 257, 265
Howard, John 56
Howard, Robert E. 61
Howard, Ron 79
Howard Award see World Fantasy ("Howard") Award
The Howling (film) 235, 238
The Howling Man (collection) 23; see also *Selected Stories* (Beaumont)
Hoyt, John 53
Hubbard, L. Ron 271
Hudson, Rock 212–3, **213**, 217–8
Huggett, Richard 131
Hugo Award 4, 9, 217
Hull, Henry 4, 85, **86**, 87, **88**
Hume, Alan 179, 183
The Hunchback of Notre Dame (1923 film) 159
The Hunchback of Notre Dame (1939 film) 94

Hungary 189–90
The Hunger and Other Stories 23
Hunger and Thirst 7, 199
Hunnicutt, Gayle 177, **178**, 179, **181**, 183, 212, 215–6
Hunt, Marsha 43
Hunted Past Reason 7, 271
Hunter (proposed series) 51
"The Hunter" (story) 192–4
Hunter, Evan 64
Hunter, John 135
Hurd, Gale Anne 79
Hurley, Karen 209, 211
Hush ... Hush, Sweet Charlotte 124
Huston, John 141–4
Hutton, Jim 27–8
Hyde-White, Alex 242
Hyland, Diana 43
Hynek, Joel 257
Hysteria 124

I Am Legend (graphic novel) 123, 184, 267
I Am Legend (1967 film) see *Soy Leyenda*
I Am Legend (novel) 5–7, 10, 118, 120–4, 149–52, 154, 187, 189, 250, 264–8
I Am Legend (2007 film) 264–9, **266**
I Am Legend: Awakening (comic book) 267
"I Am Legend, Too" 267
I Am Omega 269
"I Dated a Robot" 49
I Dream of Jeannie 201
"I Kiss Your Shadow" 61
I Know What You Did Last Summer (film) 260
I Promised to Pay see *Payroll*
I, Robot (book and film) 266
"I Sing the Body Electric!" (story) 24, 38
I, the Jury (1953 and 1982 films) 195
I Walked with a Zombie 45, 100
I Was a Teenage Werewolf 79
I Will Fight No More Forever 195
I Wish It Could Be Christmas Forever 227
Ice Station Zebra (film) 63
Icy Breasts (*Les Seins de Glace*) 197–9
Idelson, William ("Bill") 22, 26, 31
IDW Publishing 184, 262
If (magazine) 139
Ikarie XB 1 29
Il Était une Fois un Flic (There Was Once a Cop) 198
"I'll Make It Look Good" 61
Illinois 195, 212, 214; see also Chicago, Illinois
Illustrated Gazette 67
The Illustrated Man 183, 212–3, 215, 218
Image Entertainment 96
Imagi-Movies 206
Imagination (magazine) 118
IMDb (Internet Movie Database) 112, 138, 148, 207, 239
The Immortal (series) 148
Implosion 141

O Impossível Acontece 29
In Harm's Way (film) 129
"In His Image" 201
In the Line of Fire 218
"In the Nick of Time" *see* "Nick of Time"
In the Year 2889 137, 139
The Incredible Hulk (TV series) 70, 161
The Incredible Shrinking Man (film) 3, 9–17, *11*, *13*, 18, 20–1, 49, 52, 80, 184, 229–31, 235, 269
The Incredible Shrinking Teacher 17
The Incredible Shrinking Woman 16, 228–31, 234
Incubus (novel and film) 210
Independent Artists 94–6, 98
Indian Dunes, California 233
"The Indian Spirit Guide" 68
Industrial Revolution 225
Inglis, Raul 234
Inner Sanctum (1948 film) 94
Inner Sanctum (proposed series) *see Dead of Night* (proposed series)
Inner Sanctum mysteries 94
Innerspace 235
The Innocent and the Damned see Girls Town
The Innocents 96, 182
Inquisition 89
INSITE (The International Network of *Somewhere in Time* Enthusiasts) 220, 223, 226
INSITE (journal) 220, 227–8
International Network of *Somewhere in Time* Enthusiasts *see* INSITE
Internet 72, 112, 138, 148, 207, 239, 264
Internet Movie Database *see* IMDb
Into The Twilight Zone: The Rod Serling Programme Guide 233–4, 249
USS *Intrepid* 268
The Intruder (novel) 23
"The Invaders" (episode) 28, 34–5, 38, 48, 236
The Invaders (1967–68 series) 174
Invasion of the Body Snatchers (1956) 238
Invasion of the Saucer Men 137
The Invincible Six (aka *The Heroes*; 1968) 269
Iraq 261
Ireland 141, 209
Ireland, Jill 146, 148–9
"Iron Mike Benedict" 53
Irvin, Tom 249
Irving, Amy 248
Irving, Richard 52
Irwin, William 207
The Island of Dr. Moreau (1977 film) 48
The Island of Dr. Moreau (novel) 199
Island of the Animals 199
"An Island Unto Himself" 29
Israel, Lee 125
It (miniseries) 246
It Came from Hunger! Tales of a Cinema Schlockmeister 138, 140–1
It Came from Outer Space 10

It Came from Weaver Five 16, 84, 109
It Conquered the World 80, 137, 193
It Takes Two 5
It! The Terror from Beyond Space 236
Italy 92, 122, 141, 146–7, 197
It's a Gift 37
"It's a Good Life" 232–7, *236*
It's a Wonderful Life 28
It's Alive (1974 film) 138
"*It's Alive!*" (1969 film) 137–42, 185
"It's Still a Good Life" 237
Ivins, Perry 54

Jack the Ripper 166, 171
Jackson, Shirley 177, 179, 184
Jacob's Ladder 144
Jaffe, Sam 72
Jakob, Dennis 112
Jalbert, Pierre 61
Jamaica 96–7
James, Henry 96, 179, 184
James Bond (film series) 50, 132, 136, 147–8, 219, 221, 226
Jameson, Joyce 101, 104, *105*, 112–3, 117
Jamieson, Parker 271
Jane Eyre (1944 film) 34
"The Janitor Had Three Eyes" 52
Janssen, David 52
Japan 141
Jarrott, Charles 187
Jaws (film) 159, 179, 232, 240
Jaws (novel) 158, 239
Jaws the Revenge 241
Jaws III see Jaws 3-D
Jaws 3-D (aka *Jaws III*) 239–41, *241*
Jaws 2 (film) 221–2, 240–1
Jeepers Creepers 161
Jefferson, Thomas 225
Jefferson and Hamilton 225
Jenney, Lucinda 252
Jensen, Paul M. 135
Jerome, Jim 79
The Jerry Springer Show 254
Jewel of the Seven Stars 149
Jillian, Ann 41
Jim Junior 107
Jimenez, Neal 265
Joanou, Phil 74
John Harvey & Sons, Ltd. 104
Johnson, Brad 56
Johnson, Doug 194
Johnson, George Clayton 1, 3, 6, 22, 27, 45, 50–1, 201, 217–9, 232–3, 235
Johnson, John Calvin 170
Johnson, Kenneth 161
Johnson, Lamont 38–9
Johnson, Michelle 77
Johnson, Ted 167
Johnson, Tom 67, 134, 136–7
Johnson, William 16
Johnston, John Dennis 232, *237*
Johnston, Margaret 94, 97, 101
Jones, Alan 250
Jones, D.F. 141, 181
Jones, Gordon 85
Jones, Hank 127, *127–8*, 130

Jones, James Earl 248–9
Jones, Morgan 127
Josephs, Wilfred 123
Jour de Fureur see *Fury on Sunday*
Jourdan, Louis 188
Journal of the Gun Years 7, 116, 120, 270
Journey into Fear (film) 34
Journey to the Center of the Earth (novel and 1959 film) 39
Journey to the Unknown 67–8
"The Joust" 54
The Joy Luck Club (film) 254
Joy Ride 161
Joyce, Yootha 123–4
Jules Dracula 263
"Julie" 201, 203
Julienne, Rémy 148
"The Jungle" (episode) 26
Jungle Fever 254
Jurassic Park (film) 234, 258
Jurassic Park (novel) 158, 234
Justice (magazine) 147
Justman, Robert ("Bob") 65

Kafka, Franz 63
Kamen, Michael 252, 256
Kansas City 199
The Kansas City Massacre 174
Kaplan, Jonathan 79
Karen Black Like Me 206
Karig, Walter 210
Karlen, John 201, 203
Karloff, Boris 59, 70, 107, *108*, 110–2, *110*, *113*, 114, 116–7, 138–9
Kartalian, Buck 127
The Kate Smith Hour 171
Kaufmann, Maurice 123–4
Kay, Gordon 127–8
Keaton, Buster 35, 37, 39
Keir, Andrew 67
Keleghan, Peter 249, 251
Kelley, Deforest 64
Kelly, Gene 116, 148
Kelly, Jack 64
Kelly, Richard 73–4
Kelman, Rickey 35–6
Kelsey, David 228
Kemmer, Edward 47
Kemmerling, Warren 58
Kennedy, John F. 45, 155–6
Kennedy, Kathleen 75
Kennedy, Robert F. 270
Kennelly, Norman 227
Kent, April 9, 12
The Kentucky Fried Movie 230
Kerr, John 89–90, 92–3
Kershner, Irvin 52–4
Keyes, Ed 14
Keys, Anthony Nelson *see* Nelson Keys, Anthony
Khalil, Ahmed 131
"Kick the Can" 232–5
Kiebach, Max 141–2
Kill, Baby ... Kill! see *Operazione Paura*
Killers from Space 193
Kilpatrick, Lincoln 149, 151
Kim, Daniel Dae 176
Kimble, Lawrence 52
King, Diana 123

King, Jacki 228
King, Stephen 4, 31, 61, 75–6, 118, 161, 177, 206, 246
King Kong (1976 film) 229–30
King Kong (1933 film) 240
King of Kings (1961) 213
King Tut 196–7
The Kingdom of Nemo 89
"King's Garbage Truck" (column) 5
Kingsbridge Armory (Bronx) 268
Kinsey, Wayne 126
Kirby, Brian 231, 269
Kirby, Randy 192
Kirk, Phyllis 32
Kirk, Tommy 137–9
Kirsch, Robert 3
Kirschner, David 245–8
Kiss Me Deadly (film) 169, 186
Kiss Me Kate (film) 32
"The Kiss of Blood" 67
Kiss of Death (1947) 251
Kitten with a Whip 28
Kjellin, Alf 63
Kleeb, Helen 54
Kleiser, Randal 26
Klemperer, Werner 69
Klugman, Jack 42–3, 64
Klute 152
Knapp, Charles 232, 238
Kneale, Nigel 239
Kneubuhl, John 53
Knight, Eddie 130, 136
Kobe, Gail 31
Koepp, David 257–61
Koetting, Christopher 100, 142–3, 207
Koko 177
The Kolchak Papers (aka *The Night Stalker*; novel) 162, 165–7, 169, 171–3
The Kolchak Tapes see *The Night Stalker* (film)
Kolchak: The Night Stalker (comic-book series) 176
Kolchak: The Night Stalker (TV series) see *The Night Stalker* (1974–75 series)
Kona (dog) 265, 267
Konow, David 21
Koontz, Dean 5
Korda, Zoltan 87
Korean War 148
Kornbluth, C.M. 70
Korty, John 208
Koslo, Paul 149–50, 242
Kozoll, Michael 176
Kroeker, Allan 237
Kronos (aka *Captain Kronos: Vampire Hunter*; 1974 film) 182
Krueger, Christiana 141
Krull 250
k2 Productions 262
Kubrick, Stanley 33, 142, 171
Kunard, Penny 194
Kuran, Peter 232
Kuttner, Henry 249–51

La Barba, Joe 9
La Cava, Lou 101
Lacey, Laara 69
La Coste (chateau) 142

"The Lady in Red" (song) 36
Lady in White 271
"The Lady on the Wall" 54
The Lady Takes a Flyer 10
The Lady Vanishes (1938) 185
Laird, Jack 69, 210
LaLoggia, Frank 271
Lamb, Gil 37
Lamden, Derek 212, 215
Lancaster, Burt 48, 269
Lancer Books 93, 106, 117
Lanchester, Elsa 138
Landau, Martin 112
Landers, Lew 107
Landis, John 230–4, 244
Landor, Rosalyn 131–2
Landry, Christopher 217–9
Lane, Abbe 232
"Lane Change" 74
Laneuville, Eric 149–50, *152*
Lang, Fritz 45, 120
Langton, Paul 9, 12
Lanin, Jay 62
Lansdale, Joe R. 206
Lantz, Francess 5
Lanzarote, Canary Islands 216
Lao-Tzu 15
Laramie, Wyoming 56
Laredo 193
La Roche, Mary 32
Larroquette, John 232–3
Larson, Randall 133
Las Vegas, Nevada 161–2, 164–8, 172, 176
Lassell, John 52
Lassie Come Home (film) 183
Lassiter, James 265
"The Last Flight" 26–7, 53
"The Last Hour of John Butler Hickok" 56
The Last House on the Left (1972 film) 148
The Last Man on Earth (*L'Ultimo Uomo della Terra*) 111, 117–23, *117, 119, 121*, 149, 151–2, 265
The Last Picture Show (film) 186
The Last Revolution 174
The Last Rites of Richard Keene 264
Last Summer at Mars Hill (collection) 206
The Last Voyage 143
Laszlo, Ernest 52
Late Night Horror 67, 211
Latham, Louise 185
Latigo Canyon, California 62, 149
Launer, S. John 27, 29
Laura (1944 film) 79
The Lathe of Heaven (1980 film) 217
Laugh-In 229
Lautner, Georges 197–9
Lava, William 37
Lavery, Emmet, Jr. 270
Lavin, Linda 194–5
Law, Jude 48
Law & Order 148
Lawman (series) 18, 35, 39, 50, 56–9, *58*, 77, 149, 187
Lawrence, Francis 265–6, 268
Lawrence, Marc 9
Lawson, Sarah 131–3, *134*, 135
"Lazarus II" 201

Le, Myca Dinh 233
Leachman, Cloris 185–6, 237
Leacock, Philip 185
LeBorg, Reginald 94
Lee, Christopher 131–7, *131, 134*, 191, 207
Lee, Elsie 117
Lee, Patrick 73
Lee, Spike 101, 254
The Leech Woman 13, 17
The Legacy (1978 film) 132
The Legend of Hell House 78, 177–84, *178, 181*, 210
Legion of Decency 21
"Legion of Plotters" 262
Leiber, Fritz, Jr. 70, 94, 97, 100
Leiber, Fritz, Sr. 94
Leicester, William F. 117–8, 120, 123
Leigh, Jennifer Jason 228
Leinster, Murray 72
Lem, Stanislaw 214
Lemmo, Joan 209
Lenehan, Nancy 245–6
Lennon, John 195
Leonard, Hugh 67
Leonard, Nancy Hahn 207
Leonard Maltin's Movie Guide 17, 85, 89, 93, 100, 183, 242
Leonard Maltin's TV Movies 127, 185, 205, 208
Leone, Sergio 14, 123, 147–8
The Leopard see *Il Gattopardo*
The Leopard Man 45
LeRoy, Gloria 207
Lesnie, Andrew 268
Lester, Seeleg 76
Lethal Weapon (film series) 48, 242
Let's Do It Again (1953) 10
Let's Pretend 4
Levitt, Melanie E. 231
Levitt, Ruby R. 14
Levka, Uta 141
LeVouvier, Jean 209
Lewis, Al 170
Lewis, Alfred 270
Lewis, Fiona 187, 189–90, *189*
Lewis, Geoffrey 249, 251
Lewis, Ira 242
Lewis, Jerry Lee 18
Lewis, Lisa 257, 259
Lewis, Richard 77
Lewton, Val 45–6, 98, 169, 177
Leyland, Crash 234
Licht, Jeremy 232, 236, *236*
Die Liebesabenteuer des Marquis S see *De Sade* (film)
Lifeboat 126
Lifetime (network) 257
"Ligeia" 103
Lights Out 27
"The Likeness of Julie" 201, 203
Lilies of the Field 32
Lindley, Barbara 187, 190
Linington, Elizabeth see Blaisdell, Anne
The Link 270
Linke, Paul 245, 247
Linville, Larry 162, 164, 176
The Lion in Winter (1968 film) 226
Lionsgate Entertainment 262

Lippert, Robert L. 117, 120–3
Lira (production company) 197
Lithgow, John 48, 74, 76, 232, *237*, 238
"Little Girl Lost" 24, 38–41, *40*, 48
"Little Green Men" 176
"Little Jack Cornered" 57
The Little Shop of Horrors (1960 film) 80–1, 111
Little Shoppe of Horrors (magazine) 136
Live and Let Die (film) 221
The Lively Set 10
"Living Doll" (episode) 206
Lloyd, Norman 62
Locke, John 103
Lockwood, Alexander 155
"The Locusts" 215
The Lodger (1944 film) 36, 171
Lofficier, Jean-Marc and Randy 233, 249
Loftin, Carey 155, 158
Logan, Bruce 228
Logan, John 265
Logan Square (Chicago) 259
Logan's Run (novel and film) 203, 217
Logan's Run (series) 148, 203
London, Frank 44
London, William, Jr. 162
"Long Distance Call" (aka "Sorry, Right Number"; Matheson story) 26, 45–6
"Long Distance Call" (Beaumont & Idelson episode) 26
"Long Distance Call" (Matheson script) *see* "Night Call"
Long Island, New York 6, 10
"Long Live Walter Jameson" 238
"The Long Years" 216–7, 219
Longdon, Terence 212, 216
The Longest Day (film) 130
Looney Tunes (comic book series) 49
The Looney Zone 49
Looped 126
Loose Cannons 5, 242–5, *243*
Lord, Jack 67
Lord Dunsany 174
The Lord of the Rings: The Fellowship of the Ring (film) 268
Lorimar Television 201, 244, 270
Lorre, Peter 51–2, 101, *103*, 104, 106–7, *108*, 109–14, 116, 138
Los Angeles, California 3, 6, 9, 62, 68, 93, 119, 122, 149–50, 152, 156, 159, 176, 184, 192, 195, 223, 234, 246, 260, 268
The Los Angeles Times 3, 93, 156, 226, 268
The Lost Boys 48, 230
The Lost Continent (1968) 134
Lost in Space (series) 148
The Lost Missile 236
Lost Moon 258
The Lost Weekend (film) 195–6
The Lost Work of Stephen King 5
The Lost World (novels and series) 234

The Lost World: Jurassic Park 234, 258
Loughram, Derek 245–6
Louis Armstrong and His All-Stars 18
The Love Letter (film) 228
"The Love Letter" (story) 209
Lovecraft, H.P. 24, 59, 70, 79, 112, 171, 236
Lovell, Jim 258
"Lover When You're Near Me" 50
Lowe, Rob 230, 261
Lowndes, Jessica 78
Lucas, George 12
Lucas, John Meredyth 69
Lucas, Tim 92, 122
Lucasfilm 270
Lucisano, Fulvio 141, 143
"The Luggage Store" 215
Lugosi, Bela 187
Lumet, Sidney 175
Lupino, Ida 54, *55*
Lurie, Hunter 264
Lurie, Rod 264
Lusitania 222
Lye, Reg 187, 190
Lyndon, Barré 171
Lynley, Carol 162, 164
Lynn, Betty 53
Lyons, Robert F. 207
Lytton Center Theatre 100

Mac, Bernie 49
Macadams, Annabelle 137–9
MacArthur, Gen. Douglas 205
Macaulay, Charles 69
MacCorkindale, Simon 239–40
MacDonald, John D. 4
MacDonald, Prof. Leon
MacDonald, Philip 27
MacDonald, Tom 262
Machete (faux trailer) 184
Machiavelli, Nicoletta 197
Machine-Gun Kelly 87
Mack, Kevin Scott 257
Mackinac Island, Michigan 222
Maclay, John 198
MacLeish, Archibald 258
Macnee, Patrick 209, 211–2, 217
Macy, William H. 220, 225
Mad About You 32
"Mad House" 77, 201
The Mad Magician 36
Mad Max (film series) 161
Maffeo, Neil T. 199, 201
The Magazine of Fantasy and Science Fiction 3, 23, 27–8, 44, 50, 68–9, 72–3, 118, 201, 264
The Magic Land see The Wonderful Wizard of Oz
"Magic Saturday" 75
Magician's Choice 33, 61, 227
Magne, Michel 146, 148
The Magnificent Ambersons (film) 34
The Magnificent Seven (film) 54, 147
Magnum Force 31
Mahler, Gustav 226–7
Maibaum, Richard 50
Mailles, Roger 147
Main Street to Broadway 126

Maine 5, 46
The Maine Campus (newspaper) 5
Maître du Mond (Master of the World; novel) 85, 87, 89
Majestic Studios 206
"Make Me Laugh" 70
Malcolm in the Middle 186
Malibu, California 20
Malick, Terrence 130
Malta 216
The Maltese Falcon (1941 film) 169
Maltin, Leonard 129
A Man Called Horse 44
"A Man Called Ragan" 56
A Man for All Seasons (1965 film) 219
The Man from Atlantis 148
The Man from Bitter Ridge 10, 16
Man from God's Country 17
The Man from U.N.C.L.E. 66–7
The Man in Half Moon Street (play and film) 171
Man in the Shadow 18
Man of Steel: The Career and Courage of Christopher Reeve 226
"The Man Trap" 50
The Man Who Could Cheat Death 109, 171
The Man Who Could Work Miracles 3
The Man with the Golden Arm (film) 21
The Man with Two Shadows see Cold Sweat (1970 film)
The Manchurian Candidate (1962 film) 67
Mancini, Henry 9, 15
Manders, Stanley 265
Manet, Edouard 256
The Mangler (film) 75
Maniac (1963) 124
Mankofsky, Isidore 223–4
Mantell, Joe 44
Manvell, Roger 269
Manza, Ralph 53
March, Lori 29–30
Marcus, Mitch 184
Marcus Welby, M.D.
Marcy Avenue Armory (Brooklyn) 268
Margheriti, Antonio (aka Anthony M. Dawson) 123
Margulies, Stan 194
Marihugh, Tammy 42
Marineland, California 89
Marinker, Peter 212
Mario Bava: All the Colors of the Dark 92–3
The Mark of Zorro (1940 film) 116
Markham 53
Markle, Fletcher 60
Markowitz, Robert 248–9
Marks, Julian 249
Marley, John 56, 176
Marlowe, Nora 45
Maross, Joe 29–30
Marquand, Richard 132
Marquis de Sade *see* De Sade, Louis Alphonse Donatien
The Marquis de Sade see De Sade (film)

Married ... with Children 150
"Mars Is Heaven" (aka "The Third Expedition"; story) 42, 214
Mars Needs Women 139
Marshall, Frank 235
Marshall, Helene 9
Marshall, Herbert 39
Marshall, Sarah 38–9
Marta, Jack A. 156
Martell, Donna 56
"The Martian" 215
The Martian Chronicles (book and miniseries) 42, 212–9, *213–4*
"The Martians" 215, 219
Martin, Bruno 147
Martin, Homer 256
Martin, Lock 9, 12
Martin, Ross 42, 185
Martínez, Fele 17
Martinson, Leslie H. 56
Marvel Science Fiction 201
Marvin, Lee 44–5
Marx Brothers 37
The Mary Tyler Moore Show 186
Maryland 267
Masada (miniseries) 150
La Maschera del Demonio (Mask of the Demon) see *Black Sunday* (1960)
M*A*S*H (series) 164
Masi, Victor 162
Masino, Steve 85
Mask of the Demon see *Black Sunday* (1960)
Maslin, Janet 261
Mason, Buddy 112, 114
Mason, James 146–9
Masque of the Red Death (1989 and 1990 films) 112
The Masque of the Red Death (1964 film) 79, 107, 109, 141
"The Masque of the Red Death" (story) 89
Masques 50
Masques II 264
Mass Illusions (effects company) 252, 255
Massey, Anna 141–3
Master of the World (film) 85–9, *86, 88*, 105, 111, 147, 208
Master of the World (novel) see *Maître du Mond*
Masters, Todd 252
Masters of Horror 77–8
Matheson, Alison Marie ("Ali") 5, 25, 74, 76–7, 220, 225, 253
Matheson, Bertolf 31, 196
Matheson, Bettina Louise ("Tina") 6, 10, 25, 39, 253
Matheson, Christian Logan ("Chris") 5, 25, 253
Matheson, Fanny 4, 31, 61, 196
Matheson, Gladys 196
Matheson, Murray 232, 234
Matheson, Richard Christian ("R.C.") 5–6, 25, 28, 70, 74–5, 77–8, 206, 242–5, 253, 267, 269
Matheson, Robert 6, 196
Matheson, Ruth Ann 33–4, 39, 61, 93, 199, 247, 253; *see also* Ruth Ann Woodson

Matheson Mafia 3; *see also* The Group
Matheson Uncollected: Volume One 65, 210
Matheson Uncollected: Volume Two 93, 147, 201, 256
"The Matheson Years" 3
Mathews, Kerwin 212
Mathison, Melissa 232, 235
The Matrix 268
Mattei, Giuseppe 118, 122
Maurer, Lisa 239
Max Headroom (1987–88 series) 77
Maxie (aka *Free Spirit*) 211
Maximum Overdrive 161
Maxwell, Frank 31
Mayerling 147
Maynard, Kansas 44
Maynor, Asa 47
MCA Home Video 160
McCalla, Irish 18
McCalman, Macon 207
McCarey, Leo 10
McCarthy, Andrew 230
McCarthy, Joseph 59, 176
McCarthy, Kevin 232, 236, 238
McCarthy, Maggie 252
McCartney, Paul 195
McCarty, John 117, 238
McCauley, Kirby 245
McClanahan, Rue 245–7
McCloud 160
McClure, Tipp 44
McCord, Bob 33, 37, 44, 47
McCord, Kent *see* McWhirter, Kent
McCourt, Malachy 248
McCracken, Michael 232
McCutcheon, Beryl 31, 47
McDonald, Ryan 78
McDougall, Donald 54
McDowall, Roddy 177, *178*, 179, 182–3, 212, 215–6, 219
McGarvin, Dick 209, 211
McGavin, Darren 162–3, *163*, 165–9, *165*, 171, *172*, 173, 175–6, 212, 214, 216
McGee, Henry 123
McGee, Mark Thomas 80–1, 87–8, 93, 100, 116, 145
McGee, Marty 49
McGill, Michael 76
McGowan, Oliver 27
McGrath, Doug 232
McGraw, Charles 162, 168
McGruther, Michael 262–4
McLean, Bill 170
McLeod, Norman Z. 37
McMahon, Whitey 14
McQueen, Steve 22, 49, 54, *54*
McRobbie, Peter 248
McWhirter, Kent (aka McCord) 127, 129
Mecacci, Piero 118
Mechele, Tony 67
Medak, Peter 73
Medford, Don 42–3
Mediums Rare 7, 270
Medusa (aka *Twisted*; 1974) 208
Meeker, Ralph 162, 164, 169
Megowan, Don 192

Mélodie en Sous-sol (aka *The Big Grab, Any Number Can Win*) 198
Meltzer, Lewis 17, 21
Melville, Jean-Pierre 198
Melvin Purvis, G-Man 174
The Memoirs of Wild Bill Hickok 7, 227, 271
Men in Black 5
Men, Makeup, and Monsters: Hollywood's Masters of Illusion and FX 230
The Men Who Made the Monsters 135
Menzies, Mary 89–90
The Mephisto Waltz (film) 72
Mercer, Ray 78, 85, 89, 101
Mercury Theatre 34
Meredith, Burgess 231–2
Merkerson, S. Epatha 242
Merritt, Abraham 94
Messina, Emilio 197–8
Metro-Goldwyn-Mayer *see* MGM
Metromedia Producers Corporation 209
Metty, Russell 150, 152
Mexico 63, 199
Meyers, Richard 230
Meyjes, Menno 76
MGM (Metro-Goldwyn-Mayer) 17–8, 30, 39, 42, 51, 89, 171, 213, 246, 256
MGM Home Entertainment 92, 111, 161
Michaels, Bill 170
Michaels, Victoria 220, 225
Michigan 222
Midnight Express (film) 73
Midnight Graffiti 12, 16, 25, 50, 58, 60–1, 63, 72, 86, 120, 166, 185, 187, 196, 201–2, 231, 265
"Midnight of the Century" 176
Midvale 244–5
The Midwich Cuckoos 200
Mihok, Dash 265, 267
Mike Hammer (1956–59 series) 165
Milland, Ray 10, 53, 101, 117, 171, 196
Millennium (series) 176
Miller, Denny *66*, 67
Miller, Dick 232
Miller, George 161, 232–3, 238
Miller, Mark A. 92, 111, 136–7
"Millicent and Therese" 201, 203, 207, 209
"The Million-Year Picnic" 216
Mills, Juliet 64
Mills, Mort 54
Mills, Richard 123
Mineo, Sal 269
Minton, Kevin 139
Miolans Prison 142
The Misadventures of Merlin Jones 139
The Misfits 269
"Miss Belle" 68
"Miss Stardust" 75, 77
Miss Tallulah Bankhead 125
"The Mission" (episode) 76
Mission: Impossible (film) 258
Mission: Impossible (series) 193
Mr. Sardonicus 210

Mr. Terrific 17
Mr. Wrong 5
Mitchell, Bill 94, 97
Mitchell, Thomas 251
Mitchum, Jim 18, 20
Mitchum, Robert 18
Modern Library 60
Moe, Marilyn 162
Mom and Dad Save the World 5
Moment of Fear 94
Monet, Claude 256
Monkey Business (1931) 37
The Monkey's Uncle 139
The Monolith Monsters 13
Monroe, Marilyn 139
Monster of Terror (aka *Die, Monster, Die*) 59, 79, 107
Monster on the Campus 17
"The Monsters Are Due on Maple Street" 168, 233
Montana 255
Montecito (production company) 245
Monteleone, Thomas F. 231
Monterey County, California 192–3
Montgomery, Lee Harcourt 209–10
Moody, Ralph 54
Mooney, Laura 232, 235
Moonjean, Hank 228
Moonlighting 5
Moonstone Comics 176
Moore, C.L. 250
Moore, Demi 230, 257
Moore, Harry 67
Moore, Mary Tyler 52
Moore, Ted 219
Moorehead, Agnes 34–5, 38
More Classics of the Horror Film 133
"Morella" 101, 103–4, 106, 112
Morgan, Brooke 262–3
Morgan, Nancy 245–7
Morgantown, Pennsylvania 87
Moriarty, P.H. 239
Moritz, Neal 265
The Morning After (novel and 1974 film) 7, 194–7
Morricone, Ennio 256, 264
Morris, Liz 239
Morris, Oswald 187
Morrison, Jenny 257, 259, **259**, 261
Morrow, Barry 254
Morrow, Vic 61, 232–3
Morse, Barry 212, 216, 219
Mort d'un Pourri (Death of a Corrupt Man) 198
Mosconi, Remo 147
Mossad 243–4
Mostow, Jonathan 186
"Mother by Protest" *see* "Trespass"
Mother Goose in Prose 247
Motion Picture Association of America (MPAA) 121
"Mountains of the Mind" 201
The Mouse That Roared (film) 17, 231
Moviecraft 52
Movieline 254
Mower, Patrick 131–2
Moxey, John Llewellyn 72, 98, 162–4, 169
MPAA *see* Motion Picture Association of America (MPAA)

MPI Home Video 190, 210
Mrs. Miniver (1942 film) 222
Mullally, Don 176
Mumy, Bill 232, 236–7
Mumy, Liliana 237
Munich, Germany 254
The Munsters 170
Murch, Walter 270
The Murders in the Rue Morgue (1971 film) 207
Murphy, Audie 17, 129–30
Murphy, Eddie 16
Murtagh, Kate 170, 173
Museum of Television & Radio (New York) 161
"Mute" 24, 41, 43, 59
My Ambition 262
My Fair Lady (film) 45
My Favorite Horror Story 203
Myers, Stanley 212, 217
Myrtle, Robert 262
Mysterious Island (1961 film) 68, 143
Mystery Scene 7, 243–4
Mystery Tales 147
Mystery Writers of America 162

Naked City (series) 22
Nalder, Reggie 59, **59**
The Name of the Game 52, 157
"The Naming of Names" 215
The Nanny (film) 124, 182
Nardella, Marie 249
Narizzano, Silvio 123, 125
The Narrow Margin (1952) 168
NASA 213
Nashville 203
Nashville, Tennessee 123
National Lampoon's Animal House 233
National Lampoon's Jaws 3, People 0 239
The Nature of Evil 245
The Navigator: A Medieval Odyssey 254
NBC-TV 42, 48, 52–4, 59, 62, 64, 66, 68–71, 74, 94, 129, 150, 160, 174, 187, 196, 207, 209–10, 212–4, 217–9, 225, 245, 271
Neame, Ronald 269
Necromancy 182
Needham, Hal 208
Needle in a Timestack 270
"Needle in the Heart" *see* "Therese"
Neel, Roy 14
Neill, Ve 228
Nelson, Judd 230
Nelson, Ralph 32, 198
Nelson Keys, Anthony ("Tony") 130, 136
Network 229
Nevada 161–2, 164–8, 172, 176, 220
"Never Give a Trucker an Even Break" 161
Never Take Sweets from a Stranger 135
The New Encyclopedia of Science Fiction 231
New England 82, 114, 125, 162
"The New House" 71–2, 164
New Jersey 4, 196, 263

New Orleans, Louisiana 154
"The New People" (episode) 68
New Stories from the Twilight Zone 26
New World Pictures 79
New York (city) 6–7, 9–10, 53, 100, 130, 138, 146, 161, 168, 170, 174, 177, 199, 206, 242–3, 246, 260–1, 266–8
New York (state) 4–5, 27, 30, 37, 52, 196; *see also* New York (city)
The New York Daily News 168
The New York Review of Science Fiction 7
The New York Times 100, 130, 206, 260–1, 266–8
The New York Times Book Review 177
The New Yorker 4
New Zealand 254
Newall, Basil 94
Newland, John 59–61
Newman, Laraine 75
Newman, Paul 41
Newport Beach, California 54
Newsom, Ted 182
Nicholls, Anthony 94, 97
Nicholson, Jack 79, 107–8, 111–2, 202
Nicholson, James H. ("Jim") 78–82, 84–5, 87, 101, 111–4, 116, 138, 140–1, 144–6, 181–3
Nicholson, Sylvia 181
Nice, France 147, 197
"Nick of Time" 27, 30, 33–4, 47, 59–60
Nickelodeon 5
Nicol, Alex 35–6, 38
Nicole see *The French Villa*
Nicotero, Greg 78
Nielsen Media Research 217
Night and the City (1950 film) 148
"Night Call" 24, 26, 45–7, 113
The Night Creatures (unproduced script) 120, 123, 267
Night Gallery 48, 60, 68–71, 150, 156–7, 173, 210, 221
The Night Killers 173, 175, 201
"Night Meeting" 216
Night of the Big Heat (film) 135
Night of the Demon (1958, aka *Curse of the Demon*) 45, 98
Night of the Eagle 50, 94–101, **95**, **96**, **99**, 181; *see also* Burn, Witch, Burn (film)
Night of the Lepus 26
Night of the Living Dead (1968) 118, 120, 123, 133
Night of the Quarter Moon 18
Night Shapes (collection) 175
Night Slaves 31
The Night Stalker (aka *Kolchak: The Night Stalker*; 1974–75 series) 54, 162, 170–1, 175–6
The Night Stalker (film) 77, 162–71, **163**, **165**, 173, 175–6, 187, 192, 203
The Night Stalker (novel) *see The Kolchak Papers*
The Night Stalker (2005 series) 162, 176

The Night Stalker Companion 164
Night Stalking: A 20th Anniversary Kolchak Companion 164, 166–9, 171, 176, 191
The Night Strangler (film) 61, 77, 162, 169–77, *172*, 187, 192, 252
The Night Strangler (novelization) 166, 172
Nightmare (1964 film) 124
Nightmare (novel) 123–4
"Nightmare as a Child" 236
"Nightmare at 20,000 Feet" (episode) 24, 46–9, 233, 238, 244
"Nightmare at 20,000 Feet" (film segment) 48, 232, *237*, 238
"Nightmare at 20,000 Feet" (story) 47, 232, 238
Nightmare Bloodbath see *Satan's Sadists*
"Nightmare of 20,000 Tweets" 49
A Nightmare on Elm Street (1984 film) 78
Nightmares and Dreamscapes (series) 206
Niles, Steve 123, 184, 267
Nimoy, Leonard 64, 70
1984 (1956 film) 217
1941 156
"Ninety Years Without Slumbering" 22
Niven, David 21
Nixon, Richard M. 187
No Name on the Bullet 17
"No Such Thing as a Vampire" 67, 209–11, 264
"No Trespassing" see "Private — Keep Out!"
Noir: Three Novels of Suspense 7, 56, 62–3, 100, 143, 147, 149, 197, 199–200, 208–9, 269, 271
Nolan, Dani (aka Danny Sue) 52
Nolan, Danny Sue see Nolan, Dani
Nolan, Jeanette 72
Nolan, Tom ("Tommy") 53, 127
Nolan, William F. 1, 3, 6, 33, 53, 173–5, 187, 196, 201, 203–4, 209–10, 217–8, 249–51
Norden, Joe 31
Norfolk, England 112
The Norliss Tapes 174, 187
Norma Rae 92
Norry, Marilyn 78
North Hollywood, California 25
Northern Exposure 75
Northern Lights Entertainment 244
Norwegian Merchant Marine 196
Nosferatu (1922) 59, 264
"Nothing in the Dark" 38, 45–6
Nonum 269
"Now Die in It" 147
Now Is Tomorrow 52–3
Now You See It... 7, 33
Numata, Joanna 265, 267
"Number Twelve Looks Just Like You" 187
Núñez Flores, Alfonso 123
Nurmi, Maila see Vampira

Oakland, Simon 162–3, 169, 176
Ober, Philip 43

The Oblong Box (film) 143, 207
Oboler, Arch 27
O'Brian, Hugh 62
"An Occurrence at Owl Creek Bridge" 69
"Of Death and Thirty Minutes" 57
O'Farrell, Conor 257, 259
Off Beat: Uncollected Stories 33
"The Off Season" 215
O'Hara, Shirley 155
The Oklahoma Woman 80
Okola, Ingrid 262
Oldfield, Richard 212–3
Oliver! (1968 film) 136
Olivier, Laurence 87
Olson, Jean 47
O'Malley, Kathleen 63
The Omega Man 149–55, *150*, *152*–*3*, 242, 249, 265, 268
The Omen (1976 film) 48, 245
Once a Thief (1965) 198
Once Around the Bloch 68
"Once Upon a Time" 35, 37–9, 168
Once Upon a Time in America 14
Once Upon a Time in the West see *C'era una Volta il West*
One Cut to Paradise 234
"One for the Book" 27
"One for the Books" (episode) 74–5, 223
"One for the Books" (story) 50, 74
"100 Greatest Moments in TV" 161
One Step Beyond 59
O'Neill, Dick 242
Onyx Cave 138
"An Open Letter to Robert Bloch" 157
Operation Fear see *Operazione Paura*
Operazione Paura (Operation Fear, aka *Kill, Baby...Kill!*) 123
Orange County, California 83
Orca 217
O'Rourke, Heather 39
Orwell, George 62
Oscar 10, 17, 30, 32, 45, 48, 52, 73, 79, 88, 129–30, 138, 176, 186–7, 201, 203, 219, 222, 257, 266, 268; see also Academy Award
Ossian's Ride 269
Othello (play) 154
The Other Side of Bonnie and Clyde 139
O'Toole, Annette 245–7
Our Gang (film series) 144
Our Mother's House (film) 182
Ousterhouse, Corveth 137–8
Out of Africa (film) 226
Out There 50
The Outer Limits (1963–1965) 76, 87
The Outer Limits (1995–2002) 76–7
The Outer Limits Companion 76
Outrageous Conduct: Art, Ego, and the Twilight Zone *Case* 233
Outré 7, 24, 212
Outside the Law 10, 12
The Overlook Film Encyclopedia: Horror 85, 93, 100, 106, 126, 136
The Overlook Film Encyclopedia: Science Fiction 85, 231

Overton, Frank 41
Owen, Meg Wynn 67
Owens, Grant 192, 201
Oxford University 241
Oz (book series) 7, 245–7
Ozarks 138

Pacific Coast Highway (California) 171
Pacific Palisades (California) Post Office 7
Paddock, Josh 252, 255
Padgett, Lewis (pseudonym) 250
Paganini, Niccolò 226
Paget, Debra 101, 105
Pajama Party 37, 139
Pakula, Alan J. 152
Pal, George 28, 174, 195, 201
Palance, Jack 33, 186–9, *189*, 191–2, 248–9
"Pale Rider" (teleplay) see "Spur of the Moment"
Pall, Gloria 27
Palm Springs, California 174
Palmdale, California 159
Palmer, Lilli 141–3
Palmer, Randy 81, 138, 140
Palmer, Robert ("Bob") 170, 207
Panama 14
Panic in Year Zero! 117
Paramount Pictures 17
Paramount Television 270
Paranoiac 124
Paratroop Command 208
Pardon Mon Affaire 197
Paris, Anatole 146
Paris, Marie-Madeleine 146
Paris, France 135
Park City Film Music Festival 263
Parker, Alan (composer) 239
Parker, Alan (director) 73
Parker, Albert 101
Parker, Warren 37
Parkins, Barbara 72
Parkyn, Leslie 96, 98, 100
Parry, Harvey 116
Parsons, William 37
Parton, Regina 170
"A Passage for Trumpet" 43
"Passage on the *Lady Anne*" 46, 201
Passen, Lisa 17
Passion Play 7
The Path: Metaphysics for the '90s 7
Pathé Lab 101–2
Paths of Glory (film) 171
Patriot Games (film) 218
"Pattern for Survival" 118
"Patterns" (episode) 22
Patterson, Hank 54
Paul, Lee 192
Paul Blaisdell, Monster Maker 138, 140
Paulsen, Albert 61
Payne, Willie 131–2
Payroll (aka *I Promised to Pay*) 98
Pearblossom, California 159
Pearson, Syd 123
Peck, Gregory 57, 238
Peckinpah, Sam 129
Peden, William H. 11
Penn, Christopher 64

Penn, Leo 64, 74–5
Penn, Sean 64, 75
Pennington, John 187
People magazine 93
Per Qualche Dollari in Più (For a
    Few Dollars More) 148
Pereira, Gilvan 29
Perito, Nick 227
Perkins, Anthony 93
Perkins, Jack 26
Perry Mason (1957–66 TV series) 52
Persoff, Nehemiah 199
"Person or Persons Unknown" 32
"Person to Person" 264
Peter Pan (play) 220, 222
Peters, Bernadette 212, 216, 219
Peters, Virginia 170
Petersen, Wolfgang 254
Peterson, Bob 44
Peterson, Cassandra *see* Elvira,
    Mistress of the Dark
Petrie, Daniel 269
Petrie, Howard 55
Petticoat Junction 129
Peyrelon, Michel 197
Peyser, John 127–9
Pfeiffer, Michelle 254
Pflug, Jo Ann 169–70, 192, **193**
The Phantom from 10,000 Leagues 80
*Phantom of the Circus see Circus of
    Horrors*
Phantom of the Opera (1943 film)
    94
Philip Marlowe (1959–60 TV series)
    7, 22, 49, 54, 193
Philippines 141, 233
Philips, Lee 199–201
Phillips, Fred B. 78, 85
Phillips, Julia 232
Phillips, Mark 39, 64, 69–70, 76,
    151, 154
Phillips, Michael 232, 264
Phyllis 186
Pick's Disease 25
Pico Boulevard (Los Angeles) 68
The Picture of Dorian Gray (1973
    film) 187, 190
Pierce, Maggie 101, 104, 106
Pierson, Jim 194, 209
"Pigeons from Hell" 61
Pillow Talk 174
"Pilot, Not the Pilot" 48
Pine, Howard 10
Pine, Robert 127, 129
Pinocchio in Africa 5
Pioneer Square (Seattle) 170
Piranha (1978) 235, 238
The Pirate Movie 116
Pirates 116
*Pirates of the Caribbean: The Curse
    of the Black Pearl* 116
Pirie, David 100, 126, 137
Pistilli, Luigi 146, 148
The Pit and the Pendulum (1913
    film) 89
Pit and the Pendulum (1961 film) 5,
    89–94, **91**, 101, 146, 251
The Pit and the Pendulum (1990
    film) 112
The Pit and the Pendulum (noveliza-
    tion) 93

"The Pit and the Pendulum" (story)
    89–90, 93
Pitlik, Norm 127
Pittack, Robert W. 28, 46
Pitts, Michael R. 148–9
Planet of the Apes (1968 film) 149
Planet of the Apes (series) 148
*Planet of the Vampires see Terrore
    nello Spazio*
Planet Terror 184
Platinum High School 21
Playboy 35, 67, 73, 76, 155–7, 184,
    204, 210
Playboy Press 209
Playhouse 90 32
Plein Soleil (aka *Purple Noon*) 198
Plotinus 15
Plummer, Christopher 219, 221,
    223
Pocket Books 172
Poe, Edgar Allan 5, 24, 78–9, 81–5,
    88–93, 101–4, 106, 112–4, 120,
    141, 143, 146, 198, 207, 239
Point Blank 45
Pointer, Priscilla 232
"Points Beyond" 211
Poitier, Sidney 32
Polák, Jindrich 29
Polanski, Roman 67, 72, 116, 169
Police Story (1973–78 series) 50
Polish Village (Chicago) 260
Pollack, Sydney 52
Polone, Gavin 257
Poltergeist (1982 film) 39–40, 75
PolyGram Filmed Entertainment
    252–3
Ponti, Carlo 72
POP Film & Animation 252, 255
The Poppy Is Also a Flower 148
Porky's 242
Porky's II: The Next Day 242
Porter, Don 194–5
Porter, Nyree Dawn 212, 216, 219
Post, Mike 194
Post, Ted 31–2
Potter, Luce 9
Powell, Dick 9, 16, 52
Powell, Eddie 131–2, 136
Powell, William 176
Power and Light 270
Powers, Stefanie 66, **66**, 123–6
Prague, Czechoslovakia 143
Pratt, Fletcher 27
Pravda, George 187
Pravda, Hanna-Maria 187
Praxis Film Works, Inc. 239
Premature Burial (film) 79, 84, 101–
    2, 109, 112–3, 210
"The Premature Burial" (story) 102
Preminger, Otto 21, 143
Presley, Elvis 92
Presnell, Don 49
"Prey" 5, 34–5, 201, 204–5, 209,
    249
Price, Vincent 78–9, **80**, 83–93,
    86, **88**, 101–2, **103**, 104–7, **105**,
    108, 109–14, **113**, 116, **117**, 118,
    119, 120, 122, 138, 207
Pride (collection) 245
Pride of the Yankees 222
"The Prime Mover" 23

The Prime of Miss Jean Brodie (film)
    182
A Primer of Reality 7
The Prince and the Pauper (1937
    film)
"Prince of Flowers" 206
"Private — Keep Out!" 27
The Private Life of Sherlock Holmes
    131
The Private Lives of Adam and Eve
    21
Private Parts in Public Places 142
Private Secretary 28
Private Stock Effects, Inc. 239
The Private World of Arthur Curtis 31
Problem Child 247
Problem Child 2 247
Produced and Directed by Dan Curtis
    194, 205, 209, 252
Production Code 121
The Professionals 45
Profondo Rosso (Deep Red) 93
Progeny of the Adder 166
Project Unlimited 87–8
Prosky, Robert 242
Protosevich, Mark 265, 267
Pryor, Nicholas 74
PSI (unproduced pilot script) 244
The Psychiatrist 157
Psycho (1960 film) 39, 54, 81, 124,
    157, 169
Psycho (novel) 157, 208
Public Parts in Private Places 142
Pullen-Shaw, Anthony 212, 214
Purple Noon see Plein Soleil
The Pursuit of Happyness 266
Putch, John 239–40
Pym, John 16
Pyott, Keith 131

Quaid, Dennis 239–40, **241**
"A Quality of Mercy" 233
"Quarry" 206
Quarry, Robert 52
Quatermass and the Pit (aka *Five
    Million Years to Earth*) 67
The Quatermass Xperiment (aka *The
    Creeping Unknown*; film) 120–1
Queen Elizabeth (ship) 120
Queen of Blood 64
"Queen of the Nile" 201
Quiet, Please! 27
Quillan, Eddie 170
Quincy M.E. 52
Quinlan, Kathleen 186, 232, 236,
    236
Quinn, Bill 232, 234

The "R" Project 174
Rabiger, Paul 186
Racconti di Fantascienza (Tales of
    Fantasy) 72
Race Against Time 64
Rachmaninoff, Sergei 226–7
Radio Bugs 144
Rafelson, Bob 202
The Raft (Trumbull) 270
Ragona, Ubaldo B. 117, 122
Raiders of the Lost Ark 84
Rain Man 254
Raine, Jack 43

Randall, Anne 170
Randall, Sue 27
Randall, Tony 174
Rank Organisation 92
Rastar (production company) 219–20, 223
The Rat Patrol 129
Rathbone, Basil 101, 105–7, 112, 114, 116–7, 138–9
Rathbun, Mark 4, 33, 50, 52, 54, 61, 64, 127, 147, 155, 195, 211, 221, 226
Rau, Umberto 118
The Raven (1935 film) 107
The Raven (1963 film) 81, 93, 102, 107–12, **108, 110**
The Raven (novelization) 81, 93, 107, 109
Rawhide (series) 31
Ray, Aldo 10
Ray, Nicholas 213
Ray, Rebecca 194
The Ray Bradbury Theater 24, 214–5, 217
Raybould, Harry 26
Raymond, Jim B. 194
Raymond Chandler in Hollywood 54
Razzie Award 240
Rea, Peggy 162
Read, Martin 187
Real Steel 45
Reardon, Craig 231, 245, 247
"Recalled" 203
The Red Baron (1971 film) see *Von Richthofen and Brown*
The Red Circle (1970) see *Le Cercle Rouge*
Red Planet Mars (film) 193
Red Sleep 244, 269
Red Sun 147–8
Red Sundown 10, 12
Redfearn, Linda 149
Redgrave, Lynn 187
Reed, Carol 96
Reed, Oliver 100
Reed, Walter 33–4
Reedall, Mark 212
Reel Conversations: Candid Interviews with Film's Foremost Directors and Critics 120
Reemes, Dana M. 14–5, 230
Reese, Jeff 209
Reeve, Christopher 219, **220**, 222, **223**, 224–6
Reeve, Dana 226
Reeves, Michael 143, 207
La Regina (production company) 117, 119, 121
Reichmann, Wolfgang 212, 215
Reid, Craig 230
"*O Reimplante*" 29
Reiner, Carl 195
Reisman, Del 29
Reitman, Ivan 244–5
Renard, Ken 60–1
Renard, Maurice 18
Rendezvous with Rama 65
Repp, Stafford 33
Republic Pictures 87
"Requiem for a Heavyweight" (episode) 22, 32, 45

Requiem for a Heavyweight (film) 32
"Return" (story) 186, 201
The Return (unproduced script) 174
"The Return of Andrew Bentley" 59–61, **59**, 208
Return of the Frontiersman 30
"Return to Hell House" 179
Revelation (New Testament book) 151
Revenge of the Creature 10, 240
Revill, Clive 177, **178**, 179, **181**, 183–4
Revolutionary War 72
The Reward (1965) 269
Reynolds, Kathryn 201
Rhapsody on a Theme of Paganini (Op. 43, Variation XVIII) 226–7
Rhodes, Jordan 162
Rhubarb (cat) 112
Ribotta, Hector [Ettore] 118
Rice, Anne 118, 126
Rice, Jeff 162, 164–7, 169, 172, 175–6
Rich, David Lowell 48
Richard Diamond, Private Detective (TV series) 52
Richard Matheson: Collected Stories see *Collected Stories* (Matheson)
The Richard Matheson Companion 1, 3, 7, 10–1, 199, 221, 245, 269
Richard Matheson: He Is Legend 4; see also *He Is Legend* (Rathbun & Flanagan)
"Richard Matheson — Storyteller" (DVD extras) 111, 113, 117, 142, 161
"Richard Matheson: The Writing of *Duel*" 156
Richard Matheson's Hell House (graphic novel) 184
Richard Matheson's Kolchak Scripts 167–8, 172–5
Richard Matheson's The Twilight Zone Scripts 24, 32, 35–8, 43, 46, 50, 61, 73, 237–8
Richard II (play) 220
Richard III (play) 92
Richards, Brian 192
Richards, Rick 170
Richardson, Ralph 218
Richardson, Salli 265, 267
Richter, W.D. 152
Ride the High Country 129
"Ride the Nightmare" (episode) 62–3, 203
Ride the Nightmare (novel) 7, 62–3, 146–7, 149
Ridgeview, Ohio 33
Rifkin, Steve 257, 259
The Rifleman 129
Ringel, Harry 134
Rio de Janeiro, Brazil 29
"The Ripper" 171
Rippy, Leon 242
Ritch, OCee 22
Ritter, Jason 245–6
Ritter, John 196, 245–7
Ritter, Tex 247
Rivero, Enrique 111
Riviera (France) 149
Rivoli Theater 143

The Road Warrior 238
Robards, Jason 149
Robert Bloch: Appreciations of the Master 7
Roberts, Joseph 170
Robertson, Cliff 32
Robertson, Stuart 257
Robinson, Bernard 136
Robinson Crusoe (novel) 267
Robson, Mark 46–7
Robur le Conquérant (Robur, the Conqueror, aka *The Clipper of the Clouds*) 85, 87, 89
Robur, the Conqueror see *Robur le Conquérant*
Rocco e i Suoi Fratelli (Rocco and His Brothers) 198
Rocco and His Brothers see *Rocco e i Suoi Fratelli*
Rochelle, Edwin 44
Rock All Night 80
The Rockford Files 195
The Rocky Horror Picture Show 132, 226
Rod Serling's Night Gallery: *An After-Hours Tour* 70
Rod Serling's The Twilight Zone Magazine 4, 33, 74, 227, 264, 270
Roddenberry, Gene 25, 50, 65–6
Rodriguez, Robert 184
Rogan, Josh (pseudonym) 232, 235
Rogers, Linda 112
Rogers, Roy 87
Rogers, Steven 61
Rome, Italy 122–3
Romero, George A. 5, 61, 77, 112, 118, 120, 123
Roncom Telefilms 52
Ronnis, Melena 78
Rooney, Mickey 21, 241
Rooney, Wallace 35–6
Roosevelt, Theodore ("Teddy") 67
The Ropers 129
Rosemary's Baby (film) 67, 72, 133, 169, 200
Rosemary's Baby (novel) 183
Rosen, Burton 52
Rosen, Milton 127
Rosenberg, Max J. 102
Rosenberg, Stuart 41
Rosenbloom, Maxie 18, 20
Rosenman, Leonard 27
Rossi-Stuart, Giacomo (aka Jack Stuart) **117**, 118, 122–3
Il Rosso Segno della Folio see *Hatchet for the Honeymoon*
Roth, Eli 184
Roubicek, George 94
Round Up the Usual Suspects 106
Route 66 22
Rowan & Martin's Laugh-In see *Laugh-In*
Rowlands, Gena 62
Royal Flying Corps 26
Rubin, Bruce Joel 257
Rugrats 5
Rule, Janice 94
The Ruling Class (film) 73
Rumania 164, 211
Runaway Daughters 80

Rusoff, Lou 80
Russell, John 56, **58**
Russell, Kurt 186, 265
Russell, Paddy 67
Russell, Ray 3, 50, 79, 102, 177, 210
Russia 143
Russo, Tom 268
Ryall, Chris 262
Ryan, Al 206
Ryan, Eileen 31, 75
Ryan, Robert 89

Saboteur 62
Sackheim, William 261
Sadwith, James 271
Sagal, Boris 149–50
Sagal, Jean 150
Sagal, Joe 150
Sagal, Katey 150
Sagal, Liz 150
Sagansky, Jeff 188
St. Elmo's Fire 230
St. Elsewhere 211
St. Germain, Comte de *see* Comte de St. Germain
St. Louis, Missouri 77
Saint Nikolai's Cathedral 141
St. Patrick's Cathedral (New York) 268
Salem's Lot (1979 miniseries) 59, 75
'Salem's Lot (novel) 118
Salkow, Lester 122
Salkow, Sidney 117, 120, 122
Salter, Hans J. 9
Salva, Victor 162
Sammon, Paul M. 5, 9, 12, 16, 25, 50, 58–9, 61, 64–5, 72, 80, 95–6, 109–10, 113, 120, 125, 166, 185, 187, 196, 201, 203–4, 223, 231, 265
Le Samouraï (The Samurai, 1967) 198
Sampson, Robert 38
"Samson the Great" 57
The Samurai (1967) *see* Le Samouraï
San Diego, California 72, 154, 186, 221
San Fernando Valley, California 34
San Francisco, California 255
Sanchez, Paul 219
Sand Canyon, California 159
Sander, Gordon F. 174
Sanford, Donald S. 76
Sanford, Gerald 69
Sangster, Jimmy 72, 124, 176, 191
Santa Monica, California 7, 253
Santos, Michele 262
Sapinsley, Alvin 69
Sarafian, Richard C. 57, 149, 181, 183
Sarde, Philippe 197
"Sardonicus" 210
Sargent, Joseph 64, 181
Sargent, William 63
Sasdy, Peter 68
Satan's Sadists 21
Satan's Sister see La Sorella di Satana
Saturday Night Live 32, 48
Saul, John 271
Saving Private Ryan 130

Sawaya, George 127
Sawtell, Paul 118
Saxon, Aaron 107
Sayles, John 79, 83, 235
Scannell, Frank J. 9
Scapperotti, Dan 21, 246
Scaramouche (1952 film) 116
Scarborough Zoo (England) 190
Scarbury, Joey 195
The Scary Door 49
Schallert, William 9, 12, 18, 232, 236, 238
Scheider, Roy 240
Schell, Maria 212, 215
Schermer, Jules 56, 58
Schickel, Richard 12, 158
Die Schlangengrube und das Pendel (The Snake Pit and the Pendulum) 89
Schlesinger, John 203
Schlock 230
Schlock-O-Rama: The Films of Al Adamson 21
Schoenberg, Burt (aka Shonberg) 84
Schopenhauer, Arthur 18
Schorer, Mark 59–60
Schow, David J. 76, 230
Schrader, Paul 270
Schramm, David 245, 247
Schumacher, Jerry 31
Schumacher, Joel 228, 230–1, 263
Schwartz, Sherwood 17
Schwarzenegger, Arnold 265
Sci-Fi Channel (SFC) 76, 219, 261
SCI FI Wire 73
Science and Health 199
Science Fiction in the Cinema: 1895–1970 10
Science Fiction Television Series 39, 64, 69–70, 76
Science Fiction Theater 210
Science Fiction Weekly 174
Scientology *see* Church of Scientology
Scifipedia (defunct website) 7
Sciorra, Annabella 252, 254
Scorsese, Martin 74, 79, 150
Scott, Campbell 228
Scott, George C. 56
Scott, Jacqueline 155, 158
Scott, Jeff 127, 129
Scott, Nathan 35
Scott, Richard 131
Scott, Ridley 265
Scott, Simon 26, 52–3
Scotti, Vito 85
Scourby, Alexander 26
Scream 260
Scream and Scream Again 207
Scream of the Wolf 192–4, **193**
Screaming Mimi (film) 62
Screamplays 180
Screen Actors Guild 225
Sea Dreams (theme-park attraction) 239
The Sea Hawk (1940) 116
Sea World 240–1
Seattle, Washington 170, 173
"Second Chance" 209, 211, 224
Seconds (film) 171

Secret Agent (series) *see Danger Man*
Seel, Charles 155
Les Seins de Glace see Icy Breasts
Selected Stories (Beaumont) 23, 50; see also *The Howling Man* (collection)
Sellers, Peter 17
Seltzer, Walter 149–52, 154
Selznick, David O. 125
Selznick, Joyce 125
Senensky, Ralph 70
September 11, 2001, terrorist attacks 268
Serling, Carol 22, 24, 231–2, 238, 248
Serling, Rod 4, 22–30, 32–4, 36, 38–9, 43, 45, 48–50, 68–9, 76, 168, 173–4, 177, 210–1, 231–3, 236, 239, 248–9
Serling: The Rise and Twilight of Television's Last Angry Man 174
"The Settlers" 215, 219
Seven (1995) 258
Seven Arts 130–1, 134
Seven Days in May (film) 171
7 Faces of Dr. Lao 201
Seven Footprints to Satan (novel) 94
"747<in> 70
7 Steps to Midnight 7, 271
The Seven-Per-Cent Solution (film) 131
The Seventh Seal see Det Sjunde Inseglet
77 Sunset Strip 56
Seymour, Jane 208, 219, 221–4, **223**, 226
S-F 2 230
SFC *see* Sci-Fi Channel
Shadow of a Doubt 222
The Shadow of the Cat 98
Shadow on the Sun 7, 271
"Shadow Play" 26
Shadowed Places 269
Shake, Rattle and Rock 80
Shakespeare, William 32, 57–8, 106, 114, 154, 220, 246, 252–3, 257
Shakespeare in Love 257
Shalet, Diane 170
Shane (film) 129
Shannon, Harry 228
Shannon, Richard 62
Shantry, Roger 170
Shapiro, Marc 21, 256
Shatner, William ("Bill") 28, 33–4, 46–7, 59, 64–5
Shaun of the Dead 184
Shaw, Helen 232, 235
Shaw, Robert J. 62
Shawn, Dick 75
Shay, Don 151
She (novel) 133
The She Beast see La Sorella di Satana
The She-Creature (1956) 80, 137, 140
She Demons 18
Sheckley, Robert 72
Sheedy, Ally 230
Sheena, Queen of the Jungle (1955–56 TV series) 18
Shefter, Bert 118

Sheinberg, Sid 175
Sheldon, James 235
Shelley, Barbara 191
Shepard, Bill 220, 224, 227
Shepperton Studios 136
Sheridan, Lee 93
Sherman, Orville 192
Sherwood, John 13
Sherwood Oaks College 48
Shifter 244
"Shine, Little Glow Worm" 109
The Shining (1980) 259
Ship of Fools (film) 52
"Shipshape Home" 50–2
Shirley, John 226
Shock (magazine) 262
Shock Theater (TV package) 3
Shogun (novel) 18
Shonberg, Burt *see* Schoenberg, Burt
Shorr, Richard 101
Showtime (network) 76–7
Shpetner, Stan 207–9
Shrinking Lover see *Amante Menguante*
The Shrinking Man (novel) 5–6, 9–11, 14–6, 21, 120, 179, 184, 189, 228, 258
Shuler-Donner Productions 244
Shurlock, Geoffrey M. 121
The Sicilian Clan see *Le Clan des Siciliens*
The Sid Caesar, Imogene Coca, Carl Reiner, Howard Morris Special 17
Sideshow Collectibles 48
Sidney, George 32
Sign of the Pagan 189
Signet Books 145
"The Silent Towns" 216, 219
Silkwood 195
Silver, Joel 244
Silverberg, Robert 270
Silverman, Fred 218
Silverstein, Elliot 43–4
Simmons, Johnny 262–4
Simmons, Richard Alan 9, 16
Simmons, William P. 17
Simon, S. Sylvan 221
Simon, Stephen 221, 252, 254, 257; *see also* Deutsch, Stephen
Simon & Schuster 94
Simonin, Albert 146, 148
Simpson, Mickey 56–7
The Simpsons 39, 48–9, 155, 206, 236
Sinatra 270
Sinbad and the Eye of the Tiger 221
Sinclair, Robert B. 57
Singer, Mark 4
Singer, Robert 209
Singh, Mohan 131
Singuineau, Frank 94
Siodmak, Curt 150
Sirrs, Janek 265, 268
The Six Million Dollar Man (series) 170
The Sixth Sense (film) 260
The Sixth Sense (series) 61, 70, 171, 207
Det Sjunde Inseglet (The Seventh Seal) 89

Skedaddle 208
Skelton, Red 221
Skelton, Scott 70–1, 210
Skipper, Pat 245–6
Skotak, Robert 89
The Skull 142
"The Skull of the Marquis de Sade" 142
Slade, Michael 123
"Slaughter House" 175
Sleepy Hollow (1999) 258
Sliders 77
Smart Girls Don't Talk 30
Smith, Cecil 156, 196
Smith, Clark Ashton 70
Smith, Dean 192
Smith, Delos V. 207
Smith, Dick 188
Smith, Eddie Bo, Jr. 257, 259
Smith, Harkness 28
Smith, Kellita 49
Smith, Kent 162, 164, 169
Smith, Maria 228–9
Smith, Robert S. 159
Smith, Will 265–8, **266**
Smith, Willow 265, 267
Smithee, Alan (pseudonym) 149
Smithsonian Institution 206
Snake Eyes 258
The Snake Pit and the Pendulum see *Die Schlangengrube und das Pendel*
Snowfall and Other Chilling Events 72
So Weird 5
S.O.B. 38
Sobczynski, Peter 258, 260
Sohl, Jerry 1, 3, 22–3, 31, 50–1, 59, 76, 79, 155–6, 201, 206
Solar Crisis 149
Solaris (novel) 214
Sole Survivor 5
Soledad Canyon, California 159
Solomon, Ed 5
Some Like It Hot 222
Someone Is Bleeding 6, 147, 197, 199, 253
Something Outside 77
Something Wicked This Way Comes (novel and film) 218
Somewhere in Time (film) 72, 208, 219–28, **220**, **223**, 254, 270
Somewhere in Time (musical) 227
Somewhere in Time (novel) see *Bid Time Return*
Somewhere in Time and *What Dreams May Come: Two Novels of Love and Fantasy* 253–4
The Somewhere in Time *Story: Behind the Scenes of the Making of the Cult Romantic Fantasy Motion Picture* 220, 227
Somma, Joseph Michael 262
Sony Pictures Imageworks 265
The Sopranos 176
The Sorcerers (film) 143
La Sorella di Satana (Satan's Sister, aka *The She Beast*) 143
Soreny, Eve 41
Sorority Girl 81
Sorrentino's (restaurant) 221

"Sorry, Right Number" *see* "Long Distance Call" (Matheson story)
Sothern, Ann 28
Sound Beach (New York) 10
The Sound of Music (1965 film) 221
South Africa 112
South Pacific (1958 film) 90
Southern California School of Writers 3; *see also* The Group
Soy Leyenda (I Am Legend; 1967 film) 123
Soylent Green 149–50
Space (theme-park attraction) 75
The Space Children 17
Space Patrol (1950–55 TV series) 47
Spade, David 155
Spain 90, 93, 141, 213
Spain, Fay 18, 20
Spalding, Harry 122
Spanish Inquisition *see* Inquisition
Sparr, Robert T. 57
Spartacus (1960 film) 152
Speidel, William C. 170
Spelling, Aaron 242
Spencer, Roy 187
"Spider in the Web" 176
Spielberg, Steven 4, 12, 39, 51, 70, 73–6, 118, 130, 155–62, 231–5, 238, 248, 258, 260
Spielberg on Spielberg 158
Spignesi, Stephen J. 5
Spillane, Mickey 165
The Spirit (2008) 264
"Spirit Unwilling" 53
Spirits of the Dead see *Histoires Extraordinaires* (1968 film)
Spiritual Cinema Circle 221
"The Splendid Source" 155
Spotnitz, Frank 176
"Spur of the Moment" 26, 43–4
Squire, Katherine 53
Sri Lanka 257
"SRL Ad" 201
Stag (magazine) 147
Stainer-Hutchins, Michael 131
Stalling, Carl 237
Stallone, Sylvester 242
Stanley, John 101, 208
Stanwood, Michael 127
Stanwyck, Barbara 125
Star in the Dust 18
Star Science Fiction Stories No. 3 77
Star Trek (film series) 52
Star Trek (1966–69 TV series) 25, 33, 47, 50, 54, 60, 64–66, 70, 74, 148, 154, 236
Star Trek: Deep Space Nine 256
Star Trek 8 (book) 65
Star Trek Memories 65
Star Trek: The Motion Picture 65
Star Wars (1977) 84, 182, 212, 219, 249
Starburst 147, 254
Stargate Films 245, 247
Stark, Ray 219, 221
Starlog 51, 248, 256
The Starlost 148
Starr, Zoe 131
Startling Stories 75
Stears, John 212, 219
"Steel" 24, 29, 44–5

Steel, Dawn 244
Steele, Barbara 89–90, *91*, 92–3
Steiger, Rod 183
Stein, Herman 9, 15
Stein, Karen 262
Steiner, Fred 41
Steinman, Shwan 155
Stephens, Martin 182
Stepsister from Planet Weird 5
Stern, Jenna 248–9
Stevens, Darryl 85
Stevens, Morton 60, 207–8
Stevenson, Jay (pseudonym) 234
Stewart, Paul (actor-director) 38–9
Stewart, Paul (special-effects supervisor) 232
Stewart, Susan 228
Still Me 225–6
Stimson, Kenneth 192
Stine, Clifford 9, 13, 15
Stir of Echoes (film) 257–62, *259*
A Stir of Echoes (novel) 227, 253, 257–61
Stir of Echoes: The Dead Speak see *Stir of Echoes: The Homecoming*
Stir of Echoes: The Homecoming 261
Stoker, Bram 149, 186–8, 190–1
Stone, Andrew L. 143
Stone, Fred 187
Stone, George E. 37
Stone, James 54
Storm, James 192, 201
Stott, Judith 94, 97
Stout, William 174
Straczynski, J. Michael 176
Strand, Maud 220, 225
Strange, Billy 141
The Strange Case of Dr. Jekyll and Mr. Hyde (1968 film) 187
Strange Conflict 132
The Strange Possession of Mrs. Oliver 207–9
Strange Tales (magazine) 60
The Stranger Within 199–201
Stratford, Tracy 38, *40*
Stratton, Rick 249
Straub, Peter 177
Strauss, Peter 270
The Strawberry Blonde (1959 television production) 101
Streep, Meryl 254
Strock, Herbert L. 101
Strus, Lusia 257–8
Stuart, Jack see Rossi-Stuart, Giacomo
Stuart, Randy 9, 12, 17
Stuart, William L. 56
Studio 57 51–2
Studios la Victorine 147
Sturgeon, Theodore 3, 50–1
Sturges, John 54
Sturgess, Olive 107–8
Stuve, Paul 11
Suarez, Jeremy 49
Subotsky, Milton 102, 142, 212–3
"Such Interesting Neighbors" 211
Sudak, Eunice 106–7
Sudden Terror see *Eyewitness* (1970 film)
Suicide Battalion 137
Summers, Jeremy 69

Sun, Sabine 146
Sundance Institute 79
Superman (1978 film) 48, 191, 226
Superman II 191
Sutherland, Donald 123–4, 126, 230
Sutherland, Kiefer 230
Swanson, Logan (pseudonym) 61, 63, 73, 117, 120, 180, 203, 209
Swanwick, Peter 131
Swayze, Patrick 257
Sweden 141, 256
Sweethearts and Horrors 116, 138
"Sweets to the Sweet" 102
Swerling, Jo, Jr. 225
Swift, Jonathan 21
Swift, Lela 212
Sykes, Peter 134, 182
Symons, Julian 63
Syracuse, New York 246
Szollosi, Tom 5, 70, 75
Szwarc, Jeannot 68, 70–1, 221–3, 225–7, 240

Tabu (1931 film) 79
Taft, Sara 42
Tager, Aron 249, 252
Tahan, Charlie 265, 267
Takei, George 64
The Taking of Pelham One Two Three (1974 film) 64
Talbott, Michael 209, 211
Tale of a Dog 144
Tales from the Crypt (series) 209
Tales of Fantasy see *Racconti di Fantascienza*
Tales of Manhattan 103
Tales of Terror (1962 film) 81, 93, 100–7, *102, 103, 105*, 112, 147, 201
Tales of Terror (novelization) 93, 106–7
The Talisman 177
Talk to Her see *Hable con Ella*
Tallman, Frank Gifford 26
Tamahori, Lee 217
Tamblyn, Russ 18
Tanen, Ned 221
Tanganyika 9
"Tape Loop of the Unconscious: Plumbing Buchanan's '*It's Alive!*'" 141
Tarantino, Quentin 184
Tarantula 10, 13, 16
"Target of Hate" 55–6
A Taste of Evil 72
Tatopoulos, Patrick 265, 268
The Tattered Dress 18
Taurog, Norman 91
Tavarez, Alan 262
Taylor, Carlie 112
Taylor, Don 110
Taylor, Elizabeth 183
Taylor, Rod 27–8
TCM (Turner Classic Movies) 12, 158
Teenage Cave Man (1958) 81
Teenage Mutant Ninja Turtles 172
The Television Horrors of Dan Curtis: Dark Shadows, The Night Stalker and Other Productions, 1966–2006 205

The Tempest (play) 154
Tennessee 123, 139
Tenser, Tony 107
Terrell, Ken 85
The Terror (1963) 111
"Terror at 5 Feet" 48
Terror of the Doll see "Amelia"
Terrore nello Spazio (Terror in Space) 29
Tesla, Nikola 270
"The Test" (episode) see "*L'Esame*"
"The Test" (story) 72, 74
Texas 137–8, 140
The Texas Chain Saw Massacre (1974) 75, 78
The Texas Chainsaw Massacre (2003) 78
Thanksgiving (faux trailer) 184
Thanksgiving (holiday) 49, 188, 235
Thaxter, Phyllis 35–6
T.H.E. Cat 150
"The Theatre" 248
Theodore see Gottlieb, Theodore
"There Shall Come Soft Rains" 215, 217, 219
There Was Once a Cop see *Il Était Une Fois un Flic*
"Therese" (aka "Needle in the Heart") 201, 203–4, 209
"*They're Here...*": Invasion of the Body Snatchers: *A Tribute* 238
"They're Tearing Down Tim Riley's Bar" 70
The Thin Man (film) 176
The Thin Red Line (1998 film) 130
The Thing (1982) 264
Things to Come 3
Thinnes, Roy 174–5
"The Third Expedition" see "Mars Is Heaven"
"Third from the Sun" (episode) 24, 27, 29–31, 34–5, 48
"Third from the Sun" (story) 24, 27, 29–30, 50
The Third Level 210
3rd Rock from the Sun 48
30 Days of Night (graphic novel) 267
"The Thirty-First of February" 63
Thirty-Minute Theatre 67
"Thirty Minutes" 35, 56–7
36 Hours 28
This Is a Thriller: An Episode Guide, History and Analysis of the Classic 1960s Television Series 60, 94
This Rebel Age 17–8; see also *The Beat Generation*
Thomas, Dylan 227
Thomas, Michael R. 242
Thompson, Emma 265–6
Thompson, Howard 100
Thompson, Jeff 205
Thompson, Lea 239–40
The Three Musketeers (1948 film) 116
Three O'Clock High 5, 74
Three's Company 129, 247
Thriller (series) 59–61, *59*, 67, 171, 187, 207, 239
Thriller Video 210

Thrilling Wonder Stories 201
"Throttle" 161
"Through Channels" 264
Through the Golden Horn 248
Thunderball (film) 147, 219
Thurman, Billy 137–9
"Thy Will Be Done" 52–3
"Tick of Time" 22
Tigerland 263
Tigon British Film Productions 107
Tijuana, Mexico 199
Tilley, Patrick 270
Tilton, Cash 262
Time and Again 224
"Time Is Just a Place" 211
Time Killer see The Night Strangler (film)
The Time Machine (1960 film) 28
The Time Machine (novel) 211
"Time of Flight" 64, 181
"Time Out" 231, 233
Time Out Film Guide 16, 85, 89, 93, 100, 126, 137
A Time to Kill (film) 230
The Time Tunnel (series) 148
Timpone, Anthony 230
The Tingler 79
"'Tis the Season to Be Jelly" 118
To Hell and Back 15, 128–30
To Live 271
To the Devil—A Daughter (novel and film) 134
Tobias, George 170, 173
Tochi, Brian 149
Todd, Ryan 245–6
Todman, Bill 54
Toledo, Spain 90
The Tomb of Ligeia 79, 92, 103, 107–8, 112
Tomerlin, John 22, 58, 140, 187
Tomlin, Lily 16, 228–9, 231
"Too Proud to Lose" 57
Topart, Jean 146, 148
Tormé, Mel 77
Tormé, Tracy 77
Toronto, Canada 187, 249–50, 262
Touch of Evil 18, 152, 160, 162
A Touch of Strange 50–1
Tourneur, Jacques 4, 45–6, 48, 98, 112–3, 116–7, 181
Tower of London (1939) 116
Tower of London (1962) 92
Towers, Harry Alan 112
Towne, Robert 79, 111–2
Trackdown (series) 52
Trans Continental (production company) 141–2, 144
Transylvania 67, 190
The Transylvanian Library: A Consumer's Guide to Vampire Fiction 166
The Trap (1966 film) 100
Traube, Dr. Sylvia 12
"The Traveller" 201
Travis, Nancy 242–3
Treasure Island (1972 film)
Treasure Island (San Francisco) 255
"Treehouse of Horror II" 206
"Treehouse of Horror IV" 48
"Treehouse of Horror VI" 39
"Treehouse of Horror VIII" 155

Trenton Film Festival 263
"Trespass" (aka "Mother by Protest") 186, 199–201
TriBeCa (New York) 267
The Trigger Effect 258
Trilogy in Terror see Trilogy of Terror
Trilogy of Terror 34, 103, 106, 201–7, **202, 204**, 209–11, 249–52, 264
Trilogy of Terror—The Movie see Trilogy of Terror II
Trilogy of Terror II 205, 249–52
Triska, Jan 242
TriStar Pictures 242–4
Tron 40, 247
Troupe, Tom 57
Trubo, Richard 80
"Trucks" 161
Trueblood, Guerdon 239–40
Trumbull, Robert 270
"Tryptophan-tasy" 49
Tucker, Burnell 212, 215
Tucker, Jonathan 78
Turini Pass, France 198
Turley, Jim 37
Turman, Larry 196
The Turn of the Screw (1974 film) 174, 187
"The Turn of the Screw" (story) 96, 179
Turner, Brad 76
Turner, Lana 98, 101
Turner, Larry 89–90
Turner Classic Movies *see* TCM
Tushingham, Rita 100
Tutankhamun *see* King Tut
Tutankhamun: The Untold Story 196
Tuttle, William 17, 44, 47, 169–71
TV Guide 48, 65, 162, 167, 228
TV's Magic Memories 52
Twelve O'Clock High (film) 238
Twelve O'Clock High (series) 29
20th Century–Fox 68, 92, 105, 120, 130, 133, 177–8, 181–2
28 Days Later 268
20,000 Leagues Under the Sea (novel and 1954 film) 85, 89
Twice-Told Tales (film) 120
The Twilight and Other Zones: The Dark Worlds of Richard Matheson 1, 7
The Twilight Zone (1959–1964) 4, 7, 21–51, 54, 56, 57, 69–70, 73–5, 77–8, 111, 113, 157, 168, 170, 185, 187, 201, 204, 206, 211, 218, 225, 231, 233, 236–8, 248
The Twilight Zone (1985–1988) 26, 39, 49, 73–4, 76
The Twilight Zone (2002–2003) 237
The Twilight Zone Companion 23, 39, 234
The Twilight Zone Radio Dramas 49
Twilight Zone: Rod Serling's Lost Classics 49, 248–9
Twilight Zone Scripts and Stories (Johnson) 22
The Twilight Zone Scripts of Charles Beaumont, Volume One 25, 50

The Twilight Zone Scripts of Jerry Sohl 50
The Twilight Zone: The Definitive Edition 48
Twilight Zone—The Movie (film) 39, 48–9, 231–9, **236–7**, 250
Twilight Zone—The Movie (novelization) 239
The Twilight Zone: The Original Stories 21–2, 24–5, 41–2, 45, 236
The Twilight Zone: Unlocking the Door to a Television Classic 26, 38
Twins of Evil 182
Twisted see Medusa (1974)
Two Evil Eyes see Due Occhi Diabolici
The Two Faces of Dr. Jekyll (aka *House of Fright*) 136
The Two Jakes 111
"Two Shots from Fly's Photo Gallery" 226
2001: A Space Odyssey (film) 142–3, 213
The Two Worlds of Jennie Logan 228
"The Twonky" (story) 250

UCLA Parapsychology lab 244
U-I *see* Universal-International
Ullmann, Liv 146–9
Ulmer, Edgar G. 141
L'Ultimo Uomo della Terra see The Last Man on Earth
Uncharted Seas 134
Under the Bounding Main 173
Underground City (Seattle) 170, 173
The Undying Monster 36
The Uninvited (1944 film) 36
Union Army 170
United Artists 79
United Nations 148
Universal City, California 226
Universal-International (U-I) 6, 9–11, 13, 15, 18, 231; *see also* Universal Pictures
Universal Pictures 3, 9, 16–7, 69–71, 94, 96, 116, 127–30, 156, 160–1, 166, 171, 175, 219–21, 223, 225–6, 228, 230, 234, 239, 241, 261, 271; *see also* Universal-International
Universal Soldier (1971 film) 145
Universal Studio Museum 204
Universal Studios Home Video 156
University of Maine 5
University of Missouri 6, 11, 199, 201, 227
University of Nevada, Las Vegas 172
Unrealized Dreams 116, 231
"The Untouchable Divorcee" 147
L'Uomo dalle Due Ombre see Cold Sweat (1970 film)
Upcoming Horror Movies (website) 262
UPN Network 176, 237
Uram, Sue 65
U.S. Infantry *see* 8th Division, U.S. Infantry
USA Network 249–50
"Usher II" 217
Ustinov, Peter 127

Vagabond Books (Los Angeles) 260
Vahanian, Marc 68
The Valachi Papers (film) 147
Vampira (aka Maila Nurmi) 18
"The Vampire" (episode) 176
"Vampire" (R.C. Matheson story) 267
Vampire Chronicles (book series) 126
The Vampire Cinema 137
Vampires and Slayers 151, 166, 173, 189, 266
Van Cleave, Nathan 31, 44–5
Vancouver, British Columbia, Canada 78
Vanders, Warren 52
Van Doren, Mamie 17–8, 20–1
Van Dyke, Bonnie 192
Van Dyke, Dick 7, 194–6
Van Genechten, Jan 136
Van Gogh, Vincent 256
Van Patten, Dick 71
Van Patten, Joyce 74, 199, 201, 212, 215–6
Van Patten, Vincent 68, 71
Van Sickel, Dale 155, 160
Van Vogt, A.E. 70
Varallo, Nathalie 147
Varela, Rosario 257, 260
Variety 140, 191, 218
Vaughan, Peter 123–4
V.C.E. (effects company) 232
Vega, Paz 17
The Veils of Bagdad 9
Venice, California 39
Ventura, California 156
Vera Cruz 147
Vered, Annabel 228
Vermont 267
Verne, Jules 39, 85, 87–9, 216
Verneuil, Henri 198
Verreaux, Ed 232
Verschooten, Gilbert 136
Victor, Charles 89–90
Video Store Magazine 111
Video Watchdog 122
Vietnam War 225
Vigil 254
Viking Press 221
Village of the Damned (1960) 100, 200
Village of the Damned (1995) 200
Vincent Price: The Sinister Image 106
Violent City see *Città Violenta*
Vire River 61
Virginia City, Nevada 220
The Virginian (series) 129
Visconti, Luchino 198
Visions of Death: Richard Matheson's Edgar Allan Poe Scripts, Volume One 82–5, 90, 102
"A Visit to Santa Claus" 61
Vivian, Bert 131
Vlad Tepes (Vlad the Impaler) 187
Vlad the Impaler *see* Vlad Tepes
Vogel, David 77
Von Buelow, Erik M. 201, 204
The Von Metz Incident see *Loose Cannons*
Von Richthofen and Brown (aka *The Red Baron*) 79, 154

Von Sydow, Max 252, *253*, 256
Von Trapp, Captain Georg 221
Voodoo Woman 139
Voskovec, George 219, 222
Voyage to Lilliput 21
Voyage to the Bottom of the Sea (film) 201
Voyage to the Bottom of the Sea (series) 148
Voyage to the End of the Universe 29

Waggner, George 56
Wagner, Jane 228–9, 231
Wagner, Robert 126
Waiting to Exhale (film) 254
Walker, Clint 56, 192–4
Walker, Peter 31
Walker, Zena 68
Wallace, Connie 108
Walsh, J.T. 186
Walter, Elizabeth 72
Wang, Gene 54
Wanted: Dead or Alive (series) 7, 22, 49, 54, *54*, 187
War and Remembrance (miniseries) 167, 205
War-Gods of the Deep see *City Under the Sea*
The War Lord 150
The War of the Worlds (novel) 214
Ward, Al 162
Ward, Bill 116
Ward, Larry 56
Ward, Sandy 194
Ward, Simon 186–7, 189, 191
Ward, Vincent 252, 254–7
Warden, Jack 269
Warner Bros. 56, 149–54, 204, 230–1, 235–7, 265–6
Warner Home Video 154
Warren, Alan 60, 94
Warren, Gene 85, 87
Warwick, Robert 26
Washington, D.C. 166, 234, 242
Washington Square (New York) 267
The Wasp Woman (1959) 81
Watch the Skies! Science Fiction, the 1950s and Us 12
The Watcher in the Woods 182
Waters, Russell 131
Watling, Leonor 17
Watson, Larry 162
Watts, Gwendolyn 123–4
Waugh, Harry H. 104
Wayne, David 63
Wayne, Nina 170
WB (network) 176
Weaver, Dennis 155, *156–7*, 158, 160–2
Weaver, Fritz 29–31, 212, 215
Weaver, Robby ("Rob") 160
Weaver, Tom 16, 84, 88, 106, 109, 120, 122, 248
Webb, Jack 53
Webster, Mary 42, 85, *86*, 87, *88*
"The Wedding" 76
Weddle, Vernon 192
Weil, Liza 257–8
Weiner, Jack B. 194–5

Weinraub, Bernard 260
Weird Tales 60, 171, 175, 251
Weird Woman 94–5
Weis, Don 44–5, 139
Weissbach, Herbert 141
Welles, Orson 18, 34, 47, 100, 152, 160, 162
Wellman, Manley Wade 70
Wells, H.G. 3, 141, 211, 214, 234, 268
Wendt, George 220, 225
Wenger, Cliff 209
Werewolf (series) 176
WereWolf of London 4
Werewolf Women of the S.S. 184
West, Kit 186
West, Mae 41
West Side Story (film) 113
Westerfield, James 54
Westmore, Bud 9, 127, 192
Westmore, Frank 209
Westmore, Mike 201, 204
Westmoreland, Robert ("Bob") 194, 231
Westwood, Patrick 89–90
Westworld 195
Wetherell, Virginia 187, 190–1
What (1963) see *La Frusta e il Corpo*
What Dreams May Come (film) 221, 252–7, *253*, *255*
What Dreams May Come (novel) 5, 7, 68, 70, 120, 221, 244, 252–7, 265
What Ever Happened to Baby Jane? (1962 film) 106, 124–5
"What the Devil?" 27
"What Was in the Box?" *see* "Big Surprise" (story)
Wheatley, Dennis 130, 132–6
Whedon, Joss 176
"When Day Is Dun" 118
When Nights Were Bold 227
"When the Sky Was Opened" *see* "And When the Sky Was Opened"
When the Sleeper Wakes 141
When Worlds Collide (film) 195
"Where Is Everybody?" 22
"Where the Dead Are" 248
"Where There's a Will" 245
Which Witch Is Which? see *Witches' Brew*
The Whip and the Body see *La Frusta e il Corpo*
Whistling in the Dark 221
Whitby, England 190
White, Christine 47
White, David 31
White, Jesse 37
White, Will J. 29
Whitlock, Albert 91
Whitney, Grace Lee 64
Whitten, Leslie H. 166
Whittington, Dick 155, 160
Whoever Slew Auntie Roo? 62
Whybrow, Roy 177, 184
Wiater, Stanley 24, 27, 30, 32, 34–7, 41, 43–4, 50, 68, 72–4, 78, 140, 177, 199, 201, 237–8, 244
Wicker Park (Chicago) 260

Wicking, Christopher 143, 207
Wide World of Entertainment 187
Wikipedia 112
Wild, Harry 30
The Wild Angels 80, 183
Wild Bill (unfilmed Matheson script) 271
Wild Bill and His Lady 227
The Wild Wild West (series) 42
Wilder, Billy 183
Wilkerson, Guy 33
Wilkinson, Harris 262
Will Penny 152, 154
Will Rogers State Park, California 199
"William and Mary" 67
Williams, Bill 52
Williams, Chalon 257, 259
Williams, Douglas 112
Williams, Grant 9, *11*, 12, *13*, 14–15, 17, 231
Williams, Jay 270
Williams, John (actor) 171
Williams, John (composer) 88, 239
Williams, Lucy Chase 90, 92, 103, 114, 117
Williams, Patrick 248
Williams, Rhoda 38
Williams, Robin 252, *253*, 254, *255*
Williams, Steven 232–3
Williams, Tim 167
Williams, Van 56
Williamsburg (Brooklyn) 268
Williamson, Fred 17
Williamson, J.N. 5, 50
Willits, Bernie 225
Wilson, Elizabeth 228–9
Wilson, F. Paul 203
Wilson, Jack 219
Winbush, Camille 49
Wincelberg, Shimon 146, 148
The Winds of War (miniseries) 167, 193
Windust, Bretaigne 53
Winner, Michael 148
Winningham, Mare 73, 230
Winter, Douglas E. 6, 118, 178
Wintle, Julian 96, 98, 100–1
Wise, Robert 46–7, 133, 177, 213
"Witch War" 201
The Witches (aka *The Devil's Own*; 1966 film) 124, 133
Witches' Brew (1985 film) 98, 101
Witchfinder General (aka *Conqueror Worm*; film) 143, 207
"With Affection, Jack the Ripper" 171
Withers, Iva 98
Witney, William 85–7, 208
The Wiz (film) 230

The Wizard of Oz (1939 film) 172, 246
Wolf, Leonard 183, 205–6
The Wolf Man (1941) 56
Wolfshead: The Legend of Robin Hood 182
Woman 271
Wonder Woman (TV series) 26
The Wonderful Wizard of Oz 245–6
The Wonderful World of the Brothers Grimm 201
Wood, Ashley 262
Wood, Forrest 149
Woods, Sunny 207–8
Woodson, Phil 199
Woodson, Ruth Ann 6, 253; *see also* Matheson, Ruth Ann
Woodstock 150
Woolf, Gary 94
Wooll, Nigel 126
Woolman, Claude *66*, 67
Wooten, Katherine 235
The World Beyond (TV package) 138
World Fantasy ("Howard") Award 4
World Horror Convention
"A World of Difference" 22, 28, 31–2, 75
"A World of His Own" 32–3
World of Wonder 27
World Science Fiction Convention (Worldcon) 9
World Science Fiction Society 9
World War I 26, 132
World War II 6, 61, 63, 127, 129–30, 199
World War III 78
Worldcon *see* World Science Fiction Convention
Worsley, Wallace, Jr. 159
Worsley, Wallace, Sr. 159
Wotkowski, Lucas 262–3
Wouk, Herman 167
Wright, Edgar 184
Wright, Maggie 212, 214
Wright, Teresa 219, 222
Writers Guild of America 4, 57, 61, 100, 146, 151, 161, 235, 240
Writers Guild of America Award 4, 57, 162
Wyer, Reginald 98
Wykehurst Park 181
Wylie see *Eye of the Cat*
Wylie, Philip 270
Wyman, Jane 10
Wyndham, John 200
Wyngarde, Peter 94, *95*, 96, *96*, 98, 101
Wynn, Ed 32
Wynn, Keenan 32, 176
Wynn, Tracy Keenan 32
Wynorski, Jim 112

The X-Files (series) 77, 176, 217, 233, 265
X—The Man with the X-Ray Eyes 210
Xavier University 154

Yablonsky, Harold 89
Yankovic, "Weird Al" 75
Yates, Peter 250
"Yawkey" 18, 39, 57
The Years Stood Still 199
Yellen, Linda 270
Yentl (film) 248
"Yesterday" 195
"Ylla" 213
YMCA 30
York, Michael 184
York, Susannah 33
You Only Live Twice (film) 132
Young, L.E. "Buck" 127
Young, Terence 146–8
"Young Couples Only" 51–2
Young Frankenstein (film) 243
"Young Man's Fancy" 26, 35–6, 38, 44
The Young Racers 80
The Young Warriors 7, 127–30, *127–9*
You're a Big Boy Now 202
"Yours Truly, Jack the Ripper" 171
YouTube 72, 264
Yu, Ronny 246
Yugoslavia 141, 187

Z Channel 226
Zanetti, Eugenio 257
Zanuck, Darryl F. 130
Zanuck, Richard 130
Zavada, Ervin 245
Zaza, Paul 242
Zemeckis, Robert ("Bob") 76, 176, 260
Zerbe, Anthony 149–50, 152, 154
Zicree, Marc Scott 23, 26, 28, 41, 47, 234
Ziemann, Sonja 141
Zilinskas, Bernard 262, 264
Zinnemann, Fred 130
Zola, Emile 197
Zombie, Rob 184
Zontar, the Magazine from Venus 141
Zontar, the Thing from Venus 137
Zotz! (novel and film) 210
Zucker Brothers (David and Jerry) 230
Zugsmith, Albert 9–11, 15–8, 20–1, 89, 231
Zulu 143